HOT FLASH HOLIDAYS

NANCY THAYER

HOT
FLASH
HOLIDAYS

A Novel

BALLANTINE BOOKS • NEW YORK

Published in the United States by Ballantine Books, an imprint of The Random House Publishing Group, a division of Random House, Inc., New York.

BALLANTINE and colophon are registered trademarks of Random House, Inc.

Library of Congress Cataloging-in-Publication Data
Thayer, Nancy.
Hot flash holidays / by Nancy Thayer.
p.   cm.
ISBN 0-345-48551-3—ISBN 0-345-48552-1 (TR)
1. Middle aged women—Fiction.   2. Female friendship—Fiction.
3. Menopause—Fiction.   I. Title.
PS 3570.H3475H685 2005
813'.54—dc22   2005052064

Printed in the United States of America on acid-free paper

www.ballantinebooks.com

2 4 6 8 9 7 5 3 1

Book design by Susan Turner

ACKNOWLEDGMENTS

Wisdom is hope and knows no age.

My gratitude is immense for the wisdom of my editor,
Linda Marrow, and my agent, Meg Ruley.

I couldn't have written this book without the
gifts of inspiration, anecdotes, humor, chocolate, wisdom,
and oh, yes, an ankle bracelet, from my friends,
younger and . . . older. Enormous thanks to Deborah Beale,
Mimi Beman, Jill Burrill, Laurie Chatfield-Taylor,
Jennifer Costanza, Martha Foshee, Tina Gessler, David Gillum,
Kim Guarnaccia, Gilly Hailparn, Charlotte Maison,
Joan Medlicott, Margrethe Mentes, Elena Murphy, Robyn North,
Letitia Ord, Tricia Patterson, Jane Patton, Pam Pindell,
Selma Rayfiel, Susan Sandler, Laura Simon,
Josh Thayer, and Sam Wilde.

And Charley, thanks for being
better than chocolate!

CHRISTMAS

On this early December day, snowflakes sparkled down to earth like granted wishes from a magic wand.

Inside the handsome lounge of The Haven, Yule logs blazed cheerfully in the fireplace, while Presley, Sinatra, and Springsteen sang Christmas carols. Near the long casement windows, five women were looping lights around a Norway spruce so tall they had to use a ladder to reach the highest branches.

"Okay, that's the end of the last string," Marilyn called from behind the fat tree.

"Plug them in," Shirley told her.

Marilyn knelt to fit the plug into the socket.

"Oooooooh!" Shirley, Faye, Alice, Marilyn, and Polly sighed with delight as dozens and dozens of multicolored miniature lights twinkled to life.

"Now," Shirley announced, "for the fun part. How shall we do this?" Shirley was the director of The Haven, but the four other women were her best friends, practically her family, and she wanted to please everyone.

"I think we should all hang the ornaments we brought where we want," Polly suggested.

"But keep in mind," Faye added, "it will look better if the heaviest, biggest ornaments go on the bottom boughs, with the smaller ones on the higher branches." She was an artist, with an artist's eye.

"Yes, but we don't want it to look too *perfect*," Alice insisted. "We want it to look real."

"Good point, Alice," Shirley agreed. "Perfection, as we all know, isn't real."

"Sometimes it is," Marilyn disagreed, in her thoughtful, vague way. "The horseshoe crab, genus *Limulus,* for example, is perfect. Its design hasn't changed since the Triassic period, that's two hundred forty-five million years."

"Lovely," Faye said gently, amused. "Still, we really don't want to hang a horseshoe crab on the Christmas tree."

"I suppose not. Although one year we did." Marilyn smiled at the memory. She was a paleobiologist—the others teasingly called her a pale old biologist—and her grown son and her ex-husband were molecular geneticists. "Teddy was nine, and fascinated with crustaceans and fossils, so we bored holes in lots of shells, slipped colored cords through, and hung the tree with crabs, mollusks, and gastropods."

Alice snorted with laughter. "You are so *weird!*"

"Oh, I don't know," Polly chimed in. "David told me that he and Amy are hanging *only* homemade decorations on their tree. And my daughter-in-law is such a purist, she'll use *only* vegetable dyes, natural wood, straw, and such. Afterwards, they'll probably carry the tree outside and feed the entire thing to the goat."

The others laughed. As they talked, they moved back and forth from the tables and couches where the boxes of decorations were set out. Occasionally Shirley dropped another log on the fire.

The spacious room, with its casement windows, high ceilings, and mahogany paneling, seemed to glow with contentment. Once built to house a private boarding school, this old stone lodge had been abandoned for a few years. Then Shirley, with the help of her friends and a few investors, had bought it and opened The Haven, a premier spa and wellness resort with a burgeoning membership and second-floor condos for staff or friends.

She had staff (she had *staff*! Shirley, who had struggled financially most of her life, got a thrill every time she remembered that). But she hadn't wanted her staff to decorate the Christmas tree, and neither had her friends. They'd wanted to do this together. They'd agreed to bring three boxes of decorations each, and they'd agreed to do it without advance discussion or collaboration, so their choices would be a surprise.

Now they worked quickly, climbing the ladder to adorn the top, stretching left and right, standing back to appraise, kneeling to the lowest branches, murmuring to themselves, exclaiming at what the others had chosen.

Shirley was a sucker for whimsical creatures with smiling faces: elves, snowmen, Santa Clauses, cherubs, fat angels with crooked smiles and tilted halos, fairies with freckles and yarn hair.

Faye had selected expensive glass ornaments: gorgeous faceted stars, elongated teardrops and iridescent icicles, extravagantly striped or translucent balls in gleaming gemstone colors.

Polly loved to cook. She'd baked dozens of gingerbread men and women, sugar-cookie stars, leaping reindeer, trumpets and drummer boys and crescent moons, the absorbing, familiar activity bringing back memories of Christmases when her son was little. She'd decorated them with colored icing, silver balls, and sprinkles of colored sugar, and glued ribbons firmly on the back, for hanging. She'd also strung cranberries and popcorn on fishing wire and bought boxes of candy canes.

Alice, less sentimental and more practical, had chosen thirty of the skin care, cosmetic, and aromatherapy products on sale at The Haven, and tied their lavender boxes with glittering gold and silver bows.

Marilyn's contribution was a boxed set of antique ornaments from the Museum of Fine Arts, and a handmade collection of brass and enamel stars, sun, moon, and planets purchased from an Asian gentleman selling them from a rug on a sidewalk in Harvard Square.

When every ornament was hung, the five women stepped back to admire their handiwork. The mixture was eccentric, aesthetically enchanting, and wildly cheerful.

"It's fabulous," Shirley said. "Let me get my camera."

Alice said, "I'll pour the hot chocolate." She twisted the cap off a large Thermos and poured the fragrant liquid into Christmas mugs—little gifts from her to the others. Then, without the slightest twinge of guilt, she took out a can of Reddi-whip, shook it, and topped the drinks with snowy swirls of the white concoction. After that, she opened a little plastic bag, dipped her hand in, and sprinkled dark chocolate shavings on the creamy peaks.

"I brought some Christmas cookies—without the glue." Polly opened a red and green tin, and the sweet, warm aroma of butter and sugar rose into the air.

Marilyn and Faye pushed two of the more comfortable wing chairs close to the sofa so they could all sit in a half-circle, facing the tree. Shirley returned from her office with the camera and began snapping shots of the tree and its trimmers.

Shirley wore purple Tencel pants with an emerald top that flattered her auburn hair. Her earrings and necklace were miniature battery-operated Christmas lights that blinked on and off.

Faye wore scarlet trousers in a silk-and-wool weave with a matching jacket over a sleeveless white shell. A chunky choker of garnet and jade circled her neck. Her white hair was held back with a matching barrette.

Plump, auburn-haired Polly wore jeans and a bright green sweater with white snowmen she'd designed and knit herself.

Alice looked majestic in a velvet tunic and pants of swirling crimson and indigo, embellished with lavish gold embroidery. Earrings, necklace, and bracelets of heavy, scrolled gold gleamed against her dark skin.

Marilyn wore brown wool trousers and a shapeless gray sweater. She wasn't color-blind; she just kept forgetting to think about her clothing.

The five curled up on the sofa and settled into the chairs.

Shirley raised her mug. "To the holidays!"

"To the holidays!" the others toasted.

They all sipped the rich hot chocolate, and sighed in unison.

Faye focused dreamily on the twinkling tree. "This is going to be the best Christmas ever!"

Alice chuckled. "Yes, and I'm Glinda, the Good Witch of the North."

"Did you know," Shirley informed them, "in the movie *The Wizard of Oz,* Glinda, the Good Witch of the North, was played by an actress named Billie Burke when she was *fifty-three* years old?"

"You're kidding!" Polly nearly spilled her cocoa. "She looked so young! All that blond hair. The sparkling pink dress. The tiara."

"I wish I had that dress," Faye mused.

"I wish I had her magic wand," Marilyn murmured.

Alice lazily turned her head toward Marilyn. "Really. What would you do with it?"

Marilyn didn't hesitate. "I'd turn my mother back into her normal, independent self. Oh, yes, and renovate Faraday's sexual abilities."

"He's still impotent?" A former hotshot executive, Alice didn't mince words. Besides, they'd helped solve one another's problems before, and were ready to do it again, if they could.

"Always." Marilyn's tone was rich with regret. She'd only discovered the joys of sex in her fifties, and she wanted to make up for lost time.

"You need a magic wand to make his wand magic," Polly joked.

"What's going on with your mother, Marilyn?" Shirley asked.

Marilyn sighed. "My sister says she's going downhill fast. Not physically, mentally. Sharon wants me to have Mother come here for Christmas and stay indefinitely, so I can watch for signs of senility and help her decide whether or not Mother should be 'persuaded' to go into an assisted care facility."

"Hard decision," Faye sympathized.

"I know." Marilyn pinched the bridge of her nose. "Sharon

said she can't make this kind of decision herself, and she's absolutely right."

"How old is your mom?" Alice asked.

"Eighty-five. She lives in Ohio, in the same town where we grew up, only a short drive from my sister's home. I've always felt guilty that I haven't been able to help Mother as much as Sharon has. But I live so far away, and I don't want to give up my position at MIT."

"Not to mention," Alice teased, "you often have trouble keeping your thoughts in the same millennium, never mind on the same species."

"There is that," Marilyn agreed easily.

"Is Faraday spending the holidays with you?" Shirley asked.

Marilyn nodded. "He is. He's got two grown children and some grandchildren, but one lives in California and the other in Ohio."

"It's hard when your kids live so far away." Faye looked wistful. "Thank heavens, Laura and Megan and Lars are coming back east for Christmas. I can't wait to get my hands on my little granddaughter again. I hope she remembers me."

"Faye," Alice bossily reminded her, "you've chatted with her every day on your web-cam."

"Yes, but it's not the same. I want to hold her. Smell her. *Cuddle* her."

"I know exactly what you mean." Polly's son and his family lived only a short drive away geographically, but emotionally, they were on Pluto.

"Will you get to see your grandson for Christmas?" Faye asked.

"I've been invited for Christmas dinner." Polly made a face. "But it will be at Amy's parents' house, and they have piles of relatives, so I know I won't be able to hold Jehoshaphat much. Plus, they're so *virtuous*. I always feel like Mae West visiting the Amish."

"What about Hugh?" Alice, Marilyn, Shirley, and Faye all asked in chorus. Polly had been dating the handsome doctor since April, and their hopes for her were high. Polly deserved someone wonderful.

"Hugh's spending Christmas day with his children and his ex-wife." Polly mimed pulling out her hair. "The size-six, perpetually dependent, helpless little Carol."

"Well, that sucks," Shirley said. "Come have Christmas with us."

"Thanks, but actually, I've been invited to Christmas dinner at Carolyn's, and I just might go there instead."

"Oh, do!" Faye told her, impulsively. "I'll be there, with Aubrey."

"Really?" Polly brightened. "I wonder whether Carolyn would mind if I brought Hugh."

Of course she would, Faye thought silently. Carolyn wants her father to marry *you*. She shifted uncomfortably on the sofa, then leaned forward to grab a cookie. Polly had helped Carolyn during a stressful time in her life, and Carolyn, whose mother had died when Carolyn was just a child, had pounced on Polly as a surrogate mom. Polly was so good-natured and sweet, she didn't seem aware of Carolyn's intentions to match her father up with her, and if she *were* aware, Polly would be so horrified, she'd probably move to Alaska. Faye really liked Polly, the newest member of the Hot Flash Club, and didn't want to cause her any embarrassment.

Alice looked puzzled. "Faye, I thought you said Lars and Laura and baby Megan were coming to have Christmas with you."

"They're coming east, yes," Faye explained. "They're spending Christmas Eve and Christmas morning and most of the day with me. They're going to Lars's family for Christmas dinner."

Alice groaned. "Christmas is so complicated!"

"Yeah, but the food's good," Polly pointed out cheerfully.

Simultaneously, everyone reached forward to grab a cookie. They all laughed.

"I always gain ten pounds over Christmas," Faye moaned, munching.

"It's impossible not to," Alice assured her as she chewed. "It's stress eating."

Polly giggled. "Last night I ate a pepperoni pizza, a pint of ice cream, and two bags of mega-butter popcorn."

"I can trump that," Alice said. "I bought a box of expensive chocolates to take to my bridge group, and last night I sat down and ate them all."

Shirley licked a curl of cream off her spoon. "Hey, Faye. You said you think this will be the best Christmas ever. Want to elaborate?"

"Well, I didn't mean *ever*," Faye corrected herself. "The best Christmases I ever had were with Jack, when Laura was a little girl. Christmas is really about children. There's nothing like the joy on their faces, the surprise when they see all the gifts under the tree. This Christmas, Megan is three, old enough to really appreciate everything. Plus, I've moved into my darling, new little house—not that I didn't love living in my condo here at The Haven, Shirley," Faye hastened to assure her friend. "But it's so nice to have a little place all my own. I've got three bedrooms, you know, and one is for me, one is a guest bedroom, and one is for Megan! I painted the room myself—"

"—I saw it the other day," Polly told the others. "It's exquisite. A little girl's *dream* room."

"I can't wait for Megan to see it!" Faye beamed. "She's *so* clever! Do you know what she said? Laura told her to eat the crusts on her bread, and Megan said, 'Mommy, don't you know? They only put crusts on the bread so you won't get peanut butter on your fingers when you're eating the sandwich.' "

Alice was amused. "Sounds like she's going to be a lawyer like her father."

"I've bought so many presents I feel guilty." Faye searched the other women's faces. "But isn't this what Christmas is all about? Giving lots and lots of fabulous presents? Spoiling your family?"

"I think it's about making dreams come true." Shirley's voice was rich with longing.

"First of all, it's a religious holiday," Marilyn reminded them.

"And now it's become one gigantic gimmick for our consumer economy," Alice weighed in with a frown. "We're bombarded with ads and sentimental scenes of smiling families around the tree. We're brainwashed with syrupy Christmas music and completely unrealistic promises that our families will be happy if only little Johnny gets a video game or little Mary gets the right doll."

"Are things okay with Gideon?" Faye asked gently.

"Why do you ask?" Alice demanded. "Christmas *sucks,* whether I'm happy or not!"

"I sort of agree with Alice," Polly cut in. "Well, I don't think Christmas *sucks,* but I do think it's gotten far too commercialized. And it does raise unrealistic expectations."

"But where's the joy in life, without unrealistic expectations?" Shirley cried.

Marilyn cocked her head, studying Shirley. "I'm surprised at you, Shirley. I would have thought you'd tell us that Christmas is a festival of light during the darkest days. That it's about hope for new life during the coldest season of the year."

Shirley blushed. "I *do* think all that. But you know, I never got to have children, and my three former husbands were all assholes, so I never had a really *happy* Christmas before. I was never with someone I loved, who loved me in return."

"So what dreams do you think will come true this Christmas?" Alice tried to sound casual. She knew it made Shirley unhappy, but Alice distrusted Shirley's beau, that jackal Justin. She just hoped that Shirley understood that this wariness came from her protective love of her friend.

Shirley gulped. She shouldn't be nervous, she told herself. When was she going to grow up? When was she going to stop being a coward? Hadn't she proven herself enough already? She'd been the creator of The Haven, and for two years now, she'd run the spa intelligently, just as if she were a clever person with good business sense. Her friends should trust her judgment. They should be *reasonable* about her forthcoming announcement.

Yeah, and pigs would fly out her butt.

This Christmas she was going to give Justin a gift that would change his life. She was *certain* that even though he was twelve years younger than she, Justin loved her, too, just as sincerely. Her Hot Flash friends had to stop fretting. Sure, Justin was handsome, but if he *had* looked at other women—and who could blame him, they were always looking at him!—that was *all* he'd done. He was in her bed every night.

"Well?" Alice prompted. It didn't take a psychic to know Shirley was feeling guilty. Something was up. "You're giving Justin a computer for Christmas, right?"

"Of course not." Shirley faked a laugh and sipped her cocoa, stalling. "He already has one." What she was giving Justin cost a lot more than a computer.

But that was nothing compared to what she suspected he was going to give her.

"Shir–ley," Alice wheedled, trying not to sound like a mother looking at a kid with a suspicious bulge in his backpack.

Shirley stalled. "I'm spending Christmas day with Justin and his kids."

"He's got three kids, right?" Faye asked.

"Right." Shirley held up a finger as she munched another bite of cookie. "Spring's thirteen, her sister Angel is fifteen. Ben's ten; he has a different mother from Spring and Angel. The girls live in Stoneham with their mother and stepfather, and Ben lives on the Cape with his mother and grandmother. The girls don't like Ben and he doesn't like them, and Justin would prefer to have Ben on Christmas Eve and the girls on Christmas day, but Ben's mother insists on having Ben on Christmas Eve and Christmas morning, and the girls' mother insists . . . Well, you get the picture."

"And you think this Christmas is going to be about making dreams come true?" Polly looked skeptical.

And Alice looked downright disbelieving.

Shirley decided not to tell them now. Why should she, after all? Justin was the recipient; he should know about it first. She could tell them later.

"But you see," she babbled evasively, "I finally have enough money to give really cool gifts! I've never had this kind of money before—"

Alice shook her head impatiently. "You're not rich, Shirley. You're just solvent, and you're working hard for every penny you make, and don't forget, you're getting older and you need to save for the future. You *are* sixty-two."

"Thank you, Mrs. Scrooge," Shirley sniffed.

Faye, playing peacemaker, changed the subject. "Alice, are you spending Christmas with Gideon?"

Alice knew she was being headed off at the pass. But why was she so worried for Shirley when the other three seemed to be perfectly comfortable with Justin? "Christmas Eve, we're having Alan and Jennifer to dinner. They're going down to the Cape for Christmas day with her folks. Christmas day we'll spend with Gideon's kids."

"You like them, don't you?" Polly asked.

"I like them all fine." Alice let out a big fat sigh. "I don't know why I'm so *cranky* these days."

"Hormones don't take holidays," Polly said.

"It's not just that," Alice admitted. "I've gotten cranky since I've retired." Seeing Shirley's mouth twitch, she said, "All right, I was probably cranky *before* I retired. That might be why I was such a dynamite executive at TransContinent." Alice shook her head in frustration. Her boiling energy, creative vigor, and, all right, slightly anal-compulsive need to get things done right and *soon* had carried her into the top echelons of a major insurance company during the days when most women, especially black women, were thrilled to stop scrubbing corporate floors and become secretaries. Alice had been *someone*. She'd been a *force*. And she missed that.

"You need to find something to do," Shirley advised. "Something more than playing bridge."

"You think I don't know that?" Alice snapped.

"You need a grandchild," Faye said in a dreamy voice.

"I already have grandchildren," Alice reminded her.

"But they live in Texas," Faye persisted, "and you seldom see them."

Alice gave Faye a level stare. "Faye, you know children are just not my thing. Oh, I loved my sons like a mother panther when they were young, and I took good care of them, even though I worked. I've got photo albums full of smiles. But babies in general aren't my thing."

"What will you do if Alan and Jennifer get married and have children?" Polly asked.

"Let's not go there." Alice still didn't like Jennifer. And it was *not* because Jennifer was white. After all, her four best friends were white. It was more that when Alice first became aware of Jennifer D'Annucio's existence, Jennifer had been having an affair with Faye's son-in-law, Lars.

Now, Alice, she told herself, don't be so judgmental. The best love she'd had in her life had been with a married man when she was thirty-five. She didn't consider herself less trustworthy because she'd had that affair, and she refused to let herself think less of Jennifer for her affair, either. Still, she was glad handsome Lars and his family had moved to California, even as she sympathized with Faye, who was *all about* grandchildren, that her family was so far away.

"Oh, *damn*!" Marilyn flew up out of her chair.

"What's wrong?" Polly asked, alarmed.

Marilyn's words were muffled as she tugged her sweater up over her head. She clasped it to her chest for modesty, her flushed face and chest clear evidence of the problem.

"I'm so *sick* of these hot flashes!" she cried.

"Me, too," Faye commiserated. "I don't understand the *point* of it."

Marilyn hurried to a window and pressed her burning face against the cold glass. "Nature's telling us we're past childbearing age."

"Hel-*lo*! I *know* that!" Alice grumbled. "I can look in the mirror and *see* that."

"Nature designed our reproductive systems before human beings had mirrors." Marilyn grabbed a magazine and fanned her face. "It's possible that in the evolutionary process, hot flashes once served a purpose which has become irrelevant. Perhaps in fifty years, or five hundred, women won't have hot flashes."

"I can't wait that long," Polly quipped.

"I know," Marilyn lamented. "It's not just the surge of heat I hate. It's the way it derails my mind. I'm making mistakes when I teach my classes, or I lose my place, or forget what I'm saying right in the middle of a sentence. It's embarrassing."

"At least you don't gain weight simply by breathing," Faye consoled her. "Aubrey's taking me out to wonderful restaurants so often, I'm ballooning up again."

"You look wonderful, Faye," Alice assured her. "I've decided to stop fussing about my weight. I enjoy eating, and so does Gideon, and he likes me the way I am, nice and squashable."

"That's fine, as long as your health isn't affected," Shirley warned. "Statistics show that the leanest people live the longest."

"Yeah, but do they have as much fun?" Rebelliously, Alice grabbed another cookie.

Marilyn was cooling down. She pulled her sweater back on and returned to her chair. "I've decided to take a sabbatical starting this June. I keep thinking perhaps my brain is just overloaded. I mean, in the past two years my husband left me for a younger woman, I had the most fabulous sex of my life with a guy who turned out to be a creep, I met all of you and joined the Hot Flash Club and the board of The Haven, I became a grandmother, and I started dating Faraday."

"That's enough to blow your fuses," Alice confirmed.

"What will you do?" Faye asked Marilyn. "Take a trip? Write a book?"

Marilyn shrugged. "Before I can plan anything, I've got to deal with my mother. I'll have a chance to see whether she needs assisted living when she's here over Christmas."

"*Christmas,*" Shirley crooned happily.

Alice rolled her eyes. "How can you be so perpetually hopeful?"

"It's a choice, I guess," Shirley told her.

Marilyn leaned forward to skewer Shirley with a look. "Um, you might also add that you have a lover who's good in bed, and no demented relatives."

Polly chuckled. "Remember 'Old Maid,' that card game we played when we were kids?"

"Oh, yes." Faye grinned. "There were all kinds of crazy characters who came in pairs. Like Greasy Grimes and Betty Bumps. But there was just one Old Maid. The point was to be the one at the end of the game who didn't hold the Old Maid."

"Now the goal is not to *be* the Old Maid," Alice joked.

Polly brushed cookie crumbs off her bosom. "I'm thinking 'Old Maid' was a rehearsal for real life. For example, my daughter-in-law is 'Princess Insanely Possessive Prig Pot.' "

Alice laughed. "Tell us how you really feel, Polly!"

Marilyn giggled. "Yeah, and Faraday's the 'Limp Lothario.' "

"Sure, they're flawed." Shirley spoke up before the others came up with an unflattering nickname for Justin. "But we still love them. We still want them to have a wonderful Christmas."

"We can't make other people happy," Alice pointed out sensibly.

"No," Polly agreed, "we can't. But we can do everything we can to set the stage for happiness."

Faye said, "You're right, Polly. That's what I'm going to do this Christmas, for my daughter and my granddaughter and my son-in-law."

"That's what we'll all do for those we love," Shirley said.

"I'll drink to that." Alice raised her mug.

"I'll drink to that, too," Polly said, "but first, can I have more Reddi-whip?"

On the night before Christmas, all through the house, Faye wandered in her robe. It was two A.M. She was completely incapable of sleep. This afternoon, her daughter Laura, her son-in-law Lars, and her adorable baby granddaughter were arriving for the holidays. Faye was so excited she was nearly demented.

Megan was three years old now, and Faye was going to give the little girl a Christmas she'd remember always! In her exuberance, Faye had put up not one, but three Christmas trees.

The largest one was in front of the living room window. She loved the way the tree looked from outside, framed perfectly by the window, the lights shining with the radiance of home. She'd decorated it with all the ornaments she and Jack had used when Laura was a child.

The second tree was in the kitchen. Inspired by Polly's gingerbread ornaments for the tree at The Haven, Faye had rummaged around at the back of her utensil drawer and found her box of Christmas cookie cutters. All day, Faye had baked and decorated in a kind of domestic trance. She'd filled five bags of frosting with different colors and let her much-ignored artistic side go wild as she squeezed smiling faces and silly designs on sugar Santas and snickerdoodle stars for her kitchen tree.

But the *pièce de résistance* was in Megan's bedroom, where Faye had put a tiny Christmas tree in a pink pot with white bunnies. She'd decorated it with miniature lights and twenty-five fairies. There were twenty-five simply because Faye had made them all herself, out of pipe cleaners, yarn, papier-mâché, and fabric. It had been meticulous, intricate work, and by the time she'd finished the twenty-fifth fairy, her body refused to do more. Her back, arms, and eyes ached from concentrating on such minutiae. She felt as bent and twisted as an ancient Chinese peasant after years of embroidering silks. But the tree, when finished, was *magical,* a little girl's fantasy of fairies, sequins, tulle, beads, and bows.

Faye could not *wait* to see Megan's face when she saw the trees!

She hadn't ignored Laura and Lars, either. Piles of gorgeously wrapped presents surrounded the living room tree, and in the late afternoon, about twenty of Laura and Lars's closest friends were arriving for an informal holiday party. Faye was making her father's famous eggnog, which involved a sinful amount of vanilla ice cream and bourbon. The refrigerator was stuffed with cheeses and exotic olives, caviar and salmon. In the early afternoon, she'd start putting together little canapés for the party, just before she drove out to the airport.

For now, since she had insomnia, she might as well set up the dining room table for the party. Maybe that would tire her out and she'd be able to catch a few hours' sleep. She knew she was in a state of holiday hysteria. Perhaps finalizing a few more preparations would calm her down. Kneeling, she reached into the bottom of the kitchen cupboard to dig out the enormous crystal punch bowl. It hadn't been used for three years, not since her husband Jack died, and the sight of it released a flood of memories.

She and Jack had been married for thirty-five years. His death had opened the floodgates of a dark ocean in her heart, with powerful tides beyond her control and waves that pulled her under and threatened to keep her there. Her ability to paint the beautiful still lifes and scenes that had once brought her joy and some small renown had drowned in grief, too. Nine months after his death, Faye had tried to paint again, only to discover that her work was accurate, but without soul, vibrancy, resonance. She gave it up. Another enormous loss.

Thank heavens for her daughter and granddaughter and for the love of her Hot Flash friends, her lifelines to the living world.

She rose, lifting the punch bowl to the counter. Had the damned thing always been so heavy? Yes, but she'd been younger, stronger, once. At times like this, her body made her age quite clear. Carrying it over to the sink was such an effort, it brought on a hot flash. She tore off her robe, ran a glass of cold water, and held it to her forehead, trying to cool down.

The gingerbread people smiled at her from the kitchen Christmas tree. Jack would have wanted Faye to go on with her life, to savor every moment of it, to be happy. And she wanted to provide a good role model for her daughter. So she had muddled on as cheerfully as she knew how.

It had been tough, selling the house where she and Jack had raised Laura. It had been like severing the line to a gleaming yacht whose cargo was the domestic reality of her younger life—favorite fabrics, familiar wood, comforting patterns of light falling through windows—and watching it float off into the mists, gone forever.

But the money she'd been able to give Laura and Lars had helped them buy their own home. More than that, it had served as a kind of bridge away from a rough patch in their marriage. Faye would have given up anything to help her daughter.

And this past year of living in the little condo at The Haven had been good for Faye in many ways. She'd learned to appreciate new spaces, new views, new possibilities. Now that she'd settled into her own new little house, she thought she might be able to enjoy quite a few years of contentment. Perhaps, even, of happiness.

She was doing work she loved, teaching courses in art and art therapy at The Haven. She had as full a social calendar as she wanted, cheerfully punctuated at least once a month with a Friday-night Hot Flash Club dinner at Legal Seafoods.

And now she was actually dating. *Seriously* dating. It was amusing, and terrifying, too.

"What would *you* have thought of Aubrey, Jack?" Faye asked, a little startled by the sound of her voice in the silence of the kitchen. "If you want me to stop dating him, you'd better give me a sign."

She had met Aubrey Sperry this April at The Haven's spring open house, and to her immense surprise, the attraction between them had been mutual, immediate, and intense. They'd kissed the first night they met, like a couple of hot-blooded teenagers, in the parking lot of The Haven, stretching toward one another over the gearshift of Aubrey's Jaguar. His mouth had tasted like peppermints, and his fine white hair had been soft as down. His fingers along her neck, his kisses on her throat, had been as delicate and tantalizing as the first drops of spring rain, and only because she didn't want to startle him did she refrain from shouting out, "Hallelujah!" for her body did feel born again.

But a sharp rapping on the window had startled them. They'd pulled apart to find Carolyn, Aubrey's only child and extraordinarily bossy daughter, glaring at them, as if she were Aubrey's mother and was about to yank him out of the car and spank him for misbehaving.

Faye could understand Carolyn's possessive concerns. Carolyn and Aubrey shared the ownership and responsibility for the Sperry Paper Company, which had been handed down through the generations. No wonder Carolyn had freaked out when, the previous fall, Aubrey had, on a whim, married a much younger woman who had *appeared* naïve and sweet but turned out to be manipulative and mercenary.

In a way, Faye had been part of the chain of responsibility for this revelation. She, Alice, Marilyn, and Shirley, the founders of the Hot Flash Club and of The Haven, had followed their chosen life directive, which was, in a word, *Interfere*. They'd realized that four of The Haven's clients needed help, so they'd organized a special Jacuzzi/aromatherapy encounter for the women, who quickly became friends, and did what women friends have done since the beginning of time: plotted clever ways to solve one another's problems.

Aubrey's wife's deceitful scheme was destroyed, and Aubrey's brief marriage was annulled.

And Aubrey's ego was crushed. He was seventy. He'd wanted to be youthful and virile. Instead, he'd been exposed as a fool.

In their most intimate, tender moments together, Aubrey had confessed his humiliation to Faye. He did not go so far as to say that he was anxious about his possible sexual performance, but their initial adolescent lust was cooled by the realities of life and aging. Faye let him know that she could be patient. After all, she was anxious, too.

They'd been dating for almost eight months now, and had not yet progressed past affectionate kisses and fraternal hugs. But that was all right. They'd both been so overwhelmed with moving houses.

Faye had done the lion's share of sorting through her possessions of over thirty years when, the year before, she'd sold her house and pared down to the bare necessities for her condo at The Haven. She'd sold some of her heirlooms, given stuff away, and rented a storage facility for furniture with which she couldn't bear to part.

It had been fun for a while, in a clean, crisp kind of way, to live in small rooms on the third floor of a building whose grounds were groomed by professional gardeners. But quickly she realized she wanted to have her own place, with her own yard, her own flowers, her own bird feeders.

So she'd bought this little Cape Cod located halfway between The Haven, where she taught part time, and Boston, with its theater, museums, and art galleries. During the past few months, in a kind of domestic ecstasy, she'd chosen new rugs, new wallpapers, new furniture, and unpacked her treasures from the storage units, rediscovering each beloved possession with a new delight. She'd hung her favorite still life, the painting Jack had loved the most, one she'd painted only a year before his death, above the mantel in the living room. She hoped it might inspire her to return to her work.

So far, she hadn't set up her easel or picked up a brush.

But in the fall, she'd planned and planted her garden with spring blooms. Digging into the ground, crumbling rich fertilizer into the dark earth, preparing healthy beds for the plump garlic-shaped bulbs, had been a satisfying and deeply sensual experience. She felt connected to the land, as if she'd planted part of her heart among the flowers. Afterward, she was too tired for much more than a microwave dinner and an evening with a book. She didn't miss the energetic demands of sexual passion, and she very much enjoyed the daily phone conversations with Aubrey.

Aubrey's relocation had been much more complicated. He, his daughter Carolyn, her husband Hank, and their baby had lived in a magnificent, if slightly Edward Gorey–esque, Victorian mansion riding high on a hill overlooking the town of Sperry. Big as an ark, the dwelling had been built by Aubrey's grandmother at the turn of the century, when servants as well as family were housed there. Aubrey had his own wing, and Carolyn had hers, and there were common rooms, and a plucky, though overwhelmed, housekeeper, who tried to keep the pantries full and the dust at least rearranged.

But the house was dark and inconvenient. Hank had been the one to suggest they move. He and Carolyn had bought a modern, sleek, practical new house near the mill, where Carolyn was executive vice president. Aubrey, officially president but eagerly easing out of the position, letting Carolyn take over the reins, had opted to buy a handsome apartment forty minutes to the east, in the middle of Boston, on Beacon Hill, near his various private clubs and the restaurants he loved to frequent.

The process of breaking up the Sperry home, which was practically a museum, and would actually become a museum for the town, was a staggeringly exhausting endeavor. The Sperrys had antiques and oil paintings needing expert appraisal, and it all required the services of several lawyers, which of course made the process even more time-consuming. Some weeks passed when Aubrey barely had the energy to phone Faye to say hello before he tumbled into bed.

So it was no wonder they hadn't yet tumbled into bed together.

It just might prove to be a problem, Faye thought, leaning against the kitchen counter, staring out her window at the moonlight on the snow, that she and Aubrey had not been able to consummate their relationship before they remembered how old, creaky, and saggy they were. Now that they had the time and the distance to regard the matter intelligently, they both had gotten shy about their aging bodies.

Aubrey was such an elegant man, with a luxurious wardrobe and courtly manners, so meticulous about his grooming. He was actually shocked, Faye thought, to find that in spite of his rigorous personal hygiene, his body had betrayed him. Arthritis made him stoop and creak. He had to pop pills or suffer painful indigestion and even so, what he called "dyspepsia" called up embarrassing burps at inappropriate times and often, if he forgot his medicine, made him nearly double over in pain. His beautiful white hair was thinning, his pink scalp showing through, the few surviving strands at the front of his head crinkling and refusing to lie down, waving in the air like survivors from a sinking ship.

Still, he was head-turningly handsome. Faye enjoyed entering a party or the theater on his arm. More than that, she enjoyed looking at him, admiring his aristocratic profile, the way his face changed subtly when he was amused or aroused. Because she was thirteen years younger, she thought she'd be able to shut out the wailing Greek chorus of her own vanity when they ever did get around to making love—especially if they kept the lights off.

What would Laura think of Aubrey? Faye had told her daughter all about him, and Laura had assured her mother she was delighted to know Faye was dating. Aubrey was coming to the little Christmas Eve party tonight and would stay for a cozy family dinner afterward.

Faye imagined it: the four of them around the table, Aubrey charming Laura and Lars as they talked, and adorable little Megan on Faye's lap. It had been six months since Faye had flown out to

California to visit her daughter's family. Yes, they had "talked" via their web-cams almost every day, but children took shy easily. Would Megan allow Faye to put her to bed? Faye had bought a rocking chair for Megan's room. Closing her eyes, she conjured up a vision of perfect holiday happiness: rocking her granddaughter to sleep, softly singing the same lullabies she'd once sung to Laura, gazing down at her grandchild's face, while downstairs the others got to know one another over coffee and Dutch apple pie, Laura's favorite dessert.

Her thoughts lulled her. The sweet, heavy brandy of sleepiness flowed through her blood, weighing down her limbs. Leaving the punch bowl on the counter, Faye left the kitchen and, flicking off the lights as she went, returned to the living room. She lay on her side on the sofa, pulling a woven tapestry throw over her for warmth. This familiar old trick had often allowed her to sink into sleep on nights when she tossed and turned in her own bed. She knew she would sleep now, and she was so grateful.

The lights of the Christmas tree shone in the room, like dozens of bright angels keeping watch.

Faye woke to find the sun streaming in. Great! No weather problems would keep Laura's plane from landing.

She stretched, feeling wonderfully rested. Glancing at the clock, she gave a little cry of terror—she'd slept almost until nine o'clock!

Racing into the kitchen, she started her coffee, then phoned American Airlines to see whether Laura's plane had left yet. A robotic voice presented "options," but of course the option to speak with a living human being wasn't one of them. Faye had to suffer through several minutes of pushing buttons and negotiating with a system that somehow, even though computerized, managed to be as smug and implacable as a high school principal. And it *was* like being back in school; it was like taking a test. The computer had all the power. She had to concentrate fiercely on what the robot said, and if, God forbid, she pressed the wrong number, she'd flunk and have to start all over again.

The whole process was so infuriating, it made her erupt in a Mount St. Helens of a hot flash. Really, Faye thought, there should be an option for menopausal women, who could scarcely remember their own names: "If you belong to the Hot Flash Club, press *I* for *Insane* and someone will be with you instantly."

Finally she keyed in the flight number and was connected to an information bank. Laura's flight had not yet departed.

Oh, no! The plane was due to leave at nine in the morning, and it was two minutes after nine! What had happened? Weren't they going to be able to make it? There couldn't be a blizzard in California—my God! What if there'd been an earthquake?

She raced into her tiny family room and turned on the television, quickly clicking the remote control to CNN. After a few minutes of watching the news, she calmed down. No earthquake reported. No disaster in L.A. All right. Fine. Everything was fine. The plane might be late—

—because while it was nine o'clock here, it was only six o'clock on the West Coast, she remembered, laughing out loud with relief. What an idiot she was! She had to *calm down*!

She finished her coffee, then went into the dining room, found the damask tablecloth, and flapped it out—she'd always liked the way the cloth *flew* out, exuberant, like a bird delighted to spread its white wings—over the long dining room table. As she drank her coffee, she nibbled on Christmas cookies and her homemade, salted, candied pecans. Perhaps not the healthiest breakfast, but it was the holidays, hardly time even to consider dieting.

She rinsed the punch bowl and set it on the table, then brought out the punch cups, the ladle, the Christmas napkins, the pitchers for juice and sparkling water for those who didn't want punch, the plates, and the silver. She stacked Christmas CDs in her stereo player.

When the phone rang, she jumped so hard she nearly launched herself into space.

"Hello, my dear," Aubrey said. "I thought I'd check in to see if you need anything for tonight."

"Oh, thanks, Aubrey, that's so kind of you." His voice made her smile. "But I think I've got it under control. I'm just scurrying around, getting things ready for the little party."

"Then I won't keep you," Aubrey told her. "But you know I'm here if you need me. You've got my cell phone number."

She grinned like a schoolgirl. How sweet was that, to say *I'm here if you need me*! Oh, gosh, this really was going to be the best Christmas ever!

She unwrapped the twisted red, white, and green Christmas candles and put them in their tall silver holders. When the florist arrived with the flowers she'd ordered for the mantel, dining room table, and guest room, Faye was still in her robe, with so much left to do.

Hurriedly she showered and dressed, then drove off to pick up the turkey and the bluefish pâté from the health food store. She stopped at Wilson's Farm to buy apples, oranges, clementines, grapes, and several kinds of sweet rolls for tomorrow morning's breakfast. Her pantry and freezer were crammed with food already, but she wanted to have an abundance, wanted no one to be deprived of a thing.

It took her four trips to carry everything from the car to the house, and by the time she'd unpacked it all, she was drenched from a hot flash and trembling. Collapsing on a chair, she munched whatever was closest on the kitchen table. A few grapes. An onion bagel with a chunk of cheddar. She brewed a new pot of decaf with one hand while punching numbers in the phone handset with the other. Yes, the flight from L.A. had left on time, and was expected to arrive in Boston on time.

Her heart leapt with joy.

She'd better get busy! A huge pan of lasagna was in her refrigerator, dinner for tonight after the holiday cocktail party, so that was under control. It was the party itself she had to get ready for. She clicked on the radio to the classical station and heavenly Christmas music accompanied her as she chopped, diced, stirred, and spread.

Her hand was trembling. She needed something to calm her down—a glass of wine? No! She had to drive out to the airport in just—oh my God, in just one hour! She would not allow herself to impair her already excited senses. Chocolate. She needed chocolate.

From the freezer, she took a pint of Ben and Jerry's New York Super Fudge Chunk, which she'd always found worked better than a trip to the psychiatrist *and* a couple of Valium, and faster. So what if she automatically gained two pounds? It was the holidays; she had no time to worry about her weight.

She nuked the ice cream in the microwave for thirty seconds, just the perfect amount of time to get it to the perfect degree of melted richness. Digging a spoon in, she ate directly from the carton as she rushed upstairs to dress. Quickly, she removed her shirt and pulled on a Christmas sweater she'd ordered especially to please her granddaughter. Bright red, it was decorated with a scene of Santa in his sleigh, his sack bulging with presents, his white beard blowing back in the wind. The string of reindeer wrapped around the sweater, ending with Rudolph with his red nose on Faye's back shoulder.

Admiring the sweater, her eye fell on her clock. Oh, no! It was already one forty-five. Laura's plane landed at Logan at three! It would take Faye a good hour to drive there, and that would be only if the traffic was not too congested.

Hurriedly, she kicked off the ancient loafers she wore to do housework, grabbed the half-eaten carton of ice cream, and started down the stairs in her thick wool socks. Her purse was on the hall table. She'd pull on her boots, coat, gloves, and just *go*. The car keys were in—

Suddenly, she slipped. Her body was sailing in the air.

"AAAH!" she cried, throwing out her hands to grab something, *anything.* In a flash, she hit the wood floor at the foot of the stairs. Her head hit *hard* on the last step. For a moment she actually saw stars. Then everything went black.

She was dreaming of Christmas when a car alarm sounded rudely in the distance. Why was she sprawled out on the cold, hard surface of a parking lot? And who had run over her? Why wasn't someone coming to help her?

Faye opened her eyes. She was collapsed in the front hall. Her ankle hurt. Her back hurt. Over in the corner, by the umbrella stand, lay an ice-cream carton in a puddle of brown liquid.

The noise wasn't a car alarm; it was the telephone. She'd been lying here long enough for the ice cream to melt—Laura!

Faye pushed herself up. A searing pain shot through her, beginning in her neck and radiating out to her shoulders and back.

The phone continued to ring. Carefully, Faye turned her arm so she could see her watch. Three thirty-seven. Laura's plane had landed, and here Faye was, on the floor.

"All right," she said to herself in the calm voice she'd used years ago when Laura was a child, "it's going to be all right. If you can't pick up Laura and Lars and Megan, they'll simply grab a cab. They're not helpless. You need to get yourself to the kitchen, swallow a couple of aspirin, and you'll be fine."

Slowly, sensibly, she tried to roll over.

Her left ankle exploded in fireworks.

She fell back against the newel post, eyes closed, gasping with pain.

"*Shit!*" she cursed. "This isn't right. This is terrible! It's *Christmas!*"

The phone continued to ring, a shrill, demanding, exasperating sound.

Well, if she couldn't walk to the phone, she'd damn well *crawl.*

Resting her left ankle on top of her right knee, she pushed with her right foot. Awkwardly, like a debilitated seal, she scooted on her back down the hall.

Someday, she knew, she would find this funny.

Right now, she felt only pain and frustration.

Tears ran down her cheeks. The phone rang and rang. After what seemed like a century, she bumped off the wood floor and onto the tile of the kitchen. A few more shoves, and she reached the alcove where she kept her phone book and phone. The demon clamped on her neck would not allow her to sit up, so she lifted her good leg and clumsily kicked at the ringing phone until it clunked to the floor.

"Mom?" a tinny voice said.

Grimacing in agony, Faye reached over and grabbed the handset.

"Laura!"

"Mom? I've been calling for ages. We're at the airport, we—"

"Laura, I've fallen and I can't get up."

Laura laughed. For a moment, Faye was horrified. How could Laura laugh at her? Then she remembered the television ad for an alarm button one could wear around one's neck. The actress who displayed it was a little old lady who quavered, "I've fallen and I can't get up." For some reason, which at the moment completely escaped Faye, she and Laura had always laughed maniacally at this ad, and so had everyone else she knew.

"I'm not joking, Laura." Faye strained to sound firm instead of frantic. "I fell down the stairs. I've twisted my ankle, and I've done something to my neck."

"Oh, poor Mommy!"

Laura's words were muffled. Faye could hear her repeating the information to Lars.

"Listen, Mommy," Laura said, clear once again. "We're going to grab a cab to the house. I want you to hang up now and phone your neighbors. Have someone get over there—"

"Darling, I can wait until you and Lars get here."

"No, Mommy," Laura insisted. "You need to get medical attention as soon as possible. I don't want you lying on the cold kitchen floor, and if you've injured yourself, you'll need to have it taken care of as soon as possible. Who knows how long it's going to take us to get a cab here at the airport the day before Christmas? You should absolutely *not* wait."

Faye was speechless. Who *was* this person ordering her around? Three years ago, Laura had been a neurotic mass of indecision. Obviously motherhood had opened up new pathways in her brain.

"I hate to bother people on Christmas Eve," Faye equivocated. "And I haven't really gotten to know anyone well enough—"

"Then phone 911."

Who are you and what have you done with the real Laura? Faye wanted to demand. "Oh, Laura, surely that's a little dramatic."

"Mom. Can you stand up? No, right? That's not dramatic. That's real. Your health is real. Why do you think there's a 911 in the first place? I'm going to hang up now. You phone 911. I'll phone you back in a few minutes." Decisively, she clicked off.

Faye felt like a giant tuna as she lay gasping on the kitchen floor. A really *pissed-off* giant tuna. She understood that Laura was trying to be helpful, but did she have to sound so bossy? Her daughter had been so officious! She'd made Faye feel like a child. A helpless, indecisive, pathetic little child! I'll be *damned,* Faye thought perversely, if I'm going to dial 911. She wasn't exactly old, feeble, and desolate! She had a gentleman friend—although she didn't want Aubrey to see her like this, a quivering pile of helpless blubber. Well, she had her Hot Flash friends—Polly! Polly was dating Hugh, who was a doctor!

She pressed the dial button for Polly.

The answering machine came on. Cheerful Polly had taped a few measures of Christmas carols before and after her message, and Faye nearly snarled with impatience as she waited for the beep.

"Polly? It's Faye, and I've done something really stupid. I've fallen, and I think I hurt my neck, and I was wondering whether Hugh might be there, perhaps he could suggest something . . ."

Faye clicked off. Who knew when Polly would get the message? Maybe she was better, now that she'd rested. She tried to sit up. Her neck made her literally scream with pain. *Fine!* She punched Alice's number.

"Hello?"

Thank God! Alice was home. She listened to Faye's appeal, and broke into a hearty laugh. "I told you Christmas sucks! I'll be right there."

Laura called again. "Mom, we're in line to get a cab. Looks like it will be a twenty-minute wait. Did you phone 911?"

"Help is on the way," Faye dissembled. "Now, darling, I'll probably be gone when you get here, so the spare key is under the porcupine boot-scraper on the front stoop—"

"Gee, Mom, why don't you just paint a sign: *Want to burgle me? Look in the most obvious place!*"

Faye swallowed a retort. "Your beds are all made up, and the food for the party is completely prepared." Without warning, an enormous wave of self-pity swept up through her chest. She burst into tears.

"Mommy?" Laura's voice softened.

"I won't be here to see Megan see her bedroom and her little tree!" Faye cried.

"Well, of course you will," Laura said sensibly. "Your injuries don't sound life-threatening. Look, Mommy, don't worry about anything. Just focus on taking care of yourself, okay?"

"Okay," Faye agreed. She knew Laura was being kind, but her words made her feel like some kind of decrepit old invalid.

But *damn*, she *was* some kind of decrepit old invalid, if she couldn't even get up off the floor!

Really, she couldn't believe this. Not this, now, on Christmas Eve. Not with her granddaughter coming. Faye couldn't help it. She broke into serious sobs of self-pity, boo-hooing so hard it hurt her neck and her sinuses clogged up with mucus and she couldn't even get up to get a handkerchief to blow her nose.

―――――――――――

The front door banged and Alice swept into the house. From Faye's vantage point on the floor, Alice looked even taller than she really was. She wore her ankle-length mink—no one would dare spit on Alice!—and it billowed around her like a monarch's mantle as she strode across the kitchen floor.

"Good grief, honey, you look awful!" Alice knelt next to Faye. "Where does it hurt?"

"My ankle. And my neck."

"Your neck, huh? Can't take any chances with that. I'm going to call 911, get an ambulance here. Don't argue. And you're cold as ice."

In just seconds, Alice had the phone in one hand and a blanket in the other, multitasking, as usual.

―――――――――――

Four hours later, at eight o'clock on Christmas Eve, Faye was released from Mount Auburn Hospital. She'd been examined, x-rayed, ultrasounded, fitted with a soft ankle cast, presented with crutches, and enclosed in a neck brace that squeezed the flab around her jawline up, so her head seemed to be resting on a ring of Silly Putty.

"I look like a walrus," Faye complained.

"And a very pretty one, too," Laura assured her.

Alice had stayed with Faye for the first three hours, until Laura could get her husband and child settled in her mother's house. Then Laura drove Faye's car to the hospital so Alice could return to her own Christmas Eve plans.

The good news was that no bones were broken. Faye's ankle was only sprained, but sprains could be the devil to heal, the physician assured her. She had to stay off her feet.

Christmas, and she had to stay off her feet!

The bad news was that the tests had revealed Faye's neck showed signs of osteoarthritis, caused by aging. Faye moaned when the physician told her *that*. Now, when everyone asked her what had happened, she'd have to confess that she was *aging*. As if it weren't already apparent. None of her vertebrae were cracked, but she was supposed to wear her neck brace for the next few days, to support her neck and her weakened, arthritic old neck bones.

"It couldn't have happened at a better time," Laura assured Faye as they drove through the dark evening. "Lars and I are here, we can take care of you. You can lounge about in bed or on the sofa and we'll wait on you hand and foot."

"But it's Christmas!" Faye protested. She'd forced herself to be cheerful in the hospital, but now here came the tears again. She'd had the pain medication prescription filled but refused to take one of the pills until bedtime. She didn't want to be dizzy and drugged on Christmas Eve. She *had* taken two aspirin, which helped, but they didn't completely alleviate the pain. The whole time it was as if someone were pressing an iron set to "linen" up against her neck.

Laura reached over to pat her mother's hand. "Hey, remember. If Fate gives you lemons, make lemonade!"

"Oh, no!" Faye groaned. How many times during Laura's childhood had Faye given her exactly that advice? "Did that irritate you as much as it irritates me?"

Laura tossed her a grin. "What do you think?"

Faye smiled, sniffing back her tears. It was, after all, *lovely* to be in her daughter's company again. And if Laura had become, well, *assertive*, that was a good thing, a sign she'd really grown up. Faye closed her eyes, resting. She'd have some Champagne when they got home. Certainly there'd be plenty of it. The new *über*-competent Laura had used her cell phone to call everyone who was invited to the Christmas Eve party to explain Faye's fall and regretfully cancel. What a disappointment for Laura and Lars, to miss seeing their friends! And all that food going to waste!

Aubrey had been wonderful, though. He'd wanted to come to

the hospital, but Faye had asked him not to—she hadn't known how long she'd be there, not to mention (and she did *not* mention) how very much she did not want him to see her in such a vulnerable and unattractive state, carted around in a hospital gown like a suet pudding.

When Faye got the news that she was going home, she'd phoned Aubrey again, and he agreed to drive to her house so he could meet Laura and her family. So, they would manage to have, if not a *perfect* Christmas Eve, at least a pleasant one. The blow to Faye's vanity from Aubrey seeing her in a neck brace and on crutches would be balanced out by the windfall of his very presence in her life. She was so glad to have her daughter know she could attract such an elegant, charming man. She was even a little proud about it.

"Your new house is adorable," Laura said, as they pulled into Faye's drive. "Gosh, is that a Jag?"

Faye's spirits rose as they parked behind her beau's elegant vehicle. "Yes, it's Aubrey's."

"*Nice.*"

"He's nice, too." Faye smiled like a satisfied cat. It was all going to be all right. The lights on the Christmas tree twinkled gaily in the living room window. The wreath swathed in candy-stripe ribbons brightened the front door. Soon she'd be settled on the sofa with a glass of Champagne and her granddaughter on her lap and her loving family gathered all around, getting to know her delightful gentleman friend.

Laura rushed around to open the car door and assist Faye in the cumbersome task of hopping out and onto the crutches without hurting her neck or ankle. Slowly, Faye toddled up the walk, swinging the crutches clumsily, not yet used to the rhythm, feeling rather like a piece of unassembled furniture.

Laura opened the door. Faye bumbled inside. Too eager to wait to take off her coat, she clumped into the living room, leaning on her crutches, her head wobbling on its brace like a bobble-head doll.

Aubrey was standing by the fireplace, a glass of scotch in his hand. Lars was kneeling by the Christmas tree, Megan next to him, looking at all the packages.

Sweet, darling little Megan! She wore the red sweater with the white snowman that Faye had knitted for her. And a pair of jeans, and a pair of those dreadful Doc Martens boots the young seemed so obsessed with. Why would Laura buy those for her little girl? Still, it was *Megan*.

"Megan!" Faye cried with delight. She swung one of her crutches forward, hurrying toward her granddaughter.

Megan's eyes grew wide with alarm as she watched Faye lurch toward her like a creature from a sci-fi film. With a shriek, she threw herself into her father's arms.

"Honey, honey," Lars soothed. "It's Nanny. You remember Nanny. You talk to her every day on the computer phone. She gave you your pink princess doll."

Megan stared. Her lower lip quivered.

"It's the crutches." Faye hurried to make excuses for her grandchild, even though her feelings were crushed. "And the neck brace." She backed away, not wanting to traumatize Megan any more than she already had, and as she did, a fierce hot flash exploded through her. Sweat popped out on her forehead. Her underarms were ovens. Her entire body itched with heat and irritation. In front of everyone she loved, she was turning into a walking prickly pear cactus.

Dropping her crutches, she hobbled around on one foot, clawing at her coat, desperate to get out of it.

Megan gawked and tightened her grasp around her father's neck.

Laura hurried over. "Here, Mommy, let me help you."

"I'll support her while you take her coat off," Aubrey suggested.

Together, Aubrey and Laura got Faye out of her coat and onto the sofa, with her bad ankle elevated. Aubrey put a flute of cold Champagne in her hand.

"Thank you," Faye said. "Just what the doctor ordered." She tossed back a hearty slurp, then held the cool glass to her forehead.

Megan clung to her father, peering in Faye's direction from the safety of his shoulder.

"She's gotten shy recently," Laura confessed, easily curling up on the floor next to Faye. "It's not just you. I'm sure she'll come around."

"Did she see her bedroom?" Faye asked.

"Oh, yes, Mommy, it's *amazing*. Although Megan's going to sleep with us while we're here. The shy business again. I know she'll get over it, but until she does, we're allowing her to sleep with us whenever we're away from home."

"Oh," Faye said in a very small voice. "I see."

"I think Megan's hungry," Lars announced. "I wouldn't mind eating, either."

"The refrigerator—" Faye began, automatically struggling to get off the sofa and into the kitchen.

"Don't move, Mommy," Laura ordered. "I've seen the tons of food you've prepared. I'll organize a dinner for us all, here in the living room. We'll put everything on the coffee table. Lars and Megan and I can sit on the floor. It will be fun, like an indoor picnic!"

"Let's go help Mommy." Lars carried his clinging daughter out of the room.

Faye looked mournfully over at Aubrey. "I feel like a beached whale."

"You need more of Dr. Sperry's Miracle Tonic." Aubrey poured more Champagne for them both, then gently lifted her legs so that he could sit on the other end of the sofa with her feet in his lap. "Merry Christmas, Faye," he said, raising his glass in a toast.

"Merry Christmas, Aubrey," Faye echoed. She sipped the cold elixir. "Oh, Aubrey, I'm so glad you're here! But with this neck brace on, I look like—*Burl Ives*!"

Aubrey laughed. "That's all right, Faye," he assured her, patting her ankle. "I can't see very well."

Their mutual laughter made Faye relax, surrendering into the comfort of the cushions. The Christmas tree twinkled merrily, and from the kitchen floated the aromas of food being warmed. It wasn't the Christmas Eve she'd dreamed of, but it would certainly be one Faye would always remember.

3

Polly steered her car into the garage and clicked the door closed. She staggered into the kitchen, her arms full of last-minute holiday groceries. She'd probably bought too much, but better too much than too little, that was her opinion.

The light on her answering machine was blinking. She listened to the message as she took off her cap, gloves, and muffler.

Faye, asking for help!

"Oh, Faye!" Polly cried. Hurriedly, she dialed her number.

A male voice answered.

"Hello, this is Polly Lodge, I'm a friend of Faye's, she phoned—"

"Hi, Polly, this is Lars, Faye's son-in-law. Faye's gone off to the hospital with Alice. Laura's on her way there now. I'm here with Megan."

"Is Faye all right?"

"I think she will be. She fell down the stairs. Sprained or broke her ankle, did something to her neck."

"Oh, dear, and at Christmas!"

"I'll have her call you when she gets back, okay?"

"That would be great. Thanks, Lars."

Polly hung up the phone and just stood in the middle of her kitchen, miserable. *Darn it!* She had missed a rare opportunity.

As the newest member of the Hot Flash Club, she often felt like the baby sister scrambling to catch up with the big kids. Faye, Alice, Marilyn, and Shirley had met a year before Polly met them, and during that year they'd gotten up to all sorts of adventures and formed a tight bond of sisterhood. Polly was thrilled to be admitted to this casual club, but she wanted more. She wanted to be closer to all of them, or at least to one of them.

Looking down, she saw her ancient basset hound, Roy Orbison, sitting patiently at her feet, staring up at her.

"Oh, Roy!" She knelt to pet and hug him. "You're right. I can't stand here daydreaming! We've got a lot to do."

Her son, his wife, and their toddler, little Jehoshaphat, were coming to her house for Christmas Eve. Polly felt like she was preparing for a delegation from another planet.

David dwelt with his vegetarian wife Amy and their darling baby Jehoshaphat on a farm outside Boston. Amy's parents lived there, too, just up the driveway, and together they all grew vegetables and ran a precious little country store full of sour homemade jellies and scratchy hand-knitted apparel affordable only to the wealthiest and purest of souls.

Polly often wondered at the currents of fate driving her family line. Her grandparents had struggled to survive on a potato farm in Ireland. Her parents had lived as penny-pinching but respectable citizens in South Boston. Polly had gone to college, where she met and married a handsome, adventurous, unreliable travel writer and explorer. Scott got Polly pregnant, then roamed away, eventually dying in a scuba-diving accident. Polly had raised their son David alone, until she met the love of her life, Tucker Lodge, a banker. Their marriage had been a happy one. David had adored his stepfather and, after college, had gone to work in Tucker's bank. Then Tucker died of a heart attack. And David married Amy. And now Polly's son was a farmer planting potatoes on Amy's parents' farm. Was there a potato-planting gene in her blood?

Well, Polly thought as she unpacked the groceries, wouldn't it be nice if that was the explanation? Wouldn't it be helpful if, in future years, scientists isolated genes responsible for certain life choices, such as marrying someone diametrically different from one's parents? *She* had certainly done that, shell-shocking her timid, safety-loving parents when she married her first husband.

Since her son's marriage to Amy, Polly had spent hours examining her early life choices. Really, she didn't think the desire to shock, hurt, or impress her parents had played any part in her marriage to Scott. She'd been infatuated, completely *dazzled* by the man. He'd seemed so glamorous to her, and the life she'd lived with him, traveling to Peru and Mexico and the wild Newfoundland coast, had been exciting beyond her wildest dreams.

Life after the divorce had been difficult, though. She'd made her living as a seamstress, and dedicated herself to providing a happy and safe home for her little boy. When David was twelve, Polly had married Tucker Lodge. Tucker was a reliable man, a wonderful provider, and a loving stepfather. His death three years ago had devastated Polly, and she knew David mourned him deeply, too.

Was it possible that Amy and her family, so entrenched in their farm, with their smug rural virtues, were as dazzling and fascinating to David as Scott had been to Polly? Certainly David was thriving, if you could call changing from a wiry, energetic banker who liked theater and opera into a lumbering, overweight, red-faced, tractor-driving, potato-planting country bumpkin *thriving*!

Oh, Polly wouldn't care what David wore or did, if only Amy would allow her to see more of her grandson! Vegetarian Amy and her family acted as if they were civilized human beings while meat-eating Polly was some kind of Cro-Magnon creature, hooting and picking fleas off her fur. When Polly helped her mother-in-law, the year she was dying of cancer, Amy had not allowed her to see little Jehoshaphat, claiming that Polly might transmit dangerous germs. For a year, Polly had felt like some kind of leper.

The silver lining had been that she'd taken a membership at The Haven, hoping to work off some of the stress. There, she'd met three younger women who became her friends, and later, the members of the Hot Flash Club, with whom she could laugh about the gritty realities of aging. Thanks to all her new friends, she'd developed the courage to persist in her attempts to forge some kind of relationship with her grandson and his mother's tightly knit, terribly superior family.

And tonight, on Christmas Eve, Amy had agreed to come to Polly's house! This was a magnificent milestone. Jehoshaphat was fifteen months old, and he'd never visited his grandmother before.

Polly began arranging her evening's culinary offerings as artistically as possible on plain white ironstone platters.

"Let's see, I've got cheese made from the milk of goats fed by the Dalai Lama and crackers made from flour ground by French nuns during a full moon," she joked to Roy Orbison, who waddled hopefully at her feet, waiting for something to drop. "I have several kinds of fruit. I have plain nuts and salted nuts. Carrots and celery. Everything from the health food store." Because it was, after all, Christmas, she'd also used her grandmother's recipes to make the gingerbread cookies and sugar cookies David had always loved.

She carried the platters into the living room, setting them on tables out of the dog's reach.

Back in the kitchen, she surveyed the drink possibilities. From a health food store: mango juice, carrot juice, papaya juice, apple juice. Also beer, which David used to drink, and Champagne, just in case. And eggnog, whole and skim milk, sparkling and plain spring water, and a staggering assortment of herbal teas.

She glanced at her watch: five thirty. They would be here in an hour. She rushed to the living room to double-check everything. The tree's lights—the only nonorganic decoration—were glowing. Gingerbread characters grinned from the boughs, among angels, elves, and animals that Polly, who was a talented seamstress, had made from scraps of fabric. Presents for everyone lay under the tree, wrapped in paper Polly had recycled from brown paper grocery bags and tied with yarn. She was especially proud of this touch of environmental support; Amy *had* to approve of that! From the mantel hung stockings Polly had made herself for Amy, Jehoshaphat, and Polly's boy-friend, Hugh. David's stocking she'd made years ago, when he was a toddler. She'd considered giving it to Amy when they married, but quickly realized Amy would want to hang stockings of her own choosing.

She nodded admiringly at her mantel, decorated with laurel and candles. "I bought the greens myself, at Odell's farm, which is totally organic," she told her hound. "The candles are beeswax, also organic. I bought the wooden candleholders at a farm fair this fall. Can't wait for Amy to notice *them*!"

Roy snorted.

"I know, you think I'm going overboard, trying to please Amy, but come on, Roy, David's my only child. And Amy's the mother of my only grandchild!"

Her grandfather clock chimed. "Eeek!" she cried. It was time to shower and dress.

She'd laid a fire of natural woods—was there any other kind? Now she knelt to light it, so it would be blazing heartily when David and his family arrived. She clicked on the CD player, and Christmas carols rolled their golden notes out into the room. Everything was clean, dusted, polished, shining. She lit the candles on the mantelpiece. Their little flames danced, giving a lively, festive touch to the room.

"I don't think Amy can complain about a single thing," Polly assured herself.

She hurried up to her bedroom, stripped off her clothes, and turned on the bath water. As the tub filled, she stared in the mirror at her naked, sexagenarian body. She looked grandmotherly. That was appropriate. After all, she *was* a grandmother.

But she was also, to her surprise, at her advanced age, newly in love, or at least in serious like.

After Polly's mother-in-law died last year, her physician, Hugh Monroe, had asked Polly out on a date, at which point Polly, who liked to consider the glass half-full, decided Fate was getting around to balancing things out. Polly had taken good care of Claudia in her final months. She considered Hugh a kind of karmic reward. In her most sentimental moments, she even imagined that Claudia had engineered this somehow.

Hugh was so wonderful! Polly sank into her bubble bath and closed her eyes, surrendering for just a moment to the heat, the peace, and her dreams. Fragrant bubbles surged over the mounds of her round thighs, belly, and breasts.

Hugh didn't seem to mind how much Polly weighed. A jovial, energetic, portly man, Hugh liked to eat, cook, and drink. Polly hadn't discussed the philosophy of this with him, but she guessed that he alleviated the stresses of his work as an oncologist with as many vigorous sensual pleasures as he could conjure up on any given day.

She had such a good time with Hugh on their dates! He took her to elegant restaurants, but also to amusement parks where they rode roller coasters and merry-go-rounds and ate cotton candy. They'd spent a day on a small boat plunging around off Boston's coast on a whale watch—and they'd seen two whales. Polly would never forget how her heart leapt at the sight. On his next vacation, Hugh wanted to take her scuba-diving in the Caribbean, something Polly had never done, and he was trying to persuade her to take riding lessons with him. Polly wasn't so sure about that. She hadn't ridden since she was a teenager, and she had visions of swinging her hefty hind end into a saddle and the horse going "Oofh!" and fainting.

The good thing about Hugh was that she was able to confide such fears to him. When she'd confessed her equestrian vision, Hugh had replied, "Ah, Polly, any horse would be thrilled to bear your gorgeous derrière!" That night, he'd given her a full back massage that ended with kisses all up and down her spine and all over her round rear end. Until then, she hadn't realized her nerves had valiantly sneaked through the cellulite and were there waiting to receive the sweetness of his warm breath, his soft lips, like a hive when the bee buzzes back with its load of honey.

Polly smiled and hugged herself.

But enough daydreaming. She stepped dripping onto the bath mat, grabbed a towel, and began drying off. As she dressed, she could feel her courage fading beneath an onslaught of nerves.

David's wife, Amy, and her parents, Katrina and Buck, all lived and worked on the same farm. Their schedules were closely knit together, their conversation related to matters Polly didn't understand—fertilizer, insects, spinning wheels. The Andersons had lived on their land since the Revolutionary War, which indeed was something to be proud about, but the Andersons were more than proud. They were *smug.* They belonged to their own elite club with its private language and rituals, and Polly was not admitted. Last Christmas, she'd been invited for two hours only on Christmas night, to share eggnog with her son, grandson, and daughter-in-law while they exchanged presents that, Polly suspected, they never used.

Nothing Polly gave Amy and her family was ever good enough. When Polly mailed her grandson a funny card and present on Valentine's Day, she never heard whether it had even arrived. Very occasionally she was asked to baby-sit her grandson, but when she did, Amy was always just in the next room. What was *that* about?

Polly pulled on her wool slacks and the green cashmere sweater she'd knit herself. Cashmere and wool, *natural,* that ought to satisfy Amy. She sat on the edge of her bed to put on her socks and shoes. From the corner of her eye, she noticed the crystal bowl filled with Brach's Chocolate Mix that she'd brought upstairs, to keep away from Amy's critical eye.

For courage, Polly grabbed the bag, delved inside, and pulled out a chocolate-covered Brazil nut. It was especially satisfying to eat nuts, because she could crunch them. *Hard.*

The chocolate, sugar, and fat blasted into her system like a team of miniature superheroes, lifting her spirits high. She nibbled more as she brushed her red—well, *white* and red—hair and put on a bit of lipstick and eyeliner.

Any moment now, they'd be here. She'd get to hold her grandson, hand him a present, watch him as he opened it.

Where was the camera! She was standing here chewing away like a squirrel, and where was the camera?

In the kitchen? Probably.

The doorbell chimed. Polly raced down the stairs, Roy Orbison hurrying with her, his long, chubby body swaying, nearly tripping her as they went.

The air downstairs was smoky. Hadn't she pushed up the fireplace flue? She'd have to open the windows, let the smoke out. First, though, she hurried to the front door.

"David!" she cried. "Amy! And Jehoshaphat!"

Amy's brown braids were looped on the top of her head in a kind of Fräulein milkmaid look. Instead of a coat, she wore a hairy brown poncho. Jehoshaphat's chubby baby face stared over his mother's shoulder from her backpack.

They were really here! Polly was so thrilled, she nearly burst into a flamboyant flamenco. At her feet, Roy Orbison danced and barked his hoarse old dog bark. "Come in, come in."

David bent to pat the basset hound. He smelled faintly of manure and Lysol. "Mom, why is it so smoky in here?"

"Oh, darling, I lighted a fire, and I need to—" There were so many things to do at once, she couldn't finish her sentence. "Let me hold Jehoshaphat while you take off your things," she told Amy, reaching out for her grandson. Amy allowed her to lift the little boy from the backpack.

"Mom, something's wrong." David pushed past her, still in his coat.

"Darling, it's just—" Carrying Jehoshaphat, who was squirming around, looking in all directions at this new environment, Polly followed her son down the hall and into the living room.

"Jesus Christ!" David exclaimed. "Mom, call 911! The house is on fire!"

But Polly was paralyzed as she stood in the doorway to her living room. What she saw was so bizarre, her mind couldn't, for a moment, force it to make sense. Flames shot up from the mantel, where her organic greenery was crackling and popping as it burned, and her wooden candlesticks glowed orange.

"Oh my God!" Amy shrieked. Lunging forward, she snatched Jehoshaphat from Polly's arms. The little boy began to scream along with his mother as she flew back outside.

The dog, confused and frightened, stood in the middle of the hall, threw back his head, and bayed like a lost soul.

David had his cell phone out and was dialing 911.

"Hallelujah! Hallelujah! Hallelujah!" a choir sang from the CD player.

Fire, Polly thought. *Water.* Breaking out of her stupor, she ran into the kitchen, found her big lobster pot, set it in the sink, and turned on both faucets. The water ran and ran, and yet, as if she were caught in some kind of nightmare, the pot would not fill. Slowly, slowly, the level of the water rose, while black smoke drifted down the hall and into the kitchen.

Finally the pot was almost full. Polly hoisted it from the sink, turned, and started to run toward the living room. But with her first step, the water sloshed out of the pot, spilling onto her slacks and puddling onto the floor. Slipping, slithering, she almost went down.

Carefully, slowly, Polly regained her balance. She moved her legs as quickly as she could while keeping her upper torso and arms completely still, to prevent more water spilling. Arms stiff, she walked zombielike to the living room.

David was by the fireplace, poker in hand, knocking the burning greenery and blackened candleholders onto the tile hearth and into the fireplace.

"Oh, David," she cried, "be careful! Don't burn yourself!"

"It's all right now, Mom. I've got it under control. When the fire department gets here, they can check whether it got into the walls somehow, but I think we're okay."

Polly stood helplessly, holding her heavy pot of water. Above the mantel, the wall was streaked with black, and the beautiful oil painting she and Tucker had inherited from his family was scorched and curled into fragments of ruined canvas. Roy Orbison had stopped bellowing and sniffed nervously at her feet.

"Aaah, Mom, it's all right." David put the poker back in its stand. "I'll put the pot here on the hearth. In case we need it." He lifted the heavy vessel of water from Polly's hands. "Look," he said, trying to cheer her up. "The tree, the stockings, the presents—none of them burned."

Polly's lip quivered. "That's right. That's good."

"Come sit down here," David said gently. "You've had a shock."

Polly had forgotten how to move her legs.

"Mom." David put his arms around her and hugged her for a long time. "It's okay, Mom. It's really okay."

He ushered her to the sofa. Docilely, she sat. Her dog sat, too, leaning against her legs for comfort.

"I'm just going to check on Amy and Jehoshaphat." David left the room.

Because the front door was open to let the smoke escape, her son's conversation floated in with perfect clarity.

"It's okay now, Amy, come on in."

"I'm not going in there! I'm not taking my child into a burning house!"

"The fire's out."

"I'm not taking a chance. What if a spark got up in the ceiling? Everything could go at once!"

"Amy—"

"When the fire department says it's safe, I'll go in."

"Then take Jehoshaphat and sit in the car. You'll freeze out here."

Sirens sounded in the distance. Then, closer. The wails pierced the Christmas Eve air as they screeched to a stop at Polly's house. Moments later, Polly heard men speaking with her son and then two firemen stomped into the living room, garbed in rubber coats, boots, and gear.

Behind them came Amy, David, and the baby. Amy stood in the doorway, refusing to enter the room, which was just as well, because the room was crowded. Somehow the firemen were twice as big as normal persons. Roy Orbison waddled around, wagging his tail and sniffing the firemen's interesting ankles.

They checked the walls, ceiling, and hearth. They stomped upstairs and down again.

The older one, with grizzled hair, had kind eyes. "This happens more often than you'd think," he assured Polly. "Christmas candles, dry greenery, there you are."

The younger fireman said to Polly, "I notice you have smoke alarms upstairs and down. Didn't they go off?"

Polly cringed. "I took the batteries out this week. I was doing a lot of cooking, and they're so sensitive, they were going off all the time and driving me crazy."

Behind him, Amy's mouth crimped disapprovingly.

"Yeah, that happens a lot," the older fireman said. "You'd better connect them."

By the time the firemen left, all the smoke had dissipated. Polly longed to pour half a bottle of rum into a cup of eggnog and chug it down.

But instead she rallied. "Sit down, now, please. We can still have Christmas Eve," she told David and Amy. "The presents and stockings are okay. And I've made some delicious—"

"I think we'd better go home," Amy said. "The smoke gave me a headache, and heaven knows what it did to little Jehoshaphat's lungs."

"But the smoke's gone!" Polly protested, waving her arms.

"Yes, and it's freezing in here," Amy pointed out.

"It will warm up soon," Polly promised. "I'll make you some tea. I've got so many different kinds—"

With a sigh, Amy acquiesced.

The next hour dragged by. With the patience of Mother Teresa tending to the ill, Amy accepted Polly's Christmas gifts and allowed her son to touch his. The entire time, Amy darted frightened little glances at her husband, making it clear she was terrified that the house was about to spontaneously combust. She did not allow Polly's grandson to taste any cookies—too much sugar—or to drink any of the juice Polly had bought. Instead, she pulled a juice bottle from her woven bag.

Amy and David's gift to Polly was a set of woven reed place mats that Polly had seen on the sale table of the Andersons' little store over the summer. But Amy did permit Jehoshaphat to touch the set of natural wood blocks Polly gave him, and for five blissful minutes, Polly was allowed to sit playing on the floor with her grandson.

In spite of the herbal tea Polly brewed, Amy complained that her headache was growing worse.

You need caffeine, honey, you need chocolate, Polly thought. *You need a personality transplant.*

She walked them to the door, waving until their pickup truck was out of sight. For a moment, she stood looking out at the black sky with its frosty stars. All the houses up and down the block glowed with Christmas lights.

Polly returned to her smoke-stained living room. Her artistically decorated brown wrapping paper and yarn ribbons lay discarded on the floor like yesterday's trash. The present from Amy and David, the woven place mats, looked like hair shirts for a clan of masochistic dwarves. Roy Orbison sniffed through the crumpled paper and found a bit of unsalted cashew. From the CD player, the little drummer boy drummed for the fifty-ninth time that evening. Polly turned off the music.

"Merry Christmas, humbug!" she told her dog, and collapsed on the sofa.

It was only a little after eight o'clock on Christmas Eve. If only Hugh had been here! He wouldn't have let the place catch fire. Or he would have assured everyone, with his gentle physician's authority, that everything was really all right. He would have lent authenticity and gravity to Polly's gifts and food.

But Hugh wasn't here, and he wouldn't be tonight.

Tonight Hugh was spending with his grown children, their spouses, and his ex-wife, Carol.

Carol was—Polly had seen pictures—a tiny size six, and if that wasn't irritating enough, she was also a dependent little princess. Hugh and Carol had been divorced for several years now, but Carol, who had kept the house in which she and Hugh had raised their three children, was forever phoning him when the downstairs bathroom's pipes froze, or a bat got into the attic, or one of their grandchildren lost a tooth. Carol desperately needed daily conversations with Hugh, and Hugh took it all in his stride, listening to her complaints and soothing her with the same kind manner with which he spoke to his patients when they phoned. Also, he was diligent about attending his grandchildren's plays, recitals, and soccer games as often as possible. Polly admired him for this at the same time she hated how it limited their time together.

When they'd discussed their holiday schedules, Polly had thought it made perfect sense for Hugh to be with his children—and their mother—on Christmas Eve, while Polly was with her son and his family. Tomorrow, when she got to see Hugh, she would be glad to have the Carol part of Christmas behind them.

But tonight she was irrationally lonely. For a while, she indulged in a morass of negativity, imagining everyone else she knew celebrating the season in the bosom of their families. Quickly she got bored with that scenario. She'd spent too many holidays in the home of her mother-in-law, Claudia, Queen of Disdain, to believe all other families in the world were happy.

Besides, it wasn't celebrating she missed—she did a lot of that, with Hugh and with her Hot Flash friends. It was a sense of being useful, of being part of the world, that made her feel so solitary now.

But then, how useful could someone be who set her house on fire on Christmas Eve?

4

Marilyn didn't know whether her mother was truly an exceptionally pretty woman, or if it was just that Marilyn loved her so much.

Ruth came out of the guest bedroom, dressed for Christmas Eve dinner in a red wool dress and a strand of white pearls. Red lipstick brightened her pleated lips and cheerful rouge blushed her wrinkled cheeks. From her ears dangled shiny little Christmas ornaments, one red, one green. Her snowy white hair bobbed around in curls, and the bit of pink scalp showing through made Marilyn's heart ache. Her mother had had such thick hair when she was younger.

"You look great, Mom," Marilyn said.

Ruth's face lit up at the compliment. "Well, thank you, dear! I believe, no matter which God you believe in, it's important to keep rituals in your life. It helps you remember to be grateful. To reflect on the cycle of birth, life, and dirt."

Marilyn bit her lip. Ruth had been a brilliant biology professor. Now, at eighty-five, her discourse was peppered with little malapropisms. Marilyn had phoned her sister Sharon about it, and they'd agreed it was probably a result of Ruth's mini-strokes. They decided not to mention it to Ruth, who always seemed puzzled when they tried to correct her.

Ostensibly, Ruth was visiting her daughter for a few weeks, an unexceptional, ordinary thing for a mother to do. Tacitly, Marilyn was supposed to watch Ruth for signs of senility so she could share her observations with Sharon and help her decide whether or not their mother should be "persuaded" to go into an assisted care facility.

"I can't make this kind of decision by myself," Sharon had insisted during one of their many phone conversations this fall.

"I agree. You shouldn't have to," Marilyn had assured her. She already felt guilty because Sharon had remained in the same Ohio town where they'd grown up, while Marilyn had moved east for college and remained east all her life. Marilyn flew back at least once a year to visit her mother, and she sent Ruth cards and gifts and phoned her often, but that didn't compare with the time and care Sharon gave. But then Sharon, who was the older sister, and always bossy, liked to be in charge, while Marilyn, a paleobiologist and professor at MIT, craved huge quantities of solitude for her studies.

Marilyn's intellectual preoccupation was no doubt genetic, although nurture played its part as well, since both her parents, who had taught biology at a large state university, had spent much of Marilyn's childhood lying on their stomachs in the backyard, observing insects.

For a few halcyon years when Marilyn and Sharon were children, they'd been extraordinarily popular, because their parents loved to talk about nature and were full of amusing anecdotes, complete with illustrations. *The flatfish have both eyes on the same side of their heads, and the eyes can migrate from side to side! Some snakes have two heads! When the sea elephant becomes angry, his nose swells up like a balloon!*

During their adolescent years, however, their peers began to consider their parents dorky and even weird. Their father loved to tell jokes—*Two hydrogen atoms walk into a bar. One says, "I've lost my electron." The other asks, "Are you sure?" The first one says, "I'm positive."*—which made the teenagers groan and roll their eyes.

It didn't help that the professors, both of whom could describe in detail the colors of a deer botfly, dressed without any consideration of fashion. They wore clothes to keep from being cold or naked in public—the latter of which, they were always ready to discuss with the sisters' contemporaries, was practiced in other cultures.

Sharon had rebelled, becoming obsessed with clothing, hair, and current styles. She'd majored in economics and, after trying a number of jobs, had ended up as a corporate headhunter. Sharon was slick, stylish, and savvy. Marilyn had been the child who adopted her parents' ways. But Marilyn had moved away, while Sharon remained in Ohio.

So Sharon had been the one to help both parents, ten years ago, move out of their sprawling ranch house and into a small apartment in a comfortable retirement community. She had been the one to phone Marilyn when their father died, at seventy-eight, and when Marilyn flew back for the funeral, Sharon had been the one to suggest Marilyn help their mother sort through their father's possessions.

It had nearly broken Marilyn's heart to give away her father's beloved paraphernalia: the insect light traps and transparent insect-rearing cages, the beautiful ant house she'd built with him when she was a child, the Schmidt boxes filled with specimens caught and mounted with exquisite care.

"You *have* mineral hammers and rock cabinets," Sharon had argued when she caught Marilyn trying to sneak her father's into her own luggage. "I've seen your house and your lab. You don't need another bit of old equipment!" Sharon was strong-willed and assertive. They'd ended up giving anything useful to a children's museum and taking much of the rest to the dump.

Finally they had the apartment sorted out, clutter-free and airy. Ruth had been sad to see the scientific equipment go, but only because they reminded her of her husband. After retiring from teaching, she had turned her attention to other things, small things, and lots of them, including knitting, doing crossword puzzles, and compiling a recipe collection. During the past five years of her widowhood, Ruth had accumulated a rather daunting mass of clutter of her own. Her increasing inability to part with her new possessions was one of the reasons Sharon thought she was no longer fit to live by herself.

Still, Ruth could shop for herself—she didn't drive, but took the shuttle provided by the retirement community. She cooked for herself and kept her kitchen clean. She bathed daily, and her clothing was fresh and spotless. True, she was developing a tendency toward keeping her food around longer than it should be . . . the refrigerator was crammed with foil-covered packets. As with her needlework, Ruth tended to lose interest in her current meal, and being a child of the Depression, she wrapped it up and saved it for the future rather than throwing it out.

Ruth's health was good enough. She'd had a hysterectomy years before, and suffered a few very minor strokes that hadn't paralyzed her, only slowed her down. She was active; she had friends she played cards with in the lounge. Her sense of hearing was failing, she'd had cataract operations, and she needed a cane to walk because of arthritis, but still she was self-sufficient, good-humored, and happy.

And, perhaps, failing. She often forgot appointments, names, where she put something, but then, Marilyn thought, who didn't? Occasionally, Ruth's speech was jumbled. Most worrisome: she'd fallen a month ago, while stepping out of the bath. She hadn't told anyone, hadn't wanted to make a fuss. But a week later, at her annual physical checkup, the doctor had seen the bruises, still purple and yellow, along the front of her torso, and had told Ruth—and Sharon, who'd accompanied her to the appointment—that she had most probably had a transient ischemic attack, a momentary blockage of the blood supply to the brain. He'd suggested followup tests. Ruth had stalled. He'd suggested she use a walker. These TIAs were transitory, but often recurring. They were mini-strokes, the doctor warned her. They could happen anytime. Ruth had delicately rejected the walker, saying in her gentle way she would think about it, but didn't feel she needed it *quite* yet.

"I really can't tell if I want to move Mom into assisted living because it would make *her* feel better, or make *me* worry less," Sharon had told Marilyn. "You have to help me evaluate."

So Marilyn had invited her mother to visit for a couple of months, and Sharon had helped Ruth pack and board a plane, and now, here she was.

After her divorce, Marilyn had moved out of the huge Victorian where she and Theodore had raised Teddy—what a mind-warping, backbreaking project that had been! Much of her personal scientific paraphernalia and most of her books were in a storage locker until she decided where to live permanently. For the time being, Marilyn was renting a bland, furnished condo in Cambridge. She'd never been one to fuss about her surroundings or attempt coordinating curtains with carpets, and she found the small, practical space worked well for her life. Especially since she was thinking about taking a sabbatical and doing some traveling.

Now they were preparing to leave for Christmas Eve dinner with Marilyn's son Teddy, his wife, and their family.

"I've got all my presents tucked away in these big shopping bags," Marilyn told Ruth, gesturing to the bags sitting by the front door. "Where are your presents?"

"Ooops! Left them in the bedroom."

"I'll get them," Marilyn offered.

"No, no, I'm not helpless." Ruth toddled away, returning in a few moments with a large book bag. "I've got all my fits in here."

"Um, well, good, Mom!" Marilyn leaned toward the mirror in the hall, checking her hair. She looked rather messy today. Her Hot Flash friends would want to fix her up somehow, cut her hair, give her a different lipstick, brighten her up with a colorful scarf. But having her mother with her was pretty much like having a toddler around. She didn't have much free time for herself, and what time she had was often interrupted.

"What time is Fraidy coming?" Ruth asked.

"His name is Faraday, Mom," Marilyn reminded her for the hundredth time. "He should be here any minute."

She knew she sounded cranky when she talked about Faraday. Faraday McAdam was a charming man, also a scientist, always fascinating and courtly and attentive. When Theodore left Marilyn for a younger woman, Faraday's flirtation had buoyed her up, convincing her as never before in her entire life that she was attractive.

The problem was that Faraday, who at his best, when they first met, had been only a one-minute wonder, was now completely impotent.

Whenever Marilyn tried to discuss this, *gently,* with Faraday, he changed the subject, turned on the TV, or left the room. Occasionally, Faraday hinted at their living together, traveling together, marriage . . . and Marilyn dreamed of Barton Baker, the cad who had betrayed her, but also had shown her just how amazing good sex could be. Marilyn didn't want to live the rest of her life alone. But did she want to live it without ever having delicious, skin-heating, heart-thumping, artery-flushing, serotonin-surging, passionate sex again?

"Are you having a hot flash, dear?" Ruth asked.

Marilyn jumped. "I am," she replied honestly, abashed. How could she *think* of sex with her mother in the room!

As Ruth adjusted a bow on one of her presents, she said, "Marilyn, did I tell you about Jean Benedict's daughter? She's about your age, you know. Well, she ran off with her gardener to the Dutch West Guineas! It was a shock to us all, because she had been a pillow of the community. But you see, you're never too old for romance . . ."

Marilyn gaped at her mother. Had she developed a talent for mind reading?

Her thoughts were interrupted by a knock on the door.

"Here he is!" Marilyn opened the door.

"Ruth! How nice to see you again!" Faraday, large, ruddy, and jolly, made a little bow to the older woman.

Ruth smiled sweetly. "Hello, Fruity. Good to see you, too."

"*Faraday,* Mother!" Marilyn quickly corrected.

"That's what I said, dear," Ruth placidly assured her.

"Hello, Marilyn." Unfazed, Faraday leaned forward to kiss Marilyn's cheek. "Merry Christmas."

"Merry Christmas, Faraday. You look festive."

"I try," Faraday admitted modestly. Today he wore his most replete and elegant apparel: a Clan McGregor kilt in a handsome red and green tartan, perfect for Christmas; his Prince Charlie jacket with the handsome buttons on the sleeves; a tartan tie; and a dress sporran. Between his high wool socks and the hem of his kilt, his legs, massive and covered with fine red hair, were bare.

Marilyn's mother threw her hands up in astonishment. "You look wonderful! I've never seen a real live man in Scottish garble!" Ruth bent forward, peering. "I've always wondered about the purpose of that little fur purse you've got hanging down. Is it to advertise the male's reproductive equipment? Like a stag's antlers or a peacock's tail feathers?"

"Mother!" Marilyn admonished.

"Well, dear, it *does* draw the eye," Ruth calmly pointed out.

Faraday seemed amused. "It's called a *sporran,* and it's exactly as you named it," he informed Ruth. "It's a little fur purse. The kilt doesn't have pockets, so this began as a leather pouch for carrying our necessary items. This sporran is for dress only. It's made from Greenland sealskin. Everyday sporrans are usually just leather."

"And what do you wear under the kilt?" Ruth asked.

"Mother, stop it," Marilyn intervened. "Come on, let's get your coat on."

"Why shouldn't I inquire?" Ruth argued. "You're never too old to learn."

"Allow me." Faraday helped Ruth into her coat. "Marilyn tells me you taught biology. Obviously you were asking in the spirit of scientific inquiry."

"Obviously," Ruth agreed, pleased.

"So I'll tell *you.*" Faraday bent to whisper in Ruth's ear.

Ruth giggled.

Marilyn rolled her eyes but smiled. "I'll just get the presents."

She gathered up the bags full of gifts and followed her mother and Faraday out to his car. Faraday opened the trunk and set the gifts inside, next to his offering of several bottles of Champagne and wine.

"Now, then," he said, as he got behind the wheel. "Is everybody comfortable? Marilyn, do you have enough room for your legs?"

"I'm fine, Faraday." Why did he irritate her so much today? He was behaving beautifully!

Faraday started the car and they were off, driving toward Marilyn's son's house.

"I know a joke about what's under a kilt," Ruth announced.

"Mother," Marilyn said quietly.

But Faraday encouraged her. "I love kilt jokes! Let's hear it!"

"Very well. A Scotsman spends an evening in a bar and has rather too much to drink. When he leaves the pub, he passes out on the street. Two young American women notice.

" 'My,' one says to the other. 'I've always wondered what's under a Scottish kilt.'

" 'Let's look!' says the other.

"So they look, and glory be, he's naked as the day he was born. The girls giggle. Then the first one mischievously takes a blue ribbon from her hair and ties it around the man's sexual reproductive member. They run off, laughing.

"A while later, the Scotsman wakes up. Feeling something odd, he lifts his kilt, looks down, and sees the blue ribbon tied around his hoo-ha.

" 'Well, lad,' he says. 'I don't know what you got up to while I was passed out, but I'm glad you won first prize.' "

They all laughed, and the shared laughter made Marilyn relax just a little. This was the first Christmas that Faraday had accompanied Marilyn to her son's family dinner. She wasn't quite sure what this implied about their relationship. She wasn't quite sure what she *wanted* it to imply.

"Now tell me again who will be there this evening," her mother asked from the front seat.

"Well, Teddy and Lila and your great-granddaughter Irene, of course, since it's at their house. And the three of us. And Eugenie, Lila's mother."

"But not Lila's father?"

"No. They separated last year. Lila's father's gone off with a younger woman. Lila and Teddy and the baby will spend Christmas day with Lila's father. Eugenie got them for Thanksgiving this year, because I got them for Thanksgiving last year. Eugenie wanted them all for herself this Christmas, but now that she and her husband have separated, there aren't enough bits of time to go around."

"You need a computer to figure out how to divide the holidays up fairly," Ruth said.

"Or a psychiatrist," Marilyn said.

"Still," Ruth said, "there's no plague like home for the holidays."

Faraday looked in the rearview mirror and winked at Marilyn.

The evening blurred past in a flurry of kisses, gifts, Champagne, and laughter. Teddy and Lila served a veritable Christmas feast, Ruth and her great-granddaughter formed a mutual admiration society, and Faraday charmed everyone, as usual, with humorous anecdotes.

Only Eugenie, Lila's mother, cast a pall on the party. Always aloof, tonight she was especially remote, and no wonder. Poor Eugenie had had the face-lift from hell. She looked like a melted Madame Tussaud's mannequin. Marilyn could only imagine how horrible this must be for Eugenie, whose extraordinary feminine perfection had been a living advertisement for her ex-husband's plastic surgery business.

In the car on the way back to Marilyn's condo, Faraday said, "It was a grand party."

"My, yes," Ruth agreed. "Delicious food. And I got to have some time with my great-granddaughter."

Marilyn leaned forward, resting her arms on the back of the front seat. "What did you think of Lila's mother?"

Ruth took a moment to think. "Well, Eugenie's an unusual woman. She reminds me of the Portuguese man-of-war jellyfish. Beautiful, diaphanous, and poisonous."

"She was even more beautiful before she had that botched face-lift," Marilyn said.

Ruth yawned. "Well, beauty is only kin deep."

Back at Marilyn's condo, Faraday insisted on escorting the women inside, carrying their bags of presents for them.

"It was a lovely evening." Ruth turned to Faraday. "Thank you for everything."

"Yes, Faraday," Marilyn echoed, "thank you."

But Faraday showed no intention of leaving. "How about a little nightcap?"

Marilyn hesitated. She was yearning to crawl into bed with her new book on plate tectonics.

"You two youngsters can stay up, but I'm going to bed. Good night, Fairy." Ruth leaned over to kiss Marilyn on the cheek. "Good night, dear. Merry Christmas."

"Merry Christmas, Mother," Marilyn said.

Marilyn and Faraday watched Ruth toddle away down the hall.

Marilyn stifled a yawn. "I don't know if I'm up for a nightcap. I've had so much to drink tonight. All that Champagne. How about a cup of tea?"

"Actually, I don't want anything else to drink, either," Faraday told her. "I just wanted a little private time with you."

Marilyn's heart sank.

Faraday took her hand and led her to the sofa. Once they were comfortably seated side by side, he told her, "I have another present for you, Marilyn."

Reaching down, he unfastened the metal lid of his sporran.

And brought out a small black velvet box.

"Marilyn," Faraday said, his beautiful blue eyes shining. "Will you marry me?"

A hot flash that would have propelled a missile to the moon exploded inside Marilyn's body. She flushed from her belly straight up to the top of her head.

"Oh!" she cried, jumping up. "Hot flash, Faraday, excuse me!" She raced from the room.

In her bedroom, she ripped off her clothes. In her bra and panties, she went into the bathroom, ran the cold water tap, and stood over the sink, pressing cool water onto her face, letting it drizzle down her neck and shoulders. The intense sense of irritation that usually accompanied her hot flashes was multiplied by a power of ten right now. She felt wildly, almost *violently,* insane.

She gulped cold water from her hands. Soaked a washcloth with cold water and pressed it against the back of her neck. And cursed under her breath.

Damn Faraday! How could he *propose* to her! It made her feel so *cornered.* As her body temperature dropped back into the normal range, her emotions remained on Emergency Alert.

Why was she so panicked? Marilyn asked herself.

Because Faraday had pressed her into an existential corner. She cared for him. She enjoyed his company. She admired him. She shared common interests with him. But never in her life had she experienced that sweeping sense of falling in love so much praised by her Hot Flash friends. Not with Faraday, not with her husband Theodore, not even with that cad Barton, who had introduced her to the sensation of lust.

So late in her life, she *had* developed a sexual appetite. And

Faraday, who was so good, so intelligent, so charming, could not satisfy that appetite. Didn't even worry about trying. Should she refuse his proposal for that reason? Or accept it, and be thankful any man wanted to marry her at all? She was no beauty, and more than that, she was fifty-four. This might be her last and only chance to have a companion with whom to share the rest of her life. Statistically, this was a miracle. Who was she, a scientist, to defy statistics?

A gentle knock sounded at the bathroom door. "Marilyn?" Faraday whispered. "Are you all right?"

Marilyn grabbed the bathrobe hanging on the hook, pulled it on, and opened the door. "Sorry, Faraday. That was a particularly hot hot flash."

"Come sit down," Faraday told her. "I made you some chamomile tea with the valerian Shirley gave you to calm your heart."

"Oh, Faraday, how kind!" Marilyn said.

"I poured it over ice," he continued, looking pleased with himself. "So it will cool you as you drink it."

"Oh, Faraday, how brilliant!" Marilyn told him.

She allowed him to take her hand and lead her back into the living room. She felt like someone being led to the edge of a diving board. *Damn, damn, damn!* What was she going to do?

5

Alice had never been particularly interested in domestic matters. Oh, when her sons were young, she'd enjoyed the Christmas folderol, but now she was in her sixties, her sons were grown, and she didn't feel obligated to make a fuss. So this year, she'd just hung some mistletoe and holly over the doors and windows. After all, her handsome condo, in a restored warehouse on Boston Harbor, had a view like a Christmas tree itself, replete with twinkling lights from boats, cruisers, and planes going in and out of Logan Airport.

Now she slid open the glass door and stepped out onto her balcony. Her beau, Gideon, ensconced on the sofa with the remote in his hand, didn't ask why she wanted to stand out in the frosty night in her light silk caftan. He was well acquainted with her hot flashes by now.

Actually, she wasn't having a hot flash, as she leaned on the railing, breathing in huge gulps of cold, fresh air. More like a brain blip. No—more like an interior tantrum. It was as if she had a little Alice living inside her, a cranky miniature troll who was always complaining. Always wanting more.

An Id Alice.

An Id-iot Alice.

She imagined that everyone else in the whole world was probably content right now, sharing Christmas Eve rituals, anticipating tomorrow's festivities.

She wasn't.

Turning slightly, she looked through the glass door into her living room where Gideon was relaxing, zoning out as he watched television. Gideon was absolutely adorable, a great, big man who resembled the Red Sox hitter David Ortiz, or perhaps more accurately, Ortiz's father. His bald spot expanded daily, and although he tried to watch his diet because of diabetes, he still had a gut slung like a hammock holding a baby hippo. Even so, he was a gorgeous man.

And he loved Alice. Because of a prostate cancer operation, he couldn't really have sex, but Alice did her best not to mind. Marilyn's lover couldn't have sex, either. Faraday didn't have a prostate problem; he was just impotent. Alice grinned, thinking of Marilyn's complaints. God, laughter helped.

Feeling slightly less grumpy, she went back into the living room.

"Alice," Gideon said, "sit down and relax. You've been going all day."

Alice glanced around her dining area. Christmas Eve dinner was over. She and Gideon had finished clearing up. The dishwasher hummed in the kitchen. Nothing needed doing. It was nine o'clock at night.

Sighing, she collapsed onto the sofa. "I think Jennifer liked her presents, don't you?"

"Um-hum," Gideon agreed absently, his attention fixed on a taped rerun of Tiger Woods playing golf, the sport Gideon had taken up this past summer.

"And I think Alan and Jennifer were both pleased that *I* fixed Christmas Eve dinner for *them*," Alice mused aloud. Alan and his girlfriend, Jennifer, lived in the gatehouse of The Haven, a cozy cottage where they worked together, running their bakery and catering service. Because they were always slaving over an oven, Alice wanted to give them a real holiday. And she had. "I was as nice as pie to Jennifer, wasn't I?"

"Um-hum," Gideon said again.

Alice frowned. *I want him to praise me!* cried the demanding diminutive Alice, dancing up and down in frustration just inside Alice's left ear. *I want him to tell me I'm wonderful because I've gotten over my prejudice about Jennifer being white! I want him to tell me I'm a good-hearted, loving mother, not to mention a fabulous cook with the intelligence of S. Epatha Merkerson and the looks of Vanessa Williams!*

"I ate too much tonight," Alice moaned. "I look like the south end of a rhino going north."

"Drat!" Gideon exclaimed, completely ignoring his cue for a compliment.

Alice glanced at the television. Tiger Woods's ball had just missed the hole.

You've seen that exact same ball miss that exact same hole at least ten times already! Alice wanted to shout at Gideon. *You've watched every game Tiger Woods has ever played at least twenty times!*

But she kept quiet, musing on her own thoughts.

After a few moments, she said, "Did you see how much Jennifer ate? And she's still so tiny! This caftan's comfortable, but it makes me look like a camping tent with legs."

"Nonsense." Gideon's reply was absentmindedly dutiful. "You are a thing of beauty and a joy forever."

Well, that was a half-assed compliment if she ever heard one. Still, she was grateful for it. "Who said that, anyway?" she wondered aloud.

Rising, she went to her bookshelves. More and more these days, old phrases of songs and poetry popped into her thoughts. She didn't understand just why. Sometimes she thought it was because great, gaping vacancies had been left in her brain when she retired from TransContinent Insurance, and because nature abhorred a vacuum, her brain was substituting stuff she'd learned about years ago in high school and college. More likely, she was just getting senile. Whatever, she was glad people had gone to the trouble of making anthologies like her dictionary of quotations.

She sat down with the heavy tome on her lap and looked for the word "beauty" in the index. John Keats. Hm. English poet, if she remembered correctly. She turned to the quote and read aloud.

> *"A thing of beauty is a joy for ever:*
> *Its loveliness increases; it will never*
> *Pass into nothingness; but still will keep*
> *A bower quiet for us, and a sleep*
> *Full of sweet dreams, and health, and quiet breathing."*

"Oh," Alice said. "Oh."

"All *right*!" Gideon said, as Tiger's ball flew seventy thousand feet into the air.

Alice burst into tears.

That got his attention. "Why, Alice, what's wrong?"

"Oh, Gideon," Alice sobbed. "I don't know!" But she did know. And because she knew Gideon truly loved her, she sputtered, "I guess it just makes me sad, that's all. I mean, sometimes I just plain *hate* getting old! *I* was lovely once! *My* loveliness sure as hell didn't increase! I'm sagging and bagging and bloating! I'm aching and I'm getting too tired too easily, and when I'm not tired, I'm cranky and bored! Plus, I *am* going to pass away into nothingness someday, and I'm so old, that day is just around the corner!"

Gideon struggled up out of the chair, came over to the sofa, and held her for a while. When she caught her breath and dug a tissue out of her robe pocket, he said, in the kind, sensible tone of voice that had made him such an excellent high school math teacher, "Well, you know, Alice, the poem doesn't say 'A person of beauty is a joy forever.' I believe the word is a 'thing.' Like a vase."

She blew her nose. "That's a good point, Gideon."

"Plus," he added, stroking her back, "you *are* lovely, every sagging, bagging, cranky old pound of you. You're downright beautiful, Alice. And I'm changing, too. Look at me. I used to use Head & Shoulders. Now I use Mop & Glo."

She forced a laugh. How had she ever deserved such a wonderful man? And why in the hell wasn't she satisfied with her life, now that she had him in it? She gave him a long, affectionate kiss. He held her tightly for a few minutes, then returned to watching television, leaving Alice alone with her cranky thoughts.

The phone rang. She jumped for it.

"Hi, Hon," Shirley said. "How's your holiday going?"

Alice curled up in a chair, settling in for a good talk. "Pretty well, I think." She recounted the evening spent with Alan and Jennifer. Shirley wanted to know every last detail, what all the gifts were, what everyone ate. When she wound down, she asked, "How's your Christmas Eve?"

"Oh, fine." Shirley sounded oddly blue. "Justin's in his office, working on his novel. I slept a lot of the day, since nothing's going on at The Haven."

"Wise of you. You'll be glad you rested up tomorrow." Alice forced herself to sound sympathetic, and she *was,* toward Shirley. It was just that rat Justin she didn't trust. "What time do they all arrive?"

"About one o'clock. It means a hell of a lot of driving for Justin, not to mention it took the skills of a U.N. negotiator to organize a time when both his ex-wives would allow their children to be away from them on Christmas. Justin picks up Angel and Spring in Stoneham at eleven thirty. Then he'll drive to the Braintree mall to pick up Ben, who lives on the Cape. His mom agreed to bring him that far. Then, about forty-five minutes to drive back out here."

"And you're roasting a turkey?"

"I am! I'm even doing it a special way, so it will be nice and tender."

"Good for you." Alice knew that this was a sacrifice for Shirley's vegetarian heart.

"Well, I want them to like me, Alice. We see each other so seldom, and I know their mothers don't want me, the new woman, to be a part of their lives."

"No one could not like you, Shirley."

"Oh, I hope you're right, Alice. I'd like to think this was the first holiday for us as a blended family."

Alice squirmed. Shirley's romantic blindness made Alice as irritable as a cow with a bug in her ear.

Of all the Hot Flash friends, Alice loved Shirley the best. When they first met, Shirley had been a masseuse with a business sense as drifty as the smoke from one of her aromatic candles. With Alice as her mentor, Shirley had changed. She'd taken courses in management and finance. She'd stopped dreaming and actually made her dream of running a wellness spa come true. Alice felt proud of Shirley for all she'd accomplished, and protective of her, too.

Alice had been in charge of personnel for a major insurance company for most of her life, so she'd developed keen instincts for liars, schemers, and bullshitters. And Justin Quale was all of those. She just *knew* it. Alice hadn't criticized Shirley when she started dating Justin, thinking—hoping—the romance would die a natural death. After all, Shirley was twelve years older than Justin and thrilled that this man, who had a Ph.D. in literature and wanted to write novels, would choose Shirley, who had never even graduated from high school. When Shirley let Justin move into The Haven, Alice had expressed her displeasure in no uncertain terms, although when Shirley hired him to teach a writing course there, Alice hadn't made too much of a fuss.

But now, something fishy was going on. Alice could *smell* it, just as surely as she knew it when her boys were teenagers and tried to sneak past her with mint on their breath, too naïve to know she could smell the smoke on their clothes.

For all Shirley's chirpy optimism, in spite of how much she had learned about business and looked and acted like an intelligent, powerful woman, she was really quite vulnerable. In her heart, Shirley believed in fairy tales. Alice did too—as long as they were by the Brothers Grimm. Justin's princely façade covered the soul of a toad. Alice *knew* it. But what could she do?

"I can't wait for the kids to see the tree," Shirley rambled on moonily. "It's the first time I've ever decorated a tree for a family. It's on the small side, but you know my condo's cozy, a bigger tree wouldn't have worked. Besides, it's kind of cute, how all the presents sort of overwhelm the tree. I've spent *hours* wrapping each present."

"Better have a camera ready."

"Oh, I do! I've told Justin to hand the presents out one by one, so I can photograph each child opening it. I can't wait to see their faces!"

"I wonder what they'll give you."

"Oh, I don't care. Probably nothing. Christmas is all about *giving*. Oh, Alice, this is going to be the best Christmas of my life!"

"I hope so," Alice said warmly, and she meant it, but as she hung up the phone, her face was creased with worry.

6

When Shirley awoke at six o'clock on Christmas morning, her heart jumped straight from slo-mo sleep mode into speed skating.

At sixty-two, Shirley knew a racing heart was not a good thing. And come on, why was her ridiculous heart flipping around like this? She shouldn't be nervous. When was she going to grow up? When was she going to stop being a coward? Hadn't she proven herself enough already?

Gazing upon the beautiful face of her beloved Justin, who snored lustily on the pillow next to her, she told herself, "I can *do* this!"

Pulling on the filmy peach robe that set off her tousled auburn hair, she went to the window and looked out upon her domain, the elegant grounds spreading around the magnificent stone building that once had been a private school and now was The Haven. Wasn't Shirley the director of The Haven, just as if she were an intelligent person with good business sense? The rule of thumb, she'd been told, was that new businesses didn't turn a profit until the third year. This was only the beginning of their second year, and already they were beginning to show one.

More than that, she'd provided a nurturing home base for hundreds of women in the Boston area, including her best friends.

Not to mention that while doing all this, she'd continued to stay away from the seductive charms of alcohol. She'd been sober for years now. She was living proof that a person could change her bad habits.

She had all the evidence she needed that she was an intelligent, rational person, right? She should be able to trust her own judgment, right?

On the bed, Justin snorted and puffed volcanically. She'd let him sleep. He deserved it, after the way he'd made love to her last night. Shirley hugged herself. Looking at Justin made her as happy as, well, as a kid on Christmas. She *loved* Justin, and she knew that even though he was twelve years younger than she, he loved her, too, just as sincerely. Her Hot Flash friends just had to stop fretting. They didn't know all the sweet things he said to her, not to mention the sweet things he did to her!

Shirley padded into the living room and did a few minutes of sun salutations. Then she went through the dining area to the kitchen. She drank her orange juice, ate some fruit yogurt, and brewed green tea, all the time going over her plans for the day.

Because she was a vegetarian, she hadn't roasted meat for decades. But Justin's kids were coming for Christmas dinner, and that meant turkey. She'd researched ways to make it tender, juicy, and delicious. She'd bought tons of veggies. And she'd bought a pumpkin pie and a cherry pie from Alan and Jennifer's bakery, so she didn't have to worry about dessert.

She had to start the turkey now. She'd decided to put it in a brown paper bag to make it especially tender, so she turned on the oven, organized her roasting pan, and hoisted the heavy bird out of the refrigerator. It was a fresh free-range turkey from a farm. She rinsed it, then rubbed it all over with butter and olive oil. Getting it into the paper bag wasn't easy, but she managed it and slid it into the oven.

There. That much done!

She washed her hands and her few breakfast things with organic soap, setting them in the wooden rack to dry. She double-checked the living room. *Perfection.* The tree and its presents glittered. And Justin's present, her *real* present, was hidden in Shirley's purse. She'd give it to him tonight when they were alone together. Tears sprang to her eyes as she thought of how Justin would look when he saw it.

She puttered around in the dining area, spreading the holiday tablecloth she'd bought especially for the occasion, setting out the plates and silverware and napkins. For the center of the table, she'd bought a long, low arrangement of red and white carnations—not expensive, but festive.

Everything was ready for the best Christmas of her life.

At ten thirty, Shirley leaned over the bed, put her hand on Justin's gorgeous naked shoulder, and gently shook him. "Hon? It's ten thirty. You'd better get going."

"Mrrph." Justin opened his eyes. "Okay. Thanks."

As he showered and shaved, Shirley made the bed and tidied the bedroom. Another good thing she'd accomplished, she thought, was helping Justin get to see his kids more often. Both his ex-wives were angry with him, and Shirley didn't blame them, because over the years he really hadn't been very good about paying child support or showing up for scheduled visits. What they didn't understand, of course, was that Justin was an artist, a writer, a sensitive, poetic soul who just could not be bound by the rigid laws imposed on ordinary people.

Justin hurried out of the bedroom and began pulling on his clothes, his silver hair in its ponytail still damp. Shirley perched on the end of the bed, watching him. God, he was beautiful! It was Fate, really, that had brought them together. They'd met in a management seminar. It was Justin's own brother, a Realtor, who showed Shirley the run-down old estate that was now the flourishing home of The Haven. No one could tell her that she and Justin weren't *meant to be.*

"Okay, Sweetface, gotta go." Justin bent over, kissed her, and went off.

Shirley headed into the bathroom for her own shower. The

thing her Hot Flash friends just couldn't seem to get was that Justin was an *intellectual*. He had a bachelor's and a master's degree in English literature, and he'd taught at various colleges and universities, but he'd never been given tenure because the world was swamped with English professors. "Publish or perish" was the unwritten academic law, but as much as Justin had struggled, he hadn't been able to teach, grade a million papers, sit on endless committees, and still find the psychic energy to write. So when his contract at a junior college was not renewed, Justin had decided to try the business sector. He'd signed up for the management seminar, hoping to learn enough to land a decent day job. He went to work at a real estate office and tried to write at night.

It was a good plan, and Justin did work hard. No one could deny that. It wasn't his fault that the real estate deals he invested in fell through. His own brother had advised him, and his own brother had lost money, too. But his brother had a lot of money to play with; Justin didn't. While Justin had been riding his professional roller coaster on its downward plunge, Shirley, with the help of her Hot Flash friends and a few wealthy investors, had gotten The Haven off the ground. It was only natural for her to invite Justin to teach a few courses in creative writing at the spa. His classes were always filled to the max—again, a fact no one could argue with. For a while, Justin rented a condo at The Haven for a nominal amount, but that made Alice cranky, plus it was a slight—*very* slight—financial negative for The Haven, so Shirley had invited him to move in with her and they rented his condo to Star, the yoga teacher.

Finally, Justin had the emotional space and comfort for writing his novel. He'd slaved over it, Shirley knew. She'd carried endless cups of coffee to him as he sat typing away at his laptop on the dining room table. He'd written hundreds and hundreds of pages in a storm of creation. A few months ago, he'd declared the novel nearly finished. Shirley was sure the work was brilliant, although Justin was too shy to let her read the book.

Perhaps it was because he hadn't yet been able to get an agent.

It wasn't Justin's fault. The publishing world was as corrupt and difficult as the academic world. Everyone knew that. He didn't have the right contacts. He was disappointed—close to despair.

Shirley studied her body in the mirror as she dressed for the day. So many wrinkles, so many lines! Her Hot Flash friends, Polly, Marilyn, Alice, and Faye, could console themselves that no matter how used up their bodies looked, it was all right. They'd given birth to children. Their bodies *had* been used. The same could be said for the sags and wrinkles on their faces—no one had gotten through the business of motherhood without some difficulties, disappointments, and sorrows. The love, worry, fear, and labor that made them good mothers marked their faces, and because of that, they would not change a thing.

But Shirley had never had children. She had wanted children. With all her heart, she had wanted children. But it had just never been in the cards, and now the marks on her face, the long, deep lines, seemed like the tracks of tears engraved in her skin.

Which was why Justin was so important to her. She could actually help make *his* dreams come true. That was a luxury she'd never experienced. Alice, Faye, Marilyn, and Polly could close their eyes and remember all the years when their kids went wide-eyed on Christmas morning, or when they gave their kids the puppy or the kitten or the new dress or the bike they'd been longing for. The greatest joy in life wasn't getting, it was giving. Just once in her life, Shirley was going to experience that.

She couldn't wait. It really made her *shiver*. It would be wonderful, seeing the kids open their presents. But it would be a once-in-a-lifetime event on the order of a miracle to give Justin his present tonight.

She knew what Justin was giving her, and it was very important that she give him his present first. She hadn't even been looking; she'd been dusting the condo. His briefcase had been sitting on the dining room table, next to his laptop and his stack of papers. It had been open, and Shirley had carelessly glanced inside. It was crammed with student essays and handouts for his creative writing course, but wedged down at the bottom was a small black velvet box.

The sight had electrified her as if she'd been struck by lightning.

"Oh my God!" she'd whispered, covering her mouth. Justin was just in the other room. They'd been talking about marriage recently, in a playful, daydreamy kind of way. She knew Justin loved her. She knew he liked to surprise her. She danced away from the dining room table, jubilant. His Christmas present to her was an engagement ring!

"Let's wait and exchange our Christmas presents on Christmas night," she'd suggested a week or so ago. "When we're alone and relaxed."

"Good idea," he'd agreed. Today was the first holiday they were spending all together, as if they were a kind of family.

———————

At one o'clock, her cell phone rang.

"Shirley," Justin said, "Ben's mom was late getting him here. We're just leaving Braintree."

"That's fine, Hon. Thanks for letting me know!" Shirley wondered what to do about the turkey. She didn't want it to dry out, so she covered it and left it in the oven.

———————

At two fifteen, the door flew open and they all stomped in.

Angel and Spring wore low-cut jeans with cropped sweaters. Spring's hair was short, spiked, and blue. Angel's was long and curly. Both girls wore glittering gold eye shadow and thick, frosted lipstick. Shirley tried to take that as a kind of compliment, that they'd dressed up to come to her place. Ben, only ten, hulked behind his half-sisters, looking sullen.

Shirley chirped, "Merry Christmas, everyone!" Pushing a little switch, she turned on her necklace and earrings so they flashed.

Spring, the most sophisticated at fifteen, rolled her eyes. But thirteen-year-old Angel said, "Cute!"

Ben pulled off his down jacket, dropped it on the floor, and waded into the pile of presents. Grabbing one of the larger ones, he picked it up and shook it. "What's in here?"

"Well, let's all get settled and you'll find out! I thought your father could hand out—"

Ben read the tag. "Mine." With both hands, in one long, violent tear, he ripped the paper from the box. "Cool! A PlayStation 2!"

"You got PlayStation?" Spring asked excitedly. "Wow! What did we get?"

As if they operated with one brain, Spring and Angel, in sync, threw themselves at the presents, scanning the tags, tossing ones without their names over their shoulders in Ben's general direction.

"Kids, kids!" Shirley cried. "Slow down! I want to get pictures of you opening your presents!"

But the three kids were like hounds digging for buried bones. They went at the presents in a frenzy, ripping the wrapping paper, shredding the beautiful bows without so much as a glance, tossing each present aside in their hurry to get to the next one.

"We got a DVD player!" Angel trumpeted, sticking out her tongue at Ben.

"*We* already have a DVD player, dummy," Ben sneered.

"We got the coats!" Spring screamed at Angel as she opened a large box. "I told you Shirley would get them for us."

Shirley perked up, waiting for them to thank her. When they didn't, she told herself to be glad the girls assumed she would do something nice for them. That was a start, wasn't it?

"A skateboard! Awesome." Ben jumped up. "I'm going to take this outside."

"Wait!" Shirley said. "Let's have Christmas dinner first."

"Aw, crap," Ben whined. "Dad! Come on!"

"Why don't you go try it out for just a few minutes," Justin told his son. "While we get dinner on the table."

"*I'm* not helping set the table if *he's* not helping!" Spring snarled.

"No, kids, you don't have to help," Shirley hastily assured them. "Everything's done; I just have to put the food on the table."

"I'll just stay inside," Ben decided, grabbing up his new Play-Station.

"Well?" Spring demanded. "I thought you said dinner was ready. I'm starving."

Shirley was almost dizzy. The opening-presents event had been a free-for-all, over almost before it was begun. The girls were already ignoring their coats, DVDs, cosmetic kits, and other presents and sat on the sofa, fighting over the television remote control.

"MTV!"

"No, VH1!"

Ben leaned against the sofa, fingers flying over his electronic game, already lost in another world.

No one had brought her a present, Shirley realized, with a twinge of disappointment. But no one had given their father a present, either. That was just *mean*.

"I'll help you put the food on," Justin said.

She gave him the best smile she could conjure up. "Thanks."

In the kitchen, she heated the creamed broccoli, the cauliflower au gratin, the marshmallow-topped sweet potatoes, the carrots simmered in brown sugar and butter. Justin's kids all liked their veggies disguised by sauces, the sweeter the better. She dished them into serving bowls, and Justin carried them to the table.

"Okay!" Shirley said. "Now, Justin, if you'll just hold the big platter, I'll put the turkey on it."

She pulled oven mitts on and lifted out the heavy pan.

"Hey!" Drawn by the aroma, Ben stood in the doorway to the kitchen. "That smells good."

His half-sisters came to stand behind him, peering over his shoulder.

"Turkey. Cool," Angel said. "We have to eat *goose* tonight. Ugh."

"My mom's fixing leg of lamb," Ben said, making gagging noises.

"Ughghghgh!" both girls croaked.

Shirley's cheeks were hot with happiness—she'd done something *right*! She'd cooked a Christmas turkey!

Carefully she cut open the brown paper bag. The turkey was gorgeous, golden brown, steaming with heat and flavor. Justin held the platter out.

Shirley put a long fork in each end of the turkey and lifted it away from the roasting pan toward the platter.

With a kind of mushy, squishing liquid sound, most of the meat fell away from the bones, splatting in greasy pieces on the floor.

"Oooh, gross!" Ben cried.

"I'm not eating that!" Spring exclaimed.

"Me, either!" Angel echoed.

Visions of a strong gin and tonic danced in Shirley's head.

———————

Fueled by Shirley's optimistic energies, the day staggered on. Enough meat remained on the turkey to feed everyone. The kids even ate the vegetables. Justin went out to watch Ben on his skateboard while Shirley, on a whim, gave the girls a tour of The Haven. Then Justin drove the kids home, while Shirley gathered up the torn wrapping paper and bows and removed the various glasses, plates, and cups the kids had left around the place. She did the dishes and cleaned up the fallen turkey mess—what a literal pain in the back!

Now, *at last,* Christmas night was here. The condo was clean, the tree twinkled brightly, and Shirley had turned off all the other lights and set candles glowing around the room. Christmas music spilled softly from the CD player. Shirley redid her makeup and tousled her hair, wanting to look perfect for the coming perfect moment.

Justin came in, smelling of fresh air and snow. "Let me fix a drink, and we can open our presents."

"Lovely," Shirley said. "I've made myself a pot of tea."

Justin sank down on the sofa next to her. "Cheers, Shirley," he said, toasting her. "Thanks for making this such a wonderful day for all of us."

His praise touched her deeply. "I loved every minute of it."

He raised his eyebrows and grinned. "*Every* minute?"

She laughed. "The bit with the turkey was a little embarrassing."

"We'll all be laughing about it a few years from now," Justin assured her.

Hey! There was a long-range plan if she'd ever heard one. Shirley's heart swelled in her chest. She blinked back tears.

"I want to give you your present now." She bent to retrieve the little red box left under the tree. It looked like a cuff link box. She hoped he would think it was cufflinks.

Justin set his drink on the table and put the present on his lap. Carefully, he undid the ribbon and lifted the lid off the box.

Inside was a check. From Shirley to Justin. For ten thousand dollars.

Frowning, Justin looked at Shirley. "What's this?"

Shirley was practically squirming all over, like a puppy who'd just dropped his bone at his master's lap. "It's money! So you can self-publish your novel! And pay for a graphic artist to give it a dynamite cover. And in a few more months, I'm going to give you another check, so you can hire someone to help you publicize your book."

Justin looked dumbfounded. He shook his head. "Shirley, I can't take this much money from you."

"But that's how much you need. You told me so, yourself."

"Yes, but—"

"Justin, take it, please. I want to help you make your dream come true."

He ran his hand over his head. "I don't know. I just don't know."

She waited, holding her breath.

When he looked at her, his eyes were shining. "Shirley, I've never had anyone love me this much. I don't know what to say." He stood up and paced the room, walking like a man in a dream.

Then he came back to the sofa, knelt in front of Shirley, and took her hands in his. "All right. I'll do it. I'll take your money and publish my novel. On one condition: every cent I make from it comes back to you, until I pay this debt off."

"It's not a debt, silly, it's a present," Shirley reminded him.

"I'm serious, Shirley. I'm going to put it in writing. Any profit from my novel goes to you."

God, she loved this man! He had such integrity! "All right," she agreed.

He pulled her down to him and kissed her passionately. "I love you, Shirley. I love you so much."

"I love you."

Rising, he said, "God, this is so exciting! I've already investigated several self-publishing presses, but now *I get to choose*. I've got to make a list, and actually, I'd better get some information off the Net. I'll want to go to their offices, meet these people, see what they propose to give me for my money."

Shirley pulled her knees up and hugged them against her, watching Justin in his excitement.

"Oh!" Justin said, stopping midpace. "I haven't given you your present yet."

Justin reached into his pocket and brought out the small black velvet box. Returning to the sofa, he sat next to Shirley and put the box in her hand.

"This is nothing compared to what you've given me," he told

her somberly. "I'm sorry I couldn't afford something bigger. I'd like to give you a diamond as big as the Ritz."

"Silly," Shirley said, kissing him lightly on the lips. It was, after all, the thought that counted. She didn't care if the diamond was the size of a grape seed; it was still an engagement ring.

She opened the box.

And gasped.

Inside, tucked into a slot in the black velvet, lay two tiny diamond ear studs.

She couldn't help it. Tears leapt into her eyes. Ear studs, and she'd thought it was an engagement ring! For a moment, a terrible bitterness filled her mouth like an acid. She felt like such a fool for assuming it was a ring!

"Don't cry, darling," Justin said. "You're worth it."

7

Cool, elegant Carolyn's Christmas decorations were all silver and white.

"It's rather like entering a spaceship," Hugh remarked, as he and Polly went into the house.

"Polly, Hugh, lovely to see you! Merry Christmas!" Carolyn, elegant in a red cashmere dress, air kissed them both before pulling them into the living room, where a bartender offered them flutes of Champagne.

The large, airy rooms were already crowded. Hank's aristocratic and rather daffy mother, Daisy, was there, carrying her pet Shih Tzu, Clock, everywhere in her arms and talking to the dog more than to the human beings. One of Hank's sisters, Evelyn, was there, with her husband and their three young children. Ingrid, Carolyn's new au pair, drifted through the room with baby Elizabeth in her arms.

Faye was ensconced on the sofa, her legs stretched out and one ankle elevated on a cushion. Her neck brace made it difficult for her to turn her head easily, so anyone talking with her had to sit on the coffee table facing her.

Polly made a beeline for Faye. "Merry Christmas, Faye! How do you feel?"

Faye managed a smile. "Awful, to tell the truth. If I don't use painkillers, I'm in agony, and if I do use them, I'm in the Twilight Zone."

Now that she was close to her, Polly could see how pale Faye was. Wanting to cheer her up, she said, "Well, you *look* gorgeous!"

A chiming noise vibrated the air.

Carolyn tapped a glass with a knife until she had everyone's attention. "Dinner's served!"

Aubrey leaned over the back of the sofa, placing an affectionate hand on Faye's shoulder. "I'll bring you a plate."

"Thanks, Aubrey." Faye made a little shooing gesture. "Go on, Polly, fix your own plate. I'll be fine."

Polly, Hugh, and Aubrey joined the line at the table. It was set buffet style, with the food served by a smiling young caterer. Suddenly, Carolyn materialized out of thin air.

"Here, Hugh." Carolyn handed him a plate heaped with food. "Take this to Faye, will you?" Deftly she turned to Aubrey. "Father, why don't you sit at the little table by the tree with Elizabeth? And Polly, could you hold Elizabeth for me? She knows you and Father, she won't fuss with you two." Before Polly could object, Carolyn lifted her baby out of Ingrid's arms and plunked her into Polly's.

So, smoothly Carolyn paired off her father with Polly. Of course, Polly loved holding the little girl. At eight months, Elizabeth was only seven months younger than Polly's grandson, still cuddly and full of bubbles and baby babble. Aubrey clearly adored his granddaughter, holding her while Polly ate. Then Polly returned the favor, and she couldn't help it; she enjoyed talking with Aubrey, no doubt about that. He was a handsome, charming man. She told him about setting her house on fire. He laughed heartily.

From time to time, Polly glanced over at Faye, reclining on the sofa, with Hugh close by. The two were talking and laughing quite happily, Polly thought. It's just a party, she reassured herself. We're supposed to talk to everyone at parties.

After dinner, everyone settled in the living room around the Christmas tree and the fire. Aubrey stationed himself next to Faye, sitting on the edge of the sofa, occasionally touching her lightly with his hand or leaning down to whisper something that made her smile.

Hugh returned to Polly's side, his jovial face flushed and bright. "What a feast! And such fascinating people."

So everything was all right, Polly thought, with relief.

Then Carolyn and Hank brought out the Perrier Jouët Champagne. Since Elizabeth's premature birth in April, Carolyn had lost her baby weight and regained her strong, healthy blond beauty. Her father had handed over control of the Sperry Paper Company to her, they'd moved into this new house, and Carolyn was thriving. She radiated confidence and well-being. Polly felt a moment of almost maternal pride as she watched the lovely young woman.

Carolyn's mother had died when she was young, and because of Carolyn's dedication to the company, handed down matrilineally through the generations, she hadn't had a chance to keep up old friendships or develop new ones. When Polly met her last year at The Haven, Carolyn was a very isolated woman. Polly, who was cold-shouldered by her own daughter-in-law, had loved the opportunity to talk about all the things women over the ages discussed: the eccentric physical problems of pregnancy, the doubts about being a good mother. Gradually, they'd become such close friends that when Carolyn went into premature labor while Hank was out of town, she had called Polly for help.

Polly alone had been privy to Carolyn's fears and struggles. She'd helped her uncover Aubrey's new wife's devious, money-grubbing scheme. Polly had been there when Elizabeth was born. She'd spent hours helping Carolyn adjust to the demands of motherhood. She'd become a kind of second mother to the young woman.

But that didn't mean Polly should pair off with Carolyn's father, even though that seemed to be what Carolyn wanted.

Now Carolyn raised her glass in a toast. "Merry Christmas, everyone!"

They all cheered and drank.

"I want to thank my mother-in-law and sister-in-law and brother-in-law for coming to spend this Christmas with us." Carolyn looked very beautiful as one of her great-grandmother's magnificent ruby-and-diamond necklaces sparkled around her throat. "This has been a year of many changes."

"You had a baby!" chirped her five-year-old niece, and everyone laughed.

"Indeed, I did." Carolyn looked at her daughter, nestled now in her husband's arms. Leaning forward, she kissed Elizabeth's nose. "And my father and I moved from the family home, which is being converted into a museum for the town. Hank and I have turned this new house into a comfortable home, we've hired Ingrid as our housekeeper/nanny, and the Sperry Paper Company has had the best year in a decade."

More cheers.

When the noise died down, Carolyn spoke again. "And I couldn't have done it all without you, Polly." She flushed as she spoke. Carolyn was always uneasy with emotion. "You were like the mother I never had. You've taught me so much, and you've helped me so much. I wish I could adopt you as my mother, but since I can't, Hank and I would like to ask you to be Elizabeth's godmother."

It should have been a poignant moment. Instead, Polly felt like an onion dropped into an emotional Cuisinart, sliced and diced by the various needs of the others in the room. Carolyn's request made Polly's heart swell with love and sympathy—she knew how hard it was for Carolyn to show affection. She knew how much Carolyn needed a mother. And baby Elizabeth was adorable.

But if Polly agreed to be Elizabeth's godmother, that would tie her in even closer to Carolyn's family. Would it drive a wedge between Polly and Faye?

Of all the Hot Flash Club, Faye was the one Polly liked the best. She was the one with whom Polly had the most in common. They were both widowed by men they had loved. They each had one child: Faye, a daughter; Polly, a son. They wanted to be grandmothers more than Marilyn, who was obsessed with her ancient fossils, or Shirley, who had never had children and was focused on running The Haven, or professional, no-nonsense Alice.

A volcanic blast of heat exploded through Polly. She couldn't think—she wanted to pour her Champagne right down the front of her dress, *anything* to cool off!

"Polly?"

Polly blinked.

Carolyn and all the others in the room were smiling at her, waiting for her reply. What could she say?

"I—I—Why, Carolyn, it's an *honor* to be asked to be Elizabeth's godmother."

Carolyn was never shy about closing a deal. "So you accept?"

What else could she say? "I accept!"

NEW YEAR'S DAY

8

New Year's Day dawned white and frigid and only got worse, as a howling wind blew tiny stinging bits of snow, like grains of sand, against buildings, trees, and cars, and into the eyes of anyone foolish enough to brave the elements.

The Haven was officially closed, most of its windows dark. But the lights were on in the locker room, and in the beautifully tiled Jacuzzi room, the hot tub bubbled and steamed. Five women in bathing suits were sinking into the healing heat of hot water and good gossip. Although they often phoned one another, the Hot Flash Club members tried to keep their juiciest news and latest crises for an occasion when they were all together, so they could all weigh in with opinions, argue, and brainstorm. But the holidays had thrown them off schedule. They had a lot to catch up on.

Marilyn held her mother's hand until Ruth was securely seated, her head resting against the back of the tub. Ruth wore one of Marilyn's bathing suits, and Marilyn couldn't help but think she was seeing the Ghost of Christmas Future in her mother's body. Like Marilyn, Ruth was slender, and for a woman in her eighties she was in good shape, but the top of the swimsuit hung loosely over her shriveled breasts while the tummy section bulged out in a little round pudding. Ruth's skin was freckled and wrinkled, creased like tissue paper, and beneath the fragile covering, her green veins wound around her bones like vines over a trellis.

Ruth's toenails were yellow, thick, and hard as ice cubes. Marilyn had cut them for her this morning, and painted them with the polish she had in the house only because her Hot Flash friends insisted she use it from time to time.

"I've always liked my toes," Ruth had confided. "I think of them as ten friendly little companions. Hello down there!" she called. Wiggling her toes, she responded in a squeaky voice, "Hello up there!"

Okay, she's senile, Marilyn thought.

Ruth continued, "You and Sharon liked your toes, too, when you were young, remember? You used to draw faces on your toes and make little caps for them out of bits of yarn or foil."

Marilyn slapped herself in the forehead. "You're right! We did!"

Memories flooded back: Long afternoons in the Ohio summer heat. She and Sharon had spent hours painstakingly drawing faces on and dressing each other's toes, tying bits of ribbon around them as neckties or tutus. Then they'd lie side by side on the grass in the shade of a tree, holding musical revues, making their toes dance while they sang songs they'd heard their grandmother sing. "Five foot two, eyes of blue," or "Hey, good lookin', whatcha got cookin'." Did anyone sing those songs anymore?

A door opened up in her mind. Marilyn felt she could step through it and reenter those summer days, which shimmered green-golden and fresh and sounded like little girls giggling. The innocence, the happiness, the *there*ness of it all swept through her. She remembered how she'd been especially fond of one of her birthmarks, the brown one on her left thigh. It had looked like a piece of a miniature jigsaw puzzle.

"Marilyn?" Her mother's voice interrupted her thoughts.

"All done!" Marilyn stuck the brush back inside the bottle and tightened it.

Later, as they drove to The Haven, Marilyn thought how her mother was a living repository of memories. When Ruth was gone, who would remember, who would care, about Marilyn's girlish toes?

Now, as Ruth bobbed in the Jacuzzi, she kept letting her feet float up so she could admire her painted nails. Marilyn noticed how

Ruth smiled every time she saw the perky spots of pink peek up through the water. *Hello up there!* she thought.

"Did you have a nice Christmas, Ruth?" Alice asked.

Ruth's face lit up. "It was *lovely*. We spent Christmas Eve with Teddy and Lila and my adorable little great-granddaughter, Irene."

"Was Eugenie there?" Shirley asked.

"She was, indeed," Ruth answered. "We could hardly pry little Irene out of her clutch."

"And guess what!" Marilyn looked at her friends with a grin. "Eugenie had a *bad* face-lift. Very *Phantom of the Opera*." Seeing Polly's puzzled face, she hastened to explain, "I know it seems callous of me to be silly about another woman's bad face-lift, but Eugenie is so superficial and critical and such a terrible snob—"

Shirley was glad Marilyn was so chatty today. She loved her friends and, as always, loved being around them, but sooner or later she was going to *have* to tell them about her gift to Justin. She let herself sink deeper and deeper into the water, so that her mouth was submerged and only the top of her head from her nose up showed.

"You've got to tell Faye about this," Alice said. "After all, she 'worked' for Eugenie."

"I wish Faye were here now," Polly said.

"I do too." Shirley slid up out of the water so she could talk. "I told her we'd be glad to pick her up, or even go to her house so she wouldn't have to deal with traveling in a car. But she said she really needed to rest."

Marilyn frowned. "Still, it's not like Faye not to come out. I hope she's okay."

"I think she's depressed," Polly told them. "I saw her Christmas night for dinner at Carolyn's house. When we had a chance to talk alone for a while, she told me that her daughter's pregnant again."

"That's great!" Shirley looked puzzled. "That should thrill Faye."

"It does, but Faye also learned that Lars's parents are moving to San Francisco so they can be near their son and his family. Lars's mother plans to help Laura when she has the new baby, so they won't have to hire a nanny. Faye feels horribly left out. She almost started crying when she told me."

"Oh, dear, poor Faye!" Marilyn's face crinkled with worry.

Shirley tried to be optimistic. "Good thing she's got Aubrey to keep her occupied."

Polly considered holding her breath and sinking to the bottom of the tub. She wanted to share her discomfort about the whole Carolyn/Aubrey business with the Hot Flash group, but now, in the soothing intimacy of the hot tub, she decided to ignore her worries. "Yes, Aubrey seems quite smitten with Faye."

"How was your Christmas?" Shirley asked.

"Well, let's see." Polly was glad to change the subject. Playfully, she cocked her head, pretending to search her memory. "Well, I *did* set my house on fire just when my daughter-in-law arrived."

"You set your house on fire! Oh, Polly!" Marilyn's mother looked horrified.

Polly waved her hands in the air. "It's all right. No one was hurt." She didn't want poor Ruth to have a heart attack. "Some greenery on the mantel caught fire. It was quite spectacular for a few moments, but only one wall was ruined. Well, and the other walls and ceiling were smoke-damaged. Fortunately, my insurance covers it, so I'll have the living room repainted. The problem is, it gives Amy one more reason to stay away from me."

"What's the matter with that girl?" Alice shook her head impatiently. "She sounds loony."

"I know," Polly agreed. "I'll never understand why David married her."

Ruth piped up, "*I* never understood why Marilyn married Theodore. He was always such a pompous little rooster."

"We got Teddy out of the marriage, Mother," Marilyn reminded her.

Polly leaned forward. "Marilyn, what did Faraday give you for Christmas?"

Marilyn very busily adjusted the strap on her Speedo.

"Oh, boy." Alice chuckled. "This is going to be good."

"Oh, Alice!" Marilyn slapped the water in exasperation.

"Come on, out with it," Alice coaxed.

"Oh, no!" Marilyn was turning red all over. "I've got to get out for a minute." Pushing herself up, she left the steamy room.

"Those hot flashes make her miserable," Ruth told the others. "She's forever pulling off her clothes. I told her she should call herself Dixie Rose Lee."

The others looked confused.

"Gypsy!" Shirley cried. "You mean Gypsy Rose Lee."

"That's what I said."

Marilyn returned, slightly less flushed. "I'll just sit out here for a while." She folded herself Indian–style on the tiles.

"So," Alice prompted. "You were saying . . ."

Marilyn made a face. "Faraday asked me to marry him."

"Oh, my God!" In her excitement, Shirley popped up like a piece of toast. "That's so wonderful! Oh, Marilyn!"

Alice yanked Shirley back down into the water. "Calm down, Shirley. We don't know whether Marilyn accepted."

"Well, of course she did!" Shirley responded, indignant. Then she saw Marilyn's face. "Didn't you?"

"Well," Marilyn hedged. "I told him I needed some time to think about it."

"But why?" Shirley asked. "Faraday's so cute! And he's fun! And he likes all that scientific stuff you like."

"True. But—" Marilyn glanced sideways at her mother. "You know, he's got a little problem in the, um, romance department."

"Do you mean he doesn't satisfy you sexually?" Ruth asked, turning to look up at her daughter.

"Well, Mom!" Marilyn blushed again.

"I think you're right to take your time," Alice weighed in. "What's your hurry? It's not like we're young women who've got to worry about ticking biological clocks. You can't have any more children. You're not getting married to get away from home or satisfy your parents. You should only do it if you really want to."

"But if you don't accept," Polly added, worriedly, "he might be insulted or hurt. He might start seeing someone else!"

Ruth stirred in the water. "You know what they say. Marry in haste, repent in leisure wear."

"Well, look." Alice's voice took on its executive tone. "If the only thing holding you back is Faraday's sexual, um, incapacity, then be an adult and try to find a solution. There are some excellent medicines for that kind of thing."

"True. But every time I try to talk with him about this, he stonewalls me."

"Tell him it's a condition of getting engaged," Alice suggested.

Marilyn nodded slowly. "I could do that." Lifting an eyebrow, she subtly nodded in her mother's direction. "It's all so complicated."

Polly got the message and changed the subject. "So, Shirley, how was your Christmas?"

Shirley squirmed. It was now or never. Actually, it didn't *have* to be now. Actually, her financial affairs weren't really any of their business. Except, of course, they were, because her Hot Flash friends had invested, some more than others, in The Haven. It would all come out one way or the other, anyway. She just had to be brave and tell them. But she was already so filled with negative energy, so envious of Marilyn because Faraday had asked her to marry him! And envy was a destructive emotion.

"Boy, do you look guilty," Alice remarked.

Shirley considered simply sliding down into the hot water and staying there. Instead, she pushed her wet hair behind her ears. "Justin gave me diamond ear studs!"

Polly peered at the little gems. "Beautiful!"

Marilyn reentered the water. "Did his kids like their presents?"

Shirley brightened. "They did! But oh, my gosh, wait till you hear about my gourmet Christmas dinner!"

As Shirley laughingly told them about the disintegrating turkey, Alice settled back against the Jacuzzi, adjusting herself so one of the jets hit her right in a sore spot in her back. The heat mellowed her out, and she was just beginning to feel ashamed for thinking ill of Justin, when Shirley said:

". . . so I want to tell you about it. It was kind of my Christmas present to Justin, but more than that, really. Remember when I said I thought this Christmas should be about dreams coming true? How we've talked about this time of our lives being about making dreams come true? Well, you know Justin's written a novel, but he hasn't been able to find a publisher." She held up a hand. "Just wait! It's hard to find a publisher. You all just don't have any idea."

"You're right," Marilyn agreed. "I've heard some of my MIT acquaintances talk about this. It's a real struggle to find a publisher for fiction. There are so many people writing excellent books these days."

Shirley threw a grateful smile Marilyn's way. "So my present to Justin was money. Enough money for him to get his book published, and to get a good cover designed for it. And later, I'm going to give him enough money to promote and publicize it."

For a moment, the only sound in the room was the burbling of the Jacuzzi jets.

Then Alice asked quietly, "How much money did you give him, Shirley?"

Shirley's shoulders drifted up toward her ears and her voice went little-girlish. "You have to understand. He's investigated this. He's checked around. It's not cheap . . ."

"How much?" Alice persisted.

"Ten thousand dollars," Shirley admitted meekly.

Alice exploded. "Ten thousand dollars! Girl, where did you get that much money?"

"It's *my* money, Alice!" Shirley shot back defiantly. "I saved some from my salary over the last two years, and I got the rest on credit card loans."

"Are you nuts?" Alice was volcanic.

"Justin's going to repay me as soon as his book starts selling."

Alice shook her head angrily. "And what if no one buys his book? What then?"

"I don't see why you have to be so pessimistic," Shirley argued.

"I can't do this." Alice hauled herself up out of the Jacuzzi. "Shirley, if you're going to think with your crotch, I'm not going to remain involved with The Haven. I've invested too much of my own time and money to see it jeopardized."

"You're crazy!" Shirley cried. "This doesn't jeopardize The Haven! It's *my* money—"

But Alice strode out of the room, leaving behind only wet footprints on the tile and four women sitting in stunned silence.

Ruth spoke first. "Oh, my."

Shirley was white. "Should I go after her?"

Polly and Marilyn looked at each other helplessly.

"I don't know," Marilyn said. "I wish Faye were here."

"I think you should let her have time to calm down," Ruth advised. "At the retirement community, some of us tend to fly off the hamper more than others, due, I believe, to hardening of the arteries, or feeling cranky because of some physical ailment."

"But Alice is only sixty-three," Shirley said softly.

"I understand," Ruth told her. "Yet anyone at any age can be bothered by something like, oh, constipation. That can affect your mood all day."

"Talk about having your head up your ass," Marilyn said with a grin.

"Indeed," Ruth agreed.

Shirley made little swirls in the water with her fingers. "I hate starting the new year off this way."

"It will work out," Polly assured her Pollyannaishly.

Ruth held up her hands. "My fingers and toes are turning into little white raisins. I think I'd better get out."

"Let's all get out," Shirley suggested. She was about to add that they could come up to her condo for hot chocolate, but she remembered that Justin was there, working on his book, and he wouldn't want to be disturbed. "We could all drive down to Leonardo's to have some dessert!"

"Not me," Polly said. "I'm so stuffed from holiday food, I don't even want chocolate."

Marilyn had her mother by the arm as they carefully made their way up the steps and out of the tub. "I think we'd better go home and have a little rest," she told Shirley, with a slight nod toward her mother, who was unsteady on her legs, leaning heavily on Marilyn.

The locker room was oddly quiet as the four women showered and dressed. Shirley said good night to Polly, Marilyn, and Ruth, then went through the building, checking to be sure all the doors were locked and turning out the lights.

The last thing she did was to unplug the twinkling Christmas tree in the lounge. Then that room was dark as well. Outside the snow fell swiftly, quickly obscuring the footprints and tire tracks of her departed guests. Justin was upstairs, but Shirley felt all alone.

9

The second rule of the Hot Flash Club was "If you're depressed, get up, get dressed, and get out of the house."

But what if you can't?

On New Year's Day, while her Hot Flash friends communed in a hot tub, Faye lay on her living room sofa with her ankle resting on a pillow and her head wobbling in the neck brace like a soft-boiled egg in a cup. She was surrounded by new mysteries, boxes of chocolates, plates of delicious food brought to her by neighbors, the latest magazines, and a pile of DVDs.

She was very crabby.

She felt guilty for not enjoying this enforced laziness. She thought back to the years when the tasks of life had overwhelmed her, when on any given day she'd struggled to drive her little girl to school and ballet practice, organize an elegant dinner party for one of Jack's new clients, pick up the dry cleaning, help out at the church fair, and even try to grab some time in her studio for painting. Back then, she would have wept with joy at the thought of having a week to do nothing but lie around like this, eating and grazing through movies and books like a big, fat cow in a lush, green pasture.

She sort of wished she'd told the Hot Flash Club to meet here at her house today. She'd thought about it. Shirley, Polly, Alice, and Marilyn had all phoned to say they'd drive her out, but Faye had refused, insisting she didn't feel well enough to leave the sofa.

But that was only partly true. While half of her wanted to be around her friends, the other half hunkered down in a gloomy wallow of misery, and Faye just couldn't be bothered to struggle up out of it.

The truth was, she felt worthless. She felt like a kicked dog who'd crawled under the house to nurse her wounds.

This Christmas had been so terrible! Faye grabbed a handful of tissues as the tears started again.

First of all, there was her foolish fall, incapacitating her and making everything difficult for everyone else. Not to mention making her feel old and helpless! And falling down her own stairs—why, it made her seem absolutely *senile*. If she'd had to fall, why couldn't she have fallen out on the ice, a *reasonable* place to fall. She kept flashing back to the moment her foot slipped. It had been so frightening! That sense of total vulnerability, lack of control, danger—and then the painful landing and her body's refusal to move without pain.

Then, to have her own beloved granddaughter shrink in terror from her! That had bruised Faye's heart, even though she understood the cause was her neck brace and crutches. Eventually, Megan got used to them and allowed Faye to hold her, but Faye knew the rich connection of their relationship had been weakened. And during the four nights of their visit, Megan hadn't once slept in or been even slightly captivated by the magical bedroom. Kind, sensitive *Laura* had made an enormous fuss over the darlingness of the room, the fairies, the colors, the attention to detail. Laura had insisted, the last afternoon of their stay, that Faye, Laura, and Megan all spend time in the room, playing Chutes and Ladders, and she'd taken lots of photos of Megan there. Faye knew she could expect a framed picture from Laura in the mail. Laura was thoughtful that way. But Megan would not carry the fantasy room in her dreams. Megan was enchanted with space cowgirls and superheroines. Faye felt oddly embarrassed, like a gawky suitor who'd brushed his pony and polished his wagon, only to find his loved one going off with a guy in a Corvette.

Christmas dinner at Carolyn's hadn't improved her self-esteem.

Faye knew Carolyn adored Polly and wanted to pair up Polly with her father, but this hadn't seemed a real problem until the moment Faye found herself stranded on the sofa, unable to do more than observe.

Carolyn had sent Hugh to bring Faye her dinner, then organized Aubrey, Polly, and baby Elizabeth into a winsome trio. Faye pretended to listen as kindhearted Hugh chatted, but really she was watching Polly, who looked so happy, holding the baby. Polly's own daughter-in-law was such a strange little snake, wriggling between Polly and her son, keeping Polly from seeing her grandchild, that woozy from painkillers, Faye decided it seemed natural—it seemed *right*—for Polly to hook up with Aubrey. They could all be one big, happy family. They *should* be.

As she rode home from Carolyn's house on Christmas night, Faye's spirits had been lower than the road the tires rolled over, and just as flat and cold. She'd done her best to hide her depression from Aubrey, blaming her neck and ankle for her lack of witty repartee.

And then, Christmas night hit.

Shortly after Aubrey brought Faye home, establishing her comfortably on her own sofa before kissing her chastely and leaving, Lars, Laura, and Megan returned from Christmas dinner with Lars's parents. Laura put Megan to bed in the middle of the big bed in the guest room where she and Lars would join her later. Then she came downstairs for a nightcap with her mother and husband.

Lars poured a brandy for himself, a Godiva liqueur for Faye, and only a glass of water for Laura. This, coupled with Laura's weight gain, made Faye's senses flick on to Red Alert. She wasn't completely surprised when Lars said, "We have some news, Faye." Looking fondly at Laura, he announced, "We're going to have another baby. A little boy. In May."

"Oh, Laura!" Faye longed to give her daughter a big hug, but could only smile and raise her glass, struggling to move like a boar stuck in a snowdrift, every movement sending shocks of pain down her neck, into her back and shoulders. "How wonderful, darling!"

"I know, Mom." Laura had been glowing. "I'm so happy. I feel good this time, too. We haven't told Megan yet. I wanted to wait until I was five months along, just to be sure."

"Now let's see." Faye thought aloud, envisioning her daughter's house. "Will you put the baby in with Megan? You have a guest room, and there's that nice little storage room off the kitchen. Will you get a nanny?"

"We're considering that," Laura began, and suddenly she looked uncomfortable. "At first we won't need to—"

Lars cut in. "—because my parents told us today that they're moving to San Francisco! They want to be there to watch their grandchildren grow up, and they'll be able to baby-sit for us or help Laura with the baby, whatever!"

"Oh," Faye said weakly, digging her fingers into her palms, forcing herself not to burst into tears. "How wonderful for you."

Over the next two days, Faye had struggled to prevent Laura from guessing how jealous she felt, how left out. She'd laughed, joked, smiled, and chattered, and whenever Laura asked, "Are you all right, Mom? You look sad," Faye answered, "It's just the pain medication, darling. It makes me feel a bit drowsy."

But when the cab took them off to the airport, Faye sat on the sofa and sobbed.

Since Christmas, Faye had been sunk in emotional quicksand. Marilyn, Alice, Polly, and Shirley had called, offering to stop by with gossip and goodies, but she'd put them off, saying the doctor insisted she needed lots of sleep for healing. Aubrey phoned often, wanting to come by, but she gave him the same excuse.

The truth was, she'd spent the week after Christmas consoling herself and fending off complete despair by eating everything in the house. Boxes of chocolates. Tins of Scottish shortbread. Macaroni and cheese, potatoes and gravy, lasagna. Comfort food. She knew she was gaining weight, but she didn't have the energy to care.

Last night, when Aubrey insisted on coming for New Year's Eve, Faye had cautiously removed her various wrappings and braces and taken a long, hot shower. It hadn't hurt to stand on her ankle—well, maybe a twinge now and then. And her neck felt fine. For a moment, elation began to percolate in her system.

Then she stepped out of the shower and saw her body. A week of overeating, and she looked like Alfred Hitchcock. Worse, when she sorted through her clothes, she couldn't find anything that fit comfortably! She'd been wearing her caftans and loose robes for a week, and hadn't realized how her waist had thickened. Not long ago, she'd cheerfully named her stomach rolls Honey, Bunny, and It's Not Funny. Now the three rolls protruded in one giant blob like a beach ball. The zippers on her largest trousers and skirts wouldn't go all the way up. The buttons wouldn't meet the buttonholes. Her arms bulged inside the sleeves of her sweaters like puppies in a bag. Worst of all, she could see the fat accumulating on her face. Her eyes looked smaller. She was developing jowls.

She wanted to crawl under a rock. It would take a really big rock to hide her. Mount Rushmore.

She had put a caftan back on for Aubrey's visit, and wrapped her ankle to provide an excuse for not leaving the sofa. Aubrey had arrived with expensive Champagne and lobster dinners cooked at one of his favorite restaurants. They'd watched a Thin Man movie with Myrna Loy and William Powell, and at midnight, as they'd watched the ball descend in Times Square, Aubrey gallantly got down on his knees by the sofa so he could embrace Faye and kiss her soundly. She didn't wear her neck brace all evening, and when Aubrey kissed her, she felt, instead of a warm surge of sexual desire, an irritating twang of pain. Aubrey had offered to spend the night, to be there to cook her breakfast in the morning, but Faye sent him away, protesting that all she could really do these days was sleep.

Carolyn was having a New Year's Day buffet today. Aubrey was going, and he'd asked Faye to go with him, but she'd declined.

The bitter truth was that her ankle and neck were both almost completely healed, but her body and soul were shattered.

So here she was, on the first day of the year, back in her braces, useless, unloved, and fat.

Defiantly, she hobbled into the kitchen, microwaved the remains of a pumpkin pie, and covered it with Reddi-whip. Then she went back to the sofa and stuffed the food into her mouth, fast, as if she were building a wall to hold back the tears.

VALENTINE'S DAY

10

On a gloomy February morning, Polly opened the door to her sewing room and looked in.

During the past year, Polly had let her alteration and dressmaking business slide into the background of her life. She'd been so busy helping her mother-in-law, Claudia, who was dying of cancer, that she hadn't had the time or energy to do more than finish the commissions she already had. So she'd told most of her customers she wasn't taking on any new projects for a while, and naturally, they found someone else to shorten their cuffs or fit a dress for a party.

But now Polly decided it was time to try to make a little money. Her husband had left her enough in his will so that she'd never be out on the streets, but any little luxuries in life she had to finance on her own. And that was fine. She enjoyed her work.

With a can of Pledge in one hand and a soft cloth in the other, Polly went around the room, dusting off her cutting table and sewing machine and the cupboard where she kept her fabric, threads, and other sewing supplies. Should she put an ad in the local give-away paper? Or even in the *Boston Globe*? Or perhaps simply phone all her customers, or send them a charming little note? That might be better.

In the far corner of the room, several cardboard boxes were stacked. Polly stopped to consider them. She hadn't really forgotten about them; she just hadn't had time to deal with them.

In November, her mother-in-law's lawyer had phoned to say they had finally finished assessing Claudia's belongings and were ready to make distributions. Claudia had willed several boxes of clothing to Polly; when could they bring them over?

Anytime, Polly had told them, shaking her head. How like Claudia, who had been a wealthy but puritanical old bat, to will her clothing to Polly, who was much too short and plump ever to fit into her lean, lanky mother-in-law's clothing! Not that Polly would ever wear them anyway—Claudia had liked plaid wool skirts and trousers, brisk little white blouses, and severe, shapeless black dresses. Her fashion style made L. L. Bean look like Versace.

Still, Polly thought, Claudia had always invested in good quality. And if Polly wasn't going to use the clothing, she should donate it to Goodwill or someplace else where it would be appreciated.

Taking up her scissors, she cut open the top box, which had been fiercely taped and marked with her name. Folding back the four leaves, Polly looked inside, expecting to see tartan trousers and ancient wool cardigans.

What she saw was so unexpected, it took her eyes a moment to adjust.

Lace. It looked like old lace. Polly dipped her hands in and lifted out an ivory lace evening wrap. Beneath it lay several pairs of lace gloves. Beneath those was a satin packet containing dozens of handkerchiefs trimmed with all kinds of lace. Then, lace nightgowns. Lace slips. Bits of lace, and more bits.

Polly lifted an ivory lawn nightgown out and held it up to the light. It was delicate and beautiful, but ripped in several places. She took out a pale white blouse with lace cuffs and collar. The lace was lovely, but the body of the blouse was stained with dark spots.

She delved deeper into the box, coming up with a pile of lace jabots and dickeys—detachable blouse fronts popular in the early part of the twentieth century but hardly of use now. Lace fichus, scarves, veils, and tippets. How curious!

The second box was piled with lace antimacassars and doilies, lace-trimmed napkins and tablecloths. Beneath were lace pillowcases and lace-trimmed sheets—but not entire sets of sheets, and often not even the entire sheets. In most cases, the lace had been cut away, leaving only a bit of ivory linen or blue cotton attached.

The third box held more lace, and also what looked like hundreds of embroidered handkerchiefs, hand towels, pillowcases, and gloves. Again, every item was either ripped or stained beyond repair.

None of the items was particularly old. Claudia had been in her eighties when she died; perhaps the oldest item was the remnants of a christening gown that might have been hers. None of the lace was of museum quality, yet all of it was lovely. So many different patterns and kinds . . .

Trust Claudia, Polly thought with a laugh, to leave her all this stuff that was not valuable, but was too good to toss out. Probably Claudia's estimate of Polly herself.

She ran her hands over various bits of lace. Could she piece together a pretty blouse for herself? Probably not.

The phone rang, interrupting her thoughts.

"Hi, Polly!" Carolyn's voice was chipper but clipped. "What are you up to on this beautiful day?"

"I'm organizing my workroom," Polly told her. "I've decided to start up my little sewing business again."

"Oh, Polly, if you need money—"

Hurriedly, Polly interrupted Carolyn's offer. "Carolyn, I love my work as much as you love yours. And you are at work now, aren't you?"

"Yes, right. I wanted to call before I forgot. I've decided to give an intimate little dinner party at my house on February fourteenth. Can you come?"

Polly hesitated. "February fourteenth? Valentine's Day?" Carrying the portable phone with her, she walked back to her kitchen and the calendar hanging on the wall, even though she knew damned well she had nothing penciled in for that night.

As if Carolyn read her mind, she continued, "You don't have anything planned with Hugh, do you?"

Polly, who was a terrible liar, stuttered. "We–well, not for-merly."

"What?"

"I mean, not *formally*. I mean, Hugh and I usually spend time together on the weekends, and the fourteenth is a Saturday this year. But I could bring Hugh—"

"Oh, Polly, I was hoping you could come alone. Hank's *other* sister, the one you haven't met yet, will be in town that weekend with her husband, and I wanted you two to get to know each other. I want to have just a little *family* affair."

Polly closed her eyes and leaned against the wall. What Caro-lyn meant was that she wanted her father to come, but without Faye, and she wanted Polly to come, but without Hugh.

"After all," Carolyn continued, "you're part of the family now. You're Elizabeth's godmother."

Carolyn was such a forceful personality, Polly thought. All right, perhaps she was a little spoiled, too, but didn't she deserve to be? She'd lost her mother when she was only seven. And perhaps she was a little bossy, but like many younger women, she had had to learn to be assertive. She ran a large business, after all. Polly didn't want to hurt Carolyn's feelings. She cared so much for her, and was so grateful to feel valuable in, and connected to, someone else's life. Certainly her own son and daughter-in-law were not inviting her for Valentine's Day dinner.

Still, it *was* Valentine's Day! A day to spend with your lover, not your family.

"Let me talk with Hugh," Polly said decisively. "I'm not sure what our plans are. Can I call you back?"

"Sure. If I don't catch the phone, leave a message on the ma-chine."

They spoke a few more minutes. At ten months, Elizabeth was starting to crawl, which meant she also investigated minute bits of mud, fluff, or food accidentally dropped to the floor, bits so small Carolyn and Hank and the nanny couldn't see them from their vantage point. Since Elizabeth considered tasting part of her investigative skills, Carolyn spent much of her time on the floor with her, being sure she didn't pick up the wrong thing.

"Last night," Carolyn said, "Elizabeth found one of those cloth-covered rubber bands Ingrid holds her hair back with. She started gnawing on it before I could stop her, and when I took it away from her—she could choke on it so easily!—she threw such a tantrum, you wouldn't believe it!"

Actually, Polly thought, I *would* believe it. Carolyn's daughter was as strong-willed as her mother. But she kept quiet.

Carolyn said, "Oh, the other line's ringing. I've gotta go, Polly. Call me!"

"I will," Polly promised.

———————————

Polly spent the rest of the day working. She checked out prices of newspaper ads and reviewed her list of customers. Getting out her colored pencils, she played around, composing a clever little communiqué announcing her return to business. It was fun, drawing in bobbins, skirts, a measuring tape, a pincushion, and finally a wedding gown. She wrote the body of the missive on her computer, changing fonts and sizes until she found exactly what worked, then with scissors and tape, cut and pasted her drawings in the margins of the letter. She copied it on her machine and found that it came off quite nicely. She ran off fifty copies, then sat down to the less creative business of addressing the envelopes.

When she decided to stop for the day, she was surprised to find it was after five thirty. The sun was staying out longer. Spring wasn't far away. No wonder she felt cheerful!

She stretched to release the tension in her neck and shoulders, then flicked off the computer and the lights in her workroom and went through the house, turning on lights for the approaching dusk.

Her old hound, Roy Orbison, lay on the sofa, snoring like a powerboat. Usually by five thirty Roy was agitating for his dinner, but tonight he was still sound asleep. Polly gazed down fondly at the dog.

"You're getting on in years, old boy," she said softly. "And so am I."

In the kitchen, she prepared an enormous salad with tons of vegetables and heated up a big mug of chicken broth. As always, she was trying to diet, and tonight she didn't feel especially hungry. Alerted by her noise, Roy woke and joined her in the kitchen, eating his dog food as if he'd just returned from a sixty-mile run. Lucky Roy, who didn't even know the concept of dieting!

After dinner, Polly started a fire in the fireplace and curled up on the sofa with a cup of herbal tea and a fat new mystery. In January, she'd had the smoke-scorched living room repainted in pale yellow while she sewed new drapes and throw-pillow coverings from a gorgeous blue silk printed with birds, boughs, and blossoms. All signs of the Christmas Eve fire had disappeared and the room, even at night, looked fresh and cheerful.

Sometime tonight, she knew, Hugh would phone. On most weeknights he didn't visit Polly, but collapsed in his own apartment, tired from his day at the hospital. He always phoned her, though, and they talked, sometimes for hours, as current dramas reminded them of past events. One of the nicer things about being older, Polly thought, was that they had so much to tell each other, so many memories to recount.

It was almost ten o'clock when Hugh phoned.

"Sorry to call so late," he said. "I fell asleep when I got home. Just woke up a while ago, had a shower and a late meal."

"Busy day at the hospital?" Polly asked as she settled back to listen. Hugh seldom discussed his patients, having more than enough to complain about or entertain Polly with by talking about his staff, the secretaries, his fellow physicians, the hospital administration.

Polly told Hugh what she'd done during the day. Then she took a deep breath, screwed up her courage, and said, as sexily as she could without humiliating herself, "So, Hugh, do we have any plans for Valentine's Day? I noticed on my calendar that it falls on Saturday this year." Hugh was clever and creative about their dates; perhaps he'd take her to some ski resort where they could spend the entire time in the room, drinking hot buttered rum and making love. It had been a marvelous surprise to Polly, what a good lover Hugh was.

"Oh, hell, Polly," Hugh answered. "My daughter's having a Valentine's Day dinner party, just for the family."

Disappointment surged through Polly. What *was* it about this generation of children that they thought Valentine's Day was a family occasion? Polly didn't have to ask whether or not Hugh's ex-wife Carol would be there. Of course she would. It irked her that Carol would be with Hugh on Valentine's Day.

"You still there?" Hugh asked.

"Yes," Polly said, weakly.

"I'm sorry, Poll. I hate to think of you alone on—"

"Oh, I won't be alone," Polly hastened to assure him. She didn't want him ever to pity her. "Carolyn has asked me to dinner at her place that night, but frankly, I'd rather spend it with you."

"Let's have our Valentine's Day dinner Friday night, what do you say?"

"I think we've scheduled our Hot Flash Club meeting for that night, and I'd hate to miss it. We haven't been meeting regularly."

"Sunday night then?"

This was good of him, Polly knew, because Mondays Hugh worked, and Mondays were hard. "Why don't we meet here after our Saturday-night dinner parties?" she suggested. "I'll have lots of Champagne and chocolate, and all kinds of treats, so we can celebrate Valentine's Day Sunday morning. In bed."

Hugh laughed, and Polly's heart went all gooey. Hugh had a wonderful, deep, hearty laugh. She could just see him, his belly trembling, his perfect white teeth gleaming in his handsome face.

"That's a great idea, Polly. Let's make that a date."

After they said good-bye, Polly considered phoning Carolyn to tell her she could come to the dinner, but it was too late, especially since they had a baby in the house. She'd phone first thing in the morning. As Polly got ready for bed, she considered calling Faye tomorrow, to discuss this whole weird triangle they were caught up in, Polly–Carolyn–Faye. Or was it more a pentagon, because Aubrey and Elizabeth were both involved, too? Polly admired Faye so much, but she wasn't sure she could bring up the subject. It was awkward. It was terribly like high school. Oh, well, Polly thought, sliding into bed, at least that made her feel young.

11

It was February thirteenth, and Legal Seafoods was crowded on Friday night, but the five members of the Hot Flash Club were given their usual table tucked away in the far corner of the restaurant where they could chat without being overheard. They settled in, ordered drinks, glanced quickly at the menu—by now they all knew their favorite dishes—then leaned forward.

"Faye, you're here with no neck brace or crutches!" Alice observed. "How are you?"

Faye lifted a languid hand to rub the back of her neck. "I get twinges from time to time. And I think my chances for a speed-skating career are pretty much over."

"But you can always do yoga," Shirley reminded her cheerfully.

Faye flushed. "I *know* I've gained weight. Give me a break! I was hardly able to move for a month. I still have to be careful."

Shirley blinked, surprised at Faye's belligerence. "I didn't mean— Yoga's not about losing weight," she said softly.

Brightly, Marilyn asked, "So, Faye, have you been able to teach your art therapy classes this semester?"

Faye shook her head. "I had to skip the winter semester. I can hardly teach if I can't stand up or move my arms. And I hear the new art teacher is doing beautifully. I doubt if The Haven will need me again."

The other four women exchanged worried glances. Faye, being *negative*?

"Of course The Haven wants you to teach again," Shirley rushed to assure her. "Whenever you're ready."

Faye shrugged and said nothing.

Polly sagged in her chair, nearly ill with guilt. Obviously Faye was depressed. The whole Carolyn–Aubrey–Valentine's Day dinner arrangement had to be part of the cause. Could Polly bring this up now? *Should* she?

Alice turned to Marilyn. "How's your mother? Did she want to join us tonight?"

"She's fine. And there's an old movie on television she wanted to watch, thank heavens. I mean, I adore my mother, but it's nice to get away from her now and then."

"Are you managing to have any time alone with Faraday?" Shirley asked.

Marilyn folded her napkin in careful little pleats. "No, and I'm glad. I know I'm using my mother as an excuse to avoid talking with him about this marriage business, but I do have to decide about Ruth, that's the most important thing right now."

"You've had her with you for two months," Alice pointed out. "How's she doing?"

Marilyn frowned. "Well, you've seen her. She gets words confused now and then—"

"But so do I," Polly interjected.

"—and she forgets what she's doing sometimes—"

"So do I," Shirley said.

Marilyn nodded. "I know. I do, too. Sometimes I have to make a note on a piece of paper and carry it with me from one room to the other. Otherwise, I'll get distracted and forget what I came in for."

Alice laughed. "I hear you. The other day I was on a tear, looking for my reading glasses, and all the time they were on top of my head. I said to Gideon, 'Good grief, Hon, how are you going to know when I'm senile?' "

"Exactly!" Marilyn agreed, then said in an irritated tone, "Oh, *damn*!" She unbuttoned her cardigan and tore it off.

"Hot flash," Polly said sympathetically.

Marilyn nodded and fanned herself with the menu. "What were we talking about?"

"Your mother," Alice reminded her.

Marilyn shook her head. "I really don't know what to do. I love her so much, and most of the time I enjoy her company. Plus, I feel obligated to Sharon. She's taken care of our mother most of our lives. It really is my turn now. And I don't think I can just dump her into an assisted living facility because she's forgetful and deaf."

Shirley chuckled. "Speaking of deaf, let me tell you what happened in Star's yoga class yesterday. Star had some new students, older people bused over from a retirement home, seven really cute little old ladies who want to stay limber. They'd never taken yoga before, so this was their trial class. So Star put them up front and went through the poses slowly, telling them not to strain themselves. You know the routine. So she had them all seated with their eyes closed, and she said slowly, 'Feel your breath.' And one little old lady yelled, 'Feel my breasts? What kind of class *is* this!' "

When their laughter died down, Alice pinned Marilyn with one of her no-nonsense glances. "But if you didn't have to think about your mother, would you marry Faraday?"

"Honestly? I just don't know."

"Did you talk to him about the sex thing?" Alice demanded.

Marilyn blushed. "I tried to. I mean, I sat him down and told him how I felt, and suggested he get something like Viagra. He had that deer-in-the-headlights look. Trapped and tortured! Why is it so difficult to talk about this with men?"

"Because we don't want to hurt their feelings," Alice said. "Men's egos are so fragile. And their private parts are so private. Women are used to having their reproductive organs plumbed and scanned and inspected, not to mention expanded to give birth. We *have* to be more practical, less sensitive about it all."

"You know, Hugh's a doctor," Polly said. "And he's in his sixties, and has no hesitation about using an erectile dysfunction medication from time to time."

"Does it work?" Alice asked.

"Very well," Polly answered, blushing. "So, Marilyn, what did Faraday say after you suggested Viagra?"

Marilyn looked exasperated. "Nothing! He said absolutely nothing! Or, rather, he said there was a show on *Nova* right then that he wanted to watch. So we watched television, then he kissed me politely good night and left."

The waiter brought their food. For a few moments everyone was engrossed in tasting and exchanging bits with one another. Alice and Shirley, who were sitting the farthest from each other, didn't offer to give the other a taste of their dishes, which made Marilyn and Polly exchange nervous glances, while Faye continued to seem lost in her own private world.

"So, Faye." Marilyn turned to her friend. "How is Laura these days?"

Faye lifted her head and forced a smile. "She's well, thank you. She's very good about e-mailing me daily. Lars's parents are staying with them while they look for a house in San Francisco, so they take care of Megan every afternoon. That gives Laura a chance to nap. And Evelyn—Lars's mother—loves to cook, so she's been preparing dinner for everyone. Laura tells me she feels rather spoiled."

Alice tried to cheer Faye with her question. "So what are you and Aubrey doing—" She saw Polly shaking her head in rapid but slight little movements, as if she'd suddenly developed a Katharine Hepburn–like palsy, but didn't interpret the message in time. "—for Valentine's Day?"

Faye's lower lip quivered. "Aubrey's been invited to his daughter's house for dinner tomorrow night. Carolyn's sister and her family are visiting, and she wants them to have a family get-together."

"Well, that sucks for you," Alice said bluntly.

"And for me, too." The hell with it, Polly decided suddenly. The Hot Flash Club's first rule was, after all, "Don't let fear hold you back." Shoving her plate to one side, she rested her arms on the table. "I wish the rest of you could help me out here. You know I met Carolyn at The Haven. I got close to her during the time she was freaked about Aubrey's weird quickie marriage. And then I was with her when she had her baby. So she thinks of me as a kind of surrogate mother, and I have to admit I like that a lot, because my own idiot son and his demented little flying-nun wife won't let me see my own grandchild. But I have no designs on Aubrey! What am I supposed to do? Carolyn invited me to dinner there tomorrow night, to her freaking *family* dinner, and I said I'd go, even though—"

Marilyn cut in. "But what about Hugh? Don't you want to have dinner with him?"

"Of course I do!" Polly replied. "But Hugh's *kids* are having a family Valentine's Day dinner with him, all the grandchildren, and oh, yes, let's not forget, helpless little size-six Carol, Hugh's ex-wife. I don't understand these young mothers. Why can't they let us alone?" She leaned across the table and put her hand on Faye's. "Faye, I'm not romantically interested in Aubrey. You've got to know that. And Aubrey adores you. You must know that, too. I would love to find a way to straighten this tangle out."

Faye gave Polly her best smile. "That's very nice of you."

"But how?" Polly asked helplessly.

"What about talking it over with her?" Shirley suggested. "Take her out to lunch and get it all out in the open."

Alice shook her head. "That won't work. Carolyn's a determined young woman. Strong personality. Used to getting her own way."

Marilyn looked thoughtful. "Stalactites."

"Oh, boy," Alice said. "Here we go."

Marilyn shook her head impatiently. "No, *really*. Think of caves, stalactites, stalagmites, some as much as several yards long, and all formed by the slow, patient, steady dripping of high-lime-content water." She brightened. "Or, think of tiny grains of sand, which the sea has—"

"We get your point," Alice interrupted. "You think Polly and Faye should just remain firm and relentless, reminding Carolyn that Polly is dating Hugh and Faye is dating Aubrey."

"Slow and steady wins the race," Polly mused, nodding.

Alice added, "Yeah. Polly, maybe you could invite Carolyn and her husband to dinner at your house, with Hugh there, so Carolyn could get to know him, and see how much you two like each other."

Polly nodded. "I guess you're right. I hate confrontations, anyway."

Marilyn grinned. "Did you know that in some caves they've discovered stalactites that drip sulfuric acid in a kind of mucusy glue? They've named them *snottites*."

Alice pushed her plate away. "Thanks for presenting us with that image during dinner."

"Good," Shirley said mischievously, "maybe you won't gain weight tonight."

Alice glared at Shirley and bit her tongue. She was doing her best not to be a total bitch about Shirley giving all that money to Justin. Shirley ought to reciprocate and get off her back about her weight.

Defiantly, Alice said, "Maybe I *will*. Because I'm going to order a big, fat chocolate dessert!"

APRIL FOOL'S DAY

12

Marilyn and her mother sat side by side on the sofa, both in quilted robes, their feet cozy in quilted slippers. They were watching one of Marilyn's favorite movies, *I Know Where I'm Going*, made in 1940, starring Wendy Hiller as a saucy city woman trying to get to a private island off the Scottish Highlands. It was in black-and-white, slow-paced but infinitely charming, and when Marilyn curled up in bed at night, she often sent herself to sleep on fantasies of meeting the male lead, Roger Livesey. Actually, it wasn't the actor she wanted to meet but the slow-smiling naval officer he played, and since modern science posited that there were an infinite number of worlds, Marilyn allowed herself to believe, deep in her heart, that in one of those worlds she could meet just such a man, tall, gentle yet rugged, with laughter dancing in his eyes and a Scottish burr that would flutter a kilt.

"That was lovely, dear." Ruth folded up the scarf she was knitting—it was already about seven feet long, but Ruth didn't seem to notice, and Marilyn didn't want to deprive her of the familiar pleasure knitting brought. "I think I'll retire now. It's late, isn't it?"

"Almost ten o'clock," Marilyn told her. "Here, let me help you up."

Marilyn held out her arms. Ruth fastened her bony hands on her daughter's wrists, and Marilyn lifted. Ruth grunted with the effort of getting her body up on her spindly legs.

"There!" she said triumphantly. "Let me catch my breath, and then I can make it on my own."

Marilyn handed Ruth her cane, and after a few moments, Ruth tottered off down the hall to the bathroom. Marilyn watched nervously, glad that the rented condo was so small, Ruth didn't have far to walk from room to room. Marilyn put their cups in the dishwasher—they'd been drinking Postum, a drink Marilyn had forgotten existed until her mother's arrival. She wiped the kitchen counter one more time and plumped up the sofa pillows. Her briefcase was in her bedroom on her computer table, which was squeezed up against her bureau. She scarcely had room in her bedroom to turn around, but she wanted to keep the dining area free for meals with her mother, and she couldn't concentrate on her work with her mother in the room, anyway.

"All right, dear," Ruth called from her bedroom door. "I'll say good night now."

Marilyn went to her mother and bent to give her a kiss and a hug. "Good night, sleep tight, don't let the bedbugs bite."

Ruth patted Marilyn's cheek. "You're a good daughter." She went into her bedroom, shut the door, then opened it again and stuck her head out. "A jumper cable walks into a bar. What does the bartender say?"

Marilyn grinned. " 'I'll serve you, but don't start anything.' "

Ruth laughed, blew a kiss, and closed the door.

Marilyn got ready for bed herself, wondering when Mother Nature would finally blow winter away and let spring arrive. She turned on her electric blanket and bedside lamp, then went around the apartment, double-checking that the kitchen and living room doors were locked and all lights were off. In the hall she paused, quietly opened her mother's bedroom door, and peeked in. Ruth lay tucked beneath her covers like a little doll, snoring gently. Ruth was never bothered by insomnia or hot flashes ruining her sleep, one good thing, Marilyn supposed, about old age.

In her own bed, Marilyn shoved her pillows into comfortable lumps for her back and neck, picked up her book, put on her reading glasses, and found her place on the page.

Then she heard pounding at the front door.

She frowned and took off her glasses, as if that would improve her hearing.

Her heart fluttered. Who would come around at this time on a weekday night? Dear God, she hoped it wasn't Teddy—had something happened to Lila or the baby?

Too alarmed to pull on her robe, she flew to the door and opened it.

Faraday stood there, handsome in his camel-hair coat, but red in the face and reeking of alcohol.

"Faraday!"

Faraday swept off his tartan cap and waved it as he bowed. "I have come to make love to you."

"Faraday, have you been drinking?" She stepped back, allowing him to enter.

He pulled her to him. "Yes, I have indulged in an aphrodisiacal libation, and more, my dear, much more."

"What do you mean?"

Faraday chuckled maniacally as he gripped her wrist and towed her toward her bedroom. "I mean, Marilyn, *mon amour,* I have finally committed the daring deed you have so often obliquely, and gently, propelled me toward." He removed his coat and gloves and dropped them on a chair.

"I don't understand."

Faraday took Marilyn in his arms and bent to kiss her. He had always been a wonderful kisser. But no matter how inventive, patient, or persistent Marilyn was when they tried to make love, "Little Johnny Jump-Up," as Faraday called his penis, had failed to rise to the occasion.

Marilyn let Faraday lead her to the bedroom and watched him pull his thick cable-knit sweater over his head. She knew from experience not to let her body get excited, because that always led to frustration. Still, she was fond of him, so she lifted off her nightgown and slipped between the covers.

As Faraday, naked now, slid in beside her, she said, "We should be quiet. I don't want to wake my mother."

"Ah, my darling," Faraday whispered, "I don't make promises I can't keep."

"You're speaking in riddles tonight." Marilyn snuggled next to him, enjoying the animal warmth of their touching bodies. His thighs and torso were warm, though his hands and face were still cold from the winter air.

"I mean," Faraday whispered, drawing his fingers lightly down Marilyn's body, "I did what you've been wanting me to do. I saw a doctor, who prescribed a helpful medication, and I took it just before I came over here. I'm good for four hours."

"Oh, my!" Marilyn reached up and stroked his bristly bearded jaw. "Faraday. How sweet of you!"

"Have to say," he continued, "I'm a little concerned about it. Just a *little*. I mean, there are side effects . . ." Turning his head away, he belched discreetly. "To build up my courage, I, um, imbibed most of the Scotch you gave me for Christmas."

"What side effects?" Marilyn nuzzled his neck.

"Heart attack. Sudden death. Stroke. Irregular heartbeat. Increased blood pressure," Faraday recited glumly.

Marilyn raised herself up on one elbow, looking down at him with concern. She put a calming hand on his hairy chest. "But, Faraday, surely those are very rare occurrences, or the FDA wouldn't allow the drug to be sold."

"I suppose—" A ferocious yawn swallowed the rest of the sentence. " 'Cuse me. Still, there's no guarantee something won't happen to me."

"I think you're very brave." Marilyn moved her hand down his belly.

He chuckled. "You wouldn't think that if you'd seen me guzzling down the scotch. Oh, yes, and I took a few Valium, too."

Alarmed, Marilyn drew back. "Oh, Faraday, that wasn't wise!"

He would have to spend the night. She couldn't allow him to drive home with all those soporifics in his system. Her mother wouldn't be too shocked, seeing him there in the morning. "I feel so guilty," she told him.

"Now, now. That's not at all how I mean you to feel, my dear."

"But, Faraday—"

"Hush now." He silenced her with a long, amorous kiss.

Marilyn returned his kiss, hugging him tightly against her. She could feel his excitement rising, hard and long, against her abdomen, and her own heart began to pound in anticipation. The alcoholic fumes from his mouth were distracting, however; she was almost getting drunk herself, simply from inhaling his breath.

They arranged themselves together.

"Why, Faraday, I think it's working!" she whispered.

Faraday pushed himself up so that he could look down at her. "G-g-good." The word came out in a mumble. His face, always ruddy, was paler than usual, and his eyes weren't focusing correctly.

"Faraday?"

Suddenly, his mouth fell open. His eyes rolled up like a couple of struck billiard balls, disappearing beneath his eyelids. He let forth an enormous snort, shuddered all over, and collapsed on top of her.

"Faraday!"

Dear God, Marilyn thought, has he had a heart attack?

"Faraday?" She shook his shoulder.

Faraday sputtered, spraying her face, and began to snore loudly against her neck. His enormous torso sagged heavily against her as his breathing deepened. His beard and mustache scratched her chin and cheek.

"Faraday? I can't breathe." Marilyn tried to shift him, but he was a deadweight. "Faraday!" She panted, sucking in small gasps of air.

Faraday snored away, his lips smacking, his alcoholic breath streaming into the bedroom like a really bad air freshener.

Marilyn was five seven and weighed 120 pounds. Faraday was six three and weighed 230. She was strong enough, but he was so very large, and heavy, and limp.

Grunting, she pushed up with her legs and arms, straining to topple him off her, but he was as leaden as a fallen tree. She couldn't budge him.

She *really* was having trouble breathing.

What could she do?

She could call for her mother. But did she want her mother to see her like this, pinned beneath a large, hairy man like a chicken beneath a big, red bull? Absolutely not! Besides, Ruth wasn't strong enough to lift herself out of a chair, so how could *she* help get Faraday off Marilyn?

Sucking up every ounce of strength in her body, Marilyn bucked and heaved one more time. In vain. Faraday's breath sputtered against her hair. She was wheezing like an asthmatic as she strained to pull air into her lungs.

All right, Marilyn said to herself. Let's look at this sensibly. Faraday was bound to wake up sooner or later. Could she fall asleep until he did?

No, a little voice inside her screamed, *because you can't BREATHE!*

The truth was, she was getting scared. More than scared—she was on the verge of real panic, that horrible claustrophobic sense of desperate helplessness. Her left leg spasmed with cramp.

Twisting frantically, she tried to scoot out from beneath Faraday, but she was too weighted down. Frightened now, she began pounding on his shoulders and back. Faraday twitched, spluttered, and moaned, but slept on.

Tears welled in her eyes and rolled down toward her ears. Her sinuses filled with mucus and she couldn't even blow her nose, which was quickly becoming clogged. A feeling of suffocation overwhelmed her, increasing her sense of panic.

What on earth was she going to do?

Turning her head, she saw her phone on the bedside table. Stretching her arm out, she could just grasp it. She pulled it toward her.

911? Oh, Lord, how embarrassing, plus EMTs would make so much noise and wake her mother.

Who else? Who lived closest to her? Alice, who was strong! Fumbling, one-handed, she knocked the phone off its cradle. Straining uncomfortably, she punched in Alice's number, then brought the phone to her ear.

"Hello?"

"Alice, it's Marilyn."

"Are you okay? I can hardly hear you."

"I can hardly speak," Marilyn squeaked. "Listen, could you come over here right now? And tell Polly or Faye to meet you? I'm in a predicament. Faraday's passed out on top of me, and I'm trapped! I don't want my mother to find us like this. Besides, I can't breathe."

Alice sounded wary. "This isn't some kind of weird experiment, is it? Or a joke you're pulling on me?"

"Honest to God, Alice, I'm trapped and nearly smothered. Please come *now.*"

"I'm on my way. I'll phone Polly from the car."

"The key's on top of the lintel," Marilyn gasped. "Be quiet coming in, if you can. I don't want to wake Mother."

For the next twenty minutes, Marilyn labored to breathe. She developed a rhythm, putting both hands beneath Faraday's shoulders and heaving him up a few inches, using that release to inhale deeply. But her arms trembled with the effort, and soon she had to let him drop back down. She tapped his face. Lifted his eyelids. He snored on. She called his name. She pinched him, hard. Nothing worked.

At last, Marilyn heard noises at the front door. Alice and Polly burst into the room, accompanied by a surge of cold air. Alice's fur coat flew out behind her as she stormed in. Polly whisked off her wool cap and mittens and tucked them into her parka pocket.

When they saw Marilyn and Faraday, Polly's hands flew up to her face in alarm, but Alice smiled.

"*Nice,*" Alice said.

"Glad you're enjoying yourself," Marilyn wheezed. "In the meantime, I can't breathe!"

"You take that side, I'll take this," Alice directed Polly.

They stationed themselves on either side of the bed.

Alice grabbed Faraday's shoulder. "You shove while I pull," she directed Polly. "On the count of three. One—two—three."

Marilyn pushed upward with her hands. They shifted Faraday a few inches, but his body was so limp, he landed back on Marilyn like a two-ton beanbag.

"Ooof!" Marilyn huffed as his body hit hers.

"Okay," Alice said. Quickly she removed her coat and rolled up her sleeves. Polly did the same. "On the count of three again, and this time, we're going to give it our all. Ready? One. Two. Three!"

Grunting with exertion, the three women shoved Faraday's warm, limp body. With a sucking noise, he came free of Marilyn and fell on his back, flopping down like a deflated plastic raft.

Marilyn scrambled off the bed, grabbed her robe, and yanked it over her naked body, taking huge, grateful gasps of air.

"He's a fine figure of a man, isn't he?" Alice remarked admiringly as she drew the covers up over Faraday.

"He's a whale," Marilyn puffed. "I've got to pee."

"I've got to laugh," Alice said. "I'll go in the living room and stuff a pillow in my mouth."

"Are you okay?" Alice asked when Marilyn entered the living room.

"Fine. Just embarrassed. And terribly grateful—I think I could have died!"

"I wonder if that's ever happened," Polly mused. "If any woman's ever suffocated beneath her lover."

Marilyn shuddered.

Alice grinned. "You'll see the humor of it in the morning. Will you be able to sleep?"

Marilyn nodded. "I'm sure I will. I'm exhausted. I'll have a bit of brandy and stretch out on the sofa." She hugged Polly and Alice. "How can I thank you? This was beyond the call of duty."

"Honey," Alice said, "I wouldn't have missed this for the world."

In the morning, Marilyn and Ruth had risen, dressed, and were sitting at the table, eating breakfast, when they heard the bedroom door open. A few minutes later, the toilet flushed. After a while, Faraday looked around the corner.

"Marilyn?" He was white and grim. "Could I speak with you?"

"Sure. Want some coffee?"

"No!" He disappeared. She heard the bedroom door slam.

She hurried into her bedroom. Faraday was dressed, but haphazardly, as if he'd just heard a fire alarm.

"Are you okay?" she asked.

"What happened last night?" He towered over her, swaying slightly.

She felt both accusatory and apologetic. "To be blunt, you passed out. You know you shouldn't mix alcohol and drugs."

"*When* did I pass out?"

"Um, when we were just beginning to make love." She put a reassuring hand on his arm. "It's okay, Faraday. These things happen. Mother doesn't know about it. I mean, she knows you slept over, but the rest she doesn't know. It was a little frightening, really. I couldn't breathe. I had to phone Alice and Polly, they came over to help move you off me—"

"You *what*?" Faraday looked like she'd slugged him in the stomach.

"Well, I couldn't lift you off me—"

"Your friends saw me naked and comatose?" His pale face flushed crimson. "What the *hell* were you thinking?"

She was stunned by his anger. "I was *thinking*, Faraday, that I didn't want to suffocate."

"This is unbelievable." Faraday rubbed his face with both big, hairy hands. "This is a nightmare."

"Oh, Faraday—"

He shook his head furiously. "I can't believe you did such a thing. I can't believe you'd embarrass me like that."

With a face like thunder, he strode from the room, grabbed his coat up from the back of a chair, and stomped out the door.

Ruth looked up from a crossword puzzle. "Was that Caraway?"

"Faraday, Mother. Yes."

"He seemed in a bad mood."

"He was just late for a class," Marilyn lied. She didn't know whether to laugh or cry. "I think I'm coming down with a cold. I'm going back to bed."

MOTHER'S DAY

Since New Year's Day, sensitive issues had flickered around the members of the Hot Flash Club like a kind of invisible miniature lightning. Alice was irritated with Shirley for her gullibility with Justin. Shirley was protective of Justin and annoyed with Alice. Polly was trying to be supportive of Carolyn without seeming to be flirting with Aubrey; Marilyn was preoccupied with Ruth; and Faye just seemed depressed.

Still, all five of them showed up for the May board meeting of The Haven, and all five remained in the conference room when the other directors left.

Alice stripped off her suit jacket, hung it over the back of her chair, and cranked open several of the casement windows, letting fresh air sweep into the room.

"That's better," Faye said, lifting her long, white hair off her neck.

Shirley opened a cupboard and brought out a plate of brownies.

Polly bent down to her book bag and lifted up a bottle of sparkling water and five paper cups. She poured the water and passed it around. "Shirley, are you okay?"

Shirley took her place at the head of the conference table, kicked off her dress shoes, and lifted her feet up to rest on the polished mahogany. "Thanks for the water. I'm fine. Why do you ask?"

"All through the meeting, you kept making faces at me and patting your chest, like you had indigestion."

Shirley laughed. "I was trying to instant message you that your jacket's buttoned wrong."

Polly looked down at the handsome tweed suit she'd made just for these board meetings. All the buttons were off by one. "Oh, no! I was in such a hurry—"

Her chagrin at a blunder any one of them could commit made them all feel sympathetic, and closer than they had for weeks.

"Don't worry about it," Faye comforted Polly. "If anyone noticed, they probably thought you were wearing some nouveau-chic asymmetrical style."

"Yeah, at my bridge group last week, I wore mismatched earrings," Alice confessed. "When someone pointed it out, I told them it was the newest fad. They believed me."

Polly unbuttoned her jacket and realigned it properly. "Good grief. When do we admit we're too old to appear in public?"

"Never!" Shirley hit her fist on the table for emphasis. "I was just reading about Stradivarius? The guy who made all the violins? He didn't start building them until after he was fifty, and he worked into his nineties."

"But let's be realistic." As she spoke, Faye removed her indigo silk jacket and fanned her face with the minutes of the board meeting. "We *are* older. We've *got* to make adjustments. We've got to accept changes."

"True," Alice agreed. "I nearly fall off the sofa laughing when I see a TV ad depicting a silver-haired couple waltzing on a cruise ship or backpacking up an Alpine path. Gideon and I are in good health and reasonably fit, but I can only be twirled on the dance floor if I take plenty of aspirin and remember to wear a panty liner."

Faye nodded. "You're right. When Aubrey tries to climb the stairs, never mind a mountain, his knees give out on him. Not to mention, I mean, excuse my bluntness, but *any* vigorous activity makes him fart like a popped balloon."

Polly laughed. "Tell me about it! The signature scent of senior romance definitely does not come from a perfume bottle."

"Still, we've got to keep dancing," Shirley reminded them.

"You are *so* 'The Little Engine That Could,' " Alice muttered.

"So?" Shirley shot back. "You want me to be 'The Little Engine That *Can't*'?"

Alice bit off her words. "Maybe 'The Little Engine with Headlights and Brakes.' "

Quickly, Marilyn derailed them. "So, Faye, how are things working out with Aubrey's daughter?"

Faye looked strained. "Well, I haven't felt like going out a lot. This winter's been so brutal, and my ankle hurts when it's bitterly cold."

"Welcome to my arthritic world," Alice murmured sympathetically.

Faye broke a chunk off a brownie, popped it into her mouth, and chewed while she talked. "Plus, I was down and out with the flu for almost three weeks. Also, Carolyn arranged a lot of 'family vacations.' They went skiing in March and to Costa Rica for two weeks in April."

Polly spoke up. "Carolyn invited me on both trips, but I refused. I said that I wanted to spend as much time with my *boyfriend* Hugh as I can."

Faye touched Polly's hand. "I'm not blaming you, Polly."

Shirley inquired softly, "Have you and Aubrey made love yet?"

"Not yet. But it's all right." Faye's expression denied her words. "At our age, sex isn't as crucial or passionate as it was when we were younger."

"That's like saying it may not be Godiva, but it's still chocolate," Alice pointed out.

Shirley turned to Marilyn. "Have you heard from Faraday?"

Marilyn sighed. "Not since our Valentine's Day catastrophe. I've phoned him and e-mailed him, but he refuses to answer. I've tried catching him in his office at the university, but he gives me the cold shoulder every time."

Faye grimaced. "He must have been humiliated, passing out on you like that."

"I think what's worse for him is knowing that my friends saw him naked and comatose."

"I can sympathize with that," Alice said.

"I can, too," Polly said, "but at our age, we've got to have a sense of humor if we're going to enjoy sex."

"A sense of humor and total darkness," joked Alice.

"Even if it's entirely dark," Polly confided, "men can *feel* how different we are. I swear, my pubic hair is thinning out, but I'm growing whiskers on my chin!"

Alice chuckled. "Yeah, and my breasts used to feel like nice, hard pears. Now they hang down like a couple of eggplants."

"Come on, men don't love women only if they're young and beautiful," Shirley insisted. "I mean, look at Prince Charles. One of the most beautiful women in the world was his wife, and she was much younger. Still, he stayed in love with Camilla."

Alice snorted. "Camilla, that dried-up old twig."

Shirley pounced. "My point exactly."

"Is Camilla older than he is?" Polly asked.

"*Yes,*" Shirley stated defiantly. "At least a year or two."

Faye noticed Alice looking annoyed, as she always did when the subject of older women–younger men/Shirley–Justin came up. So far Alice had remained on the board, but she didn't participate as much as she once had, and she seldom spoke directly to Shirley. Faye didn't feel very close to Shirley these days, either; she was always afraid Shirley would bring up the subject of health and weight.

Polly deftly switched conversational gears. "All right, everyone, let's compare notes on Mother's Day. Who got taken out to dinner?" When no one answered, she said, "Okay, who got flowers?"

Marilyn offered, "I brought Ruth flowers. And a pretty spring sweater."

"But what did *you* get?" Polly persisted.

Marilyn shrugged. "Teddy phoned to wish me a happy Mother's Day and to tell me he bought Lila a diamond tennis bracelet. That's perfectly fine with me. I've never cared much about Mother's Day."

"Nor I," Alice chimed in. "It was fun when the boys were little, but now that they're grown, I seldom think of it. Although Steven did send me a card."

"Laura sent me a card, too," Faye said. "With new pictures of Megan."

Polly pretended to pout. "That's more than I got. David didn't even send me a card."

"That's because Amy didn't remind him to send you something," Faye said. As the others raised their voices in objection, she continued, "I know it's not right, but it's true. Women are the ones who remember to buy birthday presents, Mother's Day cards, all that sentimental stuff. I did it for Jack. I'd buy the card and put the pen in his hand and stand over him to make him sign it, as if he were six years old. Then I'd make him address the envelope. Then *I'd* mail it."

"You're right." Polly nodded, thoughtfully picking a chocolate crumb off her napkin. "Now that you mention it, I did the same sort of thing for Tucker. I'd order flowers delivered to Claudia, with a card signed, 'Love, Tucker.' "

"That doesn't seem fair," Shirley said. "*You* remembered, *you* went to the trouble of ordering flowers, and *he* gets the gratitude."

Polly snorted. "*I* could have sent Claudia a *tree* and she wouldn't have acknowledged it. But never mind." Polly's smile was slightly mischievous. "I was always glad to work behind the scenes. Because Claudia would phone Tucker and thank him for the flowers, and then Tucker would thank *me* for remembering for him." She waggled her eyebrows. "With something much nicer than flowers."

"Speaking of flowers . . ." Faye leaned forward. "I had the *best* idea the other day. I was thinking about Princess Di's death, and all those flowers people put at the gates in her honor. Remember? There were thousands of beautiful bouquets."

"It was so sad," Polly reflected somberly.

"Well," Faye continued, "what happened to those flowers? Did they all just get swept up and tossed out? Wouldn't it have been great if they'd gathered up all those flowers, dried them, put them in pretty little cloth bags, and sold them as Princess Di Memorial Potpourri?"

"That's a brilliant idea!" Shirley said. "I would have bought some!"

"Me, too," Polly said. "Gee, I wish we could do something like that. Has anyone wonderful died lately?"

Alice thought for a moment. "Rodney Dangerfield, but who would buy Rodney Dangerfield potpourri?"

Faye laughed. "Few people would have the same cachet as Princess Di."

"Or the same *sachet*," Marilyn quipped.

"True," Shirley said musingly. "The potpourri would be a kind of constant memory, and how many people do we want to think of daily?"

"That reminds me," Polly said. "I'm still trying to decide what to do with the inheritance my evil old mother-in-law left me. Boxes of beautiful lace. I'd like to use it, even though it was Claudia's."

Shirley asked, "Can you separate the material from your memories?"

"I honestly don't know. Maybe that's why I can't think of anything . . . because the memory of her snotty old face gets in the way."

Alice turned to Marilyn. "Speaking of old people, how's your mom?"

"She's adorable." Marilyn played with her brownie, crumbling it into little pieces. "And I'm glad for her company, now that Faraday's no longer in my life."

"I sense a *however* in there," Alice said.

Marilyn looked around at her wonderful friends. She loved them so much. Yet she knew they all thought she was odd, and probably, she was. Certainly she couldn't speak to them about the matter closest to her heart.

Marilyn believed in the Loch Ness Monster. She was sure that Nessie was a descendant of the plesiosaurs, enormous, flippered marine reptiles that lived in the Mesozoic Era. Almost daily, science discovered new creatures in unexplored jungles and on the sea floor. It was possible, it really was, that the long, narrow, freshwater lake, averaging four hundred fifty feet in depth and more than a thousand feet in some places, could hide a plesiosauroid.

To know Nessie existed had been Marilyn's lifelong dream. Too weird for her to share even with her Hot Flash friends, it was her own private mystery, as much a part of her as her scientific work or her maternal love or her sexual desires or her affection for her friends. It was the bedrock of her soul.

The more Marilyn learned about scientific matters, the more science unearthed facts about the universe, the more firmly she believed in God. She could not believe life was random. From the vastness of the starry cosmos to the nearly unfathomable worlds living inside one drop of water, an awesome order prevailed, and everywhere hints were hidden that sent man off on adventures his greatest imagination could not forsee. The universe was too beautiful, and too intricate, for man ever to come to the end of his searching.

The older she got, the more urgently she yearned to begin her own private quest.

"Earth to Marilyn," Alice prompted.

Marilyn's shoulders slumped. "I've taken a sabbatical. My courses end next month, then I'll be off for a year. I was hoping to go to Scotland for a couple of weeks, just by myself. But I don't think I can leave my mother alone. And I don't want to ship her back to my sister's just for two weeks."

"Hire someone to live in," Alice advised. "A practical nurse or someone like that."

Marilyn made a face. "I don't know. I'd feel awful, hiring a stranger to stay with her. She wouldn't say anything, but I know it would hurt Mother's feelings." She shrugged. "It's all right. I can go another year."

"Don't be silly!" Faye said. "Ruth can stay with me."

Marilyn looked at Faye. "Oh, I can't ask you—"

"But I'd love to have her," Faye insisted. "What do I have a guest room for, anyway? It's not like my own daughter is planning any visits. It would be good for me, Marilyn, really, it would."

"I'd help," Polly offered. "I mean, if Faye needs to go out of town, or has a date with Aubrey, or whatever, I can always take Ruth out to dinner or come sit with her. I think Ruth's a hoot."

Marilyn was dumbfounded. Had she had a minor brain warp and told them how important this trip was to her? She was so shocked she was speechless.

"I'll bring her out here for some yoga," Shirley added. "We'll keep her busy."

"I've got season tickets to the symphony," Alice chimed in. "Gideon doesn't like to go to them all. I'll take her in his place."

Tears welled in Marilyn's eyes. "I can't believe you'd all really do this for me."

"Please," Alice chided. "You'd do the same for any of us."

Shirley took Marilyn's hand. "Isn't this your dream?"

Marilyn nodded. "It's the trip I've dreamed of for years." She frowned. "I should warn you. Ruth can be irritating. She says the same thing over and over again, and it takes her *forever* to move two feet. And she's practically deaf, and you have to repeat stuff a thousand times. And she—"

"Marilyn." Faye's voice was decisive. "We're doing it. We're taking care of Ruth. So make your plans. Two weeks, even more— we'll all do just fine."

Marilyn looked radiant. "You are all so wonderful! Oh, wow! I'm so excited!" She looked serious again. "But we're going to have to break this to Ruth gently. You should all come over to the apartment and visit, so she gets used to you."

"We can do that," Faye said. "It's going to be fun."

FOURTH OF JULY

The sun shone down on a perfect day: sunny, clear, and hot. Divine picnic weather.

Shirley bustled about on the large slate patio off The Haven's kitchen door, carefully setting, right in the center of each picnic table, a bowl of red, white, and purple-blue petunias with a cute little American flag in the middle. She felt festive in red cropped pants, a blue-and-white striped jersey, and red espadrilles. And her earrings were so clever—they looked like firecrackers!

All around The Haven, the grounds spread like green velvet. The gardener had mowed the grass two days ago, and now, at the far end, by the beginning of the walking path, Justin was stabbing croquet wickets into the ground. They'd already set up the badminton net.

Shirley paused for a moment to gloat.

A few years ago, she'd been lonely and just a hair above down-and-out. Now she was the director of this flourishing business, *plus* living with a literary genius who loved her enough to stop his important work and help her with the humble manual labor of preparing for this party.

It hurt that her friends didn't trust Justin, but their faith in *her* encouraged her to have faith in *him*. And he'd worked so hard over the past few months, and accomplished so much! He'd researched and assessed various self-publishing companies, finally choosing The Hemingway Group. Wasn't that the most elegant name! It gave Shirley shivers. The Hemingway Group was based in Boston, which was an asset, Justin informed her. This company not only knew how to package Justin's novel, but how to market it. They had contacts with the media. They were planning an extensive publicity campaign for the book's publication this fall. Justin went in about once a week to meet with Dee Sylvester, who had helped edit the book and was working with graphic artists to create the *perfect* cover. She'd promised Justin that this book would explode on the book-reading public, zoom to the top of the bestseller list, and bring editors from New York publishing houses pounding on his door.

Shirley couldn't wait until the fall! *Then* her friends would come crawling to her with apologies for not believing in Justin. Especially Alice!

Alan and Jennifer strolled up the long drive from their cottage, once the gatehouse for the property. Instead of paying rent, they helped out whenever The Haven had an open house or some event needing food. They'd helped Shirley prepare the food for today's party, but they were also guests, part of the Hot Flash Club's extended family. They greeted Shirley with a kiss on the cheek, then set to work.

Alan asked, "Shirley, is the bar good here?"

"That's fine." Shirley slid a rubber coaster under one of the tables to level it. "If you want to bring the ice out, I'll get the glasses."

They set up the bar, then wheeled out the state-of-the-art barbecue grill. Shirley was a vegetarian, but Alice and the others had protested that not having hamburgers and hot dogs on the Fourth of July was not only bizarre but practically un-American, so of course she gave in. She was also providing a full bar, even though she was a recovering alcoholic. Everyone else enjoyed a beer or wine, or a cool g-and-t; but she didn't crave the stuff at all these days, when simple air was like nectar.

"Hello!" Polly came around the corner of the building, her boyfriend Hugh following. "Oh, this is beautiful!"

Like Shirley, Polly had red hair, but Shirley kept hers dyed auburn, partly because Justin was so much younger than she, but also because it made her feel she looked less dated when she faced her board of directors. Shirley would never say this, but she was pretty sure she looked younger than Polly, who was letting the white grow in among the red and who also carried more weight than she. Shirley was naturally slender, and years of yoga kept her limber, while Polly was endowed with a more feminine kind of frame, with a substantial bosom and hips. Still, Polly looked lovely in her polka-dot sundress and the straw hat she wore to keep her freckled face from sunburn.

"Hello, Polly! Hello, Hugh!" she called, and the party officially began.

As the sun rolled high in the sky, the guests played croquet and badminton, strolled along the walking paths Shirley had created in the woods, and lounged about on the patio, nibbling appetizers and chatting.

Sometimes Shirley found her new work stultifying: running the spa, dealing with paperwork and administrative details. Just this week, she'd had to listen to Elroy Morris, the buildings and grounds manager, explain why they needed a new septic system—honestly, what could be more boring! And it was so expensive! She'd had to review the insurance with their rep; thank God Alice sat in for that, even if she had taken off right afterward, still too cranky about Justin to spend even a minute alone with Shirley. And then there were the endless problems with staff, illnesses, taxes—sometimes Shirley wanted to pull out her hair. She missed her massage clients, missed the immediate magic of feeling people relax beneath her hands, soothing away their knots and kinks, bringing balm to their souls.

Yet Shirley knew The Haven provided a sanctuary for many more women than she could handle alone. This was a little universe, where women could retreat from the real world, relax, heal, and renew.

Justin was playing badminton with Hugh, so Shirley joined her friends at a picnic table beneath the shade of a striped umbrella. Ruth had come with Faye, which was good for them both, because Carolyn had wanted her father with *her* for the Fourth of July, so Aubrey wasn't there. Polly sat next to Alice, and Gideon was on Alice's other side, so Shirley felt buffered from her critical friend.

Alice was talking with Ruth. "Have you heard from Marilyn?"

Ruth lit up. She looked very cute in her red, white, and blue sweater, with a little matching bow in her white curls. "I have! Just yesterday! She phoned to say she'd arrived in Edinburgh safely. She stayed there a couple of days to get over her jet sag. Then she rented a little car, and drove on the left side of the roads, all the way to Loch Ness! She said she misses you girls terribly." Ruth counted on her fingers. "She said Shirley would love all the Celtic magic potions and jewelry. Faye and Polly would love all the woolen shops. And Alice, you would have kept her from screaming every time she drove around the traffic circles they call 'roundabouts' over there."

"Sounds like she's having a wonderful time," Shirley said. "I'm so happy for her."

"Shirley?" Alan approached the table. "It's after five. Shall I start the hamburgers?"

"Not yet. Why don't you and Jennifer join us for a while?" Shirley looked around. "Where is Jennifer?"

"Oh, she's, um—" Alan looked nervous. "Putting final touches on a salad, I think. I'll check."

Poor Alan, Shirley thought. He loved Jennifer, and Jennifer loved him, and of course he loved his mother, and Alice adored him, but there were tensions between Alice and Jennifer. It was one of the frustrating things about Alice, who seemed perfectly content and comfortable being the only black woman in the Hot Flash Club yet worried that Jennifer, as a white woman, would somehow bring harm to Alice's son.

Alan went off, swinging his spatula. Alice leaned forward. "Faye, I love your outfit."

Faye smiled. "Thanks. I made it myself." She touched the lacy inset on her pale blue tank top. Over it, she wore a gauzy shirt of a darker blue that obscured her plump arms and draped smoothly over her rounded tummy and hips.

"You make most of your clothes, don't you, Faye?" Polly asked.

Faye nodded. "I do. I designed my own little outfits when I started having hot flashes. I got tired of pulling sweaters off over my head. I knew I needed layers. So I made up patterns for myself: tank top, shirt with short sleeves, jacket with longer sleeves. Of course in this hot weather, I leave off the shirt."

"And you make them in such wonderful colors," Shirley said. "And centering the first layer with bits of lace or embroidery like you do is so clever!"

"I wish you'd show me how to make them," Polly told Faye. "I think I told you, I have boxes of old lace my mother-in-law left me. I want to throw them out, because she was such an evil old queen, but I can't make myself do it. So they're just sitting in my sewing room, gathering dust."

Ruth set her wineglass on the table. Her white curls bobbed on her wobbling little head. "You should team up. Use Polly's lace and Faye's designs and make a whole lot of these pretty little outfits. I'll bet you could sell them and make money."

Shirley nearly jumped out of her chair. "Oh, my God! You could sell them here at The Haven! Hot Flash clothes!"

"Hot Flash *fashions*," Alice amended.

Polly and Faye looked at each other wide-eyed.

Polly, whose sewing business was on idle, thought: *I could use the money! But Faye doesn't need money.* "Well . . ."

Faye thought: *This might be fun, and it would give me something creative to do, now that I can't paint.* "Maybe . . ."

Shirley said, "If you two did start a little business, Carolyn would *have* to see that you're not about to be driven apart by her machinations."

Alice looked excited. "I could do the bookkeeping for you. It would be fun for me."

Faye hesitated. "I don't know. I like to sew for myself, but I've never sewn for anyone else."

"But I have!" Polly reminded her. "That's what I *do*! And just think, wouldn't we be great models to set the patterns? We're both plump, and our weight has sunk down around our equatorial zone like that of a lot of women our age—except for you, Shirley—"

"And Marilyn," Shirley added.

Faye cocked her head, considering. "What if we make them and they don't sell?"

Polly laughed. "Then we wear them ourselves! We'll have a fabulous wardrobe!"

Polly's enthusiasm was contagious. Faye grinned. "All right! Let's do it!"

Shirley jumped up and hugged Marilyn's mother. "Ruth, you are a *genius*!"

Ruth beamed. "Well, girls, since it was my idea, I'll buy the first outfit!"

"Oh, no," Faye retorted. "Since it was your idea, you get the first one free."

"Nonsense," Ruth told her. "You'll never make any money if you give things away. Right, Alice?"

"As your business manager," Alice said, "I concur with Ruth."

From down the road, at a house inhabited by a family of five, came the pop of firecrackers, sounding like applause.

———

A little later, as the enticing aroma of barbecued burgers floated in the air, Alan announced that dinner was ready. Everyone helped themselves at the long table set with rice salad, potato salad, romaine and endive salad, chickpea salad, and piles of fresh sliced veggies. Alan remained at the grill, cooking more burgers, and Jennifer kept an eye on the food, whisking empty bowls into the kitchen and bringing back refills.

"Enough!" Shirley told Alan. "They've all had seconds and thirds. Sit down and eat with us. You two are guests today, not staff!"

"Oh, we're fine," Alan told her. "We'll sit down in a minute."

"Well, you'd better. Jennifer looks wiped out. Is she sick?"

A strange look of terror flashed over Alan's face. "She's fine," he muttered.

When dark fell, Alan and Jennifer finally pulled up chairs to join everyone else as they waited for the fireworks to begin. Last year, Shirley had noticed that the adjoining town held a fireworks display that bloomed so high in the sky it was easily visible from the grounds of The Haven.

"How perfect is this!" Shirley was so pleased with herself. Everyone was relaxed. They all had a drink in their hands, iced tea, or coffee, or sparkling water. "I think we should toast Alan and Jennifer, our fearless chefs!"

"Hear! Hear!" Gideon said, raising his cup.

"Hoorah and thank you!" cheered Faye.

There was just enough light for Shirley to notice how Alan glanced at Jennifer, who nodded her chin just half an inch.

"Um, this might be a good time," Alan said, his voice slightly shaky, "for us to make an announcement."

Shirley clutched her hair with both hands. "Oh, no! You two haven't gotten a better job somewhere else?" She loved having the two live in the gatehouse; it made The Haven seem more homey.

"Not at all," Alan assured her. Reaching over, he took Jennifer's hand in his. "Jennifer and I are going to have a baby in December." He took a deep breath. "So we got married last week."

Silence fell. Shirley could hear birds twittering in the trees. In the distance, a motorcycle roared.

Shirley could scarcely summon up the courage to look at Alice. When she did, she saw that Alice wore her implacable, executive, *mess-with-me-and-I'll-rip-your-guts-out* look.

"Alice?" Faye said softly.

"Alice." Gideon put a restraining hand on Alice's arm.

Alice felt paralyzed, but her thoughts were racing. Alan had gotten married without telling her. Without inviting her to attend. They were having a baby, even though they knew how hard life could be for mixed-blood children. And he was announcing this now, in front of everyone, instead of coming to her first? Alice felt betrayed and humiliated. She felt like everyone else thought she was some kind of monster. She was aware of her friends staring at her hard, as if they were using the force of the gaze to press her back in her chair. She wanted to go into a padded room, knock her head against a wall, and scream till her throat was sore.

"I didn't know about this," Shirley assured Alice.

"No one did," Jennifer said. "My parents are furious that I'm living with Alan. They'll probably disown me now."

Alice gasped. Jennifer's parents disapproved of her son? How *dare* they! Alan was a *wonderful* man, intelligent, hardworking, kindhearted—

Ruth touched Alice's arm. "Remember. *Carpe diem.* Squeeze the day."

"Mom?" Alan interrupted her thoughts. "Aren't you going to say anything?"

Alice swallowed. For some bizarre reason, perhaps because she'd spent her life working in a corporation, reading and writing and living by rules, a register appeared in her mind, clicking along like a David Letterman list. Oddly, these were not corporate rules, but the rules of the Hot Flash Club:

1. Don't let fear rule your life.
2. When you're depressed, get up, get dressed, and get out of the house.
3. Celebrate every chance you get.

Rule number three—that was the one she wanted now. It lay in front of her like a path.

She smiled. She tried to *beam*. "Congratulations!"

The surprised delight on her son's face was a blessing.

Alice felt the air around her shift, as everyone released held breaths. "We should celebrate!" Alice hoped the others didn't hear the wobble in her voice. "Shirley, is there any Champagne around?"

"Yeah, there is, but it's not really *good* Champagne."

"Could we break it out?" Alice turned to Alan and Jennifer. Jennifer was crying quietly, smiling at the same time. Alan looked like he was going to faint. The sight nearly broke Alice's heart. "I hope you two will let us throw you a party."

"Could we invite our friends?" Alan asked.

They had friends? Alice's head spun. Of course they had friends! Alice had just never met them or heard about them, because she'd held Jennifer and Alan at arm's length.

Alice smiled. "Of course you could invite all your friends!"

Shirley said, "I'll get the Champagne."

Faye jumped up. "I'll get the glasses."

Jennifer said, "I—I—I have to go to the ladies'." Shyly, she confessed, "Since I've been pregnant, I have to pee all the time."

"Honey," Alice said, "I hear you."

She sank back in her lawn chair, exhausted, vaguely aware of all the others rushing in and out of The Haven's kitchen.

Gideon leaned over and whispered in her ear, "You did good, Alice."

"Thank you. My brain feels like a bath mat."

"Here's the Champagne!" Shirley called, her arms wrapped around bottles.

"And here are the glasses!" Faye followed, carrying a tray.

Everyone rose as Shirley and Justin and Faye opened the bottles, aiming out toward the garden. With a satisfying popping noise, the corks exploded. Champagne surged up in a froth of bubbles. They filled the glasses and passed them around.

Alice raised her glass in a toast. "To Jennifer and Alan!"

"To Jennifer and Alan!" everyone chimed.

With a noise like thunder, fireworks burst in the sky.

When Marilyn woke on the Fourth of July, she lay still and smiling in her unfamiliar bed, allowing herself to savor the moment. She was here!

She was in Scotland, on the very shore of Loch Ness!

She'd found this little B&B on the Internet, made reservations, flown to Edinburgh, and driven here all by herself. She felt brave. She felt like a woman on a pilgrimage.

She jumped up and pulled on her khakis, sweatshirt, and hiking boots. She ran a brush through her sensible chin-length hair, which, she noticed, needed another touch-up. The white was showing through the auburn. She shrugged. Who cared? She'd worry about that sort of thing when she was back home. She fastened her money belt around her waist—a stylistic faux pas that would make her Hot Flash friends shriek with horror—grabbed her room key, and headed down the stairs for breakfast.

The dining room was small and oddly decorated, with a red-and-green tartan rug and orange-and-pink floral wallpaper. The delicious aroma of coffee curled from the urn on the sideboard.

A young, Nordic-looking couple glanced up from their table. "Good morning."

"Good morning," Marilyn replied.

She poured herself a mug of coffee and sat next to the window. Through the lace she could see the green hillside rising upward, and a steady rain pouring down.

That was all right. She'd brought a good oilcloth raincoat,

knowing that it would rain at least half the days she was here, if not all of them. It was mild outside, nearly seventy, and once she started walking, she'd warm up quickly.

The vigorous, ruddy-cheeked owner of the B&B, garbed in a flowered, frilled apron, took Marilyn's order for a full breakfast, returning with a plate of scrambled eggs, sausage, fried mushrooms, a potato scone, white toast, and a mysterious blob of brown. Marilyn ate quickly, eager to start her day.

The Nordic couple went out. A man came in. He was around Marilyn's age, bald except for a rim of gray hair, spectacled, lanky, and lean. Like Marilyn and the young couple, he wore hiking clothes. He greeted Marilyn with a nod and a smile, then sat down at the remaining table, opened a folder, and took out a sheaf of papers. Marilyn strained to read them—it was an unbreakable habit of hers, spying on other people's work—but they were too far away.

She'd finished her breakfast, except for the odd brown substance. Now she decided to try it—why not? When in Rome, after all. She tasted a forkful—*hm*. Perhaps onions and pureed corned beef?

"Pardon me," the man asked from across the small room. "But do you know what that is?" He had a marvelous Scottish accent.

Marilyn hesitated. She didn't want to seem like an ignorant tourist. But actually, she *was* an ignorant tourist, so she confessed, "I have no idea."

"Blud pudding."

"Excuse me?"

"Blud pudding. Blood and suet and seasonings."

"Ah." Marilyn put her fork down. "Thank you for telling me."

"Some develop a taste for it." His eyes sparkled.

"Yes, well, perhaps not for breakfast." Washing down a big swallow of coffee, she rose. "Have a good day."

"Aye, you, too."

Back in her room, she checked her pack: bottles of water, some trail mix, a chocolate bar, maps, tissues, and sunglasses, in case the weather changed. She pulled on her rain jacket, skipped down the stairs, and went out into the Loch Ness day.

———————————

For twenty-three miles, Loch Ness cut like a narrow knife blade through the Great Glen dividing the north of Scotland from Inverness to Fort William. Geologists knew the loch lay in a fault line active since mid-Devonian times, 400 million years ago, but on this lovely summer day, Marilyn forgot all that, as her senses exulted in air softened by a gentle rain, the tantalizing azure sparkle of the water, and the emerald hills rising steeply on either side. She was here, now.

Leaving her car in the B&B lot, she strode downhill and along the road toward the Loch Ness Monster Exhibition Center. It was hardly a scientific headquarters, but she wanted to tour it nonetheless, and she was not disappointed. Ignoring the souvenir shop with its Nessie dolls and mugs, she focused on the sketches and detailed accounts by witnesses who'd testified to the creature's existence over the years. St. Columba saw the monster in A.D. 565. Would a saint lie? In 1987, a million-dollar sonar exploration called Operation Deepscan found evidence of a mysterious moving mass larger than a shark. And most recently, a member of the coast guard discovered with his own sonar an enormous underwater cavern, which he called "Nessie's Lair." A professor at Harvard and MIT had also spent years searching for the creature.

Crowds shuffled past the exhibits and clogged the passageways. Most of them were families with children hugging soft stuffed toys of a friendly, smiling, slightly goofy Nessie. This wasn't a sweet cartoon character invented by Disney, Marilyn wanted to remind them.

Leaving the throngs, Marilyn returned to the fresh air. Just on the other side of A82 and down by the loch was Castle Urquhart, a stony ruin set on a small promontory. Marilyn wished its stones could talk.

The rain had stopped, and shafts of sun striped the landscape.

Marilyn wanted to lean against the rocks and stare out at the blue waters, but a busload of senior tourists arrived, clucking like chickens as they fluttered down to the castle, so she dug out her map, planned a route, and set off walking.

Paths wound up- and downhill, through forests and bogs, past streams and rivulets. Marilyn wandered along, taking her time, never getting too far from a view of the lake. Occasionally, she thought of her Hot Flash friends, or wondered how Ruth was doing, and whether her granddaughter was over her cold. Sometimes she thought of Faraday, and wondered whether she'd ever be with a man she loved.

But mostly she let her mind drift through the ages. She thought about the geology of this land, the metamorphic schists underlying the hills, the altered limestones, the shattered granite. She imagined the last Ice Age, just a geological moment ago, when this great glen was occupied by an enormous glacier. Everything would have been white then, blindingly white beneath the sun. She thought about the moving on and holding of time, how it never stopped but often saved.

She loved the ache in her legs from all the climbing up and down the lumpy, uneven, tufty hills, so unlike the flat streets of the city where she worked. She felt she was breathing differently, seeing more, hearing more clearly. She felt her body sparkle as her lungs pulled in new air, skimming through her blood like transparent vitamins.

In her excitement, she forgot to eat. It was nearly four in the afternoon when she felt her physical system plummet. Shaky, tired, and weak, she collapsed on a rock on the edge of the loch while she munched her trail mix.

Today there was no wind, so the loch lay still, except for the occasional wake caused by a boat. Some enterprising soul motored by, his launch loaded with tourists fishing off the side or taking pictures or gazing through binoculars. Marilyn sat watching for over an hour, but not a ripple disturbed the surface.

When she'd regrouped, she rose and headed back to her B&B. She showered, then collapsed on the bed for a nap, waking two hours later with a rumbling stomach.

Outside it was still light—the sun stayed up past nine o'clock in the summer. She went down to the front hall to study the brochures and decide where to eat.

The Scotsman she'd met at breakfast this morning was there. He wore jeans and a flannel shirt and smelled of the same soap Marilyn had just used in her shower.

"Hello," he greeted Marilyn. "Did you have a good day?"

"It was *bliss*," Marilyn told him.

"Are you a Nessie hunter?"

She hesitated. She didn't want him to think she was just some kind of superstitious cryptozoologic nut. "I'm a paleontologist, actually. I teach in Cambridge—the American Cambridge—and I study trilobites, which are—"

"Trilobites, you say! Indeed! I know what they are. I'm a paleo-artist."

"Get out!" Marilyn exclaimed.

"But it's true." He held out his hand. "Ian Foster."

Marilyn looked at his hand as if it were made of diamonds. "*The* Ian Foster? You've done the restoration drawings of the plesio-sauria?"

"That's right."

"Oh, my gosh!" Marilyn had to restrain herself from going into adolescent shrieks. "Oh, what a pleasure to meet you! What are you doing here?"

"The same thing as you, I imagine, taking a little holiday, going for walks, airing out my poor old brain." Folding his arms, he leaned against the wall. "I've just finished a critical analysis of existing and dependent phylogenies via cladistic methods."

"How fascinating!" Marilyn was too enthralled to be shy. "I'd love to hear about it."

The Nordic couple came through then, muttering to each other in guttural tones. They stopped to say hello, then passed on, out the door.

Ian looked at Marilyn. "Listen, would you like to join me for dinner? There are several fairly decent restaurants in Inverness, which is only about fifteen miles from here."

"I can't think of anything I'd rather do!" Marilyn told him, adding to herself, *Except wait on the banks of the loch, watching for Nessie.*

———————————

They sat together at a small table in a large pub, eating fresh trout, drinking Scots lager, and talking about paleontology like reunited old friends.

Thin and gawky, Ian was not a handsome fellow. His Adam's apple protruded sharply, bobbing up and down as he spoke, and pouches bagged beneath his dark eyes, slightly hidden by his heavy glasses. His forehead bulged out, and his bald head stuck up from his rim of hair like an ostrich egg from a nest. But his hands were beautiful, his fingers long, lean, and supple, and he had nice, even white teeth. Something about him was very attractive to Marilyn. Perhaps she was high on simply being here, but the longer she spoke with Ian, the more she wanted to touch his elegant hands. She even found herself fantasizing about pressing her lips to his, and she didn't feel the slightest bit guilty, because Ian was widowed, with a grown son living in Australia.

After dinner, they ordered fresh berries for dessert. Wanting to linger, they asked for cheese and crackers, and after that, they had a brandy. Finally, they left the pub and drove back along the loch to the B&B. It was raining again, so for a while they sat in Ian's car, talking, until the windows misted over and Marilyn shivered—she assumed from the damp. They ran inside to find the lights were dim, the common rooms empty, the building hushed.

Ian looked at his watch. "It's almost midnight."

"Oh, dear. We should go to bed," Marilyn said reluctantly.

"How much longer are you here for?" Ian asked.

"Ten more days."

"Well." He hesitated. "Would you like to join me tomorrow? We could hire a boat to take us out on the loch. Have a little picnic."

"Oh, that would be wonderful!"

He smiled at her enthusiasm. "Good, then. I'll see you at breakfast." He held out his hand and shook hers. "I'm awfully glad I met you, Marilyn."

"Yes," she said, flushing. "Me, too."

In all her life, Marilyn had never experienced the kind of happiness she felt over the next few days. In her twenties, she'd married Theodore for three reasons. First: she knew she was a science nerd, too engrossed with her studies to be attractive to most men. Second, the time was right. Third, Theodore had been the one to ask her. But during the long years of her marriage, her own scientific interests had been overshadowed by her husband's brilliance, and by his lack of interest in anything that didn't further his own career or studies. Then he left her for a younger woman.

She'd shared common scientific interests with Faraday, but she'd never felt like she felt right now with Ian: as if they were two halves of a whole, two pieces of one jigsaw puzzle, best friends who'd been waiting all their lives to meet.

Ian made her laugh. She made him laugh. Often they said the same word at the same time. They walked at the same pace—they were so comfortable together.

Ian was from Edinburgh. He taught at the university there, and he was an ardent Scotsman. One day when the rains poured down, he drove her to visit Cawdor Castle, where Shakespeare set *Macbeth* and where, after a delicious lunch, Marilyn got to lean on a fence and gaze to her heart's delight at a herd of shaggy red-haired Highland cows. But mostly they hiked the hills around Loch Ness, sharing lunches from their backpacks, talking, or silently enjoying each other's company.

The night they met, Ian had shaken her hand when they parted. The next night, he pressed a gentle kiss on her forehead. The third night, he kissed her cheek. By the fourth night, Marilyn thought she'd hit him with a full-body tackle, wrap her legs around his hips, and clutch him like an octopus if he didn't get a little more passionate—and he either read her mind or sensed her urges, because that night he pulled her to him and kissed her heartily.

"Oh, my!" she sighed when he released her.

They were sitting in his little car, rain singing down all around them.

He pulled back, studying her face as well as he could. It was late. They could only barely see each other's face.

"Marilyn," he said softly. "What shall we do? I'd like to take you to bed, but we're both practically strangers, and you're going back to the States in a few days."

Her mouth had gone dry. Her heart was thudding. "I think you should take me to bed."

Quietly, they crept into the B&B and up the stairs to Marilyn's room. They locked the door. Ian put his arms around her and they pressed against each other, all up and down. This kiss was different from the others, rougher, warmer, more urgent. Marilyn wanted him inside her so much she was afraid she'd explode.

They pulled the covers back and fell on the bed with all their clothes on. As they kissed each other's mouths and eyes and faces, Marilyn unzipped her denim skirt and wrenched it off while Ian unzipped his khakis. Ian rose up on his arms and Marilyn tilted her hips up. He slid inside her, fitting as perfectly as the loch outside fit into the glen. Marilyn felt her eyes go wide with surprise as her body adjusted to this delicious intrusion. Ian moved slightly, and they both groaned. He lowered his head and brought his mouth down to kiss her. She clutched him to her and kissed him back. They rocked together slowly, letting the tension build. Something loosened inside her. A landslide of sexual pleasure rode through her pelvis. Clutching him for dear life, Marilyn surrendered to a force she'd never known her body contained.

After a while, she opened her eyes to see Ian smiling down at her.

"Okay?" he whispered.

She nodded. He moved again, quickly now, and she felt his own release inside her. When he fell against her, drained, she hugged him to her while tears tracked down her face.

"Do you know," he whispered, stroking her hair away from her face, "we're both still wearing our shoes."

She laughed as she cried.

Over the next week, Marilyn made love more than she ever had in all her life. Even if she added together all the times she'd ever had sex with her husband or that cad Barton or Faraday, she thought the sheer quantity surpassed them—and the quality! My God! She'd never realized! They made love in her room and his, in his car and in hers, standing up in a forest, lying down in a valley, and every time she wept with joy. When they hiked, they held hands. When they drove to a restaurant, she kept her hand on his thigh. When they ate, they sat next to each other, or twined legs under the table. She was giddy with sensuality. She ate more than she'd ever eaten, she drank more wine, she sang when she showered, she laughed about nothing. She felt like a teenager—no, she felt like some kind of angel.

"Look," Ian told her on the eighth night, "I've got to go back to Edinburgh tomorrow. I've got several professional matters to attend to."

"I'm leaving for home in three days," Marilyn told him. "Tomorrow night will be my last night here."

"Do you fly out of Edinburgh?"

"Yes."

"Then spend the last night with me at my house. I'll take you to the plane."

Marilyn began to cry. "Oh, damn, Ian. I don't want to be away from you."

"Can you rearrange your schedule? Stay a little longer?"

"I wish I could. But I've left my mother with friends, and I can't impose on them any longer."

"I understand. Well, look. I'll come visit you, how's that?"

"Oh, will you? When?"

"I'll have to check my calendar. Perhaps sometime in early September."

"That's so far away!"

"We'll e-mail every day," he promised.

As Marilyn watched Ian drive away that sunny morning, she felt as if she were watching a lover go off to war or sail away to conquer new lands. She wanted to sob with grief. She felt as if her skin were being ripped from her body.

But the day was beautiful, and the hills surrounding the loch were filled with hikers who saluted her with good cheer as they stomped past. She couldn't allow herself to stand weeping like an escapee from an institution for the demented, so she blew her nose, packed her backpack, and went out for a long hike around the lake.

That night she had dinner at the B&B, too weary to care about eating a gourmet meal. She couldn't taste anything, anyway. She lay on her bed, staring at the ceiling, remembering every word Ian had said, every kiss he'd pressed against her. She cried some more.

Her mind was in turmoil. Was she in love? If she was, was Ian? Certainly he seemed to feel as strongly as she did.

Now she wished her Hot Flash friends were here. She longed to talk all this over with them. Since she couldn't, she tried to imagine what advice they'd give.

Faye and Polly and Shirley would all probably say, *Lovely, Marilyn, we're so happy for you!* But levelheaded Alice would give her a look. *Girl,* Alice would say, *I'm glad you had fun, but don't try to make it into more than it is. Anyone who wants to base her future on sexual attraction is a fool.*

Thinking of her friends calmed Marilyn's nerves. She lay in the dark smiling, and her tears dried up and disappeared.

But her friends weren't through talking to her yet. She couldn't tell which one it was—maybe it was all of them—but a voice in her head said quite clearly, *We thought you were on a pilgrimage, Marilyn. We thought this trip was about making your childhood dream come true, not about getting laid.*

Although, they continued, *getting laid is nothing to sneeze at!*

She was restless. Marilyn tied her sneakers, grabbed up her fanny pack and a sweater, and went back out into the Scottish night.

It had not rained all day, and it was not raining now. A moon, not quite full, rode high in the sky, the occasional cloud sailing slowly across its face. The air smelled fresh, of grass and wild garlic and clover, as Marilyn sauntered down the long bank toward the loch's edge. There was no breeze. The deep waters of the loch slumbered, dark beneath the sky, dark to their depths.

It was midnight, but cars still passed on both sides of the loch, their lights flashing off and on like signals as they wound over the curves.

She crossed the road, heading toward the loch, going slowly, for the land was boggy and uneven, perfect for turning ankles. As she walked away from her B&B and the road up the hill to other hotels, the civilized world retreated. Nature closed around her.

It felt good to walk. Concentrating on each step soothed her nerves. She came to a small, sheltered cove overhung with trees, dense with bushes, and settled into a gap just her size at the water's edge. She could almost dangle her feet in the water. Instead, she drew her knees up, wrapped her arms around them, and gazed out at the loch.

She thought: *Ian.*

She shivered, remembering his touch, his breath, his body, his laughter.

Even if she never saw him again, the time she'd shared with him was a revelation. Love *did* exist. *Love at first sight* did exist. Even for a woman in her fifties, miracles could happen.

She knew her Hot Flash friends would scoff. They'd tell her there are no such things as miracles. Life doesn't give you miracles, they'd remind her. You're a scientist, for heaven's sake, they'd adjure. Be rational. Be skeptical. Be logical.

Her sensible side took over: Don't dream of a future with this man, this Ian. He lives in Scotland, you live in the United States. The past week was lovely; be grateful for that much. Don't expect anything more. For heaven's sake, you know nothing about the man, really. For all you know, he has a wife tucked away back home, or a mistress or two.

Marilyn idly watched the sleeping dark water as her mind tempered the past week's sensual richness with the astringency of common sense. In a lecturing way, her mind presented the facts: She'd been fortunate all her life. She had a healthy son, and now a healthy granddaughter. She had wonderful friends and work that fulfilled her. She was middle-aged, too old for miracles.

Why was she suddenly so greedy? She'd never been greedy before. She'd settled for a lackluster marriage, believing it was the best she could do. She'd accepted her junior position at the university with gratitude, not dreaming of anything more. Perhaps it was the influence of her Hot Flash friends, who got her to change her hair and clothing (when she remembered to), assuring her she could be more than plain, she could be actually *pretty*. Pretty, even at her age. Yes, it was her Hot Flash friends who caused her to be greedy—why, it was Shirley who said these should be the days of Dreams-Come-True.

But of course, they couldn't really mean that. At their advanced years, they knew that life could disappoint as much as it could thrill, and they were lucky if life didn't bring hurt or even grief.

But *still,* a small voice in Marilyn insisted, still good things can happen. We can change ourselves for the better. We can meet men and fall in love, and they can fall in love with us. We can—

Something moved in the water.

Marilyn blinked.

Perhaps twenty yards out, in the middle of the loch, the water stirred, sending concentric ripples with a shushing sound to the shore.

Above, a cloud passed over the moon, dimming the night, and then it floated off, and the loch stretched away, exposed in the clear air.

A swelling bulged from the surface of the water.

Marilyn held her breath.

Gradually, in a stately, steady manner, the shape broke through the water to reveal itself as a heavy, almost equine, arrow-shaped head supported by a narrow neck. Up it rose, one foot, two feet, three, four—

"Oh!" Marilyn whispered, trembling with excitement.

—ten, twelve feet at least, the neck extended from the long humped body that breached the water's surface, sending waves rolling to the land. With infinite grace, the neck turned, dipping the head this way and that, as if the creature were scanning the area. For a moment, Marilyn saw the liquid gleam of an eye.

The creature tilted her head back, exposing her throat to the sky, bending slowly to the left and right like a sunbather soaking in the rays. A low hum emanated from her, a satisfied sound, almost a purr. Then, in one sudden movement, like a duck or a bird, she bent her head to brush intently at her side, as if she were any kind of normal beast scratching an itch.

Tears streamed down Marilyn's face.

The beast, at least forty feet long, slowly swam a few feet, stopped, and turned its neck warily. Again it navigated down the middle of the loch, as if out for a stroll.

I should do something! Marilyn thought. I should take a picture or call someone!

But she couldn't take her eyes off the creature. She was paralyzed with awe.

Then, across the loch, the double lights of a moving car glittered, and with a smooth, fluid plunge, the creature dove, disappearing beneath the loch's surface.

The car passed, its red taillights flickering, then vanishing. Marilyn waited, but the water was smooth now, as if a hand had passed over it, leveling all wrinkles.

Marilyn was trembling all over, and after a few moments, she realized she was freezing cold. The night air was cool, and she was, she knew, in shock.

Still, she waited, watching.

She waited over an hour, hugging herself while her teeth chattered, but the creature did not return. Finally, reluctantly, she went back to the hotel.

In her room, her mirror reflected her face, flushed with excitement. Using the little in-room service, she brewed a cup of hot tea and drank it down without tasting it. The tea warmed her and brought her to her senses. She looked at her watch. It was almost four in the morning. She felt as exhausted as she had just after giving birth to her son. She fell on her bed, pulled the spread over her, and sank into a dreamless sleep.

LABOR DAY

16

On a steamy afternoon at the end of August, the Hot Flash Club, plus Marilyn's mother Ruth, gathered at Polly's house. Polly handed out glasses of iced tea sprigged with mint, then asked, "Is everyone ready?"

"Ready!" Marilyn, Ruth, Alice, and Shirley chorused.

"Behind door number one!" Polly waved her arms like Vanna White. "Our first design!"

The double doors between the living and dining rooms flew open. Faye stepped out. She posed, one hand on her hip, the other at the base of her neck. Her thigh-length russet jacket covered a pumpkin shirt over a tank top inset with leaves embroidered in emerald and garnet.

"Oh my God! It's gorgeous!" Shirley cried.

Alice applauded. "Double wow."

Ruth held out her hand. "Let me feel that material. Is it Velveeta?"

"Washable velour." Faye walked around the room so everyone could feel the fabric.

Polly hurried into the dining room. She returned, pulling a rack of clothing.

The others jumped up and sorted through the selection.

"The colors are all autumnal because they'll go on sale in September," Faye explained. "If they sell well, we'll start on Christmas and winter colors right away."

"How many sizes did you make?" Marilyn asked.

Polly answered. "We've got twenty finished, in all. Three each of size twenty down to size ten, and one each of size twenty-two and twenty-four."

"Hey," Shirley protested. "Then they're all too big for me!"

"You don't need to wear this style," Alice told her. "You don't have any bouncing blubber to cover up."

Faye and Polly signaled each other with their eyes. Faye whisked into the dining room.

"But you *should* wear one of these ensembles," Polly said, "because you're the director of The Haven, and it would be great advertising, so—"

"TA—DA!" Faye came out with her arms full. "We've made one for each of you."

Polly lifted two of the garments from Faye and helped distribute them to each woman.

"Oh!" Shirley clapped her hands in delight. "You made mine purple!"

"It's Panting Pansy, actually," Faye told her. "We're naming each color. With a Hot Flash Hyacinth shirt and a Melted Mallow tank top."

"Here, Ruth." Polly approached the older woman. "This is yours."

Ruth tottered to her feet, beaming. "You girls didn't have to make one for me. I'm past the hot flash stage, after all."

"But of course we had to make one for you! You're the one who came up with the idea!" Polly reminded her.

"Let's just try the jacket on for now." Marilyn helped Ruth slide her arms in.

"This is just *lovely.*" Ruth smoothed the sea green material over her hips. "This Friday I'm going to a lecher. I'll wear it then."

"*Lecture,*" Marilyn enunciated in a whisper over Ruth's head.

Alice slipped into her jacket. "Feels like butter. And the color's delicious."

"Mad Marigold jacket," Polly announced. "With Sizzling Scarlet shirt and Crazy Carrot tank."

Alice went out into the hall to check herself in the long mirror. "Good grief, Gertrude, this flows like water!"

"That's because we made a yoke across the shoulders and lots of little tucks." Faye ran her hands along the back stitching.

"I predict these will be a raging success!" Alice said.

Polly disappeared, returning with a chocolate cake. "*Now* we have to make a few business decisions. We thought we should have a little nourishment to help our brains."

"What a beautiful cake!" Ruth said. "Did you make it, Polly?"

"Oh, no. Haven't had time to bake, with all the sewing. I bought it at The Haven's bakery." Polly and Faye bustled around, bringing out teacups, coffee cups, spoons, and napkins.

Marilyn reached out for a plate. "Alice, your party for Jennifer and Alan was a great success."

Alice smiled. "Thanks. I enjoyed meeting their friends."

Faye spoke around a mouthful of cake. "And Alan and Jennifer look so happy!"

Polly turned to Shirley. "How's Justin's book coming?"

Shirley lit up. "It will be published in October. Speaking of parties, we're planning a *huge* event."

Alice cast a worried glance Shirley's way. "Have you read his manuscript yet?"

Shirley bristled. "Not a single word. Justin says he wants it to be a surprise." Defiantly, she added, "The publishers swear it's going to be a bestseller."

"Lovely," Polly smoothly interposed. *"Now."* She set her empty plate on the table and clapped once, briskly. "Time for business. We agree these outfits are fabulous, right? Show of hands? Okay, we want to have these outfits in The Haven's gift shop in September. First, we have to have a name for our business."

"So we can sew in the labels," Faye explained.

"What are the possibilities?" Alice asked.

Shirley waved an enthusiastic hand. "Havenly Yours! Heavenly, Havenly, get it?"

"I was thinking Wisely Woven," Polly suggested.

"But they aren't *woven*," Marilyn pointed out.

"Hot Flash Fashions?" offered Alice.

"Mmm . . ." Faye tilted her hand back and forth in a so-so response.

Marilyn had an inspiration. "What about Crones' Crafts?"

"No!" Polly objected immediately. "*Crone* has too much of a negative connotation."

"So does 'hag,' " Shirley reminded them. "And 'hag' comes from the early Greek phrase 'Haggia Sophia,' meaning goddess of spiritual wisdom."

"What does 'crone' come from?" Faye asked.

Ruth spoke up. "It's from the Scottish for 'withered old ewe.' "

"Eeeuuwe!" cried Polly.

"Ancient wisdom has divided the life cycle of a woman into three parts: Maiden, Mother, Crone. Crone's wise, and possesses knowledge of ancient secrets." Shirley stirred sugar into her tea as she spoke. "Crone is definitely associated with old age and death. The crone's colors are black. She's sometimes called 'The Dark Mother,' because she knows the secrets of passing over into death."

For a moment, everyone in the room was quiet.

Faye said, thoughtfully, "We're all going to be crones someday."

"With all the advances in technology and medicine," Marilyn added, "we'll probably live different lives from the older women before us."

"True," Alice said, "but still, if we're lucky, we're going to get really old."

"And not necessarily really wise," Shirley added, with a grin.

Faye turned to Ruth, clearly the oldest among them. "What do you think?"

Ruth deliberated. "I think 'Crones' Crafts' is cute." As she spoke, she turned the rings on her liver-spotted, wrinkled, bony old hands. "But technically, girls, you're none of you crones, not yet.

I'm a crone." She held up her hand in a "stop" sign. "*Please*. I'm eighty-three! It's been a couple of decades since I've had hot flesh. I'm not sad, scared, or embarrassed, so please don't you be. I'm just saying, I vote for 'Hot Flash Fashions,' not 'Crones' Crafts.' "

"But I'd like to get the word 'crone' back into our vernacular. If we *use* it, it will become something people won't dread," Shirley protested. "I mean, look at you, Ruth. You're old, as you said, but you're not shriveled, toothless, and scary."

Ruth laughed. "You haven't seen me naked!"

Shirley continued, "I think part of the mission of The Haven is to present new ways of looking at all the ages of womanhood."

"Well put," Alice said. "I'm impressed by your argument, Shirley."

Shirley blinked, thrilled to have Alice compliment her.

"And," Alice continued, "I still think your suggestion, Havenly Yours, is the best. It's clever, and it advertises The Haven."

"Let's take a vote," Polly decided. "All in favor of Hot Flash Fashions, raise your hands."

Ruth raised her hand.

"Crones' Crafts?"

Shirley raised her hand.

"Havenly Yours?"

Marilyn, Polly, Faye, and Alice raised their hands, and then Ruth said, "Can I change my boat? I choose Havenly Yours, too."

"Then Havenly Yours it is," Polly told them.

17

"It's amazing," Shirley said to Justin on Labor Day as she looked out the kitchen window at the green grounds of The Haven. "Sometimes I actually believe there's hope for humanity."

Justin plunged a corkscrew into a bottle of wine. "And that would be because . . ."

"Well, look." Shirley waved her hands toward the window. "Alice has made Jennifer sit on the recliner, while she and Gideon help Alan set up the tables. Not to mention that everyone decided to make this a potluck, so I wouldn't have so much work to do."

"Doesn't take much to thrill you, does it?" Justin smiled to take the edge off his words. He'd had his teeth whitened, and he was tan from playing tennis, so his smile was like a million watts.

Shirley was too happy to let the tone of his voice bring her down. As the publication day of his book drew near, Justin was becoming nervous, short-tempered, and cranky. She didn't blame him. He was, after all, an artist, naturally sensitive, and worried about the event of a lifetime.

"Here come Carolyn and Hank and their baby. I know Carolyn's father is bringing Faye! I just wish Carolyn would *get* it, that Faye and Aubrey are a couple. Faye and Polly spent all summer sewing together. They're such good friends now. Polly—"

"*Your* name should be Polly," Justin growled. "Pollyanna." Carrying the wine bottle and his glass, he went through the door.

Poor Justin, Shirley thought. Then she brightened. "Oh, my gosh! Here's Marilyn with her Scottish lover!" She raced outside.

The summer heat lay heavily across the day, frizzing hair, driving everyone into the shade of the patio where the tables were set out. Shirley fluttered from person to person, kissing, hugging, loving them all.

She wondered, just a *little,* in her secret and critical mind, just what it was Marilyn saw in this Ian fellow who had come to visit her for a couple of weeks. He was bound to be brilliant, but gee, he was a funny-looking guy, all elbows and knees and Adam's apple. Shirley thought Faraday had been much handsomer, and sexier, too.

"I'm verra pleased to meet you," Ian told Shirley. "I apologize for not shaking your hand, but as you can see, both hands are full." With his chin, he motioned to the large bowl he carried.

"Mother made her famous hot potato salad." Marilyn was absolutely glowing with happiness. And she wore a darling frou-frou filmy yellow dress that made her look divinely feminine. "And I made curried chicken salad."

"I'll take your bowl," Shirley told Ian, "and you can help Ruth get settled."

Ruth chuckled. "I like the division of labor. You girls take the food, I'll take the man." She fluttered her eyelashes flirtatiously, looking adorable in a dress covered with hummingbirds, with a hummingbird hairclip in her white curls.

"Madam." Ian held out his arm. "May I?"

Ruth clutched it and winked at Shirley. "Little does he know, I'm as stable as a horse."

"Your mother looks good," Shirley whispered to Marilyn as they carried the food to the long table.

"She has good days and bad," Marilyn said. "Some days she's really foggy and forgetful. Today she's in great shape."

Polly and Hugh appeared with plates in their arms.

"Cold paella salad," Polly announced.

"Tuna tonnato," Hugh told Shirley, setting a brightly colored dish on the table. "We've got an apple pie in the car. I'll just fetch it."

Faye strolled up. "My gosh, look at all the food! No dieting today."

"It's a holiday," Shirley reminded her. "It's illegal to diet on holidays."

"Is that a Hot Flash Club rule?" Polly asked. "If not, I move that we vote it in!"

It was too hot to play badminton or even croquet, so everyone lolled around chatting until Shirley announced that all the food and guests were there. Alice told Alan to move the sun umbrella to the left, so it would more completely shade Jennifer, and Jennifer told Alice to put her feet up on the end of her recliner.

We're a lucky group, Alice thought now, surveying her friends over the rim of her gin and tonic. We're an unusual group—five women of a certain age, each with her own beau. Polly and Hugh. Faye and Aubrey. Alice and Gideon. Marilyn and Ian.

Shirley and Justin.

Justin was the youngest, and by far the handsomest. He had all his hair, and no belly sagged over his belt. Alice looked around the party for him and spotted him in fervent conversation with Carolyn. Carolyn's husband Hank, who was pretty cute himself, was busy taking their daughter for a toddle on the grass, and Justin had pulled his chair so close to Carolyn's that their knees were just an inch away from touching. As Alice watched, Carolyn smiled, blushed, and shook her hair away from her face demurely, as if Justin had just paid her a compliment. Which, no doubt, he had. Justin knew Carolyn was wealthy. He was probably buttering her up. But Carolyn was a businesswoman, not an easy mark. Alice wasn't worried about Carolyn.

Alice looked around for Shirley. Dusk was just beginning to

fall, softening the light and moderating the heat. Shirley was with Marilyn and Ian.

"Let me show you the walking paths before it gets dark," she said. Shirley escorted them toward the woods.

Alice watched the three stroll away. Gideon and Hugh were engaged in a fierce discussion of the Red Sox.

Alice stood up. She was half-surprised by the direction her thoughts were carrying her legs, but as she strolled unnoticed into the kitchen of The Haven, she decided that somewhere in her unconscious mind she'd been plotting this all along.

Just waiting for the right opportunity.

Alice wanted a peek at Justin's novel. Shirley might be shy about reading it, but Alice wasn't.

In the kitchen, Alice took a moment to let her eyes adjust to the different light. Then she hurried.

She knew the layout of The Haven well. She'd examined every inch when Shirley was considering buying it, and during the past two years, Alice had made her way countless times past the back corridor leading to all the offices, into the great foyer, and up the handsome staircase to the second floor where the private condos were. She'd been in Shirley's condo often, although not since Justin had moved in.

Shirley's condo was at the end of the building. The door was open. Not just unlocked, but wide open. Good.

Alice stepped inside. Quickly she scanned the place. It was so very *Shirley,* with lavender walls hung with paintings of nude goddesses. Batik cushions spilled across the sofa. Candles and incense holders sat on every table.

A short hallway led to the bathroom and two bedrooms. Alice peeked in. On the left, a violet paisley duvet covered a bed. A man's robe was tossed over a chair.

Alice went into the other bedroom. Aha! This was clearly Justin's study, where he was writing his purportedly brilliant novel.

Two walls were lined with shelves filled with books. A handsome desk sat in front of the window, a computer humming on top of it. Filing cabinets stood in front of the fourth wall.

Quickly, Alice surveyed Justin's desk. Well, well, he was a very tidy boy. She saw a calendar blotter, blank notepad, pens, tape dispenser, stapler, paperweight, Post-its, and telephone, but that was all. No sign of the precious novel.

She crossed the room, stuck her head around the corner into the hall, and listened carefully. No sounds on the stairs. Good.

Approaching the filing cabinets, she yanked open a drawer, swiftly flipping through the files, which had been carefully labeled in a firm hand: *Correspondence/Agents. Correspondence/Publishers.* Those held only polite letters of rejection. Files of newspaper and magazine clippings and online essays about how to get published or how to survive the trials of refusals filled the rest of the drawer. Alice felt a twinge of sympathy for Justin.

It didn't last long.

She opened the next file drawer. It was crammed with lesson plans, sample tests, essays, and handouts from his days of teaching English. Another drawer held the boring paperwork of everyday life: a car insurance folder, passport information, receipts for tax purposes.

One more drawer. Alice pulled.

It wouldn't open.

Ha! This drawer, no doubt, held the priceless manuscript.

She tried gently enticing the drawer open. It didn't work. She yanked hard. It wouldn't open.

Her heart was pounding. How long had she been away from the party? She should have noticed the time when she came in. She hurried to the window and looked out—everyone was occupied, talking and laughing; no one was looking around for her. Justin was still smarming around Carolyn.

Okay. Alice forced herself to take a deep breath. Plunking down in Justin's office chair, she wiggled the mouse. The computer brightened and came to life.

She took a moment to study the icons on the screen, then opened the word-processing program. Clicking on the folder "C," she learned it contained correspondence. Appropriate.

Could the folder named "N" possibly contain the novel?

Only one way to find out.

With a trembling hand, Alice clicked. Dozens of files marched down the screen. She moved the cursor to "Title" and clicked again. Her heart drummed in her ears.

Spa Spy, a novel by Justin Quale.

The words leapt out at her so fast, Alice gasped. She'd found it! She'd found his novel! Her heart went pit-a-pat.

Hang on now! It was called *Spa Spy*? That didn't sound good.

She closed that file and opened the one labeled "Chapter One."

She read the first page. He wrote well. It read fast. But . . . Alice was literally on the edge of her seat as she scrolled hurriedly down to the middle of the chapter.

"Oh, no," she whispered. Stunned, she clicked and tugged the mouse, speeding the cursor through succeeding chapters.

Spa Spy seemed to be about a group of women who ran a wellness retreat for wealthy older women. Everything was rosy—until the second chapter, when it was revealed that spy holes had been placed in strategic spots in the walls of the locker room, Jacuzzi room, and massage therapy rooms. The managing group were using the spy holes to photograph and tape-record certain of their wealthiest clients, with blackmail plans in mind. The director's lover, a handsome man who bore a remarkable resemblance to Justin, was trying to foil their scheme.

"Oh, no!" Alice cried again.

Her heart contracted fiercely as the full horror of it hit her. Justin had appropriated details of The Haven. Anyone reading this trash would immediately withdraw their membership. Even if there was the standard disclaimer about this being a work of fiction bearing no relation to any living person, it would still kill The Haven's business. Shirley would be devastated.

And heartbroken. When Shirley realized what Justin had done, she would know the truth about the man she believed loved her . . . Alice's own heart cracked at the thought.

A searing pain shot from Alice's chest into her left arm. She clutched her arm, groaning.

What—?

What was happening?

She couldn't get her breath. An immense pressure weighed against her chest—dear God! She was having a heart attack!

She tried to reach for the telephone, but only managed to knock the handset off before crumpling to the floor. She was aware of a suffocating pressure and a burning pain—and then it all went black.

"So that's the main walking path," Shirley told Ian as they came out of the shadowy forest onto the grassy lawn.

"It's wonderful," Ian said. "So many varieties of deciduous trees!"

Ian and Marilyn were holding hands and lingering in the shelter of the woods, as if the tree bark were amazingly interesting, which, Shirley thought, it just might be to this pair of scientific brains. Probably they wanted to press their noses up against the tree trunks, searching for bugs.

More likely, they wanted to remain hidden in the woods so they could kiss.

"I've got to run into the kitchen and get some candles," Shirley told them.

"Need help?" Marilyn called dutifully.

"No, thanks!" Shirley grinned as she fairly skipped across the lawn.

Everyone seemed to be having a good time. Gideon and Hugh were still deep in discussion, probably solving the Red Sox pitching problems. Jennifer, Alan, and Ruth were sitting with Carolyn and Hank, who bounced his daughter on his knee. No doubt they were talking about babies. Faye and Aubrey were at the far end of the grounds, playing croquet.

Where was Alice?

She spotted Justin slinking into the kitchen.

Something about the way he moved worried her. He looked so . . . *furtive.*

She hurried onto the patio. "Just getting some candles," she tossed over her shoulder.

The kitchen was dark, cool—and empty. Shirley went through into the foyer just in time to see Justin's feet disappearing up the great front staircase.

She followed.

Where was he going? Why did she feel so nervous? Her palms were sweaty! Her heart was pounding! This was ridiculous! The poor man probably just wanted to take a pee.

But there were restrooms on the first floor, close to the kitchen.

Well, then, maybe he'd spilled something on his shirt and went to change it. Or something, *anything*—why was she so spooked?

She flew up the stairs after him.

At the end of the hall, the door to her condo was open, providing a direct shot into the foyer and down the little hall leading to the bedrooms.

Justin was standing in the hall. He was just standing there, staring. Staring into his own study. Not moving. Why would he do that? He looked oddly *satisfied.*

"Justin?" Shirley called.

He turned his head and saw her coming toward him. In a flash, he disappeared into his study.

"What's going on, Hon?" Shirley asked, hurrying into the condo and down the hall.

She turned into Justin's study. Justin was hurriedly moving the computer mouse—and Alice was collapsed on the floor!

"Alice?" Shirley ran into the room and threw herself down. "Oh, my God, Alice!"

Alice lay curled on her side, unconscious.

"Justin! Call 911! Alice is—I think she's had a heart at-tack!" Shirley turned Alice on her back. Alice flopped like a doll. She wasn't breathing. "Oh, God, oh, Alice!"

Justin was speaking with 911. Shirley shoved the window up and screamed down at the backyard. "Hugh? HUGH! Come up here, please! Alice had a heart attack!"

Startled faces stared up at her from the patio. She dropped to the floor and began CPR on Alice. Shirley's hands were shaking— her entire body was trembling as if it were about to shatter—but she forced herself to concentrate.

Kneeling, she pinched Alice's nose tight, covered Alice's mouth with her own, and blew. Once. Twice. Three times? She couldn't re-member how many times to breathe!

Alice didn't respond. Shirley put her hands between Alice's breasts and shoved down hard. Once, twice, three times—she knew she had to do it fifteen times at the rate of one hundred per second, or was it one hundred times at the rate of fifteen per second?

She blew again in Alice's mouth. Alice had a mole by her left eyebrow. She'd never noticed that before. She moved back to her chest and pumped. Beneath her tangerine chiffon poncho, Alice's chest remained still.

Suddenly Hugh was there, kneeling next to Shirley. "I'll pump. You breathe." He began to count aloud. Quickly they synchronized their efforts.

In a blurry kind of way, Shirley was aware of the others crowding into the room, asking how Alice was, what they could do to help. Justin bent down to unplug his computer, then lifted it off the desk and left the room with it in his arms.

"Mom?" Alan fell to the floor next to his mother. "Is she okay? What can I do?"

"Just give her room to breathe," Hugh told him. "We're doing what we can."

"The ambulance is here!" Faye called.

"She's got a pulse," Hugh said.

"Should we stop now?" Shirley asked.

Two EMTs ran into the room.

The closest hospital was Emerson in Concord. The ambulance tore down The Haven's driveway, siren blaring. The rest of the party followed in various cars. Since Justin had disappeared, Polly tucked Shirley into the back of Hugh's Range Rover and sat with her, keeping a comforting arm around her.

"Justin was just standing there," Shirley sobbed. "Just *standing* there, looking."

Hugh spoke up from the front seat. "Not everyone knows how to give CPR."

"Then he should have yelled out the window like I did. Phoned 911. Run back downstairs and grabbed you. *Something.*" Shirley couldn't stop shaking.

"Take some deep breaths," Polly told her.

Shirley tried, but her thoughts kept exploding. "And then, when I was giving her CPR, Justin was removing his computer from the room! As if he had something to hide!" She covered her face with her hands and wept.

At the hospital, the Hot Flash friends and their beaux clustered in a waiting room for what felt like an eternity. Shirley repeated her story over and over again, how she'd followed Justin, how sneaky he'd looked, and then how creepily he stood there staring into his study, looking alert and somehow *satisfied*. How Alice had lay unconscious, her face void of her formidable personality.

"If she doesn't recover, I won't be able to live with myself," Shirley whispered.

"She'll recover," Faye promised, because anything else was unthinkable.

———

Hugh returned to the room, a physician in a white coat at his side. Everyone knew at once that Alice hadn't died—both men were smiling.

"Alice is awake," the physician informed them. "She suffered a mild cardiac infarction. We have her on an anticoagulant, and we're going to run some tests on her to find out exactly what the problem is. She'll be in the hospital for a couple of days at least. Who's her next of kin?"

"I am!" Shirley cried eagerly, then added honestly, "Well, I feel like I am."

"I am," Alan insisted.

"I am," Gideon bellowed.

The physician smiled. Pointing to Alan, he said, "We need you to sign some forms." He looked at Shirley. "You must be Shirley. Come with me. She wants to see you. But only for a moment, you understand."

———

Enthroned on a high white hospital bed, an oxygen tube snaking into her nose, IVs dripping into her arms, Alice lay beneath white sheets, sleeping.

"Alice?"

Alice opened her eyes. Seeing Shirley, she turned her hand over, palm up. Shirley grabbed it with both hands.

"Oh, Alice!" Tears ran down Shirley's face, plopping on her shirt. "Oh, honey, I'm so glad you're okay."

Alice's face grew serious. "Shirley. Must tell you." Her voice was whispery, strained. "Justin's novel? It's called *Spa Spy.* It's— bad. You can't help him publish it."

A nurse entered the room. "Ladies? What are we doing to get the patient agitated?"

"Alice." Shirley bent close to her friend. "Don't worry. I promise you, Justin Quale and his novel are on their way out of my life."

"But—" Alice struggled to explain.

"Tell me the details later. I know all I need to know now."

"How—?" Alice's face creased anxiously.

Frantically, Shirley wondered how she could reassure her. "Justin gave The Hemingway Group ten thousand dollars this spring. I mailed them a check for ten thousand more last week. First thing in the morning, I'm calling the bank and canceling the check. Next thing, I'm throwing all his stuff out on the lawn."

Alice smiled and relaxed into the pillows. "Sorry, kiddo."

"I love you, Alice!" Shirley bent down and kissed her friend. "I'll spend the night here."

"Tell Alan and Gideon I'm okay." Alice closed her eyes. "Just really tired."

The other members of the Hot Flash Club volunteered to come with her, but Shirley insisted she needed to do this herself. So they arranged a schedule for sitting with Alice—Gideon and Alan would spend the night at the hospital; Polly and Faye would arrive early in the morning to take over; Marilyn would relieve them in the afternoon; and Shirley would join Marilyn whenever she was through with Justin.

Through with Justin.

When Shirley returned from the hospital, it was almost midnight. Someone had brought the food in from the patio, but empty plates and glasses were still scattered outside and the kitchen was in chaos. She checked her answering machine—perhaps Justin had phoned to ask how Alice was—but there were no messages.

Glad to have a use for her nervous energy, Shirley buzzed in and out the kitchen door, carrying trays of plates, utensils, and used paper napkins in from the patio. She sorted, tossed, rinsed, and stacked, until all that was left to do was turn on the dishwasher.

Its hum was comforting in the huge kitchen. It sounded kind, almost concerned.

"All right, now you're getting weird on me," Shirley said aloud, because that's what Alice would say.

She turned off the lights and set the alarms. She climbed the stairs to her condo—the door was still wide open. She looked in Justin's study. No Justin. No computer.

Still too restless to sleep, Shirley decided to pack Justin's clothes. It was a melancholy task, and as she folded his white terry-cloth robe, the tears began.

Perhaps she'd suspected just a *little bit* that he didn't love her. She could believe he'd pretended to because she provided free lodging and food, not to mention funds for the publication of his book.

But she'd never dreamed his novel was titled *Spa Spy*! It had to be based on The Haven. Oh, her poor clients would feel so invaded! Was she hopelessly naïve? She brought his robe to her face and sobbed into it, letting it absorb her tears.

The robe smelled so good. It smelled like Justin.

The worst thing, the very worst, was the memory of Justin standing there in the hall, alert, *waiting*. He'd been looking at Alice, collapsed on the floor, and had not done what any normal person would do. He had not run in to help her. He'd just stood there, watching, as if waiting for her to die.

She sobbed harder, in huge, heaving sobs that produced frightening noises, like some kind of jungle rampage. So what? No one was here to hear her.

That was all right. The pain of his betrayal hurt so much—but it was pain she had to bear alone. She'd never had a baby, but she'd heard other women talking about the agony of labor. Even though husbands, lovers, doctors, nurses, midwives, or coaches were with them, they all had to endure the pain in their bodies alone.

Shirley had to endure this pain alone. She could do it, she thought, if she could consider it a kind of labor, like giving birth to herself—a new and, *dear God, please,* less gullible self.

"Shirley?"

She woke. Sun streamed in through the windows. She was lying on her bed with Justin's robe in her arms. Her eyes were swollen and crusty. Her mouth was dry.

Justin leaned in the bedroom doorway, handsome in a crisp white button-down shirt with the sleeves rolled up over his tanned arms. He looked perfect. Shirley sat up, aware of her own disarray. Wrinkled clothing, hair no doubt sticking up in all directions, skin blotched from sleep.

"Is Alice all right?" Justin asked.

Shirley nodded, yawning. She needed a shower and a gallon of peppermint tea.

"Thank God." Justin sat down on the bed. "I was so worried." He tried to pull her into his arms.

"Don't, Justin." Wearily, Shirley put both hands on his chest and pushed him away. "Don't bother pretending. We both know it's over between us."

He looked shocked. "What are you talking about?"

"Oh, Justin." She gazed at his handsome, immoral face. "You didn't try to help Alice. She was dying, and you grabbed your computer and left."

"But you've got to understand!" Justin sputtered indignantly. "All those people—my work is private—"

"Your work is shit," Shirley told him. She dropped the robe on the floor and stood up. "We're through, Justin, and as far as I'm concerned, your work is no longer any concern of mine. I'm stopping the check to The Hemingway Group. And I want you to move out."

Justin jumped up, genuinely alarmed. "You can't do that! Shir', I'm so close to publication!"

"Yeah," Shirley spat, "publication of a novel called *Spa Spy?*"

"Shirley, it's a work of *fiction.*"

"How dumb do you think I am?" Shirley demanded, immediately adding, "No, don't answer that. I don't want to know."

"Shirley. Please." He approached her, once again trying to take her in his arms. "Let's talk about this. Let's talk about *us.*"

Shirley looked up at his handsome, smug face. Her hesitation sparked triumph in his eyes.

She stepped back. In a firm, level voice, Shirley said, "Justin. Leave. I mean it. Pack your clothes and leave. It's over."

He tried to grasp her hand. She wrenched away from him. She hurried into the bathroom and slammed the door.

Sometimes Justin had joined her when she showered, soaping her back, pressing her against the tiles as he kissed her.

Today, she turned the lock on the door and took her shower alone. The sound of the water obscured any pleas he might have tried to make.

The warm water rinsed her clean.

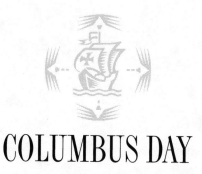

COLUMBUS DAY

19

The tang of fall lanced the air on the Friday night beginning Columbus Day weekend. The five members of the Hot Flash Club hurried from the parking lot into Legal Seafoods, hugging themselves for warmth. The restaurant was crowded, but they were still seated at their favorite table.

"Alice," Marilyn said, "you look *amazing*. You, too, Faye. And you, too, Polly."

The three women glowed. When Faye and Polly had heard about the lifestyle changes Alice's heart attack was forcing her to make, they had decided to join her, partly for moral support, partly to prevent something similar from happening to them. So they'd all been on the same diet, and attended the same yoga and exercise programs.

"I've only lost eight pounds," Alice said as she unfolded her napkin. "Five in the hospital, three since."

"But it's only been six weeks," Polly reminded her. "We're supposed to lose it *gradually*."

"Do you feel better?" Shirley asked.

Alice nodded. "I hate to admit it, but I do. I think the exercise and yoga's helping my arthritis. I'm less stiff."

"Yes, well, *I'm* having trouble with—" Faye stopped talking because suddenly the waiter was there. When everyone had given her order and the waiter left, she continued. "*Gas,*" she whispered. "All these vegetables I'm eating have me as bloated as the Hindenburg. After dinner, you could hang Firestone ads on my side and float me over football stadiums."

"Me, too!" Polly chimed in. "I never used to have gas, and now I have it all the time! It's so embarrassing! Especially since the worst time is night, when Hugh and I make love. I'm so busy trying not to pass gas, I can't enjoy myself!"

Shirley looked thoughtful. "But *men* aren't timid about it. They love to let it rip."

"Men consider farting an art form," Alice agreed. "I swear, Gideon will walk through the condo to find me, as if he's presenting me with a gift or performing some kind of symphony."

Polly laughed. "I know. Hugh does that, too. But it wouldn't be the same if I did it. It just doesn't seem *feminine*."

Marilyn nestled her chin in her hand, squinting as she thought. "Perhaps it was once some primitive form of communication. You know how male mammals fight for control of the females? They fight, and bellow, and snort. Well, perhaps the male who could produce the most powerful scent and the most terrifying sound announced his supremacy."

"In that case, Gideon would win, believe me," Alice chuckled.

"It's all natural." Shirley squeezed the lime slice into her sparkling water. "Your body at work."

"It's not just farting," Faye said. "It's acid indigestion, too."

"Hugh likes to speak his belches." Polly imitated him in a bullfrog rumble. *"Helllllllo. Goooood-bye."*

"I get acid indigestion, too," Alice told Faye. "It kind of scares me, actually, every time I get heartburn. I mean, I'm afraid I'm having another heart attack."

Shirley patted Alice's hand. "Hon, that's not going to happen. You're on Plavix. You're doing everything your doctor advised with lifestyle changes. When you get heartburn, just remind yourself that's a sign that you're eating all the great crucifers and fiber that are keeping you healthy and strong."

Alice shook her head. "It's hard to think that way when there's a Bunsen burner flaring up between my breasts."

"You should get a prescription antacid," Polly advised her.

"More *pills*!" Alice looked despairing.

"Alice, I take tons of pills." Faye counted on her fingers as she named them. "Blood pressure medication, which also helps heart arrhythmia. I've been on that forever. Cholesterol medication. Aspirin for mild arthritis. Pills for bladder control. Allergy medication during allergy season, which seems to be just about the entire year. Antacids. Vitamins and extra calcium."

"Is that all?" Shirley was surprised. "I thought you were taking those omega-3 fatty acid supplements I told you about. Really, you should all take them. Didn't I give you the literature?"

Polly nodded. "We all read it. But I'm like Faye. I hate to depend on so many pills. Doesn't seem natural."

"Well, that's just crazy," Shirley argued. "That's like saying you won't use the phone or drive a car. We're fortunate that so many researchers are finding supplements that keep us healthy and active."

Marilyn laughed. "I read there's a new medication to help stroke victims. It dissolves blood clots, and it comes from the saliva of vampire bats. Isn't nature amazing?"

Alice shuddered. "That's just too weird."

Polly said, "We probably don't *want* to know where most of our medicine comes from."

"If you want to take fewer medications for arthritis," Shirley advised, "talk to the nutritionist at The Haven. I know certain foods are great anti-inflammatories. Ginger, turmeric, celery. Debbie carries a range of supplements and natural medicines in the shop."

The waiter set their meals before them—everyone had fish and steamed broccoli.

Alice tasted her salmon. "How's the shop doing?"

"We've still got a limited inventory," Shirley told her. "We need to work up a complete business plan before we invest in a lot of stock."

"Speaking of business plans . . ." Faye's eyes sparkled with merriment.

"What?" Alice demanded. "I can tell by your face this is going to be good."

"Oh boy." Polly looked like she was going to crawl under the table.

Faye smirked. "Well, you know, Polly and I talked with several banks about getting a loan to start Havenly Yours. For industrial sewing machines, materials, salaries, et cetera."

"Go on," Shirley coaxed.

"So our first meeting was yesterday, with Third National in Lincoln . . ."

"Wait! Wait!" Polly interrupted. "Remember, I've never done a business meeting before! Tucker used to do all that kind of stuff."

Faye grinned. "So Polly and I made the appointment. I met Polly at the bank. She looked very efficient in a tidy little cream pantsuit. We were shown into the vice president's office. Evan Krause. Our age, *terribly* serious."

"Talks like his jaw's wired shut," Polly added. "All the charm of a robot."

"So we sit down in his terribly serious office and pull out our folders and go over the business plan with him. And Evan doesn't see one of the figures—" Faye swallowed a snicker.

"—the health benefit package," Polly added. She was turning red.

"So Polly gets up, leans over his desk, and points to the line in our figures. And as Polly leans over, there's her rear end staring right at me." Laughter bubbled up around her words. "And it looks like five or six little brown *pellets* are dangling from her bum."

Marilyn, Shirley, and Alice gawked at Polly. Polly put her napkin over her head.

"I'm thinking what *are* those things?" Faye put her hands to her heart in mock shock. "They looked like little . . ." She glanced around to be sure no one was near. ". . . *turds*!" She snorted, trying to contain her laughter.

"I'm *so* dying of embarrassment," Polly mumbled behind the napkin.

"So Polly sits down again. But I can't concentrate. All I can think of are those little brown nuggets and how they could be on the *outside* of her clothing!" She rocked with suppressed laughter. "So she and Ichabod Banker are *staring* at me, which sends me into a hot flash, and then I *really* can't think. Oh, Jeez," Faye interrupted herself. "Just *thinking* of it is giving me a hot flash!" She grabbed her water glass and pressed it against her neck.

Polly removed the napkin from her head and carried on. "So to make a long and painful story short, we did not do a very professional job of presenting our business plan. I couldn't understand why Faye was so scattered. I had to do all the talking, while Faye sat there twitching like she was being inhabited by aliens. So the Robot Banker says he'll take it under advisement and let us know—"

"And we stand up and Polly leans over to shake his hand." Faye exploded with laughter. "And I look at her chair, and those five little brown pellets are lying there! Ahahahaha!" Tears streamed down her cheeks. "Like she'd laid five little brown eggs!"

Her laughter was contagious. They all howled. It was like junior high.

"What *were* they?" Marilyn choked out.

"Well, I was nervous, you have to understand!" Polly held out her hands, pleading. "While I was driving to the bank, I ate a bag of chocolate-covered peanuts. For the endorphins for courage and tranquillity. You know! I gobbled them down like mad. I guess some of them fell onto my seat and rolled down and got attached to my trousers."

"And when she scooted around during our presentation, they brushed off her clothes and got stuck on the fabric of the chair!" Faye finished.

Alice wiped tears from her eyes. "And I thought I had problems when the underwire in my bra broke free when I was in a business meeting."

Marilyn blew her nose. "So did you get the loan?"

Polly nodded her head eagerly. "We *did*!"

For some reason, this set them off again. They laughed so hard Alice stuffed her napkin in her mouth to stifle herself and Shirley's breath turned into little mouse squeals.

Finally, they settled down.

"My stomach hurts," Faye sighed.

"Why weren't you there, Alice?" Marilyn asked. "I thought you were doing the accounting for Havenly Yours."

"She is," Polly explained. "But her doctors want her to avoid stressful situations. They said she can work at home, or at The Haven, with us, but nowhere else."

"Which is a shame," Alice added, "because I could have *handled* that banker."

"But it's good for us," Polly told her, "to learn how to do that sort of thing." She patted her own shoulder. "I mean, I did manage to stay calm, cool, and collected. I did manage to present the business plan as if I actually had a brain. I'm really proud of myself, Alice, for doing something that's as easy as breathing for you."

Marilyn asked, "Alice, are you still allowed to play competitive bridge?"

Alice made a face. "Nope. Too stressful. They want me to wait a few months."

Polly decided this was a good time to ask her question. She turned to Shirley. "What's happening with Justin?"

Shirley rolled her eyes. "I haven't heard from him since the day after the Labor Day picnic."

"And his book?" Faye asked.

"Not going to happen. When I withdrew the second check and they knew no more money was coming, The Hemingway Group pulled the plug on publication."

"But what about the first ten thousand dollars Justin gave them?" Polly asked.

"Gone. The Hemingway Group kept that. I knew they would; it was in the contract Justin signed with them."

"Do you miss him?" Faye asked gently.

"Of course I do!" Shirley's eyes went moist.

Polly leaned over to give Shirley a little hug. "You'll meet someone else."

"I doubt it." Shirley dug a tissue from her purse and blew her nose. "In fact, I don't even want to. I've decided I'm going to be chaste."

Alice snorted. "Yeah, right."

"Oh, *stop* that!" Shirley elbowed Alice.

Faye turned to Marilyn. "How's Ian?"

Marilyn's face went blissful. *"Wonderful."*

"It must be hard with him on the other side of the Atlantic," Polly said.

"It is. I miss him so much. But we e-mail each other several times a day, and we call each other a lot. And actually, since you asked—" Marilyn bit her lip.

Faye read her mind. "You want us to take care of Ruth while you visit him?"

"Could you?"

Polly and Faye nodded eagerly. "Sure," said Faye. "Ruth's adorable."

"Oh, you two are so wonderful! I don't know how I'll ever be able to thank you!"

"We both want to be bridesmaids at your wedding," Polly said.

Marilyn's face fell. "I don't know if that can ever happen. I mean, his work is in Edinburgh, and mine's here. Plus, there's Ruth. She's doing all right, living with me, but I couldn't move her to another country; it would be too hard on her."

The waiter arrived to take their dessert orders. Virtuously, they all ordered fruit bowls.

"While we're all here," Faye said, in a more serious voice, "I'd like to discuss something with you all, before we meet with the entire board of directors of The Haven. Polly and Alice and I have been discussing the employee benefit package for Havenly Yours. We think we'll need to hire six women."

"After we get it set up, Faye doesn't want to be involved with the day-to-day business," Polly told the others.

"I enjoyed making the first round of outfits," Faye explained. "It was challenging, and it was fun working with Polly. But I really don't enjoy sewing that much. I couldn't do it all day. And I wouldn't be any good, supervising others sewing, but Polly's made her living as a seamstress. She'd know what to do."

"So we're thinking four women at the sewing machines," Polly continued. "One woman at the cutting table. One to sweep, clean, carry, et cetera. We've already talked with some women we'd like to hire." She looked at Alice, who took over.

"They're friends of the women who clean The Haven. They're all Hispanic immigrants, and they're all young and eager to work. And they all have children."

"And we thought," Polly went on, "that since The Haven is so large, it would make sense to have a day-care room for the children. That would mean paying another employee to work as a caregiver, but the salary would be minimum wage."

"I really believe in having day care on the site." Alice automatically reverted to corporate-speak. "I was the one who pushed through child care at TransContinent Insurance, and it made an enormous difference to the welfare and productivity of our employees."

"I think it's a great idea," Shirley said.

"I do, too," Marilyn agreed.

Alice looked satisfied. "Good. We'll add it to the business plan. It's a surprisingly small sum, and I think it will pay off in employee satisfaction."

Shirley scoffed. "What you mean is, you're a big ol' softie, and you like the idea of making life better for workingwomen."

Alice smiled. "If you want to put it that way. But the directors will like it better it we phrase it in more businesslike terms."

"I'm going to miss working with you, Faye," Polly said.

Faye squeezed her hand. "I'll miss working with you."

"What are you going to do?" Shirley asked. "Want to teach art at The Haven?"

Faye shook her head. "I don't think so. Maybe in the winter. I'm in a kind of restless mood these days."

"How are things with Aubrey?" Marilyn asked.

Faye played with her fork. "Oh, I'm still seeing Aubrey. We have a date every weekend, and we have a great time. Symphony. Ballet. Theater."

"But Carolyn keeps her father on a pretty tight leash," Polly added. "I thought she'd realize, when Faye and I spent every day all summer sewing together, that we're good friends. I've hinted in every way possible that I really like Hugh and have no interest in Aubrey. I've invited Carolyn and Hank to dinner several times, at my house, with me and Hugh, just the four of us, and I do everything but sit on Hugh's lap to make it clear that we're a couple. But Carolyn keeps inviting me to her house for dinner, and *not* inviting Hugh, and inviting Aubrey, but not Faye. I've started turning her down. I don't know what else to do!"

"She's a very stubborn young woman," Faye pointed out.

"Well, I'm a very stubborn *older* woman!" Polly retorted.

Shirley asked, "Faye, have you invited Carolyn to your home?"

Faye shook her head. "Carolyn's so standoffish with me. I know she dislikes me, or at least wants her father to be with Polly instead of me. I guess I'm just being cowardly—but no," she changed her mind midsentence—"I'm not cowardly. I just don't have the energy to deal with her."

"Have you considered taking antidepressants?" Alice had been wanting to ask this question for some time now.

Faye closed her eyes. "I have. But I'm already taking so many pills." Seeing all the concerned faces, she said, "Don't look so glum! I'm not suicidal! I'm just—restless."

"Or *resting,*" Shirley suggested. "It's only been three years since your husband died. Plus, you're grieving over the loss of your daughter and granddaughter. Even though they're alive and well, they're on the other side of the continent, and really not part of your life. You know how sometimes you get a cold because your body wants to make you stop racing around and spend a few days in bed? Maybe this is the mental equivalent."

"Maybe," Faye agreed. "I do feel kind of empty. Like a well, drained."

"Maybe *you* need to take art therapy," Marilyn suggested.

"Shirley's got a point," Alice weighed in. "You used to paint. I've seen your paintings in your house. They're amazing. I'd love to buy one of your still lifes."

"I stopped painting after Jack died." Faye's face fell. "I *tried* to paint, but everything just was stale, *blah.* I think I've lost it, you know? Whatever my gift or talent was, it's dried up and vanished with my hormones."

"Are you sure?" Marilyn pressed. "You won't know until you try."

Faye fiddled with a button on her jacket. "I'll think about it." Wanting to change the subject, she turned to Alice. "How's Jennifer?"

"She's getting big." Alice beamed. "She's been wonderful to me since the heart attack. She's made so many casseroles, I never have to cook. The food's healthy, too. She's got a little problem with edema, so we're both on low-salt diets. I call her every day to remind her to lie down, put her feet up, and rest."

Shirley reached across the table to take Alice's hand. "Did I ever tell you how much I admire you for the way you've handled Alan's marriage?"

"Thanks, Shirl'. I guess I'm so used to giving commands and manipulating things to fit some work directive, I had to learn how to relax and accept what life throws my way. And thank heavens I met all of you. I couldn't have done it without you." Worry flittered across her face. "The damned thing is, now that I've let myself be open to Jennifer, I really like her. More than that, I *care* for her. When Steven's wife had their kids, they were living in another state, and I was glad to be a grandmother, but they were distant, I was busy with work, and I didn't get as involved. Now that I see Jennifer several times a week, I'm actually getting excited about this coming baby, and nervous as hell every time she tells me her feet are swelling."

Polly nodded. "I often thought that expression, 'Love means never having to say you're sorry,' really should be, 'Love means never feeling safe.' "

"No, no!" Shirley objected. "Remember, we're not going to let fear rule our lives!" She turned to Alice. "I have a number of herbal remedies for edema. Ginger's really good and can be used in all kinds of recipes. I'll make up a list you can give her."

Marilyn looked at her watch. "It's late. I should get home to Ruth."

"Give her a kiss for me," Faye told her. "And make your reservations for Scotland. I'm looking forward to spending time with her again."

"Me, too," Polly said.

"But don't leave until after next Tuesday," Shirley reminded Marilyn. "We've got The Haven's board of directors' meeting."

"Right." Marilyn beamed euphorically. "I'll make my reservations for Wednesday morning! I can't wait to see that man again!"

HALLOWEEN

20

"That was a lovely excursion!" Ruth leaned heavily on her cane as she and Faye came in from the cold.

"Glad you enjoyed it. Let me take your coat, Ruth, and then I'll light the fire."

"Thank you, dear." As Faye hung their coats in the closet, Ruth slowly toddled into the living room. "I just love this house. It's like a little bit of heaven."

Faye smiled. "I'm not sure I'd go that far."

But Ruth's praise made her see the room with fresh eyes, appreciating the opulent colors, rich fabrics, and harmonious arrangement of furniture. As Faye moved around her home, lighting the fire, turning on the lamps, setting the kettle to boil, she realized she was more content than she had been for a while, perhaps for months. It was pleasant, having Ruth around. It was not simply that Faye was less lonely; it was more as if her pleasures were doubled, because she saw how Ruth enjoyed the simplest events and objects of everyday life.

Faye stuck her head into the living room. "Ruth, what kind of tea would you like? Earl Grey or apple cinnamon?"

"Apple cinnamon, please, dear." Ruth's voice was muffled. She had established herself at the far end of the sofa, slipped off her shoes, and pointed her gnarled feet out toward the fire. Her head was bent almost inside her knitting bag as she burrowed around, retrieving her needles and yarn.

Faye hummed as she prepared the tea tray. She loved it when

Ruth called her "dear" or "sweetie." It made her feel young again, and very little could do that these days. She was reminded of her grandmothers, especially her mother's mother, who had smelled like lilacs and willed Faye some beautiful brooches and elegant gloves. By herself, Faye drank from a mug, but Ruth was a guest, so Faye brought out her grandmother's Limoges teapot and cups, and Ruth was thrilled with the thin china and its translucence. Setting the quilted tea cozy, patterned like a plump cat, over the steaming teapot made having tea more of an *event*. It made her stop rushing through her day and relax. She experienced it all more fully: The spicy aroma of the tea. The dollhouse charm of the silver spoons, tea strainer, sugar tongs, cups and saucers. The clarity of the peaceful moment.

"Well, isn't this just beautiful!" Ruth exclaimed as Faye set the tea tray on the low coffee table. "It's like being in one of Sargent's still lifes! Look at the way the firelight gleams on the silver."

Faye served the tea the way Ruth preferred it, with one lump of sugar, and handed it to her, then settled back in her armchair to toast her own feet at the fire. "Would you like me to put on some music?" This was Ruth's second night at Faye's. Ruth had been thrilled to see Faye's CD collection of classical symphonies, and yesterday evening they'd listened to Sibelius's Fifth Symphony.

"Not just yet, dear," Ruth said. "I'm rather enjoying hearing the wind howl. It makes me feel so smug, sitting here, warm by the fire. Besides, don't we need to go over the final arrangements for the party?"

"Oh, right." Faye pulled a pad and pen from her purse, tucked her fire-warmed feet up under her, and flipped the pad open.

At Ruth's instigation, Faye had decided to give a "Come as Your Favorite Person in History" dinner party on Halloween weekend. She'd drawn clever invitations and mailed them out, planned the menu—chili, jalapeño cornbread muffins, a green salad, and a Hot Flash cake—and was in the process of making decorations. Construction paper, scissors, and glue were spilled across the dining room table in various states of transformation into moons, black cats, witches, and ghosts.

Faye read over the list. "I've got everything for the dinner except the salad bits. I'll get those on Friday. Oh, and we have to decide on costumes for ourselves. Who are you going as, Ruth?"

"Madame Curie," Ruth announced decisively. "Not only did she discover radium, she worked with her husband, had two children, and won *two* Nobel Prizes. Oh, yes, and after she was widowed, she was involved in a scandalous love affair." Ruth smiled. "A real rain essence woman. Who will you be, Faye?"

Faye rearranged her legs beneath her. "I haven't decided."

"Why don't you come as one of the early women painters?" Ruth inquired. "Mary Cassatt? Rosa Bonheur?"

Faye looked deep into her teacup. "I don't paint anymore, Ruth."

"Yes, you've said." Ruth contemplated the large, gilt-framed, luminous still life above the fireplace, a bouquet of summer flowers. "You create such beauty, Faye. You have such talent. What a pity you've given up!"

Faye bit back a flash of anger. "It's not that I've 'given up.' It's more that *it* gave *me* up after my husband died." Tears burned her eyes. "I did try. But nothing I did looked right. Everything was just bland. Lackluster."

"I understand."

The quaver in Ruth's voice made Faye look at her. "Are you all right, Ruth?"

"Oh, yes, dear, I'm fine." With a trembling hand, Ruth set her cup on her saucer. "It's just that I was trying to build up the courage to ask you a favor, but now . . ."

"What is it, Ruth?" Faye leaned forward, concerned.

"Oh, it's just silly." Ruth paid great attention to her knitting needles, her knobby fingers tangling the yarn.

"Maybe, maybe not," Faye said sensibly. "Tell me, and I'll decide."

Ruth peered shyly at Faye. "I was hoping you might paint my portrait."

"Oh." This was the last thing Faye could have imagined Ruth would ask.

Ruth blushed with embarrassment, her twisted hands fluttering in the air, as if she were trying to shoo her request away. "I know, it's ridiculous of me even to think of such a thing. I mean, no one paints portraits of old biddies like me. Well, unless they're someone *important,* like Queen Elizabeth or Elizabeth Trailer."

"It's not that—" Faye protested.

"It's just that all my life I've longed to have my portrait painted. Conceited of me, I know. I'm certainly not beautiful. I never was beautiful. But now that I have a great-granddaughter, I'd like to leave her something to remember me by, and a portrait gives a person so much more dignity than a photograph, don't you think? I mean, I'm not *someone* to the world, but I could be *someone* to my great-granddaughter. I'd like to give her—what do I mean? An illusion? Something to dream by." Ruth smoothed the loose flesh of her liver-spotted, bony hand. "Silly old woman," she muttered to herself.

Pity pierced Faye's heart. It felt much like a cupid's arrow, stinging as it filled her, like an enormous invisible IV, with a kind of hopeless love and longing. Faye knew exactly what Ruth meant, because Faye thought the same kind of thing about her granddaughter Megan. She wanted to provide a kind of *message* to this child of her blood and love and history. Perhaps it was a desire bred in one's DNA, as tightly knit as the yarn in Ruth's endless scarf.

Faye swallowed a sip of tea, washing down the lump in her throat. "Well, Ruth, if you didn't mind that it's not a *good* portrait—"

Ruth looked up, her face childish with joy. "You'll do it?"

"Of course I will."

Faye didn't have a studio in her new home. When she'd bought the house, she was sure she'd never paint again. So the morning after Ruth's request, Faye walked through all the rooms with a judgmental eye, looking for the best natural light. Megan's bedroom won hands down, having the most windows and a northern exposure. With a mixture of sadness and satisfaction, Faye set about tacking plain white sheets up over the childish murals she'd painted. She rolled up the flowered rug and shoved it under the bed. She moved all the furniture into one corner, opening up a space large enough for her easel and the chair where Ruth would pose.

She wrestled the armchair in from her bedroom and placed it in the light, then asked Ruth to try it out for comfort.

"It's comfortable enough," the older woman said. "But I don't feel right, with my hands empty."

"Let's get your knitting!" Faye turned to go out the door.

"No," Ruth said firmly. "Knitting isn't right. And I don't want to be just sitting here, like a lump on a frog."

Faye blinked. "Well, then—I've got it!" Suddenly she was excited, as ideas swarmed into her mind. "We'll create a kind of scientific tableau. I'll have to borrow someone's microscope, and—and—"

Ruth understood at once. "Faye, that's a brilliant idea! We'll search Marilyn's storage locker. She's got her old microscope there, and all kinds of equipment. I think she's saved some of her early nature corrections, too."

The next day, Ruth accompanied Faye as she rushed around, lugging paraphernalia from Marilyn's locker, carrying a kitchen stool up to the bedroom, balancing a small end table on two encyclopedias to make it the right height. Finally she had the scene set: Ruth, wearing a shirt and glasses, bent over what could pass as a lab table, a microscope at her right hand, a pen, pad, ruler, scale, beakers, and collection jars at her left. Just behind her, on another table, lay several birds' nests, a mineral hammer, a specimen box, a pile of books, and a pair of binoculars. Before she began, Faye took a few Polaroid shots to show Ruth, who was delighted with the tableau.

"This is the real me!" she said. "Thank you, Faye."

Ruth was supposed to move to Polly's for the last five days of Marilyn's trip, but Faye asked Polly if she would mind if Ruth stayed at her house, because of the portrait, and Polly gladly agreed. She had her hands full, running Havenly Yours. Still, Polly insisted on providing dinner. Sometimes she arrived with carry-out food; sometimes she brought groceries and cooked in Faye's kitchen.

In the autumn evenings, the three women sat together, lingering over pork roast stuffed with apples and onions, or scallop bisque and pumpkin bread, indulging in a glass or two of wine, enjoying the light of the candles Polly set on the mantel and the table. Storms shook the windows as the play of shadows cast a dreamy mood. Polly and Faye asked Ruth about her life, and Ruth regaled them with bits of history, the years vanishing from her face as she talked.

"Oh, yes, I had fun as a young woman. I got to wear tipsy hats covered with glitter and beads to nightclubs. Black wool suits with huge splatters of rhinestones on the lapels. Bright red lipstick. Shoulder pads. I danced at The Stardust and The Blue Moon, and—don't tell Marilyn this, she might be upset—I promised five different men I'd marry them."

Polly and Faye were shocked.

"Well, dears, it was because of the war, don't you know. Those brave young men, going across the ocean to a foreign land to fight, not knowing whether they'd come back. I wanted to give them hope. I wrote them long letters and sent them parcels of food I'd cooked myself and gloves and socks I'd knit myself."

"Did you ever—" Polly hesitated, wondering how to ask this politely. "Were they ever, any of them, um—your lover?"

Ruth looked puzzled. "No, dear. I didn't have a brother. I did have a sister." Her face brightened. "Anyway, toward the end of the war, I met Marilyn's father. I knew at once he was the man for me. We married six weeks after we met."

Later, after Ruth had toddled off to bed, Faye whispered, "Perhaps Ruth needs a hearing aid."

"Perhaps," Polly agreed. "Or perhaps," she grinned, "she just didn't want to answer our question."

Wednesday evening, Alice lifted a gold circlet from its box. She was dressing to go to the new, noncompetitive, pleasantly low-key bridge group she and Gideon had joined. Last week, for her birthday, her daughter-in-law Jennifer had surprised her with a dinner party and a gift Alice would never have expected: an ankle bracelet.

"I'm too old to wear an ankle bracelet!" Alice had protested, but secretly, she was pleased. She'd never worn an ankle bracelet before.

Now she bent to fasten it around her ankle. Its delicate links and tiny dangles gleamed playfully. She couldn't help smiling. No one could see it beneath her long trousers, but *she* knew it was there.

During the evening, she remembered it and felt oddly pleased. Her poor old aching feet might be bumpy with bunions and misshapen from years of wearing pointed high heels, they might be tucked away in comfortable, sensible sneakers, but her ankles were still trim and attractive. In fact, her legs were still good. She wanted to go shopping. She would buy some skirts and show off her legs! Distracted by such thoughts, Alice played bridge so badly she and Gideon lost most of the rubbers, but she didn't really mind.

Although Gideon kept his apartment, he spent most nights at Alice's, and when they returned from bridge they got ready for bed, even though it was not quite ten o'clock. Usually she enjoyed this comfortable routine, but now as she pulled on her warm flannel pajamas, the ankle bracelet sparkled at her. She felt oddly—*playful.*

Gideon was already in bed with a book, his pillows stuffed up behind him. Alice's book and glasses lay waiting on her bedside table. Alice lifted the covers and slipped in next to him.

"What do you think about Faye's Halloween party?" she asked.

"Sounds like fun," Gideon responded absentmindedly.

"I mean, who do you think you'll go as?"

Gideon lay his book on his lap. "I'm not sure. My favorite person in history? I don't know. I admire so many men. Frederick Douglass, I guess."

A hot flash hit Alice. Kicking off the covers, she pulled her legs up and wrapped her arms around her knees. The bracelet glinted around her ankle—a little beacon.

"You know who I'd really like to pretend to be?" Alice was surprised at how difficult it was to confess this to the man with whom she shared so many intimacies. "Cleopatra."

Gideon peered over the top of his glasses. "Cleopatra!"

"She's not the woman I admire most, but she would be so much *fun* to impersonate. I always thought she was so glamorous and mysterious. Not to mention brilliant and cunning. She ruled Egypt. She seduced Antony with her beauty." Suddenly Alice was completely mortified—to think she could masquerade as Cleopatra! "I've got to get some water."

In the bathroom she filled a glass, then held it to her neck, cooling off. *Alice, you really are an idiot,* she scolded herself.

She couldn't even look at Gideon when she got back into bed. "Anyway," she began briskly, "I suppose—"

"You know, I'd love to go as Marc Antony," Gideon announced, to her complete surprise.

"You're kidding!"

"No, I'm not. As a kid, I used to fantasize about being a gladiator. I wouldn't want to be Caesar—he got assassinated. But I could really enjoy being Antony, especially if you were Cleopatra."

"Oh, Gideon!" Alice giggled. "This could be fun!"

Over the next week, they indulged in a kind of Egyptian-history orgy. On the DVD player, they watched the movie starring Elizabeth Taylor and Richard Burton. Inspired, intrigued, they spent a day at the Egyptian rooms at the Museum of Fine Arts. Getting into the spirit of things, they ate in several Middle Eastern restaurants. They visited costume shops, trying on different possibilities, unable to suppress their pleasure as the age-old, childish game of dress-up made them envision themselves anew. They brought home books and videos about Egyptian tombs and treasures. They discussed the possibility of traveling to Egypt to view the pyramids.

Because Gideon had been a schoolteacher before he retired, he suggested they read Shakespeare's *Antony and Cleopatra* aloud in the evenings. At first Alice felt awkward, even silly, but soon the power of the story, told in Shakespeare's intense, opulent language, drew her in. When they read of the extravagant barge with purple sails and silver oars bearing Cleopatra to Antony, Alice was captivated. She closed her eyes and allowed herself to be carried away when Gideon, in his deep, sonorous voice, read the famous lines: "Age cannot wither her, nor custom stale Her infinite variety; other women cloy the appetites they feed, but she makes hungry Where most she satisfies."

The night of Faye's Halloween party, Alice stood in front of her bedroom mirror, scowling. She'd insisted on sharing a bottle of wine with Gideon as they dressed. It was one thing to try on costumes in privacy, quite another to appear in front of other people, especially her friends, masquerading as one of history's most glamorous women. And at her age!

"Ready?" Gideon stepped out of the bathroom, adjusting his armor.

Alice wore a gold lamé tunic, cut low. A heavy half-circle collar of faux gold and turquoise gleamed against her chest. On her head was a wig of hundreds of beaded tight black braids that made tantalizing clicks as she moved. Set in the wig was a gold crown centered with an asp. Snake bracelets wound up her bare arms. On her feet she wore jeweled sandals, and just above, her ankle bracelet. She'd painted her toenails gold.

Gideon wore a white tunic that ended just above his knee. Leather straps of Roman sandals wrapped all the way up his calves, exposing his sturdy, masculine legs. Over his chest he wore a light, metallic shield. A red cape hung from his shoulders. A gold laurel wreath circled his head.

"Alice, I swear, you make a dynamite Cleopatra."

"Thanks. You're a pretty snazzy Antony."

"I like your wig and the headpiece." As Gideon spoke, he brushed his fingers against her neck. The beaded braids whispered. "And the eye makeup, well, it suits you, Alice."

She'd borrowed a book from the library and copied the long, slanted black lines that exaggerated the size and shape of her eyes. "Thanks, Gideon." She leaned against him, studying their reflections in the mirror. "But you know, I've learned something. I'm glad I live now, even as a humble wage-earner, rather than back then, even as queen."

Gideon grinned. "Because we've got movies, air-conditioning, and chocolate?"

"Well, yes, but also because we've got deodorant, soap, and antibiotics. Did you know, Gideon, in centuries past, people used to have wigs for their pubic hair? Called merkins. Because people had to shave off their hair because of lice, or lost it because of syphilis."

Gideon shuddered. "You know the strangest things."

"Marilyn told me." Alice accepted his embrace, her hair clicking, her tunic whispering as she moved. Wrapping her arms around him, she leaned her head against his chest. "And remember, Cleopatra lived only thirty-nine years." She hugged her sturdy, stocky friend and lover. "Plus, she never knew *you*."

Gideon tightened his arms around her and kissed the top of her head. "Alice. What a very nice thing to say!"

"This was a brilliant idea!" Queen Guinevere told Zelda Fitzgerald as they stood side by side in Faye's living room, holding cups of mulled apple cider spiced with cinnamon and cloves and just a soupçon of rum.

"Thanks." Faye surveyed her party with pleasure. "Too bad Marilyn's not here."

"Oh, I don't know," Polly said. "I'm pretty sure Marilyn is quite happy to be in Scotland with Ian."

Lucille Ball swept up to them, a cup of alcohol-free cider in her hand. "Faye, this is so much fun! And thanks for inviting the board members of The Haven."

"I'm delighted to do it," Faye told Shirley. "I'd like to get to know some of them better. Like old Nora Salter. She's so cool, coming as Agatha Christie."

Polly leaned in to say, *sotto voce*, "Look at her over there on the sofa, head to head with Madame Curie. I'd love to know what they're talking about."

Faye grinned. "It's a good bet they're not discussing their bunions."

"I had a hard time deciding who I wanted to be," Shirley confessed. "If you want to know the pathetic truth, I wanted to come as Cinderella. I've always wanted to be Cinderella . . . in her ball gown, *not* in her apron days! But since I'm Prince Charming–less, I settled on Lucille Ball."

"You won't be Prince Charming–less long," Faye predicted.

"I'm not so sure about that," Shirley told her, adding, "Now that I'm single, I can really empathize with you, Faye. You were so brave, dating all those men we forced you to go out with last year. We *thought* we were doing the right thing."

"You probably *were* doing the right thing," Faye admitted. "I needed to have a few starter boyfriends. It helped me realize a bad date wasn't the end of the world, and it certainly made me appreciate Aubrey!"

"I see that his daughter and her husband are here." Shirley turned slightly, and kept her voice low. "That's good, right?"

"Oh, absolutely. She's *got* to see how much of a *couple* Polly and Hugh are—"

"Queen Guinevere and King Arthur!" Polly, who had overheard them, made a little curtsy. "And you and Aubrey are F. Scott and Zelda Fitzgerald. So different!"

"The Fitzgeralds were Aubrey's idea," Faye informed them. "He wanted to get his father's old tux out of the closet. And Polly helped me pull together this flapper costume. I must say I love the way it skims my waist, and shows off my legs. And all the long ropes of pearls camouflage my stomach."

"You look smashing," Polly told her.

"Well, I probably look more like Eleanor Roosevelt than Zelda Fitzgerald, but it's still fun to dress up."

Shirley adjusted a button earring pinching her ear. "I think you both have your hands full, trying to have your way against Carolyn's wishes."

The three women nodded ruefully. Carolyn had come as Superwoman, her husband as Superman.

"What are you three gossiping about?" Cleopatra swept up to them.

"Geez Louise!" Shirley exclaimed. "You look like a million dollars, Alice."

"It's true," Faye agreed. "You make a gorgeous Cleopatra."

"Yeah, and you're absolutely radiant!" Polly gushed.

Jennifer and Alan approached. Because Jennifer wasn't feeling terribly energetic these days, they hadn't given much thought to their Halloween personae but simply cut holes in white sheets, made halos of aluminum foil, and came as angels. Now Alan had a supporting arm around Jennifer's waist.

"This is a great party, but we're going to leave," Alan said.

Alice's eyes flew to Jennifer. "Are you all right?"

Jennifer looked embarrassed. "Oh, I'm fine, really. I just have a bit of a headache." Turning to Faye, she said, "Your party is wonderful, Faye. So clever. And the food's delicious."

"Thanks." Faye looked concerned. "I hope you're not coming down with a flu."

Alice put a gentle hand on Jennifer's forehead. "You don't feel like you have a temperature."

Jennifer's halo slipped down over one ear. "Oh, I'm fine, I'm sure. It's just this headache, and I'm having a little problem with swollen ankles."

"Have you mentioned this to your doctor?" Alice asked.

"Oh, sure. It's all right. I'll be better when I lie down." Jennifer waved her hand dismissively.

"Elevate your feet," Faye and Polly simultaneously advised.

"And Alan," Alice said to her son, "you wait on her hand and foot, okay?"

Alan made a comic bow. "Absolutely."

All four women walked Alan and Jennifer to the door. They stood on the porch, waving good-bye, so they were all together when an old truck pulled up and Polly's son David and his wife Amy stepped out.

"Amy! David!" Polly was over the moon. She didn't think they'd actually deign to come. "How wonderful to see you both!" She introduced her friends to her son and his wife.

Faye smiled invitingly. "Let me show you both to the drinks table. We've got spiked apple cider, and plain cider, too. And let me guess who you are—"

"Ma and Pa Kettle?" Alice's eyes glinted mischievously. "The Beverly Hillbillies?"

"No!" Amy's mouth pursed with displeasure. "We're Charles and Caroline Ingalls!"

Polly looked puzzled. "Um . . ."

"From *Little House on the Prairie*!" Amy looked offended.

"Of course!" Faye rushed to appease the stern younger woman. "That would have been my first guess! I'm so glad you came. How is little Jehoshaphat?"

Polly took a deep breath. Faye's question was perfect. Amy and David both lit up like lamps, chatting away as fast as they could, describing their son's latest prodigal achievements.

Finally their conversation ran down and they just stood there, holding a glass of alcohol-free cider, looking slightly puzzled and not particularly interested in their surroundings.

"Come meet Teddy and his wife, Lila," Alice invited, in a fit of inspiration. "They have a little girl about your son's age." Linking arms with Amy and David, she led them into the living room, making a funny face over her shoulder at Polly, Faye, and Shirley.

Beautiful Lila had come as the gorgeous seductress Delilah, with a slinky, revealing gown, bracelets high on her arms, and heavy makeup. Teddy wore a shield, white tunic, and leather thongs. He'd pulled a bare wig on over his own thinning hair in order to look like Samson after he was shorn, and the result was surprisingly attractive. Together, he and his wife looked exotic and sexy.

"Maybe introducing them isn't such a good idea," Polly murmured. "Amy is such a little prig, and Lila looks so sensual."

"Wait and see," Faye soothed Polly.

"And don't expect a great friendship to develop," added Shirley, who was feeling rather pessimistic these days. "They couldn't be more different."

Polly helped herself to another cup of spiked cider. "Amy is so damned *pure*. She'll think gorgeous Lila looks like a harlot, and probably drag poor David from the party."

"You're wrong!" Faye whispered to Polly. "Turn around! Look!"

Polly obeyed. The wholesome farm couple and the glamorous biblical lovers were retrieving photos from pockets and purses, passing them around, babbling and bonding as they shared pictures and anecdotes about their children.

Alice returned to fill her own glass of cider. "Well, Faye," she grinned, "I think we can safely say this party is officially a success." Her eyes dropped. "Although I am a little worried about Jennifer."

"She'll be fine," Faye assured her.

"I hope so," Alice said fervently.

THANKSGIVING

The afternoon sky loomed low and gray, threatening rain. As Alice and Gideon drove along the winding country road, a cold, intermittent wind flickered and gusted, making the fallen leaves heaped in the gutters suddenly skitter and jump like small, darting creatures. Tree boughs, bare and brittle, clattered and dipped toward the car like the living trees in *The Wizard of Oz*.

It made Alice's nerves itch. She was cranky, when she knew she should be grateful. Damn it, she *was* grateful. She counted her blessings every night as she fell asleep, and reminded herself of them during the day, every day.

First, her sons were happy. Steven, down in Texas, communicated with her more than ever now that e-mail existed, and in January, Alice and Gideon both were going to visit Steven's family, which she hadn't done in years.

And Alan—well! Alan loved running the bakery and catering service—something Alice had never *dreamed* he would do, although given how much *she* loved food, why was she so surprised? And she had to admit, Alan was in love with his wife, and Jennifer obviously loved him deeply. They had only one more month to wait for the birth of their child—and here Alice's breath caught in her throat.

Jennifer had been diagnosed with preeclampsia and ordered to remain in bed for the rest of her pregnancy, which was why Alan was cooking the turkey but Gideon and Alice were bringing most of the Thanksgiving dinner out to the caretaker's cottage at The Haven. Alice had researched preeclampsia on the Internet, and what she'd learned had terrified her. It was a serious condition involving high blood pressure, protein in the urine, water retention, headaches, severe nausea, rapid heartbeat, and other uncomfortable and life-threatening problems. The child could die—or the mother.

Dear God, please let Jennifer and the baby be okay, Alice prayed. It was so frustrating for Alice not to be able to *do* something, to *fix* this problem, to take charge! That was what she'd done all her life both at home and professionally, but now she was utterly helpless. And it was driving her totally nuts!

She felt her heartbeat accelerate. Damn it! Deep breaths, she reminded herself. Deep, deep breaths. Shirley had said to breathe right down to her asshole. And think positive thoughts.

All right then. Well, she was healthy, more or less, as long as she took her medicine and exercised regularly and watched what she ate, although the thought of limiting caloric intake during Thanksgiving and Christmas seemed to her like some kind of sadistic joke. Go back to the Gratitude List, she told herself.

Well—*Gideon*! This burly, sweet man driving the car was a wonderful companion, friend, and lover. They had great fun together, playing bridge, attending movies and the symphony, or just lounging around the apartment, reading, listening to music, watching TV. And his health was good these days.

And her friends were amazing. She'd never had such close friends since her school days. She loved the sense of belonging to a group, especially this group, which made her laugh and kept her involved with the real world. She'd been afraid of retirement, fearing she'd feel useless, but with them she had more than enough work to do. She was on the board of The Haven, plus she'd helped get the business side of Havenly Yours set up, although she'd refused to take on the full-time job of bookkeeper.

Now she thought perhaps that had been a mistake. Because with all the richness in her life, Alice still felt a kind of gap, something not sharp enough to be called pain, something more like a sense of longing. She didn't feel *complete* yet. And she *had* felt complete for great hunks of her life, especially when she was working and raising her sons. But work and intellectual stimulation didn't fill that void these days; she'd given it her all, and still, even when immersed in calculations for some budget, she'd raise her head from her computer and gaze at the sun on the windowsill, and sit very still, almost *listening*, as if she'd just heard someone whisper her name.

"Alice?" Now Gideon actually did call her name, tugging her back into the present. "We're here." He undid his seat belt and peered at her. "Are you okay?"

"Oh, I'm fine. Just daydreaming." Impulsively, she leaned over and kissed his mouth. "I love you, Gideon."

"And I love you, Alice," Gideon replied with a smile, "but at the moment it's the aroma of the pumpkin pie that's making me drool."

"Fickle!" Alice scolded playfully. "Okay, let's go eat."

Alan came out of the house, hugged his mother, shook hands with Gideon, and helped them carry in the casseroles and pans.

Alice set the large, wooden salad bowl on the kitchen counter. Without taking off her coat, she hurried into the living room to see Jennifer, who reclined on the sofa in loose pants and one of the Havenly Yours jackets Alice had given her.

"Hello, honey." Alice bent down to kiss Jennifer's cheek. "You look beautiful!" But Jennifer's face was far too flushed, and she clearly was uncomfortable. "How do you feel?" She perched on the coffee table so she could take her daughter-in-law's hand. "Tell me true."

Jennifer smiled. "I'm glad to see you, Alice. Poor Alan's so worried, he's buzzing around me like a drunk mosquito. With you here, he'll calm down."

Alice cocked her head. "I'm sure he will. But you didn't answer my question. How are you?"

Jennifer's face grew serious. "I'm okay, I think. It's best if I just lie here, not moving, but that makes me feel like such a wimp. But if I try to do anything, the nausea and headaches start up again."

"How's your blood pressure?" Alice picked up the little home monitor lying on the table.

"We just took it. It's okay. Elevated, but not dangerous." Jennifer shifted impatiently on the sofa. "It's so boring, just talking about my health!"

"Hello!" Gideon came into the room, bending to kiss Jennifer's cheek. "You look like the bell curve, lying there."

"I feel more like a hot air balloon," Jennifer joked in reply.

"Take your coat off, Mom," Alan suggested. "The turkey's ready. I thought we'd all fix our plates and bring them in here, so Jenny won't have to move."

"Good idea." Alice squeezed Jennifer's hand.

In the kitchen, she tossed the salad while Gideon poured three glasses of wine and one of water. As Alan lifted the small turkey onto the platter and began slicing it, Alice watched him out of the corner of her eye. He was moving just a bit too quickly, just as he'd rushed them into eating now instead of enjoying a relaxing few moments of conversation. He was anxious, of course he was; he wanted to get this day over, and the next, and every day until his child was safely brought into the world. *Slow down,* Alice wanted to advise him, but she kept her mouth shut. The last thing he needed was a nagging mother.

Back in the living room, Alan adjusted Jennifer's pillows, lifting her into a sitting position so she could eat. He brought her a tray with a small plate of food, placed a pillow beneath her feet, then stood back to scrutinize her.

"Sit down, Alan." Jennifer flapped her hands at him. "Enjoy your turkey!"

The baby wasn't due until late December. Alice dutifully lifted her fork to her mouth, but worry dulled her senses. Jennifer wasn't going to last another month; that was obvious. Perhaps she and Gideon shouldn't have come; perhaps their mere presence was elevating Jennifer's blood pressure just that little bit more. Should they leave? God, what could she do?

"Did you know," Gideon said conversationally, "Faye's flown out to California to have Thanksgiving with her grandchildren?"

"Oh, I'm so glad," Jennifer said. "I know Faye misses her daughter a lot."

Thank God for Gideon. With the focus off Jennifer, Alice's own blood pressure dropped. She added, "Laura invited her out there for two weeks. Lars's parents, who've moved out there, are going on a cruise, so Faye will have Laura and Megan and the new little baby all to herself."

"Who's Aubrey spending Thanksgiving with?" Alan asked.

Alice snorted. "Who does Aubrey spend *every* holiday with? His daughter Carolyn. She's such a spoiled brat! She *insisted* that Polly come, too, because Polly's Elizabeth's godmother."

"Then where's Hugh having the holiday?" Jennifer inquired.

"With his kids, which means with his clingy little ex-wife Carol."

"I wonder," Gideon mused, sipping his wine, "which is worse, to be involved in family conflicts or to be without a family, like Shirley."

Alan took a bite of Alice's salad. "Good, Mom. Where's Shirley spending Thanksgiving?"

"With Marilyn and Ruth." Alice thought for a moment. "I'm not sure whether Marilyn and Ruth will be seeing Marilyn's granddaughter today or not. There's another difficult daughter-in-law."

"It's not Lila who's difficult," Gideon corrected her mildly. "It's Lila's mother, Eugenie."

Alan looked thoughtful. "Whatever happened to that guy Marilyn was dating—Faraday?"

Alice and Gideon exchanged glances. Alice had told Gideon about Faraday passing out on Marilyn, and they'd shared a good laugh, but it would be uncharitable to gossip about it. Although it was pretty funny.

Gideon said, "Faraday and Marilyn broke up. Too bad, because he was a good guy."

"Yeah," Alice added, "but Marilyn was never in love with him like she is with this Ian guy. With him, she's really found the love of her life, and she deserves some happiness. She was such a dutiful wife, I think she believed marriage was the same for everyone, sort of like plain bread, necessary but tasteless. With Ian, she's getting the bread PLUS a great big helping of strawberry jam."

"Trust you to use a food metaphor," Gideon teased Alice.

"Alan?" Jennifer's weak voice interrupted their lighthearted banter. "Alan—I'm going to—" Shuddering, she vomited all over her plate and her clothes.

In a flash, Alan was at her side. "Jenny, honey—"

Alice hurried into the kitchen, returning with a roll of paper towels and a wastebasket. Alan handed her Jennifer's plate and used a towel to wipe his wife's face.

"Alan." Jennifer's eyes were wide. "I feel . . . terrible. I'm so dizzy, and I've got a pain in my side, and my head . . ."

"Hospital," Alice said. "Now."

Alan supported Jennifer's head in gentle hands. "Is that what you want?"

Tears streamed down Jennifer's red face. "Yes. Please. Oh, Alan, I'm so frightened!"

"I'll call 911," Alice said.

"Maybe it would be faster if we drove her there," Alan said.

Alice bit her tongue just one millisecond to keep from yelling. In as calm a voice as she could muster, she said, "An EMT would know what to do right away. They'd be able to give her an IV. But whichever way you two want—"

"Ambulance," Jennifer said. "Please."

Toward evening, the sky finally split apart, showering the New England area with thin, sharp raindrops that promised to change to sleet at any moment. Inside Marilyn's condo, it was warm and peaceful. Marilyn had roasted a turkey and set the table with a white cloth, china, and silver. Shirley had brought lots of vegetable dishes and a gorgeous centerpiece she'd made from autumn leaves and a few hardy roses and mums from the grounds of The Haven.

So much beauty, Shirley thought, such luxury! She refused to let herself mope simply because she wasn't with Justin. Because she wasn't with *any* man.

She'd wakened cranky, and grumbled through her lonely morning in her empty condo in The Haven's enormous edifice. Today the old stone building's elegance and solidity made her feel shabby and temporary. How had it happened, that of the five Hot Flash Club women, she, Shirley, the only one who couldn't have alcohol, was also the only one who didn't have a man? It wasn't fair! She was in the best shape of them all, with her limber, slender body. And she liked sex and loved men more than the others, too; she was sure of that. Plus, the other four all had children and grandchildren to love. Shirley didn't have any of that. She just felt so *rejected* by Fate!

Still, she'd forced herself to dress up and drag her unwanted, pathetic old body over to Marilyn's condo, and she was going to be a regular little ball of good cheer if it killed her.

And now that she was here, she was glad. She loved Marilyn, even if Marilyn had just returned from Scotland where she no doubt screwed her brains out with that man she adored, and Ruth was always a pleasure to be around. Shirley helped Marilyn carry in the food, and then took her place at the laden dinner table.

"Well, here we are!" Ruth wore a dark green sweater patterned with autumn leaves. She looked around the table, her wrinkled old face radiant with pleasure. She beamed at Shirley and Marilyn. "The three little figs!"

"Pigs." Marilyn sliced a tender strip of meat off the turkey breast and lay it, with its golden brown, salt-and-pepper–speckled skin, on her mother's plate.

"The three graces, I would say," Shirley amended.

Ruth glanced up from a bowl of sweet potatoes. "Just who *were* the three graces?"

"Goddesses from early Greek mythology," Shirley told her. "I can't remember their Greek names, but they stood for um, let me think: Brilliance or Splendor was one. Joy. And something like Optimism."

"Would you like sweet potatoes?" Ruth held out the bowl. "Were they young or old?"

"Young, I think."

Ruth spooned pecan-onion-apple stuffing onto her plate. "But with names like that, they could be any age, right?"

"Sure," Shirley agreed. "Why not?"

Ruth took a bit of creamed spinach. "Oh, Shirley, this is delicious." She nibbled on her roll, then observed, "Not many girls named Grace anymore."

"Fashions change." Shirley helped herself to the stuffing Marilyn had made especially for her, in a pan, with butter instead of turkey drippings. "Not many are named Shirley, either."

"Nor Ruth," Ruth said. "Nor Vagina."

"Regina," Marilyn quietly revised, using the British pronunciation.

Ruth cocked her head. "And they name girls such strange

things these days. Like that beautiful actress with the big lips—
Harlot Johnson."

"Scarlett Johansson," Shirley said quietly, flashing a smile at
Marilyn.

Marilyn didn't respond to Shirley's smile, which made Shirley
feel awful for just a moment. Did Marilyn think Shirley was making fun of Ruth? But now that Shirley paused to really look at Marilyn, she realized that Marilyn looked tired. Old. Absolutely *dragged
down*, a look Shirley saw in the mirror all too often but had never
before seen on Marilyn.

"Marilyn," Shirley said, "I haven't spoken with you since you
went to Scotland. How was your trip?"

"Oh, it was fine." Marilyn didn't lift her eyes from her plate.

Shirley hesitated. "Oh. Well, how's Ian?"

Marilyn made a noise, an odd little moan. Still she would not
meet Shirley's eyes. "He's fine. He's busy with his work." Her chin
trembled. "I'll just get some more gravy." Lifting the gravy boat,
she disappeared into the kitchen.

Bastard! Shirley thought, suddenly flaming with anger. Men
were all alike everywhere; you couldn't trust any of them. Oh,
Shirley knew all too well the signs of a woman betrayed.

Ruth patted Shirley's hand to get her attention. "Two termites
walk into a bar. What do they say?"

"Um—" Shirley forced a smile. "I don't know. What do they
say?"

"Is the bar tender here?" All the wrinkles on Ruth's face lifted
up as she smiled.

"Very funny," Shirley chuckled.

"Oh, I've got lots more of those. Marilyn's father always had a
slew of wonderful jokes. His students loved him."

Marilyn returned, her face composed, but guarded. Now that
Shirley took a moment to study her friend, she realized that Marilyn, who had never been a clotheshorse, looked more—more down-

right *dowdy* than Shirley had ever seen her. Her gray sweater hung on her—why, Marilyn had lost weight! Shirley sent an urgent glance of concern toward her friend, who shook her head slightly and leaned over her mother. "More gravy, Mom?"

"Thank you, dear. I was just telling Cheryl about your father. He was so handsome, wasn't he? And as smart, I swear, as Allen Einstein. He could have gone on for a Ph.D., but he loved teaching high school–age students. So did I. We spent so much time concocting experiments!"

What could Shirley do to help Marilyn? God, Marilyn looked so tired! She looked *whipped*. Ruth was looking at Shirley expectantly. "Tell me about them," Shirley urged.

Ruth's face lit up. For the rest of the meal, she recounted the pleasures she'd shared with her husband, creating ant houses and aquarium tanks, sweeping nets and rearing cages for the butterflies, moths, caterpillars, turtles, reptiles, and lizards studied in the classroom. Equally fascinating to Ruth and her husband were water fleas, leeches, roaches, and bats. Well, Shirley thought, this explains a lot about Marilyn.

"Mother," Marilyn said, when she could get a word in, "would you like any more turkey? Or stuffing?"

"Oh, no, dear, thank you. I'm full." Suddenly Ruth's rosy face sagged. "In fact, I believe I'm just a little tired. All this chattering away I've been doing . . ." She looked at Marilyn, confused.

Marilyn took her mother's hand. "Would you like dessert now, Mother? Pumpkin pie?" When her mother didn't answer right away, she suggested, "Or perhaps a little nap? Wouldn't a little rest feel good?"

"Yes, dear. That's a good idea." Ruth's voice quavered, and when she tried to rise from her chair, her arms trembled.

Marilyn and Shirley jumped to assist her up.

"It's awful, getting old." Ruth shook her head. "I hate being dependent."

"You're not dependent, darling," Marilyn assured her. "For heaven's sake."

Together they accompanied the older woman into her bedroom. With a sigh, Ruth subsided gratefully onto her bed. Marilyn unfolded the light blanket at the foot and spread it over her mother. Then she and Shirley went out of the room, pulling the door almost closed.

"She'll sleep for about thirty minutes, then wake up all bright and bushy-tailed," Marilyn whispered.

"Fine with me. I'll help you with the dishes. I need to move around, after eating so much."

Shirley could tell that Marilyn was preoccupied, so they worked in companionable silence as they cleared the table, rinsed the dishes, and stacked them in the dishwasher.

"Coffee?" Marilyn asked.

"Not yet. I can wait till your mother wakes up. But tell me, Marilyn, what's wrong?"

Marilyn looked guilty. "Oh, dear. I didn't mean to spoil your Thanksgiving."

"Nonsense. This is a perfectly fine Thanksgiving. But I can tell something's not right. Is it Ian?"

Marilyn's face flushed bright red. Bringing her hands up, she covered her face, but Shirley could *feel* the misery emanating from Marilyn in a dark aura.

"Is it another woman?" Really, Shirley thought, that wouldn't be completely unreasonable. Marilyn and Ian lived an ocean apart.

But Marilyn shook her head. She grabbed for a paper towel. Her face was streaming with tears.

"Oh, honey." Shirley put her arms around Marilyn. "Oh, Marilyn."

"He a-a-asked me to marry him," Marilyn sobbed.

Shirley drew back. "And that's a bad thing?"

"No, of course not! But he wants me to live with him, in Edinburgh. And I can't, Shirley, I just can't. I can't leave my mother." Wrapping her arms around her stomach, she folded nearly in half as she wailed soundlessly. "Oh, Shirley, I love him so much!"

Sympathetic tears welled in Shirley's eyes. "Here, Hon, sit down." She grabbed a clean water glass and poured some wine into it. "Drink this. Come on. Take a sip."

Marilyn sank onto a kitchen chair, took the glass, and drank. She closed her eyes and sat very still. "God. I'm sorry. I didn't mean to be such a drama queen."

"You couldn't be a drama queen if you tried." Shirley pulled another chair up close, so she could hold Marilyn's hand. "Come on, Marilyn, let's think this through. There's got to be a solution."

"There's not. Really, there's not. I've thought about nothing else the past two weeks. Sharon's husband's ill. Cancer. It's serious." Marilyn shook her head. "And here I am, blubbering about myself."

"You deserve to blubber if you've met the love of your life and you don't think you can live with him."

"Well, *Sharon* can't take care of Mother. She's been the responsible one all her life. It's my turn now. And I can't put Mother into some kind of—of—*place*."

"Why not?" Shirley demanded.

"Oh, Shirley, come on. Ruth's not gaga. She's not incapable. She's just slightly . . . *frail*. Forgetful, sometimes, but usually she's great. I'd feel like a monster if I put her in an assisted living facility."

"But there are all kinds of facilities, Marilyn," Shirley argued. "Where Ruth could be safe, and have friends her own age, and medical or any kind of assistance at the touch of a bell."

"I couldn't do it, Shirley. She calls assisted living facilities 'finishing schools.' And she's so happy here. She was such a good mom to me and Sharon. If she were a little more incapacitated, or a lot more forgetful, then maybe . . ." Marilyn shook her head violently. "No. I need to keep her here with me."

"And lose the love of your life?" Shirley cried.

Marilyn closed her eyes and sagged against the chair. "What else can I do?"

Shirley glanced at the bottle of Burgundy. It seemed to be singing her name in dulcet tones, assuring her that if she'd just take a little sip, or maybe two, this terrible sympathetic pain in her heart would ease. She jumped up and paced the floor.

"There's got to be some solution. Damn it, where's the chocolate?"

This brought a wan smile to Marilyn's face. "The solution would be chocolate?"

Shirley hurriedly rifled through Marilyn's cupboards until she found a bar hidden in the back. Tearing off the wrapper, she broke it open, handed a piece to Marilyn, and bit into a piece. Her mouth was flooded with soothing, stimulating, glorious, dark sweetness.

"Did you know," Marilyn mumbled, licking her lips, "cacao trees can develop diseases called 'swollen shoot' and 'pod rot'?"

Shirley's laughter was laced with relief. If Marilyn could joke at a time like this, she'd be okay. "I'm not surprised. I always thought there was something sexual about chocolate, and of course it would be masculine." She broke off another piece and handed it to Marilyn. "Now. Let's consider our possibilities. For one thing, you and Ian could continue seeing each other. Lots of people have transcontinental marriages, why not have a transoceanic one? I mean, for God's sake, Marilyn, you have gobs of money, why not spend it? You could hire a live-in caretaker, someone your mother would get to feel safe and comfortable with, and then you could visit Ian every other month, and he could come over and visit you every other month. Yeah!" Shirley nodded enthusiastically, pleased with her idea.

"It wouldn't be fair," Marilyn said. "Not to Ian, not to me. For one thing, we both have work to do, professional commitments, classes to teach. But actually, Shirley, we've discussed this kind of possibility, and we just can't feel good about it. Ian wants to be *married.* He wants to buy a home and share every day of his life with a wife. He wants domestic *permanence,* and I can understand that." Tears spilled down her face. "I want him to have that. I love him so much, and he's been so lonely, and he's such a lovely man. He wants to plant a garden with someone, and have dinner parties with friends, not pack up a suitcase every month and spend half his time with me suffering from jet lag. And I feel the same way."

"What if—"

Ruth toddled into the room, leaning on her cane. Her white curls were flattened on one side of her head from sleeping, and her pink scalp shone through. Her face was flushed and her lower lip trembled.

Marilyn sprang up. "Mom, are you okay?"

Ruth reached out and grabbed Marilyn's shoulder with one clawlike hand. "Oh, dear, I'm so embarrassed, I feel so terrible." Looking completely mortified, she whispered, "I wet the bed."

Marilyn patted her mother's arm. "That's all right, Mom. I'll help you change clothes, and I'll change the sheets. It won't take a minute."

"*I'll* put on the coffee," Shirley chirped, "and warm up the pumpkin pie!"

Marilyn and her mother slowly left the room.

Ruth looked up at her daughter. "I think it's because I had so much to eat and didn't wee before I took my nap."

"I'm sure that's the reason," Marilyn agreed.

"I don't wet the bed often," Ruth insisted.

"No, Mom, of course you don't."

By the time the two women came into the living room, Shirley had set out a pot of decaf coffee, and cups and plates for the pie. She helped Marilyn lower Ruth into a chair and set up a little table next to her. Marilyn served the pie.

When she'd finished her helping, Ruth set her plate down. "Sherry," she said brightly, "did I ever tell you about my husband? He taught science in high school. He was as smart as Albert Feinstein, but he loved teaching more than research. We spent so many happy hours together, making peppermints for our students. We taught them to build sweeping nets, aquarium tanks, insect traps . . ."

Shirley smiled encouragingly as she listened to Ruth, but what she heard was the melody of Marilyn's sorrow.

Was she happy, or not, was life easy, or hard? *It's all relative,* Polly reminded herself on Thanksgiving Day, then laughed at her pun.

Hearing her laugh, Hank, seated on the sofa next to her, cast a puzzled glance her way. Everyone gathered here at Carolyn and Hank's for Thanksgiving dinner had been discussing world affairs, which were certainly nothing to laugh about.

Polly thought quickly. "Elizabeth," she mouthed to Hank, who looked over at his daughter. His face softened with adoration. The toddler, in pink padded corduroy rompers Polly had sewn for her, sat on the floor, concentrating very hard on putting a rectangular block of wood into a round hole.

They were having drinks before they went in to dinner. Polly tossed hers back like a private dick in a tough-guy novel. She wished she *were* a private dick in a tough-guy novel, or at least had some of his guts.

She had just come from an afternoon Thanksgiving feast with David, Amy, little Jehoshaphat, and Amy's parents, Buck and Katrina. Their wine was homemade and so sweet Polly felt little crystals of sugar clinging to her teeth like barnacles on oyster shells. The "turkey" was tofu, shaped, flavored, and baked into a curdled mass resembling, in texture and taste, a rubber rug pad. The conversation revolved around the farm, which was fine, but no one bothered to ask Polly one single question about her life. In fact, no one had particularly talked to Polly at all.

David was distracted. He'd kissed her when she arrived, then immediately run out to the barn. His favorite Border collie was having her pups today, so throughout the meal, David excused himself to check on her. Amy was also preoccupied; Jehoshaphat was coming down with a cold. He was irritable and fussy. Nothing Amy did could keep the little boy from whining, writhing, squirming, and now and then bursting forth in a full-scale tantrum. Amy looked frustrated and embarrassed by her son's behavior but allowed no one else to interact with him.

Polly left before dessert—pumpkin pie served with a homemade dessert wine, which Polly was sure would be even sweeter than the syrupy swill they'd had during dinner. It pleased her to tell them she had another dinner party to attend—proof that *someone* wanted her company!

But as she drove away from the farm, her body had sagged with disappointment and with fatigue from keeping a forced smile on her face for two hours. How different it would have been if Hugh had been with her just now! He would have lifted an eyebrow or twitched his mouth in silent humor or commiseration. As they drove away, he would have said, "Well, we've done our duty at the Bumpkin Banquet, now let's go to my house and treat ourselves to my best brandy!"

But Hugh was having Thanksgiving with his children and his ex-wife, and Polly was here at Carolyn's, where she was very much wanted, but where she didn't especially want to be.

Carolyn, sweeping around the room in a saffron cashmere dress that made her blond beauty glow, was beaming. Her little family was here—Hank and baby Elizabeth, Aubrey, and now Polly. Faye was safely on the other side of the continent. Carolyn didn't bother to ask about Hugh.

Am I getting to be a cantankerous old biddy, or am I allowing myself to be pushed around? Polly wondered. The Bible said to love one another. The Beatles said love is all you need. Stephen Stills said love the one you're with. She did love Carolyn and Elizabeth, but she loved her son more, and would certainly have loved her grandson if she'd had half the chance.

Perhaps the solution was tangled up in the definition of love. Perhaps, like sins, there were loves of commission and loves of omission. You did lots of committing when your child was a baby—nursing, rocking, feeding, bathing, sheltering, soothing. Later, attending recitals, driving to soccer practice, holding the line on disciplinary rules about curfew. But with a grown child, so much of love involved omission. Letting go. Shutting up. After all, if David had become an Air Force fighter pilot or, like his father, a wild adventurer who disappeared into foreign countries for years at a time, Polly would have gotten on with her own life and been grateful for an occasional sighting.

So, she admonished herself, she should just stop sniveling and enjoy the day. Here she was, in a gorgeous home, with people she cared for deeply. She hadn't been part of her grandson's birth, but she had been right there for Elizabeth's. The little girl's paternal grandmother, wealthy, batty Daisy, lived far away, and when she came to visit, she never put down her bug-eyed little dog long enough to hold Elizabeth—which was probably a good thing, because Daisy, adorable as she was, was also so scatterbrained she might forget whom she was holding. Maybe, Polly thought, when she was really old, she'd look back to see that she'd been absolutely essential in Elizabeth's life.

And maybe the fabulous Champagne Carolyn was serving was blissing Polly out.

"Dinner's ready," Carolyn announced.

Polly went with the others into the dining room. Carolyn had set out place cards. Polly was not surprised to find her place next to Elizabeth's. She helped Hank establish Elizabeth safely in her handsome wooden highchair.

"Yummy-yummies for our tummies," Polly babbled to Elizabeth.

"Lolly yummy!" Elizabeth shrieked gleefully, and threw her hands up over her head, waving her fat little fists in the air. Elizabeth had a name for Polly—*Lolly*, while Jehoshaphat, four months older, hadn't seen his grandmother often enough to give her a name.

The table had gone quiet. Polly looked around. Everyone was smiling, waiting.

"What?" Polly said.

Carolyn inclined her head toward a gold foil packet lying at the head of her place.

"Oh! A present? What fun! When can we open them?"

"No time like the present!" Carolyn punned, beaming.

Polly picked up the packet and untied the golden bow, aware of Aubrey, across the table, performing the same act.

Inside was a British Airways round-trip ticket to London and a printed itinerary. Ms. Polly Lodge had reservations at the Ritz in London, from December 20 to December 31. Polly looked up, baffled. "I don't understand."

Carolyn clapped her hands with glee. In her highchair, Elizabeth mimicked her mother.

"We're all going to spend Christmas in London!" Carolyn announced. "We've booked tickets for the best plays, and we'll have Christmas dinner at the Ritz! I've made reservations—"

Polly couldn't hear the rest. From deep within her belly, a cyclone of sizzling intensity swirled, so furious and powerful, Polly couldn't tell whether it was a hot flash or her own pure indignation. She took a drink of water to calm herself, but her pulse flared in her neck and her heart pumped so hard she could feel it shake in her chest.

"—so divine!" Carolyn said. "If it snows, it will—"

"Carolyn." As if she'd been body-snatched, Polly looked down from the ceiling to observe herself rising from the table. "Forgive me, but I can't accept this. I *won't* accept this. I am dating Hugh Monroe, and *he* is the person with whom I want to spend my Christmas holiday." Interesting, how the words came from her boiling body with cold, clipped clarity. "My best friend, Faye, has been dating your father for over a year now, and if anyone should accompany your little family to London, it is she. Faye is a wonderful woman, as you would know, if you ever gave her a chance."

"Oh, Polly, silly," Carolyn trilled, laughing. "Sit down. Don't be so dramatic."

Polly met Carolyn's eyes. "It seems the only way I can get through to you about this, Carolyn, is by being dramatic. You should know by now, it's not in my nature. But you've ignored every kind of hint I've given about my relationship with your father." She turned to Aubrey. "Aubrey, you are a charming, handsome, wonderful man. I don't know, however, how intelligent you are, because you let Carolyn walk all over you. If you want Faye to be with you, you've got to be forceful with this beautiful daughter of yours." She looked back at Carolyn. "I'm going home now. And I hope the next time you invite me to your house, you'll tell me to bring Hugh."

"Oh, Polly!" Carolyn seemed more amused than upset.

Hank jumped up and followed Polly to the door. As he took her coat from the closet and slid it over her arms, he said, "Polly, you're trembling. Are you sure you want to drive right now?"

The conflagration had reached Polly's face; she knew she was crimson. "I'll be fine." She was verging on tears and needed to get out of the house.

Wanting to run to the car, Polly forced herself to walk, keeping her back straight, her head high. She settled into her little gray Volvo, grateful for its nestlike snugness. The amiable vehicle smoothly rolled out of the driveway and onto the road even though Polly's foot quaked on the pedal.

She looked in the rearview mirror. Carolyn's house grew smaller, then disappeared as other houses came into view.

"HA!" Polly expostulated triumphantly.

Then she burst into tears. Then she burst out laughing. As she stopped for a red light, she imagined people in the car next to her looking over to see a madwoman, laughing and crying at the same time. Oh, well, she thought, who would be surprised? It was Thanksgiving, after all, another family holiday!

Really, she was proud of herself. She had put her foot down firmly to Carolyn and it was about time. For if Carolyn really wanted Polly to be godmother to Elizabeth, she'd better welcome the *real* Polly; she'd better allow Polly to be herself.

"And now, Missy," Polly asked herself aloud, because if she was already laughing and crying, why not talk to herself as well? "What would the real Polly Lodge like to do right now?"

The answer came fast and certain.

She wanted to be with Hugh. She was proud, overwhelmed, excited. Her body was enormously *awake*. She wanted to use this energy; she wanted to make love. She wanted to grab Hugh Monroe and kiss him like he'd never been kissed before.

So she headed toward his place. The daughter who was hosting the Thanksgiving meal had small children, so their plan was to eat early. Hugh might not be home when Polly arrived, but he might be, and if not, Polly had the key. She could slip in, *undress,* and surprise him when he arrived. Ah, what a delicious plan!

Since his divorce from Carol, Hugh had lived in an apartment on elegant Commonwealth Avenue, near the Boston Public Gardens. The magnificent building, staid and formal, was part of a block of row houses with marble stoops and neoclassical friezes and gargoyles above the doors. Parking was often a problem, but this evening the streets were empty and Polly easily found a spot.

No lights shone from Hugh's windows on the second floor; he wasn't home yet. Good. That would give her time to get ready.

Her key ring jingled as she opened the street-level outer door. She climbed the wide, curving stairs to the second floor and let herself into his apartment. It could have been a formal, stultifying place, with its acres of walnut paneling and its marble or parquet floors, but during his divorce, Hugh had given all his parents' antique furniture to his children or Carol. This new home he'd furnished with simple, expensive, modern pieces.

The front door opened into the enormous living room, dominated by a chocolate leather sofa facing a huge plasma television. Most of the walls held shelves of books, and one wall was almost entirely windows looking out onto the street.

Polly hung her coat in the closet. Humming, she crossed the expansive living room and closed the drapes. She didn't want the neighbors to see what she was about to do. Some logs were laid in the fireplace, so she knelt to light them. As the flames caught hold and grew, they threw out a romantic golden glow.

In the kitchen, she lingered at Hugh's wine rack. Did she want wine, or Champagne? Champagne. She had a lot to celebrate. Hugh always kept some cold in his refrigerator, and she opened it now, laughing when the cork exploded across the room. She poured herself a glass.

She emptied ice into a silver bucket and set it on the living room coffee table, nesting the bottle in the ice to keep it chilled. She brought in a flute for Hugh and a little bowl of nuts for herself, since she had eaten little at her vegetarian son's, and nothing at Carolyn's.

Sipping Champagne, she went into the bathroom and undressed. She was quite satisfied with her body, she decided, studying it in the mirror. The dieting she'd done in comradeship with Alice had indented her waistline, and with her full hips and heavy breasts, she had a luxurious hourglass shape. Her bulging belly made it clear that time and gravity had sifted most of the sand to the bottom, but because Hugh always made it clear that he loved every ounce and inch, she tried to carry her ass like an asset.

She brushed her teeth. Carefully, she redid her makeup. She brushed her hair. She considered wrapping a towel around her—she couldn't remember when she'd last, if ever, walked naked around her house, let alone anyone else's—but decided to go *au naturel*.

In the living room, the fire was crackling and gleaming, throwing out so much heat she was quite comfortable in her naked state. Sinking onto the sofa, she tried several poses, imagining which would be the most seductive.

"Here I am," she will say. "Your dessert."

Plumping up a couple of throw pillows, she established them under her head, then reclined on her side as if posing for a portrait. Her breasts hung low. So did her belly. When she heard the door open, she would rearrange all her bits. For now, she picked up the remote control and flicked on the television.

Polly waited an hour, fed two more logs to the fire, ate all the peanuts, drank half the Champagne, and peed twice.

Finally she heard Hugh's key scratch the lock. Quickly she ran her hands through her hair, mussing it. She positioned herself just so, head on hand, smiling at the door, one leg lying against the leather, the other bent at the knee, providing Hugh with a glimpse of what he privately called her "honey-well." The firelight danced. The room had grown hot, but that was fine. It made her nipples expand. Hugh liked that look.

"Here we are!" Hugh stepped into the room. By his side was a beautiful younger woman, her arm linked through his, her long blond hair falling against Hugh's shoulder.

"Oh!" said the woman.

"Oh," said Hugh.

"Oh!" cried Polly. Frantically she grabbed a throw pillow and held it over her naked torso. Of course, it was too small to cover *everything*.

Hugh began, "Polly—"

"No, no!" Polly babbled. Jumping up, she snatched the other pillow, and holding both pillows over her front, she ran past Hugh and the woman, shamefully aware of all her jiggling, lurching blubber. She scurried down the hall and into the bathroom, where she dropped the pillows and yanked on her clothes. She didn't bother to put on her pantyhose, but stabbed her bare feet into her shoes.

All she wanted in the world was to get out of there, now! Blood pounded through her body, making her completely deaf and nearly blind, but she moved as fast as she could, vaguely aware that she was sobbing. Throwing back the bathroom door, she raced down the small hall and spotted her purse where she'd left it on a table.

Hugh and the woman were in the living room. The woman had taken a chair. Hazily, Polly heard Hugh say to the woman, "Just wait here a moment—"

She didn't waste time taking her coat from the closet, but snatched up her purse, yanked open the door, and raced down the long, curving staircase so fast she slipped and nearly fell.

"Polly!" Above her, Hugh materialized, his ruddy face concerned. "Wait! Let me explain!"

But Polly flew out the door, down the street, and into her blessed Volvo. She was shaking so hard, it took her several tries to stab the key into the ignition. Finally, she connected, started the engine, and accelerated onto the street. Weeping, she drove home, so sick with humiliation and despair that she was halfway there before she thought to turn on the heater.

26

"Mrs. D'Annucio?" Alice gripped the phone so tightly she thought she'd leave permanent indentations in the plastic. She was on the hospital pay phone. Her cell phone only worked outside, and she didn't want to be too far away from the operating room.

Deep breaths, she reminded herself. "This is Alice Murray. I'm fine, thank you. I'm calling about Jennifer. No—she's—" For a few moments, Alice bit her tongue and tapped her foot, until the other woman stopped spitting out words.

"I'm calling because Jennifer is in the operating room right now, having a C-section. She—" Again, she listened to the other woman's shrill voice. "Yes, I know it's a month early, but you know she has preeclampsia—"

A barrage of sound hit Alice's ear. Alice inhaled so hard she was surprised she didn't suck the phone down her throat. No wonder Jennifer hadn't told her mother about her health problem. The woman didn't stop talking long enough for anyone to tell her anything.

"It's a medical condition involving high blood pressure and it's dangerous to the mother and the child—"

Alice held the phone away from her ear while Jennifer's mother screamed, "Oh, my God!" thirty or forty times.

The line was muffled. Alice heard rustling noises and arguing voices. Then a man's voice came over the phone.

"This is Jennifer's father. Where is she now?"

Alice spoke fast. "She's in Emerson Hospital in Concord. She's in the operating room. They're doing a C-section. Alan's with her. She was awake when they wheeled her in. I think they're planning to give a local anesthetic."

"We'll get in the car and come up at once. We're on the Cape, so it might take about two hours, depending on traffic."

"We'll be here." Alice doubted that he heard her, because his wife was in the background, screaming.

"Could you take our cell phone number and phone us if you know anything?" Mr. D'Annucio asked.

"Of course." Alice dug around in her shoulder bag, pulled out a pad and pen, and wrote down the information. She was surprised at how it helped, having *something* to do.

She returned to the waiting room. Gideon sat on a turquoise vinyl couch, thumbing through an old issue of *Newsweek*.

"Her parents are on their way up," Alice told him.

"That's good." Gideon patted the seat next to him. "Sit down, Alice."

"In a minute." She stayed on her feet, pacing the maternity-ward waiting room like a caged panther.

"Alice, come on and sit down," Gideon pleaded. "You're recovering from a heart attack, for God's sake. You know you're not supposed to get agitated."

Alice reached the end of the room, wheeled around, strode toward the opposite wall. "I'm supposed to get exercise, too," she reminded him. "So let's just call this exercise." She clenched her fists and opened them nervously. "I just wish I could *do* something."

"It's not going to help Jennifer if you have another heart attack," Gideon soberly reminded her.

"I'm not going to have another heart attack! I'm going to—oh!" Alice slapped herself in the middle of the forehead. "I know what I should do! I should call her best friend, Maya, remember, who came to the party we threw for Alan and Jennifer this summer? And what were the other girls' names? Two of them were married—Alisa and Morgan—but I think Maya was only engaged. Now, what were their last names?"

"Why don't you wait until Jennifer's out of surgery?" Gideon suggested. "You don't want everyone rushing down here."

"Well, if *I* were Jennifer, I'd want my friends to know!" Alice argued.

"But they're all having their Thanksgiving dinners," Gideon pointed out.

Alice stopped pacing, folded her arms, squinted into the distance, and debated Gideon's line of reasoning. "I understand where you're coming from," she told him. "I won't ask them to come down here, not unless they volunteer. But I want them to know what's going on."

"You want them to worry about something they can't do anything about?" Gideon asked.

"But they *can* do something," Alice insisted. "They can *worry*."

Gideon exhaled noisily, like a principal with a recalcitrant child. "And their worry is going to help Jennifer?"

"Yes," Alice told him decisively. "Worry is a kind of prayer. It *helps*. Maybe it's a female thing, but it's what I feel is true, and it's what I'm going to act on. If *I* were Jennifer's friend, I would want to know."

She rushed to the nurses' station, borrowed a phone book, and made a list of phone numbers. The mental effort it took to remember Jennifer's friends' last names provided a moment's ease from her own anxiety. *God,* she thought, *I hope I'm not relieving my fear by passing it off onto these young women.* She stopped, searched her soul, then made the phone calls.

She was just hanging up for the last time when she saw her son striding down the hall toward the waiting room. For a moment, her legs went so weak, she nearly fell.

Then she saw his face.

"Alan?" The word came out in a croak.

"We have a daughter, Mom," Alan said. "Five pounds, one ounce."

That even one tiny ounce could be measured against the enormity of all their hopes and fears made Alice burst into tears. "How's Jennifer?"

"She's got a headache. She's going to have to stay in the hospital for a few days. She's not out of the woods yet, but she's going to be okay." Alan wrapped his mother in a tight bear hug. "It's okay, Mom."

"I'm so glad!" Alice dug a tissue from her pocket and blew her nose.

Gideon came out of the waiting room. Alan told him the good news while Alice pulled herself together.

"I phoned Jennifer's parents," Alice told her son. "And all her friends."

"And CNN and all the major networks," Gideon joked.

Alice made a face at him. "Her parents are on their way. I'd better phone them and Jennifer's friends again."

"Want to see your granddaughter first?" Alan asked.

Alice staggered backward, amazed. "Can I?"

"Sure. Come on." Alan wrapped a supporting arm around his mother and led her down the hall.

They passed through a swinging door into a room so bright it seemed like heaven. Jennifer lay on a high table, as white as the sheets covering her. Her eyes were closed. But when Alan and Alice came to her side, she opened them.

"Look who's here." She adjusted herself slightly on her bed, turning so Alice could see the very small person bundled in her arms.

Alice bent over and gently pulled the blanket back from the baby's face. Her eyes were swollen nearly shut. Her tea-colored skin was blotchy, and her vulnerable scalp was covered with a few black curls.

"Oh, my," Alice breathed. "She's *beautiful*."

"We think so," Jennifer agreed. Reaching out, she took her husband's hand. "Her name is Alice."

CHRISTMAS

27

Shirley was in her office at The Haven on Monday afternoon when her phone rang.

"Shirley? This is Hugh Monroe."

"Oh, hi, Hugh, how are you?"

"I'm well, thank you, but I'm concerned about Polly. Have you spoken with her recently?"

Shirley thought for a moment. "Not since last Wednesday. Have you—"

"I've tried to phone her for three days now, and her line's always busy."

"How odd!" Polly frowned. "Have you called Carolyn? Polly spent Thanksgiving with her and the Sperrys."

Hugh made an ambiguous coughing noise. "Well, I saw Polly—briefly—Thanksgiving night, but that's a good suggestion. I'll call Carolyn right now."

"I'll check in with Alice and Marilyn, see if they've heard from her," Shirley told Hugh. "Faye's out in California with her daughter. Hugh—" She paused. "Is there any reason to worry? I mean, I don't want to pry, but did you two have a fight or something?"

Again, the ambiguous cough. "Not a fight, no. More of a . . . *something*."

"I see," Shirley said, although she didn't. "I'll call you back after I talk with Alice and Marilyn."

"Alice? It's Shirley. How are you?"

"Still in *heaven*. I'm just leaving for the hospital to visit Jennifer and baby Alice."

"Well, listen, just tell me, have you spoken with Polly in the last few days?"

"Um, no, actually. I tried to call her several times to tell her about the baby, but I've always gotten a busy signal. Why? Is something wrong?"

"I don't know. Hugh just called. He can't reach her, either."

"Well, damn! That's weird. Have you talked to her son?"

Shirley snorted. "Yeah, like *he* would know."

"I think Polly was going there for Thanksgiving . . ."

"Yeah, and to Carolyn's after that. Hugh says he saw Polly briefly Thanksgiving night."

"*Briefly.*"

"Yeah. I'm not sure what that means. I asked if they had a fight, and he said they had a *something*."

"Oh-oh. Sounds worse than a fight."

Shirley clutched the phone tight. "But even if they did have a fight, or broke up, or *something*, Polly wouldn't do anything *rash*, would she?"

"Of course not. Polly's sensible, optimistic—"

"But you *know* how the holidays can make you crazy. I mean, it's hard to be alone at Christmas, and her son and his wife aren't exactly loving, and if she and Hugh broke off—"

"I'm going over to her house."

"Wait, Alice. Let me see what Hugh says after he talks with Carolyn."

"You can call me on my cell phone. I'm driving over there now."

"Shirley?" Hugh's voice was taut with concern. "I spoke with Carolyn. She said Polly was very emotional on Thanksgiving. Made a bit of a scene and stormed from the house without taking a bite of her Thanksgiving meal, Carolyn said. She's been trying to phone her without any success."

"I spoke with Alice. She hasn't talked with her, either. She's driving over to Polly's house right now. Listen, Hugh, I don't want to pry, but . . . did you and Polly break up?"

"No, no, no," Hugh insisted. "Nothing like that." He hesitated. "Well, maybe it was something like that. I mean, not on my part. We had . . . a misunderstanding, Shirley. I don't want to say more without talking to Polly about it first. It's kind of a sensitive matter."

The hair on the back of Shirley's neck stood on end. "Oh, God! I'm going over there."

"I'll meet you there."

"She keeps a key hidden in a metal box behind the drainpipe next to the garage."

"I know."

"I'll check in with Marilyn from my cell phone."

"Marilyn? Listen, have you talked with Polly in the last few days?"

"No . . ." Marilyn's voice trailed off as she turned her head from the phone. "It's Shirley, Mother." Her voice was clear again. "Why? You sound worried."

"I *am* worried. Hugh phoned and he hasn't been able to get hold of her, and he saw her *briefly* on Thanksgiving night, and Carolyn said Polly was *emotional* and Hugh said he and Polly had a *something*. He wouldn't give any details."

"Oh, dear. That sounds bad. Have you—okay, Mother. Shirley, Mother says hello."

"Tell Ruth I say hello."

"Mother, Shirley says hello. Have you spoken with anyone else?"

"I called Alice. She's been trying to reach her, and so has Carolyn."

"I think I'll drive over there," Marilyn said.

"I'm on my way right now. And Hugh is, too."

"Yes, but I think I live closer to her than you do. What?" After a pause, Marilyn said, "Mother wants me to tell you it's always darkest before the silver lining."

Heat broke out over Polly's body, so intense it made her stomach heave as she lay twisted in her disgustingly damp and tangled sheets. With weak arms, she fought to shove the covers away. The movement made her stomach roil—desperately she flung her head over the side of the bed and barfed violently into the lobster pot sitting on the floor. How did that get there?

Her head was thick with heat and nightmarish blips of sound and color. Orange, purple, worms, swollen masses of—she barfed again. This time only a thin stream of liquid trailed out, burning her mouth as it came.

Collapsing back among her pillows, she touched her forehead with a shaking hand. She was sick. Really sick. Flu, probably. She'd been wallowing in her bed like an overwrought sow for—how long? She couldn't figure it out. She remembered coming home from Hugh's, weeping hysterically and shaking with cold, or with cold and emotion. She'd wept—she'd *howled*—she'd been so out of control she'd scared herself. She'd drunk some brandy, but vomited it all up immediately.

She *hated* vomiting, but it did clear her head momentarily. Her memory flashed vivid bits, out of sequence. She must have pulled herself together enough to get herself to bed, because she could remember morning sunshine streaming in through the windows and Roy Orbison sitting by her on the bed, whining pitifully. Dutifully, she'd risen, wrapped her robe around her (when had she put on her nightgown?), and gone downstairs. The kitchen door had a dog flap, so she didn't have to worry about putting Roy Orbison out.

She'd filled his food bowl to overflowing, grabbed the lobster pot, and staggered back up to bed.

Now she was *cold,* so cold her skin was covered in goose bumps. Chills rippled up and down her body like icy fingers on piano keys. She grabbed for the covers, the movement stirring up a rolling ocean in her stomach. She clutched the blanket to her chin.

"Where's a damn hot flash when you need one?" she whined.

Her voice came out in a croak.

Great, she had laryngitis, too.

Roy Orbison thought she'd called him. With a giant leap, he landed on the bed. The impact of his weight made the bed rock. Oh, God, she was so dizzy! She needed to get to the bathroom, but she felt too sick to move. Roy licked her arm. She managed a feeble pat on his head. Good old loyal companion.

Speaking of companions, why had none of her friends called? How much time had gone by? One day? Two? Well, Faye was in California, visiting her daughter. But why hadn't Marilyn phoned, or Alice or Shirley? Not to mention Hugh. She had been sure he would phone her to apologize, to explain, to—to *something*! He was a gentleman, after all; he wasn't a monster. She could understand how he would dump her in order to be with that lovely young woman. Men did it all the time. She hated it that he'd betrayed her, but she was astounded that he hadn't phoned to somehow attempt to make her feel better about it.

She was so thirsty! Her throat burned. She could actually feel her esophagus drying out like a sponge left in the sun. Out of the corner of her eye, she saw a can of ginger ale on her bedside table. Feebly, she reached out for it, brought it to her parched lips, and discovered it was already empty. When had she drunk it? For that matter, when had she brought it upstairs?

"Oh, boo hoo," she cried helplessly, as tears slid down her face. How did her body manage to produce moisture everywhere except where she needed it?

Next to her, Roy Orbison suddenly sat up. He cocked his head. Then he leapt off the bed and skittered out of the room. She heard his nails clicking busily as he went down the stairs.

Probably he was going to eat again. All Roy's best ideas involved eating. Polly sank into her pillows, a blubbery, pathetic mass of nausea and discomfort. In a moment, she'd get herself to the bathroom, and then she'd phone someone . . .

She heard voices. Several voices, all talking at once. Oh good, now she was hallucinating.

The voices got louder. Steps sounded on the stairs. Who . . . ? A burglar? Maybe someone was coming to murder her. She felt so sick she almost didn't think she'd mind.

"Polly!"

Alice exploded into the room, followed by Shirley, Marilyn, Ruth, and Hugh. Waves of cold air swept in with them, making Polly shiver. They radiated health, energy, and good humor as they gathered around her. She was aware of how she must appear, with her hair clumped with sweat and sticking out all over, her nose red, her eyes puffy, her lips chapped, her breath foul.

"Polly!" Shirley sank onto the bed, touching her cold hand to Polly's hot forehead.

"I'll empty this." Marilyn grabbed the lobster pot and disappeared into the bathroom.

Alice was fixing something on the bedside table. "Polly, you moron, you left the phone off the hook."

"Polly." Hugh peered over Shirley's shoulder. He was so handsome, his blue eyes so full of concern! "Polly, that woman was my niece."

"Oh, honey," Ruth cried, "you're sick."

"Oh," Polly sighed, closing her eyes. "I'm so glad."

I am *not* nervous, Faye assured herself as she waited for her guest to arrive. I'm an independent, intelligent woman, and if necessary, I can be stubborn. Or even *rude.*

To remind her guest that she was a professional artist—something Faye had almost forgotten after her husband's death, something she'd almost *lost*—she remained in the clothes she'd pulled on this morning: jeans with an elastic waist, a white cotton tank top, and a long, loose blue denim shirt, everything spotted here and there with ruby and celadon oils from painting Ruth's portrait. Her long hair was pulled back in a clip. Her nails, which she'd grown long during the past year when she wasn't painting, were clipped short again, the way she liked them when she was working. She wore no makeup. Now, at the last moment, Faye rushed upstairs and put on a touch of blusher and lipstick.

As always, a pause in front of a mirror led to a confrontation with her inner nag, who sounded very much like Joan Rivers. *For God's sake, look at you! You've gained back the weight you lost! Your skin is blotchy! Haven't you ever heard of exfoliation? And why are your eyes so puffy?*

"Stop it!" she scolded herself, and ripping her attention away from the mirror, she went back down the stairs—slowly, so she wouldn't fall—and into the kitchen to turn the burner on under the teakettle.

She took out the flowered Limoges teapot that had belonged to her grandmother and filled it with loose leaves of Earl Grey. Running her hands over the rounded belly of the pot, she admired its classical lines, delicate painted flowers, and brilliant gilding. All her life she'd intended to pass this tea set down to Laura.

During her visit to San Francisco this Thanksgiving, Faye had realized that Laura would never use this pot. Would never *want* to use this pot. The life Laura and Lars lived was so different from Faye's. Streamlined. Urban. Modern. And, it seemed to Faye, centered around electronic equipment. Lars and Laura were always on the computer or cell phone. Megan, at four, spent what to Faye were inappropriate amounts of time in front of the computer and television. Or else she was shipped off to the expensive, elite neighborhood preschool, while her little brother, only six months old, dawdled in a playpen at the accompanying nursery. Lars worked endless hours, and Laura also worked, in her own way, keeping to a rigorous exercise routine with her trainer at the local health club, supervising the live-in housekeeper/baby-sitter, attending committee meetings for the chicest charities, and planning cocktail and dinner parties for Lars's partners and potential clients.

It amazed Faye how different Laura was in San Francisco from the way she'd been just three short years ago, when Megan was still an infant. Laura had been depressed and overwhelmed with the responsibilities of motherhood. Now, somehow, she'd found herself; she'd entered that kind of "I am woman, hear me roar" phase that Faye could remember from her early days as a young mother. Laura had had her thick, long hair, for so many years tumbling to her shoulders, sheared into a kind of skullcap that made her eyes huge. She had lost more weight than Faye considered healthy, and racing around in her tight, rather athletic-looking clothing, she resembled a young boy, or an elf.

And she was radiantly happy.

The children were thriving, Lars looked at Laura with adoration, they were all having great fun—and their lives were so *different* from Faye's!

They loved California. They'd never return to the East Coast.

As Faye flew home from her visit, she'd leaned her head against the window of the huge humming plane, considering all this, trying to come to terms with the truth of it, struggling not to feel rejected, or disappointed, or solitary. Or, admitting she *was* solitary, but capable of making this phase of her life into one she not merely survived, but actually enjoyed. After all, she had her friends, she had a beau, and now, again, thanks to Ruth, she had her work.

The thought of Ruth's portrait, waiting for her in the little bedroom/studio, lifted Faye's spirits. The picture was finished; Faye had had it framed, and was keeping it until Christmas, when Ruth would present it to Marilyn.

It was a good portrait.

Somehow, as if a spell had been lifted, Faye was painting again. Really working.

Just before Faye left for San Francisco, while she was getting ready to take apart the little scene she'd set up, her attention had been captured by the way the light fell on the birds' nests in Ruth's portrait. The scratchy texture of the nests and the subtle, varied hues of the dried grasses challenged her. An image appeared in her mind—a still life of the nests, juxtaposed with fresh flowers. Daffodils? No. Something autumnal. Mums? Perhaps a sheaf of bright mums, lying on their side, their fluffy petals silky against the crisp grass of the nests—that would be fun to try to capture. During her stay in California, the thought of that still life nestled against her heart like a gold locket.

So that was what she was returning to: her work. It had always been part of who she was, why she lived, and now it had regained its place in her life. This year, she hadn't bothered to put up a tree in the kitchen. The little blue spruce in the living room was much smaller than any she'd ever had before. Since she'd been home, she'd been absolutely *high*, full of energy, eager to get to work every day, obsessed with thoughts of building a real studio in her back garden, so interested in her work that she considered Christmas a kind of interruption.

Three days ago, Carolyn Sperry had phoned and asked if she

could meet with Faye. Regarding a *business proposal,* she had added, mysteriously.

Of course, Faye, always polite, had agreed, but she'd thought, *Egad! Now what?* She knew Carolyn wanted Aubrey to date Polly, but would she be brazen enough to offer Faye money to stop seeing her father? What else could she mean by a business proposition?

As Faye set out the teacups, cream and sugar bowls, and silver spoons on the tray, she saw that her hands were shaking.

"I liked it better last year," Alice mused thoughtfully, as she reclined on a sofa in the lounge of The Haven, cuddling her namesake in her arms. She drove out almost every day, to take care of baby Alice so Jennifer could take a bath or a nap.

Shirley, kneeling on the floor amid a crackling muddle of wrapping paper, paused to study the Christmas tree. "I know. Me, too. It's bigger than last year's tree, so all the ornaments are there, but it still lacks something."

"Maybe we should hang some tinsel?" With the tip of her finger, Alice pushed back the blanket around the baby just a millimeter, so she could see all of her smooth, curving cheek.

Shirley watched Alice gaze adoringly upon her granddaughter. "Maybe some pacifiers and booties?" she teased.

"Maybe," Alice cooed.

"Oh, Alice!" Shirley laughed.

Alice looked up. "What?" She focused. "No, hey, I heard you. I mean it. What if we hung little bits on the tree that symbolized what we're celebrating this Christmas? Pacifiers would be *cute*! And some lacy tags from Havenly Yours. And since Marilyn went to Scotland, she could hang bagpipes, or little Loch Ness Monsters . . ."

"Are you nuts? You know Marilyn broke it off with Ian because of her mother. That's certainly nothing to celebrate, and as for me—I could hang, um, let me see, what have I achieved this year—oh, *I* know! A broken heart!"

Alice's face fell. "That's not *all* you've achie—"

Shirley waved her hands. "I'm sorry, Alice, forgive me for being such a pill." Pushing aside a roll of wrapping paper, Shirley lay back on the floor, stretching, closing her eyes.

"You're not a pill." Alice said everything in a light, breathy voice, so she wouldn't wake the infant in her arms. "But you're not at 'The End,' either. You're just kind of at a station, waiting for a train."

"I don't know." Shirley allowed herself to be honest. "It's been over three months, Alice, since Justin hit the road."

"Since you righteously kicked his nasty ol' ass out of here," corrected Alice.

"Whatever. Since I've been with a man." Self-pity struck her. She sat up, as if she could physically move away from it, grabbed a present, centered it on a square of paper covered with dancing reindeer, and grabbed the scissors. "I wish I could be the kind of woman who doesn't need a man!"

"Well, you are, in many ways." Alice leaned sideways, stretched out an arm, and grabbed her cup of tea from the table. "I mean, you're professionally and financially self-sufficient. It's not like you lack meaning in your life."

"I know. I know." Shirley measured a length of scarlet ribbon and snipped. "Still . . ."

"Still, you're happier with a man around." The baby squirmed and squinched up her face. Alice loosened the blanket around little Alice's feet and retucked it.

"Yes, who isn't?" Shirley said, defensively.

"I'm not arguing."

"That's a first," Shirley muttered under her breath.

Alice just smiled. "All right, we've named the problem. What can we do about it?"

"I wish I knew!" She reached for another box.

"Let's see." Alice tapped her lower lip with one long, red nail. "If I met Gideon at the symphony, and Polly met Hugh at the doctor's, and Marilyn met Ian while traveling, then how . . ."

"Sounds like there's a light-bulb joke in there," Shirley chuckled.

Alice brightened. "I know! Remember last year? We all found one single man for Faye to date."

"Yes, and remember last year? When none of them worked out? Faye met Aubrey at our open house, by accident."

"Hm." Alice subsided against the sofa. "You're right. Well, then, let's think of places where you could meet a guy."

Shirley set a present under the tree. "Not here, because mostly women come here."

"Okay, how about a bookstore?"

"Right. I'll just lounge around the auto repair section."

"That's not a bad idea."

"Actually," Shirley said, as she cut along another roll of paper, "I'm kind of off books in general, after Justin."

"Understood. What kinds of clubs could you join? Or maybe you could take some courses. Remember, you met Justin when you took that business management seminar."

"That might work. But not until after the first of the year. So that's another month without getting laid."

Alice pointed a finger at Shirley. "Is that all you want? Think about it. Remember how old you are. Men your age, our age, aren't going to be as lusty as younger men."

"So I'll date younger men."

"I don't think that's smart. You seem to get in trouble with younger men. Besides, Shirley, men are already, naturally, *psychologically* younger than women. You were dating Justin, who was fifty, which was sort of like dating someone, oh, forty-two, but if you date someone sixty-three, he'll be fifty-five."

"Maybe psychologically or intellectually, but sexually, to date a man who's fifty, I need to date a man who's forty." Confused, Shirley threw up her hands. "Look. I'll date anyone any age, but first I have to *meet* someone, and I don't seem to be doing that!"

Alice leaned her head against the sofa and closed her eyes. "We're two creative, intelligent women. We ought to be able to find a solution. I mean, even a hundred years ago, women answered ads as mail-order brides, so—" She sat up, swung around, set her feet on the floor, and faced Shirley. "I've got it. We'll sign you up on an online dating service. Match.com or something like that."

Shirley looked at Alice. "Hmmmm."

"It's brilliant!" Alice said. "Tell me it's not."

Thoughtfully, Shirley twirled a strand of hair. "I'm not so sure about *brilliant,* but it could be fun . . ."

"Let's go try it out now!" Alice said, getting to her feet.

"But I'm not through wrapping—"

"Oh, you can do that later! Come on!" Alice clopped away across the parquet floor, and in her arms, little Alice made kissy movements with her mouth as she slept.

"Your house is really lovely," Carolyn told Faye as she settled on the sofa by the fire. Carolyn was clad in a snug-fitting camel pantsuit that set off her sleek blond hair. She looked chic, young, and terrifying.

"Thank you." Faye finished the tea ritual and handed Carolyn a cup of steaming Earl Grey. She felt like a hippo entertaining a gazelle. Leaning back in her chair, she aimed for a pose of relaxed confidence, but even though Carolyn had seemed friendly so far, Faye knew that if she tried to lift her cup off its saucer, everything would chatter like teeth in the Arctic.

"Delicious." Carolyn sipped her tea, and with steady hands, returned the wafer-thin cup to its saucer. "Faye, I'll get right to the point. I think the Christmas card you sent us is absolutely beautiful. And when I was here for your Halloween party, I saw your paintings. Aubrey told me you did wonderful work, but I had no idea. Your paintings are exceptional."

"Thank you." Faye's infinite relief sparked off a hot flash.

"Sperry Paper is hitting hard times," Carolyn continued. "We've got so much competition these days. We produce premier-quality, personal stationery, but we're looking for ways to branch out. I'd like to put out a line of note cards, with your paintings reproduced on the front. Some of what you've already done would work well for what I have in mind. But I'm hoping you wouldn't be averse to creating a few scenes especially for our purposes. Holiday scenes, for example, and occasion scenes. Birthdays. Anniversaries. That sort of thing."

Faye was stunned. If she'd been standing, she would have fallen down. As it was, she was overwhelmed, her brain short-circuited with shock.

Apparently Carolyn was used to causing this sort of response. "I've mentioned it to Father, by the way, and he thinks it's an excellent idea." When Faye still didn't speak, Carolyn shifted on the sofa, crossing one sleek leg over the other. Her hand fiddled with the heavy gold chain around her neck—the only sign that she might be nervous herself. "I realize I haven't been what you might consider welcoming over the past few months. I apologize. My father's been very happy since he's been dating you, and I want you to know I'll stop trying to match him up with Polly. I can be stubborn and I like to have my own way, but I know when it's time to quit."

"I don't know what to say," Faye admitted. *Deep breaths,* she reminded herself.

Carolyn's cell phone rang. She reached into her handsome leather briefcase and shut it off. "I don't want you to feel pressured about this. Obviously, this business arrangement stands completely apart from your relationship with my father."

Faye finally managed to speak. "I'm so glad. I like your father very much. And I'd like to be your friend, too—" She noticed Carolyn's slight flinch. "—although I realize, what with your baby and running your business, you don't have much time for friendships."

Carolyn smiled. "Sometimes I can be a wicked, cold bitch, I know."

"That's all right," Faye assured her. "I've met worse. And I like your idea about the note cards. I've just started painting again. When my husband died, I—lost interest for a while. But now, well—would you like to come up to my studio to see the still life I've set up? And I've got some old paintings stored there as well. You might want to look through them, to see if you like something, to give me an idea of the sort of thing you've got in mind."

"I'd love to see them." Carolyn stood up, eager.

Faye stood up, too, and when she set her cup and saucer on the table, her hands were as steady as if she were holding a brush.

Marilyn was dreaming. It was Thanksgiving, or perhaps Christmas—some holiday. She was at a party with her Hot Flash friends, and all their acquaintances, and lots of other people, too. Glamorous men and women laughed and drank Champagne. Marilyn's mother clutched her arm tightly, afraid of getting lost in the crowd. Suddenly, they were all called in to dinner. Marilyn found her place card next to Ruth's at a table with a few strangers in a room annexed to the main room. Slices of turkey lay on her plate, but nothing else. Marilyn sneaked a look around the corner of the door into the other room, where her friends sat at a long table laden with bowls and platters of delicious, aromatic food: creamed onions, chestnut stuffing, garlic mashed potatoes, cranberry sauce.

"Could I have some mashed potatoes, please?" Marilyn whimpered.

No one even noticed her.

Marilyn woke up with a start. It was seven in the morning. She could hear Ruth fumbling around in the bathroom. She covered her eyes with her arm, letting the dream sift back into the recesses of her brain.

"Okay, now," she said aloud. "That was just pathetic."

Tying her striped bathrobe around her, she headed into the kitchen to start breakfast. She liked coffee; Ruth liked tea.

Cold rain streaked the windows, and even in this well-insulated building, she could hear the wind moan. Flicking on the television, she curled up in a chair and waited for the Weather Channel to give the local forecast. She never used to watch TV in the morning, or during the day at all, and only rarely watched it in the evening. She had so many research articles to read, or students' papers to grade. But Ruth liked to have the television on all the time, and now that Marilyn was on sabbatical, she had no papers to grade or committee reports to read. She was supposed to be doing her research, but going to her lab made her squeamish these days, afraid she'd run into Faraday. She'd seen him several times since he broke off with her, and he'd always been polite, but clearly it was uncomfortable for them both.

"Good morning, dear!" Ruth toddled into the living room, clean, clothed, and fragrant with lavender cologne. She pecked a kiss on Marilyn's cheek, then went into the kitchen to pour a cup of tea. "What's on the schedule for today?" Ruth stirred milk into her very strong tea and added a teaspoon of sugar.

"I was thinking we'd get our tree." Marilyn put a couple of eggs on to boil. "But it's going to rain all day, perhaps turn to snow. Maybe we'd better wait until tomorrow."

"If it snows later on, we could get it then. It's always fun to choose Christmas trees in the snow." Ruth dipped her spoon into the sugar bowl.

"You've already put your sugar in," Marilyn told her.

Ruth giggled. "Oh, did I? I guess I have a sweet heart."

"Sweet tooth," Marilyn murmured as she popped bread into the toaster.

They settled down at the table, their eggs in their little cups, the clever egg-slicing device next to Ruth's plate. It made Marilyn smile to watch her mother attend to the opening of her egg. It was a moment of pleasure and concentration for Ruth as she carefully fit the aluminum ring over the top of the egg and snipped the shell, then neatly lifted off the top bit of egg, revealing the shimmering yellow yolk inside the solid white.

"Perfection!" Ruth said, as she did every morning. She sprinkled salt and pepper on the egg, dipped in her spoon, and nearly purred with pleasure.

This is a moment in a life, Marilyn told herself. *This is a good moment in a life that deserves lots of good moments.*

She ate her own egg without much noticing its flavor. All food seemed bland these days. All life seemed bland—bleak.

Mentally, Marilyn slapped herself. "So, Mom," she said brightly, "let's go to the Museum of Science!" Her mother loved going there.

"Well, dear, actually, I was thinking I'd like to stop in at the local Senior Citizens' Center." Ruth dipped a tip of her whole-wheat toast into the eggshell, soaking up every last bit of buttery yolk.

Marilyn stared. "The local Senior Citizens' Center—is there such a thing?"

"Oh, yes. On Hawthorne Street. Open every day from nine to five. Sometimes in the evenings, too, if they have a speaker."

"How did you find out about this?" Perhaps Ruth had been scammed by a telemarketer when Marilyn was out . . .

"It was in the *Boston Globe*. There was an article about it last week. It looks like fun. They've got bingo, and arts and crafts, and dances, and programs."

"Well, great!" Marilyn felt oddly rejected. She felt all snarly inside. Here she'd changed her life in order to take care of her mother, and her mother had made other plans.

Ruth peered over her glasses at Marilyn. "You'd better get dressed, sweetheart. It's rather late in the morning to be in your robe. You don't want to acquire slovenly rabbits at this age."

"You're right, of course." Marilyn set her dishes in the sink and went off to get dressed for the day, which suddenly loomed emptily before her.

In her bedroom, she listlessly pulled on trousers and a sweater, vaguely aware her Hot Flash friends would scream at the mismatched colors, but unable to give a damn. What would she do with herself after she dropped her mother at the Senior Citizens' Center? How much time would she have? An hour? Two? Three? She allowed a mild surge of resentment to surface before reminding herself it didn't really matter—she didn't care whether she went in to the lab or not. Her work seemed so unimportant these days.

She forced herself to move forward. "Okay, Mother. Let's get our coats on."

She held Ruth's coat for her, then pulled on her own, choosing the ugly, puffy down one her friends hated, because she was in such an ugly, puffy mood. Ruth gathered up her purse and gloves, Marilyn locked the door, and together they took the elevator down to the lobby.

"You wait here," Marilyn instructed her mother. "I'll bring the car around, then come in and get you."

"I can walk to the car myself, honey," Ruth objected.

"Of course you can, but I'd feel better if you'd wait for me. The rain's turning to ice."

"All right, dear," Ruth said agreeably.

Marilyn ran through the bitter wind to her car in the condo lot. It was one of those bleak, gray days when clouds drained the world of color. In her hurry to get inside the car, she hit her shoulder, *hard*.

"Damn!" She dropped her head onto the steering wheel. Deep breaths, she told herself. Take deep fucking breaths! Get your act together, Marilyn. You're not the only woman making sacrifices on this planet. Think of Shirley—she's carrying on without Justin.

When she'd regained a bit of self-control, she drove around to the front of the building. Just where she needed to park the car, at the end of the sidewalk leading from the condo, a taxi was stopped, its exhaust spiraling up through the rain like smoke from a chimney. A man stepped out of the cab, pulled up the hood of his raincoat, took the two suitcases the driver handed him, and ran for the condo. He disappeared inside.

Marilyn waited until the taxi drove away, then pulled up and parked in the empty space. She switched on her hazard lights and turn indicator, then ran through the streaming rain.

In the lobby, Ruth stood dry and perky with her red-and-green striped Christmas muffler, matching cap, and mittens. She was chatting with the man in the raincoat, her face bright and animated. In contrast, Marilyn felt drenched and soggy.

"Ready to go, Mother?" Marilyn asked, straining to sound cheerful.

"Not just yet, dear," Ruth said. "Look who's here."

The man in the raincoat turned.

Marilyn's knees went weak.

"Ian?"

"Hello, Marilyn." Ian was smiling from ear to ear.

"What are you doing here?" Her brain couldn't assimilate this new information. It was like trying to fit a cookie cutter in a jigsaw space.

"I've just come from Boston University," Ian told her. "I'm taking a position there."

"You are?" Marilyn felt herself stagger backward. She put a hand out against the wall to stabilize herself.

"I didn't want to tell you until I knew for sure." Ian put his hands on Marilyn's shoulders, steadying her. "I'm moving here. And while I didn't envision asking you in exactly such a time and place, once again, I'm asking you to marry me."

"Oh, Ian!" Marilyn's heart flowered like a poinsettia.

From behind Ian's shoulders, Ruth said, "There's always light at the end of a prayer."

Steam wreathed the heads of the Hot Flash Club as they lounged in the fragrant Jacuzzi.

Alice's tense muscles were melting like butter in the soothing warmth. "Shirley, this was a brilliant idea."

"Thanks! I thought we could all use a little relaxation time."

Shirley had invited them for Christmas Eve lunch at her condo. She'd surprised them with a beautifully served salad of field greens and chopped vegetables, and a concoction of mixed fruits. Sparkling water was the only beverage, and dessert was, instead of food, a nice long soak in the Jacuzzi.

Faye patted her bulging belly. "I really appreciate this, Shirley. I've been eating so much—you know how it gets during the holidays—everything's so rich. People drop off gifts of chocolates or homemade fudge or—"

"Pecans!" Polly chirped. "Those wonderful salted, candied pecans!"

"I made a *bûche du Noël*," Alice told them. "Needless to say, I ate half the icing while I put the thing together."

Marilyn looked surprised. "A *bûche du Noël*? That's pretty ambitious."

Alice stretched her limbs like a contented cat. "I've really got the Christmas spirit this year."

"Yeah, you should see her tree," Shirley said enthusiastically. "It touches the ceiling. And the *presents*! It's like Santa's workshop in her living room."

Alice grinned. She didn't feel the slightest bit abashed. "Well, a baby needs so much! And I got quite a few little goodies for Jennifer—you know how emotional young mothers are."

"Oh, and old nonmothers aren't?" Shirley teased.

"I got you a few things, too," Alice assured her. She told the others, "Shirley's spending tonight with us. I didn't like the thought of her being alone on Christmas Eve and Christmas day."

"Plus," Shirley added enthusiastically, "while the turkey's roasting and Gideon's watching football, I'm going to access my site on match.com and show Alice all my prospective suitors."

"How many do you have?" Polly asked.

"Twenty-two!" Shirley giggled. "I don't know when I've had so much fun!"

"Speaking of beaux . . ." Marilyn pulled up the strap on her bathing suit. "Ruth has a man in her life!"

"How wonderful! Where did she meet him?" Faye asked.

"At the Senior Citizens' Center. His name is Ernest Eberhart. He's just her age, and very cute. And wait till you hear how they met! They were in line to go into the cafeteria, and Ernest was in front of Ruth. He was using a walker, and he turned to Mother and asked her to pull his pants up."

The other women gasped in surprise.

"Well, you see," Marilyn explained, "he'd just gotten out of the hospital, and he'd lost weight during an operation, so his pants were loose. This was his first time out in public with a walker. He was afraid that if he took his hands off the walker, he'd lose his balance and fall. So he asked Ruth to just hitch up his pants."

"What did she do?" Polly asked.

"She reached over and yanked up his pants with both hands. Then she said, 'This is the first time any man has ever asked me to pull his pants *up*.' "

They all shrieked with laughter.

"The saucy thing!" Faye chuckled.

"That Ruth is my role model," Shirley said.

"Well, Ruth and Ernest and their group are pretty impressive for their age." Marilyn laughed. "Ruth told me a story, and it's *true*. Ernest's best friend, Harold—I haven't met Harold yet, but my mother has—anyway, Ernest's friend Harold went to the doctor this week. He's eighty-six and hasn't been feeling up to snuff. The doctor told him he has cancer, and has only a year or so to live. 'In that case,' Harold said, 'I want a prescription for Viagra.' "

"Good for him!" Alice cheered.

Shirley looked thoughtful. "What's that saying? It's better to travel hopefully than it is to arrive."

"Speaking of traveling," Marilyn looked at Polly and Faye. "When do you leave?"

"We're flying down to Florida tomorrow morning," Faye said. "Aubrey and me, Polly and Hugh."

"The guy who dreamed up this Christmas Getaway Cruise was a genius," Polly added. "When I dropped off my presents to Amy, David, and Jehoshaphat yesterday morning, I was in such a hurry I didn't have time to feel rejected by them."

"At least Carolyn's changed, don't you think, Polly?" Faye asked.

"Oh, absolutely," Polly agreed. She told the others, "Carolyn and her family—everyone except Aubrey—left for London yesterday. And the evening before, Carolyn gave a dinner party. She invited Faye and seated her next to Aubrey. She told me to bring Hugh, and she placed us next to each other."

"So your Thanksgiving temper tantrum worked!" Shirley said.

Polly objected, "I wouldn't call it a *temper tantrum* . . ."

"You're right," Shirley agreed. "That makes it seem irrational. I just meant you stood up for yourself and what you wanted. Sometimes that's hard to do."

"Sometimes it's hardest to do with members of your own family," Marilyn added.

"Speaking of families," Faye said, "it was such a good idea, Shirley, to have that Christmas party for the families of the employees of The Haven. Everyone enjoyed it so much."

"I think I enjoyed it most of all," Shirley said. "I had so much fun buying presents for all those little kids—and when they saw the tree! And opened their presents! They were genuinely thrilled. All those darling faces." She patted her chest. "Makes me tear up."

"This time last year," Faye said in a musing tone of voice, "you wanted it to be a Dream Come True Christmas."

"I still do," Shirley admitted. "I suppose I always will."

"You're an incorrigible optimist," Alice declared.

"But sometimes you're right," Marilyn told Shirley, smiling. "I'm living proof of that."

"Have you and Ian found a house yet?" Faye asked.

Marilyn shook her head. "Oh, with Christmas and all, we've had to put the search on hold. We'll have more time after the first of the year."

"How does Ruth like Ian?" Polly asked.

"She adores him. But she still insists she'll only live with us as long as she has a private apartment. She says we need our privacy and she needs hers."

Alice said, "Lots of places have mother-in-law apartments these days."

Marilyn nodded. "Good thing. There are about thirty-eight million women over fifty in the United States today. I don't know how many of their mothers are alive and kicking, but it's got to be quite a few. Fathers, too. Anyway, if Ian and I find a house we like that doesn't have one, we can always build an apartment on."

"Have you decided on a wedding date?" Shirley asked.

Marilyn smiled dreamily. "Not yet. Don't worry. I wouldn't dream of getting married without all of you in attendance!"

Alice waved her fingers. "Prunes!"

Shirley nodded. "Right. Time to get out."

The five women climbed out of the Jacuzzi, went into the locker room, took quick showers, then pulled on their warm winter clothing. They'd entered the Jacuzzi separately, and now as they dressed together, they noticed they were all wearing the same thing: hot pink sweatshirts printed across the bust with the logo "Havenly Yours," given to the five by the employees of The Haven and Havenly Yours.

"Look!" Shirley called. "Someone should take our picture!"

"No camera!" Faye faked a pout.

"That's all right," Alice said. "We'll wear these again, in the new year, when someone else is around to get all five of us together." She glanced at her watch. "Oh-oh, it's late! I've got to run."

Shirley said, "You go ahead, Alice. I've got to get some stuff from my apartment. I'll be at your place soon."

"Merry Christmas, everyone," Faye said as she tucked her hair into a red wool fedora decorated with a green sprig of holly.

"Merry Christmas!" the others chorused.

They pulled on caps, and gloves, and mufflers, and coats. They hugged and kissed, and grabbed up their purses. Chattering and laughing, they rushed out of The Haven to their cars and their busy lives.

And snowflakes drifted down around them like snippets of celestial lace.

NANCY THAYER is the author of sixteen novels, including *Custody, Between Husbands and Friends, An Act of Love, Belonging, Three Women at the Water's Edge,* and *Everlasting,* which was a Main Dual selection of the Literary Guild. Her work has been translated into more than a dozen languages. Her first novel, *Stepping,* was made into a thirteen-part series for BBC Radio, and her ghost novel *Spirit Lost* has been optioned and produced as a movie by United Image Entertainment. In 1981 she was a Fellow at the Breadloaf Writers Conference. She has lived on Nantucket Island year-round for twenty years with her husband, Charley Walters.

ABOUT THE TYPE

This book was set in Sabon, a typeface designed by the well-known German typographer Jan Tschichold (1902–74). Sabon's design is based upon the original letter forms of Claude Garamond and was created specifically to be used for three sources: foundry type for hand composition, Linotype, and Monotype. Tschichold named his typeface for the famous Frankfurt typefounder Jacques Sabon, who died in 1580.

STANDOFF

AT

STANDING ROCK

The Story of
SITTING BULL

and
JAMES McLAUGHLIN

Patricia Calvert

▲ ▲ ▲

TWENTY-FIRST CENTURY BOOKS   BROOKFIELD, CONNECTICUT

TO WENDY SCHMALZ, MY AGENT,
WITH GRATITUDE AND AFFECTION.
P.C.

Acknowledgments

I wish to acknowledge in particular the careful work of the late Louis L. Pfaller, O.S.B., member of the Benedictine Assumption Abbey in Richardton, ND, who catalogued James McLaughlin's extensive correspondence and preserved it on microfilm. Later, the North Dakota Heritage Center, 612 East Boulevard, Bismarck, ND 58505-0830, fell heir to this material, where it is now available to researchers. The personnel at the Heritage Center were more than gracious in providing access to the McLaughlin Collection, making this book possible. I also wish to pay homage to the early work of Stanley Vestal, and to Robert M. Utley's later extensive research on the history of the Sioux.

Published by Twenty-First Century Books
A division of The Millbrook Press, Inc.
2 Old New Milford Road, Brookfield, CT 06804
www.millbrookpress.com

Cover photographs courtesy of National Archives (Sitting Bull) and State Historical
Society of North Dakota (Major James McLaughlin #A1356)
Photographs courtesy of State Historical Society of North Dakota: pp. 6 (#A2250), 14
(#A1356), 21 (#A4518), 40 (#310g), 49 (#189-D), 56 (#A5195), 88 (#C1424), 114 (top
#22H90), 130 (Fiske 1525); North Wind Picture Archives: pp. 26, 64, 80; Smithsonian
Institution: pp. 34 (#3195-G), 114 (bottom, #52835); Library of Congress: p. 72;
Saskatchewan Archives Board: p. 96 (top, #R-A859); Montana Historical Society, Helena: p.
96 (bottom); National Archives: p. 104; Culver Pictures, Inc.: p. 123

Library of Congress Cataloging-in-Publication Data
Calvert, Patricia.
Standoff at Standing Rock / Patricia Calvert.
p. cm.
Summary: Parallel biographies of Sioux leader Sitting Bull
and Indian Agent James McLaughlin show how the respresentatives
of their two nations came into conflict as their cultures clashed.
ISBN 0-7613-1360-5 (lib. bdg.)
1. Sitting Bull, 1834?–1890—Juvenile literature. 2. McLaughlin, James, 1842–1923—Juvenile
literature. 3. Dakota Indians—Kings and rulers—Biography—Juvenile literature. 4. Dakota
Indians—Wars—Juvenile literature. 5. Indian agents—Biography—Juvenile literature. 6.
Standing Rock Indian Reservation (N.D. and S.D.)—Juvenile literature. [1. Sitting Bull,
1834?–1890. 2. McLaughlin, James, 1842–1923. 3. Hunkpapa Indians—Biography. 4.
Indians of North America—Great Plains—Biography. 5. Indian agents.] I. Title.
E99.D1   S58   2000
978.004'9752'0092—dc21   [BBB]   00-024729

Contents

PORTRAIT OF SITTING BULL TAKEN AT THE STANDING ROCK
INDIAN RESERVATION, 1883

1

FREE AS WIND ACROSS THE GRASS

Tatanka Jyotanka,
he miye!
Sitting Bull, J am he!
SITTING BULL

*C*hildren were greatly valued among the Sioux, who believed that sons and daughters were gifts from Wakan Tanka, the Great Spirit. Such faith ensured that the baby born in March 1831 to chief Tatanka Iyotanka and his wife, Her Holy Door, would be warmly welcomed.

The birth occurred on the south side of the Grand River in present-day South Dakota near Many Caches, so called because it was where the Sioux often cached, or stored, winter food supplies in the soft clay banks above the river. The boy was to be his parents' only son, making him especially precious. He joined a six-year-old sister, Good Feather, and a few years later a second sister, Brown Shawl Woman, was born.

In the beginning, the baby was called Jumping Badger, although everyone in the tribe knew it was a temporary name. Sioux boys weren't given a permanent name until adolescence, when some worthy deed or unusual omen indicated what it should be. But the name Jumping Badger didn't stick. Even as a small child the boy was cautious. If he was given a bit of meat to chew, he held it in his chubby fingers and examined it carefully before putting it in his mouth. Soon, he was nicknamed Hunkeshni, or Slow.

The baby's cradleboard was suspended from the horn of his mother's saddle whenever the camp was moved, which happened often because the Sioux were hunters and traveled constantly in search of game. When he was older, Hunkeshni was put in a willow basket supported between two poles pulled behind his mother's pony. By the time he was three, Slow rode behind Her Holy Door, his arms wrapped about her waist, his legs curved snugly around the belly of her horse. That curve eventually became a permanent bow, causing the boy to seem shorter than he actually was.

Slow enjoyed all the games his friends played. *Che-hoo-hoo* was a wrestling game, and *hu-ta-na-cu-te* was similar to ice hockey. Sleds were made from buffalo ribs lashed together with leather thongs, and the hoop game—guiding a willow-stick hoop into an opponent's safe zone—became one of Slow's favorites. In summer there were pony races, and boys sharpened their skill with bow and arrow by killing small game such as squirrels, grouse, and rabbits. Slow was an expert marksman, and in spite of his nickname became an accomplished runner as well. Among Slow's friends during those happy, free-as-wind-across-the-grass days were Gall, Thunder Hawk, Crow King, and Strikes the Kettle. They would be with Slow many years later during what became the most famous Indian fight in Western history, the Battle of the Little Big Horn. Strikes the Kettle was especially loyal, and stood at his friend's side on the day of his death.

At the time of Slow's boyhood, the western Sioux, collectively known as the Lakota, were divided into seven council fires, or seven distinct tribes, which shared a common language and customs. They were the Oglalas (Scatters Their Own), the Brules (Burned Thighs), the Miniconjous (Planters by Water), the Two Kettles (Two Boilings), the Sans Arcs (Without Bows), the Hunkpapas (Campers at the Opening of the Circle), and the Sihasapa (Blackfeet). The latter should not be confused with the Blackfeet of the northwest.

Slow's family belonged to the Hunkpapas, one of the smaller groups, who camped and intermarried with the two other small tribes, the Sans Arcs and Blackfeet. Their homeland was the grassy plain west of the Missouri River below the mouth of the Muddy Water, the Yellowstone River. It was an area rich with game such as buffalo, deer, and elk, and was crisscrossed with streams and rivers that furnished ample water and fish like trout and bass. Groves of pine, cottonwood, and willow were scattered throughout the region, supplying the necessary fuel and shelter to survive through hard prairie winters.

Slow's family was wealthy by Sioux standards, wealth being counted mostly in horses. When he was a grown man, Slow proudly recalled that his father "was very rich, and owned a great many ponies in four colors." The boy's people had an attitude about wealth that was unique to Indian culture: It was not meant to be hoarded. Greed and personal acquisitiveness were not honored. Rather, a wealthy man was expected to share what he had with others in the tribe. Four was a holy number to the Sioux, and the four virtues most admired, in order of their importance, were bravery, fortitude, generosity, and wisdom.

According to Sioux belief, "A man must take pity on orphans, the crippled and the old. If you have more than one of anything, you should give it away to help those persons." Even after he became a chief, the boy once called Slow was particularly admired by his people for the charity he practiced.

If wealth were counted in ponies, another animal exerted an even more powerful influence over the lives of the Lakota Sioux. The buffalo, which for more than a century had covered the western plains like a great brown blanket, provided all the essentials of life—food, shelter, and clothing. The staple of the Sioux diet was buffalo meat; the hide of the buffalo was used to make tipis, bedding, and even furniture. Clothing for men, women, and children was fashioned from its skin; its sinews and tendons were used to make thread, bowstrings, and bindings of every kind. Its blood was used for paint, its hooves to make glue, and its horns to make spoons, cups, and ornaments such as necklaces, bracelets, and earrings.

The movement of the buffalo herds dictated when Slow's people moved their camps, and whenever a large harvest of buffalo was taken the camp was filled with good-natured laughter and the fine smell of cooking meat. The women and girls spent days scraping hides with knives made of bone, then worked them until the skins were velvet-soft. Meat was hung on willow racks to dry in strips. Later, the strips were pounded into a paste, mixed with fallow, and called pemmican. It could be preserved and packed in *parfleches*, or leather bundles, when camp was moved again. At such times there was plenty of *wasna*, a favorite Sioux dish made of shredded buffalo meat mixed with wild berries and bone marrow. When buffalo herds were plentiful, life was good for the whole *tiyospaye*, or band; when they were scanty, everyone suffered equally.

Because the buffalo was so important to the Sioux in practical terms, it became a focus of their social and religious life as well. A young man could do nothing better in the eyes of his peers than prove himself as a hunter. Slow did so by the age of ten, when he killed his first buffalo calf.

Next to hunting, the primary activity in the life of Sioux men was waging war on their enemies, chief among whom were the Crows, or *Hohes*. The aim of war was threefold: to take a few scalps, capture horses, and count coup. *Coup* was a word the Sioux had borrowed from early French traders to describe one of their war customs, the aim of which was not to slay a foe but to demonstrate personal courage. It consisted simply of striking an enemy with a coup stick or other object—even one's hand— then crying out, "I have overcome this one!"

In the summer of 1845, when Slow was fourteen years old, having already proven he was a capable hunter, he sought a chance to prove himself in war. When a group of about twenty Sioux warriors, including Slow's father, set out in search of Crow scalps and ponies, they were greatly annoyed when Hunkeshni insisted on joining them.

Slow's parents urged their son not to be so headstrong, but he ignored their warnings. He was a sturdy boy, not overly tall for his age but powerfully built and confident of his abilities. So, mounted on a gray horse streaked with red, his body painted yellow, Slow rode away with the war party.

On the third day out, the Sioux warriors surprised a group of about a dozen Hohes along the banks of the Powder River, near the border of Crow country. In the melee that ensued, Slow struck one of the enemy, knocking him from his horse. One of the older Hunkpapas rode in and finished off the unlucky Hohe; only four Crows escaped the Sioux war party that day.

When the Hunkpapas returned to camp, Slow's father hosted a great feast for his son, as was customary to honor a boy who had entered manhood. During the festivities, his father gave away Slow's gray horse plus four others to needy members of the tribe.

The young man was covered with black paint, the color of victory, and a white eagle feather was tied upright in his hair, a sign that he had counted his first coup. His father presented him with a fine bay horse and a rawhide war shield painted red, green, blue, and brown. On the last day of his life, that shield was still in Slow's possession.

Then the mounted youth was led through the camp so he could be congratulated by every man, woman, and child. Most important, his father proved his admiration for his son by bestowing his own name on the boy—Tatanka Iyotanka, Sitting Bull. To avoid any confusion in the future, he adopted the name Jumping Bull for himself.

Tatanka Iyotanka ... Sitting Bull. The name carried with it an image of the animal that was sacred to the Sioux, calling to mind the reaction of a buffalo bull after it had been mortally wounded. The bull would settle back on its haunches, then turn, snorting, to face its attacker, its great dark head lowered, undefeated until its final breath.

Many years later, when historian Stanley Vestal interviewed several elderly Sioux warriors while preparing a biography of Sitting Bull, he asked what men Sitting Bull had admired as he was growing up. The question was met with silence. At last, one old man spoke up: "Sitting Bull did not imitate any *man*; he imitated the buffalo." He referred to the deep respect the Sioux held for the buffalo—a strong, stubborn animal that wasn't afraid of any enemy.

Thus did the boy named Slow pass into history on a joyous summer day in 1845 when he was fourteen years old. In his place was born a young man called Sitting Bull, who later inspired terror in the hearts of his foes by charging into battle with the cry: "*Tatanka Iyotanka, he miye!* Sitting Bull, I am he!" It was a name destined to be mentioned anytime that Indians or whites gathered to speak of the four virtues of the Sioux—bravery, fortitude, generosity, and wisdom.

2

YOUNG MAN FROM THE NORTH

I arrived in Minnesota in 1863, with two strong, bare hands...

JAMES McLAUGHLIN

*I*t is ironic that so much is known about Sitting Bull's boyhood—a Native American who spoke no English and left behind no records in his own hand—but so little about the early days of James McLaughlin, the man who would prove to be the Sioux chief's final adversary. In movies and novels, Indians often are portrayed as inscrutable, but from several points of view, James McLaughlin could be considered the more inscrutable of the two.

Although more than 30,000 pages of James McLaughlin's correspondence are preserved on microfilm at the Heritage Center in Bismarck, North Dakota, precious few of them pertain to his growing-up years. Whereas Sitting Bull left behind an elaborate oral history that was faithfully recorded by newspaper reporters, missionaries, and military archivists, McLaughlin was tight-lipped about personal matters and family affairs. Nevertheless, a persistent biographer can tease out a few bits of information from the jottings that exist.

McLaughlin described his earliest days in a brusque, nononsense manner in a single sentence in his autobiography, *My Friend, the Indian:* "Born in 1842, in the province of

PORTRAIT OF INDIAN AGENT JAMES McLAUGHLIN
TAKEN IN 1878

Ontario, of Irish and Scotch ancestry ... I arrived in Minnesota in 1863, with two strong, bare hands, and entered into an apprenticeship for a career among the Indians by becoming acquainted with many of them and of their mixed bloods at St. Paul, Mendota, Wabasha, Faribault, and other places in that frontier state."

Fortunately, McLaughlin's principal biographer, Father Louis Pfaller, a Benedictine monk from Assumption Abbey in Richardton, North Dakota, later was able to glean a few additional nuggets of information from the tiny notebooks that McLaughlin kept, as well as from his letters to relatives, friends, and government associates.

McLaughlin's father, Felix, was born in Northern Ireland on July 29, 1807. His mother, Mary Prince, was born at Gretna Green, Scotland, on May 8, 1806. As a child, Mary moved to Belfast, where later she met and fell in love with Felix McLaughlin. The couple were married on June 29, 1828, a month to the day before Felix's twenty-first birthday, and emigrated to Canada the very next morning. They settled in Roxborough township at the eastern end of the province of Ontario, near the town of Cornwall, directly across the St. Lawrence River from the border of New York state.

Ten children were born to the McLaughlins, beginning with Mary in August 1829 and ending with the birth of John twenty years later, in 1849. On February 12, 1842, the McLaughlins' seventh child, a boy, joined a brood that eventually included six girls and four boys. He was named James. His parents apparently believed that they had run out of suitable middle names, because they didn't give him one. For the rest of his life, McLaughlin had to fend off the wish of others to give him at least an initial—an H. or a J. or a B.—but he remained plain James to the end of his days.

In the year of McLaughlin's birth, far away on America's western plains, a Sioux boy named Hunkeshni was already eleven years old, and had gained honor in his tribe by killing his first buffalo. Nearly fifty years later, when both boys were long since grown to manhood, their paths would cross on the bleak prairie near Fort Yates in Dakota Territory, only a few miles from Grand River where Sitting Bull was born. The result would be dramatic, and even today remains a subject of controversy among historians.

James—not only did he not have a middle name, but it seems that he was never the sort of boy that others might call Jim or Jimmy—attended a country school in the tiny village of Avonmore, and graduated from eighth grade in 1857, at age fifteen. The family was devoutly Catholic, and church attendance was a regular habit that James maintained throughout his life. There was no high school in the village of Avonmore, so James was apprenticed to a blacksmith for a period of three years in the nearby larger town of Cornwall.

Blacksmithing was a worthy trade in a day when farm tools, wagon parts, and railway locomotives were crafted from iron, and it guaranteed that James would be able to make a proper living for himself. However, McLaughlin wasn't trained simply as a hammer-and-tong sort of blacksmith. He studied the basics of machinery, which included the mechanics of sawmills and gristmills. In order to have succeeded as well as he did later in life, he must also have become a skilled reader and writer, because his penmanship and grasp of grammar were far superior to what would have been expected from an ordinary eighth-grade graduate in that day.

Forty years after his apprenticeship, McLaughlin commented about his blacksmith training in a letter to a superintendent of Indian schools: "The blacksmith's trade, to become a first class mechanic, requires time ... being only acquired after long practice and a determination to master the trade. Iron workers, very different from wood workers, have no patterns or forms to follow or guide them, but must depend upon the trueness of the eye in turning out their work." That training did more than make young James a good blacksmith; it made him a shrewd observer of the world around him.

At age eighteen, after his apprenticeship was completed, McLaughlin traveled and worked throughout the provinces of Ontario and Quebec but found nothing that suited him on a permanent basis. He had a strong belief in his own abilities, however, which was matched by a sense of adventure, and he turned his eyes to the southwest.

In the 1860s young men in Canada were talking not about the opportunities in the Canadian provinces but about the ones south of the border. The fast-growing, exciting twin towns of Minneapolis and St. Paul, along the Mississippi River in Minnesota, which had become the thirty-second state in the American union in 1858, beckoned to many.

From early photographs, one can envision the sort of twenty-one-year-old fellow who descended from the train in St. Paul on April 13, 1863. One early commentator described young James McLaughlin as "very tall," but information in government archives indicates that he was actually just a bit more that 5 feet 6 (168 cm) in height, and much inclined toward the thin side. He dressed nattily, his thick hair was jet black, his beard well-trimmed, and his glance had a piercing intensity that set him apart. No doubt he made a favorable impression on those he met on that spring day.

Blacksmiths were in demand in such a bustling state, and James quickly found work. James had been a devout churchgoer at home and probably joined a church soon after his arrival in Minnesota. Perhaps that's where he first became acquainted with Mrs. Joseph Buisson, a part-Indian widow of almost sixty years, who had been married to a well-respected white Minnesotan. In due time, the widow introduced James to one of her daughters, a pretty, petite, dark-eyed girl named Marie Louise, who had been born the same year as James. On January 29, 1864, within a few months of their meeting, the couple were married.

Marie Louise was no ordinary girl, and her entry into James's life was destined to shape his career and his place in American history in a way that neither of them could have foreseen. Marie's grandmother, Istagiwin, or Brown Eyes, was a member of the Mdewakanton Sioux tribe. In 1796 she married a Scottish fur trader, Duncan Graham, who had emigrated to America to work for the Hudson's Bay Company and later the American Fur Company. One of her five children, a daughter named Mary, became the wife of Captain Joseph Buisson, a Mississippi riverboat captain and trader. Mary, in turn, became the mother of Marie Louise on December 8, 1842.

One of seven children, Marie learned the Sioux language and customs from her half-Indian mother. At age fourteen she was sent to a Catholic convent at Prairie de Chien, Wisconsin. There, she was educated in the religious and cultural customs of whites, as were her sisters Harriet and Mary Jane. Three of her brothers became riverboat captains, like their father.

Marie's mother often spoke of being homesick for the land of her forebears, which was located near a certain mysterious lake in what was then called Dakota Territory. The Sioux name for the place was Minnewaukon, meaning "the lake where spirits dwell," which had been mistakenly translated by whites as "Devil's Lake."

James McLaughlin could not have suspected it was a place that would play a pivotal role in his own life. His wife's unique background would profoundly determine the opportunities that were presented to her husband. The life choices made by the young Canadian, stemming in large measure from the connections that Marie Buisson brought to their marriage, would make him a successful blacksmith as well as the best known—and sometimes most controversial—Indian agent in the United States.

3

BECOMING
AN
OLDER
BROTHER

*J was still in my
mother's insides
when J began to study
all about my people....*
SITTING BULL

Sitting Bull had proved his courage in battle when he counted coup on a Crow enemy when he was only fourteen years old. Then, in 1846, when he was fifteen, he was struck in the foot during a skirmish with twenty Flathead Indians north of the Yellowstone River, further enhancing his reputation as a warrior. When the Sioux returned to camp, another celebration was held. This time, a red feather was added to the white one that Sitting Bull wore upright in his hair, indicating he had been wounded in battle.

Success in war meant a young man was eligible to join an *akicita*, or a secret warrior society. The most prestigious of such societies among the Sioux were the Strong Hearts, and after joining it Sitting Bull first became a bonnet wearer, then a sash bearer. Sash bearers went into battle with a stake and rope, staked themselves to the ground, and were expected to remain on the field until cut loose by a comrade or killed. The headdress worn by members of the Strong Hearts consisted of a buffalo-horn cap decorated with a flowing tail of eagle feathers.

Within that society was a smaller, even more select group called the Midnight Strong Hearts, which Sitting Bull was invited to join. Among the other members were Gall and Crow King, good friends from his boyhood. Throughout these years Sitting Bull was especially noted for his daring horsemanship and took pride in owning fast ponies. He became expert at flattening himself against one side or the other of his mount, thereby presenting a hard-to-hit target to an enemy.

As Sitting Bull grew to full maturity, he attained the physique that would make him such a compelling presence. His head was large, his shoulders broad, his torso thick and barrel-like. He was slightly less than 6 feet (183 cm) tall but seemed shorter because of his bowed legs. He wore his hair braided on one side but let it fall loose on the other, and painted the center part of his scalp dark red. His eyes were piercing and shrewd; his mouth was a wide, thin slash in his face. He was imposing indeed, and all who met him did not quickly forget him.

In 1851, when he was twenty years old, Sitting Bull was married for the first time. His bride was a girl named Pretty Door (some historians contend that she was called Light Hair). The site of the marriage was at a camp along the Powder River, and afterward the pair left on a hunting trip. As the newlyweds traveled across the prairie, Sitting Bull killed two buffalo and an antelope, so the couple made camp in a thick grove of cotton-woods. Pretty Door set about skinning the animals and slicing the meat in strips to dry. According to an account that Sitting Bull gave later, their tranquility was disturbed by a Crow warrior, whom Sitting Bull swiftly wounded with an arrow. Worried that other Hohes might be lurking nearby, the couple packed up and hastened back to the larger Sioux camp.

In 1856, as a man of twenty-five, Sitting Bull performed his first dance in honor of Wi, the sun. Sun Dances usually were performed once a year, in the Moon of Chokecherries—June—and lasted twelve days. During the first four days, some of the

SITTING BULL'S ADOPTED SON ONE BULL, SON OF
SITTING BULL'S SISTER GOOD FEATHER

ceremonies concerned the chastity and fertility of the women of the tribe; during the second four days instructions were given to the men who had announced that they wished to perform the Sun Dance.

During the final four days, a dance circle was made, a dance pole was raised, and the dancing commenced. Wooden skewers were inserted through a dancer's skin, then beneath the chest or back muscles. The participant was suspended from the dance pole by rawhide thongs, where he remained until his flesh tore, releasing him from his ordeal. The ritual seems like torture—and it certainly must have been—but participants transcended their pain by achieving a trancelike state. Sitting Bull danced several times during his life, and a nephew, White Bull, remembered that his uncle's body bore deep scars on the back, chest, and arms.

In 1857, Pretty Door gave birth to Sitting Bull's first son, but died soon after. When the boy was four years old, he died as well. To replace his lost son, Sitting Bull adopted One Bull, the son of his sister Good Feather, and raised him as his own.

That year was marked by two other important events in Sitting Bull's life. As the result of his success in war, his close friends Gall, Black Bird, Brave Thunder, and Strikes the Kettle nominated him to become a war chief. Sometime later, his name was put before a gathering of warriors near his birthplace at Grand River, who approved his nomination to become a tribal chief, a position beyond even that of war chief. When the entire tribe gave their approval, Sitting Bull, at age twenty-six, had reached the top of the Hunkpapa warrior hierarchy.

The Crows and Lakotas had always been each other's favorite targets, and women and children of the enemy often were not spared in battle. One day when Sitting Bull and his companions came across the camp of a family of five—a Crow warrior, his wife, and their three children—four of the group were swiftly slain. The oldest child, a stocky lad of twelve, witnessed the slaughter of his kin, and when the Hunkpapa warriors turned on him, he must have believed his own time had come. He did not cry for mercy but turned to the one man among the enemy whose face seemed to reflect pity. He addressed Sitting Bull simply as "older brother."

Sitting Bull, who had no brothers, was stirred by the boy's words. "Let him live," he told his companions. "I have no brother. I take him as my brother." There were noisy objections, but Sitting Bull prevailed and took the boy into his tipi. He was clothed, his face was painted, and a feast was held in honor of the fact that he would be known henceforth as Sitting Bull's brother. When the boy's Crow relatives discovered what had happened, they tried to arrange his release. The boy declined. Because of his refusal, he was sometimes called Stays Back. He became a brave warrior and remained loyal to Sitting Bull until the final day of their lives, when they faced death side by side.

In yet another fight with the Crows at an encampment on the Cannonball River near Rainy Butte, an important chapter in Sitting Bull's life came to a close. The Hunkpapas were attacked by a war party of fifty Crows, and during the fracas—so violent that it resulted in the death of six good war ponies due to overheating—Jumping Bull, Sitting Bull's father, was killed. Sitting Bull ran down his father's attacker, slew him, and hacked his body to pieces in a fit of grief. Then several Crow women and children were captured and taken back to the Hunkpapa camp, where they were to be killed the following day.

But when morning came, Sitting Bull's bitterness had softened. "Treat them well and let them live," he told his people. "My father was a man, and death is his." It was then that his newly adopted son, Stays Back, became formally known by the name Jumping Bull, in honor of Sitting Bull's father. Later, the captured Crow women and children were given horses and told to return to their people.

Sitting Bull had become a successful hunter and warrior, but to be considered a *wichasha wakan* (wichasha meant "man"; wakan meant "holy"), had long been one of his private goals. "I was still in my mother's insides when I began to study all about my people," Sitting Bull once told a reporter from the *New York Herald*. "I studied there, in the womb, about many things. I studied about the smallpox, that was killing my people—the great sickness that was killing the women and children."

Rather than look outward, a Sioux male who wanted to become a holy man looked inward and learned how to interpret dreams, to have visions, and acquired an ability to prophesy the future. For the Sioux the whole world was a church, and all living creatures—from the largest buffalo to the smallest mouse, including all inanimate objects such as rocks, trees, rivers, and clouds—were sacred. From them, it was believed that a man could gain wisdom and strength.

For many Sioux youth, the road to becoming a *wichasha wakan* began in adolescence, with the pursuit of a vision. A boy went out alone to the hills or the plains, without food or water, and fasted until a vision came to him. Dreams and visions usually were private matters that weren't openly discussed, but according to Robert Higheagle, Sitting Bull must have had one of the most important kind, a dream about a thunderbird. Higheagle recalled that Sitting Bull had painted lightning streaks on his face, the mark of a person who had experienced such a dream.

Another bird—the common prairie meadowlark, much smaller and hardly mythic—became especially meaningful to Sitting Bull. A story was told by One Bull about how his uncle once tended a wounded meadowlark that in gratitude offered him many words of advice. Sitting Bull then told his companions that this particular bird could impart wisdom to any Sioux who was patient enough to listen. Toward the end of his life, Sitting Bull received a second message from a meadowlark. On that occasion, the bird warned him of the fate awaiting him at the hands of his own people.

The boy once called Slow would need all of his skills as a hunter, warrior, and holy man in order to deal with an enemy far more dangerous than the Crows. That enemy was the *wasichus*, the men with pale faces, who were appearing in ever-greater numbers in Indian country. At the time of Sitting Bull's birth in 1831, the white population of the United States was approximately 11 million; 2 million were nonwhites. Only 3,000 Hunkpapa Sioux were counted among the 2 million. By the middle of the century, the white population of the United States numbered more than 23 million, and the demand for territory to settle became intense. East of the Mississippi River, some Indian tribes had already been driven off their ancestral lands and forced to live as prisoners on reservations.

However, such numbers or events were unknown to the Hunkpapa. The Sioux were yet unaware of the danger that lay ahead. They looked about their vast domain and observed that all was as it should be: There were still plenty of buffalo; the prairies were free and unfenced; life was as it had always been. In twenty-six short years, from 1851 until 1877, all that would change.

AN EARLY 1870S VIEW OF ST. PAUL, MINNESOTA

4

THE LAKE WHERE SPIRITS DWELL

*I have a very good double
rig for such a trip,
with an extra saddle pony....*

JAMES McLAUGHLIN

Six months after his marriage to Marie Buisson, James McLaughlin moved his bride to a home in the village of Owatonna in southern Minnesota, an area of rolling countryside dotted with small homesteads. On November 9, 1864, the day after Lincoln's reelection, a daughter Mary was born, only to die in infancy. The arrival of a second daughter, Clara, in January 1866, cheered the young parents, but she died before her second birthday.

In Owatonna, McLaughlin applied for U.S. citizenship and after four years moved to the village of Wabasha, along the banks of the Mississippi, where Marie had been born. The village was named after her great-grandfather, Chief Wabasha, and because it was located conveniently downriver from St. Paul (population 20,000) and Minneapolis (population 13,000), James hoped the booming activity of the twin cities would create a steady trade.

James quickly formed a new partnership with John Hunter. Their motto, "We do all kinds of Blacksmithing with neatness and dispatch," didn't generate a flood of business.

Desperate to provide for his wife and the healthy baby boy who had been born in January 1868, McLaughlin finally took a job as a traveling salesman. The new baby was christened James Harry, and was called Harry by his family.

McLaughlin traveled as far as Iowa, Kansas, and Missouri, selling jewelry, watches, tools, and kitchen utensils. Rural folk had no stores nearby in those days, and McLaughlin surprised himself by doing very well. But the life of a traveling salesman meant that he was separated from Marie, so when he went on the road again in 1869 he took his wife and year-old son with him. Soon, McLaughlin was able to buy a better team and a brand-new wagon.

He still did smithing, however, and when the family returned to Minnesota in 1870, James resumed his trade again. The year was notable for another event: McLaughlin made a brief comment to himself in one of his many small notebooks: "Mother died at 20 minutes past 10 o'ck on Friday, AM August 5, 1870." It was in keeping with James's reticent nature that he made no further remark regarding how he felt about the loss. By contrast, a few years earlier, far away near a place called Rainy Butte, a man named Sitting Bull had reacted with murderous rage to the death of his parent.

Earning an adequate income continued to be difficult, and to supplement his blacksmith's wages McLaughlin hauled water for neighbors, clerked in local stores, and added carpentry to his skills. Finally, he applied for another job as a salesman, this time with a New York firm. He postponed accepting the position, however, because of the birth, in November 1870, of Imelda, the only one of the McLaughlins' daughters to live to adulthood. The delay in taking the new job would change the course of her father's life.

Two months after Imelda's birth, McLaughlin learned from his wife's uncle, Alexander Faribault, a purchasing agent at Fort Snelling, that Major William Forbes had recently been appointed the agent for the U.S. government's new Indian reservation at Devil's Lake in Dakota Territory—the same Devil's Lake that Marie's mother had spoken about with such nostalgia—and was looking for men to accompany him.

Faribault urged James to apply. With two children and a wife, twenty-nine-year-old McLaughlin realized that he needed to look to the future. He knew what such a position could mean: As a government employee, he would finally have a regular income. Therefore, early in 1871, he wrote directly to Major Forbes:

"I am a blacksmith by trade. Can do anything in that line," he stated in his typical, no-nonsense way. "I have a fair knowledge of most kinds of business. If you should have anything in that line ... or need any person to assist in trading with or supplying the Indians & have not already [got] another person, I would like to go with you. References given if required. P.S. I have a very good double rig for such a trip, with an extra saddle pony."

Later, McLaughlin discovered that he had much in common with the man who became his boss. Both men had married granddaughters of the Scottish fur trader Duncan Graham. Forbes, like McLaughlin, also had emigrated from Canada, was a devout Catholic, and was of Scotch-Irish ancestry as well. He had arrived in Minnesota thirty years earlier and worked as a clerk for John Jacob Astor's famous American Fur Company. He became fluent in the Sioux language, and built up a relationship of trust with Indians who came to trade.

However, the Great Sioux Uprising of 1862, in which Forbes played a role, had turned whites and Sioux against each other and destroyed Astor's fur trade. Forbes then volunteered for duty with a Minnesota detachment in the Civil War, where he attained the rank of major.

When Forbes returned to Minnesota in 1866, then a man in his fifties, his health and spirit seemed broken. General Henry

H. Sibley, who was to become Minnesota's first governor, knew of Forbes's previous good relationship with the Sioux and urged him to apply for the position as Indian agent at the newly created reservation at Devil's Lake, which had come into being as the result of President Ulysses S. Grant's "Peace Plan." It was more than helpful that Forbes's oldest daughter was married to Captain John Patterson, the post commander at Fort Totten, near the reservation.

The Indians who were to occupy the reservation had told officials through their chief, Tio Waste (Little Fish), that they didn't want a stranger as their agent but would be willing to accept a man such as Forbes, whom they remembered well from his days as a trader with the American Fur Company. Forbes then took Sibley's advice, got the job, and quickly let it be known that he wanted to develop a staff to take with him to Fort Totten, located several miles from Devil's Lake. The fort, about 70 miles (112 km) south of the Canadian border, had been built in 1867 to provide protection for settlers traveling overland from Minnesota to Montana Territory, and would serve as an initial base of operations for the new agency. When Forbes received McLaughlin's letter, it must have seemed like a perfect chance to hire exactly the sort of man he was looking for.

When McLaughlin got word in March 1871 that Forbes had accepted his application, he hastily tidied up his affairs in Minnesota and prepared to enter the Department of Indian Affairs. His motives upon entering government service were practical: He needed a job, applied for one, and got it. It paid a mere $720 per year, or $60 a month, but the income would be steady and there was the lure of advancement.

Forbes immediately put McLaughlin in charge of buying supplies such as food, clothing, and farm tools to be given to the Indians, then of transporting such items out to the new reservation. James apparently imagined that because he had married into a part-Indian family he was well prepared for the job that lay ahead. Later, he admitted in his autobiography, "I see now that I was not nearly so well equipped for life among the Indians as I thought I was when I mounted a horse and navigated a bull-train of twenty yoke of cattle and ten wagons out through the streets of St. Paul in the early morning of July 1, 1871."

The journey took a month, and must have been a challenge for Marie, with two small children to manage. In his cryptic manner, McLaughlin recorded the kind of reception he got from the 700 Indians at the reservation: "I was welcomed in such a fashion as might be expected by Indians who did not know what [to expect] from the new institution. They were not exactly cordial."

The Indians' lack of enthusiasm was understandable. For more than a year, they had been without adequate food or clothing. Colonel Phillipe Régis de Trobriand, commander of the Middle District of Dakota Territory, strongly denounced the conditions he found at the site in 1868. The hundreds of Indians gathered around Fort Totten lived "like dogs from the scraps of the garrison kitchen. In the winter they are more numerous, attracted by the hope that provisions will be distributed ... they live from hand to mouth and from day to day." Often, the Indians had to kill their horses for food.

The only dwellings at the reservation were a few decaying buildings once occupied by soldiers from the fort. Marie settled in one of them with her children. McLaughlin organized some of the Indians into woodcutting parties in the nearby woods, and by November 1871 they had collected enough logs to build two sound buildings. The Indians themselves continued to live in their buffalo-hide tipis as they had in times past. Before activities could get into high gear, disaster struck: Four days before Thanksgiving, both the carpentry shop and blacksmith shop burned to the ground. Fortunately, the smithing equipment was salvaged.

Indians were put to work harvesting the corn, potatoes, and turnips that Forbes had urged them to plant earlier in the year.

When Forbes and McLaughlin returned to St. Paul to buy winter supplies, Forbes purchased a set of gunmaker's tools. He had been successful duck hunting around Devil's Lake, and considered that guns would help the Indians to supplement their meager food supply. With a blacksmith on his staff, he was certain that the guns could be properly maintained.

But McLaughlin turned out to be much more than a blacksmith. Forbes's age and Civil War experiences had left him with a variety of health problems, and he was grateful for his energetic young employee's eagerness to handle all the necessary outdoor work.

It didn't take Forbes long to discover that McLaughlin also had a deep interest in what he himself was committed to: giving the Indians an education beyond teaching them how to hill potatoes and cultivate corn. The Indians had much to learn. McLaughlin noted that when they came to the agency for rations, they gladly accepted the sacks of flour that were distributed—then emptied the contents onto the ground so the sacking material could be more quickly made into clothing.

It's unlikely that James McLaughlin, not yet thirty years old, guessed in the autumn of 1871 that he was embarking upon a life among the Indians that would last until the day of his death fifty-two years later in Washington, D.C. It was a career that would bring him fame and honor. It also brought infamy—all of it connected with a man he had yet to meet—Tatanka Iyotanka, or Sitting Bull.

5

INDIANS MUST STAND ASIDE

...we wish you to stop the whites from traveling through our country, and if you do not stop them, we will.

HUNKPAPA CHIEFS

In the first third of the 1800s, most of the *wasichus* known to Sitting Bull and other Sioux were traders like those at Fort Pierre. The fort, originally built in 1832 by the American Fur Company, was located on the west bank of the Missouri River, near the point where the Bad River emptied into it in the present state of South Dakota. The Indians called it "the place of wornout fences," because the stockade walls resembled a broken-down fence.

The traders were mostly French Canadianieskas or mixed bloods, men of mixed Indian and French Canadian heritage. They were a rough bunch—coarse-mannered and heavy drinkers—who didn't make a good impression on the Sioux or arouse any special anxiety. In fact, the Plains tribes soon got accustomed to bartering goods with *wasichus* at the string of forts up and down the Missouri—Fort Clark, Fort Union, Fort Berthold, as well as Fort Pierre. They traded for items that made life easier—for example, metal tools that could be used in place of bone knives and awls; iron cooking utensils to replace clay pots and basketware; and most important, guns and ammuni-

HER HOLY DOOR, SITTING BULL'S MOTHER; SITTING BULL; AND HIS
OLDEST DAUGHTER, MANY HORSES, IN A PORTRAIT DATED 1883

tion to be used instead of bows and arrows. The Sioux had learned that rifles were of great advantage on a buffalo hunt.

There was a risk in lingering too long around places such as Fort Pierre, however. Whiskey was easily available; diseases such as smallpox, measles, and cholera were prevalent; and the chastity of Indian women wasn't respected by the whites. In addition, the Sioux didn't always get along well with some of the other tribes who came to trade—the Arikaras, for instance, as well as their despised enemies, the Crows.

By midcentury, neither the Lakota Sioux as a group nor Sitting Bull as an individual perceived that the whites were developing an agenda: to settle the western plains and even beyond, all the way to the Shining Water, the Pacific Ocean. It wasn't long after Lewis and Clark returned from their fact-finding mission in 1805, undertaken at the behest of President Thomas Jefferson to find an all-water passage to the Pacific, that statesmen in Washington conceived of a policy they called Manifest Destiny. That policy became an attractive means of satisfying an increasing demand for land as immigration from Europe continued, a demand that was matched by a decreasing amount of land available for settlement east of the Mississippi. Tribes such as the Chesapeake, Potomac, Pequot, Montauk, Mohawk, and Seneca already had been driven off their homelands.

Manifest Destiny held that it was the duty—perhaps even a God-given right—of white settlers to acquire all lands beyond the Mississippi. It was Jefferson's dream, and later presidents fully upheld it. The fact that in the eastern United States, settlement by whites frequently meant that Indians had to be forcibly removed or resettled on parcels of land designated by white men in Washington was not regarded as an ethical problem.

For example, on May 28, 1830, President Andrew Jackson signed the Indian Removal Act, designed to sweep the Cherokees from their rich farmland in the trans-Mississippi area so it could be appropriated by whites. As a result, General

Winfield Scott rounded up the hapless Cherokees in the autumn of 1838 and marched them along what came to be called the *nunna da ult sun yo*, or the "trail of tears," to a new home on western reservations. Winter came on and the Cherokees were poorly dressed and badly fed; one out of four died before they reached their destination in Arkansas and Oklahoma.

The victorious conclusion of the Mexican-American War in 1848 meant that a national policy regarding the western territories could be developed in earnest. The U.S. government turned its full attention to the Plains. Only twenty years later, an editorial in the *Cheyenne Daily Leader*, confidently summed up what Manifest Destiny really meant:

"The rich and beautiful valleys of Wyoming are destined for the occupancy and sustenance of the Anglo-Saxon race.... Indians must stand aside or be overwhelmed by the ever increasing tide of immigration [which has] pronounced the doom of extinction upon the red men of America."

Of course, neither Sitting Bull nor other chiefs of the seven council fires knew anything about what the whites called Manifest Destiny. Therefore, when the government called for a "peace treaty" meeting with the Plains tribes in September 1851, to be held at Fort Laramie along the North Platte River, the Sioux, Cheyenne, Arapaho, Shoshone, Crow, Assiniboine, Arikara, Mandan, and Hidatsa readily agreed to attend.

Sitting Bull must have listened attentively as boundaries were described by the white men who came from Washington for the discussions. The government wanted, among other things, the Indians (1) to cease to make war on each other, and (2) to agree to allow white settlers to proceed peacefully along the Platte River Road, used by those who were headed for the farmlands of Oregon and the goldfields of California.

In addition, the tribes would be required to confine themselves to particular territories. For the Sioux, that meant an area defined by the Heart, Missouri, White, and North Platte rivers. In return for agreeing to terms of the treaty, the Indian tribes would be guaranteed annuities of $50,000 a year for fifty years (a period that was later reduced to fifteen years by the U.S. Senate).

Not all the tribes signed the treaty. Sometimes, even members within a tribe were divided on whether to sign or not sign. The Hunkpapas were more unified than most in their opposition, because young men—such as Sitting Bull himself—weren't willing to give up making war on their traditional enemies, a custom that had deep cultural roots. Nor would they promise to desist from harassing a wagon train now and then if it suited them.

Matters came to a head for both Indians and whites on a hot August morning in 1854. An inexperienced West Point graduate, John Grattan, took thirty men and descended on the camp of Brule chief Conquering Bear. He demanded loudly that a brave named High Forehead, who had been accused of stealing a cow from a Mormon wagon train, be turned over to him immediately.

When Conquering Bear didn't hand over the culprit as speedily as Grattan thought he should, the young officer lost his temper and ordered his men to fire into the peaceful gathering with canon and rifles. Later reports suggested that Grattan had been drinking, accounting for his poor judgment. Conquering Bear was killed, whereupon the outraged Brules and their Oglala cousins turned on the soldiers and killed them all. Grattan, who once foolishly boasted he could whip the entire Sioux nation with twenty good soldiers, never had a chance, and the incident became famous as the Grattan Massacre.

In response, the government dispatched General William S. Harney to Indian country, and for the first time the Sioux witnessed their women and children being shot or taken captive by the whites. Later, Harney earned the name "Mad Bear" for his behavior in an attack on Chief Little Thunder's camp, and when a new treaty conference was held in March 1856, the presence of the Sioux was demanded, rather than requested. Among other things, this treaty declared that the chief of each tribe would henceforth be appointed by Harney himself. For the Hunkpapas, Harney said that Bear's Rib would be considered their official spokesman.

The decision astonished the Sioux. How foolish of a white man to think he could dictate who would or would not be a chief for any tribe! A chief earned his position only after performing many brave deeds, not because some white man wrote his name on a piece of paper. Harney's treaty ultimately was ineffective, because the U.S. Senate didn't approve it; nevertheless, Bear's Rib took his position as a government chief seriously and worked earnestly for peace. In the spring of 1862, when a steamboat carried annuities to Fort Pierre, 3,000 Sioux gathered to receive their share. But Bear's Rib confided to the government agent, Samuel Latta, that not all members of his tribe approved of taking such annuities, that his life had been threatened as a result. Bear's Rib asked that no other goods be sent; just the same, on June 6, two Sans Arc braves carried out the warnings made against him, and shot Bear's Rib dead near the gates of Fort Pierre.

Six weeks later, ten Hunkpapa tribal chiefs—chosen by their own people, not by any white man—sent a letter to Pierre Garreau, the agent in charge of Fort Berthold. "We notified the Bear's Rib yearly not to receive your goods," the letter said. "He had no ears, so we gave him ears by killing him. We now say to you, bring us no more goods.... We also say to you that we wish you to stop the whites from traveling through our country, and if you do not stop them, we will. If your whites have no ears, we will give them ears."

When the Sioux continued to harass travelers and attacked a steamer headed up the Missouri to Fort Benton in Montana Territory, General Henry H. Sibley, who had crushed the Great Sioux Uprising in Minnesota in September 1862, was sent west to quell the upheavals along the Missouri. General Alfred Sully also was called into action, and thus began the Wars of the Plains, which lasted until the death of Sitting Bull himself in 1890.

Fort Rice had been one of Sitting Bull's favorite targets in his efforts to oust the whites from Indian country, but when the building of Fort Buford began along the future border between North Dakota and Montana in the summer of 1866, it aroused his wrath like none of the other forts. To the Sioux, this one represented the deepest penetration into their world, and they bitterly resented its presence. Fifteen short years later, in 1881, Fort Buford would play a melancholy role in Sitting Bull's life.

Another territorial insult came in 1864, when John Bozeman devised a shortcut to the Montana goldfields, soon named the Bozeman Trail, which cut through the heart of the Indians' favorite buffalo-hunting country. Three new forts were built along the gold miners' trail—Fort Reno, Fort Phil Kearney, and Fort C.F. Smith. Once upon a time, the Sioux had been unaware of the whites' agenda, but now their eyes were open. If the *wasichus* wanted war, the Sioux vowed to give them war.

Not all was war and politics, however. In 1865, after the death of his first wife, Pretty Door, Sitting Bull took two wives, a common practice among the Sioux. With Snow-on-Her, the elder, he had two daughters; by his younger wife, Red Woman, he had a son. In addition, his widowed mother, Her Holy Door, lived with him, as did his sister Good Feather and her son, One Bull, whom Sitting Bull had earlier adopted as his own. Jumping Bull, his adopted Crow brother, was included in the family as well.

Sitting Bull, now thirty-four years old, was nearly at the height of his power among the Sioux, and one of his most trusted advisors was his mother, Her Holy Door. He regularly sought her opinion in important matters. "You must be careful how you act in war," she counseled, pointing out that his large family would be devastated if anything happened to him. Sitting Bull, still as cautious as he had been in his cradleboard, took care to heed her advice.

MARIE McLAUGHLIN, WIFE OF JAMES, STRADDLED
TWO WORLDS – THAT OF HER INDIAN HERITAGE AND
THE WHITE WORLD SHE MARRIED INTO.

6

WE WERE
ALMOST FROZEN

*Mr. James McLaughlin ... is
general Overseer in every branch of
labor carried on at this Agency... it
would be impossible to replace him.*
MAJOR WM. FORBES

At Devil's Lake, Forbes put McLaughlin to work building log homes for Indian families to replace their traditional buffalo-hide tipis. He believed that living in dwellings that couldn't be picked up and moved at the whim of their owners was an essential part of subduing the Sioux.

It was an arduous task to first fell the trees, then saw the logs into the proper lengths by hand, so McLaughlin requested that equipment for a sawmill be ordered to facilitate the job. Forbes finally got permission to purchase what was needed, and was pleased with the fine work that McLaughlin turned out, which included not only homes for the Indians but also tables, chairs, and beds. Consequently, Forbes requested that James's salary be increased from $60 per month to $75. This additional money must have been welcome as James's family was growing—another son, Charles Cyprian, was born on August 22, 1872.

It was no easy matter to convert a formerly wandering, buffalo-hunting people—"the wildest of the prairie people," in Forbes's words—to a sedentary lifestyle. It became clear that some kind of leverage would have to be applied to keep the Indians from accepting handouts without performing certain duties in return. Therefore, Forbes declared, "No goods, provisions, groceries or other articles, except materials for the erection of houses, shall be issued to the Indians unless in payment of labor performed or produce delivered."

He devised a reward system whereby the Indians were induced to work more diligently at farming. In return for their labor, they would be given money to buy extra goods and supplies—all kinds of food, cooking utensils, and clothing. It seemed always necessary to prod them, however, because this way of life was not congenial to the Sioux temperament. Farming was considered "women's work"; doing the same thing day after day did not strike former warriors as a manly way to live.

Once, when Forbes and McLaughlin returned from a trip to St. Paul to buy supplies, they discovered that the Indians had done nothing in their absence. Disgusted, Forbes informed his wards that although he had returned to the reservation with plenty of new goods, they would "lay on the shelves until [the Indians] had earned money, or checks, by their labor to procure them.... You never saw such a revolution as I caused among them. Every man is now busy with his scythe, ax, or hoe," he reported to General Sibley. Nevertheless, Forbes had a sincere fondness for his charges, noting that "my Indians are good fellows, and I would hate to lose them." McLaughlin, too, would come to regard the Sioux as "my Indians" and sometimes as "my children."

Forbes, knowing that order must be maintained on the reservation but that a police force recruited from among the Indians themselves would be more respected by other Indians, deputized men whom he considered worthy. The policemen were called *ceska maza*, or "metal breasts," because of the badges they wore.

Once the Indians had been contained on reservations, the ultimate object of Grant's Peace Policy was to educate them so they would be able to live successfully in the white man's world. They not only must be taught manual skills such as farming, cattle raising, and carpentry, but also the basics of reading and writing. Such abilities would be necessary if they hoped to survive in a world where buffalo no longer provided the essentials of life.

In May 1873, when Congress appropriated $5,000 dollars for a reservation school, Forbes sent McLaughlin to St. Paul to buy building materials and hire brickmakers, bricklayers, and carpenters. James wasted no time getting a two-story, 40-by-60-foot (12-by-18-m) school building erected. Major Forbes reported that the Indians themselves were excited by the project, and in July 1873 a cornerstone was laid for what was named St. Michael's School. Two of Forbes's cousins belonged to the order of the Grey Nuns in Montreal. He appealed to them to send teachers and in 1874 four Sisters—including Sister Lajemmerais, a qualified nurse—agreed to come to the reservation to teach at a yearly salary of $150 each, plus room and board. The Sisters stressed that they would instruct girls and boys up to the age of twelve, but after that the boys must become the responsibility of male teachers.

The Grey Nuns arrived in Jamestown on October 28, 1874. It was a cold, sleety day, and they expected to be met by James McLaughlin. However, due to a misunderstanding about the date of their arrival, the disconcerted Sisters found themselves alone at the train depot. They were even more unnerved on not being able to find lodging in Jamestown.

Someone suggested they could stay at the nearby fort, but an officers' party had been planned for that evening, and Captain Patterson decided that the presence of four nuns would dampen the merry time the officers expected to have. The Sisters ended up huddling together in the railroad pump house, where they slept on straw with only horse blankets to protect them from the cold. It's easy to imagine that they might have felt they'd been foolish to have accepted an offer to teach at Devil's Lake.

Two days later, Forbes and McLaughlin arrived with horses and wagons and the long trip to the reservation was finally begun. In a journal kept by the nuns, Sister Allard described the first day of their journey: "... the deep snow and fierce wind [meant] we traveled only twelve miles. The horses were exhausted. We were almost frozen, especially Sr. Lajemmerais.... Mr. James McLaughlin, our driver, took off his fur coat and gave it to Sister. It was done with so much kindness that the favor was accepted."

Since the school itself was 7 miles (11 km) from agency headquarters, and inasmuch as the Sisters' residence was not yet habitable, the nuns were housed temporarily at McLaughlin's home. Another entry in the nuns' journal noted: "This gentleman really loved and was devoted to the Sisters [and his wife] received us with the greatest politeness and kindness." Marie McLaughlin had her hands full, because a third son, John Graham, had been added to the family on June 29, 1874.

The winter of the nuns' arrival turned out to be one of the worst in many years. Forbes observed that temperatures "averaging 25 below zero for five weeks [were] too severe for cattle even under shelter." The Grey Nuns found themselves ministering to so many Indians who were ill with whooping cough that finally Dr. James Shaw was called to help treat the 1,000 Sioux at Devil's Lake. Forbes himself, whose health hadn't been robust, became ill and often complained of dizziness. The doctor assured him it was probably "nervous frustration" that caused his symptoms.

On Christmas Eve of 1874, Forbes noted in a letter to General Sibley that only twelve Indian children were enrolled at St. Michael's. He blamed that fact on interference by the Sioux medicine men, whom he believed exerted a negative influence over the Indians. "But I will beat them, and soon will give you a glorious account of our progress," he promised.

Only two months later, enrollment had more than doubled, to twenty-nine students. Both Forbes and McLaughlin were pleased. But it wasn't necessarily the Indians' enthusiasm for education that prompted them to send their sons and daughters to St. Michael's; instead, they knew it was a place where their children would be properly fed.

The depth of Forbes's hostility toward medicine men was readily absorbed by young McLaughlin. "*I will beat them*," Forbes had said of the tribal medicine men, as if they were engaged in some sort of battle. Of course, Forbes's opinion was common for the time. Most whites had little regard for Indian customs or beliefs. It was assumed that the only way Indians could be rescued from the plight that faced them was if they adopted the ways of whites, which included learning manual skills, being taught to read and write, and perhaps most important of all, by becoming Christians.

When Forbes's four-year appointment came to a close he reapplied for the position, even though he continued to complain of dizziness and poor appetite. He was justifiably proud of what he had been able to accomplish at Devil's Lake, and was eager to continue his work. He wrote to the *St. Paul Pioneer Press* early in 1875: "There are now 102 families living in good houses ... my people have been comfortable, having had plenty of food, fuel, and clothing. In short, I do not think a more contented and happy people can be found."

Forbes didn't take all the credit himself. He realized that he had made a very wise choice in accepting young James McLaughlin's application four years earlier, and when he applied to the Commissioner of Indian Affairs for operating funds in 1875, the Major requested an increase in salary for the man who had become much more than a blacksmith, this time to $100 a month.

"He is general Overseer in every branch of labor carried on at this Agency," Forbes wrote. "He is conversant with all branches of mechanics necessary ... and works when required as a blacksmith. He also attends to running the mill, sawing, and making bricks, lime and such.... I am satisfied it would be impossible to replace him.... I have to acknowledge that I am indebted to him a good deal."

Forbes also noted that Mrs. McLaughlin was "an estimable woman," an able translator of the Indians' language (for which she was paid $400 a year), and "the right sort of influence among them." One historian, however, was not as charitable toward Marie McLaughlin. In his estimation, she had "a consuming and calculating ambition and little else. [She] strove constantly to rise above the 'accident' of her birth as part Indian, and to achieve what she regarded as her rightful social place among the exclusive coterie of officers' wives." The writer's bias was obvious: being part Indian, Marie McLaughlin ought to have known better than to consider herself equal to the white wives of the military officers at the agency.

Forbes's continuing poor health was noticed by visitors to Devil's Lake, and McLaughlin certainly was aware of it himself. Being a prudent man, he kept one eye on the future: He wisely made a copy of Forbes's praiseful letter to the Commissioner of Indian Affairs for his own file. In the event something happened to his superior, he knew he would need it as a recommendation in the event he applied for the position of agent himself.

7

ARE YOU WITH US?

The whites provoked the war...the cruel, unheard of and wholly unprovoked massacre at Sand Creek...shook all the veins which bind and support me.

SITTING BULL

$\mathcal{J}$n the autumn of 1864, Cheyenne chief Black Kettle moved his band to Fort Lyon in Colorado. The commander of the fort, Major Edward "Tall Chief" Wynkoop, was well liked by the Indians, who believed he would treat them kindly as cold weather came on and game became scarce. Not long after their arrival, however, Wynkoop—who had fallen into disfavor with military officials in both Colorado and Kansas because of his tolerant attitude toward Indians—was replaced by Major Scott J. Anthony.

Major Anthony led Black Kettle to believe that his people would be safe at Fort Lyon, and readily gave them permission to make a permanent camp 40 miles (64 km) from the fort, along the dry bed of Sand Creek. Until extra government food supplies could be ordered, Anthony also gave the Cheyennes permission to hunt buffalo in the area. The Indians were unaware that no sooner had they left the fort than Anthony informed his superiors that a large band of Indians were about to settle at Sand Creek, adding that he would keep them quiet until additional troops could be sent.

Colonel John M. Chivington, a former Methodist minister named by Governor Evans of Colorado as commander of the territorial volunteers, was sent in response to Anthony's message. A tall, barrel-chested man, he had no love for Indians. "Damn any man who sympathizes with Indians!" he once exclaimed to another officer. He considered it a white man's duty "to kill Indians, and believe it is right and honorable to use any means under God's heaven to kill Indians."

Early on the morning of November 29, 1864, Chivington, whose special interest previously had been organizing Sunday schools in gold-mining camps throughout the West, fell upon Black Kettle's sleeping camp with a force of 1,000 men. There were about 600 lodges in the Indian village; more than half were occupied by old men, women, and children because the hunters had been given Anthony's permission to go off to hunt buffalo.

When the alarm was sounded by some Indian women who had risen early, Black Kettle got up quickly. Believing that his people were safe, he tied an American flag and a white surrender flag to a pole and raised it high, calling out to the villagers that there was no need to panic. Nevertheless, the volunteers opened fire from two directions. A hundred families were slaughtered, mostly women and children. The Sand Creek Massacre was followed by scalpings and horrible mutilations of Indian women by the soldiers. Their brutal acts, which were explained partly by the volunteers' heavy drinking during the long night ride to Sand Creek, left a stain on American history that exists to the present day.

In the spring of 1865, when some of the Sand Creek survivors straggled northward—starving, with few ponies, wearing only the clothes on their backs—they were welcomed among their cousins, the Sioux. The Cheyennes told Sitting Bull what had happened, how White Antelope, an old man of seventy-five years, had been shot dead as he approached the soldiers with his hands raised, crying out in plain English, "Stop, stop!"

OFFICERS ROW AT FORT BUFORD

The Cheyennes vowed to Sitting Bull, who by this time had been a Sioux war chief for eight years, that they would never again trust the *wasichus*. "We were told that white men would not kill women and children, but now we have lost all faith in white men," said a Cheyenne chief. "We plan to strike the whites all along the Platte, and after that the settlements to the west," he vowed. "Are you with us?"

Sitting Bull had already taken a hard line against white invasion of Sioux lands. His position was supported by that of Tashunka Witko, or Crazy Horse, an Oglala chief several years younger than he but already a strong leader, who also believed the *wasichus* must be driven out of Indian country.

What the Indians probably didn't know, or couldn't appreciate at the time, was that a long, bloody battle the whites had been waging against each other—the Civil War—had finally ended on April 9, 1865, with the surrender of General Robert E. Lee at Appomattox, Virginia. The end of that war freed many soldiers for duty in the West to fight Indians. The Sioux couldn't have guessed that such a convergence of historical events would spell the doom of their old way of life.

Not all the chiefs were hardliners like Sitting Bull and Crazy Horse, however. By 1868, even widely admired warriors such as Red Cloud of the Oglalas began to talk of a peaceful settlement of disputes between Indians and whites. In addition, many Lakotas had become accustomed to the easy life that could be lived near the forts, and were called "stays-around-the-forts," or "friendlies." Only about one third of the Sioux sided with Sitting Bull and Crazy Horse, who were considered to be leaders of the war faction and were labeled "hostiles."

Young Bear's Rib, whose father had been appointed a chief by the whites only to be assassinated by his own people at Fort Pierre in 1862, became a spokesman for the peace faction. "We realize that the whites go wherever they want to, that nothing can stop them ... we can no more drive them away than we can a wall of solid rock," Bear's Rib said. Sitting Bull, however, had come to mistrust the whites even more than before, partly because of the growing presence of forts throughout Indian lands. He bitterly resented the fact that buffalo herds were being scattered, that large stands of timber were cut down to satisfy the demands of whites, and that there seemed to be no end to the long lines of settlers' wagons.

President Abraham Lincoln had signed the Homestead Act in 1862, and once the Civil War was over there was nothing to stem the tide of settlers who were eager for cheap land. By 1868, Indians saw emigration into their territories increase dramatically. Whites who wanted to start their lives over after the war turned their faces west, and were assisted by the extension of railroads like the Union Pacific and roads like the Santa Fe Trail and the Bozeman Trail, an emigrant road to the Montana gold fields.

It must have seemed to Indian eyes that the flood of *wasichus* would never stop. While Indians like young Bear's Rib continued to counsel for peace, Sitting Bull and Crazy Horse argued more fervently that a line had to be drawn to protect the remaining Indian lands. It soon became equally clear to men in Washington that something had to be done to settle the escalating violence between whites and Indians.

Another peace commission was convened in 1868 at Fort Laramie in present-day Wyoming. The Oglalas, led by chief Red Cloud, who had been victorious at the battles of Fort Phil Kearny and Fort C.F. Smith, agreed to attend. It was more difficult to persuade leaders such as Sitting Bull or Crazy Horse to participate, much less sign an agreement, so the U.S. government called on a Jesuit missionary, Father Pierre De Smet, to press its cause and make sure that all the chiefs came to the treaty meeting.

In May 1868, Sitting Bull's dramatic response to rumors of peace was to attack one of his favorite targets, the hated Fort

Buford, a foray that resulted in the death of two civilians. The Hunkpapas then moved on to Fort Stevenson, but finding the garrison alerted for trouble, they went on to Fort Totten, at Devil's Lake. Only six years later, a young blacksmith named James McLaughlin, newly associated with the Department of Indian Affairs, would arrive at "the lake where spirits dwell" to begin his career as an Indian agent.

Sitting Bull returned to his camp along the Yellowstone River only days before De Smet was due to arrive for his conference. The camp was large, numbering 600 lodges, and included other bands such as those led by Black Moon and Four Horns, Sitting Bull's uncle. Sitting Bull's old friend Gall was also present. Father De Smet was well known among the Sioux and held in high esteem, so on June 18, 1868, a greeting party was organized to welcome the priest. A translator accompanied De Smet, making it possible to record Sitting Bull's remarks.

"The whites provoked the war; their injustices, their indignities to our families, the cruel, unheard of and wholly unprovoked massacre at Fort Lyon [Sand Creek]... shook all the veins which bind and support me," Sitting Bull said. "I rose, tomahawk in hand, and I have done all the hurt to the whites that I could."

When the priest rose to speak to the gathering, he urged the Sioux to "bury all your bitterness toward the whites, forget the past, and accept the hand of peace which is extended to you." De Smet offered to leave his personal emblem of peace with the Sioux, a flag bearing an image of the Virgin Mary on it, surrounded by glittering stars, as a token of goodwill.

Sitting Bull reluctantly agreed to "remain hereafter a friend of the whites," yet the words were hardly out of his mouth before he reconsidered and added that he might have forgotten a few things. Yes, he would remain a friend of the whites, he repeated, but would never sell any part of his country. He demanded that whites stop cutting wood along the Missouri

River, and that all the forts be abandoned. Sitting Bull's words were cheered by his people, making it clear to De Smet that chances for peace weren't likely.

The peace commissioners waited impatiently for the Sioux to arrive at the treaty site on July 2, 1868, the date set for the signing of an agreement. The Sioux (it isn't documented that Sitting Bull was among them) didn't really understand what it meant to sign a treaty. For example, it became plain in the speech given by Gall, who had been sent by Sitting Bull to represent the Hunkpapas, that he didn't comprehend that the treaty had not taken into consideration the main Sioux grievances: that the forts must be abandoned, that whites must stop traveling through Indian lands, and that steamboats must cease plying the waters of the Missouri. Nevertheless, Gall was the first of the chiefs to "touch the pen."

Even some of the whites did not fully realize what the document contained. From the standpoint of the peace commission, the aim of the treaty was to establish the Great Sioux Reservation, which later became the states of North and South Dakota. An agency would be established; clothing and food would be issued to Indians for a period of thirty years; schools would be built to prepare the Indians to lead an agricultural life. The treaty also required that the signers give up all rights to occupy any land outside of the area designated by the reservation agreement, and that they would give up making war on each other.

Sitting Bull would never have agreed to such terms, nor, as Gall decided later when he reflected on it, did his signature bind him to do so either. Therefore, only two months later, the Hunkpapas boldly raided Fort Buford again, stole 250 head of cattle, and left three soldiers dead.

Sitting Bull's uncle, Four Horns, was the principal chief of the Hunkpapas and had been a Shirt Wearer since 1851. As he grew older and felt his powers waning, he realized that strong leadership was critical for all Lakotas at this time in their history. Four Horns decided to give up his leadership role and relinquish it to his nephew. Moreover, he proposed that Sitting Bull be made a supreme chief over all seven Sioux tribes.

Such elevation to power had never been considered necessary before; now the man and the moment seemed fated to meet. Sitting Bull was youthful and vigorous at thirty-eight; he had wide experience in war, in the hunt, in spiritual matters, and in tribal politics. Increasing encroachment by whites into Indian country demanded such a leader.

Four Horns energetically promoted his nephew's ascendancy to the new position over all the tribes. The Blackfeet, Miniconjous, Sans Arcs, and their cousins the Cheyennes agreed with Four Horns's plan. Some of the other nontreaty tribes were slower to accept Sitting Bull's role, but gradually rallied around him. Sitting Bull was supported by Black Moon and Crazy Horse, and together these Indian tribes became known as "hunting bands," because they rarely appeared around any agency. Instead, they continued to live off the land as had their fathers and forefathers.

Wooden Leg, a Cheyenne, summed up Sitting Bull's role: "There was only one who was considered as being above all the others. This was Sitting Bull. He was recognized as the one old man chief of all the camps combined." However, it meant that the Sioux were divided, because Red Cloud of the Oglalas and Spotted Tail of the Brules, the largest Lakota tribes, chose the reservation way of life for their people, believing it was the best hope for survival. To his dying day, Sitting Bull steadfastly maintained that it was not.

As Sitting Bull rose to a new position of power, James McLaughlin was about to take up life as a blacksmith on a newly established reservation at Devil's Lake. He and Sitting Bull had their own views on what was a proper course for the Sioux, views that were poles apart. Sitting Bull was determined to preserve the freedom his people had known for generations; McLaughlin knew the world was changing, that the Sioux would have to change with it. In ten years, the two men would meet for the first time at a place not far from where Tatanka Iyotanka had been born at Many Caches.

ORPHANED EARLY IN HER LIFE, EMMA CROW KING WAS
RAISED BY THE McLAUGHLINS.

8

DEATH AT
DEVIL'S LAKE

I will do my best to abolish…
all kinds of Superstitions
…medicine dances for feasts,
Sundances, and etc.…

JAMES McLAUGHLIN

*A*lthough Major Forbes assessed his progress at Devil's Lake in glowing terms in early 1875, by midyear he decided to apply for the position of Inspector of Agencies, a job that paid better, and, he hoped, had lighter responsibilities. In June he noted in his letter of application to General Sibley that matters at Devil's Lake were "in fine condition … especially as everything looks favorable for a good crop." He again referred to not feeling well.

One month later, it became obvious to James McLaughlin that the agent's health had taken a turn for the worse. The young overseer confessed to Forbes's relatives in Montreal: "I fear for his recovery. If anything should happen to him, there are many, very many who will miss him; however, while there is life there is hope." In this case, hope was tethered on a short rope. Forbes died suddenly on July 20, 1875.

Upon the death of his superior, McLaughlin as *de facto* head of the agency had as his first job to arrange the transportation of Forbes's body to St. Paul for burial. His second, self-appointed but equally urgent, task was to begin the process of securing the agent's position for himself.

Since the agency was under the jurisdiction of the Catholic Church, McLaughlin knew that his name must be put before the office of Catholic Missions in Washington, D.C., which would then submit his application to the Commissioner of Indian Affairs. The man to do that for him was Bishop Seidenbush, at the Vicariate of Northern Minnesota, whose headquarters were in St. Cloud. McLaughlin wasted no time getting in touch with him.

"I have the advantage of being born and raised a Catholic," he wrote on the very day of Forbes's death. "Accordingly, if ever agent, I will do my best to abolish polygamy & eradicate from my agency all kinds of Superstitions there existing, viz., *medicine dances for feasts*, *Sundances*, and *etc.*, for I know that polygamy & Supersitious practices are not only adverse to political, but also to Christian civilization, this last being the only true, real & efficacious civilization."

McLaughlin's clear and forceful declaration (the italics in the letter were his own) indicated a certain insensitivity to beliefs that were deeply held by the Sioux. Medicine dances, and the performance of the Sun Dance in particular, were integral to the Indians' way of celebrating their relationship to the world. To their way of thinking, the practice of polygamy (marriage to more than one woman at the same time) was not a libertine act, nor was it offensive to the Great Spirit. Rather, a man took more than one wife only if he were confident he could provide for her and any children they might have.

It could be said that McLaughlin exhibited a closed mind about what constituted a "true, real & efficacious civilization." Yet it must be remembered that he was a product of his time and culture. McLaughlin wasn't alone in believing that sacred Indian beliefs must be completely stamped out—they were often labeled "foolish" and "heathenish" by whites—and that Indians must fully adapt themselves to the white man's ways. McLaughlin earnestly believed that if the Indians were to be rescued from the perils awaiting them in a changing world—starvation and disease, to name the two most immediate ones—they would be best served by trading worn-out customs for the successful ones of white men.

McLaughlin, now thirty-three years old, with four years of sound experience behind him, collected many letters of recommendation, wherein men such as General Sibley, Lieutenant Colonel L.C. Hunt, the commander at Fort Totten, and Senator S.J. McMillan praised his abilities. Among his other attributes, the letter writers pointed out that McLaughlin was the first choice of the Indians themselves to take Major Forbes's place. Dr. James Shaw joined the chorus of supporters, noting that McLaughlin was industrious, honest, and in particular did not partake of alcohol, which frequently was a serious problem among Indian agents on other reservations.

After returning from Forbes's funeral in St. Paul, McLaughlin continued to administer the affairs of the agency—not a difficult task, since he had assumed many of these duties before Forbes's death—and settled down to wait for news from Washington. When no word came, James renewed his application for Forbes's job. Then a stunning blow fell. Officials announced that a total stranger had been named as the new superintendent of the Devil's Lake agency. In fact, he had been appointed on the very day that Bishop Seidenbush's letter promoting McLaughlin's candidacy had arrived in Washington.

To James McLaughlin's dismay, twenty-six-year-old Paul Beckwith, a native of St. Louis, arrived at Devil's Lake on September 10, 1875, to assume Major Forbes's duties. The fact that Beckwith's uncle was a good friend of General Charles Ewing, a commissioner on the Catholic Missions board that approved the appointment, no doubt contributed to the choice of such a young, inexperienced man.

Beckwith hadn't been at Devil's Lake long before he realized everyone was severely disappointed that McLaughlin hadn't been selected for the position. Due perhaps to nervousness or naiveté, one of Beckwith's first acts was to fire Frank Stone, a $35-a-month wagon maker at the agency, and replace him with his own brother-in-law, William Chard, at a salary of $60 per month. He requested permission to discharge the agency clerk, Jane Forbes, the deceased Major's daughter, whom he accused of falsifying agency records, hinting that she had done so at McLaughlin's bidding. In her place, he intended to hire his own wife, Martha, and increase the clerk's salary by 25 percent.

On the surface, McLaughlin maintained a steely calm. On the inside, he boiled with outrage. He called Beckwith "a Catholic for the occasion," pointing out to Bishop Seidenbush that the new agent's relatives on his wife's side of the family were all Protestants. McLaughlin declared that Beckwith intended to "work more for himself and his family than for the Indians." James soon learned through the grapevine that Beckwith had decided that to gain the confidence of the Indians he would need to discharge former employees of the agency and hire an entirely new staff loyal to him and no one else. As soon as warm weather arrived, he planned to discharge the Grey Nuns as well.

Beckwith might have been young and impulsive, but he wasn't a complete fool. He wrote to General Ewing, suggesting that his conflict with McLaughlin could be resolved if McLaughlin were sent farther south to become the agent at the Standing Rock reservation. He noted that the Indians there were an especially "wild set," and that McLaughlin had the sort of experience needed to handle them.

At the same time, Beckwith realized that McLaughlin had no intention of allowing himself to be transferred, and was determined to remain at Devil's Lake. As a result, Beckwith threatened that if he were forced to give up his position in favor of McLaughlin he would go "to the President ... and prevent any person connected with the Agency ever becoming agent." His message to McLaughlin was plain: If I can't have this job, neither can you.

In February 1876, Beckwith reported to the Commissioner of Indian Affairs that he hoped to be granted additional funds at the agency by reducing the number of employees. In particular, he believed that the position of overseer—the job that McLaughlin had held since 1871—ought to be abolished immediately. Beckwith pointed out that although he couldn't charge McLaughlin with any specific crime, he accused him of influencing "the Indians against my authority." He hinted that McLaughlin stocked his own home with flour, sugar, and pork that were intended for the Indians' use, and requested permission to "discharge him for the good of the service." To further solidify his own position, Beckwith decided that it also would be wise to remove Marie McLaughlin from her position as the agency interpreter and promptly did so.

In disgust, McLaughlin referred to the youthful Beckwith as "the boy," and the two men settled down to wage a war of words. Each dispatched a blizzard of letters to Washington in attempts to fortify his own candidacy. Finally—since Beckwith had, indeed, been officially appointed head of the agency—he decided to put an end to the matter with a single bold stroke. On April 2, 1876, he fired McLaughlin and gave him three days to remove himself, his wife, and his four children from the premises. McLaughlin responded by leaving immediately for St. Paul to plead his case in person. It would be three months before he returned.

The Indians, who had been silent witnesses to the power struggle between the two white men, declared they also would leave the reservation and wouldn't return until McLaughlin did. In small groups, they vanished across the prairie that surrounded Devil's Lake, leaving their crops untended, their log houses empty. This turn of events increased fears among the white settlers throughout the region, who believed that the Indians might revert to their old predatory habits of attacking farmsteads, stealing cattle, and wreaking other kinds of havoc.

For the next three weeks, McLaughlin traveled throughout Minnesota, building support for his candidacy. He vowed not to return to the Devil's Lake agency until he could go "clothed with authority to order Beckwith off as he did me." At last, under increasing pressure from Washington, which included General Ewing himself, Beckwith resigned on April 29. He agreed to vacate his office by July 1. In early May, McLaughlin heard that the U.S. Senate favored him for the position of superintendent. Belatedly, Beckwith admitted, "McLaughlin ... will make a good agent, and I am glad he is to fill the place. We both have been laboring under a mutual mistake."

On June 8, 1876, the Senate confirmed McLaughlin's appointment, and on the evening of July 2, he returned victoriously to Devil's Lake. Two days later, Beckwith departed, taking with him many of the agency's records and left food supplies depleted. McLaughlin quickly ordered new rations of sugar, flour, and coffee, and when word got out that Beckwith was gone, the Indians began to drift back from the countryside.

McLaughlin must have heaved a sigh of relief. He had successfully concluded a long, nerve-wracking battle to save his career. At last, he was officially the agent at the lake where spirits dwell. He hadn't had time to digest the news about a bloody confrontation that took place a few days earlier, on June 25, 1876, not far from a river called the Little Big Horn, out in Montana territory.

It, too, had ended successfully—in that case for two of the most famous Sioux chiefs in American history, Sitting Bull and Crazy Horse—and would be remembered as the Custer Massacre. The result of that debacle would have far-reaching consequences for both Indians and whites, and would bring James McLaughlin and Sitting Bull face to face at the very place that young Paul Beckwith had hoped to dispatch his adversary—at Standing Rock.

9

BLUECOATS FALLING INTO CAMP

*... save me and give me all
my wild game
animals ... so that my people
will have enough food this
winter ...*

SITTING BULL

In the Laramie Treaty of 1868, the Paha Sapa, or Black Hills, considered by the Sioux to be a sacred place where they could go to speak to their gods, were not viewed by the whites as having any particular commercial value. As a result, the Black Hills were included in the Great Sioux Reserve. The treaty, signed by President Ulysses S. Grant, promised that the Paha Sapa would be "set apart for the absolute and undisturbed use and occupation of the Indians ... [and] the United States now solemnly agrees that no persons ... shall ever be permitted to pass over, settle upon, or reside in the territory."

Such an agreement was reassuring to the Indians, but in 1872, only four short years after the treaty was signed, rumors began to circulate among the whites about vast stores of gold in the Black Hills. The Sioux themselves had long known there were gold deposits in the Paha Sapa, but were confident that the terms of the treaty would be honored.

Perhaps the Sioux, Cheyenne, and Arapaho ought to have known better. After all, the Bozeman Trail had been carved through the heart of Indian country so whites could reach the Montana goldfields, and the Platte River Road was used by

MAJOR GENERAL GEORGE ARMSTRONG CUSTER

goldseekers headed for California. The Indians underestimated the powerful attraction of gold for white men, who were willing to risk almost any danger to acquire the precious metal.

When Red Cloud of the Oglalas, one of the signers of the Laramie Treaty, complained to Grant about the appearance of whites in the Black Hills, the president assured him that he "would prevent all invasion of this country by intruders." Nevertheless, in the summer of 1874, 1,000 bluecoated soldiers from the Seventh Cavalry under the command of General George Armstrong Custer descended on the Paha Sapa. Custer stayed for two months, and had several newspapermen with him, along with naturalist George Bird Grinnell. In her memoirs, Martha Jane Canary, better known as Calamity Jane, claimed to have been included in the mission, too.

The Sioux knew the yellow-haired general all too well, and had ample reason to despise him. It was Custer who had fallen upon Black Kettle's camp along the Washita River early on the foggy morning of November 27, 1868. The Cheyenne chief had survived Sand Creek four years earlier, but fate was not as kind this time. When Black Kettle, his wife riding double behind him, was approached by the soldiers, he raised his hand in a sign of peace, but he was shot off his horse. Seconds later his wife also was killed. In addition to killing 103 Cheyennes and taking 53 women and children captive, Custer—called Pehin Hanska, or Long Hair, by the Sioux—fired into the tribe's pony herd, slaughtering several hundred animals.

When Custer announced on July 30 that gold was indeed present in great quantities in the Black Hills, the news was duly reported by the press. "From the grass roots down it was 'pay dirt'," proclaimed a Chicago newspaper. Thousands of gold-hungry whites descended like locusts on the sacred Paha Sapa. Custer was indifferent rather than insulted when he heard the Indians called him a thief, and had named the route he followed into the Black Hills the "Thieves' Road."

Custer advised the War Department in September 1874 that the Indians "neither occupy nor make use of the Black Hills," and the area ought to be immediately thrown open to white settlement. "I shall recommend extinguishment of Indian title at the earliest moment practicable for military purposes," he added.

Sitting Bull was incensed by the activity of the goldseekers. "We want no white men here," he insisted. "If the white men try to take [the Black Hills] I will fight them." But even more than Sitting Bull, it was young Tashunka Witko, or Crazy Horse, who most detested the presence of the whites. Ten years younger than Sitting Bull, he had been born in the Black Hills in the Moon of Ripe Plums—August—in 1841, which made the place even more special to him than to other Sioux. His hatred of goldseekers was increased by the fact that a few years earlier his younger brother, Little Hawk, had been killed by gold miners along the Yellowstone River.

A certain segment of American public opinion, centered mostly in the East, strongly objected to the intrusion of whites into the Black Hills. Partly in deference to such objections, a new treaty conference was called in September 1875, to review the status of the Black Hills, during which the government made an offer to buy the land from the Indians. When word of the plan was relayed to Sitting Bull, he stooped to take a pinch of dust from the ground. "I do not want to sell any land to the government," he warned, "not even as much as this."

The conference was one of the largest ever assembled, totaling hundreds of tipis and about 20,000 Sioux, Cheyenne, and Arapaho. When it became clear that the Indians wouldn't sell the beloved Paha Sapa, the U.S. government offered to buy only the mineral rights. As Senator Allison of Iowa put it, if the Indians would be willing to "give our people the right to mine in the Black Hills ... we will make a bargain for this right. When the gold or other valuable minerals are taken away, the country will again be yours." Chief Spotted Tail of the Brules was indignant. He said the senator's proposal made it sound as if the Indians were being asked to "loan" the Paha Sapa to the whites for a while.

The Sioux were offered $400,000 a year for a lease on the Black Hills. It would have been a bargain for the government, inasmuch as gold worth more than a half-billion dollars was eventually extracted from the area. However, the Indians were united in their refusal to sign any agreement that encroached on their sacred territory. As Crazy Horse put it, "One does not sell the earth upon which the people walk."

On November 3, 1875, President Grant met secretly in Washington with senior military advisors and Indian affairs officials to work out a plan to resolve the Black Hills crisis. Two decisions came out of that meeting: (1) miners would be discouraged, but not prevented, from going into the Black Hills to search for gold, and (2) all Indian hunting bands—those that refused to live on reservations or to accept government rations—would be compelled to turn themselves in to the nearest established agency or be considered enemies of the United States. Shortly after the meeting, a reservation inspector suggested that it would be wise to "send troops against them [the Indians] in winter, the sooner the better, and whip them into submission."

Faced with a stalemate, the U.S. government decided to cancel the terms of the Laramie Treaty outright, and to seize the land after offering what was deemed to be a "fair equivalent of the value of the hills." The hunting bands were notified that they must report to government agencies by January 31, 1876. If they refused, they would be considered lawbreakers and the army would be sent against them. Runners were dispatched to the camps of Sitting Bull and Crazy Horse and all other chiefs of hostile bands to advise them of the new law.

If the situation hadn't held such deadly implications, the Indians' response to the demand to show up on the reservations would have been almost comical. The runners came back to report that the bands had received the message with good humor but replied that because hunting was good they were far too busy to comply. Instead, they offered to come back in the spring to discuss the matter further. Unfortunately, they failed to understand that a decision had already been made; from the government's point of view, there was nothing further to discuss.

On the morning of March 17, 1876, when the ground was covered with snow and the temperature was stuck at forty degrees below zero, soldiers mounted on white horses under the command of Colonel J.R. Reynolds descended on a camp of about a hundred tipis belonging to Northern Cheyennes, Oglalas, and Miniconjous that was situated along the Powder River only a few miles from the Wyoming border. Scantily clad men, women, and children scattered for safety, and finally the warriors were able to return the soldiers' fire. By noon the soldiers, with four dead and six wounded, left the village after burning many tipis and capturing half of the Indians' herd of horses.

Desperate for food, shelter, and clothing, the Indians sought safety first in the camp of Crazy Horse. However, his band was small and couldn't accommodate the needs of so many refugees, so in April 1876, Crazy Horse packed up and led everyone to Sitting Bull's camp. There, Sitting Bull lived up to his famed reputation for generosity: Robes, blankets, tipis, clothing, food, and horses were swiftly provided to the newcomers. "Oh, what good hearts they had!" recalled one of the destitute Cheyennes.

The Powder River attack served to awaken the hunting bands to the seriousness of the U.S. government's determination to force them onto reservations. As warm weather returned to the Plains, the combined tribes—joined now by bands of Brules, Sans Arcs, Blackfeet, and more Cheyennes—moved north in search of new grass for their ponies, fresh game for the hunters, and to escape pursuit by other troops.

Sitting Bull was acknowledged as the overall leader of the assembled tribes, numbering 460 lodges, or about 3,000 people, 800 of whom were warriors. Crazy Horse was recognized as one of several lieutenants. One of the Sioux later explained why no one voiced objections to Sitting Bull's position. "He had come now into admiration by all Indians as a man whose medicine was good ... as a man having a kind heart and good judgment as to the best course of conduct."

In May, Sitting Bull prayed to Wakan Tanka to "save me and give me all my wild game animals and have them close enough so my people will have enough food this winter.... If you do this for me I will sun dance two days and two nights and will give you a whole buffalo."

In the first week of June, Sitting Bull performed another dance in honor of Wi, the sun, while the camps were pitched near Rosebud Creek in eastern Montana. During the ceremony, he received a vision from the Great Spirit. In it, Sitting Bull saw soldiers, as numerous as grasshoppers, falling headfirst into the Indians' camp. He interpreted the dream to mean that bluecoats soon would attack but the Sioux would be victorious over them.

The first opportunity for a fight came on June 17, 1876. Indian spies—called "wolves"—reported that General George Crook had arrived on the Rosebud. Sitting Bull and Crazy Horse counseled the young men against hasty action, but the warriors' blood was up and they wouldn't listen. Finally, both chiefs accompanied their men toward Crook's camp. Sitting Bull, his arms still swollen and crusted with the wounds of his recent Sun Dance, didn't participate in the actual fighting.

In the battle that ensued, the Indians—fueled by courage brought on by Sitting Bull's vision—fought with a daring that surprised Crook and his staff. When the dust cleared, Crook retreated, declaring that victory was his, but amazed by the fact that the Indians, with a force that he estimated to be only half the size of his own, had inflicted so much damage.

Now that their whereabouts were known, the Indians immediately moved camp about 8 miles (13 km) farther to the valley of the Little Big Horn River. Over the next several days, the encampment increased in size with new arrivals of Indians who'd left the reservations, and soon numbered 1,000 lodges and 7,000 people, 1,800 of whom now were warriors. The valley of the Little Big Horn River—called the Greasy Grass by the Sioux—offered plenty of grass, good water, and thickets of cottonwood trees for shade during the hot summer days. Sitting Bull's lodge, situated near the cottonwoods, was a crowded household. Both of his wives were with him, as were his mother, two teenage daughters, a son, two stepsons, his sister, and his newborn twin sons.

Thirteen-year-old Black Elk, who later became a famous chronicler of Indian life, was swimming with companions in the Little Big Horn at noon when the first alert of soldiers headed toward the camp was sounded. This time, it wasn't Crook who pursued them; it was the man they called Long Hair—Custer.

Pehin Hanska had divided his regiment, keeping the largest command—about 225 men—for himself, and sending 175 men, including about 35 Arikara scouts, with Major Marcus Reno and another contingent with Captain Frederick Benteen. His aim was to overwhelm the Indians with a three-pronged attack. When Custer learned that the Indian camp was much larger than expected, he sent messengers back to tell the other companies to hurry to his aid, not realizing that Reno's forces had already run into Indian trouble and had suffered serious losses or that Benteen's men were later pinned down by the enemy and were unable to move.

Custer was not prepared for the onslaught of nearly 1,000 Indian warriors led by Crazy Horse that swarmed over the position he had staked out for his troops on the long slope of Medicine Tail coulee. The Indians' swift charge scattered the cavalry horses, which carried off the troops' ammunition.

Confused, the bluecoats panicked. As an Indian woman who saw the battle remarked, the scene was like "driving buffalo to a good place where they could be easily slaughtered." Crazy Horse made a daring charge into the soldiers' midst, and other warriors, roused by his good medicine, grew even braver.

It has been estimated the battle of the Little Big Horn lasted about an hour, perhaps less. When it was over, not a single bluecoat was left alive. Yellow-haired Custer himself was dead. White Bull, Sitting Bull's nephew, said that twenty-seven Indians were killed, but the number probably was closer to forty. Everything had taken place just as Sitting Bull's vision had predicted.

Sitting Bull was labeled a coward by some whites for not taking part in the actual battle. However, his Sun Dance wounds were still painful, so he had remained behind to organize the escape of the women and children. A Cheyenne warrior, Wooden Leg, had no such criticism, and summed up his respect for the Hunkpapa chief: "He had a big brain and a good one, a strong heart and a generous one.... I have never heard of any Indian having spoken otherwise of him."

The Indians celebrated their victory with feasting and dancing, but Sitting Bull was haunted by foreboding. He was forty-five years old, and had seen a great many ominous changes in the Sioux way of life. In spite of the defeat of a despised enemy, he regretted the deaths of so many men, and urged his people not to rob the bodies of the fallen bluecoats. When they disobeyed, he foresaw what it meant. "Henceforth you shall always covet white people's belongings," he warned.

AN ENGRAVING FROM A BRITISH NEWSPAPER SHOWING A GHOST DANCE

10

AT THE CROSSROADS

...he is so much vilified and written up in the newspapers [that] it is to a certain extent disgraceful to be known as an Indian agent.

JAMES McLAUGHLIN

$\mathcal{M}$cLaughlin hardly had time to pick up the pieces after Beckwith's departure before he was faced with what the Custer Massacre might mean to the agency he had just taken charge of. Rumors circulated that hostiles from the larger Standing Rock agency to the south—named for its single tall column of limestone rocks—were preparing to go on the warpath. Devil's Lake would be one of their likely destinations, because many Sioux brethren were located there. Since the garrison at Fort Totten had been reduced to only thirty-five soldiers, McLaughlin was understandably alarmed.

Nevertheless, he kept a cool head; behaving calmly under duress was one of the personal qualities that served him well throughout his life. When nothing out of the ordinary took place at Devil's Lake, McLaughlin decided on August 10, 1876, to join the Grey Nuns and students from St. Michael's for a picnic at Devil's Heart Butte, about 10 miles (16 km) from the fort.

No sooner had the group commenced to eat when two riders galloped up, warning that painted Sioux in full war regalia had left Standing Rock and were headed in the direction of Devil's Lake. Picnic baskets were hastily repacked and everyone rushed back to the safety of Fort Totten. McLaughlin took charge of ten rifles and ten revolvers and asked for volunteers to scout the surrounding countryside for signs of the approaching hostiles. One hundred Indians answered the call and twenty were selected for the job, but twenty-four hours later nothing suspicious had been sighted. The warning apparently was only a rumor. Similar stories surfaced for the next several months, but nothing came of them either. The new year dawned peacefully with a final addition to the McLaughlin family. James and Marie's fourth son and last child, Rupert Sibley, was born on December 10, 1876.

Although McLaughlin hadn't served in the military, the Indians addressed him as "Major," probably because they were so accustomed to calling his predecessor by that title. McLaughlin himself always signed his name simply as James McLaughlin and never pretended to have any official military rank. In time, however, most whites also called him Major, and historians frequently refer to him that way, too.

McLaughlin's day-to-day concerns were more mundane than the dramatic and bloody events that had taken place farther west. He had a school to run, crops to plant, the challenge of convincing a nomadic people to settle in one place, and—unlike Forbes—he had no loyal assistant to help him. The most well-meaning agent had to work daily to overcome the attitude of former warriors toward manual labor. As soon as new grass appeared on the prairie each spring, Indian men were eager to resume their wandering ways.

Just as Forbes had done, James continued to use rewards—in the form of wagons, oxen, tools, or furniture—as a means of encouraging men to do better at farming. He urged an increase in the number of acres of wheat planted, with an eye toward eventually establishing a flour mill at Devil's Lake. In 1880 his dream came true, and on December 16 he was able to describe to Father Brouillet one of the earliest mills in Dakota Territory.

"Our mill is a perfect gem and works to perfection. The Indians are highly pleased with it....Their delight at having flour ground by their own mill, from wheat of their own raising, being almost unbounded. This will be a great incentive to them in cultivation of larger fields next year."

There was one job that Indian men didn't have to be cajoled into doing, because it was rather like their old roving life. Hauling freight across the prairie from Jamestown, 85 miles (137 km) south of the reservation, or from Grand Forks, 90 miles (145 km) to the east, became a sought-after job. Basic supplies such as coffee, tea, sugar, salt, and tobacco had to be regularly delivered by teams and wagons, in addition to ordnance for Fort Totten.

McLaughlin took pride in how well students were doing at St. Michael's school. Girls had progressed in reading, writing, gardening, sewing, and various domestic skills. However, the Grey Nuns came close to abandoning their jobs in 1877 as the result of an order handed down by the Commissioner of Indian Affairs. Rather than continuing to regard St. Michael's as a boarding school, the commission decided it should be designated a day school, and the nuns' wages were decreased accordingly. The four Sisters plus their five helpers would be allowed the meager pittance of $1,250 per year to be divided among them, and would be required to supply their own food and clothing.

McLaughlin vigorously objected, and gave several reasons why he considered the new plan a mistake. (1) No student lived closer than 3 miles (5 km) to the school, and some as far away as 12 miles (19 km). (2) There wasn't enough warm clothing available for all children to be properly dressed when traveling long distances in freezing weather. (3) Indian parents opposed any kind of school, and a change of policy might encourage them to keep their children home altogether. (4) The Indians' eating habits were irregular, but if children were boarded they would be guaranteed better diets.

Even if the majority of students had not lived so far from the reservation, the Major argued, it still was best to remove them from their native environment so they could more easily be educated without interference from reluctant parents or uncooperative medicine men. Eventually, McLaughlin was successful in his defense of the boarding-school system, and the former arrangement was retained.

Each year a few more children came to St. Michael's. Enrollment might have been larger if both parents and children had felt more comfortable with the idea of learning the white man's ways, but often the children were even more fearful than their parents. When a man named Wiokiya visited agency headquarters with his eleven-year-old son in tow, McLaughlin wanted to know why the boy wasn't enrolled at the mission school. At the mere mention of school, the boy took off across the prairie like an antelope. His father laughed.

"There he goes," he told McLaughlin. "If you can catch him, you can have him." McLaughlin dashed after the boy, caught him after a 3-mile (5-km) chase, and put him in school. The boy became a fine pupil, took the name Ignatius Court, and later studied in Illinois and Indiana.

McLaughlin understood how difficult it was for Indian children to learn English, so when he discovered that Reverend Alfred S. Riggs, a noted authority on educating the Sioux, had published *The English and Dakota Reader*, he ordered twenty-eight copies for the modest sum of $28.20. The book contained side-by-side illustrations of English and Sioux words and sentences, but to McLaughlin's great disappointment the Commissioner of Indian Affairs informed him that such texts could not be used. Then, as now, bilingual education was a subject of controversy.

Soon, general enrollment at St. Michael's grew until it was necessary to add two new wings to the school, one of which served as a hospital. When the Grey Nuns were first hired, they had made it clear they wouldn't teach the older boys, who often were rowdy and hard to discipline, but Father Bonin, the agency chaplain, didn't want to teach them either. Therefore, two monks were recruited as teachers, Brother John Apke and Father Claude Ebner. A log building was built nearby to house the older boys and the monks. Adjacent to the dormitory was a 60-acre (24-hectare) plot where the boys were taught farming skills.

In McLaughlin's day, it was accepted that Indians couldn't be brought into the modern world unless they abandoned the last vestiges of their old traditions. Contemporary sociologists might argue the point, but almost no one did in that era. Consequently, in November 1877, McLaughlin notified the Indians at Devil's Lake that the practice of feasting and dancing must cease immediately. He warned that any chief who sanctioned either type of celebration would be removed from office. When Chief Little Fish organized a dance outside the borders of the reservation, only twenty-seven Indians attended. Little Fish concluded that he had made a mistake in judgment, apologized to McLaughlin, and pleaded not to be deprived of his chieftainship. McLaughlin replied that he would have to "make an example of him and all those who took part in the dance" by placing them last in line for the regular issue of government rations.

McLaughlin, now earning a yearly salary of $1,500, had never been overpaid, but he learned in the spring of 1878 that Congress intended to reduce the salaries of all agents and that his would be cut to $1,200. He advised his superiors that he would be forced to resign because he couldn't support a wife and five children on such a sum. When church officials were informed of McLaughlin's decision to leave, $300 was obtained from mission funds, and James agreed to remain on the job.

McLaughlin was troubled by more than the pitiful salary paid to Indian agents, however. He was pained by the reputation of men doing the sort of work he considered to be vitally important to the welfare of so many needy human beings. He wrote to Father Brouillet to voice his sentiments:

> How few know the arduous and trying duties of an Indian Agent. The public are ever ready to believe everything reflecting upon him. He may toil hard and do that which is laudable and receive but little encouragement and no recognition ... he is so much vilified and written up in the newspapers and a great ado made about the most trivial and often well meant matters that it is to a certain extent disgraceful to be known as an Indian Agent.

It was true that for many years Indian agents had been held in contempt, partly because many of them were poorly chosen. Henry Whipple, an Episcopal missionary among the Sioux, declared that agents were "often men without any fitness, sometimes a disgrace to a Christian nation; whiskey sellers, barroom loungers, debauchees." The opinion of General Philippe de Trobriand was equally gloomy: "The agents of the Indian Bureau are nothing more than members of a vast association of thieves who make their fortune at the expense of the redskins and to the detriment of the government."

When a year passed and Congress failed to raise agents' salaries, McLaughlin arranged to sell property he still owned in Minnesota because he needed cash to go into business. He intended to become a trader, a job that paid much better. Again, church officials begged him not to leave; again, he postponed his decision.

Overall, the agency at Devil's Lake under McLaughlin's supervision was regarded as a model of how a good reservation should function. Compared with others around the country, Devil's Lake was peaceful and quiet. The situation at Standing

Rock was quite the opposite. Perhaps because it was much larger and many Indians who had participated in the Custer Massacre were located there, it proved much harder to manage. (Young Beckwith had been right: They were a "wild set.") Although the Commissioner of Indian Affairs had rejected Beckwith's suggestion to transfer McLaughlin to Standing Rock, the idea now gained support among officials in Washington. Father Brouillet advised the Major to be "prepared at any moment to move" to the more troubled reservation.

News soon filtered out from Standing Rock that Father Stephan, the acting agency head, who, though honest to a fault, didn't get along well with the military commanders at Fort Yates, was willing to resign if someone such as McLaughlin took his place. Both General Sherman and General Terry supported McLaughlin's transfer because they knew of his excellent rapport with military personnel at Fort Totten.

In April 1880, McLaughlin made a trip to Fort Yates to assess the wisdom of accepting the new assignment. He liked what he saw, and five months later bade farewell to the Indians at Devil's Lake, with whom he had worked for almost ten years. As soon as his children recovered from measles, McLaughlin traveled by train to Bismarck, where the family boarded the steamer *Sherman*, and headed down the Missouri toward their new life at Fort Yates.

As McLaughlin stepped off the steamer on September 10, 1881, eager to assume his new position at Standing Rock, Sitting Bull and his followers were hustled on board. They had surrendered to the U.S. government two months earlier at Fort Buford. The group was considered dangerous, and was destined to be imprisoned 200 miles (320 km) south at Fort Randall, along the border between South Dakota and Nebraska. The two men met briefly, and the Major's assessment of Sitting Bull indicated that he had already made up his mind about the chief: "...he had an evil face and a shifty eye."

AN ILLUSTRATION BY FREDERIC REMINGTON ENTITLED *THE DEFEAT OF CRAZY HORSE BY COLONEL MILES, JANUARY, 1877*

11

NO PLACE TO HIDE

... when there are no more Buffalo or game, I will send my children to hunt and live on prairie mice.

SITTING BULL

To the Sioux, George Armstrong Custer was a hated enemy. He was the man who commanded the massacre at the Washita, who laughed about the Thieves' Road, who advocated the elimination of Indian rights in the Black Hills. But to whites, Custer was an American hero: He was the golden-haired "boy general" of the Civil War, who had galloped his horse up Pennsylvania Avenue to the White House on May 23, 1865, a scarlet kerchief around his neck, to celebrate the end of that long, bloody conflict. The nation was outraged by the fate he had met at the hands of savages, and demanded a swift accounting.

Sitting Bull realized what lay ahead for his people after the Little Big Horn. "Friends, we can go nowhere without seeing the head of a white man," he said. "Our land is small, it is like an island in a lake. We have two ways to go now—to the Land of the Grandmother, or to the Land of the Spaniards." To the north was Canada, the Land of the Grandmother, so called because it was ruled by Britain's Queen Victoria; to the south was Mexico, the Land of the Spaniards.

From his headquarters in Chicago, General Philip Sheridan—already famous for his remark that "the only good Indian is a dead Indian"—pledged to wage a policy of "total war" against the perpetrators of the Custer Massacre. He felt that those bands of Indians that insisted on clinging to the old ways had caused the young general's death and they became the targets of his wrath.

Sheridan's strategy called for the building of forts all through the heart of buffalo country, plus the constant pursuit of the Sioux until they finally surrendered unconditionally. He also intended to impose strict control over all existing Indian agencies, to disarm any fugitives who turned themselves in to such agencies, and to confiscate all Indian horses. Without ponies, there would be no chance that the Sioux or their relatives could repeat their stunning victory along the Little Big Horn.

In August 1876, within days after the Custer Massacre, Generals Terry and Crook gathered along the Rosebud River, their combined armies totaling 4,000 men. They would have pursued the hostile Indians immediately, but heavy rains resulted in deep mud, preventing them from speedily moving such a large force of men, horses, and equipment.

However, the Indians had already broken camp and moved on. After the battle along the Greasy Grass, their most immediate concern was finding fresh game and new pastures for their large pony herds. Sitting Bull took his Hunkpapa band, along with some Miniconjous and Sans Arcs, to Killdeer Mountain. Another large group split off and followed Crazy Horse toward the Black Hills.

But very soon the Black Hills became forbidden territory. Congress prohibited funds from being allocated to any of the friendly Indians until they signed a treaty giving up all rights to the Paha Sapa. Mindful that winter was coming on, the threat of rations being withheld forced the nonhunting Sioux to sign away their sacred land.

The forts that Sheridan wanted to build couldn't be started until summer, but he intended to keep the Indians on the move throughout the winter and scare off the buffalo as well. By spring, he believed that Sitting Bull's people would be starved into submission. General Nelson A. Miles, called Bear Coat by the Indians because he wore a long overcoat trimmed with bear fur, was dispatched to Indian country. He set up camp at the mouth of the Tongue River, where he expected to winter his men while carrying out Sheridan's policy of continual harassment. Miles became a familiar figure to the Indians, and had much in common with Custer: He was only four months older, also served with distinction in the Civil War, and was every bit as ambitious as Custer had been.

Of course, Bear Coat wasn't the only one who could pursue a policy of harassment. In October, Sitting Bull and his warriors attacked a wagon train in eastern Montana, shot some of its mules, and stampeded the rest. But when the wagon master re-formed the train of eighty-six wagons and proceeded on his journey with an escort of two hundred soldiers, Sitting Bull knew there was no way he could compete with their weapons and endless supplies of ammunition.

Therefore, he discussed with his chiefs the advisability of arranging a meeting with the whites, and one was scheduled with the help of a part Indian interpreter, Johnny Bruguier, a mixed blood who had recently taken up with the Sioux. The meeting took place on a sunny but very cold October day. Sitting Bull arrived accompanied by a dozen of his chiefs, shabbily dressed, clutching a buffalo robe close around himself to ward off the chill. When Miles demanded a return of the mules that had been stampeded from the wagon train earlier in the month, Sitting Bull retorted that Miles should then bring back the buffalo that had been scared out of the country.

Both Miles and Sitting Bull made their positions clear: Miles demanded unconditional surrender, while Sitting Bull insisted that the troops withdraw from the Yellowstone country so that Indians could hunt and trade freely as in the old days. Tempers flared, and the discussions ended without a resolution. A second meeting was held, but the results were no better. Miles warned that a failure to surrender would be considered a hostile act, obligating him to attack. Sitting Bull refused to bend, even though some of his chiefs advised him to do so. In the following skirmish, one Indian was killed and two soldiers were wounded.

Miles wrote to his wife on October 25, 1876, four months to the day after the Custer battle, and described with a degree of sympathy the man he'd just met. "He has a large broad head and strong features. He is a man evidently of great influence and a thinking, reasoning being. I should judge his great strength is as a warrior. I think he feels that his strength is somewhat exhausted and he appeared much depressed."

The Indians headed east toward the Yellowstone, with Miles still in pursuit. One of Sitting Bull's nephews, White Bull, a Miniconjou, disagreed with his uncle about what course the bands ought to follow, so White Bull disengaged himself from the larger group and set out for the north, toward Missouri River country. The defection of his much-loved nephew increased Sitting Bull's sense of isolation. Even in the best of times, cold weather was hard on the Plains, but the winter following the massacre at the Little Big Horn was the worst that any of the Sioux could remember. Under Sheridan's policy of harassment, the need to move camp often meant that the effects of the harsh weather were even more punishing. Food supplies ran low; ponies became as thin as smoke as they pawed feebly through the snow in search of a few blades of grass.

Many of the hunting bands turned themselves in—including White Bull's—but the thought of a life of confinement still was more than Sitting Bull could bear. Historians have considered that he was unrealistic, yet the chief had some company:

Crazy Horse also was determined to remain free, and kept his band of Oglalas on the move, even though his people began to perish in increasing numbers from starvation and cold.

On November 25, five months after the Custer debacle at the Little Big Horn, more than 1,000 cavalrymen under the command of Colonel R.S. Mackenzie attacked the Cheyenne camp of chiefs Dull Knife and Little Wolf in a canyon near the Powder River. The inhabitants of the camp of 200 tipis were driven from their lodges. Their supplies of clothing, food, cooking utensils and ammunition was set afire, their pony herd of 700 was captured by the soldiers, and thirty Cheyenne were killed.

The temperature dropped to thirty degrees below zero as the Cheyenne fled through the snow; eleven infants froze to death in their mothers' arms. Three weeks later, the destitute hostiles staggered into Crazy Horse's camp on the upper reaches of the Tongue River, where they were taken in. It was becoming clearer to the hostile bands that there was no place to hide.

During the first week of December 1876, Miles sent soldiers out under the command of Lieutenant Frank Baldwin to pursue the hostiles. Miles had struck a deal with Johnny Bruguier, the interpreter that Sitting Bull had recently befriended. Bruguier was facing a murder charge for killing a man in a drunken brawl, and Miles promised to help him evade punishment if he would reveal where Sitting Bull was camped. To save his own skin, Bruguier became a paid informer, enabling Baldwin to attack a new camp that Sitting Bull had established far up the Missouri in northwestern Montana. The troops seized thousands of pounds of dried meat, several hundred buffalo robes, and many horses. It was a devastating loss, which, in the dead of winter, couldn't be recouped.

By February 1877, Sitting Bull could see only one way out of his predicament: He headed for the Land of the Grandmother. Other small bands of Sioux had already fled to Canada, making it an even more attractive sanctuary. Chiefs Red Cloud and

Spotted Tail, who had long since surrendered and now lived on reservations, urged Sitting Bull to give up his fight, but he stubbornly refused.

By mid-April, he arrived at the Big Bend of the Milk River in northern Montana, not far from the Canadian border. Even when news came that Crazy Horse had surrendered at Fort Robinson in Nebraska on May 6, 1877, accompanied by nearly 1,000 followers and 12,000 ponies, Sitting Bull would not abandon his dream of leading his people back to the old days, the old ways. Instead, Sitting Bull took his followers across the *chanku wakan*, or sacred road, into the Land of the Grandmother. He was hungry, discouraged, and desperate—but still free.

Sitting Bull told Canadian officials: "I am looking to the north for my life, and hope the White Mother will never ask me to look to the country I left....Not even the dust of it did I sell [and] I will remain what I am until I die, a hunter, and when there are no more Buffalo or game, I will send my children to hunt and live on prairie mice."

12

LOOK AROUND YOU—EVERYWHERE

In a few years the buffalo will
be gone and the footprints
of the deer will be seen no more
among your valleys.
JAMES McLAUGHLIN

*M*cLaughlin arrived at the Standing Rock agency at a difficult time in its history. Many of the inhabitants were the very warriors who had wiped out Custer and his bluecoats five years earlier. They had spent part of that time as exiles in Canada along with Sitting Bull but, unlike their chief, had returned to the United States the same year the Major himself arrived at the reservation.

Rain-in-the-Face summed up the bitter sentiments of many when he declared:

> The yoke of the Great Father is degrading.... I do not want to be treated like an ox or a child. The lands on which our forefathers lived and on which I was born are filled with buffalo, but I am forced to live like a squaw while the white man can hunt as much as he likes. I do not like the men the Great Father sends to us. Their tongues are not straight. Flowers grow out of their mouths, but their hearts are filled with hate.

McLaughlin called a council soon after his arrival, and at one o'clock on the appointed day several thousand members of various bands—Hunkpapas, Blackfeet, Sans Arcs, Mineconjous, and Oglalas—gathered to hear what their new agent had to tell them. A reporter from the *New York Evening Telegram* recorded what was said. Rain-in-the-Face, who complained so bitterly about being treated like a child, couldn't have been pleased by what he heard:

> I occupy the same relation toward you that a father does toward his children, and as the first thing that is necessary on the part of children is obedience, so I look to you to willingly obey me and listen to the commands of the government.... I don't expect you to become independent farmers and cattle raisers all at once.... But look around you—everywhere. In a few years the buffalo will be gone and the footprints of the deer will be seen no more among your valleys. You must prepare to live without game. It is for this that I come from the Great Father.

McLaughlin promised that he intended to treat members of the different tribes equally. As soon as cold weather came, he told his listeners, plenty of blankets and rations would be provided for everyone, a promise that was greeted with enthusiasm. He urged the tribes not to compete with each other nor perpetuate past jealousies, but to unite and work for the welfare of all.

At the conclusion of his remarks, John Grass, a chief of the Blackfeet Sioux, rose to express his approval. "Take a look at the new father," he advised. "His words are very good and it is your duty to think that his tongue is straight." Long Soldier was more reserved. "You say you will assist us," he reminded McLaughlin. "Many have told us so, but I hope you mean it."

Although McLaughlin had assured the gathering, "to your past mode of life I have no objections," one of his first acts was to abolish the tradition of the Sun Dance. He also objected to the Scalp Dance, the Kiss Dance, the Buffalo Dance, and the Horse

A COUNCIL AT THE STANDING ROCK INDIAN RESERVATION.
McLAUGHLIN IS SEATED AT THE TABLE.

Dance. The only ceremony he permitted the Indians to continue was the Grass Dance—but warned that it could be performed only on Saturdays.

To take the sting out of his opposition to ceremonial dancing, McLaughlin later announced that, since the winter of 1881–1882 had been a long, hard one, a buffalo hunt would be held in the spring. He added, perhaps to the Indians' surprise, that he intended to go with them. On June 10, 1882, about 2,000 Indians headed west from Fort Yates in search of buffalo. Two days later, mounted on a fine gray horse loaned to him by chief Crow King, McLaughlin set out to join them.

At the beginning of a hunt, the Indians played a game they believed could predict if hunting would be good. The Major described in his memoir, *My Friend, the Indian*, how the ceremony in which he took part was conducted. Three freshly cut bushes were propped up 10 yards (9.1 m) apart in an area arranged in front of spectators. Taking turns, contestants on horseback galloped in front of the crowd and tried to knock down all three bushes. If no bushes were knocked over, "the hunt might as well be abandoned," McLaughlin wrote. If one bush were knocked down, so-so success was predicted; if two bushes were knocked over, the hunt would be fairly successful; if all three were knocked down, many animals would be killed. The new agent rode down all three bushes, to the enjoyment of the Indians.

The omen was accurate: 5,000 buffalo were killed during the hunt, which lasted several days. At the beginning of the hunt, McLaughlin let it be known that he would like to take a live buffalo calf back to his children. After the first day, he was exhausted and slept so soundly that he awoke in the morning to discover that all the hunters were back on the prairie—but around his tent, tied to stakes, were twenty-two buffalo calves!

The practice of farming didn't go as smoothly for the Indians as the familiar pursuit of hunting buffalo. During

McLaughlin's first two years at Standing Rock, the region was hit by frequent drought, scorching wind, blight, and early frost. While the Indians weren't responsible for nature's whims, McLaughlin laid part of the blame for crop failures on them. He noted that in the spring they commenced tilling and planting energetically enough, but then quickly lost interest in tending their plots. "...a number of fields have been neglected by the owners," McLaughlin wrote in a report to the Commissioner of Indian Affairs. "This careless indifference, so peculiar to the Indian, is perpetuated by the 'free ration system,' and can only be remedied by compelling all able-bodied Indians to render an equivalent in labor for the subsistence and clothing issued to them."

Although the harsh climate of Dakota Territory indicated that garden crops would always be hard to raise, making it more sensible for the Indians to become full-time cattle raisers, McLaughlin believed that such a vocation had its drawbacks. Caring for cattle was "but a small remove from the hunting life of the wild Indian and . . . will perpetuate that nomadic spirit and love of roaming without any of the comforts of a fixed abode." A recognition of the Indians' nomadic spirit and wanderlust showed that he was aware of what had once been an integral way of life for generations.

Nevertheless, the Major held close to his heart an inflexible definition of what the most powerful "civilizing" influences were. In a letter to Captain George Brown on April 25, 1883, the Major listed the issues as he saw them: (1) Indians must learn to identify themselves as individuals. (2) Indians must learn to take personal responsibility for their actions. (3) Indians must be weaned away from their tribal affiliations. (4) Indians must learn to live in permanent homes rather than pursue their wandering habits. In short, the Indians must become something other than what they were. They must cease to be Indians; they must learn to be white men in thought, habit, and deed. To

McLaughlin and to other whites the solution was simple; it must have seemed quite otherwise to the Indians.

McLaughlin was pleased to record that he had traveled 550 miles (885 km) around the reservation, and had visited each of the 1,180 families for whom he was responsible. The trip also gave him an opportunity to observe the deplorable condition of the roads, and he soon required every able-bodied man on the reservation to work a few days each year at road- and bridge-building.

In 1881 approximately 1,500 acres (607 hectares) of land were under cultivation at Standing Rock. By 1891, ten years after his arrival, McLaughlin proudly reported to the Commissioner of Indian Affairs that 5,000 acres (202 hectares) were under cultivation, plus 110 acres (46 hectares) that were tended by the pupils of the two agency boarding schools.

> The crops, which are not yet all harvested, are estimated as follows: Wheat, 5,225 bushels; oats, 21,000; corn 15,150 bushels; potatoes, 10,600 bushels; onions, 650 bushels; beans, 660 bushels; turnips, rutabagas, beets, carrots, etc., 11,300 bushels; melons, pumpkins and squash, 53,500 bushels and the hay cut and stacked will approximate 5,000 tons.

It was an achievement that both he and his "children" could be proud of.

McLaughlin modified his views on cattle raising, and by 1891 the Indians owned 5,000 beef cattle, 500 of which were cows with calves at their sides. "The grass is excellent this season and the cattle will go into the winter in good condition," McLaughlin noted. He was a meticulous record-keeper, and was pleased to report that the Indians had sold $21,134.76 worth of beef and $3,850 of stove wood. The total sales from all activity at the reservation was $39,138, a fine record indeed.

McLaughlin was successful in coaxing more and more of the Indians out of their tipis and into log homes, which didn't necessarily induce Indian women to improve (in his opinion) their housekeeping habits. As a result, he created the position of Matron of Domestic Economy, and hired Mrs. Lucy B. Arnold to fill it. After some time on the job, Mrs. Arnold documented what she'd accomplished:

> I can safely say I have found the majority [of women] making efforts to cultivate neatness & civilized habits, as far as the accommodations of the houses afford. Their houses generally consist of two rooms & an entrance way used in winter as a place for their water barrels, & a refuge for the many dogs, which are still kept as an article of diet.... So far I have found it impossible ... to induce them to keep a fresh cow about their residences [but] a great many keep chickens and even pigeons.

Some of the Indian settlements at Standing Rock were 50 miles (80 km) or more from agency headquarters, and McLaughlin concluded that it would be desirable to establish churches in as many of those settlements as possible. The step was necessary "not because they are thirsting after knowledge or seeking enlightenment...[but because] I do not know a single full-blood Indian here who is a Christian and after the children leave our school they take on the indifference of their parents and rarely attend church." McLaughlin did not confine his interest merely to Catholic missionaries, but was supportive of the efforts of Episcopalians and Congregationalists as well.

As much as Christianizing the Indians, McLaughlin believed—as he had at Devil's Lake—that education was of critical importance. When he arrived at Standing Rock, of 763 children between the ages of six and sixteen, only 100 were in school. At the end of his service at the reservation, more than

600 Indian boys and girls were attending. Day schools were built in the more remote settlements to accommodate children who were unable to attend at Fort Yates.

A government school inspector who visited Standing Rock commented that McLaughlin was "always watchful for the interests of the Indians, mingling kindness, firmness and tact." Even more important, O.H. Parker noted that the Major seemed "to know every man, woman and child on his reservation.... I wish we had more agents such as James McLaughlin."

It disturbed McLaughlin that soldiers from nearby Fort Yates corrupted the morals of some of the Indian women. He wrangled permission from Washington to evict "squawmen" from the reservation, and got the cooperation of the commander of the fort to prohibit his men from sneaking off to visit the Indian camps. As Forbes had done earlier, McLaughlin also established an Indian police force to keep order. Such men took pride in their jobs, and even though their salary of $8 a month was pitifully small, they energetically patrolled 200 miles (320 km) of reservation border, keeping white smugglers, timber thieves, and cattle rustlers at bay. A Court of Indian Offenses was established, whose judges were selected from among the Indians themselves. The sentences handed down usually consisted of fines, community service, and occasionally imprisonment.

In his introduction speech in the summer of 1881, McLaughlin told the Indians that the Great Father in Washington "sent me to take care of you and to labor in your interests. I intend to do my duty like a man." The Major lived up to his pledge. Under his administration, the Sioux and their cousins at Standing Rock slowly loosened their attachment to the old ways. With tentative steps, they began to enter the white man's world.

13

GRANDMOTHER CHANGES HER MIND

I surrender this rifle to you through
my young son ... I wish it to be
remembered that I was the last man
of my tribe to surrender....
SITTING BULL

*A*bout 1,000 people, their lodges ragged and old, crossed the Canadian border with Sitting Bull. The shabbiest lodge of all belonged to the chief himself. Then, in the first spring days of May 1877, knowing that his people were finally beyond the reach of the bluecoats, Sitting Bull's spirits lifted. The weather warmed, the grass in the Land of the Grandmother turned green, and thickets of trees on nearby Wood Mountain leafed out. It was tempting to believe that life might be good again.

At their camp at Pinto Horse Butte, the Sioux met with a delegation of redcoated North-West Mounted Police, led by Major James M. Walsh, commander of the nearby fort. As British citizens, the Canadians were generally sympathetic to the plight of the Sioux. That point of view was reflected by Sir William Watkins's assertion in British Parliament shortly before the Battle of the Little Big Horn that if war occurred it wouldn't be caused by the Indians as much as it would be the outcome of the Americans' breach of the Laramie Treaty of 1868. *The New York Times* scornfully reported Watkins's comments under a headline that read, "HAW!" Even Charles

JAMES M. WALSH OF
THE NORTH-WEST
MOUNTED POLICE

COLONEL NELSON
"BEAR COAT" MILES

Dickens, author of such classics as *Oliver Twist* and *The Tale of Two Cities*, weighed in with his opinion: "If the Americans don't embroil us in war before long it will not be their fault."

As he spoke to Major Walsh through an interpreter, Sitting Bull recited a long list of injustices he believed the United States had committed against his people. Walsh replied that the Sioux were safe now in Canada, and as long as they behaved themselves the Grandmother would protect them. However, he warned the new arrivals that they must obey Canadian law; if any Sioux crossed back over the U.S. border to steal or cause other mischief they would be held accountable.

If Sitting Bull had any doubt about Major Walsh's determination to enforce Canadian law, it was dispelled when White Dog and two companions rode into camp leading several horses that Walsh recognized as stolen animals. Without blinking an eye, the Major placed White Dog under arrest. As the startled brave was about to be clapped in leg irons he protested that he had not stolen the horses, they had simply been wandering loose on the prairie. He offered to turn them over, whereupon Walsh relented. It was a lesson Sitting Bull took to heart: The redcoats played fair, but they insisted on obedience.

Major Walsh—whose critics didn't doubt his good intentions—was, like Bear Coat Miles, considered to be somewhat like George Armstrong Custer in his love of attention. Nothing pleased him more than to be referred to by American newspapers as "Sitting Bull's boss." In any case, he brought to his relationship with the refugees a sympathetic attitude, and worked hard to establish a spirit of respect with Canada's most famous exile. Over time, Sitting Bull came to trust Major Walsh more than any white man he had ever known.

Before the month was out, three emissaries from the United States followed Sitting Bull across the border and requested an informal meeting with him. One was a Catholic priest, Father Martin Marty, from the Standing Rock agency and a friend of

James McLaughlin. William Halsey was an interpreter from the same agency, and John Howard was a part-time scout for Bear Coat Miles. In a different time and place the Sioux might have killed Halsey and Howard, but they clearly remembered the rules that Major Walsh had laid down. At first, Sitting Bull refused to meet with the trio. It was only after Walsh—whom the Sioux called Long Lance—agreed to take part in the talks that he conceded to parley.

Walsh and the assistant commissioner at the nearby fort, Lieutenant Colonel Acheson G. Irvine, held a preliminary meeting with the three American visitors. Walsh made it clear that the Sioux could remain in Canada as long as they abided by the laws that had been explained to them. Finally, on June 2, 1877, Sitting Bull joined the council after receiving repeated assurances from Walsh that he was safe. Then he told the Americans bluntly: "Why would I return [to the U.S.]? To have my horses and arms taken away?... I have come to remain with the Grandmother's children." He left no doubt that, having gotten across the border, he intended to stay where he was.

Irvine described Canada's notorious fugitive in observant terms: "He is a man of somewhat short stature, but with a pleasant face, a mouth showing great determination, and a fine high forehead. When he smiled, which he often did, his face brightened up wonderfully."

Although Irvine might have been impressed by the chief's smile, exile weighed heavily on Sitting Bull, and he often lapsed into a melancholy mood. He had once been a powerful chief, the supreme leader of the seven council fires, looked up to by all the Lakotas. Now, he said, he was "nothing." He grew increasingly bitter toward the Americans, and fancied that peace talks were only efforts to get him back to the United States, where he would be hanged.

Five months later, in a second attempt to resolve the problem, the U.S. government dispatched an official commission to

Canada, headed by General Terry, to urge the Sioux to return to the American side. Sitting Bull and the other chiefs steadfastly refused to do so. No doubt Sioux distrust was hardened by news that Bear Coat Miles was now pursuing Chief Joseph and his band of Nez Perce. The Nez Perce, like the Sioux, resisted being confined to a reservation in Idaho, and Chief Joseph fled with 800 lodges toward the Canadian border, hoping to find the same kind of refuge that Sitting Bull had found.

When Sioux scouts brought word that on September 30, 1877, Miles had trapped the starving Nez Perce in the Bear Paw Mountains of Montana, only 40 miles (64 km) from the Canadian border, the Sioux listened with narrowed eyes. Upon his surrender, a beaten and demoralized Chief Joseph delivered one of the most-quoted speeches in Indian history. It was recorded by Lieutenant Charles Wood, who resigned from the army not long after; his experience with Chief Joseph spurred him to become a lawyer and advocate of social justice for disadvantaged people. Chief Joseph said:

> I am tired of fighting. It is cold and we have no blankets. The little children are freezing to death. My people, some of them, have run away to the hills, and have no blankets, no food; no one knows where they are—perhaps freezing to death. I want to have time to look for my children and see how many of them I can find. Maybe I shall find them among the dead. Hear me, my chiefs! I am tired; my heart is sick and sad. From where the sun now stands I will fight no more forever.

Personal grief over the death of one of his sons contributed to Sitting Bull's unwillingness to attend the second council at Fort Walsh. Even after he agreed to participate, his fears were again aroused by the appearance in camp of stragglers from Chief Joseph's band who had managed to escape Miles's soldiers. White Bird, with a party of fifty men, forty women, and many children, arrived in Canada. The condition of the starving, wounded Nez Perce women and children prompted the Sioux to ask Major Walsh how he could expect them to enter any discussions with men who would do such a thing.

The Major encouraged Sitting Bull to at least hear what the Americans had to say, and the Sioux chief finally agreed. The council, with what was officially called the Sitting Bull Commission, took place on October 17, 1877. A newspaperman, Jerome Stillson of the *New York Herald*, recorded that Sitting Bull arrived wearing a dark shirt with white dots, black leggings with red stripes down the sides, a cap of fox fur, and what Stillson called "a quiet, ironical smile." He shook hands warmly with the Canadian emissaries, but pointedly refused to do likewise with the Americans.

The Americans' terms, communicated through General Terry, were familiar: (1) Return to the reservations that are set aside for you. (2) Surrender your arms and ponies. (3) Begin a new way of life dependent on farming. Sitting Bull refused. Other chiefs and several women made speeches. The decision was unanimous: There would be no return to the United States. When word drifted north that Crazy Horse had been killed on September 5, 1877, at Fort Robinson, only four months after his surrender, the Sioux were convinced that they had made the right decision.

Politics has never been a simple art. The Sioux believed they had won a victory by boldly stating they would never leave their adopted country, which meant that Canada was now responsible for their welfare. It wasn't exactly what the Grandmother's government had bargained for. When several hundred of Crazy Horse's followers deserted Fort Robinson to join Sitting Bull in the spring of 1878, it meant that refugees from the American side of the border numbered nearly 6,000 people.

If buffalo had remained as plentiful on the prairies as they had once been, both the Sioux and the Canadians might have managed, but Canada had its own Indians to worry about—the Blackfeet, Blood, Piegan and Cree tribes, among others. The northwest Blackfeet (not to be confused with the Blackfeet Sioux) had long been enemies of the Lakotas and fiercely resented competition for the dwindling buffalo herds. It was inevitable that young men from Sitting Bull's camp would drift across the border into Montana in search of meat, even though such forays had been forbidden by Major Walsh. Sitting Bull himself wandered south to hunt. In July 1879, Bear Coat Miles took action against the trespassers, and in an ensuing encounter, Sitting Bull killed a Crow scout, Magpie, and captured his horse. Such blatant misconduct, added to diminishing food supplies and the animosity of Canada's own Indians, caused the Canadians' attitude toward Sitting Bull and his followers to cool. Soon, officials began to urge the Sioux to return to their homeland.

Finally, in May 1880, Sitting Bull's nephew and adopted son, One Bull, crossed the border and went to Fort Buford to ask under what terms Sitting Bull would be allowed to return to the United States. The answer was the same as it had always been: Give up your arms and your ponies and settle on a reservation. Major Walsh, a staunch supporter of Sitting Bull's cause, had been transferred to Fort Qu'Appelle, leaving Sitting Bull without an advisor, while the officer who replaced Walsh worked actively toward ridding Canada of a guest who had overstayed his welcome.

In the autumn of 1880, Sitting Bull met with interpreter Edward Allison to discuss surrender. Other chiefs—Little Hawk, Big Road, and Rain-in-the-Face among them—had already drifted south. Sitting Bull became increasingly isolated, and when his old friend Low Dog also headed south in April 1881, Sitting Bull realized that the time had come for him to do the same.

In April 1881, Canadian officials were relieved when Sitting Bull packed up part of his camp and seemed prepared to leave. Among those left behind were Sitting Bull's oldest daughter,

Many Horses, of whom he was especially fond. But Sitting Bull didn't head for Fort Buford on the other side of the border, where he was supposed to surrender to American authorities. Instead, he went 200 miles (320 km) north, to Fort Qu'Appelle, where Major Walsh was stationed.

This time Walsh couldn't help, and when Sitting Bull learned that in his absence Many Horses had married a man he didn't approve of and had been transported to the Standing Rock reservation, the weary chief bowed to the inevitable. In July 1881, he surrendered at Fort Buford—the very fort on which he had inflicted so many raids in happier days. Accompanying Sitting Bull were his mother, sister, and two wives, plus a second pair of twin boys born in Canada in 1880 (the first pair of twin sons were born just before the Battle on the Little Big Horn). The chief was suffering from a severe eye infection, and carried one of his most treasured possessions—a fine Winchester rifle. He motioned to Crow Foot, one of his five-year-old twins, and instructed the boy to hand it to Major David H. Brotherton, then declared:

> I surrender this rifle to you through my young son, whom I now desire to teach in this manner that he has become a friend of the Americans.... I wish it to be remembered that I was the last man of my tribe to surrender my rifle. This boy has given it to you, and he now wants to know how he is going to make a living.

Sitting Bull had composed a song about the end of his life as a free Indian, roaming the prairie at will:

> *A warrior I have been,*
> *Now it is all over;*
> *A hard time I have.*

But the hardest times were only beginning.

14
TWO ROADS
BECOME ONE

…Sitting Bull will never again cause any trouble…
his influence is very limited now…
JAMES McLAUGHLIN

…if the Great Spirit has chosen any one
to be the chief of this country, it is myself.
SITTING BULL

S itting Bull's ten-day stay at Fort Buford ended when he and his followers boarded the *Sherman* and headed for the Standing Rock reservation, 280 miles (450 km) down the Missouri River. Their first stop came two days later, on July 31, 1881, when the steamer tied up at Bismarck. Sitting Bull's companions donned their finest outfits for the occasion, but he wore plain blue pants, a white shirt that was none too clean, his only decoration the scarlet streaks painted on his face. He also wore a pair of smoked glasses that someone had given him to protect his infected eyes.

Sitting Bull had never been in a white man's town before, and when he saw a railroad car he asked to see it move. When the engineer obliged, the chief declared he would rather walk than take any chances with the iron monster. At the Merchants Hotel, Sitting Bull and some of his chiefs were treated to ice cream, and were astonished that such a cold dessert could be made in spite of the hot weather. During his exile in Canada, a trader, Gus Hedderich, had taught Sitting Bull how to sign his name, and when spectators at the hotel

SITTING BULL AND MEMBERS OF HIS FAMILY UNDER
GUARD AT FORT RANDALL IN 1882. THE WHITE WOMAN
AND CHILD ARE UNIDENTIFIED.

asked for his autograph, a witness reported that he obliged "with grace."

After reboarding the steamer on Sunday evening, the journey downriver was resumed. Sitting Bull and 190 followers disembarked at noon on Monday. Distraught that Many Horses wasn't at the dock to meet him, as well as by the turn his life had taken, Sitting Bull lamented: "This is the first time I have had to surrender and give up." Running Antelope comforted his friend, saying: "Brother, don't weep, everything will come out all right."

Two days later, Many Horses arrived. "We both cried," Sitting Bull said of their reunion, yet his spirits were lifted.

Instead of proceeding directly to the fort, however, the Sioux languished on the banks of the Missouri in the blistering summer heat because officials in Washington suddenly grew fearful about the danger of integrating the most notorious Sioux chief in history into the population at Standing Rock. Officials also were concerned about the new demographics of the Plains, which had changed in ways that Sitting Bull could never have guessed when he was a boy and rarely saw a white man. Prior to the Custer Massacre, there were about 5,000 whites in Dakota Territory, but by the time Sitting Bull left the Land of the Grandmother, 17,000 miners were prospecting in the Black Hills, 117,000 homesteaders had spread themselves across Dakota Territory, and towns dotted the prairie. By 1885 the number of settlers would double. Could a notorious holdout like Sitting Bull be safely included in the new landscape?

No, Washington finally concluded, and a month later, on September 6, 1881, Sitting Bull and his band were ushered back to the steamer and taken 300 miles (480 km) farther downriver to Fort Randall, on the border between the present-day states of South Dakota and Nebraska. The chief was dismayed, but there was no arguing with the bayoneted rifles that soldiers from Fort Yates were prepared to use if trouble erupted. If Sitting Bull recalled White Antelope's hopeful words, they must have sounded hollow indeed.

▲ ▲ ▲

McLaughlin was forty-one years old and had been head of the Standing Rock agency for less than two years when Sitting Bull was moved back from Fort Randall to take his place with other Sioux. The Major's formerly lean frame had thickened at the waist; his black hair now was iron gray. McLaughlin had always been a serious-minded person—almost humorless, one could say—and wore his authority with an unsmiling dignity. He fully supported the chief's transfer to Standing Rock, telling the Commissioner of Indian Affairs that he had "the utmost confidence in the good intentions of Sitting Bull." He suggested that it would be best if the move occurred early enough in spring so the chief and his people could begin planting crops.

By no means was McLaughlin intimidated by articles that had appeared in major newspapers such as the *New York Herald* and the *Chicago Tribune*, or in magazines like *Harper's Weekly*, which often tended to make a hero out of the chief. He took special pains to explain his own views to Sitting Bull when the chief stepped off the steamboat *Behan* at Fort Yates on May 10, 1883. Later, he described the points he made in a letter to the Commissioner of Indian Affairs.

First, he assured Sitting Bull that "he and his people would receive their proportionate share of all goods and supplies that came to this agency for distribution among the Indians; that he would be assisted and encouraged in every way possible with the means at my disposal, and be treated in all respects in the same manner as the other Indians of the agency, but that he must not expect anything more than others [who were] equally deserving.... I thereupon carefully and clearly explained to him his status, together with the rules and regulations governing the Indian service, which I informed him I should endeavor mildly but strictly to enforce." McLaughlin added wryly, "He did not visit me again for several days."

No doubt Sitting Bull needed time to reflect on the Major's words. It must have been a struggle to come to terms with his new "status," as McLaughlin put it. Nevertheless, when two agency employees were sent out to check on Sitting Bull a few days later, the chief was found working diligently in the 12-acre (5-hectare) field about 4 miles (6 km) from the fort, which had been set aside for him and his followers. When he was asked if he found the work difficult, the chief quietly replied, "No," and indicated that he was eager to become a farmer.

Three months later, however, McLaughlin described to the Commissioner of Indian Affairs the type of man he believed he was dealing with. The harshness of his report seems startling. Sitting Bull was "an Indian of very mediocre ability, rather dull," he wrote. "I cannot understand how he held such sway over or controlled men so eminently his superiors in every respect, unless it was his sheer obstinacy and stubborn tenacity."

McLaughlin wasn't finished. "He is pompous, vain, and boastful," he complained, "and considers himself a very important personage...[because] he has been lionized and pampered by the whites since the Battle of the Little Big Horn.... However, I firmly believe that Sitting Bull will never again cause any trouble, he having been thoroughly subdued; moreover, his influence is very limited now, and I hope to be able to turn what little he has toward the advancement of his people."

It's hard to say why James McLaughlin took such a sudden dislike to Sitting Bull, because there were many Indians at Standing Rock whom he admired a great deal. One of them was Gall, Sitting Bull's friend from boyhood, who had also fought at the Little Big Horn. Unlike Sitting Bull, Gall yielded more readily to the demands of the white man's ways and was regarded approvingly by McLaughlin as being a "progressive." (Once, uncooperative Indians such as Sitting Bull had been labeled "hostile"; now they were called "nonprogressive.") The Major respected John Grass too, and to the end of his days he never understood why the chief couldn't follow the footsteps of such men.

Except for his kindly treatment by Major Walsh in Canada, Sitting Bull was often frustrated by the whites' lack of respect for his position as the chief of all the Lakotas. Therefore, in August 1883, when the U.S. Senate sent a delegation to Standing Rock to assess how things were going, Sitting Bull met them in council fully determined to make the visitors recognize his importance.

"Do you know who I am?" he asked, nettled by what he perceived as their indifference to his role. "Do you know who I am?" he demanded again, his voice rising. When he didn't get a satisfactory answer, he declared angrily, "I want to tell you that if the Great Spirit has chosen any one to be chief of this country, it is myself." Proper acknowledgment still was not forthcoming, so he cried out, "You have conducted yourselves like men who have been drinking whiskey!" With that, he stalked out of the meeting, beckoning to his companions to follow with a wave of his hand.

After several minutes of reflection, Sitting Bull realized that he had overplayed his hand, and returned to the gathering. "I am here to apologize for my bad conduct," he said, yet felt obliged to remind the delegation, "I have always been a chief," suggesting that he wished to be treated like one.

The chairman of the committee, Senator Henry L. Dawes of Massachusetts, was a sympathetic advocate for Indians' rights, and took a tolerant attitude toward Sitting Bull's outburst. Senator John Logan from Illinois, however, a former major general in the Civil War, was outraged. "You were not appointed by the Great Spirit," he snapped when Sitting Bull returned to the meeting. He declared that the chief had "no following, no power, no control, and no right to any control." Logan demanded Sitting Bull's arrest, but McLaughlin—always cool in a hot situation—urged the senator not to make an issue of the incident.

A month later, Sitting Bull's ruffled feathers were smoothed when he traveled north to Bismarck with McLaughlin and 300 other Sioux to help celebrate the laying of a cornerstone for the new capital of Dakota Territory. Former President Ulysses S. Grant was present for the occasion, as was the president of the Northern Pacific railroad. Most of the Indians camped south of the railroad tracks, but Sitting Bull was put up at the Sheridan House with other notable guests, which bolstered his self-esteem. As he had done on his first visit to Bismarck, he sold autographs for from $1.50 to $2.00 each, and came home with $150 in his pocket.

It was the beginning of the kind of public exposure that caused McLaughlin much concern. Sitting Bull was regarded by whites as a drawing card at public events, and received many invitations to appear at local fairs and other gatherings. Even Father Joseph Stephan, whose position McLaughlin had taken at Standing Rock, requested Sitting Bull's presence in Jamestown for a church fair in November 1883. McLaughlin turned down the invitation, perhaps because he didn't want Sitting Bull to become more pompous and vain than he already considered him to be. When a Major Newell asked if Sitting Bull could appear in an exhibition, McLaughlin crisply replied on February 14, 1884, that it would be detrimental to the successful management of other agency Indians to witness "the most disaffected Indian leader of modern times ... paraded around the country and lionized by the public."

However, Sitting Bull's curiosity about whites had been whetted by his exposure to their habits and customs, and he requested an opportunity to see more of the white man's cities. When he discovered that McLaughlin planned a trip to the Minnesota state capital in March 1884, Sitting Bull requested a chance to go with him. McLaughlin agreed and justified the decision to the Commissioner of Indian Affairs by noting that if Sitting Bull could see for himself the comforts enjoyed by the whites, he would realize that, by working hard and becoming educated, Indians could have the same advantages.

McLaughlin arranged not only for Sitting Bull to make the trip but also for the chief's favorite nephew, One Bull, to accompany him. The Major himself took along his oldest son, sixteen-year-old Harry. For ten days the party enjoyed the sights of St. Paul, which included three evenings spent at theatres, a visit with railroad magnate James J. Hill, a tour of the pressroom of the *Pioneer Press*, and a visit to a shoe factory, where Sitting Bull was presented with a pair of shoes made especially for him. As far as the chief and One Bull were concerned, however, the highlight of the trip was a visit to the fire department, where a demonstration was given of a response to a fire call. The sound of the clanging bell, the sight of firemen sliding down a pole, the speed with which the fire horses were harnessed, ending with a mad dash out the station door so enchanted the two men that they insisted on a repeat performance.

For a time, McLaughlin was pleased with the results of the trip, because afterward Sitting Bull visited him often to reminisce about the wonderful sights he had seen. "His eyes have been opened," McLaughlin wrote to T.M. Stevenson in May 1884. "What influence he has is being turned in the right direction and the recent trip to St. Paul has been largely instrumental in bringing this about."

Reports of Sitting Bull's appearance in St. Paul spawned requests from others, among them John Burke, Buffalo Bill Cody's representative, who came to Fort Yates hoping to get permission for the chief's participation in the Wild West Show. McLaughlin declined, saying that he believed the Indians needed to concentrate on growing and tending crops, not on becoming celebrities.

However, both McLaughlin and his wife encouraged Sitting Bull to accept an invitation to appear at the Minnesota State Fair in September 1884. At first, the chief was reluctant, perhaps believing that he had seen quite enough of the white man's world. Finally, he agreed, providing six of his followers and two women could accompany him. Young Harry McLaughlin was again included in the party, and Marie McLaughlin—called "Mother" by many Indians at Standing Rock—acted as an interpreter. But the year was notable for an event that caused Sitting Bull much sorrow: the death of his mother, Her Holy Door.

William Cody hadn't given up the idea of getting Sitting Bull for his show, and petitioned the Commissioner of Indian Affairs to allow Sitting Bull a chance to become part of the Wild West Show. The Commissioner refused. Not to be put off, Cody obtained a letter of recommendation from General William T. Sherman. This time, Sitting Bull didn't have to be encouraged to leave Standing Rock, because he understood that the trip would give him a chance to meet the Great White Father, President Grover Cleveland.

McLaughlin grudgingly assented, and on June 12, 1885, Sitting Bull began a four-month tour with Cody's Wild West Show in Buffalo, New York. His contract guaranteed him $50 a week, a $125 bonus at the end of the run, and the right to keep all the money from sales of his autograph. On June 23 the chief did indeed meet President Cleveland, to whom he slyly observed that although he believed McLaughlin was a good man, he trusted the president more. Sitting Bull was especially taken with one of the show's other stars, young Annie Oakley, and nicknamed her "Little Sure Shot." At the end of the tour, Buffalo Bill gave Sitting Bull the gray circus horse the chief had ridden in his performances, plus a wide-brimmed white hat, both of which the chief kept until the day of his death.

McLaughlin hoped that such experiences would make Sitting Bull more amenable to following the white man's path, but noted in a letter written one month after the chief's return from his Wild West appearances that he had become "a great nuisance." The Major complained about Sitting Bull, saying that the chief was

> working against our schools and will not send any of his children, and tries to influence others, and is very pompous and insolent; it may therefore be necessary for me to adopt stringent measures with him.... In the near future I may be obliged to arrest him and confine him to the Guardhouse. I will only do so, however, as a last resort, when persuasive powers fail.

McLaughlin also criticized the way Sitting Bull squandered the money he had earned in the Wild West Show. He considered it foolish that the chief hosted feasts for his friends and family and gave them many gifts. However, that was precisely what Sitting Bull and the Sioux believed was the proper way to use one's wealth—to give it away. McLaughlin was convinced that the chief's sharing of good fortune was an affront to his own authority and undermined his efforts to guide the Sioux in the proper direction. Consequently, when John Burke wrote in 1886 to request Sitting Bull's participation in another Wild West Show, McLaughlin replied that it wasn't advisable for the chief to do any more performing, because he was "too vain and obstinate to be benefitted by what he sees, and makes no good use of the money he earns, but spends it extravagantly."

In 1887, Sitting Bull moved his followers from the spot that McLaughlin had picked for them near Fort Yates to a place 40 miles (64 km) away toward the southwest, along the Grand River, very close to where he had been born at Many Caches fifty-six years earlier. Agents from other reservations, including L.F. Spencer of the Rosebud agency, soon joined McLaughlin in the belief that Sitting Bull's independent behavior fomented discontent that infected other agencies. In a telegram to the Commissioner of Indian Affairs, Spencer didn't mince words: "Arrest Sitting Bull and permanently remove him from Indian Country. He is a constitutional disturbance."

Such complaints caused McLaughlin to worry more than usual, so he sent a delegation of Indian police to Sitting Bull's new camp. However, all was quiet at the site, and he reported to the Commissioner that the chief had not been off the reservation, that "there is nothing unusual in his actions ... the old man has been behaving himself very well."

As time passed and no sign of discord came from the camp on the Grand River, McLaughlin felt relieved. He became so satisfied with the conduct of his famous ward that a year later, on April 9, 1888, he described Sitting Bull's behavior as "all that could be desired." Two roads had become a single path: On one side walked an iron-willed, reform-minded white man; on the other a proud but powerless Indian. In spite of their differences, each had preserved his half of an uneasy peace at Standing Rock.

ABOVE, CHIEF GALL,
CHILDHOOD FRIEND OF
SITTING BULL, AT THE
TIME OF HIS SURRENDER;
AND RIGHT, IN 1888 AT
STANDING ROCK
RESERVATION, WHEN HE
WAS A FAVORITE OF
McLAUGHLIN.

15

A BOMB
IN BLANKETS

...to the Standing Rock Indians, who protected the interests of the Great Sioux Nation...great praise is due.
JAMES McLAUGHLIN

I would rather die an Indian than live a white man.
SITTING BULL

The Sioux Act was introduced in Congress in the spring of 1888, and McLaughlin was at first favorably impressed by what he heard. When he had a chance to study the bill, however, he was disturbed by what he discovered. The act would create six separate reservations—Pine Ridge, Rosebud, Cheyenne River, Standing Rock, Crow Creek, and Lower Brule—out of the former 11-million-acre (4.5-million-hectare) Great Sioux Reservation. Indian families would be allotted a mere 160 acres (65 hectares) each, and the remaining land—about 9 million acres (3.6 million hectares)—would be termed "surplus" and sold to white settlers at $0.50 per acre.

At one time or another, the Sioux had roamed at will through the present states of Minnesota, Iowa, North and South Dakota, Wyoming, Montana, Colorado, and Nebraska. Territory had been surrendered in various treaties, and still more in the Black Hills treaty of 1876. Although McLaughlin considered it his duty to move the Indians toward accepting the white man's way of life, he vigorously took their side in regard to ceding more land by the Sioux Act. He expressed concern about the new legislation to the Commissioner of Indian Affairs.

"In the event this bill becomes a law," he wrote, "I trust that the interests of the Indians will be carefully guarded and all conditions of the agreement fully explained and clearly made known to them through competent and honest interpreters." He pointed out that in previous treaties the government didn't fully inform Indians of their rights, which not only worked to their disadvantage but put the government in a bad light as well.

McLaughlin knew that he wielded no special power in Washington; he was simply an agent on a reservation in far-off Dakota Territory. He decided that the best course of action was to be politely unhelpful in assisting the government to obtain the necessary signatures—three fourths of all adult male Indians—that would allow the bill to become law.

For several years, Sitting Bull had lived quietly along the Grand River, enjoying his family. His nineteen-year-old daughter Walks Looking left a son to be raised after her sudden death in 1887. Many Horses also presented him with grandchildren, as did his adopted sons One Bull and Jumping Bull. His ten-year-old daughter Standing Holy, born two years after the Battle of the Little Big Horn, had become his current favorite. The old chief was almost content. "The farther my people keep away from the whites, the better I shall be satisfied," he told Mary Collins, a Congregational missionary, adding, "I would rather die an Indian than live a white man." Not surprisingly, he adamantly opposed the Sioux Act from the moment he heard about it. He had vowed long ago never to surrender even a pinch of dust of Indian land and wasn't about to begin now.

The commission that arrived at Standing Rock in July 1888 to collect the required signatures included its chairman, Captain Richard Pratt, head of the Carlisle Indian school in Pennsylvania, Judge John Wright of Tennessee, and Reverend William Cleveland, a Protestant missionary to the Sioux and a cousin of President Cleveland. As head of the Standing Rock agency, McLaughlin was eligible to become an *ex officio* member of the commission, but excused himself because he believed privately that the treaty was grossly unfair to the Indians.

For a month the commissioners haggled with the Sioux, who, when they realized that McLaughlin didn't support the bill either, refused to sign. After obtaining only twenty-two names—among them was Gall's—the delegation moved on to the Crow Creek and Lower Brule reservations, where results were equally dismal. A reporter from the *Bismarck Tribune* asked Sitting Bull how he felt about the Indians who had signed. "Indians!" the chief snorted. "There are no Indians but me!"

Pratt dissolved the commission in disgust, telling officials in Washington they should pass the bill into law without the Indians' signatures. Such a high-handed course was deemed inadvisable; instead, notices were sent to the agents of the various Sioux reservations inviting them and selected Indian delegates to Washington to help draft a new bill. Among the ten Indians whom McLaughlin took from Standing Rock in October 1888, were Sitting Bull, Fire Heart, Thunder Hawk, and Bear's Rib, plus Louis Primeau as an interpreter.

Later, McLaughlin confided to Father Marty what the ordeal in Washington was like:

> My work with that Commission was a very trying one [but] to the Standing Rock Indians, who protected the interests of the Great Sioux Nation, by refusing to ratify the act, great praise is due. They ... discussed the bill in connection with the old treaties in such an intelligent manner that the Commissioners were unable to meet their arguments.... They stood firm for their rights to the end.... No act in my past life ... gives me greater satisfaction than our stand in this matter.

In the revised Sioux Act, 9 million acres west of the 102nd meridian were surrendered by the Indians at a price of $1.25 per acre—a sum that Sitting Bull argued for in a two-hour speech—rather than $0.50. Parcels of 320 acres (130 hectares), not 160 acres, were allotted to each Indian male. Forty-six chiefs, including a reluctant Sitting Bull, signed the new document.

A month later, the election of 1888 changed everything. Benjamin Harrison, a Republican, became president, and demanded that a new bill be drafted. He was supported by the newest states admitted to the Union, which would benefit most from settlement by whites—North and South Dakota, Montana, and Washington. A major change was that land would be sold for $1.25 per acre only for three years, then the price would drop to $0.75, and finally back to the original $0.50.

The Indians were not without advocates, however. The National Indian Defense Association dispatched Catherine Weldon, a young widow, to Standing Rock to assist the Sioux in their resistance to the act. McLaughlin had opposed the first bill, but realized that the latest one might be the best deal the Indians could hope for, and didn't welcome her interference. Newspaper articles suggested that the attractive widow fell in love with the aging Sioux chief and called her "a white squaw." Headlines jeered: "She Loves Sitting Bull," and "A New Jersey Widow Falls Victim to Sitting Bull's Charms"—rumors that outraged strait-laced McLaughlin but amused Sitting Bull.

General Crook, who had pursued the Sioux prior to Custer's defeat, was one of the three commissioners of the new delegation that came in July 1889 to gather signatures. His approach, as reported in the *Weekly Argus*, a Fargo newspaper, was devoid of tact. Instead, the general heaped ridicule on the hapless Sioux.

"When I left you eleven years ago I thought by this time you would be much further advanced than you are now," he taunted. "I feel you are satisfied to loaf on and do nothing and let the government feed you. Then [at the Little Big Horn] you were brave men....You are not brave men now but squaws, and the government will have to send dolls and rattles to amuse you." One can imagine the shame that a warrior like Rain-in-the-Face felt on hearing such words come out of a white man's mouth.

The Crook commissioners started collecting signatures at the other reservations first, leaving Standing Rock until last because of Sitting Bull's opposition. They lacked only 600 signatures to meet the three quarters needed for ratification. McLaughlin declared that he would need three days to line up signers, and urged Crook to meet the demands of Indians at Standing Rock to receive payment for the ponies that were confiscated back in 1876, plus an extension of school provisions that were promised in the Laramie Treaty of 1868.

The Major arranged a secret night meeting in an abandoned building 5 miles (8 km) from Fort Yates to discuss the new act with Indian leaders such as John Grass, Gall, and Mad Bear, all of whom he considered progressive. Sitting Bull, who had been called "a dynamite bomb in blankets" by reporters, was excluded. McLaughlin explained that if the Sioux didn't sign now, the government might go ahead and take their land anyway, just as it took the Black Hills. This might be their last good chance to wring concessions from the commissioners, he warned. The following morning, after the concessions asked for were met by Crook, the signing proceeded.

When Sitting Bull and his followers appeared unexpectedly and tried to break up the gathering, McLaughlin ordered the Indian police to keep them at bay. He had no intention of letting the signing process be disrupted at the last minute. Sitting Bull made it clear that he believed that those who had touched the pen—among them his oldest friends, Rain-in-the-Face, Black Bird, Catch the Bear, and even his nephew One Bull—had betrayed the best interests of the Sioux. He reminded them that the government had never honored its promises and wouldn't do so now.

It didn't take long for his prediction to come true. Only two weeks after the signing, the heads of the various agencies, including McLaughlin, were informed that beef rations for the Indians would be reduced by several million pounds per year. This reduction combined with several years of crop failures, brought the Indians near starvation. As if that were not enough, disease such as measles, whooping cough, and influenza were rampant on several reservations.

In February 1890, another promise was broken: The land the Indians had surrendered was opened to settlement without any boundary surveys, as had been promised in the Sioux Act. Among the Indians, a sudden death was considered a bad omen, so when news came that General Crook had died unexpectedly, the Sioux took it as a sign of further bad luck. Reverend Cleveland, who had participated in the first attempt to gather signatures, later recalled a prophetic remark to him made by an elderly Indian: "They [the whites] made many promises ... they never kept but one. They promised to take our land and they took it."

At his camp along the Grand River, Sitting Bull brooded as winter dragged on. As he pondered the meaning of the sudden death of General Crook, perhaps he remembered an earlier omen he had received. After he arrived at Standing Rock in May 1883, and the reality of permanent confinement had settled upon him, he rode alone onto the prairie, picketed his pony, and sat down to reflect on his fate.

Sitting Bull told his nephew One Bull what happened next. He heard a voice call to him, and turned to see that it was an old friend, a meadowlark. The bird spoke in Sioux, as it had done in his boyhood. "The Lakotas will kill you," it warned. The vision of bluecoats falling headfirst into camp had come true. Sitting Bull must have wondered if the meadowlark's prediction would, too.

16

A PROPHECY FULFILLED

Sitting Bull is a man of low cunning,
devoid of a single manly principle....
JAMES McLAUGHLIN

...you imagine that, if I were not here, all the
Indians would become civilized, and that, because
I am here, all the Indians are fools.
SITTING BULL

When rumors about the appearance of an Indian messiah came to Standing Rock, Sitting Bull, approaching his sixtieth birthday, was skeptical. Even when Kicking Bear and Short Bull took eleven men from the Pine Ridge and Cheyenne agencies and went to Nevada to investigate the story for themselves, he made no effort to join them. Instead, in the spring of 1890, Sitting Bull welcomed his white friend Catherine Weldon back to his camp on the Grand River.

The previous year, Mrs. Weldon and her son Christie lived in a cabin about 25 miles (40 km) away; this time, they moved in with Sitting Bull's family. As before, James McLaughlin resented the widow's meddling, nor was he pleased when she told him, "I honor and respect Sitting Bull as if he were my own father ... nothing can ever shake my faith in his good qualities." When she asked permission to establish a school near the Grand, the Major denied her request, so Mrs. Weldon busied herself teaching Indian women domestic skills. Since she was an artist of modest talent, she also painted the chief's portrait.

When stories of the Indian messiah reached McLaughlin, he paid closer attention than Sitting Bull had. In Nevada, a Paiute Indian named Wovoka claimed to have had a vision in which a messiah—a red one, not a white one—appeared before him. The Christ-like savior predicted that soon all whites would be banished from Indian country. A thick covering of fresh earth would miraculously cover the prairies, burying the *wasichus* and their towns. Herds of buffalo, wild horses, and all kinds of game would return, and long-dead ancestors would come back to life. Indians would once again hunt, sun dance, and move their camps without asking any white man's permission. To bring the millennium about more quickly, Wovoka urged Indians to participate in a Ghost Dance ceremony, and to wear magical red ghost shirts that would protect them from soldiers' bullets.

McLaughlin noted in a letter to the Commissioner of Indian Affairs in April 1890 that his first concern was "the Sitting Bull element, that chiefly reside in the more remote settlements along the Grand River." He spent nineteen days traveling to all corners of Standing Rock to assess for himself the danger created by the messiah story. He was reassured by what he found, and reported on June 18 that although there were certain malcontents "who cling tenaciously to the old Indian ways," there wasn't anything to be concerned about. Nor did McLaughlin have any doubt in mind whom the malcontents were: Circling Hawk, Black Bird, and especially Sitting Bull. Removal of such Indians from the reservation "would end all trouble or uneasiness in the future," he declared.

As Indians on other agencies began to perform the Ghost Dance, Sitting Bull finally became curious himself. He asked McLaughlin for permission to travel to the Cheyenne agency to learn more about the messiah stories, but the Major refused. Sitting Bull was determined, however, and without telling McLaughlin, he invited Kicking Bear and Short Bull to his home on the Grand River.

SITTING BULL AND SHOWMAN BUFFALO BILL CODY POSED
FOR THIS PORTRAIT IN 1885.

The Major was incensed when he discovered that proponents of the Ghost Dance craze had arrived at Standing Rock. He warned the commissioner, "There is now considerable excitement and some disaffection existing among certain Indians of this Agency." Then, in the bluntest language possible, he described the culprit who was responsible.

"Sitting Bull is [the] leading apostle of this Indian absurdity; in a word, he is the Chief Mischief Maker, and if he were not here this craze ... would never have gotten a foothold at this Agency." McLaughlin had done his best to put up with Sitting Bull, but now he unleashed a verbal attack that did no justice to himself or his adversary.

> Sitting Bull is a man of low cunning, devoid of a single manly principle in his nature or an honorable trait of character.... He is a coward and lacks moral courage ... and is the most vain, pompous and untruthful Indian that I ever knew ... a polygamist, libertine, habitual liar, active obstructionist and a great obstacle in the civilization of these people.

Since he believed no good would come of the visit by Kicking Bear and Short Bull, McLaughlin sent a detachment of thirteen Indian police to escort the intruders off the reservation. He notified Sitting Bull that his "insolence and bad behaviour would not be tolerated," and was convinced anew that the only solution to the problem was to remove the chief from Standing Rock. "I would respectfully recommend the removal from the reservation and confinement [of Sitting Bull] in some military prison ... sometime during the coming winter and before next spring opens," he advised the commissioner. McLaughlin had mentioned arrest before; now he pressed for it.

The Major and Mrs. Weldon had never agreed on the subject of Sitting Bull, but she objected to the Ghost Dance as strongly as he did. She called Kicking Bear a "false prophet and cheat," which soon cost her Sitting Bull's friendship. "I have turned my former friends into enemies, & some feel very bitter toward me," she confessed. "Even Sitting Bull's faith in me is shaken, & he imagines that I seek his destruction, in spite of all the proofs of friendship which I have given him for many years." The breech between the aging chief and the young widow widened, and she decided to leave Standing Rock. Sitting Bull himself drove her to the dock along the Missouri where a steamer waited. Just before boarding, her son Christie stepped on a nail; he died on the boat from tetanus, and Mrs. Weldon never returned to Sioux country.

Heads of other agencies became agitated as winter drew near, partly because white settlers throughout the area were growing more alarmed by the Ghost Dance rumors. P.P. Palmer of the Cheyenne agency reported that even though his Indians had been forbidden to perform the Ghost Dance, they continued to do so. After the inflammatory contents of McLaughlin's letters to the Commissioner of Indian Affairs were made public, fears intensified. President Harrison stepped forward to do whatever was necessary to prevent an Indian uprising, beginning with the dispatch of additional troops to Fort Yates.

When McLaughlin discovered that another Ghost Dance was about to take place at Sitting Bull's camp, he decided to go there himself, in hopes of talking sense to those who had gathered. He arrived on Saturday, November 15, 1890, as the dance was in progress. The participants, some of whom wore ghost shirts, had already danced themselves into a trancelike state. The Major realized that attempts at conversation at such a time were pointless, and retreated to the home of his most loyal policeman, Lieutenant Bull Head, 3 miles (5 km) from the Sitting Bull settlement.

Early Monday morning, McLaughlin returned to visit Sitting Bull. The chief emerged from an *inipi*, a sweat lodge, built near his log home, and greeted the Major with a handshake. McLaughlin pointed out how much had been accomplished for the Indians in their new way of life, and warned that it could all be destroyed if the ghost dancing continued. Sitting Bull had a suggestion. "Go with me to the agencies to the West," he invited McLaughlin, "and let me seek for the men who saw the messiah.... I will demand they show him to us, and if they cannot do so I will return and tell my people it was a lie." The two men parted with the issue unresolved; they never met again.

General Nelson Miles, Sitting Bull's old foe from the days along the Canadian border, believed he had a solution to the problem of a peaceful arrest of Sitting Bull. He appealed directly to a man with whom the chief was on good terms: Buffalo Bill Cody. Miles wrote to Cody in late November, authorizing him "to secure the person of Sitting Bull and deliver him to the nearest Commanding Officer of the U.S. Troops."

On Thanksgiving Day, 1890, Buffalo Bill arrived in Mandan, North Dakota, with three friends, Dr. Frank Powell, "Pony Bob" Haslam, and G.W. Chadwick, and proceeded toward Standing Rock. However, officers at Fort Yates suspected that Cody wouldn't share the honor of capturing the chief with the military, and conspired to appeal to the showman's well-known love of liquor by inviting him to the officers' club and getting him so drunk that he would forget his mission.

When McLaughlin learned of Cody's presence, he telegraphed Washington, requesting that the arrest order for Sitting Bull be rescinded immediately. "William F. Cody has arrived here with a commission from General Miles to arrest Sitting Bull. Such a step at present is unnecessary and unwise as it will precipitate a fight which cannot be averted.... I have matters well in hand ... can arrest Sitting Bull by Indian police without bloodshed.... Request immediate answer."

The answer was four hours in arriving, during which time Cody—none the worse for having imbibed heavily the evening before—set out for Grand River with a wagonload of gifts for Sitting Bull, much of it consisting of candy, which he knew the chief was fond of. He was accompanied by eight newspapermen, to whom he remarked that he was about to embark on "the most dangerous undertaking of my career." It's not clear why Cody never reached Sitting Bull's camp. Apparently he was told that the chief had left Grand River headed along a different route, causing Cody to switch roads hoping to intercept him, only to miss him altogether.

When an answer to McLaughlin's telegram came, it contained the words he hoped to read: "...make no arrests whatever, except under orders from the military." For the moment, a standoff had been averted.

McLaughlin wrote to Sitting Bull in early December, ordering all dancing to stop, whereupon the chief dictated a reply to his son-in-law Andrew Fox: "God made you—made all the white race, and also made the red race—and gave them both might and heart. You should say nothing against our religion, for we say nothing against yours. You don't like me because you think I am a fool," he accused McLaughlin, "and you imagine that, if I were not here, all the Indians would become civilized, and that, because I am here, all the Indians are fools." Sitting Bull also insisted he would go to Pine Ridge to learn more about the Ghost Dance.

McLaughlin received Sitting Bull's answer at agency headquarters at 6 P.M. on December 12, 1890, and dictated a swift reply: "My friend, listen to this advice ... do not attempt to visit any other agency at present."

Two days later, when spies reported that the obstinate chief was making plans to leave anyway, two troops of cavalry started a night march to Sitting Bull's camp on the Grand River. McLaughlin alerted Lieutenant Bull Head, adding an ominous postscript to his letter: "You must not let him escape under any circumstances."

At 4 A.M. on December 15, as an icy drizzle fell on the prairie, more than forty Indian police and volunteers proceeded toward Sitting Bull's home. In the cabin where the chief lived were the elder of his two wives and his fourteen-year-old son Crow Foot, the boy who had surrendered his father's rifle at Fort Buford. Also present were his nephew's wife, Red Whirlwind, and two elderly Indian men who had participated in the recent Ghost Dance. The rest of the chief's family were asleep in a small cabin nearby.

As dawn broke, the camp along the Grand River was roused by the sound of rapidly approaching horses. The Indian police pounded on the door of Sitting Bull's cabin and forced their way in. Sitting Bull rose from his bed, and the Indian officers shoved him toward the door, causing Sitting Bull to reproach them for not allowing him to dress properly. His wife hurried to the other cabin to get the clothes he requested. When he was shoved again, Sitting Bull exclaimed, "Let me go! I'll go without any assistance."

But an accusation from Crow Foot caused Sitting Bull to hesitate. His son cried out, "You call yourself a brave chief [but] you are allowing yourself to be taken by the *ceska maza!*" After a moment of reflection, Sitting Bull told the police, "*Mni kte sni yelo. Tokel eca maya nu ta neci ecun po.* I am not going. Do with me what you like."

The police had saddled Sitting Bull's horse—the same gray horse that had been a gift from Buffalo Bill—so that a quick departure could be made. It was not to be. Catch the Bear, Sitting Bull's longtime friend, came forward and urged the crowd that had gathered: "Let us protect our chief."

As some of his other followers begged Sitting Bull to go quietly, Catch the Bear suddenly raised his rifle and shot Lieutenant Bull Head, striking him in the side. As he fell, Bull Head drew his own pistol and shot Sitting Bull, whereupon Red Tomahawk, another member of the Indian police, also fired at Sitting Bull, striking him in the head. Strikes the Kettle, one of Sitting Bull's most loyal supporters, in turn fired at Red Tomahawk. The three men—two Indian policemen and Sitting Bull—fell together in a bloody heap just beyond the cabin door.

The ensuing struggle, lasting only moments, left eight Indians dead, including Sitting Bull's adopted son, Jumping Bull, and Catch the Bear, who had fired the first shot. Young Crow Foot, who dashed back into his father's cabin, was discovered hiding under some blankets. "Do not kill me," the boy cried. "I do not want to die!" His plea went unheeded; he was clubbed with a rifle butt and shot several times. Among the dead Indian police were Hawk Man, Afraid of Soldiers, and Little Eagle. Shave Head and Bull Head were mortally wounded and died later.

A distraught Indian, whose brother had been one of the slain Indian police, seized a neck yoke lying nearby and smashed the head of Sitting Bull, disfiguring it badly. Someone slashed the large portrait on the cabin wall that Mrs. Weldon had painted of the chief. Outside, in the cold December drizzle, the gray circus horse stood saddled, waiting for the rider who would never mount it again. A few days later, fifteen peeled willow sticks were driven into the ground around Sitting Bull's cabin, marking the spot where each man had fallen. The meadowlark's prophecy had been fulfilled.

MAJOR JAMES McLAUGHLIN, TOWARD THE END OF HIS LIFE,
GREETING INDIAN PARISHIONERS ON THE STEPS OF THE FORT
YATES CATHOLIC CHURCH.

17

A LONG LIFE
YET TO LIVE

To the men of my time was appointed the task of taking the raw and bleeding material which made the hostile strength of the plains Indians, of bringing that material to the mills of the white man.... The duty was not always congenial; it sometimes led to things and places I should not have elected to seek out.

JAMES McLAUGHLIN

School at Fort Yates was dismissed on the afternoon of December 16, 1890, so everyone could witness the arrival of the dead and wounded from the camp along the Grand River. The injured were taken to the hospital, then the frozen bodies of the Indian police were unloaded from a wagon. Sitting Bull's body, on which the others had been stacked, was removed last and taken to the "dead house" behind the hospital.

Sergeant Shave Head, knowing he was about to die of the abdominal wound he had received, asked that his wife be called so they could be married in the white man's way; he died fifteen minutes before she arrived. Lieutenant Bull Head, also mortally wounded, died two days later after great suffering. No white men lost their lives in the standoff. The Indian police, except for Little Eagle, who was buried along the Grand River, were laid to rest with full military honors in the Catholic cemetery at Fort Yates.

On December 17, Sitting Bull—considered a pagan—was wrapped in canvas, placed in a pine box, and buried in a remote corner of the post cemetery. For many years his grave was poorly tended, and because the states of North and

South Dakota soon argued about who owned the chief's bones, the site was vandalized several times. Some historians believe that whatever bones are in the grave today do not belong to Sitting Bull, that he is buried elsewhere in an unmarked spot. In life, he'd never wanted to live any closer to the whites than he had to; in death, he might have gotten his wish.

When James Walsh, the former major who had befriended Sitting Bull in Canada and now employed by the Dominion Coal, Coke, & Transportation Company of Winnipeg, heard about the chief's death, he said: "I am glad to learn that Bull is relieved of his miseries, even if it took the bullet to do it." Walsh knew the chief well enough to realize death had freed Tatanka Iyotanka of the humiliation caused by living as the white man's prisoner.

The day after Sitting Bull's death, the *New York Herald* reported:

> There was a quiet understanding between the officers of the Indian and military departments that it would be impossible to bring Sitting Bull to Standing Rock alive, and that if brought in, nobody would know precisely what to do with him....There was, therefore, cruel as it may seem, a complete understanding ... that the slightest attempt to rescue the old medicine man should be a signal to send Sitting Bull to the happy hunting ground.

James McLaughlin was taken aback by the furor that the chief's death created, and wasn't prepared for the criticism leveled at him. Headlines in Eastern newspapers used words and phrases such as "Murder!", "Foul Play!", and "Investigate McLaughlin!" Rumors abounded—that Sitting Bull's death was a planned assassination, just as the *Herald* suggested; that Officer Bull Head was drunk when he rode to the Grand River; that McLaughlin personally plotted the chief's death. No evidence to support any of those claims has ever been found.

In death, Sitting Bull became more famous than ever before, and his meager possessions were much sought after. Buffalo Bill purchased the gray circus horse from Sitting Bull's widows, and it appeared in his Wild West Show at the Chicago World's Fair in 1892. The chief's cabin and the slashed portrait painted by Catherine Weldon eventually became the property of the North Dakota Heritage Center in Bismarck. His Winchester rifle, the war shield he had carried since he was a boy of fourteen, and other personal effects became valuable collector's items.

Two weeks after Sitting Bull's death the final chapter of Plains Indian life was written at a place called Wounded Knee. Chief Big Foot of the Miniconjous, considered to be a "fomenter of disturbances" just as Sitting Bull had been, tried to take his people—including several members from Sitting Bull's band—to safety at the Pine Ridge reservation. He was intercepted by bluecoats under the command of Major Samuel Whitside, who saw that Big Foot was ill with pneumonia, his blanket stained with blood due to severe lung hemorrhage. Whitside ordered a wagon brought up so the chief could travel more comfortably.

As evening fell, the Sioux were herded toward *Chankpe Opi Wakpala*, or Wounded Knee Creek. The bluecoats counted the Indians assembled—120 men and 230 women and children—and tents and rations were issued to them. On Monday morning, December 29, 1890, in an atmosphere of mutual distrust, the Indian men were asked to surrender their arms to prevent an incident like the one that had resulted in Sitting Bull's death two weeks earlier.

A hot-headed young man named Black Coyote—he was said to be deaf and might not have understood the gravity of the situation—held his rifle aloft and declared he had "paid money for it" and did not want to give it up. When he was seized from behind the weapon discharged harmlessly in the air, but within seconds, the Seventh Cavalry, Custer's old outfit, returned the fire. Almost simultaneously, the Sioux warriors who had not yet handed over their arms shot back. Afterward, one tally listed 102 young men and women, 24 old men, 7 old women, 6 boys under age eight, and 7 babies under age two among the Indian dead. Because many Sioux died later, the total count has been estimated at 300 or more killed. The Seventh Cavalry lost 25 men and 39 wounded, many by gunfire from their own ranks.

Before the Indian bodies could be removed from the battle-field, a freezing blizzard shrouded them in snow. On New Year's Day, the dead—frozen into grotesque positions—were stacked in a pit and buried in a common grave. Years later, Black Elk, who had been swimming in the Little Big Horn river on the day of the Custer Massacre and who became a noted historian of his people, reflected on what happened at *Chankpe Opi Wakpala*: "And so it was all over. I did not know then how much was ended.... A people's dream died there. It was a beautiful dream." Two lines from a poem by Stephen Vincent Benét summed up the tragedy with equal poignancy:

> I shall not be there. I shall rise and pass.
> Bury my heart at Wounded Knee.

Sitting Bull's death, combined with those at Wounded Knee, ended the Indian wars. James McLaughlin still had a long life to live, however, and while he regretted the circumstances sur-rounding Sitting Bull's death—in particular the deaths of the Indian policemen, whom he had admired—he made no secret of the fact that the chief's passing made life at Standing Rock eas-ier. Sitting Bull had been right: McLaughlin hadn't liked him. His presence had been a constant threat to the Major's deeply held conviction that he—not an old medicine man who dreamed of past glory—knew better what was truly in the Indians' best interests.

One of McLaughlin's private challenges in the following years was educating his four sons and a daughter on an agent's meager income. He told his superiors that he was once again considering leaving the Indian service for an occupation that paid better. However, he struggled along until his sons were established on ranches of their own. When he was mentioned as a candidate for the U.S. Senate from North Dakota, he declined the honor; a job in politics wasn't what he had in mind.

Then, in 1895, he was called to Washington and advised that President Cleveland intended to name him Assistant Commissioner of Indian Affairs. It was a desk job, not the kind that McLaughlin believed suited him, and he declined that, too. But when the position of inspector of all U.S. Indian agencies was offered, he accepted. Of course, it meant moving to Washington and being home even less than he had been before, but he believed he could continue to carry out the kind of work that meant so much to him.

▲ ▲ ▲

Over the next twenty-eight years, McLaughlin erased whatever taint of scandal over Sitting Bull's death had tarnished his otherwise fine reputation by being a good a friend to Indian tribes throughout the nation. Ironically, one of his first inspections was at the agency where he had started his career, at the Lake Where Spirits Dwell. He spent four days traveling around Devil's Lake, increasingly displeased with what he saw. Indian children were not attending school regularly; homes were not properly furnished; polygamy was permitted. He outlined a program of reform to the agent in charge that required the dismissal of any employees who wouldn't enforce it. The century was about to turn, and McLaughlin was more convinced than ever that as Indian men and women stepped into it they must be encouraged to forsake the ways of their ancestors.

At the Tongue reservation in Montana in 1906, McLaughlin spent a week visiting as many of the 1,400 Cheyenne there as he could. Living conditions were poor, and he displayed a sympathetic understanding of Cheyenne temperament by noting that they were a "proud-spirited" people who had "many notable traits of character and can be led by moral suasion, but will not brook coercion." As he spoke, perhaps he reflected on his relationship with Sitting Bull, a man who couldn't be coerced either.

Relocation of tribes that were dissatisfied with the reservations they had been assigned to was a thorny problem as the twentieth century commenced. One of McLaughlin's dilemmas centered on Chief Joseph, who longed to return to the Wallawa Valley of Oregon, the original home of the Nez Perce. The old chief was "quite intelligent and exceedingly shrewd," McLaughlin observed after traveling with him for several days throughout the region. But whites in Oregon had sworn revenge on the Nez Perce for their uprising in 1877, so he concluded that relocation was not in anyone's best interest. Chief Joseph, who had almost outwitted Bear Coat Miles along the Canadian border more than a quarter of a century before, died in 1904 without setting foot in the Wallawa Valley again.

When relocation of the Mission Indians came up, however, McLaughlin vigorously supported their desire to be placed somewhere other than the harsh, hostile scrap of ground they had been confined to in the Agua Caliente area of California. "First the Indian occupied the fertile valleys and rich agricultural lands but gradually has been pushed back until now there is nothing left for him but barren hills," he wrote. "Out of these they endeavor to make a living on land which the white man would not accept as a gift."

He finally located a site that he thought would suit the Mission tribe—it had enough tillable land and water for their needs—but the Commissioner of Indian Affairs didn't approve it. A Los Angeles newspaper derided the choice as "the judgement of a tenderfoot." McLaughlin remarked bitterly that he felt "keenly the manner in which my selection was ignored—but I am even sorrier for the poor Indians, whose comfort and prosperity are lessened thereby."

McLaughlin's job took him to forty-five states, put him in touch with all major tribes in the country, keeping him out of Washington much of the time. His only daughter, Imelda, married in 1895 but died unexpectedly four years later. Marie never joined the Major in Washington but continued to live near Fort Yates, seeing her husband only when he returned for brief visits. She became so lonesome that Emma Crow King, an orphaned Indian girl whom the McLaughlins had adopted, interrupted her schooling and moved back home.

In 1907 the Chicago, Milwaukee, and St. Paul railroad founded a town in South Dakota and named it McLaughlin in the Major's honor. It was a pleasing recognition, and Marie soon moved there, along with son Charley. In 1910, short of funds as always, McLaughlin published his autobiography, *My Friend, the Indian*, hoping it would fatten his bank account. Initial book sales were lively, but his royalties came to only $800.

The four McLaughlin sons had received a good upbringing, but the Major was sometimes disappointed in their behavior. He scolded John in 1908 about his drinking habits and inability to manage money properly (he "squandered" it, McLaughlin complained, the same accusation he had aimed at Sitting Bull long ago!), which resulted in the young man getting a reputation as a ne'er-do-well. A few months later, John died of a broken neck after a fall from a horse. Five years later, Harry died; only Charley and Sibley outlived their parents.

In 1921, McLaughlin was honored at Fort Yates for fifty years of continuous service among the Indians. Later that year, he went home to Ontario for a rare visit with his brother Felix, and returned feeling ill with a cold. Nothing kept him from work, however, including the serious back injury he got while trying to hoist a car out of the mud on an inspection trip to the Fort Berthold reservation in North Dakota.

On the morning of July 28, 1923, after several weeks of hard work on the collection of annuities the government owed to the Santee Sioux, eighty-one-year-old McLaughlin arose in his apartment at the National Hotel in Washington feeling wearier than usual. A friend called a doctor, and two hours later, when a nurse delivered the medicine that had been prescribed, she found McLaughlin dead. He had always said that he "wanted to wear out, not rust out." Unlike Chief Joseph, he got his final wish.

James McLaughlin was buried on August 3, 1923, in the family plot at McLaughlin, South Dakota, where his two sons and only daughter were buried. Toward the southwest, not far as the crow flies, his famous adversary, Sitting Bull, had died thirty-three years earlier. Among the honor guards at the funeral were some of the Indian police who had participated in the attempted arrest of the last Sioux chief to give up his rifle—Bear's Ghost, George Flyingby, Otter Robe, Shoots Walking, and Tall Bull. As an epitaph, McLaughlin's own words fit him best, demonstrating that in spite of the stormy relationship he had with Sitting Bull he was a man of insight and compassion, who understood the Indian in sympathetic terms.

▲ "The history of treaty-making with the Sioux is the history of treaty-making with all the Indians. The treaties were made for the accommodation of the whites, and broken when they interfered with the money-getters."

▲ "To the men of my time was appointed the task of taking the raw and bleeding material which made the hostile strength of the plains Indians, of bringing that material to the mills of the white man, and of transmuting it into a manufactured product that might be absorbed by the nation without interfering with the national digestion. In doing my part toward bringing about this transmutation, I went to the Indian, instead of sitting in my office and waiting for the Indian to come to me. The duty was not always congenial; it sometimes led to things and places that I would not have elected to seek out."

▲ "I am not an apologist for the Indian ... but I do know that the sins of the Indians are traceable to the avarice, the cruelty, the licentiousness of the white man."

▲ "We took away from him his hunting-grounds and put him on a reservation. This reservation was generally located in a country unavailable for the use of the white man of the early day. It was not poor land, except by comparison with the richer territory surrounding it, and it was held to be good enough for the Indian."

▲ "I believe I came to understand Indian human nature....I believe the Indian was a man before outrage and oppression made him a savage. I have known him as a savage, a fighting man, in the pride and insolence of his strength; I have known him as a sage in council, then as a beggar with the pride starved out of him."

Sitting Bull and James McLaughlin were neither saints nor sinners. They lived in tempestuous times, their lives entangled in ways that neither man anticipated and, as McLaughlin himself admitted, "led to things and places I should not have elected to seek out." Sitting Bull—who'd lived by the Sioux code of bravery, fortitude, generosity, and wisdom—would have expressed agreement with one of his ironical smiles. Each man's vision was based upon his upbringing, education, and experience. Each man was strong-willed, accustomed to commanding respect, and determined to lead the Sioux toward a different day. That Sitting Bull and James McLaughlin had radically different opinions about what that new day should be like cannot detract from the integrity of either man.

Source Notes

p. 12: Vestal, Stanley, Sitting Bull: Champion of the Sioux (Norman: University of Oklahoma Press, 1989), p. 3.

p. 12: State Historical Society of North Dakota, The Last Years of Sitting Bull (Bismarck: North Dakota Heritage Center, 1984), unpaged.

p 15: Utley, Robert M., The Lance and the Shield: The Life and Times of Sitting Bull (New York: Henry Holt & Company, paperback edition), pp. 11-13.

p. 17: McLaughlin, James, My Friend, the Indian (Boston: Houghton Mifflin Company, 1926), p. 8.

p. 19: McLaughlin Collection, Letter to Supt. of Indian Schools, Sept. 4, 1901, Roll 24, Frames 742-744.

pp. 20-21: Pfaller, Louis, James McLaughlin: The Man With the Indian Heart (New York: Vantage Press, 1978),p. 380.

p. 22: Utley, Robert M., The Lance and the Shield: The Life and Times of Sitting Bull (New York: Henry Holt & Company, paperback edition), pp. 18-22.

p. 25: Vestal, Stanley, Sitting Bull: Champion of the Sioux (Norman: University of Oklahoma Press, 1989), p. 49.

p. 29: Eriksmoen, Curtis G., The Career of Major James McLaughlin Before His Prominent Years: The Period Prior to His Appointment to the Standing Rock Reservation. (Grand Forks: University of North Dakota, Master's Thesis, 1967), p. 11.

p. 30: Eriksmoen, p. 12.

p. 31: McLaughlin Collection, Rough draft of letter (Notebook 1), Roll 16, Frames 5-6.

p. 31: Eriksmoen, Curtis G., The Career of Major James McLaughlin Before his Prominent Years: The Period Prior to His Appointment to the Standing Rock Reservation. (Grand Forks: University of North Dakota, Master's Thesis, 1967), p. 28.

p. 32: McLaughlin, James, My Friend, the Indian (Boston: Houghton Mifflin Company, 1926), p. 8.

pp. 35, 37: Brown, Dee, Bury My Heart at Wounded Knee: An Indian History of the American West (New York: Holt, Rinehart & Winston, 1970), p. 189.

p. 38: Utley, Robert M., The Lance and the Shield: The Life and Times of Sitting Bull (New York: Henry Holt & Company, 1993, paperback edition), pp. 44-46.

p. 39: Utley, p. 49.

p. 43: Pfaller, Louis L., James McLaughlin: The Man With the Indian Heart (New York: Vantage Press, 1978), p. 26.

p. 44: Pfaller, p. 20.

p. 45: Brown, Dee, Bury My Heart at Wounded Knee: An Indian History of the American West (New York: Holt, Rinehart & Winston, 1970), p. 83.

p. 46: Brown, p. 89.

p. 48: Brown, p. 84.

p. 50: Chittenden, Hiram M., and Alfred T. Richardson, Life, Letters, and Travels of Father Pierre-Jean De Smet, Vol. 3 (New York: F.P. Harper), p. 912.

p. 54: Pfaller, Louis L., James McLaughlin: The Man With the Indian Heart (New York: Vantage Press, 1978), p. 28.

p.55: Eriksmoen, Curtis G., The Career of Major James McLaughlin Before His Prominent Years: The Period Prior to His Appointment to the Standing Rock Reservation (Grand Forks: University of North Dakota, Master's Thesis, 1967), p. 42.

p. 57: Eriksmoen, p. 45.

p. 58: McLaughlin Collection, Roll 16, Frame 137.

p. 58: McLaughlin Collection, Roll 16, Frames 193-194.

p. 60: Utley, Robert M., *The Lance and the Shield: The Life and Times of Sitting Bull* (New York: Henry Holt & Company, 1993, paperback edition), p. 145.

p. 61: Brown, Dee, *Bury My Heart at Wounded Knee: An Indian History of the American West* (New York: Holt, Rinehart & Winston, 1970), p. 277.

p. 62: Brown, p. 280.

p. 62: Brown, p. 284.

p. 69: McLaughlin Collection, Rolls 1 and 19.

p. 70: Pfaller, Louis L., *James McLaughlin: The Man With the Indian Heart.* (New York: Vantage Press, 1978), pp. 43-44.

p. 71: McLaughlin Collection, Roll 19, Frames 302-309.

p. 71: McLaughlin Collection, Roll 19, Frames 417-419 and 455-456.

p. 75: Manzione, Joseph, *I Am Looking to the North for My Life: Sitting Bull, 1876-1881* (Salt Lake City: University of Utah Press, 1991), p. 133.

p. 77: Utley, Robert M., *The Lance and the Shield: The Life and Times of Sitting Bull* (New York: Henry Holt & Company, 1993, paperback edition), p. 173.

pp. 79-81: Utley, p. 182.

p. 81: The *New York Evening Telegram*, Dec. 9, 1881.

pp. 82-83: Pfaller, Louis L., *James McLaughlin: The Man With the Indian Heart* (New York: Vantage Press, 1978), p. 70-72.

p. 83: McLaughlin Collection, Roll 20, Frames 131-136.

pp. 84-85: Pfaller, Louis L., *James McLaughlin: The Man With the Indian Heart* (New York: Vantage Press, 1978), pp. 78-79.

pp. 86-87: Manzione, Joseph, *I Am Looking to the North for My Life: Sitting Bull, 1876-1881* (Salt Lake City: University of Utah Press, 1991), p. 38.

pp. 86-87: Manzione, pp. 47-48.

pp. 90-91: Brown, Dee: *Bury My Heart at Wounded Knee: An Indian History of the American West* (New York: Holt, Rinehart & Winston, 1970), p. 328.

p. 93: Utley, Robert M., *The Lance and the Shield: The Life and Times of Sitting Bull.* (New York: Henry Holt & Company, 1993, paperback edition), p. 232.

p. 97: McLaughlin Collection, Letter to Commissioner of Indian Affairs (Notebooks), 48-49.

p. 98: McLaughlin Collection, Roll 20, Frames 179-180.

pp. 99-100: McLaughlin Collection, Roll 20,Frames 210-222.

p. 100: McLaughlin Collection, Roll 1, Frame 6; Roll 17, Frame 103

Page 101-102: McLaughlin Collection, Roll 20, Frames 386-389

p. 102: McLaughlin Collection; Letter from L. F. Spencer to Commissioner of Indian Affairs, Oct. 20, 1887, RG 75. No. 27986-1887.

p. 102: McLaughlin Collection; Letter to Paul C. Blum, April 9, 1888, Roll 20, Frames 745-746.

pp. 105-106: Pfaller, Louis L., *James McLaughlin: The Man With the Indian Heart.* (New York: Vantage Press, 1978), p. 110.

pp. 106-107: McLaughlin Collection; Letter to Fr. Marty, Feb. 23, 1889: Roll 20, Frames 813-186.

p. 107: Pfaller, Louis L., *James McLaughlin: The Man With the Indian Heart* (New York: Vantage Press, 1978), p. 124-125.

p. 112: McLaughlin Collection, Letter to Commissioner of Indian Affairs, Oct. 17, 1890, Roll 21, Frames 369-381.

pp. 112-113: Pfaller, Louis L., *James McLaughlin: The Man With the Indian Heart.* (New York: Vantage Press, 1978), p 134.

p. 113: McLaughlin Collection, Roll 21, Frame 438-445; 457.

p. 113: Pfaller, Louis L., *James McLaughlin: The Man With the Indian Heart.* (New York: Vantage Press, 1978), p. 143.

p. 115: Utley, Robert M., *The Lance and the Shield: The Life and Times of Sitting Bull* (New York: Henry Holt & Company, 1993, paperback edition), p. 298.

Page 116: Utley, pp. 300-302.

p. 118: McLaughlin, James, *My Friend, the Indian* (Boston: Houghton Mifflin Company, 1926), p. 3.

Page 121: McLaughlin Collection, Roll 22; Frames 209, 236, 305, 308, 330, 418, 423-428.

p. 122: Pfaller, Louis L., *James McLaughlin: The Man With the Indian Heart* (New York: Vantage Press, 1978), p. 203.

Page 124: McLaughlin Collection, Roll 14, Frame 5; Roll 26, Frames 821-834.

p. 124: *Washington Sunday Star*, July 29, 1923.

p. 125: McLaughlin, James: *My Friend, the Indian* (Boston: Houghton Mifflin Company, 1926), pp. 3-4.

Index

Thou Shalt Not Grill

**Other Pennsylvania Dutch Mysteries
by Tamar Myers**

Thou Shalt Not Grill

A Pennsylvania Dutch Mystery
with Recipes

Tamar Myers

NEW AMERICAN LIBRARY

New American Library
Published by New American Library, a division of
Penguin Group (USA) Inc., 375 Hudson Street,
New York, New York 10014, U.S.A.
Penguin Books Ltd, 80 Strand,
London WC2R 0RL, England
Penguin Books Australia Ltd, 250 Camberwell Road,
Camberwell, Victoria 3124, Australia
Penguin Books Canada Ltd, 10 Alcorn Avenue,
Toronto, Ontario, Canada M4V 3B2
Penguin Books (N.Z.) Ltd, Cnr Rosedale and Airborne Roads,
Albany, Auckland 1310, New Zealand

Penguin Books Ltd, Registered Offices:
80 Strand, London WC2R 0RL England

ISBN 0-451-21113-8

Printed in the United States of America

PUBLISHER'S NOTE
This is a work of fiction. Names, characters, places, and incidents either are the product of the
author's imagination or are used fictitiously, and any resemblance to actual persons, living or
dead, business establishments, events, or locales is entirely coincidental.

For Genny Ostertag, with gratitude.

Acknowledgments

I'm a lousy cook. However, it is my pleasure to share the recipes included in this book. I am indebted to Sharon and John Wilkerson for their Grilled Grouper recipe and Jim and Jan Langdoc for their Beer Butt Chicken recipe. A special thanks goes to Damon Lee Fowler for the other recipes in the book, all of which came from *Damon Lee Fowler's New Southern Kitchen*, published by Simon & Schuster, New York, 2002.

1

I seldom discover feet protruding from the top of my washing machine. Forgive me, then, if I assumed the worst. Besides, jumping to conclusions is my only form of exercise.

My heart leaped into my mouth. Given the length of my scrawny neck, that is quite a trick. At any rate, there have been enough murders at my full-board inn to satisfy a multitude of morticians. Of course, murder is always tragic, but somehow it becomes even more so when it happens in your home. To put it plainly, a corpse in my Kenmore was not going to be good for business.

Forcing my heart back down my narrow gullet, I approached the machine for a closer look. The shoes were cheap. Some kind of shiny plastic. The pant legs looked plastic as well, and they didn't droop down the legs like real pants would. Then I noticed the little tube that protruded from one ankle. It looked just like the valve on the air mattress I sometimes use to float on when I swim at Miller's Pond.

"Buzzy Porter," I said through clenched teeth.

The man lived up to his name. He had been my guest for only an hour, and already this was his third stunt. The first was when we shook hands in my lobby and I got the shock of my life. I mean that literally. The little gadget hidden in his palm packed a punch that nearly lifted me out of my brogans. His second stunt was to take advantage of my state of confusion and slap a sign on my back that read KISS ME, I'M GORGEOUS. This gag might have worked on someone who is used to being manhandled. But I felt his hand, as hot as a branding iron, burning its way, first through the paper, then my dress, and finally my sturdy Christian underwear.

Perhaps I should have been flattered by the word "gorgeous," but it is so far from the truth as to not even be funny. Of course, my fiancé, Gabriel Rosen, would disagree with that, but he is blinded by love. My point is that I have no illusions about who I am.

One of the things that I am is opinionated—although I prefer to use the word "informed." I have been known to inform others of their failings, in hopes that they will mend their ways and in the end make the world a better place. It was high time Buzzy Porter did his share to help.

I found the prankster supine in the parlor, but hardly resplendent in faded shorts, a torn T-shirt, and bright orange flip-flops. In Grandma Yoder's day, there wouldn't have been a piece of furniture comfortable enough upon which to sprawl. Not only did Grandma believe that reclining was inherently evil, but it was her policy that guests—all of whom were friends and neighbors— should not stay more than two hours. Three straight-back chairs and one lumpy Victorian love seat enforced that policy.

My guests, on the other hand, pay through the nose for an "authentic" Pennsylvania Dutch experience. Some even take advantage of A.L.P.O.—Amish Lifestyle Plan Option—whereby they pay extra for the privilege of performing chores. None, however, are willing to risk hemorrhoids, and in recent years I've been forced to supply a comfy couch and several well-padded armchairs. But no La-Z-Boy recliners. Grandma's ghost wouldn't sit still for that.

"Mr. Porter," I said, after praying for patience, "you will find your toy in the kitchen trash can, should you wish to retrieve it."

He had the audacity to feign ignorance. "What toy is that?"

"On second thought, maybe I should keep it. I have a foster daughter who might get a kick out of it."

That got his attention enough to make him sit. "No, no, I'll go get it. But first, would you like a piece of gum?"

"No, thank you."

He held out a packet labeled Floozy Fruit. "Oh, come on, Miss Yoder. Take a piece."

"Mr. Porter—"

"For your foster daughter," he said. "Maybe she'd like a stick."

"All right," I said just to shut him up. Between you and me, I eschew gum chewing. It's not the substance itself I detest, but those people who chew like cows chomping on their cuds. Worse yet are the folks who attach used gum to the undersides of tables, or leave it to sizzle on hot sidewalks, where it invariably finds its way to the soles of my shoes.

I reached for the gum. But no sooner did my digits touch the pack, than a spring-loaded contraption came out of nowhere and snapped closed on my index finger. I felt like a mouse that had been trapped.

"Get this thing off me at once!" I roared.

"Gotcha!" Buzzy let go of the gum pack and slapped his thighs. At least he was entertained.

I ripped the offending gadget off my finger—it really wasn't on all that tight—and dropped it down the front of my dress. I have not been blessed in the bosom department, and where there was once room for a Siamese kitten, there was now plenty of room for a fake pack of gum. Frankly, if the little spring went off again, there was nothing for it to grab.

"Mr. Porter, one more prank, and you're out of here. And don't even think about asking for a refund. In fact, I have half a mind to charge you for what will surely be the onset of my first gray hair."

"Okay, okay, I hear you. But don't I at least get my trick back? It cost me twelve ninety-nine."

I may be a simple Mennonite innkeeper, but the Good Lord gave me a head for business. The Bible instructs us to nourish our talents, and I try to do so on a daily basis.

"Ten bucks even," I said.

"Aw come on, Miss Yoder. That's not fair."

"I'm going to count to ten, and then the price goes up to twenty."

"But, Miss Yoder—"

"You'll still be saving almost three dollars in the event you want to go out and buy yourself a new one."

"Miss Yoder—"

"That's my name all right. Don't wear it out. One, two, three—"

He whipped out his wallet so fast it was a blur. When my eyes had adjusted I studied the two bills he proffered. I even walked over to the window and held them to the light. They looked genuine, but I was, after all, dealing with a irrepressible jokester.

"If the ink on these disappears," I warned him, "I'll know where to find you."

"Yes, Miss Yoder," he said. Perhaps the smirk on his face was accidental.

My name is indeed Yoder—Magdalena Portulacca Yoder—although it won't be that way for long. Sometime next year I plan to marry Dr. Gabriel Rosen. Gabe the Babe, as I like to think of him, lives across Hertlzer Road in an old farmhouse. My intended is a retired M.D., an urban refugee from the Big Apple. For some reason he decided that my hometown of Hernia, Pennsylvania, population 1,978.5 (Selma Graber is five months pregnant) would be the perfect place to try his hand at writing mystery novels.

I, on the other hand, have local roots that extend to China. My Amish ancestors founded Hernia in 1804, my family having first settled in the eastern part of the state in the early seventeen hundreds. I am related to all the first families: the Yoders, of course, the Bloughs, the Hostetlers, the Seilers, the Zugs, and a host of others. In this south-central Pennsylvania valley we have inbred to the point that I am, in fact, my own cousin. Give me a sandwich and I constitute a family picnic.

However, I do not qualify as a family *reunion,* and that is a good thing. Hernia was about to celebrate its bicentennial—Hernia Heritage Days we were billing it—and Amish and Mennonite exiles were pouring into town like bees to the hive at dusk. My inn, The

PennDutch, had been booked solid for more than two years in advance. This is not unusual, mind you, because the rich and famous have long used my establishment as a "quaint little getaway," to quote *Condornest Travels*.

In fact, it was in this very magazine that the town council had placed an advertisement, hoping to draw at least some of its dispersed back home to celebrate the birthday bash. For the record, I had been firmly against this ad, on the grounds that it might draw *too* many people, and as a result our hamlet would turn into another Lancaster. And judging from the buzz in the biz—and by that I mean other hoteliers in the county—we were in for quite a crowd. Of course, that didn't surprise me. What surprised me was that none of *my* expected guests appeared to be of the faith. They certainly didn't have the right names.

After I left Buzzy Porter—certainly not one of our kind—I mulled over this phenomenon. Perhaps this week's guests were merely run-of-the-mill tourists with exceptional foresight. I would have asked Buzzy his motive for visiting, had he not immediately given me the shock of my life. Oh well, the next guest to arrive was going to get grilled like a wienie at a Girl Scout cookout. A wienie that had broken off the stick and landed in the coals where it . . .

The jarring sound of my doorbell brought me back to reality. "Let the grilling begin!" I cried.

2

The couple that stood at my door looked as if they had already been grilled. Perhaps over a very hot fire. He was as bald as a cantaloupe, and his exposed skin, where not covered by freckles, was only a shade or two lighter than the poinsettia my sister gave me for Christmas. He wore faded overalls over a mostly white shirt. At least the yellow stains spreading from his armpits matched the clump of hair that sprouted above the top button of his collar and the eyebrows the size of sparrow wings.

She, on the other hand, was deeply tanned, but her blue eyes had faded to the point that their color was in question. Her sun-streaked brown hair was short and as dry and coarse as kindling. The hideous twigs were held in place by tortoiseshell barrettes that begged to be released from duty and thrown in the nearest garbage receptacle.

Because I charge exorbitant prices, I normally get an exclusive clientele. After all, there is no limit to the amount of abuse folks will tolerate, just as long as they can view it as a cultural experience. The more you charge them, the better deal they think they are getting. At any rate, the couple standing before me didn't look like they could afford a night in a Motel 6, much less my esteemed establishment.

"May I help you?" I ask charitably.

He proffered a chapped paw. "We're the Nortons. Chuck and Bibi."

She nodded vigorously. I assumed it was in agreement, although it's possible she was trying to dislodge the ugly doodads from her do.

"You should have a reservation for us," he said. He spoke in flat tones that hinted of one the square states far to our west.

While I like to think that I have a mind like a steel trap, it is more likely made from unadulterated iron. It seems to have been rusting up on me quite a bit lately.

"Ah yes, the Nortons."

"From Inman, Kansas," she said, sounding worried.

Inman, Kansas. That rang a bell. So it wasn't a square state but a rectangular one. Sort of like Pennsylvania, but a great deal flatter. My family is no longer Amish, but Mennonite, and many of our number have migrated to Kansas, particularly to the Inman area. When I'd received the Nortons' request for lodging, I had made a mental note of their hometown, hoping to play "Mennonite geography" with them when I saw them.

Alas, Norton is neither an Amish nor a Mennonite name. But a buck is a buck, is it not?

"Koom on een, dears," I said. "Velkommen to zee PennDutch." Most guests, by the way, get a kick out of my fake German accent.

The Nortons showed no reaction, although Chuck did step aside to allow Bibi to enter first. She strode in on sturdy brown legs, but didn't give my quaint decor a second look.

"When do the festivities start?" she asked, preempting my grilling session.

Already it was time to ditch the accent. "The tractor pull and pig chase are tomorrow. The hay-baling contest and Bake-Off are the day after. So is the cow auction. And then Wednesday—well, that's the big day. The actual anniversary. At noon we dig up the time capsule. After that we have the town picnic up on Stucky Ridge."

"Fireworks?" Chuck Norton asked.

I shook my head. "We Plain People aren't really into that."

"How far is it back into town?"

"Four point two miles, but you're not going to find another

place to stay. I'm the only game in town, and you won't even find a room over in Bedford, which is the nearest real city. Everything's been booked for months."

"Oh no, we're not looking for another place." The frumpy woman was as nervous as a mouse in a cattery.

"Mother likes to walk," Chuck Norton explained.

"Your mother!" I cried in amazement. "Why, she doesn't look but ten years older than you."

"She's my *wife*. Mother is what I call her."

Bibi Norton was too tanned to blush. "And I call him Father. We have twelve grown sons, you see."

Father Chuck slipped a thumb under an overall strap. "And all of them wheat farmers like Mother and me."

"You don't say." This is my newest response when, in fact, I have nothing to say. I'm sure the world can use twelve more wheat farmers, but for one couple to have a dozen offspring seems to be taking to excess the biblical commandment to be fruitful and multiply. Perhaps this is just sour grapes on my part, seeing as how I am forever doomed to be as barren as the Gobi Desert.

I checked in the Nortons. They declined A.L.P.O. and expressed no interest in the history of my charming inn or its engaging proprietress. In short, they promised to be as much fun as a mammogram. At least on the plus side, they were strong enough to carry their own luggage to the top of my impossibly steep stairs. Otherwise I would have had to schlep their bags up myself. My elevator, which is barely larger than a bread box, has been on the fritz ever since two contestants from a pie-eating contest decided to do the mattress mambo in that minuscule space.

"Third room on your right," I called after them.

They didn't even have the courtesy to respond.

I was still filing the Nortons' paperwork when the front door slammed open. Without looking up I knew exactly who it was and had a pretty good idea what had happened. My foster daughter has at least one hormone-related crisis a day.

"Boy trouble?" I asked.

"I hate him!" But instead of stomping off to our room—we share one when we have guests—Alison collapsed on the floor like a winter coat that had slid off its hanger.

"Jimmy?" I asked, careful to keep my tone neutral. Jimmy was her boyfriend du jour, and I did not approve of him in the least. She had just turned thirteen, and he was seventeen. Of course, she wasn't allowed to date, but I couldn't stop them from seeing each other at school. What's a pseudomother to do, except pray that they broke up?

"Don't be a dingus, Mom. Of course it's Jimmy. Do you know what he had the nerve to do?"

"What?" It was all I could do not to jump and shout for joy. Because the check-in counter hid my feet, I did a little shuffling dance. Yes, I know, it's a sin to dance. I would just have to repent of it later.

Alison pulled herself up into something resembling a sitting human being. "He went out with Carrie Sanders, that's what. On a real date! In a car and everything. And you know what?"

"What?"

"It's all your fault."

"Mine?"

" 'Cause you won't let me date. Carrie's mom lets her."

"How old is Carrie?"

She shrugged. "Who cares? I hate her."

"Is she older than you?"

"Okay, so she's a junior, but so what? Jimmy is the only man I'll ever love—except that now I hate him."

The parlor door opened and Buzzy stepped into the foyer. When he saw Alison, he smiled. In those few seconds he was transformed from a clown into a rather handsome young man.

"Sorry, Miss Yoder," he said. "I didn't know you had company."

I shook my head. "This is my daughter, Alison. She lives here. Alison, this is Mr. Porter."

"Hey," she said.

"Care for a piece of gum?" he asked.

"Yeah." She looked at me defiantly. Alison has a habit of discarding her used gum wherever she happens to be when she tires of it. Usually it ends up on the floor or, at best, stuck to the bottom of a piece of furniture. Pleading and scolding have had zero effect on her, so lately I'd been making her chew it outside.

Buzzy winked at me and held out the bogus pack. Apparently that old gag isn't popular in Minnesota from whence Alison hails, because she shrieked in surprise. When she saw that it was just a trick, she shrieked with laughter.

"What else do ya got?" she asked. From the look on her face it was clear my newly dumped daughter had developed an instant crush on the bothersome Buzzy. Needless to say, I was about as thrilled as I'd be if my prize hen, Pertelote, took up with a fox.

My next guests, Buist and Capers Littleton, more than made up for the Nortons' lack of social graces. This couple hailed from Charleston, South Carolina, which is the nation's capital of good manners. I know this for a fact, because I've been there. The folks in that fair city are always polite to your face, even if they hate your guts. While this isn't my style, I appreciate being the recipient of consideration, no matter how insincere.

The Littletons had driven twelve hours just to attend our bicentennial. Even though they must have been as tired as hookers after a Shriners' convention, they trotted out their good manners the minute they set foot in my inn.

"Oh, what a lovely place," Capers cooed, adding two syllables to the final word.

"But it isn't half as lovely as you," Buist purred. He appeared to be looking at my feet.

I beamed. "And for only twenty dollars more a day, you can experience an authentic Amish lifestyle by pitching in with the chores."

"Oh what fun," they exclaimed in unison.

I doubted, however, that Capers was capable of any real work.

She was a tiny thing with lacquered nails. Her bottle-blond bob was lacquered as well. Her dress was linen, that curious choice of the idle rich, who claim to like this fabric for its cooling properties, yet invariably wear outfits lined with some man-made unbreathable material. The end result is that folks who could well afford a maid, walk around as wrinkled as a Chinese shar-pei, and smelling like a wet dog too.

Buist Littleton wasn't nearly as rumpled in his blue and white seersucker suit, although his jacket was undoubtedly lined as well. In fact, he looked rather dapper, what with his bow tie and white buckskin shoes.

The couple appeared to be in their mid-thirties, although their driver's licenses pegged them at a full decade older. A good sunscreen, I've learned through observation, can do almost as much to preserve the appearance of youth as can a surgeon's scalpel.

As it turned out, I need not have worried about carrying their cases upstairs. Buist was far too much of a gentleman to have allowed that.

"Miss Yoder," Capers said, as she turned to follow her husband, "do we dress for dinner?"

Needless to say, I was properly shocked. I had to catch my breath before answering, during which time I couldn't help but picture Buist in the buff. Frankly, it was an intriguing sight.

"Of course," I rasped. "I do not allow naked people in the dining room. Or in my inn altogether, unless, of course, they're bathing—"

"Ma'am," Buist said with a twinkle in his eye, "I believe what my wife meant was, do we need to change into evening wear?"

I must confess that I learned one of life's most useful lessons not from kindergarten, but from my cat. Alas, I had to give my poor pussy away on account of my foster daughter's allergies, but not before the feline had a chance to teach me the importance of staying cool. Whenever you miscalculate a distance, or commit some other attention-grabbing blunder, just pretend you *meant* to do it.

"Gotcha!" I said, borrowing from Buzzy.

"Very good," Buist said, and then he and Capers pretended to laugh. Like I said, the folks from Charleston are nothing, if not polite.

"By all means, put on the dog."

"I beg your pardon?"

"Dress to the nines. Even the tens, if you want."

They smiled happily. I smiled as well, knowing that I would encourage all my guests to gussy it up, except for Buzzy. That would fix his wagon good.

I know, a good Christian should be above such spiteful thoughts, but I am only a saint-in-training. In fact, every now and then I find myself in sinners' rehab. With any luck Buzzy Porter was going to get a taste of his own medicine come dinner.

3

I had good reason to believe that at least one from among my next batch of guests would need no coaxing to play dress up. The trio arrived in a stretch limousine. Luxury cars are not unusual in Hernia, thanks to the caliber of my clientele, but they impress no one. Amish are known as the Plain People, and most Mennonites I know run a close second in the race for modesty. True, we have a few Methodists and Presbyterians in town, as well as two Jews—even a lone Episcopalian—but over the years folks have become blasé about celebrities roaming our streets.

The locals certainly were not going to drop their teeth over an actress like Octavia Cabot-Dodge. When her manager, a Ms. Augusta Miller, had called to make the reservations, she'd made a point of emphasizing the woman's stardom. Now, I don't watch movies, and gave up on TV when *Green Acres* reruns went off the air, but even I knew that Ms. Cabot-Dodge was a has-been. I remembered reading an article—*Peephole* magazine, I think—that said the actress's biggest achievement was staying in seclusion for forty years. Before going into hiding she'd managed to do three movies, one of which won her an Oscar, and two that were complete bombs. She might still have succeeded as an actress, but she was reportedly impossible to work with. According to the magazine—and I read this rag only when I'm in the checkout line at the supermarket—the fallen star was hoping to gain notoriety by her absence. Apparently she'd succeeded to a point, or the editor at *Peephole* would have passed on the piece.

While I, for one, wasn't going to open my peephole and spill the beans, I doubted that she really wanted her privacy. If that was the case, why had she shown up in a limo? My hunch—and a hunch from a woman is worth two facts from a man—is that the faded film star had run out of funds and was planning to stage a comeback. Whatever her reasons for her ostentatious arrival, just as long as she cooperated and dressed for dinner, her secret was safe with me.

When she stepped out of the stretch she was already dressed to the eights. From her narrow shoulders hung a green satin creation that fell just short of being a ball gown. It went too far to qualify as a mother-of-the-bride dress at a formal wedding, yet atop her head perched a very matronly, not to mention dated, green pillbox hat. Even from a distance I could see that her face was swathed in green netting. It may be true that rolling stones gather no moss, but apparently stagnant stars do.

Trailing behind the down-on-her-luck diva was a frumpy woman of advancing years and a bespectacled chauffeur in an ill-fitting uniform. I pasted a cheery smile on my face and opened the door.

"Gut marriye," I brayed. "Velkommen to zee PennDutch."

"Good morning," Octavia said in a voice a full octave lower than mine. "I suppose you know who I am."

"Well, you must be—"

"Octavia Cabot-Dodge." She said this loud enough so that the Babester, had he been standing on his porch across the road, could have heard it.

"Magdalena Yoder," I said. "I'm the proprietress."

She sniffed. "I hope this festival of yours is all it's been cracked up to be."

"Of course, dear. Folks in Hernia love a good time. Just last month we had a mock funeral for Orville Humpheimer's two-headed calf. There was even a drawing—the winner got veal chops—but I didn't win, which was fine with me, since I don't eat veal on principle. Except that Orville's calf died of natural causes. Seems it got one head stuck in a barbed-wire fence—"

"Is there a porter for my bags?"

"At your service, dear. Although I'm sure your chauffeur would do a far better job. Last time I dropped one of the cases down the stairs and it split wide open, like a melon on a sidewalk. You wouldn't believe what that woman had inside."

"Stanley," she said, without turning her head. "Get the bags."

The chauffeur, who was barely more than a teenager, stepped forward boldly. "I'm not just a chauffeur," he said, looking directly at me. "I also rappel."

"Don't be so hard on yourself, dear," I said kindly. "Nobody gets to choose how they look."

The lad rolled his eyes behind his wire-rim frames. Besides being repelling, he was impudent.

I might have said something to correct the young man, but the dowdy diva did it for me. He rolled his eyes again, but sauntered off to do as he was bid.

It was time to drop the phony accent. "Come on in," I said, "before the flies do."

Octavia Cabot-Dodge placed a tiny foot on the first step leading to my porch, but then removed it. She immediately put the other foot on the step and removed it. She repeated this behavior seven times. It was like watching someone do step aerobics. Finally she put her first foot on the second level. From then on she progressed normally. In the meantime I observed that her shoes, which had at one time obviously cost a great deal, were rather scuffed.

"This is my personal assistant, Augusta Miller," she said, upon reaching the porch.

Assistant? I was sure Ms. Miller had introduced herself as the actress's manager. Well, perhaps a personal assistant and a manager were one and the same. Despite five years of dealing with the herd from the Hills, the ways of Hollywood remain beyond my ken.

The woman whose job description was in question mumbled something unintelligible. I thought best not to pursue the matter and attempted to usher the ladies in, but again, Ms. Cabot-Dodge did her little dance. This time over the threshold. I pretended to look away, but you can be sure I counted. As before, eight was the magical number.

Once inside both ladies scrutinized the foyer, which, by the way, does double duty as my office. "This floor looks new," Augusta said. "The wallpaper too."

"Well, they are," I said. "Relatively."

"Either they are, or they aren't," Octavia said.

"They're less than two years old," I wailed.

"How old is the inn? Your brochure said it was a historical Pennsylvania Dutch farmhouse."

My cheeks burned. "It is! I mean, almost. The original house was blown to smithereens by a tornado, but I rebuilt this place to look exactly like it was."

"Why, that's false advertising," Augusta muttered.

One thing I've learned from my teenybopper foster child is that when the going gets tough, change directions. "Would either of you like to avail yourselves of A.L.P.O.?"

Octavia recoiled in horror. "Dog food?"

"Oh, no. It's my Amish Lifestyle Plan Option. You see, for just twenty dollars more a day, you get to do chores—like clean your own room." No sooner had the words escaped my mouth, than I realized they were a mistake. Obviously the woman couldn't afford such an extravagance, even if she did arrive by limousine.

Much to my surprise, however, a glint appeared in her eyes, shining though the veil of green like twin beacons through fog. "Is that it? Just cleaning one's room?"

"By no means. There's the barn to muck, the chicken house straw needs replacing—"

"Sign up my assistant," she said, the glee in her voice quite evident. "The chauffeur as well."

Augusta gave her employer a look that would have turned grapes into raisins, had there been any lying around. I had the feeling she was going to give Octavia a piece of her mind as well, but Stanley the chauffeur stumbled up the steps under a load of suitcases that a dozen Sherpas would have been hard-pressed to manage.

I moved to help the lad, but Octavia stopped me by laying a withered hand on my bare arm. "Stanley can manage, Miss Yoder. If he needs help, my assistant will be glad to do it."

Her assistant shot her another glance capable of drying fruit. Since dried apricots are a favorite snack of mine, I made a mental note to tote some fresh ones with me for the next few days. Now that I no longer carry a kitten in my bra, there is plenty of room for goodies.

I smiled at Augusta, then turned my attention to Octavia. "Dinner is normally at six, like the Good Lord intended, but because today is Sunday, it will be a half hour later."

Octavia nodded. "Where does the help eat?"

"My cook, Freni, is an Amish woman. She prefers to eat in the kitchen."

"I meant *my* help."

"Why, in the dining room with everyone else."

"Well!" Octavia said in a huff, but Augusta was grinning like the Cheshire cat.

It was time to hustle their bustles through the registration process before it came to fisticuffs. I even risked Octavia's wrath by helping the hapless Stanley schlep the rest of the mountain of suitcases up my impossibly steep stairs. To be honest, I did it just because I knew it would irk her. You see, I had already made up my mind I was going to side with the help this time.

When one is as successful a proprietress as I am, one can afford to make up any rules that one wishes. Therefore, I choose not to rent my rooms by the day, but by the week. Guests must arrive on Sunday between the hours of three and six. Theoretically this gives them plenty of time to attend the church of their choice earlier in the day, but the truth is most of the folks, all of whom are blessed just by virtue of the fact they can afford my rates, have not darkened the door of a church or synagogue since they were children. At any rate, guests must check out by noon the following Saturday.

They may, of course, leave earlier, but they will not get any money refunded. To the contrary, those who depart before the agreed-upon date are subject to a fine. S.A.L.E., I call it. Suckers Always Leave Early.

In fact, I have a whole string of fines that I am free to impose at will, because they are all delineated in the fine print on my brochures. Guests arriving after the six p.m. Sunday deadline are charged a late arrival fee. And believe you me, I was extremely irritated at twenty after six when all but one of my guests had gathered in the parlor, waiting to be ushered into the dining room. The holdout had yet to arrive on the premises. Never mind that we were all dressed in our best clothes. I, for one, was looking pretty spiffy, if I must say so myself. I'd polished my brogans, put on a freshly laundered prayer cap, and my blue broadcloth dress was one that I'd worn only a handful of times. Much to my disappointment, even Buzzy had cleaned up pretty well.

"You certainly look handsome," I said. I was not being flirtatious, mind you, merely kind. Compared to the Babester, Buzzy at his best looked like a comic strip character with his finger in a socket. According to my sister, Susannah, some men actually work at getting their hair to stick out in all directions.

"Thank you, Miss Yoder. Do you like my flower?"

I didn't. It was obviously a fake. But a compliment is a blessing one bestows upon another person, and should not be construed as a lie.

"It's lovely," I said graciously.

"Smell it," he said.

"I beg your pardon?"

"It's a gardenia. It has a really nice scent."

I decided to bless Buzzy further by pretending to smell his flower. "Mmm," I murmured, but all I could smell was the odor of Buzzy's aftershave.

"You need to lean closer, Miss Yoder. This is a new variety. They say it smells like lemon."

I leaned closer. "Smells just like Pledge," I said, to show that I was a good sport.

"You really think so?"

"Aack!" I shrieked, as Buzzy's blossom squirted water directly into my left eye.

Buzzy roared with laughter. He even slapped his thighs—although he should have been slapping his own face. The only thing stopping me from doing so was my genes. My Amish and Mennonite ancestors have been professing pacifists for almost five hundred years and it's all I can do to swat a fly.

Fortunately Buist Littleton was not a pacifist. Au contraire, I hear that the Civil War is still being waged in his fair state.

"Apologize to the lady," he said in a quiet, authoritative voice.

Buzzy appeared puzzled. "Excuse me?"

"You heard me, sir. Apologize to her."

Buzzy stopped laughing. "All right, you don't need to make a federal case out of it." He looked at me with all the sincerity of a televangelist. "I'm sorry, Miss Yoder. That was childish of me. Will you forgive me?"

The Bible says to forgive seventy-seven times, and Buzzy had offended me only fourteen times since setting foot on my property—not that I was counting. The only other human being to irritate me so many times in such a short space of time was my brother-in-law, Melvin Stoltzfus.

"Sure," I said, to set a Christian example.

"Shake?" He offered me his right hand, which looked to be empty of battery-powered devices, but my parents didn't raise a complete idiot.

"How about we just nod our heads, dear?"

"Yeah." He seemed actually eager for the change of custom.

I nodded my head, and he nodded his head. But he didn't stop. He nodded faster and faster until his noggin was vibrating like the paint mixer at the Home Depot over in Bedford. Then—and if swearing wasn't against my religion, I'd swear this was true—his head spun all the way around, as if it weren't even attached at the neck. So bizarre was the sight that both Octavia and Augusta gasped like drowning turkeys—I've heard a few of those, by the way. Even Buist was shocked into silence, but Capers, bless her genteel heart, almost gagged. Apparently Chuck and Bibi Norton were used to such sights down on the farm, because they barely blinked.

Stanley Dalrumple, the youthful chauffeur, scowled behind his wire-rimmed glasses. "The guy's a show-off," he said as Buzzy Porter's head shimmied to a stop.

Buist found his tongue. "It was just an illusion. The human body is not capable of such movement."

"Linda Blair did it in the *Exorcist*," Augusta ventured.

"That was a movie," Octavia snapped. She licked her lips, which, although painted, were as dry as cornflakes. "Did you know they wanted me to play her part?"

Augusta snorted. "Nonsense. Linda Blair was a teenager and you were—"

Octavia had changed to a forest green satin gown. She was hatless and therefore without a veil. Her dark eyes bored into her assistant.

"Too good for the part," Augusta said, finishing her sentence.

I glanced at my trusty Timex. "Dinner is now served. Our one remaining guest will just have to fend for himself when he arrives. The rest of you will find place cards at your assigned spots. Of course, none of us will begin eating until after grace has been said." I glared at Buzzy. "And you, young man, will behave yourself. Is that clear?"

"As clear as your best crystal," he said with a smirk.

Since I don't own any crystal, I found that to be a strangely foreboding remark.

4

My cook is also my kinswoman. Although she is eighteen years my senior, a cursory glance at our tangled family tree could produce the conclusion that she is my very much older, identical twin sister. Never mind that we look nothing alike. While I am tall and skinny enough to be a cell phone tower, dear Freni Hostetler is short and squat. She wears glasses, not to mention the fact that as an Amish woman, she dresses in distinct garb. Although my modest dresses and white organza cap set me apart from most of our tourists, I am clearly not of her faith.

The word Mennonite is derived from the name of a Roman Catholic priest, Menno Simons, who became a fervent supporter of the Anabaptist movement and formally left the Church in 1536. The Amish are named after Jacob Amman, who believed the Mennonites were too liberal, especially in regards to the doctrine of shunning unrepentant members. Amish who leave their church will often, but not necessarily, end up as Mennonites. This is what happened in my family two generations back.

Freni's interpretation of scriptures is, in a word, more strict than mine. She refuses to work on Sundays, and I respect that. As a consequence, our dinner that night had all been prepared the day before. It was not, however, a repast to be sneezed at.

My massive dining-room table groaned under the weight of food: platters of cold roast beef and smoked ham, bowls of chicken salad, tuna salad, potato salad, three-bean salad, green pea salad, and tossed salad, deviled eggs, chunky apple sauce, corn relish, pickled beets, pickled cauliflower, watermelon rind pickles, dill pickles and sweet pickles, and homemade bread. In the kitchen waited two shoofly pies, an apple pie, a custard pie, and a chocolate cake with fudge icing. Except for the tuna, none of the victuals came from a can. Any guest who went hungry was too picky for his or her own good.

When I threw open the pocket doors that opened to my dining room, Chuck and Bibi Norton's sun-faded eyes lit up at the sight of my bountiful table. "My, my," Bibi said, "someone has certainly gone to a lot of trouble."

"It all looks absolutely delicious," Capers said.

Everyone else nodded, including Buzzy. "Looks just like the salad bar at Shoney's," he said. I think he meant it as a compliment.

There was a bit of milling about as the guests found their seats. The handsome and mannerly Buist was seated on my right. Stanley Dalrumple had the honor of sitting on my left. Bibi's place was next to Buist and across from Augusta Miller. Chuck, alias "Father" Norton, was on her left. Buzzy was to sit on Bibi's right, and Alison had whined her way to Buzzy's right, which put her on Capers's left. The end of the table was reserved for the declining diva.

As for the missing guest—I still didn't know if it was male or female—he or she would sit across from Alison on Chuck's left. If the mystery diner didn't show up before the food was gone, he or she was just plain out of luck.

At any rate, Buist, ever the Southern gentleman, pulled out my chair for me. To my amazement everyone waited until I was seated before following suit. My point is, I was safely ensconced in my seat when the puerile prank was pulled. I am merely an opinionated woman, not crude, so I shall not describe the noise I heard in detail. Suffice it to say, it was as if one of my guests had already consumed an entire bowl of three-bean salad. By the look of surprise on Augusta Miller's face, followed by one of utter mortification, my guess is that Buzzy had left a whoopee cushion on her chair.

Of course, Alison howled. Her high-pitched yips would have summoned dogs from three counties if I hadn't given her the business. She shut up immediately, but reserved the right to glower back at me.

The second Alison shushed, Chuck Norton scraped his chair on the floor. I wouldn't have thought a sturdy, beef-fed farmer like Chuck could think so fast—I certainly couldn't.

"Miss Yoder," he said, louder than normal conversation would require, "if you put some little rubber tips on these chair legs, they wouldn't make this noise. Save them from getting worn, too."

I smiled. "Really? Well, I'll have to look into that." Alison fought to stifle a giggle, while both Buzzy and young Stanley grinned behind their napkins like foolish schoolboys. "Mr. Porter, dear," I said, without missing a beat, "would you like to say grace?"

The grin widened. "Excuse me?"

"Thank the Good Lord for providing us with this food. And for making it so available to us, that we don't have to drive all the way into Pittsburgh in search of a Shoney's."

"Can do," he said, which was not the answer I was expecting.

He started to say something else—perhaps he even began his prayer—but I interrupted him. The Good Lord expects us to pray with our eyes tightly closed and our hands folded. Not like the Episcopalians. I know for a fact that at least one of them prays with her eyes wide open. The Lord also expects us to offer prayers, the length of which are in direct proportion to the time it took to prepare the food. The minimum requirement is that the blessing be long enough to allow hot food to become cold and cold food to warm up to room temperature. Anything shorter than that smacks of ingratitude.

When I was sure everyone had their eyes tightly closed and their hands folded, I ordered Buzzy to begin. However, to enforce the Lord's rules, I kept my peepers open. Just as Buzzy began his second attempt, I saw Octavia and Augusta exchange glances. Since both women were emitting icy stares, I felt confident that Buzzy's prayer, no matter how interminable, would not contribute to our food spoiling. Still, I had no choice but to clear my throat and force the women to behave.

"Go ahead now, dear," I said to Buzzy, when the women were under control.

Eyes tightly closed, he smiled. "Rub-a-dub-dub. Thanks for the grub. Yay, God!"

All eyes flew open, all mouths as well. Stanley Dalrumple snickered, but Alison had lived with me long enough to be properly shocked. If not, she faked it well.

"Mr. Porter," I said sharply, "what kind of prayer was that?"

"The kind we used to say in college."

"Was this a school for heathens?"

Stanley snickered again.

"Mr. Porter, I asked you a question."

"It was a state school," Buzzy mumbled.

"Why am I not surprised?" It was a rhetorical question, meant to buy time while I considered my options. What if the prankster's prayer hadn't taken, like a vaccine gone bad? In that case we would be eating unblessed food. Yes, I know, folks do it all the time, but look at the state the world is in.

On the other hand, I couldn't very well ask the man to pray again, because that would be like second-guessing the Good Lord. In the end I decided to leave the problem in God's capable hands, but just to let the Lord know I didn't approve of Buzzy's irreverence, I sighed loudly. Meanwhile my guests waited with their forks poised.

"Dig in," I finally said. "Bon appétit!"

They dug, some much deeper than others. In fact, the way Chuck Norton helped himself to the meat platter, I was afraid I might have to run out and kill the fatted calf. I mean that literally.

But poor Chuck had taken only one bite of ham when his face turned the color of a good pickled beet and his eyes began to bulge. "Brrrgh," he said, his mouth quite full.

"What was that, dear?"

"Auugh."

Bibi sprung to life. "Father is choking! Please, somebody, do something."

My heart pounded. "Does anyone know the Heimlich Maneuver?"

The rest of my guests shook their heads in horrified amazement as Chuck tried futilely to dislodge the ham. Thank heavens I had read enough books to have a basic understanding of what needed to be done. There are perhaps better teachers than fear, but no better motivators. Fearing that Chuck might actually choke on my ham and die—not to mention a potential lawsuit filed by his devoted wife, Bibi—I flew into action.

I may be tall, but I'm scrawny. Still, I had enough adrenaline coursing through my veins to hoist an elephant and fling it over my shoulder. I yanked the farmer out of his chair and squeezed his middle like I was a python and he was my dinner. Of course, I did it a lot faster than a real python would. The upshot was that Chuck's dinner shot across the room, barely missing Octavia's head, and landed on the floor with a splat.

Chuck gasped a few times, as he fought for words. "Why, that's not ham at all. That's rubber."

So much for gratitude. "Mr. Norton, I assure you that this establishment serves only the finest cuts of meat."

"No!" He coughed. "I don't mean that it's tough—it's rubber."

I raced over to the regurgitated repast and prodded it gingerly with the toe of my brogan. It had the same texture as my shower mat.

"Buzzy Porter!" I bellowed.

The wise guy winced. "He was supposed to chew it—not inhale it."

"That's beside the point." I gestured to Chuck Norton. "Do you wish to press some sort of charges?"

"Well, I—are you a police officer, Miss Yoder?"

"Gracious no. But the Chief of Police is my brother-in-law." There was no need to tell him that my sister's husband and I get along as well as children and bathwater.

"I'm sorry," Buzzy blurted. "Like I said, he wasn't supposed to swallow it."

I nodded to Chuck. "It's your call, dear."

Bibi Norton looked anything but dowdy when she was angry. "Let's do it, Father."

Buzzy blanched. "Hey, wait. Maybe we can make some kind of a deal."

"You could have died," Bibi reminded her husband.

Buzzy turned to me. "Please, Miss Yoder."

I have a kind heart, but I'm about as sentimental as a Chinese snakefish. There was, however, something in the young man's voice that made me believe him. *This* time.

"Okay, let's say we cut you a deal. You'd have to stick to it, or suffer the consequences."

"Sure, anything."

Bibi's faded eyes grew bright with emotion. "But we didn't agree to a deal."

I gave her a patient smile. "If your husband presses charges, Buzzy here could end up in the slammer. But it would probably be for only a few days—maybe just overnight, or until someone bails him out. In the meantime, who knows what little gags he has already laid in place. It's more than likely he has already short-sheeted your beds. There could be spiders in your showers, water balloons above your doors—this young man is capable of anything."

"Miss Yoder, are you suggesting we just let him go? My husband could have died."

"No, I'm not suggesting that—although I might suggest your husband cut his food into bite-size pieces and chew first. Now, where was I?"

"You were about to cut a deal with this hooligan," Octavia Cabot-Dodge said. Since grace, she had opened and folded her napkin eight times.

"Ah yes. I suggest that we require young Buzzy here confess to everything he has done, in exchange for immunity. Because I assure you, there are things we don't know about that will rear their ugly heads. Then we give him exactly half an hour to undo his dastardly deeds."

"And if he doesn't?" Plain Bibi Norton was out for blood. Seeing as how I didn't have an electric chair at my disposal, perhaps I could let her throw my toaster in Buzzy's bathwater.

"Then it's back to plan A. We call the cops."

"Man, that's no fair," Alison said. She stamped a foot under the table.

I swallowed back my irritation. "It's quite fair. It's all up to Buzzy, isn't it?"

Everyone nodded except for Alison, Stanley, and Buzzy.

"Mene, mene, tekel, parsin," I said.

They stared at me like I was missing grain in my silo, prompting Alison to come to my defense. "That's Pennsylvania Dutch, ya know."

I thanked her with a smile. "Actually, it's Babylonian. It's from the Bible. It's the handwriting on the wall." I mustered a stern look for Buzzy. "The writing is for you, dear. You have exactly one hour."

Buzzy didn't even excuse himself from the table. He just got up and slunk from the room. I would like to say that the rest of the meal was enjoyable, despite Alison's accusing stares. Alas, that is not the case. Augusta and the diva conducted their own ocular warfare, while Chuck continued to inhale his food without chewing. Stanley smirked his way through dessert. Had it not been for a smattering of pleasant conversation between myself and the cultured Capers, we might well have resembled your typical American family.

As for Buist—he jumped to the top of my short list the second time his foot made contact with mine. The first time he did it, I passed it off as an innocent mistake. I have long legs, and given the size of my tootsies, you can be sure that I have, at times, strayed into someone else's territory. But this was no accidental touching. Buist Littleton's foot was pressed firmly up against mine, and whenever I moved mine, his followed.

Perhaps then you can understand why a confirmed pacifist would slide her fork under the protective cover of the tablecloth and give him a gentle jab. Unfortunately, the Southern gentleman's only response was a grin. Well, a gal's gotta do what a gal's gotta do, so I made like I was testing one of Freni's roasts for doneness.

Buist gasped and his eyes glazed over, but this time he moved his foot. The rest of the guests were too caught up in their own scenarios to notice our little drama—except for Capers.

"Darling," she drawled, "remember the vacation we took to Aruba?"

Buist paled as the glaze left his eyes. "Yes, of course, sugar."

"Keep remembering, darling." The ice in her voice could have cooled a Charleston summer.

For a moment neither of them spoke. "Aruba?" I prodded. "I have always wanted to go to Aruba. Please, tell me more."

"It's a lovely island," Capers said, and then cleverly put a piece of shoofly pie in her mouth.

Dinner was essentially over. Before I excused the guests I invited them to help me clear the dishes and, should they be feeling stressed, contribute a few stitches to a quilt I keep stretched across a frame in a corner of the room. The quilt is generally a big hit with guests, and it is a win-win situation, because the subsequent sale of their handiwork adds coins to my coffers. This particular evening there were no takers for either task.

Theoretically I could have forced the A.L.P.O. guests to help me with the dishes, but I was suddenly in the mood for solitude. I let the guests drift off to the parlor, where they waited out the appointed hour, while I labored and contemplated a new wrinkle in my life.

5

John and Sharon Wilkerson's Grilled Grouper

1 cup olive oil
2 tablespoons minced onion
3 tablespoons grated Parmesan
   cheese
1½ teaspoons dried basil leaves
1½ teaspoons dry mustard
1½ teaspoons dried oregano leaves
1½ teaspoons sugar

4 teaspoons salt
2 teaspoons pepper
½ cup red-wine vinegar
2 tablespoons fresh squeezed lemon
   juice
4 grouper steaks or 2 large
   grouper fillets

Combine first nine ingredients in a blender and process for 30 seconds. Add vinegar and lemon juice; process for an additional 30 seconds. Transfer sauce to a large bowl.

Dip fish into sauce to generously cover. Grill fish over hot coals 10 minutes on each side or until fish flakes easily when tested with a fork. Baste frequently with prepared sauce.

Remove fish to a warm serving platter and serve immediately.

SERVES 4 TO 6

6

Actually, the new wrinkle in my life was a face full of wrinkles. Gabriel Rosen, my gorgeous hunk of a fiancé, had surprised me on my birthday by announcing that his mother would be living with us—after the wedding, of course. For the record, I don't do the horizontal hootchy-kootchy unless I'm hitched. And please, no reminders that I was an inadvertent adulteress by virtue of unwittingly marrying a bigamist. That was then, and this is now, as Alison is fond of saying. Besides, Aaron, snake that he was, talked me into doing far worse things than the mattress mambo. Once we even danced—standing up!

Now where was I? Oh yes, Gabe's mother. Don't you agree that he could at least have discussed his intentions with me first? But no, he announced this arrangement right in front of her. What was I to do? Grin and bear it?

Well, I'd grinned until my face nearly split in two. Frankly, I didn't know how much longer I could take it. Ida Rosen was opinionated, demanding, overbearing—at least that's how she treated me. Gabe she treated like he was still a little boy. In the blink of an eye my dearly beloved went from batching it to living a life of pampered ease. Ida did all his cooking, cleaning, and laundry. That I could almost understand. But whenever he went out she insisted on knowing where he was going, and why. In cool weather she made him wear a jacket. Once I even saw her cut his meat!

I had to quit obsessing about Ida Rosen. Just thinking about her was making my skin itch under my sturdy Christian underwear. To take my mind off my misery, I washed the dishes by hand in scalding water. Still unable to rid my brain of frightening images of my future mother-in-law, I started to scrub the kitchen floor. This was, of course, an exercise in futility, since Freni keeps the place so clean that germs die of starvation. Nevertheless, I had worked my way halfway across the room, when the doorbell rang. That's when I discovered, much to my dismay, that I had trapped myself by an expanse of wet floor.

"Would someone please get the door?" I hollered.

No one responded, and the bell rang again.

"Doesn't anyone hear the doorbell?" I bellowed. After all, the front door is much closer to the front parlor than it is to the kitchen.

The bell rang a third and fourth time in rapid succession.

"Darn," I said, which is as bad as I can swear.

Because I was still expecting one last guest, I had no choice but to answer it myself. I was not, however, a happy hostess when I flung open the door. In my mind I saw Ida Rosen, her face screwed up in a disapproving look. It took me a few seconds to adjust to reality. Unfortunately my mouth works faster than my mind.

"Now what is it?" I snapped.

"Is this the PennDutch Inn?" a small voice asked.

I stared. Standing on the porch was a beautiful Japanese girl. I knew her nationality because it was written on the reservation card. What I hadn't known until then was her gender, thanks to a rather difficult name.

"Miss Mukaisan?" I did the best I could with the pronunciation.

She bowed from the waist. I followed her example, which prompted her to bow again. After the fourth round we both gave up.

"My name is Teruko Mukai," she said, "but everyone calls me Terri."

I hate being wrong. "Are you sure? I know there was a 'san' in there someplace."

She smiled. " 'San' is a title—like mister or miss. We attach it to the end of the name. But in English, I think, you would hyphenate it."

"Then you may call me Yoder-san. Velkommen to zee—" I stopped my silly charade. After all, the girl spoke perfect, unaccented English, and she hailed from the other side of the globe. "Yes, this is the PennDutch Inn. And you're a mite late, dear."

She smiled again. "I'm sorry Yoder-san, but this is a very big country. I had no idea Pennsylvania was such a long state. And the traffic out of New York City—"

"New York? Is that where you drove from?"

"Oh no. I took a cab from Kennedy International Airport."

"You *what*?" But there it was, pulling out of the driveway and onto Hertlzer Road.

"I'm afraid he was not happy with my tip, but that was all the cash I had."

"Don't worry, dear. I take most credit cards, and there are banks over in Bedford." She was a mere slip of a girl, so it was easy to glance behind her. "Where is your luggage?"

Terri's hands flew to her face. "The cab!"

I was faced with two choices: hop in my car and chase down the cab, or call the Hernia police. I'm a fast driver for a Mennonite, but what if the cabdriver refused to pull over? Or what if he did pull to the side of the road, and he was armed and still in a cantankerous mood? On the other hand, dealing with the local authorities was less appealing than a liver-flavored milkshake. The chief is my nincompoop brother-in-law, and the only other officer is his spoony sidekick, Zelda Root. Working together they could possibly find their way out of a paper bag—if given both directions and a string to follow.

"Darn," I said for the second time that night, and ran inside to make the call.

No one answered at the station, so I called Melvin at home. My sister, Susannah, picked up.

"Susannah! Put Melvin on the phone, please. This is an emergency."

My sister giggled. "I can't, Mags."

"Is he there?"

"Oh, he's here all right, but he can't come to the phone."

There was no time for nonsense. "Then take it to him."

"We don't have a portable, silly. You know that. Besides, he hates being disturbed when he's—uh—you know."

"Put him on *now*."

Susannah sighed loudly and let the phone drop. Then I heard her voice in the background, followed by a whoosh of water. Finally Melvin picked up.

"Yoder, this better be good. I still haven't read the comics."

"Melvin, listen to me. You need to take the cruiser and chase down a cab."

"You're nuts, Yoder," he said and hung up.

I know I should make allowances for Melvin, given that he was kicked in the head by a bull when he was a teenager—one that he was trying to milk—but not only is he a nincompoop, he's arrogant. Besides, I'm not really sure he's human. He looks just like a praying mantis, with eyes that move independently of each other and a bony carapace. The Bible commands us to love our neighbors, but it says nothing about loving insects.

Still, the man wields power in our small community, and one must give unto Caesar what is his. For the sake of Teruko Mukai I would grovel to the man who once sent his favorite aunt a gallon of ice cream by UPS. I punched redial.

My sister picked up after the first ring. "Susannah's house of perpetual love."

"Susannah!"

"Oh, Mags, I'm only pulling your leg. You know we have Caller ID."

"Put Melvin back on the phone."

"He doesn't want to speak to you."

"This is police business."

"But—"

"I'll cut off your allowance for a month." When our parents

died—squished in a tunnel between a milk tanker and a truck full of state-of-the-art running shoes—they left the farm in a trust to me. I was instructed to make sure my sister was cared for, but she was not to be given her inheritance outright until such time that she proved she was a mature adult. That was eleven years ago, and Susannah is now thirty-six. Enough said.

Susannah didn't hesitate. "Melkins," she called, "Mags is insisting."

He got on the line with remarkable rapidity. "Is this extortion, Yoder? Because if it is—"

"Shut up, dear, and listen. One of my guests—a Japanese lady—took a cab from New York. He dropped her off here, but then drove away with her luggage. He was angry at her for not tipping well, and I think he means to keep her stuff. By now he's probably halfway to Bedford."

"But, Yoder, I'm in my pajamas."

"Then throw a coat on. Just think, this time you'll have a good excuse to drive fast with the siren on."

"Hmm. Okay, but you better not be making this up."

It was my turn to hang up. Then I comforted Terri Mukai. The poor woman had been privy to my conversation, and being somewhat brighter than my brother-in-law, she was clearly concerned about his competence.

I'm convinced the Good Lord doesn't mind a white lie if it's meant to comfort someone. "Don't worry, dear," I said. "The man's an expert at what he does." An expert at irritating me, that's what.

The reason there hadn't been a helpful response from the parlor when the doorbell rang is most of my guests had gone to bed early. Freni's cooking has a tendency to produce that effect. Plus, as I've observed, traveling can be very tiring. What surprised me is that Alison had hit the sack as well. I don't have a television—I have long since given away my black-and-white—but that doesn't stop her from begging to stay up late.

At any rate, the Littletons were still awake; I could tell by the light under their door. When they heard me show Teruko Mukai to her room, they popped out to say hello. The Charlestonians were still dressed, by the way. Even though it wasn't their business, I shared with them the sad fate of Miss Mukai's belongings. I thought of it as a preemptive strike, lest the new arrival put an even worse spin on the story. It wouldn't do to have my charming Southern guests think that we Yankees were nothing but a bunch of cutthroats and thieves.

Upon hearing the sad tale, Capers Littleton gave Miss Mukai a hug and then held her at arm's length. "You know, darling," she drawled to the new arrival, "you and I are about the same size. I'm sure I could find a few things for you to wear."

"Please, Mrs. Littleton," the young woman protested, "I do not want to trouble you."

"Oh, it is no trouble. I insist. I always travel with twice as many clothes as I need. Don't I dear?"

Buist nodded vigorously. "That's a fact."

"There then, it's all settled," I said.

Teruko Mukai bowed deeply to show her appreciation. "Americans are very kind," she said.

I waited patiently while Capers retrieved a fresh nightgown and a set of casual clothes for the following day, and then I showed the girl her room. Her basic toiletries I supplied myself. Half my guests leave their brains at home when they go on vacation, along with half the things they mean to pack, so I am well stocked with the essentials. Usually I charge my guests by the item, but in Teruko's case I decided to make an exception in the interest of international goodwill. Finally, the girl was settled in and I was able to totter off to bed myself.

Although Alison complains loudly when she has to share my room, the child is starved for affection and doesn't really mind. Many times she stays in my room a few extra days on her own volition. I enjoy her company too. The only real downside is that she somehow manages to hog my king-size bed—oh, and she thrashes about like a shark out of water.

Sure enough, the girl was sprawled across both sides, snoring as loud as a chain saw. "Move over, dear," I said and pushed her to the halfway mark.

She rolled back to where I'd found her. I pushed her again, and before she could react, I threw myself on the empty spot. A moment later the back of her hand connected with my nose. I have the prominent Yoder nose—one deserving of its own zip code—and I know it's an easy target, but it's just as sensitive as any other schnoz. Being bonked on it hurt like the dickens.

Because I knew the child meant no harm, I gently moved her arm away and then protected my face with my pillow. That turned out to be a good move, because four inches of feathers helped to muffle the sound of her snores. Eventually I fell asleep, although I dreamed I was on the Nina with Christopher Columbus. The ship was pitching, and every now and then the yardarm would smack me on some vulnerable part of my body. Just as I was lecturing the famous explorer on how to provide better guest services, his cell phone rang. And rang.

"Chris, dear, pick it up."

"But Magdalena, carina, it's your phone you hear."

"It is?"

That's when I awoke to find my bedside phone ringing. I glanced at my alarm clock. Five a.m. on the dot. Unlike my sister, I do not have Caller ID. Since the only folks who have my private number are family or close friends and they would all be asleep now—well, except for Babs who, given the time difference, could still be partying—I panicked.

"What happened?" I blurted.

"I didn't catch the cabdriver, that's what."

"Melvin! You woke me at five in the morning to tell me you failed at your job?"

"I didn't fail, because there never was a cab. It's time to face it, Yoder, you're getting senile."

"Good night, Melvin."

"Yoder, I'm not calling about the stupid cab, anyway."

"Susannah? Is something wrong?"

"Something's wrong, all right, but it has nothing to do with my Sugar Boo."

"Spit it out, dear. You've got to the count of three. One—"

"There's been a murder."

7

"What?" I sat up straight in bed.

"Yoder, are you getting deaf now too?"

"I heard what you said. What does it have to do with me?"

"The name Buzzy Porter ring a bell?"

"Loud and clear. What about him?"

"He's the victim, and I found one of your room keys in his pocket."

"But that's impossible. Mr. Porter is upstairs—asleep."

"He's sleeping all right. The kind you never wake up from."

"Stay right there. Don't hang up!"

I thundered up my impossibly steep stairs and pounded on the prankster's door. "Mr. Porter, are you in there?"

There was no answer, so I tried the knob. It was locked. This meant I had to thunder back downstairs and grab my key ring from atop my bureau. I took a second to holler into the phone.

"Stay!"

By the time I got back to Buzzy's room, every other door along the hallway was opened. Glassy-eyed guests stood mutely on their thresholds, waiting for the night's entertainment to continue. Ignoring them, I fumbled with the keys, and when I got the door unlocked, I flung it open with such force that the stopper broke, allowing the doorknob to punch a hole in the wall. If by chance Buzzy was still among the living, he would pay for the repairs.

And the nerve of the guy. He was lying in bed, sleeping as peacefully as a teenager—Alison excepted. I ripped off the lazy man's covers.

"Pillows!" I roared. There was nothing in the bed but pillows and bunched-up clothes.

"Yoder-san," Terri said, appearing suddenly in the doorway, wearing Capers's nightgown, "is there a problem?"

"Not now, please."

I pushed past her and thundered down the stairs yet one more time. "Melvin," I barked into the phone, "you still there?"

"No, Yoder. I'm in Las Vegas."

"Spare me the sarcasm and describe the corpse."

"You didn't say please, Yoder."

"Please. Pretty please with sugar on top," I added to appease him.

"That's better. Okay, the guy's about five ten—dark hair. His driver's license pegs him at thirty-five."

"That old, huh?" The Buzzy I knew had appeared younger than that, but his juvenile personality might well have contributed to the illusion of youth. "Melvin, where is he?"

"Stucky Ridge."

"What?"

"I swear, Yoder, you need to get your hearing checked."

"I can hear just fine, thank you. But what would someone from out of town be doing up on Stucky Ridge at this hour?"

"Beats me. Ron Humphrey found him about half an hour ago."

"What was Ron doing up on the ridge? It's still dark, for crying out loud."

"Jogging. He's practicing for some kind of marathon. Says running up the ridge is the best kind of training."

"That figures." Ron is Hernia's sole Episcopalian and, next to the Babester, our most liberal resident. It is no secret that he drinks wine and other alcoholic beverages. He even has a satellite dish. I'd heard rumors that he belongs to a gym over in Bedford, an idea which, frankly, baffles me. I am convinced that the Good Lord programmed each of us with a finite number of heartbeats at birth.

Use them all up, and you die. Exercise, then, is a waste of heart-beats. Unfortunately, I'd just wasted an inordinate number of heartbeats going up and down the stairs.

"Yoder, you know I never ask for much—"

"Beans, Melvin."

"You swore!"

"So I did. But you're always asking for favors."

"Yes, but the election is only weeks away. I don't have time to work on this case. You know that."

My brother-in-law has delusions of grandeur. He's running for a position in the state legislature, but with at least one of his eyes on the White House. Susannah is already planning what color to wear at the inauguration. The style of the dress is the same as every other one in her closet: Fifteen feet of filmy fabric draped loosely around her tail-thin body. One's first impression is not of a sari, but a half-wrapped mummy. Of course, Melvin will never make it that far, but in the event he does, my biggest fear—besides the ruination of our country—is that my beloved sister will catch her death of cold on the reviewing stand.

"Melvin, dear, I'm not a police officer. Assign the case to Zelda."

"Yoder, you've helped me before. Besides, Zelda is going to have her hands full directing traffic for Hernia Heritage Days."

"I'm afraid that's your problem, not mine."

"Magdalena, please."

I couldn't believe my ears. This was the first time the miserable mantis had ever used the *M* word. As long as I've known him, which is to say his entire life, he has called me Yoder. Okay, so maybe he didn't call me Yoder when he was a baby, but as soon as he learned to speak—about age six—he's used only my last name, and always with a hint of derision.

"What did you say?"

"You heard me."

"Say it again if you want my help."

"M-m-magdalena."

I sighed. "Okay—but I'm only going to *help* you. You have to do the bulk of the work yourself."

"Sure, Yoder. Anything."

"Ah, ah, ah!"

"I mean Magdalena."

"That's better. But get this straight, dear—I have official duties to attend to in the next few days, and I plan to keep my commitments."

"Whatever you say, Magdalena."

"And you're going to have to take orders from me. Do you think you can handle that?"

During the ensuing pause my beloved country elected its first female President—a black Jewish woman with a Spanish surname. "Yeah, yeah," he finally grumbled. "I can handle it."

"Good. Because my first order is that you don't touch anything until I get there."

"But I—"

"Already did?"

"You hadn't given me any orders yet."

I sighed again. "Well, stop touching. Have you called the coroner?"

"No."

"The morgue?"

"The morgue?"

"Never mind. I'll be right there."

One can see Stucky Ridge from my front porch, but getting there took me fifteen minutes. That's because I had to first put on some clothes, and then I had to parry anxious queries from my guests. Also, this local landmark is more of a mountain than a ridge, and the road to the top winds like an uncoiled Slinky.

Melvin hadn't said where the murder had occurred, and I was hoping against hope that I would find him on the picnic table side and not the cemetery. Settlers' Cemetery is where my parents are buried, and it's spooky enough at high noon on a bright summer day.

To my immense relief my nemesis was on neither side of the

ridge, but in a copse that straddles the middle and serves as a divider between these two key areas. I could see the flashing blue lights of the cruiser as soon as I crested the ridge. What I couldn't figure out was how he had managed to get the car into the dense woods. I cruised down the road that leads past the picnic area, and finding no access, started down the cemetery lane. That's when Melvin came charging out of the trees waving a flashlight.

I rolled down my window. "How on earth did you get the cruiser in there?"

"You go past the cemetery—all the way to the end, and make a sharp left. But don't worry about that. Leave your car where it is and follow me."

I did as I was bid. "What's with the road back there? I never knew it existed."

"It's not a real road, Yoder. It's a way the teenagers get their cars in the woods."

"Why would they do that?"

"To have sex, Yoder—and to drink. You should see all the empty beer cans and discarded condoms."

That was a shocker. I knew that amorous couples parked in the picnic area—the Babester and I once exchanged a chaste smooch there—but it never occurred to me that someone would go all the way, so to speak, in a public place. Stucky Ridge was beginning to sound a lot like Sodom and Gomorrah.

I trotted gingerly behind Melvin. Should I accidentally step on something unpleasant, the Hernia Police Department was going to owe me a new pair of brogans. When we'd gone about thirty yards I could see Ron Humphrey standing next to the cruiser. A few more yards and the corpse was visible, facedown and illuminated by the headlights.

"Hi, Ron," I said. But I was looking at the dead body. Even from the back I could tell it was Buzzy.

"Hello, Miss Yoder. Just so you know, I had nothing to do with this."

I nodded. The young man is a computer programmer who lives in Hernia but works in Bedford. Other than the fact that he drinks alcohol—in church, no less—and believes in infant baptism, and is a fairly recent arrival in town, I have nothing against him. By all accounts he's a hardworking, taxpaying citizen, who involves himself in civic affairs. He isn't married, but the grapevine has it that he's heterosexual. My hope is that he will marry a Mennonite woman who can show him the error of his ways.

Now, where was I? Oh yes, Buzzy Porter's trunk and extremities appeared to be unmarked. However, the back of his head was covered with blood, and there seemed to be a slight depression at the crest.

"Has either of you touched the body?" I asked.

"I already confessed, Yoder. Of course I touched the body. How else could I tell if he was really dead?"

"Good point. But did you move it?"

Melvin's left eye was trained on the corpse; his right eye stared into mine. It gave me the willies.

"Yoder," he snarled, "what was I supposed to do, run over him?"

"I beg your pardon?"

"You can't back up in here. You've got to make a loop to get out, and he was right in the way."

There is no use in beating a dead horse—or a rationally challenged arthropod. "Show me exactly where you found him," I said to Ron Humphrey.

He led me about ten feet past the cruiser. "Here, I think."

I studied the surrounding area with a flashlight I borrowed from Melvin. As Melvin had warned, the ground was littered with empty cans, bottles, and unmentionables. There was even a brassiere hanging from a bush. Size 36C.

There was, however, no indication of a struggle, although I did find splotches of dark blood on fallen leaves. Most of it was concentrated where Ron had pointed, but there seemed to be a trail as well. In my opinion there was nothing more I could do until the world below awoke. But since the sky to the east was beginning to brighten, it wouldn't be long.

"Melvin, did you call the sheriff?"

"You know I can't do that."

There was no need for him to elaborate. Sheriff Hobson thought the same way I did about Melvin's investigation skills. Besides, due to the optimistic attitude of the founding fathers, Stucky Ridge was well within the city limits. Technically, it was Melvin's bailiwick, unless he sought outside help from the county. With the election three weeks away, that wasn't going to happen.

"But you finally called the coroner?"

"Yes. He should be here any minute."

"Good. I'm going to give Ron a ride home, then I'm coming right back. You wait here for the coroner."

"Alone?"

I couldn't blame the guy for sounding nervous. "Play the radio."

Melvin followed us to the edge of the copse. When I looked in the rearview mirror he appeared poised, as if at any second he would break into a run and beat me down the mountain.

"So, Ron," I said in a voice as smooth as Freni's chocolate silk pie, "do you often jog up the mountain in the dark?"

"Yeah."

"No kidding? Why?" Perhaps it was some weird Episcopalian ritual.

"I'm practicing for a marathon."

"That's what Chief Stoltzfus said. But why in the dark?"

"Because then I don't have to worry about cars. It takes me thirty-five minutes to get up here, twenty to get down. By then it's just starting to get light, so I run around the high-school track fifty times."

I gasped. "Don't you realize you're using up all your heartbeats?"

"Excuse me?"

"Never mind, dear. So tell me about this morning. What time did you start?"

"I keep my alarm set at four thirty—except for this morning. I got up a little earlier on account I have to get to work early because of a virus that's shut down two of our biggest clients."

"Feed a cold and starve a fever."

"This is a computer virus, Miss Yoder."

"I knew that." Show me where it's a sin to lie in one's own defense. "So, dear, do you normally run through the woods?"

"No, ma'am. I run to the end of the picnic area, touch the last table, and then start down. But tonight—I mean, this morning—I saw a light in the woods, so I decided to investigate."

"You didn't think that could be dangerous?"

He chuckled. "Miss Yoder, I moved here from Boston. What could possibly be dangerous in the woods out here?"

"Too bad you can't ask the victim that."

"Yeah, well, that definitely changes things. Anyway, I was hoping for a sighting."

"Of what? Teenagers doing the—never you mind."

"Trust me, Hernia kids never stay out that late. I was hoping it was an alien spacecraft."

That didn't surprise me coming from an Episcopalian. If he read his Bible—the King James version, of course, because that's what the Good Lord Himself reads—he wouldn't find anything about little green men from Mars. Come to think of it, he wouldn't find anything about computers either. I squelched my impulse to lecture the lad by stepping on the gas.

"Miss Yoder, you really know how to drive."

We squealed around a turn. "So you entered the woods. What happened next?"

"The light went out and I heard a thud. Then someone running through the brush. There must have been a car parked on the cemetery side, because the next thing I heard was a car tearing down the mountain—about as fast as you're driving now."

I took that as a compliment. "Tell me about the thud. Do you think that was the sound made when Buzzy Porter was hit on the back of the head?"

"No, ma'am. This was off to the side, and it sounded more like something hitting a tree."

I shuddered. How could the boy possibly discern between the sounds of something whacking a skull, as opposed to a tree? Perhaps it was knowledge he picked up playing those video games young folks are so fond of.

"Then what did you do, Ron?"

"Well, I have this little flashlight I take with me when I run in the dark"—he held up an object no larger than a pen—"and I picked my way over to where I thought I'd seen the light. That's when I almost stumbled over the body. Man, it was awful. I couldn't believe what I was seeing at first. But as soon as I got it together, I called Chief Stoltzfus on my cell phone."

"You carry that with you wherever you go?"

"Doesn't everyone?"

Cell phones. That's another *c* word you won't find in the Bible. I always leave my cell phone in the car.

"Weren't you scared," I asked, "waiting alone there for Chief Stoltzfus to arrive?"

"Not really. Like I said, the car took off. If it came back I would have made a beeline straight down the side of the mountain. Sure it's steep, but the car couldn't follow."

I wouldn't want to stand guard over a corpse in a copse, especially one so close to a cemetery. No doubt about it, I would have hoofed it back down the mountain to meet Melvin halfway. One had to admire the young man in spite of his bizarre belief in aliens.

"Thanks for your help in this matter, dear."

"No problem. And if you want to know who did it, just ask."

8

It's a good thing I make my passengers wear seat belts. I braked so hard my probing proboscis came within a millimeter of reinventing itself on the steering wheel. But instead of my past fleeting before my eyes, I saw my future. With a bit less beak, and in the right light, I could pass for Meryl Streep. Then think of all the opportunities that would lay before me. I could leave my sheltered life in the hills of Hernia and move to the hills of Hollywood. Of course, I'd have to give up my religion, and maybe the Babester, but if Mel Gibson or Harrison Ford came along . . .

"Miss Yoder, you all right?"

I shook myself into reality. "I'm fine, dear. I was just lost in thought. It was unfamiliar territory. For a second there I thought you said you knew who killed Buzzy Porter."

"Drug dealers, that's who."

I stared through the easing darkness. "You know that for a fact? How?"

"It just stands to reason. A man, alone, gets murdered in a remote location, it's night—what else could it be?"

I felt as let down as Susannah must have felt when she discovered the truth about Santa Claus. At least I was a mature woman with a job to do, whereas she was barely out of her teens at the time.

"I'll keep your theory in mind," I said charitably.

"Oh, it's a fact. You'll see."

I didn't have much to say to him the rest of the way to his house, except to inform him that I would probably be in touch with him again soon. The second he hopped out, I pressed the pedal to the metal. And why not? The town's only squad car was up on Stucky Ridge. Besides, there still wasn't a soul stirring—if you discount the mob of marauding raccoons that were just getting off work. Somehow I managed to miss all of them.

When I got back on top it was barely light enough to read a newspaper. Melvin was standing in the open, silhouetted by the rising sun. His arms and legs looked unusually spindly, and his head was enormous. Perhaps Ron's original theory of aliens had been the correct one. If so, our town's theological pundits were going to have to do some quick thinking. Because God had only one son to sacrifice for the sins of the world, any visitors from outer space were either sinless, or doomed. No matter how you looked at it, it was a sticky wicket.

I rolled the window down. "You looking for a ride, mister?"

"Very funny, Yoder. You bring me coffee and doughnuts?"

"No."

"Then what took you so long?"

"You didn't want me to speed, did you?"

He waved aside my question with a sticklike arm. "Bad news, Yoder. The coroner called. There's been a pileup on the turnpike. We have to handle this ourselves."

"You call Hernia Hospital?"

"The ambulance is on its way. They've agreed to let us keep the victim in the morgue."

That was a minor miracle. Hernia Hospital is a private institution and really nothing more than a glorified clinic run by the autocratic Dr. Luther and his imperious sidekick, Nurse Dudley. If I were asked to rename them I would pick Dr. Mean and Nurse Meaner. I much prefer to drive the twelve twisting miles into Bedford for my medical care. And yes, I would still feel that way if I wasn't banned from the premises.

"What are the strings, dear?"

"No strings."

"Beans."

"There you go, swearing again. Okay, so I promised to take the ambulance in for a tune-up and lube job. You happy, Yoder?"

Of course I wasn't happy. A man had died, for pity's sake.

Now that it was light I could see just how much Melvin had destroyed the crime scene by moving Buzzy's body. Still, it appeared to my untrained mind that the prankster had not been killed at the site where he was found, but moved there afterwards. Or least he had been badly wounded at some other location. I found a streak of blood on a low-hanging leaf about a yard away, and a splotch of blood on the ground about ten feet from that. Then the trail, if that's what it was, disappeared.

"Melvin, you wait here for the ambulance. I'm going to get help."

"Don't be crazy, Yoder. That boyfriend of yours is a doctor, but he can't work miracles."

"The help isn't for Buzzy," I said through clenched teeth. "It's help with the investigation."

I didn't stick around to hear Melvin's ranting. No doubt he felt threatened, but he'd only feel foolish when he saw who I had in mind.

Doc Shafor is a retired veterinarian. He is also an octogenarian whose libido got stuck on high sometime during his twenties. But most important, he is the only person I know in Hernia who owns an honest-to-goodness bloodhound.

As I suspected, he was up and about at that hour. In fact, he was in the process of cooking breakfast and had a hard time hearing my knock over the sound of sizzling bacon. When he finally opened the door, his face lit up.

"You're just in time, Magdalena."

"Doc, I can't stay for breakfast. I just—"

"Sure you can."

"No, really. There's—"

He grabbed my arm with gnarled fingers that had not lost their strength. "Whatever the problem is, it will keep until after we eat. I've made scrambled eggs with cheese, bacon, two kinds of sausage, hash browns, fried apples, and biscuits from scratch. And not drop biscuits either, but rolled."

"Man does not live by bread alone," I said and sailed into the house on a wave of aromas.

"Good call."

"But I'll have to eat and run. I'm here on police business."

I followed Doc into the kitchen. There were two place settings on the table, but I knew the extra one was not intended for me. Although Doc's been a widower for thirty years, he hates to eat alone. He even cooks like he's cooking for two. After we'd loaded our plates, I could have fed the guests back at the inn with what remained on the stove.

"Magdalena," he said when we were seated, "you're still a fine-looking woman."

The way his eyes appraised me, I felt like a horse. I suppose that was fitting, because after the Good Lord made me He didn't break the mold. Instead He made an exact copy, slapped a saddle on its back, and yelled giddyap.

"Thanks, Doc—I think. You're looking pretty good yourself."

"Is that a come on?"

"Gracious, no. You know I have a beau." I knew Doc too well to be shocked.

"I hope you realize that if this thing with that New York doctor doesn't work out—well, I'm willing to be more than friends."

It was time to switch to the world's second most deliberated topic. "These are the best biscuits I've ever eaten."

"It was my wife's recipe. After Belinda passed, I had no choice but to learn how to cook. Say, you in the mood for some scrapple?"

"I'd sooner eat ground glass. Doc, I have a question to ask you."

"Ask away, but I have a hunch the answer is going to be eight inches."

"Excuse me?"

"You want to know how far I keep the biscuits from the top of the oven, so they don't burn on top. Right?"

"It's a favor, Doc, not a cooking tip. You still own that bloodhound?"

"You mean Blue? Yeah, she's out back. I have to keep her outside full-time now because she's incontinent."

"Does her sniffer still work?"

Doc winked. "She let me know you were coming, Magdalena. That's how I knew to set two plates."

"Right. Doc, you think I could borrow Blue?"

"Don't see why not. This the police business you were talking about?"

"Yes. There's been a murder up on Stucky Ridge."

"Anyone I know?"

"I don't think so—he was a guest of mine. There seems to be a trail of blood. I was hoping Blue could follow it."

"Have another sausage link, Magdalena. You can't do police work on an empty stomach."

I did as my mama always told me and listened to my elders.

There was nothing wrong with Blue's sniffer. She tore through the woods like a hyperactive child on an Easter-egg hunt. I needed that extra sausage just to keep up. Her first stop was the spot where Melvin had found Buzzy. By then both the body and the bumbling chief were gone.

Blue snuffled the saturated ground and then charged off on the trail I'd begun. She, of course, had much better success. She led us out of the woods to the picnic side of the ridge and didn't stop until we'd reached a place that is popularly called Lovers' Leap. Believe me when I say no lovers have ever leaped to their deaths from that spot. There is a sheer vertical drop of about fifty feet to the closest ledge, but the enormous trees below would prevent anyone from falling more than twenty feet without being snagged by branches. About the best a forlorn lover could expect is a slew of broken bones and multiple abrasions.

This is the highest spot on Stucky Ridge and is marked by a concrete pillar that notes the elevation—a mind-boggling 2,801 feet. I know that sounds puny by Rocky Mountain standards, but for us Hernians it's a nosebleed height. At any rate, the numbers on the pillar are almost illegible, thanks to the graffiti painted on it by generations of expressive teenagers. Because this is our town's most significant landmark, it is also where the time capsule is buried.

No one knows for sure how deep the metal box lies, or even whether it is under the monument, or just next to it. All that is known for sure is that the box was buried in 1904 and was meant to be dug up a hundred years later. Because the marker is in such bad shape, it is the town council's plan to replace the old one after the successful retrieval of the capsule on Wednesday.

"Land o' Goshen," I panted as we neared the spot. "Would you look at that!"

Doc moves sprightly for a man his age and caught up with me seconds later. Together we stared at the scene of devastation.

The marker had been toppled, its base broken into pieces by something—possibly a sledgehammer—and the ground where the pillar stood had been excavated to a depth of four feet. The hole had a diameter of a little more than two feet. At the bottom was a rectangular imprint. Clearly, whomever was responsible had gone straight for the treasure and gotten what they were after.

But Blue wasn't done yet. She stood at the edge of Lovers' Leap and howled like the hound of the Baskervilles. Doc had to pull her back and then temporarily muzzle her with his hands.

"Bet you anything," he said, "the tools are down there, below the trees."

"Yes. But why drag the body all the way into the woods? Why not just throw it over the edge too?"

"Don't have any idea," Doc said. "You're the expert."

"I'm not an expert," I wailed. "I am merely competent."

He winked. "I bet you're more than that."

"Doc, please, this is serious business. I need to think of possible scenarios."

He released Blue's muzzle and told her to sit. Having had a good workout, she lay instead on a pile of dirt.

"Okay, Magdalena, how about this? Your corpse—what was his name?"

"Buzzy. Buzzy Porter."

"Yeah, so Mr. Porter thinks the time capsule is worth stealing—maybe it contains some damning evidence that he's privy to—and so he comes up here in the dead of the night to dig for it. But someone else wants it too. They clobber Mr. Porter over the head and then plan to bury him in the woods. If they just threw him over the edge, he'd get caught up in the trees, but a shovel would most likely slip right through. Anyway, the murderer is about to dig a shallow grave when that Episcopalian kid—what's his name?"

"Ron Humphrey."

"Yeah, so that kid comes along and the murderer takes off. But first he throws the tools over the cliff."

"Why not just put them in his or her car?"

He shrugged. "Like I said, you're the expert."

I poked a finger under the organza prayer cap that covers my bun. My scalp was itching, which for me is either a sign of inspiration or untreated dandruff.

"But, Doc, it could also be that the killer was here first, and Buzzy surprised him."

He grunted agreement. "Any idea how an out-of-towner would know where to look?"

"I haven't gotten that far." I peered into the hole. Its sides were absolutely vertical. "But I can tell you that it was a square-point shovel, not a round one."

He stepped closer, and Blue got up to look with him. "You're right about that. Now, who do you know in this county who owns a square-point shovel?"

I couldn't help but laugh. Looking for a square-point shovel in this county would be like searching for a particular fragment of fodder in a haystack. Virtually all the farmers, and half the townsfolk, own square-point shovels.

"My point exactly." Doc stepped sideways and draped an arm

around my shoulder. In order to do so he had to reach up, so it wasn't the smoothest of moves.

"While we ruminate on the perplexities of this unfortunate incident, why don't we go back to my place? I'll make you lunch." He gave me a squeeze.

"Doc, it's only nine o'clock—oh my gracious! I'm supposed to announce the tractor pull at ten and I haven't even spoken to any of my guests today. Freni's going to be hysterical that I wasn't there for breakfast, and Gabe—"

He squeezed me again. "I've always liked a woman with purpose. Tell that people doctor of yours he's a lucky man."

We turned to go, but not before Blue took one last sniff of the breeze that was blowing toward us from Lovers' Leap. It was a cool morning, but that's not why I shivered.

9

A fuming, flailing, frantic Freni is a fearsome thing. Although she's stout with stubby arms, when she becomes agitated she waves them so fast I'm afraid she'll achieve liftoff. Believe me, I have no desire to learn what it is Amish women wear under their skirts.

The moment I stepped through the outside kitchen door, Freni flew at me. "Ach, Magdalena, where were you?"

"I'm afraid it was police business, dear."

She flapped to a stop. "You got another traffic ticket, yah?"

"I'm afraid it's worse than that."

My friend and kinswoman stared at me through lenses as thick as the bottoms of Coke bottles—well, back in the days when they were made of glass. "Murder?"

"Yes, but—"

"English, yah?" To the Amish, anyone not of the faith is referred to as English. Even my Japanese guest would be considered English. No doubt this custom derives from the fact that it was the English who were in control of this country when the Amish first arrived in the early 1700s.

"So the victim was English, dear. What of it?"

Freni crossed her short arms beneath an ample bosom. Her stomach is ample as well, so it wasn't an easy position to assume.

"Was the English a guest?"

"Unfortunately, yes."

"Then I quit."

I struggled not to smile. Freni has quit her job as chief cook and bottle washer eighty-nine times in the last six years. When she reaches a hundred, I'm going to give her a plaque. It will read WORLD'S MOST FICKLE COOK. When she asks what "fickle" means, I'll tell her it is a synonym for "valuable." She'll think "synonym" is a spice and will be too confused to question me further.

"The murder didn't happen here at the inn, Freni. It happened up on Stucky Ridge."

"I still quit."

"But you can't! I have eight remaining guests to feed, the murder investigation to attend to, and my festival duties to perform." In addition to announcing the tractor pull, I was scheduled to award the prize in the greased pig contest. These honors were bestowed on me because I am the most inbred, yet articulate, resident of our burg. The prize, by the way, was two hundred dollars, and the winner got to keep the pig.

"Magdalena, these guests of yours are running me crazy."

"You mean 'driving,' dear."

"Yah, that's what I said. At breakfast, the old one who thinks she is a movie star wants her eggs poached, instead of fried. Then she wants me to put them on muffins with bacon and Holland sauce so they are a benediction."

"Ah, you mean eggs Benedict."

Her eyes, made all the more beady by the lenses, bore into mine. I knew when to quit.

"Tell me everything, dear."

Freni unfolded her arms so that she could take a deep breath. "Well, she is not the only one who gives me trouble. The Japanese English says she wants raw fish for lunch." She made a face. "Magdalena, who ever heard of eating such a thing?"

The Amish I know love fish, but it has to say Star-Kist on the label. "It's called sushi, dear. Did you tell them that you are in charge of the menus?"

"Yah, but there is much complaining." Now that her arms were free she untied her apron. "Magdalena, if I want this complaining, I can get it from Barbara."

Barbara Hostetler is Freni's daughter-in-law. Because the Bible commands it, they love each other in a general sort of way, but not a smidgen more. The truth is, Freni resents losing her only son to another woman's affections. Never mind that this woman, a "foreigner" from Iowa, has supplied the Hostetlers with three bouncing babies. And all in one fell swoop too.

I nodded gravely. "Yes, maybe it is a good idea for you to take some time off. Barbara was telling me just the other day how homesick she still gets. She's thinking of having her mother come and stay for a month."

"Ach! Then I unquit."

The best thing was to pretend our little tiff had never happened. "Where's Alison?"

"That nice couple from Charlesville, they take her to watch that silly tractor game."

I had nothing to gain by correcting her geography. Besides, it was already twenty to ten. If I didn't put my lead foot to good use, the tractor pull would be delayed.

I got there in the nick of time. The pull was to be held on Main Street, which really is the main drag in town. At the corners of Main and Elm sit the First Mennonite and Covenant Presbyterian churches. Across from them are the police station and Yoder's Corner Market, a small grocery selling dusty, overpriced goods. I don't own it, by the way. It belongs to my cousin Sam, who has the same designs on me that Doc Shafor has. Sam, however, lacks Doc's charm.

It is only a ten-minute drive from my inn to the center of town, but thanks to an overwhelming turnout of spectators, I had to park over on Kingdom Come. This is the name of a real street. It gets its moniker from the Baptist Church at the corner. At any rate, I was out of breath, and perhaps a mite out of sorts, when I arrived at my post. I certainly was not in the mood to be ambushed.

"Hi, babe," my fiancé said, as he appeared out of nowhere and grabbed my arm.

"Gabe!"

He hugged me close.

"Vell," somebody harrumphed, "this is certainly not the appropriate place for this kind of behavior."

At first I thought the disembodied voice belonged to my dear, departed mama. The poor woman is obviously not enjoying her stay in Heaven. If she was, she wouldn't find so much time to bother me. Perhaps the golden streets are too slippery—after all, Mama never did have a very good sense of balance.

"Really, dear," I whispered, "perhaps you should get back to your harp lessons." Mama also had a tin ear.

"You see what I mean, Gabriel? The voman's meshuga."

That's when I realized the voice was coming from below. Mama was definitely not spending eternity in that direction. My heart sank when I saw who it was.

"Mrs. Rosen, I'm afraid I didn't see you."

"That's because you're too tall, Magdalena. Like a bean stalk, if you ask me. But not to vorry. I hear they have surgery for that kind of thing nowadays."

"Somehow I don't think so."

"Tell her, Gabriel."

"Yes," I said, "tell *her* she's been reading too many tabloids."

My beloved didn't say anything, caught as he was between a stalk and a hard place.

"So," Mrs. Rosen said, putting her fists on her hips—at least that's what it looked like from way up here—"you're not going to stick up for your mother?"

Gabe flinched. "Ma, I refuse to take sides. You know that."

"Then you're taking her side."

"Ma!"

I flashed Ida Rosen a triumphant look and made my way to the reviewing stand. There were three seats on the rickety wooden platform, and they were already occupied by the dignitaries of the day. Apparently I was meant to stand. Sitting ramrod straight in the middle seat was Sam Yoder, in front of whose store the event was taking place. To his right sat Reverend Richard Nixon, pastor of the First and Only True Church of the One and Only Living God of the Tabernacle of Supreme Holiness and Healing and Keeper of the Consecrated Righteousness of the Eternal Flame of Jehovah. The good man was going to open the ceremonies with an invocation. To Sam's left sprawled Betty Baumgartner, a Hernia teenager who had been asked to sing the national anthem. Betty's claim to fame is that she made it to the top one thousand finalists in a TV show called *American Idol*.

I've been blessed with a good pair of lungs, so this was not my first time as an announcer. "Ladies and gentlemen, please bow your heads for a word of prayer."

Hats were doffed and heads were bowed, but the leader of the church with thirty-two names delivered more than a word. After asking God's blessing on the crowd, he prayed for the safety of the contestants, then launched into a long list of petitions that included requests for good weather, bountiful crops, and contrite hearts. So far so good, but unfortunately his mental needle got stuck in the repentance groove.

I gave the man a nudge to move things along, but the needle skipped and landed in the fire and brimstone band of his vinyl record. This is when the reverend, who evokes a taller and ganglier Abraham Lincoln, threw his arms in the air and waved them about with all the grace of a marionette manipulated by a drunken puppeteer.

"Repent!" he thundered, "or suffer forever the fiery horrors of hell. Behold, the last days are upon us—"

I tugged on the tails of his frock coat. "A simple 'amen' would do nicely now, dear."

He pulled away. "—your throats will close up with unquenchable thirst, your lips will blister like the scales of a shed snakeskin—"

What was I to do? There were Presbyterians in the audience for pete's sake, and they might not appreciate the reverend's perspective on their future home—not to mention Ron the Episcopalian.

Or Gabe and his mother for that matter. I was left with no choice but to punch the preacher in the soft spots behind his knees and watch him topple like the tower of Babel. Fortunately, Sam has good reflexes and caught the pontificating pastor before he could hurt himself.

I poked Betty Baumgartner. "Belt it out, dear."

Alas, the child was agog with wonder at what I had done, and when that finally passed she burst into shrill laughter. It was turning out to be a typical Hernia celebration.

"This may be your last chance at fame, dear. I hear there are talents scouts in the crowd."

Betty sobered instantly and grabbed the microphone. " 'Oh say can you see—' "

My mouth fell open. I assure you that I was not the only one to lose control of their jaw muscles. The girl was so off-key it would be impossible to find one note on a piano to match. I did the kind thing and prayed that she would forget the words and be forced to stop.

Half my prayer was answered. "—by the rocket's red glare in the dawn's early light—"

Just as I was leaning forward to give her a merciful punch behind the knees, somewhere across town a dog howled. It sounded a lot like Blue. Seconds later another dog joined in. Then another. It was the crowd's turn to laugh.

I grabbed the microphone from a blushing Betty. "Give the girl a big round of applause, folks."

Sam, bless his lecherous heart, clapped first. Then, one by one, the others joined in. A beaming Betty bowed dramatically before I pushed her gently aside. She plopped in her chair and picked up a pop she'd been guzzling.

"Everybody ready for the tractor pull?" I yelled.

The response was deafening. Hernians love their tractor pulls. Even the Amish, who eschew the use of such modern machines, seem to have no objection to observing this competition. The crowd was sprinkled with black bonnets and straw hats. In fact, some of the more enterprising women had set up stalls on the fringes where they sold homemade cheese and preserves. One entrepreneur had brought with her a small propane stove and was frying snitz pies, a greasy pastry filled with dried apples and a thousand calories.

I'm sure every community has their rules and regulations, but ours are simple. The contestants must be eighteen or over, and the machines they operate must belong to them. The playoffs are between pairs, who chain their tractors back to back and try to pull their opponent over a line. Think of it as a tug of war on steroids.

It can be a dangerous sport—chains sometimes snap, tractors rear like bucking broncos and can veer off course—and is normally not played on city streets. But deep down Hernians are a wild bunch, many of whom long to run before the bulls in Pamplona. Besides, Main Street is exceptionally wide, and the high-school stadium was being readied for the greased pig competition.

"First off we have Danny Gerber and 'Dirty Bob' Troyer. Danny—on my left—is driving the souped-up Massey Ferguson his dad gave him for graduation. Danny dear, did you ever finish your community service for having sprayed 'I Love Tina' on the overpass south of town?"

The crowd roared their approval and Danny gave me the thumbs-up sign.

"Dirty Bob," I said, "time to pick on you next."

The crowd roared again.

I wasn't being nasty by any means. Everyone in town calls Robert Troyer by his nickname. In fact, he's proud of it. This rather handsome man dropped out of high school his senior year when his father died. In order to support his mother and two little sisters, young Robert got a job at a garden center over in Bedford. The place was called the Onion Patch at the time. The new employee was not afraid to get his hands dirty and today, ten years later, he owns the store. You guessed the rest—it's now called Dirty Bob's.

"If you win this round," I deadpanned, "you also win a free manicure at Selma's House of Beauty."

The crowd went hysterical. Even though he now has a dozen employees, Dirty Bob still digs with his hands. He feels he needs to set an example, and when one is transplanting delicate seedlings, that's the only way to do it. It's certainly no secret that Dirty Bob has dirt embedded beneath his nails that no soap and water will reach.

"Dirty Bob will be driving a John Deere that he rebuilt by himself and—"I gasped as a couple of dormant brain cells kicked back to life and I had a mini-epiphany. "Uh, ladies and gentleman, Sam Yoder will be taking over as announcer."

"What?" Sam was on his feet in a nanosecond. "Magdalena, what the heck are you saying?"

Actually, Sam used a worse word, but as I already had a hand over the microphone, only belching Betty—her pop was long gone—heard him. "Sam, if you be a dear and do this one favor for me, I'll make your fondest wish come true."

"My house or yours? If it's mine, we'll have to pick a time when Dorothy's not there."

I was disgusted but not shocked by my cousin's proposition. He stopped being a Mennonite the day he married Dorothy, a liberal-leaning Methodist. I'm not saying that all Methodists cheat on their wives, merely that the town grocer's apple had fallen far from the tree. One might say that it rolled into another orchard altogether. In cases like that, one can expect just about anything to happen.

"Samuel Nevin Yoder, you should be ashamed of yourself. What would your mama say if she could hear you talking like that? More to the point, what will your wife say when I tell her?"

"You wouldn't dare tell Dorothy, because it would hurt her."

I sighed. "If you were a little boy, I'd turn you over my knee right now and spank you."

"I love it when you talk dirty, Magdalena."

The crowd had begun to buzz impatiently, and at least one of the contestants was revving his engine. I uncovered the mike.

"Hold your horsepower," I barked. I turned to Sam. "Look buster, what I had in mind was free advertising for your store. Between pulls you get to announce your overpriced specials. A head of wilted lettuce for one ninety-nine. That kind of thing."

"It's a deal," Sam said.

I practically threw the microphone at him. Thanks to Dirty Bob, all I needed to do was to make one phone call and I could prove whether Buzzy Porter had been the one to dig up Hernia's time capsule or had surprised someone else in the act.

10

Grilled Chicken Breasts with Eggplant, Creole Style

2 lemons
2 whole boneless chicken breasts,
    skinned, split, and trimmed
Salt and whole black peppercorns
    in a pepper mill
1 medium eggplant (about ¾
    pound)
¼ cup all-purpose flour

1 large egg, well beaten, in a wide,
    shallow bowl
1 cup fine cracker crumbs or
    matzo meal, spread on a plate
3 tablespoons melted unsalted
    butter or extra-virgin olive oil
1 cup Creole Sauce
2 tablespoons chopped parsley

Grate the zest from 1 of the lemons and then juice them both through a strainer. Put the chicken breasts in a shallow nonreactive stainless steel or glass bowl and sprinkle them with the grated zest, a large pinch of salt, and several generous grindings of pepper. Pour the lemon juice over them, turning them several times to coat them, and set aside to marinate for 30 minutes (or as much as 8 hours or overnight, covered and refrigerated).

Wash the eggplant under cold, running water. Peel and slice it crosswise into 8½-inch-thick slices. Lightly salt both sides of the eggplant slices and put them in a colander set in the sink or over a plate. Let them stand for 30 minutes. Meanwhile, prepare a charcoal grill with coals and light it. When the coals are glowing red and lightly ashed over, spread them and position a rack about 4 inches above them. Let the rack get very hot. Or preheat the oven broiler at least 15 minutes before you plan to use it.

Wipe the eggplant with a paper towel and pat dry. Lightly roll each slice in the flour, shake off the excess, then dip it in the egg, coating all sides. Lift it from the egg, allowing the excess to flow back into the bowl, and then roll it in the crumbs or matzo meal. Shake off the excess and put the breaded eggplant on a wire rack.

Lift the chicken from its marinade and pat dry. Spread it on a platter in one layer and lightly brush it and the eggplant with butter or olive oil. Put them both on the grill (or on a broiling rack under the broiler), buttered side toward the heat. Grill/broil until the chicken breasts and eggplant slices are browned on the side toward the heat, about 3 to 4 minutes. Brush lightly with butter or oil, turn them, and grill/broil until the chicken is cooked through and the eggplant is tender and browned on both sides, about 3 to 4 minutes longer, depending on how hot the fire is. The eggplant may be ready a little before the chicken. Place the eggplant on a warm platter, lay a chicken breast over each slice, and spoon Creole Sauce (see Chapter 15) over them. Sprinkle with parsley and serve at once.

SERVES 4

11

Lucky for me Melvin has a perennial zit the size of Zimbabwe on his backside. Susannah has told me far too much about this condition, which she fondly refers to as "my Sugar Buns's auxiliary brain." Up until now I've been a good Magdalena and stifled my impulse to ask how she knows which brain is which. At any rate, after escorting Buzzy's body to the morgue, my nemesis hung out in the hospital waiting room until Dr. Luther had the time to lance the police chief's eruption. Dr. Luther may well be meaner than a tick-covered snake, but he's a competent surgeon, and my brother-in-law survived the operation with his real brain intact. He was, however, in a particularly foul mood.

"What now?" he shouted into his cell phone.

"How do you know it's me?"

"Yoder, I'm not in the mood to play your silly games. It's you, isn't it?"

"Yes, but—oh, never mind. Melvin, dear, I need you to do me a big favor."

"I'm not going snipe hunting with you again, Yoder. Twice was enough."

"Melvin, I want you to look under Buzzy Porter's fingernails and tell me what you see."

"You're an idiot, Yoder."

"Just do as I say, or come election day you'll be lucky to get two votes."

"Like I said, you're an idiot. Susannah can't vote twice."

"Quit calling the kettle black and look under Buzzy's nails. Call me back the second you do so."

Melvin muttered something uncomplimentary, but I could hear him shuffle off to do as I'd ordered. On the way to the morgue he stopped for an ice cream—possibly in Beijing, China. When he returned my call he belched before speaking.

"So I looked at his nails. What about them?"

"Are they dirty?"

He sighed. "Now you tell me."

"Melvin, all you—"

"Hang on." He walked back to China for the chocolate syrup and whipped cream he'd forgotten. "They're clean, Yoder. So what?"

"Then he didn't dig up the time capsule."

"What time capsule?"

"That's right, you don't know. *The* time capsule—you know the one up on the ridge, by Lovers' Leap? The one we're supposed to open on Wednesday? Well, it's missing."

To say that Melvin was miffed at me for withholding information is an understatement. He ranted and raved and invented some curses that even a fallen Baptist is unlikely to know. He went so far as to suggest that I engage myself sexually in a position that is anatomically impossible to achieve (don't ask me how I know). Of course, Melvin was right for feeling this way. But did he have to be so rude?

In my defense, I hadn't intended to keep him in the dark. I'm so used to him being an utter incompetent, that it just didn't occur to me to fill him in. For that I ought to be ashamed.

"I'm sorry," I said for the zillionth time. "Really, I am."

"You ought to be, Yoder. Besides, why would anyone want to steal that thing?"

"Maybe if we could figure out the answer to that, we could figure out *who* took it. Oh well, at least we know it wasn't Buzzy."

"Oh yeah? How do we know that?"

"Because you can only dig so far with a shovel. Then you have to get down on your hands and knees and dig around the box with your fingers to get it loose."

Melvin snorted. "This Buzzy guy could have started the digging and then the other guy surprises him and finishes the digging. Clean nails don't mean nothing."

"Anything."

Melvin made another trip to Beijing—this time for nuts. "You have a hearing problem, Yoder? I said 'nothing.' "

"That's a double negative, dear. Anyway, I want you to check his pants. Especially the knee area."

"Check them yourself," he said and hung up.

My first impulse was to lose my temper. But fearing that I might never find it again, I wisely decided to take Melvin's suggestion. If you want something done right, do it yourself—even if it means scrutinizing a dead man's pants.

I was halfway back to my car, trotting past the gorgeous Victorian homes on upper Elm Street, when I ran into Stanley Dalrumple. I mean that literally. Arms and legs went flying in eight different directions, although all the limbs belonged to me. On the plus side, I learned that I could always have a second career, hiring myself out as a human threshing machine. The downside was that I when I finally landed, I skinned both palms and the tip of my nose.

Stanley, who is slight of stature, appeared none the worse for wear. "Miss Yoder, are you all right?"

"No, I'm not all right. My hands hurt, my nose hurts—why weren't you looking where you were going?"

"I was looking. You were the one who ran into me. You looked really zoned out—kind of like a zombie."

"Well, I have important things to think about."

Stanley snickered. "Yeah, I bet you do. Like what slop to feed us for lunch."

"Excuse me?"

The young man knew he was no match for my lacerating lingua. "Never mind," he mumbled.

But it was too late. My hackles were hiked and I needed to let off steam. Otherwise my eardrums might blow, taking half the town with them.

"For your information, buster, Freni Hostetler is one of the best cooks in the county. And not that it's any of your business, but I had my mind on a murder case I've been asked to solve."

The corners of his mouth twitched as he struggled to keep his sarcasm in check. It was a losing battle.

"Did the victim eat Miss Hostetler's cooking?"

"As a matter of fact, yes. The victim was Buzzy Porter."

Stanley Dalrumple didn't even blink behind his wire-rimmed glasses. "That figures."

"You don't seem surprised."

"The guy was a jerk."

"I seem to recall that you found him amusing."

"He was still a jerk."

"Mr. Dalrumple, I don't know about Hollywood, but here in Hernia being a jerk is not sufficient cause to murder someone."

He stared at me with all the emotion of a snake. "Miss Yoder, are you some kind of policewoman?"

"You might say that."

He showed no reaction. "I'm not a suspect, am I?"

"I never said you were. But until I can prove who the killer is, everyone is a suspect."

"I guess this means you're going to want to ask me some questions."

"You guessed right. And now is as good a time as any."

He sighed. "Well, if you must know, I wasn't just at that stupid tractor pull."

The sound of the cheering crowd in the background made that obvious. Besides, he was headed from the opposite direction when I ran him down. While it is possible a man his age would be strolling about town to view all our fine architecture, it was about as likely as Freni dancing naked at Wednesday's picnic. I decided to return his blank stare and hopefully make him nervous enough to tell me the whole truth and nothing but. Alison says I give her the willies when I do this. Believe me, I've had plenty of practice.

Stanley Dalrumple caved like an overmined coal shaft. "Okay, so I was out looking for some weed. Big deal."

It was my turn to snicker. "You won't find any weeds in these lawns. This is the high-rent district."

He had the audacity to laugh. "Not that kind of weed. I'm talking about pot. Cannabis. You know, the kind of weed you smoke."

I gasped. "You won't find that either. This is Hernia, not Harrisburg."

"Ha, you'd be surprised, Miss Yoder. I'm pretty good at sniffing it out—no pun intended. Had to learn how to find it quick after nine eleven, what with airport security being what it is. Was going to pick me up some in Pittsburgh, but the old bag didn't give me a minute to myself."

"Old bag? By that you would mean Octavia Cabot-Dodge, the down-on-her-luck diva?"

"Yeah, whatever."

I realized with a start that the upstart must have been successful in his search for illegal stimulants. Otherwise, he wouldn't be returning to the pull so soon.

"Where is it young man? Hand it over."

He finally blinked. "Do you have the authority to arrest me?"

"What if I said 'yes'?"

"You don't, do you?"

If Alison talked to me that way I'd ground her. Maybe even make her copy a page from the dictionary. The one on respect. Young people these days have no respect for their elders, which is one of society's major failings, if you ask me. In my day we had to respect even the people we loathed—which is not to say I hated Granny Yoder. It's just that I had great respect for her cane, which met my backside on more than one occasion. I know, today that would be called child abuse, and rightly so. But I don't think I'm any more screwed up than the average person, do you?

Lacking any way to discipline the impudent youth, I waggled

a finger at him—presidential style. "You will not be smoking that stuff on my property. If I so much as smell one molecule of suspicious smoke, I'm calling someone who does have the power to arrest you. Is that clear?"

"Yeah, yeah. You done lecturing now?"

"Not quite. If you offer any drugs to my foster daughter, Alison, I'll see that they not only lock you up, but throw away the key."

"If you say so."

That last comment irritated me from the tips of my stocking-clad toes to the core of my bun. "I still have a hard time believing you found marijuana in Hernia."

Stanley's smile seemed almost genuine. "Met this kid in the crowd. Could tell right away he was a pothead. Followed him back to that house." He pointed at a yellow Victorian with white gingerbread trim. It's always been one of my favorites.

"That's impossible. That house belongs to Andrew and Lydia Byler. They're the salt of the earth. Their son, David, is—describe this kid, please."

"No prob. Red hair, a million freckles. Looks like he could open a bottle with his teeth."

"That's him!" I said in dismay.

To his credit, young Stanley did not rub it in. "Miss Yoder, I'd be happy to share my stash with you."

"What?"

"A couple of tokes and you'll be feeling real mellow. Come on, try it. You look like you deserve to chill out for a while. This stuff is guaranteed to make you feel like you're floating on a cloud."

"It really does that for you?" The truth is I'm so high strung I can fly a kite on a windless day. To my knowledge, the only time I've ever felt totally relaxed—and I mean all the way back to when I made my first appearance as a six-pound, seven-ounce, squalling bundle of annoyance—is when I inadvertently drank a pitcher of mimosas. What would be so wrong about feeling that way again? Perhaps the Good Lord created the cannabis plant so that we could enjoy its benefits.

Stanley dug into his pocket and withdrew a plastic sandwich

bag filled with what looked like dried oregano. "Oh yeah, it really does that. When you're on this, you won't give a shoot about your problems."

He actually used a stronger word than shoot, and the shock of it brought me back to my senses. "Get behind me, Satan," I cried.

If someone from the *Guinness Book of World Records* had been watching, I would have earned a spot on those pages for having broken the land speed record for a human being. When I got to my car I was panting so hard I had to wait a full five minutes before I could drive.

As I've stated before, Hernia Hospital is a misnomer. Think of it as a twenty-four-hour clinic where Amish women come for births that are too complicated for midwives to handle, and where children receive stitches after falling off bicycles and skateboards. There is a small surgical unit on the premises, but the only time it was ever used was when Veronica Saylor had a bunion removed. That event made national news because the bunion was shaped like Elvis Presley's head, and Dr. Luther, who performed the operation, refused to turn the growth over to his patient. Veronica sued and won custody of her former body part. She later sold the hunk of inflamed tissue on eBay for eight thousand dollars.

Of course, I wasn't visiting the hospital to get my skinned palms and nose treated, but to get another look at Buzzy Porter. Well, at least his clothes. At any rate, you can imagine my surprise when I entered through the front door and found Alison and the Littletons sitting in the minuscule lobby.

"What's wrong?" I demanded.

The Littletons jumped to their feet, but Alison remained seated, just as pale as Granny Yoder's ghost.

"I'm afraid she has stomach pains," Capers said. Her charming Charleston accent failed to make the words less frightening.

I flew to my foster daughter's side. "Where, exactly?"

Alison groaned and pointed to the lower right quadrant of her abdomen.

My darling, and only sometimes obnoxious, child had appendicitis. I was beside myself with concern. Fortunately, I am beanpole thin, and two of me occupy very little space.

"Has the doctor seen her?"

Buist Littleton shook his head. "There was a nurse—Dudley, I think her name was. Said she'd be right back, but it's been almost fifteen minutes."

I glanced at the receptionist on duty—Thelma Umble. Bless her heart, the poor gal has the intelligence of a gerbil and the personality of an artichoke. Or is it the other way around? I had always hoped she would catch one of Melvin's eyes and that he would marry her instead of Susannah. After all, the hospital receptionist and the Chief of Police were not only double first cousins, but third cousins five different ways—or was *that* the other way around? Anyway, when my sister's marriage to the mantis became a fait accompli, I had to adjust my thinking. The descendants of this Umble-Stoltzfus union would have been genetic wildcards that might have eventually threatened national security.

Pasting a friendly smile on my mug, I waltzed over to the receptionist's desk. I don't mean that literally, mind you, ever aware that dancing is a sin.

"Thelma, dear, what's keeping Attila the Hun so long?"

Perhaps I should mention that Thelma is a natural blonde who dies her hair brown. "Ooh," she squealed, "is this a riddle? I just love riddles."

"Sorry, but this isn't a riddle. I just want to know what's taking that battle-ax of a nurse so long."

"I heard that!" Nurse Dudley has a voice that can be picked up by a seismograph—one all the way out in California. She also possesses the stealth of a Siberian tiger.

I am not exaggerating when I say I jumped out of my shoes—well, one of them anyway. A word of advice: a snoop should be just as careful about mending her stockings as she is about wearing clean underclothes.

"Nurse Dudley," I gasped, "how very nice to see you."

"Miss Yoder! Didn't I tell you to never set foot on these premises again?"

"Well, technically, it's only one foot. And then just my big toe, which is unfortunately poking through that hole." I shoved the offending foot back into its brogan.

"Get out of my hospital," the battle-ax bellowed, as fine cracks appeared in the plaster on the walls.

"Not until Alison gets help. And besides, I came here on police business. You don't want to be cited for obstructing justice, do you?"

Nurse Dudley knew that I often functioned as the mantis's mind, but she didn't have to like it. She scowled so deeply one could have planted corn in the furrows of her brow.

"Very well. I'll have the doctor see her in a minute. But first, what is this police business all about?"

"I need to see the corpse that was brought in this morning."

The furrows grew so deep I could have planted onion sets in them. "This better be on the level."

"As level as my chest." I said it soft enough so that Buist Littleton wouldn't hear. Of course, it's no secret that I'm a carpenter's dream, but why advertise it to men, even if I am engaged and he's married?

Nurse Dudley saw her opportunity to pounce and grinned in triumph. "You are as flat as a board, so I'll take that as a yes." You can be sure she didn't whisper.

I blushed as I addressed the Littletons. "Please stay with Alison for a minute." I turned back to Nurse Dudley. "How do I get to the morgue?"

She handed me a ring with just one key on it. "You'll need this. Go through those swinging doors, make a left, and it's the door at the end of the hall. The storage unit has only three drawers and he's in the middle one. There's a box of surgical gloves just inside the door if you need to touch him."

I shivered at the thought. I shivered again when I entered the ice-cold room. But I went numb with shock when I opened the middle drawer.

12

The body before me was not only stark naked, but it had once belonged to someone other than Buzzy Porter. As soon as I could react, I closed the drawer and mumbled an apology. Nurse Dudley was going to pay for her practical joke. I didn't know when, but I did know how. She and Dr. Luther liked to golf together. I'd seen the pair on many occasions, whacking the little white balls early Sunday mornings at the Bedford Country Club. At that hour they were the only ones on the course. I didn't belong to the club, by the way, but had to drive by it on my way into town to buy doughnuts for the Sunday school class I teach. (There is nothing wrong in bribing fifth and sixth graders into being cooperative.)

At any rate, I would make it a point to get up extra early one Sunday. A couple of bags of marshmallows scattered about the greens should prove frustrating, especially if my hunch was right and the confections swelled up from the dew. Then we'd see who laughed last.

Still mumbling, I opened the top drawer, which slid out far too easily. It was empty. I jerked open the bottom drawer, and it came nearly all the way out, knocking me flat on my bony behind.

"Ding dang darn!" I said. If I didn't mend my ways soon, I would surely turn into a potty mouth.

The drawer had come at me so fast because, like the top one, it was empty. I glanced around the room, which was barely more than a cubicle. An icy cubicle. There was nowhere else to look for a corpse. I tugged the middle drawer open again, and risking blindness, scrutinized the body more carefully. Primarily the face.

I had been able to immediately discern that the body wasn't Buzzy's, because the last time I saw him he had dark hair. The body in front of me was blond—everywhere, including the eyebrows. The eyes were closed, but the patrician shape of the nose was familiar. In fact, it looked a lot like Ron Humphrey's nose. I leaned in closer, breathing in the sickly sweet smell of death. It *was* Ron Humphrey in the drawer.

Anticipating my collapse, I voluntarily connected my derriere with the concrete floor. I don't know how long I sat there—maybe five minutes—as I screwed up my courage to continue my investigation. When the time was right I struggled to my feet, all the while giving audible thanks to the Good Lord for creating me with such big ones. With enough warning, and if I planted my tootsies just right, I could fall asleep standing up. Anyone who doubts my ability to do so should ask Reverend Schrock. It's been said that even the Almighty falls asleep during his lengthy prayers.

But before taking my lock-kneed position, I did something I never would have imagined. I donned a pair of the surgical gloves. Alas, there were no masks visible in the room, or else I would have worn one as well.

A closer look involved the support of every inch of my tootsies. Ron Humphrey's body was a waxy blue-gray, almost translucent in appearance. If it weren't for his distinctive proboscis and somewhat unusual hair color, I would have never recognized the man. Death is more than the absence of life; it is the absence of essence.

As an Episcopalian, Ron had existed on the fringes of our close-knit community. He and I had locked horns on a few occasions, mostly over alcohol-related issues, but we were not enemies by any means. I found him to be affable and generally very well informed. To my knowledge, everyone in Hernia regarded the young man as a hardworking citizen, deserving of the same respect afforded everyone else. He had no enemies that I knew of.

I gingerly touched one arm in a farewell gesture. It felt cool through the thin layer of latex. This meant nothing from an investigative point of view, especially since I had just taken the corpse out of cold storage.

"Good-bye, Ron," I said, since I was totally alone with the body. "I'm sure some Episcopalians find their way into Heaven, and if you're one of the fortunate ones, please say hello to my mama and papa. But if you run into Granny Yoder—well, even up there I suggest you run the other way."

Of course, Ron didn't respond, so I got right down to business. There appeared to be no unusual marks on his head. His chest looked fine as well—wait a minute. There was a small dark gray hole just below his left nipple. I hadn't spotted it at first, given that it was hidden by a mat of curly blond hair. If my hunch was right, the lad had been killed by a bullet through the heart.

Dead folks seldom cooperate when you try to turn them, and Ron was no exception. I managed to pivot him onto his right shoulder so that his back was off the floor of the drawer at a forty-five-degree angle. There didn't seem to be an exit wound, although his dorsal skin was a pale purple, a sign that blood had begun to collect there. I poked his shoulder blade with a gloved finger. Ron's skin blanched at the point of contact.

I set him down and removed the gloves. I am not skilled in forensics, but I had learned all I needed to know. At least for now. After saying a prayer for wisdom—and a second, backup prayer for patience—I strode off to find the two people who could give me some answers.

It was a slow day at Hernia Hospital, and I found the first of my targets in the staff lounge, polishing off a glazed doughnut. Nurse Ratchet—I mean Nurse Dudley—looked a bit glazed herself. It was a pleasure to disturb her sugar-induced reverie.

"You've got the wrong body in there," I barked.

Nurse Dudley fumbled with her doughnut before dropping it in the lap of her pristine uniform. As any sensible person would do, she snatched up the morsel and popped it in her mouth. She also swore at me, which is just plain not nice.

"What are you doing in here anyway?" I said. "Where is my Alison?"

It was no surprise that she spoke before swallowing. "The brat's gone home."

"Home? But she had appendicitis!"

"She had a bad case of indigestion, that's what."

"Indigestion?"

The ill-tempered woman arranged her sugar-coated lips in what was supposed to be a triumphant smile. To me it looked more like she was trying to imitate a cat swallowing a canary. Unfortunately, the poor bird was still visible in her mouth.

"Dr. Luther knows how to deal with snotty delinquents. Right away he got her to confess that she'd eaten six fried apple pies and two funnel cakes. Miss Yoder, don't you believe in teaching your foster child the basics of nutrition?"

Alison has more faults than the State of California, but nobody gets to criticize her except for her birth parents. And, of course, me. My hackles were hiked so high at that point, I could have won a Louisiana cockfight with a ten-foot rooster.

"She is most certainly not a delinquent! There is no school until Thursday." I prayed for more patience before continuing, but I've learned that it is best not to wait too long after that prayer, lest it really come true. "You'd know that little fact, dear, if you had a child of your own. Oh, and one more thing—apple pies *are* a balanced meal, just as long as you drink plenty of milk."

The nasty nurse has enviable bosoms—actually, she is top-heavy altogether—and she had to struggle to maintain her balance as she stood. "Get out of my hospital, Yoder!"

"*Your* hospital? I was always under the impression that Dr. Luther was in charge."

"Out!" she bellowed through a spray of sugar flecks.

Although she was advancing on me like a bull in heat, I did the knee-lock thing again and stood my ground. "Well, since it is your hospital, maybe you can explain why you have the wrong body in your matchbox-size morgue."

Some people can feign bewilderment, but I honestly think Nurse Dudley lacks the guile to do so—although she definitely has the bile. She scrunched her forehead in genuine astonishment.

"What do you mean the wrong body? There is only one in there."

"I know that. But the body in there belongs to Ron Humphrey, not Buzzy Porter."

"Hernia's Ron Humphrey? That cute Episcopalian boy?"

That was, by the way, the first nonconfrontational sentence I'd ever heard her speak. Her sudden passivity, and the fact that her skin was as pale as Buzzy's when I first saw him in the woods, confirmed my hunch. The woman was rude and incompetent, but she wasn't hiding anything.

"Follow me," I said.

It was a silly thing to say. Nurse Dudley bolted for the morgue, with yours truly close on her thick foam rubber heels. When she stopped in front of the drawer, I nearly ran into her. Her rear end is very well upholstered, so I wouldn't have been hurt by the collision, but there is no telling what she might have done to me afterwards.

She panted like a spent sprinter for a minute before finding a voice. It certainly wasn't hers. Nurse Dudley sounded like a grade-school girl in a screaming contest.

"It *is* Ron Humphrey!"

"That's what I said."

"But it wasn't him when they brought him in. I mean—"

"I know what you mean. Somebody switched bodies, right?"

"Right. Magdalena, you do believe me, don't you?" It was the first time she'd ever used my Christian name. This was turning into a banner week for me.

"Let's say I believe you, what possible explanation could there be for this?"

She shrugged shoulders that would have looked at home on a

quarterback. "I just know I had nothing to do with this, and neither did Dr. Luther. We've been together all morning—well, not *together* together, but when we didn't have patients we were taking advantage of the lull to take inventory."

"Are doughnuts on the list?" I know that was wicked and unfair of me, but the woman had been a thorn in my side for many years.

"One has to take a break sometime."

The tiny room had two doors. I pointed to the one I had yet to use.

"Where does that go?"

"That's our rear exit door."

"But it isn't marked. And what kind of cockeyed committee would issue a permit for a building in which one has to exit through the morgue?"

She didn't hesitate. "You should know. You were on it."

I swallowed my irritation. It's one of the ways I maintain my weight.

"You should have that marked," I said. "And you know, don't you, that it needs to be unlocked at times when people are in the building?"

"It is unlocked—that's why I gave you a key. We only lock the inside door to the morgue."

I sighed. Nurse Dudley and her doctor compatriot both had the reasoning power of teenagers. On the other hand, their illogical minds had given me the edge that I needed to secure their cooperation. At least for the near future.

"I hope you realize, Nurse Dudley, that if someone reports this violation, the county can shut you down."

"It can?" Her tone was actually respectful.

"You bet your bippy, dear."

"What do we do about it?"

"Either leave this door unlocked"—I pointed to the door that led back into the hall—"or have a contractor put in a new outside door somewhere else. But if that's the case, clear the plans first with the planning committee. In any event, you'll need to erect a proper exit sign."

"That's it?"

"Pretty much—oh, but I need to speak to the ambulance crew before I leave."

"You just did."

"I beg your pardon?"

"Magdalena, you know that we're not really a hospital—not in the traditional sense."

"You mean not accredited."

"Whatever. But we do the best we can to meet the needs of the community. Why, next year we're thinking of hiring another doctor and maybe two more nurses."

"Good for you, dear. But what did you mean by saying I'd already spoken to the ambulance crew?"

"Like I've been trying to explain, we can't afford to keep a standing crew. When the call came in this morning we hadn't opened yet, so Dr. Luther and I answered it ourselves."

"Isn't that illegal? Aren't paramedics supposed to be specially trained?"

She snorted, then caught herself by clapping a man-size mitt over her mouth. "You can't get any more trained than Dr. Luther," she finally said.

"Nurse Dudley, in addition to contacting the planning commission, I'd contact a lawyer and ask him or her to check on all the necessary regulations for running this sort of enterprise."

"That means you're not going to snitch?"

"No, I'm not going to snitch."

"Promise?"

"I promise."

"Then get out of my hospital, Miss Yoder!"

I held up my skinned hands. "But I'm wounded. I need medical care."

"Out, before I throw you out!"

"Promises are made to be broken," I said over my shoulder. It was wise to retreat while I still had the upper hand—even if it was missing part of its epidermis.

I tried calling Melvin on my cell phone. While I despise it when other people steer with one hand, I always seem to have a good excuse. And what could be more important than a body switched in a minimorgue? Besides, I have exceptional hand-eye coordination, if I must say so myself. The only person who ever beat me at jacks when I was a little girl was Gertrude Plank—and she had seven fingers on her right hand.

But our Chief of Police was simply unavailable. Even the 911 number didn't work. I had no choice but to swing by the station and wait for a warm body to show up. In the meantime I dialed home.

"Jimmy, is that you?" a girl's voice said.

"Alison?"

"Mom?"

"Sweetie, you're supposed to answer 'PennDutch.' "

"Sorry mom. Hey, do ya mind getting off the phone, because Jimmy said he was gonna call right back."

"Are we talking about Jimmy Mast, who, as we've discussed a million times, is far too old for you?"

"He's seventeen, which is only four years older than me."

"Yes, but at your age you have to figure the difference out in dog years. Think of Jimmy as being twenty-eight years older than you. That would make him forty-one."

"Gross. That's ancient. No way I'm gonna date anyone that old."

There was no point in reminding her just then that she wasn't going to date anyone—period—until she was older. At least not for another two dog years.

"Sweetie," I said as sweetly as I could, "did you have anything to eat at the tractor pull this morning?"

"Man! Somebody busted me, didn't they?"

"I'm afraid so."

"And them Southerners seemed like such nice people."

"It was Nurse Dudley, dear."

"Figures. Oh well, go ahead and yell at me, Mom."

"I'm not going to yell, Alison. I think you already learned your lesson. Now, put Freni on the phone, please."

"I can't."

"Why can't you?"

"She quit."

"What? She just unquit a few hours ago."

"Yeah, but you see, that nice Japanese lady and them farmer hicks—"

"You mean the Nortons, dear."

"Whatever. They went into Bedford and came back with fancy groceries and the Japanese lady is going to make everyone lunch. Something called terry yucky. Oh, and she had to buy herself some new clothes too, on account of you."

"It's not my fault that cabdriver hasn't been caught. And by the way, that's teriyaki, dear."

"Whatever. Mom, do I have to eat it?"

"No." Normally I would have said 'yes'—both to teach her a lesson about gorging on pastries and to expose her palate to a wider range of tastes, but I was miffed that my guests had commandeered the kitchen.

"Cool. Mom, you're the best."

"Remember that the next time you're tempted to say I'm the meanest mom in the whole wide world."

"Yeah, yeah, whatever."

"Alison, dear, did you still want to go to the greased-pig chase this afternoon?"

"Nah. I want to hang out here. My stomach still hurts."

"Okay, but Jimmy does not come over. Is that clear?"

She mumbled something unintelligible.

"I said, is that clear?"

"I heard ya. And anyway, he can't come over because he's going to be in that stupid pig race."

"It's not a race, dear. It's a chase."

"Whatever. Can I go now?"

"Yes, dear," I said. My tone was still sweet, even though my patience had been stretched as thin as phyllo dough.

Frankly, I was glad my charge had decided to stay home. It was time to take my investigation of Buzzy Porter's death to the next level. I decided to skip the police station and go straight to the heart of Hernia's law-enforcement team.

13

Zelda Root is our only full-time police officer other than Melvin. She's a short thing with enormous breasts, no hips, and matchstick ankles. In other words, the poor woman is shaped vaguely like a rooster, except that a cockerel has only one breast, and Zelda has almost no feathers. But few people ever notice Zelda's intriguing physique, not if they get a gander at her head first. Her bleached hair is short and worn in spikes, like greasy porcupine quills. As for her face—don't get me wrong; there is nothing inherently homely about it. The fact is Zelda applies her makeup with a trowel, making even Tammy Faye seem like a minimalist. For years there were rumors that Jimmy Hoffa was alive and well and living in Hernia, disguised by layers of Maybelline.

Since there had been no sign of Zelda downtown, I had a hunch I'd find her at home. Sure enough, her beat-up 1978 blue Oldsmobile was parked in the carport adjacent to her vinyl-sided bungalow. Zelda never uses her front door, so I knocked on the side kitchen door. Almost immediately I could see Zelda through the unobstructed pane. She was teetering toward me on heels as spiky as her hairdo. The second she saw who it was, her puttied face began to crumble.

"Now what?" she said, opening the door just a crack. I could barely fit my nose through the space, for crying out loud.

"Zelda, dear, aren't you going to invite me in?"

"Magdalena, this is my day off."

"It is? Melvin said you would be directing traffic, and whatever else it took to keep those unruly Amish and Mennonites in line."

She shrugged, precipitating a shower of spackle speckles on her broad shoulders. "I put in my application to take today off last year. Melvin okayed it."

"I'm not questioning that, dear. But he probably wasn't remembering the festival. It's been planned for years. A hundred years to be exact."

"That may be, but I'm not working today. I have more important things to do."

"Like what? You're not even enjoying the festivities. Why, the tractor pull must be half-over by now."

"Yes, but the pig chase isn't until this afternoon."

"And you plan to watch that?"

"I don't plan to watch, Magdalena. I plan to win the competition. The price of meat has been skyrocketing lately."

"Get out of town!" I have my sister, Susannah, to thank for that worldly expression.

She sighed, and I had to dodge a minor dust storm. "Okay," she said, "you might as well come in. You're like a bulldog, Magdalena, you know that? Once you get your teeth into something, there is no shaking you loose."

"I'll take that as a compliment, dear."

She opened the glass storm door and I sailed in. I'd been in Zelda's house dozens of times, so I didn't even wait for the invitation to plop my bony behind in one of her neon orange beanbag chairs. Just as quickly, I hauled my patooty out of the legumes.

"Zelda, do you have company? I hear voices in another room."

Zelda blushed. I could tell, because the cracks on her face, the ones from which putty had fallen, were red.

"That's the radio you hear."

"I don't think so. One sounds a lot like Mary Lehman."

"No, it doesn't."

"And the other one sounds like Esther Rensberger."

"No, it doesn't."

"Zelda," I said sternly, and gave her my best "mom" look.

"All right, I give up. But you had no business stopping by here without calling." Without further ado she led me to her guest bedroom.

The two aforementioned ladies were seated cross-legged on the floor in front of an open closet. A long low table occupied this narrow space. Atop the table was a framed photograph of the menacing mantis, Melvin Stoltzfus, flanked by two flaming candles. Three yellow roses, laid in a straight line, defined the front of this makeshift altar.

Esther Rensberger was the first to her feet. "This isn't what it looks like."

I gave her the look. "Oh?"

"We weren't actually worshipping him."

Mary Lehman is on the heavy side and had to kneel before standing. "She means we don't pray *to* him. We just pray for him."

"But we do sing hymns," Esther said. Although she's in the choir at my church, Beechy Grove Mennonite, her singing voice has been known to make tomcats commit suicide. Reverend Schrock insists that she has a right to be in choir and cites Psalm 100 to support his stand.

"Just not church hymns," Mary said, between pants.

A glance at Zelda's crumbling facade confirmed that our town's policewoman was mortified. She knew I was aware of the shrine she maintained in my brother-in-law's honor, but that was all. Trust me, I wouldn't have dreamed—not in a zillion years—that there could be three people in Hernia this kooky.

I was both appalled and intrigued. "Ladies, please sing one of your hymns."

"They're not really hymns," Zelda muttered. "They're more like odes."

"Then honor me with your one of your odes."

"Magdalena, you're mocking us, aren't you?"

"*Moi?* How can I mock unless I have all the facts? What exactly goes on in this room?"

Zelda and Mary exchanged meaning-packed glances, but Esther stepped right up to the plate. "We affirm that Melvin Stoltz-fus," she said, as if reading from a document, "is the most hand-some, charming, and intelligent man in the Commonwealth of Pennsylvania."

"You really believe that?"

"He's God's gift to women," Mary cooed.

Zelda uttered a soft "amen."

I treated them all to my most withering look. "God gave that gift to my sister, Susannah. If you want to be recipients, you need to find yourselves another man. Besides, you've got it all wrong. Melvin Stoltzfus is the *least* handsome, charming, and intelligent man in the state."

"Infidel!" Mary shouted, shaking a pudgy fist in the air.

"Blasphemer!" Esther grabbed a rose and hurled it at me. Her aim, like her voice, was far off the mark.

I pinched one of Zelda's elbows with my talons and hauled her back to the kitchen. "Your friends are nuts, you know that?"

"Magdalena, don't be rude."

"Keep them away from caramel, because they could easily end up as PayDay bars."

She glared at me through faux lashes so thick I couldn't see the whites of her eyes. "Why did you come here anyway?"

"Police business, dear. I'm afraid there's been another murder in town. Two murders, actually."

"The PennDutch?"

"No! Why does everybody assume that?"

"Face it, even Jessica Fletcher wouldn't spend the night there."

"Who is she?"

"Never mind. Who are the victims?"

"Well, a man named Buzzy Porter, for one. He was a guest of mine—but the murder happened up on Stucky Ridge. The second victim was Ron Humphrey."

Zelda teetered on her stilettos. "*Our* Ron Humphrey?"

"I'm afraid so."

"Where did that happen?"

Although Zelda has a decade on Ron, they were well acquainted. Our town has a small closely knit singles group with the disgusting name of Hernia Hotties. When Zelda isn't mooning after Melvin, she attends the functions and, I am told, can be quite the flirt. It was obvious from her fractured face that the news of Ron's death was hitting her hard, so I guided her to one of the beanbags and pushed her gently down. She offered no resistance.

"I don't know where it happened, dear, but I found him in the morgue at the so-called Hernia Hospital. It was supposed to be Buzzy's body in that drawer, not Ron's. I can only conclude that somebody switched them."

"Dr. Mean and Nurse Meaner?"

You see? I'm not the only one who feels this way about the malevolent duo who run our town's only health care facility.

"Yes, but Nurse Meaner swears they know nothing about the switch. Zelda, this time I'm inclined to believe her."

She shook her head in dismay, and chunks of foundation—one the size of New Jersey—flew in my direction. I deftly dodged the Cover Girl comet.

"But he was such a nice young man," she sobbed.

I squatted beside her and patted her awkwardly on the shoulder. I am genetically incapable of displaying any more affection. Seeing how Zelda is a distant cousin of mine, I'm sure she understood.

"Yes, he was. And even though he was Episcopalian—well, I'm sure the Good Lord makes exceptions from time to time."

Zelda turned to look at me. The Jamaican bobsled team could do their practice runs in the ruts she presented.

"Does Melvin know about this?" she asked.

"He knows about Buzzy. I've been trying to reach him to tell him about Ron—but I can't locate him. That's why I'm here."

"Do you know where *she* is?"

"I assume you mean my sister. And no, I don't know where she is. But she isn't home. I thought maybe the two of them were out raising campaign money, and had clued you in."

I had to dodge several asteroids when she shook her head again. And it may just be my imagination, but I thought I heard the faint cries of miniature Jamaican bobsledders as they plunged to their deaths.

"We never speak about what he does with *her*. Magdalena, you're always coming up with bizarre theories. Do you have any idea why somebody would kill Ron Humphrey?"

"He was the one who discovered the first body. Maybe the killer was hiding and saw Ron Humphrey at the site—although why he or she didn't just kill Ron then . . ." I shrugged. "Murder never really makes sense."

"Yes, it does."

Oh yeah, smarty-pants? That's what I *wanted* to say. Instead I arranged my equine features into what approximated a smile.

"Would you like to explain this murder, dear?"

"I'll give it a try," she said, without batting a false eyelash. "But first you have to start at the beginning."

I pointed with my chin to the guest bedroom. It sounded like a hive of bees had invaded Zelda's house.

"Oh, don't worry about them, Magdalena. Now they're reciting the One Hundred and Seventy-seven Virtues of Melvin the Magnificent. It usually takes us an hour."

I would have retched, had not my overtaxed nervous system already consumed all the fuel I'd stoked it with at Doc's bountiful breakfast. Instead, I rolled my peepers like a petulant teenager. If Mama were right, and one of them stuck in a strange position— well, at least Melvin the Magnificent and I might finally see eye to eye.

"Okay," I said, "I'll start from the beginning. But I'll need some snacks. Got any chips and dip? No pun intended."

"Very funny, Magdalena." But Zelda has Mennonite blood flowing through her veins, and a satisfying midday munchie was soon to follow.

"It's very simple," Zelda said, as soon as I was finished with my account. "The murder of Mr. Porter was not premeditated. The perpetrator didn't have a gun, so he or she sneaked up on this guy and bashed him on the back of the head with the most lethal thing he or she could get his or her hands on—in this case a shovel. But you see, even if the perpetrator was immediately aware that he or she had been observed, there was nothing they could do about it then. I mean, you can't sneak up on somebody when you've been spotted. Magdalena, even you should know that."

If Zelda's homemade molasses cookies hadn't been so good, I would have objected to her statement. "Yes, but the person who killed poor Ron Humphrey *did* have a gun. Are you suggesting there are two killers?"

"Of course not. The perpetrator *then* got a gun and shot Ron."

I cogitated on that while the cop cult in the next room chanted their ode. They were up to virtue number ninety-three, which was about Melvin having the wisdom of an owl. A bird brain beats an insect brain in the pecking order of intelligence, but sometimes one has to settle for the second-best insult.

"Amen to that!" I shouted.

Zelda snatched the plate of cookies away. "Your sarcasm is not appreciated, Magdalena."

"Sorry, dear," I said in hope of more treats. "But even if your theory is right, what would be the motive? What is so special about a time capsule? Even if it were to contain some deep dark secrets of the past, well"—I laughed pleasantly—"that was a hundred years ago."

My hostess risked losing the rest of her makeup to give me a vastly overblown look of incredulity. "Some things can never be forgotten, Magdalena."

"No fair! I didn't know Aaron was already hitched when I married him."

"Maybe so. But the capsule didn't have to contain something negative to make somebody want to dig it up. Maybe there's something positive in there—like maybe a treasure map."

"Don't be silly, Zelda, we're hundreds of miles from an ocean." Too late I remembered the cookies.

"I didn't mean a pirate's treasure, Magdalena. But you've heard the stories."

"Stories?"

"You're being coy with me, Magdalena."

"But I'm not! I don't know what you're talking about."

She cocked her head, precipitating a sudden shower of spackle. "Well, well, well. Imagine Magdalena Yoder not knowing about Hernia's hidden treasure."

14

"So clue me in," I cried.

She took her sweet time in responding. Meanwhile the voices in the guest room informed me that Melvin's one hundred and thirteenth virtue was virility. They didn't stop there, but went on and on about what a studmuffin he was. After listening to this litany of lascivious praise, I would either have to poke out my mind's eye, or never look in my brother-in-law's eyes again.

"I can't remember any details," she finally said, "but it was something my grandmother prattled on about. Something about there being this enormous fortune hidden somewhere around town. I remember looking for it when I was a little girl—digging in the garden with my mother's spade. Of course, I never found it. Later on I learned that my parents thought it was all a bunch of hooey. Only the old folks took it seriously."

Zelda's parents, like mine, had long since left their earthly bodies. There was no sense in talking to her mother. My mama on the other hand, does talk to me from her celestial perch—but she never says anything I want to hear. "Magdalena, are you still slouching? Put your knees together, child. Do you really think you ought to be driving such a fancy car? Don't marry that man, Magdalena— you'll regret it if you do." You see what I mean?

No, what I needed to do was to consult one of our town's old-timers. But who? Harriet Berkey was one hundred and four, but she suffered from dementia. Irma Yoder, a distant cousin, was almost that old, but she had a tongue that could slice cheese. Come to think of it, a lot of Hernia's elderly women had rapier-sharp linguae. Perhaps it was something in the water. Much safer to question an elderly gent.

But who? Wilbur Neubrander was pushing the century mark, but he had a reputation for letting it all hang out. Literally. I have not been privileged to witness this display, but from what I hear, I haven't missed much. Donald Rickenbach was ninety-five, but had already migrated to Florida for the winter season. That left Meryl Weaver, Doc Shafor . . .

"Toodle-oo," I said, springing to my feet.

Zelda scrambled to her feet as well. "You can't go, Magdalena."

"Of course I can. Oh, those cookies were delish by the way—although next time you might consider adding a tad more ginger."

"But Esther and Mary are just about to reach the one hundred and nineteenth virtue. That's when they have to do a little dance called the Shake-and-wag-your-heinie-poo."

It was the perfect excuse for me. "Dancing is a sin," I cried, and fled the den of iniquity.

Old Blue must have been on the ball again. Doc met me at the end of his drive. He had his thumb out like a hitchhiker. I stopped and lowered the passenger window.

"Going somewhere, mister?"

"Yeah, straight back up this drive, where we're going to have ourselves a nice lunch."

I gestured for him to get in. "Doc, I came to talk, not eat."

"There's no reason we can't do both, is there? I'm making pork chops, macaroni and cheese—not the kind from a box, but the real stuff with lots of extra-sharp cheddar—green-bean casserole, and wilted-endive salad with bacon dressing. And, of course, fresh-baked rolls. For dessert there's blackberry cobbler, or we can hand crank some ice cream. Better yet, we'll put the ice cream on the cobbler. What do you say to that?"

"Doc, do you always eat like this?"

"Folks as blessed as we are who only eat to live, and not the other way around, are missing half of life's pleasures."

I didn't dare ask what the other pleasures were. "Okay, count me in on lunch, just as long as I can ask you a serious question."

He made me wait on the shop talk—as he called it—until my second helping of warm cobbler. The mound of rich, high-in-butterfat ice cream was melting like an iceberg at the equator, and I tried in vain to catch all the sweet rivulets with my spoon. Finally I gave up and stirred them into the black goo.

"Doc, have you ever heard of buried treasure in Hernia?"

"You mean like a pirate's treasure?"

"Not a pirate's treasure, but nonetheless, something very valuable." I slurped a spoonful of blackberry cream. "Sounds silly, doesn't? But Zelda Root claims it's true. Says the old folks—her grandmother, for one—used to talk about it all the time."

"Oh, that." He took a huge bite of his dessert just to torment me.

"Well? Speak with your mouth full if you have to. I won't fine you for doing so. I promise."

He chewed twenty times before swallowing. "It's not a buried treasure, it's a huge parcel of land back in the old country."

"Switzerland?"

He nodded. "You're a descendant of Jacob Hochstetler, the patriarch, aren't you?" He used the original German pronunciation.

"Of course. Mama was a Hostetler. You know that. And Papa was descended from Jacob in at least two ways."

"Do you own the bible?"

He didn't mean *the* Bible, by the way. The *Descendants of Jacob Hochstetler,* originally published in 1911, remains the most comprehensive genealogy devoted solely to the offspring of this important Amish settler. Written decades before the invention of the first computer, it lists nine thousand coded individuals, all of whom are cross-referenced. Jacob was born in 1704, but it has been estimated that now, three centuries later, close to a hundred thousand people can claim him as an ancestor.

"Yes, Mama passed her copy down to me. What about it?"

"It mentions the treasure."

"No kidding! I thought that book was just a bunch of begots."

Doc laughed. "There's a lot of interesting family history in there. But the treasure stories—and there are a number of variations—are conjecture. The version I heard from my daddy isn't even in the book."

"Tell it anyway!"

"Well—" He reached for his spoon, all the while grinning like a Cheshire cat on steroids.

I slapped the utensil out of Doc's hand. "Tell it now, or I'll never eat another bite of food in this house again."

Doc sobered instantly. "Daddy's version had it that our ancestor Jacob was forced from his land by the Swiss authorities, who considered him a threat because of his religious convictions. To avoid accusations of outright theft, they made Jacob sign a document that said they were leasing his land from him for the next two hundred and fifty years—a quarter of a millennium. At the end of that time his descendants were free to claim it, if they provided proof of kinship. Of course, poor Jacob had no choice but to sign the paper."

I sighed. "I'm sorry for what happened to Jacob, but I don't see of what importance that is today. I mean, how is a few acres of bucolic Swiss countryside such a big deal? It certainly isn't worth killing for—not that anything is."

Doc shook his hoary head. "And I always thought you were a dreamer. Well, let me tell you why this would be such a big deal—*if* it were true. According to the oral tradition in my family, those few acres were really hundreds of acres, and what's more, they were located in what is now the heart of Bern."

"Switzerland?"

"No, Berne, Indiana. Of course, Switzerland. Magdalena, the Hochstetler fortune, as described by my daddy, would be worth millions. Maybe even billions."

I pushed my lower jaw back into speaking position. "And all one has to do is show kinship?"

"That, *and* provide the lease."

"Which, of course, nobody can do—wait just a minute!" I had to wait as well, because my heart was pounding so hard Doc's pork chops were doing the rumba in my belly. I tried to breathe deeply, but couldn't get air past my esophagus. "What if," I finally managed to say, "the lease document has been buried in the time capsule all these years?"

Doc slapped his knee. "That's my girl. There's your famous imagination. Unfortunately, that scenario is just not possible."

"Why not?" The truth be told, the task of locating the missing time capsule had taken on an exciting new dimension. Yes, I am well-fixed financially, but one can never have too much moola. I mean, think of all the charitable donations I could make with that Swiss fortune. And so what if one or two of the donations were to myself?

Doc grinned. "I can read your mind, Magdalena. And that's what I like about you—you're honest with yourself. But it's not going to happen. If the lease document were buried in the time capsule, don't you think someone else would have dug it up years ago? Maybe even a century ago?"

"Poking pins in my balloons is not going to get you into my bloomers—not that anything would," I hastened to add.

"On the other hand," Doc said just as quickly, "each branch of the family seems to have its own tradition. Local folks either discount the story these days, or assume that the document—if it ever existed—is lost in the annals of history. But it's possible that some of the family branches that moved away had traditions that involved the capsule, or they created their own stories. Family histories, if not well documented, tend to morph from generation to generation, and usually in a favorable direction. That's one of the reasons so many people claim to have royal blood."

"You'd think that trend would have reversed itself in recent years."

"Touché. Magdalena, was the time capsule mentioned in any of the ads the town council placed in magazines?"

"No. There wasn't room for everything. And we still managed

to go over the budget. Although we did mention the tractor pull—but only because Sam insisted on it, since it was going to be held in front of his so-called grocery. We made him chip in some of his own dough for that."

"So any descendants that don't live around here, the exiles so to speak, had no clue we were going to dig up the capsule?"

"None." I caught my breath. "Uh, well, I did send my guests an e-mail of the complete schedule and current weather conditions."

"When was this?"

"About three days ago. I wanted it to reach the Japanese guest, in case she didn't check her e-mail when she traveled. Except at the time I didn't know if she was a he, on account of the name."

Doc licked the last of the cobbler from his spoon. "This isn't much to go on, but you might take a closer look at your guests. Do you think any of them might own the bible?"

I had to laugh. "If any of them have even a drop of Hochstetler blood, I'll eat my prayer cap."

Doc scraped the empty spoon futilely around the inside of his bowl. "I'll make you a bet, Magdalena. If one of your guests turns out to be kin, you have to eat supper with me every Saturday night until Christmas. If they don't—"

"You know Mennonites don't wager."

"I'm not betting money. What's the matter, you afraid you're going to lose?"

Don't throw down the gauntlet in front of me unless you're prepared to lose. "You're on, buster."

"Good. And what is it you want from me if you win—theoretically, at any rate, since it ain't going to happen?"

"You date Gabriel's mother."

The color drained so thoroughly from the octogenarian's face that I worried I'd gone too far. Three corpses in one day was more than even I, the doyenne of death, could handle.

"I beg your pardon?" he rasped.

"You heard me. You have to date Mrs. Rosen—and I mean take her on a *real* date. Maybe bowling in Bedford and then out to dinner. Or just a nice ride in the country. You could even show her the lights of Hernia from Stucky Ridge."

My friend shuddered. "You know I'm a ladies' man, Magdalena, but that woman is like a bucket of ice water. Make that a million buckets. Heck, the National Park Service ought to ship her out West to put out forest fires."

"Are you backing down?"

He shuddered again. "No. As a matter of fact, I've already started to plan the menus for our future feasts. Next time we'll start out with a nice oxtail soup—"

By the time I got to my car, he hadn't even gotten to the main course. Perhaps I should have lingered, because just hearing Doc talk about food can pack on the pounds, and the Good Lord knows I could use a little extra ballast.

I fled. If I lost this bet Gabriel was going to be jealous, which is not altogether a bad thing, but if I won, I might well be able to permanently pawn his mother off on the good-hearted veterinarian. She might have dampened his ardor with her abrasive opinions, but the woman could cook up a storm. Maybe even a tornado. If her flank steak didn't rekindle Doc's flame, then all his talk was just that.

If I hadn't been in such a hurry to purge my future mother-in-law from my life, I wouldn't have come so close to taking the lives of two pedestrians.

15

Creole Sauce

2 pounds ripe tomatoes (preferably plum or Roma type), or 2 cups canned Italian tomatoes, seeded and chopped, with their juices
2 tablespoons extra-virgin olive oil
3 large or 4 medium shallots, or 1 medium yellow onion, split, peeled, and chopped
1 medium green bell pepper, stem, seeds, and membranes removed, chopped
1 small carrot, peeled and chopped
1 clove garlic, lightly crushed, peeled, and minced

1 small red hot chili pepper such as cayenne, serrano, or jalapeño
A bouquet garni made from 1 leafy celery top, 2 bay leaves, 2 large sprigs thyme, and 1 large sprig parsley
2 ounces lean salt-cured pork or country ham, in one piece
½ cup dry white wine or medium dry sherry (such as amontillado)
Salt
1 large or 4 small scallions or other green onions, thinly sliced

Creole sauce is an important element of many cuisines of the African Diaspora of the Americas and comes in many variations, from the simple *salsa cruda* (raw sauce) of the Caribbean to the suave, complex *sauce creole* of New Orleans's French Quarter. It is an indispensable accompaniment for Grilled Chicken Breasts with Eggplant, Creole Style (Chapter 10), and enhances almost any fried vegetable, seafood, or poultry.

(If you are using canned tomatoes, skip to step 2.) Bring a large tea kettle full of water to a boil. Put the tomatoes into a heatproof bowl and slowly pour the boiling water over them until they are submerged. Let them stand for 1 minute, drain thoroughly, and refresh them under cold running water. Core them and slip off the peelings. Working over a wire sieve set into a large bowl, split the tomatoes in half crosswise, and scoop out the seeds into the sieve. Discard the seeds and roughly chop the tomatoes. Add them to the collected juices in the bowl and set aside.

Put the olive oil, shallot or onion, green pepper, and carrot into a heavy-bottomed sauce pan and turn on the heat to medium high. Sauté, tossing frequently, until the shallot is translucent but not colored, about 4 minutes. Add the garlic and sauté until fragrant, about a minute more. Add the tomatoes, hot pepper (left whole), bouquet garni, ham, and wine. Bring the liquids to a boil, then reduce the heat to medium low and simmer, stirring occasionally, until the tomatoes break down and the juices are thick, about an hour.

Taste and add salt if needed. Stir and let simmer for another minute or so to allow the salt to be absorbed into the sauce. Turn off the heat. Remove and discard the hot pepper, bouquet garni, and ham or salt pork. The sauce can be made up to this point several days ahead. Cool and refrigerate in a tightly sealed container.

Just before serving, reheat the sauce over medium-low heat. Stir in the scallions and serve at once.

MAKES ABOUT 2½ CUPS

16

"I'm so sorry," I cried, mortified at what had nearly transpired.

"That's okay, darling," Capers Littleton said. "You sprayed us with a little gravel, that's all. It's really no big deal."

"But it is a big deal. I wasn't paying attention to the road. I may as well have been yakking it up on my cell phone. Ladies, again I apologize." It doesn't hurt to go overboard sometimes, especially if it can prevent lawsuits.

Terri Mukai bowed slightly. "Perhaps it is my fault. I am not used to cars driving on the wrong side of the road."

"This *is* the right side, dear, both literally and figuratively." I smiled pleasantly so as not to undo my apology. "May I offer you ladies a ride?"

They exchanged glances before Capers answered. "We're on our way to the pig chase."

"Great! So am I."

That was not a lie by any means. But since these two were on my list to interview, I would take a little longer to get there. And where they were coming from was the first question I'd ask. By my reckoning, they were less than a mile from the base of Stucky Ridge and on the side over which the murderer had quite possibly thrown the shovel. What's more, they were on the opposite side of town from Hernia High, where the pig chase was to be held.

"Thanks, Miss Yoder." Capers opened the front passenger door and gestured to Terri to get in, but the younger woman insisted that she would climb into the back. For several wasted minutes I was privy to a battle of manners: Miss Magnolia Blossom versus Miss Cherry Blossom.

We natives of the Keystone state have a different take on politeness. "Both of you hop in the back or you're going to walk."

They clambered in.

"Sorry, Miss Yoder," Capers panted.

"*Gomen nasai,* Yoder-san. I am sorry too."

"Think nothing of it, dears. Oh, by the way, what brought you to this far corner of Hernia?"

"The fall color," Capers said, without missing a beat. "I can't get enough of it. Back home we get just a touch, and it isn't until much later in the season."

It seemed like a reasonable explanation, but I had a lot more to ask. Although shedding a future mother-in-law is not as important as finding a killer—possibly even a pair of them—it still ranked high on my list of priorities. I decided to drive slowly and make some unnecessary turns, in order to give me more time.

"Well, ladies," I said to my captive audience, "I'm sure you must find our ways very strange."

Terri nodded vigorously. "Yes, you Americans are very strange."

"I wouldn't be calling the kettle black, dear. I meant our Amish and Mennonite culture—not Americans in general. Mrs. Littleton, are there any questions you'd like to ask?"

"Why, yes," she said, stretching the two words into five syllables. "I was wondering what you thought of the movie *Witness.*"

I clucked, not unlike my favorite hen, Pertelote. "I don't go to movies. Too much sin on the silver screen to suit me. The Amish don't watch movies either, but I heard that they hated this one."

"How could they hate something they hadn't seen?"

"Well, maybe hate is too strong a word. Anyway, they were very unhappy that Harrison Ford, who was dressed like an Amish man, committed an act of violence."

"Yes, when he struck the boy who was taunting them. I thought that might be the case."

"Ah, so you're familiar with our ways."

"Not really. Just what I've picked up from movies."

In desperation I resorted to trotting out the first thing folks asked me when I visited Charleston, South Carolina, on my vacation a year or two back. "Who are your people, dear?"

She smiled, grateful to be given the chance to impress me. "Well, my mama was a Capers—that's where I got the name, and her mama was a Rutledge, and her mama was a Pinckney, and her mama was a Moultrie and—"

"And your papa—I mean, daddy?"

"Daddy was a Calhoun, and his mama was a Hostetler—"

"Did you say Hostetler?" My heart sank. It's not that I minded eating supper with Doc all those times, but on whom was I going to palm off the pint-size pest that was my future mother-in-law?

Capers blushed. "Yes, just like your cook's name. Miss Yoder, I can't help that I have some Yankee blood." She clapped a manicured hand over her mouth, no doubt thinking she had offended me.

"Don't worry, dear. We were not all lucky enough to be full-blooded Yankees. Please tell me about your grandmother who was a Hostetler."

"I'm afraid there isn't much to tell. She died before I was born, and Daddy never liked to talk about her—well, anyway, all I really know is that she was from up here someplace. When I saw the ad in *Condornest Travels* I thought this festival of yours would be the perfect opportunity for me to explore my roots."

"But you were too embarrassed to reveal your connection, am I right?"

"Guilty as charged, Miss Yoder." She hung her well-groomed head in shame.

I tried not to see red. It is, after all, the color of harlots. There is nothing wrong with Yankee blood, except when it recycles too often within the same circles. The exact thing, I've heard, happens some places in the South.

"How about you, Miss Mukai? Do you have local ancestors lurking in your family tree?" It was a long shot, I know, but I seem to hit my targets easier when I can't see them. And now that I'd already lost the bet with Doc, I had nothing to lose by her answer.

"I am afraid I do not understand the question."

"Are you somehow related to the Hostetler family, or any of its spelling variations?"

Thanks to the rearview mirror, I could see that my Japanese guest looked like she'd bolt from the car at any second. I pressed the pedal to the metal. With Melvin off doing who-knows-what, and Zelda taking the day off to practice idolatry, who was there to cite me for speeding?

"Miss Yoder," Terri said, after it was clear there would be no escape, "in my country it is best to be one hundred percent Japanese."

"That doesn't answer my question, dear. Do I call you cousin, or not?"

She squirmed. "Yes, I have this Hostetler blood."

"You don't say!"

Capers patted her companion's arm. "Darling, was your grandfather a GI?"

"Don't be silly, dear," I said on Terri's behalf. "Mennonites don't go to war."

Terri shook her lovely black hair. "Oh, but he was a soldier. However, he was not a Mennonite, but of the Amish faith."

I pulled the car over to the side of the road. "Why, that's just ridiculous. The Amish don't go to war either."

"That is true, Miss Yoder, but my grandfather left his people to join the American army. He believed it was not right for others to die in his defense, if he was not willing to help protect his country."

"He fought against Japan?"

"Yes. He was also part of the occupying force after the war. That is how my grandmother met him. When he was released from duty my grandfather remained in Kakogawa and taught English."

"So that's why you speak such lovely English," Capers cooed in her inimitable style. The next time I served squab, I would think of her.

"Yes, Capers, although I do not think my English is so hot—

that is the word, am I right? It is my mother who speaks excellent English. I do not think you would tell the difference between her and Miss Yoder, although perhaps my mother is more gentle in her manner."

"Miss Mukai," I said irritably, "can we get back to the part about your grandfather being a Hostetler? Was he from this part of the state?"

She shrugged. "It was a place called Homes County."

"There isn't any Homes County—ah, *Holmes* County. That's in Ohio."

"But there are many Amish there, yes?"

"More than anywhere else in the world. Did he tell you any interesting stories?"

"Oh yes, Miss Yoder. He told me about the Indians who killed his grandmother of many generations. They stabbed her in the back and took her hair—I cannot remember the word for such a thing."

"Scalped, dear."

Capers patted her new friend's arm again. "Aren't these family legends fun?"

"Oh, but this is no legend," I assured her. "The Hostetler—only it was Hochstetler back then—family was attacked by the Delaware during the French and Indian War."

Terri cocked her head. "Were you there, Miss Yoder?"

"Not hardly, dear. It happened in the 1750s."

Capers winked at me. "I read someplace that the elderly are respected in Japan."

I glared at Capers. "I doubt if even in Japan folks live to be two hundred and fifty years old."

"I did not mean to offend, Miss Yoder. Like Capers, I too have come to Hernia to learn my family's history."

I was at a loss as to how to proceed. I couldn't very well ask the women what they knew about a buried treasure and expect an honest answer. But I could create a legend of my own that would be too enticing for them not to pursue.

"Ladies, I'm sure you have both heard about the family treasure." I paused just long enough to be interrupted which, alas, I wasn't. "Personally, I think the legend is a bunch of hooey. And I ought to know. The treasure is really a large parcel of land in Switzerland, but the deed is supposed to be buried somewhere on my farm. When I was a little girl I must have dug up every square inch—except for under that pile of *haufa mischt*."

"What's *haufa mischt*?" Capers asked.

"Horse manure," Terri whispered.

I glanced at the girl through the rearview mirror, but already she was gazing out the window, looking every bit as composed as a geisha. Since I do indeed have a hefty pile of road apples, as the locals call them, to turn under the soil before the winter rains begin, I decided to carry my little deception one step further. And bear with me, please. Deceiving a murderer—and now that I knew both women had a local connection, they were as guilty or innocent as anyone else in the community—is not a sin. The sort of lying the Ten Commandments warned us about, concerns false testimony against neighbors, not against a pile of *haufa mischt*. Au contraire, the *haufa mischt* was in the middle of a clover field, and Psalm 23 says quite clearly the Good Lord Himself tells us to "Lie . . . in green pastures."

"I keep a pitchfork hanging on the wall just inside the barn," I said. "Along with my other tools. I keep meaning to turn all that potential fertilizer under so it can decompose, but something always comes up. Perhaps when I get around to doing my chores I'll find the deed to that Swiss property. Wouldn't that be ironic?" I laughed pleasantly. "The key to a billion dollars hidden beneath a dung heap."

"Miss Yoder," Capers said the second I closed my yap, "I don't mean to be rude, but it's only five minutes to three, and that's when the pig chase is supposed to start."

I responded by giving the ladies a taste of what Hernians are capable of, should they decide to really hustle. When we arrived at the stadium Terri was the hue of seaweed and Capers the color of cottage cheese. Together they averaged out to a nice mint green, just the shade I planned to paint my bedroom someday.

• • •

Of course I got them to the stadium on time. Never mind that they had to sit in the car until they stopped shaking before attempting to climb the bleachers. I had no problem vaulting up the steps to the announcer's box. The problem waited for me at the top.

"Well, folks, if it isn't our most illustrious citizen, Magdalena Yoder. Now that she's here I guess we can start."

There were a few guffaws and a smattering of applause before I got the crowd under control with a glare that would have shriveled Attila the Hun. Then I glared at Lodema Schrock, my pastor's wife. The woman was totally unqualified to announce a pig chase. The only reason we'd picked her to do the job is that stadium's sound system is notoriously unreliable, and Lodema has a voice capable of waking the dead three counties over.

Reverend Schrock's wife is meaner than Attila and was unaffected by my glare. "Today we have twenty-three contestants—unless Magdalena wants to enter the competition instead of awarding the prize. If so, you'll be *chasing* the pigs, right Magdalena?"

"Don't push your luck," I growled.

The preacher's pesky partner seemed oblivious to the fact that I donate more money to our church than anyone else. "Folks, she just said she'd enter. How about a round of applause for Magdalena Portulacca Yoder, pig chaser extraordinaire?" Not a soul dared clap, but Lodema dared push me further. "Oops, I just remembered. She can't be chasing pigs; she's engaged to a man of the Hebrew faith. Pork is forbidden in that religion, isn't it, Magdalena?"

I snatched the microphone out of her sweaty little hand. "For your information, Dr. Rosen's religion is the same one Jesus practiced. And Jesus, by the way, chased a whole lot of pigs."

"He most certainly did not!" Like I said, the woman didn't need amplification.

"Perhaps you should read your Bible, dear. In the Gospel of Mark, chapter five, Jesus chased two thousand pigs into the Sea of Galilee."

"Jesus didn't chase those pigs. They were possessed by demons."

"Which Jesus chased from a man. It's all the same."

"Are you trying to rewrite the Bible, Magdalena?"

The crowd gasped in unison. A hunch from a woman might be worth two facts from a man, but heresy from a woman—well, that was practically unheard of in Hernia. I was going to have to dance (and I mean that metaphorically) fast to save my reputation.

"Not only will I chase those pigs, Lodema, I'm going to win this contest. And I'm going to donate the prize money to the Hernia Widows and Orphans Fund."

"We don't have a Widows and Orphans Fund."

I fished in my otherwise empty bra for a handful of twenty-dollar bills. "We do now."

The crowd roared its approval.

Perhaps I've never been a people pleaser, but it's never too late to start. I thrust my hand into the other cup. Alas, my desperate digits encountered nothing but air. Not wanting to disappoint my fans, I held up my purse. It doesn't contain cash, since a bag can be snatched, but it does contain my checkbook.

"And I'll write a check for a thousand bucks as soon as this contest is over."

"Write it now," Lodema shouted.

The crowd cheered its support.

I whipped out my checkbook. "I'm sure Lodema will be happy to match this donation."

"How dare you?" she whispered. "You'll pay for this, you know." She raised her voice a zillion decibels. "I'm only a poor pastor's wife. You're on the church board. You know how much money my husband makes. We can barely afford to put bread on our table."

"Then why not eat cake?"

Please believe me, those were not my words. Okay, so maybe they were. But there were other words interspersed between them. Lots of other words. You see, the school's notorious sound system sided with Lodema and refused to amplify most of what I said, broadcasting only the offending words. Of course that didn't stop the crowd from turning on me. I even heard boos from the Who's Who of Hernia society.

"Shame on you," Herman Middledorf yelled. Because the man is the school principal, he was in the box with us. You can bet the P.A. system cooperated then.

"Yoder, you should apologize to the preacher's wife." The directive came from Wanda Hemphopple, owner of the Sausage Barn out by the turnpike. She's kin to Lodema, and her lungs are the envy of scuba divers.

Lodema Schrock looked like she'd won the lottery. "What do you have to say now, Magdalena?"

I shoved a fist in my mouth in order to prevent a foot from going in. One can choke on size elevens.

17

Pig chase rules are very simple, but Lodema still botched them. Herman Middledorf had to explain everything to the crowd a second time, in his principal voice, which made the contest seem more like a punishment than a fun-filled event.

"There are now twenty-four contestants, and fifty pigs. When I fire the starter gun, the pigs will be released from that covered holding pen over there. The contestants must wait until they hear the gun before they can cross the ten-yard line—for those of you who don't bother to come and support our games, that's the third white line you see in front of the north goal."

Although his less-than-rapier wit drew only a few laughs— probably all from teachers—the principal beamed. In fact, he stood there so long, beaming silently, that I envisioned a new career for him. Herman Middledorf could be the world's first human lighthouse.

"Move it along, dear," I said kindly, when his audience began buzzing with impatience. "I, for one, don't have all day."

Herman cleared his throat loudly into the microphone in order to silence the throng. Since many of them had, at one time or another, been his students, most obeyed.

"There are two objectives in this pig chase. The first is to be the one who catches the first pig. The contestant who does that gets a hundred bonus points. The second objective is for the contestants to catch as many pigs as possible. And each pig is worth fifty points. When he or she has caught a pig, the contestant will carry it back to the holding pen—the gates will be closed again, although the cover will have been removed. The contestants are to lift their pigs over the sides of the pen and deposit them gently on the ground."

The crowd howled with laughter at this image, but I cringed. The term "pig" generally refers to younger swine, those not yet ready for the market, but even these can still weigh well over a hundred pounds. The last time I tried to lift something that weighed that much, I did not deposit it gently on the ground. Just ask my ex-pseudohusband, Aaron. He claims to have suffered from back pain the rest of our honeymoon.

Herman, energized by the crowd's response, resumed his lecture with vigor. "Coach Neidenmeir will keep track of each person's tally. When all the pigs have been caught and returned to the pen, the one with the highest score wins." He paused. "Oh, did I mention that the pigs just happen to be greased?"

By now the crowd had grown too impatient to give anything back. "Start the chase, start the chase, start the chase . . ."

"You better get down to the starting line," Lodema hissed. "You don't want to miss this chance to play with pigs."

I shot her a new look I'd recently learned from Alison and then hustled my bustle down the bleachers to take my place at the far end of the starting line. The contestants were much friendlier than the spectators, and for good reason. I was, after all, no competition. The others were all high school and college kids—well, except for Zelda Root and Chuck Norton.

Zelda and I didn't exchange words because she was in the middle of the lineup, busily tying her shoes. I was dumbstruck yet pleased to see that she was wearing high-heeled platform shoes that laced up her sinewy calves, almost all the way up to her much-abbreviated skirt. But the second the cat let go of my tongue, I had a question for Chuck.

"What on earth are you doing here?"

His broad freckled face widened even more as he grinned. "Howdy, Miss Yoder. Thought I'd have me a little fun this afternoon. Being a farmer, I've had me some experience chasing pigs." I glanced at his trademark overalls. "No doubt you have. Where's your lovely wife? Doesn't she want to try her hand at catching a pig or two?"

"Nah. Bibi had her some shopping to do."

"You old farts need any help?" an impertinent youth yelled down the line at us. I recognized the voice as belonging to Jimmy Mast, Alison's recent beau—the one she'd decided she hated.

Of course, all the young contestants thought Jimmy's remark was hilarious and whooped it up like a flock of cranes. Even Chuck chuckled. So as not to be seen as the elderly flatulence I'd just been accused of being, I forced my lips into a lopsided grin.

"It might be you needing the help, Jimmy Mast. One of my great-grandpas was struck by lightning one day when he was feeding his hogs. Fell right into the pen. By the time my great-grandma found him, the hogs had eaten away his face and one of his ears."

"Ooh, gross!" A teenage contestant by the name of Brandy bolted for the safety of the stands.

"She's just putting us on," Jimmy yelled, but the girl ignored him.

"She's talking smack," a boy said. His accent identified him as Lenny Coldiron, a recent emigrant from the big city with no farming connections.

"Actually, she's got a point," Chuck said, much to my surprise. "Them animals can be dangerous. Especially if they're scared. I once seen a—"

"Take your marks," Herman hollered, and held the gun aloft. The P.A. system was working just fine at the moment, by the way. When Herman finally fired the pistol—I'm convinced he was torturing us in the interim—the amplified explosion sounded like one of the cannons in the Overture of 1812. It's a wonder I was the only one who screamed.

At least I wasn't the only one who stayed put. No one, not even Chuck, put as much as one toe over the line until Coach Neidenmeir opened the gates. Even then only a few of the older boys inched cautiously forward. Jimmy Mast was not among them.

"Here them pigs come," Chuck said. "You better brace yourself, Miss Yoder. Them porkers can weigh a fair amount."

The brave boys stepped back in unison.

I steeled myself for the onslaught of swine. Although the gates to the pen had been flung open, I didn't see any pigs. Finally Coach Neidenmeir tore the canvas top off the pen. A split second later the crowd exploded with laughter.

"Why, them aren't nothing but farrow pigs."

"I beg your pardon?"

"Baby pigs. Just look at them."

I looked. Even though I always ate my veggies, especially carrots, I must have been the last person in the stadium to see the small swine. Finally I got my peepers to focus that far.

Chuck was right. They were no bigger than large house cats. Spotted things that didn't even come up to my knees. They clustered nervously, unwilling, or unable, to face their would-be captors.

"This is ridiculous," I said.

No sooner were those words uttered than the unexpected happened. Coach Neidenmeir, using a push broom, literally swept the piglets out into the open stadium. Once in the open and separated from their litter mates, the little ones panicked and darted, squealing, in fifty directions.

Simultaneously, the contestants diverged in twenty-three directions. Some of them were squealing as well. I was a late bloomer, which is the only reason I can offer for why I was so late in getting started. Most of my competitors were over the fifty-yard line and in contact with the little critters, before I even moved. But believe me, I wasn't scared.

I was, however, annoyed. Zelda's disciples had infiltrated the stands, and had apparently brought reinforcements.

"Zelda! Zelda! Zelda! *Melvin!* Zelda!"

"Cut it out!" I hollered, although it was just a waste of breath.

Turning my attention back to the contest, I noticed that while the others had no trouble catching up with the piglets, once they grabbed the squealing tikes, they were unable to hold on. Of course! The babies had been greased. By this point the crowd was laughing so hard they mercifully drowned out the cult of Melvin.

I pondered the situation. What could I possibly do different? I wasn't young and lithe like the kids, I didn't have the strength of Chuck, or the moral support Zelda had. But surely I had some small advantage—besides my shnoz (I certainly wasn't going to spear the little darlings).

Then it hit me. I'm not claiming the answer came straight from the Lord, but it did come out of the blue, and after all, that's where Heaven is. And by the way, Heaven is directly over North America, quite possibly even centered over Hernia. I heard that straight from the lips of Reverend Schrock. When the Rapture occurs, faithful Christians in Australia and other southern hemisphere locations are going to have to do some fancy maneuvering in order to catch up with the main flock.

My revelation was simply this: I was wearing a dress. As every well-brought-up woman knows, a proper dress has a skirt that extends below the knees and does not fit tightly. Such a skirt can come in very handy for carrying things, although one must take care not to display one's sturdy Christian underwear.

The first piglet slipped through my hands like fog. But on my second attempt I managed to flip the little rascal into my skirt, gather the material into a sort of sack, and sprint to the enclosure— all without losing the precious cargo. The crowd started cheering just as I lowered the piglet, *gently,* into its pen.

By the time I deposited the third little pig, the good folks of Hernia were chanting: "Yoder! Yoder! Yoder!"

I waved to my fans.

The crowd roared in response, although I'm quite sure I heard two boos coming from the reviewing stand. But the latter only served to stoke the fires of my resolve. Within ten minutes I managed to catch and safely deliver every single piglet. By the time the last squealing swine made contact with the grass inside the enclosure, the crowd was on its feet, and the noise it made was deafening. A few folks even threw plastic cups and sandwich wrappers at me—in lieu of roses, I'm sure. For a few minutes I felt like I had single-handedly won a championship football game.

"Beginner's luck," Zelda shouted in my ear, before teetering off to an exit.

The din of the crowd abated only when the faulty P.A. system finally cooperated with Lodema's lungs. "Magdalena," she thundered, "seeing as how you're so rich, I'm sure you'll be returning your prize pig in order to save our beloved town a little money."

"In a pig's ear!" I shouted in return.

Alas, my response was almost as loud as her badgering. It might surprise you to know just how fast a crowd can turn, although no doubt they were egged on by the thumbs-down Lodema Schrock and Herman Middledorf were giving me. But despite the rain of lunch and snack accouterments, I took my time in selecting the perfect piglet—one that looked like it would grow into just the right combination of ham, bacon, pork roast, and chops. Oh, and four nice pickled feet.

Alison's jaw dropped when she saw the squirming youngster. "Oh, Mom, is that for me?"

"In a manner of speaking, dear."

"Donna Wylie has a pet pig, and it's just the coolest thing." My foster daughter threw her arms around me and the swine, dirt and all. "Thanks, Mom. This is the best present I ever had."

I struggled to disengage myself from her embrace. "But, dear, this little fellow is not going to be a pet. When he grows up he's going to be breakfast, lunch, and dinner."

It took a minute or two for my words to register. "Ya gonna *eat* him?"

"We both are. That's where bacon comes from, and you love bacon."

She stared at me. "Ya sure?"

"Positive."

"Man, then I ain't ever gonna eat that stuff again."

I couldn't help myself. "And veal comes from calves. And, of course, hamburger is ground up cow muscle, with some fat thrown in. Steak is—"

Alison clapped her hands over ears. "Ya don't need to say any more, because from now on I'm a vegetarian."

"But you love hamburgers. And hot dogs."

Her hands weren't soundproof. "So? I still ain't eating them. And you can't make me."

I read somehow that the wise parent knows when to pick her battles. I'm sure Mama didn't teach me that lesson, because I didn't dare cut my hair or wear trousers until the day she died. I still don't do these things—Mama has a habit of turning over in her grave with such force that, if harnessed, the power could supply all of Pittsburgh's electrical needs. But I, Magdalena Portulacca Yoder, was not about to follow in my mama's boat-size footsteps, even if they did match mine.

"Okay, you can become a vegetarian, but make sure you get enough protein."

Her eyes registered disbelief, but she shook her head in mock nonchalance. "No prob. Stacy at school is a vegetarian, and she gets all the protein she needs from peanut butter and eggs."

"Good for Stacy. But you might want to substitute beans for eggs." Perhaps it was mean of me, but I couldn't help it. You see, one of Alison's favorite foods was fried-egg sandwiches slathered with ketchup.

"How come I shouldn't eat eggs?"

"Because eggs come from chickens, and chickens are definitely meat."

"Yeah, but eggs ain't. They're just eggs."

"They're potential chickens, dear. You don't think they develop into cabbages, do you?"

She stomped her foot. "Ah, man!"

The piglet squealed loudly, startling me so much I dropped him. He wasn't hurt, mind you, because he landed on my foot. I hopped around on one size eleven while Alison chased my future pork roast around the ground floor of my inn. The two of them disappeared into the kitchen—an appropriate place, I thought—but when they emerged a few minutes later, Alison was cradling the pig like he was a baby.

"Oh, Mom, I just love him. I'm gonna name him Babe, just like that pig in the movie."

"But Babe is what Gabe calls me! And sometimes I call him Babester."

"Yuck. But that don't have nothing to do with this. *He*," she said, planting a kiss on the swine's snout, "is gonna be named after that movie. And, Mom, I promise to walk him every day. I'll even bathe him so he don't stink—although Donna Wylie said her pet pig didn't never stink. Please, Mom, pretty please? You'll make me the happiest girl in the whole world."

My heart has a higher melting point than most, but already I could feel it trickling down around my intestines. How could I refuse to give this child the gift of pet ownership?

"There will be no need to bathe or walk him, dear. He can have that paddock on the east side of the barn. The corner by the barn is always nice and muddy."

"But, Mom, he's gonna live inside."

"Over my dead body." Over my mama's dead body as well. I was surprised the ground hadn't started to shake.

"Hey, no fair! Donna Wylie gets to keep her pig inside."

"The Wylies aren't Mennonites."

"What's that supposed to mean?"

"They lack the clean gene," I said as kindly as possible. "Besides, you should be glad I'm even agreeing to let you have him for a pet at all."

"That mean ya ain't gonna kill him when he gets big?"

"Not so long as you take full responsibility for taking care of him. Because if you don't, I'm changing his name from Babe to Ham."

Alison's face went through multiple transformations. In the end she settled on a huge smile.

"You're the best mom I ever had, ya know that? I mean my real mom woulda never even let me keep him."

"Really?" Alison's "real" mom was the wife of Aaron Miller, my ex-pseudohusband. She lives in Minnesota with Aaron. The couple was unable to control the child, so a judge gave Alison the choice of living with me, or reform school. I got lucky. I would like to say that I never think of the woman, and that I certainly do not compare myself to her, but if I said that—well, I'd be lying. How can I not compare myself to the woman my Pooky Bear never divorced, and into whose perfumed arms he ultimately returned?

"Yeah, really," Alison said. "Mom, ya can be kinda dorky, ya know that?"

"I'll take that as a compliment."

"But I love ya anyway."

Before I had a chance to faint, she reached up and planted a kiss on my bony cheek. It may have been totally accidental, but I'm sure I felt a pair of whiskery pig lips as well. I managed to lock my knees into place.

"I love you very much too, dear."

"Gross, Mom, don't get mushy."

"But you just said—"

"Sheesh! 'Love ya' and 'I love you very much'—they ain't the same. The first one ya say to your mom, but the other one is for your boyfriend. Don't ya know anything?"

I shook my head. Not only was I feeling mushy, I was positively high on love—conditional though it may be. With the exception of Freni, the Babester, and my sister, I couldn't think of any others who truly loved me. So you see, it was euphoria that clouded my judgment, just as surely as if I'd drunk a pitcher of mimosas.

"Oh, what the haystack. You can keep him inside—for now. But when he gets bigger we'll have to negotiate. In the meantime, ask the Wylie girl how she housebroke her pig, and I expect you to quickly and thoroughly clean up any mess."

Alison's eyes glowed with appreciation. Undoubtedly she would have slipped into pure mushiness had the front door not opened with a bang. While she tried to soothe the startled swine she cradled, I glared at the intruder.

"You better to learn to knock," I growled.

18

"Whatever you say, Yoder." But Melvin was not about to apologize. He swaggered up to us like he owned the place. I wouldn't be surprised to learn that he believes someday he'll own the inn, by virtue of his marriage to Susannah. If so, what he's forgotten is that arthropods—even extraordinarily large, two-legged ones—don't live as long as humans.

"What is it you want?" I snapped.

"See ya guys." Alison took the opportunity to flee the room before my irritation with her "uncle" escalated to the point that I took my feelings out on her and reversed my decision on the pig.

Melvin hadn't even bothered to greet his niece. "Yoder, I'm here on official business. We need to talk."

That was for certain. "Melvin, have you been drinking those garlic milk shakes again?"

"They're garlic soy shakes, Yoder. And I just finished one. What about it?"

"Well, unless you want to be responsible for manslaughter, I suggest we repair to the parlor, and sit on opposite sides."

"For your information, thanks to those shakes, I haven't had a cold in three years."

"That's because the viruses die before they can even get close to you."

Without further ado I led the way into the parlor and closed the door tightly behind us. Then I straightaway picked the most comfortable seat for myself. My bony butt is far more sensitive than his crusty carapace—well, it usually is. Melvin winced when his newly recontoured derriere connected with the hard seat of one of Grandma's straight-back chairs. He ended up reclining on one buttock, which somehow caused him to look like he was sitting straight.

"Indeed," I said, "we do need to talk. I've been trying to reach you for hours. Where have you been?"

"Don't be a dingus, Yoder. I just said I was working on a case. In fact, I'm about to make an arrest."

"You are?" I was too astonished to be sarcastic.

"That's what I said. You deaf, Yoder?" He barreled ahead before my sarcasm gene could kick in. "Who's your worst enemy?"

"Melvin, I think you're capable of many things—perhaps even metamorphoses—but murder is not one of them."

"Not me, you idiot. I'm talking about Lodema Schrock."

My blood raced with excitement. Oh what schadenfreude I'd feel if only it were true. How sweet life would be once my pious pastor's partner was put in the poky. What joy to know that the tart-tongued gossip would never be free to harass me again. There was just one thing wrong with this picture—Lodema Schrock was even less likely to commit murder than Melvin. At least she had a modicum of brains to stop her.

"What's your evidence, Melvin?"

He arranged his mandibles into what approximated a sneer. "Well, I dropped by the reverend's house this morning. Wanted to ask him if he'd say a few words over the deceased—you know, like the Catholics do. Read him his last rites, that kind of thing. Anyway, the reverend was home, working on next Sunday's sermon, but Lodema was out."

"So?"

"So, she was out running. Practicing for the marathon—just like Ron Humphrey."

"Which means?"

He sighed, and the scent of garlic sailed across the room to assault my nostrils. "Yoder, it's a good thing you're not the one in uniform." He tapped his head with a hairless knuckle to indicate that I wasn't the brightest bulb in the chandelier. "It's as plain as day. The two of them were in cahoots. Together they killed Mr. Porter, and then while she made off with the time capsule, he distracted us by pretending to find the body."

"I see. You're saying that Lodema Schrock, who has all the upper-body strength of a rubber chicken, ran off with a chest that might well have weighed thirty or forty pounds? Perhaps even more, if all the things that are rumored to be in it really exist."

"Looks can be deceiving. I bet you some folks would be surprised to know that I can bench-press two hundred."

"Doughnuts?"

"Very funny, Yoder. I asked the reverend where exactly his wife was running, he said he thought she'd gone running in the direction of Stucky Ridge."

"I see. But tell me this, Melvin. Why would Ron and Lodema be in cahoots? They hardly know each other. And why would they wait until now to steal the time capsule? Why not take it a year ago? Or two years ago? Or in Lodema's case—since she's supposedly so strong—why didn't she swipe it ten years ago, before Ron moved here? Then she could have kept what's in it all to herself?"

Melvin's left eye was spinning like a pinwheel in a hurricane, while his right eye appeared to be studying a dust bunny under my chair. After all, I don't claim to be the most thorough of housekeepers.

"Yoder, consider this your opportunity to learn at the foot of the master. The two of them are lovers. She waited until now because—dang it, Yoder, I'm the one who's supposed to be asking the questions."

I disguised my smile by pretending to yawn. "Melvin, dear, what I was trying to reach you about is this—Ron Humphrey is dead."

Both eyes stared at me. "*Dead* dead?"

"Possibly even triple dead. I examined his body in the morgue myself."

While he processed this shocking information (a stranger might have concluded that he'd slipped into a coma), I wrote up a mental shopping list. With Freni in quit mode, I would have to dart into Bedford and pick up some those frozen dinners I've heard so much about for the last forty years. The weather was still mild, and with any luck, my guests might not object to eating cold food. I also needed to buy some toilet tissue, laundry detergent, and bar soap. It might surprise you to know that finicky guests insist that their Lifeguard not have any previous lives.

Melvin groaned as he emerged from his reverie. "Yoder, these murders are going to ruin my chances of being elected to the legislature."

"Maybe, maybe not. It depends on how quickly we solve them."

"Believe me, Yoder, I don't want to move in with you any more than you want me to. Probably less."

"What?"

"Oh, didn't I tell you? I've decided to retire from the department at the end of December. Although, maybe I should resign right now, so I can throw all my energy into the election."

"Why on earth would you resign?"

"Susannah wants to start a family, and she doesn't want me in a dangerous job. So if I lose—well, there's no way we can afford our house payment. Because face it, Yoder, I don't have many other skills."

"Not to worry, dear. Your mother still lives on the family farm. She has oodles of room."

He shook his head so vigorously I thought sure it would snap free from his spindly neck and fly across the room in my direction. If so, I'd have to scramble to catch it. A noggin as hard as Melvin's can do serious damage to one's walls.

"Mama's selling what's left of the farm," he said. "She's says it's time for her to move into Rosewood Manor over in Bedford—that's if she can afford it. She's borrowed against the equity so many times there's almost nothing left. Heck, Susannah was supposed to talk to you about this. You know, about making up the difference in case Mama can't afford the rates."

His words sent a jolt of terror through me, one that started in the tips of my cotton-clad toes and ran to the top of my organza prayer cap. I'd be happy to pave the way for Elvina Stoltzfus in her so-called golden years, but I'd rather get hitched to Saddam Hussein than share my home with the mantis and his mate.

"Don't give up so soon, Melvin! Besides, you'd hate it here. We now have a pig in residence."

"Don't be so hard on yourself, Yoder."

He was deadly serious, but I chose to ignore the comment. I'd just had a brainstorm, and since that region is becoming increasingly arid, I needed to act on it as soon as possible.

"Why don't you two move in right now on a trial basis?"

"Uh—"

"I mean it. You'd have to sleep right here in the parlor on a rollaway, but that shouldn't be a problem. This batch of guests goes to bed early, and you two are night owls, right? Of course you'd have to do chores. I'm not a sexist, so I don't care who does what—but someone has to run into Bedford this afternoon and do the shopping. Meanwhile the other can be cleaning the bathrooms in the rooms of those who opted out of A.L.P.O. Oh, and you'll find a pile of dirty laundry in the—"

"Forget it, Yoder. My Sweetykins and I have far too much pride to be manual laborers."

"So you're not going to quit after all?"

"Don't be ridiculous. I was just kidding about moving in."

"Good. So maybe now we can talk about the switched bodies."

"You're nuts, Yoder, you know that?"

"Call me Macadamia, but if you don't hush up and listen to what I have say, you'll be scrubbing toilets before you can spell my new name."

The miserable mantis was suddenly as mum as a politician on a polygraph.

"So you're one hundred percent positive that the corpse you delivered to the morgue was Buzzy Porter?"

"Like I said, Yoder, you're nuts. From the time you left, until the ambulance arrived, I didn't leave the body alone for a second."

"Yes, but did you ride with it to the hospital?"

"Of course not. I drove the cruiser down."

"But you saw Dr. Mean and Nurse Meaner unload the victim, right?"

"Yeah." He shifted in his seat to alleviate the pain Granny's hardwood chair was inflicting on his bottom. "Yoder, we got ourselves a big problem on our hands, don't we?"

"The biggest, dear. Perhaps we should call the sheriff in on this one. Maybe even the F.B.I. I mean, kidnapping a corpse has got to be a federal crime."

The look of abject terror on my brother-in-law's face was almost touching. No doubt he believed that if we sought outside help, his reputation would suffer. But au contraire. The good folk of Hernia have no delusions about their chief's competency. If he asked for outside assistance, the majority of us would view it as a sign of latent intelligence.

"Okay, okay, we don't need to call the sheriff—at least not yet. I believe that both murders are tied to the time capsule box, and"—I lowered my voice so that there was no chance Alison could hear us, should she be trying to listen in—"I think that at least one of my current guests might be involved."

He rolled an eye, but refrained from commenting.

"I'm also convinced that the motive is a treasure—in a manner of speaking—the key to which is a document that has been in that box all these years."

"You mean the Hochstetler fortune?"

It's a good thing I don't wear dentures, or I would have had to waste precious time rinsing them off.

"You know about this fortune?"

"*Supposed* fortune, Yoder. Anyone with any brains knows that it's crap."

"Do tell."

"It's supposed to be in a cave, you know. I looked for it all the time when I was kid. Been inside every cave and abandoned mine shaft in Bedford County but never found a damn thing. Nothing, zilch, nada."

"Don't swear in this house, Melvin." My words may have been chiding, but my tone wasn't. Frankly, I was intrigued. I'd known the police chief his entire life, and I had never pictured him doing childlike things. Childish, yes, but not childlike. The image of a large-headed little boy tramping around in the woods looking for caves was almost endearing. "Did you do this by yourself?"

"Don't be mean, Yoder. You know I didn't have many friends. Of course I was alone. Almost died one day too, on account of those caves can be dangerous. Once, when I was about nine, I slipped inside a cave on some mud and knocked myself out. I have no idea how long I was unconscious, but when I came to I was seeing double and had a lump on my head the size of my fist. It wasn't until the swelling finally went down that the doc noticed an actual depression. Here, you can still feel it."

He was out of his chair and headed my way before I could stop him. "Bull!" I shouted.

He retraced his steps. "I'm not lying, Yoder. Susannah sometimes parks her gum there when she goes to sleep."

"I believe you have the dent, but it was caused when that bull kicked you. You know, the one you were trying to milk."

"Don't be ridiculous, Yoder. I didn't milk the bull until high school."

I smiled, vindicated. "Melvin, did your family tradition mention a specific cave?"

He gave me a look that would have withered a water-logged cactus, had there been one in the room. "There is only one tradition, Yoder. You ought to know—seeing as how you think you know everything. Mama said the right cave was the one at the bottom of Stucky Ridge. Her mama's mama's mama told her that. I only looked in the other caves because I couldn't find—"

"There's a cave at the bottom of Stucky Ridge?"

Melvin smiled, looking rather vindicated himself. "So you don't know everything."

"Quel surprise." I glanced at my watch, which, by the way, is a conservative Christian model. "Do you know what time it gets dark now?"

"When the sun goes down, of course. Although in the summer it sometimes stays light a while longer."

"Stay right where you are," I ordered.

"Can I at least sit in your chair?" he whined.

I said he could. Then I hurried off to find Alison. Alas, the child was happily bathing the pig named Babe—in my bathtub! I made a mental note to invest in Purell stock, but refrained from lecturing her just then.

"I'm leaving a note on the dining room table. The guests are supposed to make their own supper, but they have to pay extra for the privilege. You, of course, don't have to pay. In fact, if you cook something for them—like maybe scrambled eggs and toast—I'll double your allowance this week. And in case I'm not back at your normal bedtime, put yourself to bed. And no, you may not go over to a friend's. I need you here tonight. Any questions, dear?"

Alison seemed remarkably unperturbed by my instructions. She kissed Babe on his pink, plasticlike snout before answering.

"Can Donna Wylie come over to see him?"

"If one of her parents does the driving. I don't want to come back and find Jimmy here."

"Mom, you're so silly. Who needs boys when I've got him?"

Oh, the wisdom of youth. I planted a kiss on the back of Alison's head and sized Babe's head up for head cheese—it would take a few years—and then skedaddled. My bothersome brother-in-law just might have accidentally babbled some useful information. It was time to go spelunking with the Stoltzfus.

19

Tourists like to think that Hernia is all gingerbread Victorian houses surrounded by neat Amish farms. The truth is we have a slum, albeit a rather small one. There are two streets on the south end of the town that we locals shamefully refer to as Ragsdale. I know it's a sin to judge others on their lack of material possessions, and I promise to repent for even sharing this bit of information. And not that it's a valid excuse, but the habit was ingrained in us as children.

When Susannah and I were girls (at separate times, of course), our school bus used to stop in this part of town to take on students. It was common knowledge among us children that the Ragsdale kids were a breed apart. Some of them sported tattoos, many of them smoked, and on at least three occasions Miss Proschel, our bus driver, had to confiscate knives. Like many other stereotypes in this world, Ragsdale's reputation was based on both fact and fancy.

The neighborhood remains poor, but frankly, today I feel safer walking through it than I do visiting Foxcroft, our newest subdivision. Foxcroft, by the way, is where Susannah and Melvin live, in a house that can be distinguished from its neighbors only because my sister ignores the covenants and hangs scarlet drapes at the windows. Anyway, in the last five years since its establishment, Foxcroft has seen a homicide, eight cases of nonlethal domestic violence (that have been reported), four break-ins, and a rash of mailbox bashing. In that time period Ragsdale has been virtually crime free.

Melvin and I drove separately, agreeing to park in front of the "Block House." This residence is locally famous because the Strubleheimers, who own it, have eighteen wheelless vehicles up on concrete blocks. Most of the cars lack glass panes and are therefore home to numerous small mammals. When this unsightly collection began, the animals were primarily mice and rats. Over the years the rodents have been replaced by cats. At one point the feline population was so large that it rivaled that of the Roman Coliseum, or so experienced travelers tell me. Recently some of our more wealthy citizens, yours truly included, have been sponsoring the spaying and neutering of these mousers. The furry explosion has halted, although occasionally one still sees a kitten or two playing in the shade of the mounted wrecks.

One might think the town could do something about this eyesore, but alas, the Strubleheimers have a grandfather clause that dates back to the days when a Strubleheimer ancestor ran a repair shop for Model A Fords. It is said to have been the first in the county. And anyway, the sad truth is that as long as the mess doesn't spill out of Ragsdale and into Hernia proper, most folks don't care. The only complaints we on the town council get are from tourists who accidentally stray from the official sightseers' route, the one marked Highway to Heaven on our giveaway maps.

Melvin and I picked this spot to rendezvous because the Block House sits at the end of Tar Shingle Alley, the closest one can drive to this flank of Stucky Ridge (the portion directly below Lovers' Leap). My brother-in-law assured me that there was an actual path that wound among the rusting hulks and into the tangle of woods that hugs the base of this outcrop. As a boy, bent on discovering treasure, he was forced to run through the maze of vehicles, and not because the supposed Ragsdale bullies were after him, but because of the giant rats. If he is to be believed a rat the size of Robin Williams—but not quite as hairy—knocked him down one day, bit his ears, and probably would have eaten them had not our hero remembered that he had one of his mother's cookies in his pocket.

He fed the confection to the rodent, which immediately toppled over dead. *That* part of the story I believe.

As soon as I got out of the car on that otherwise pleasant September afternoon, the scent of ammonia nearly overwhelmed me. I would either have to beef up my contributions to the spaying fund or start feeding the cats Elvina Stoltzfus's cookies. Of course I am joking, but it was no wonder that Blue's sniffer had gone berserk when he stood at the edge of Lovers' Leap.

"Melvin, do you think any of them have rabies?"

"Don't be such scaredy-cat, Yoder. I got bit by a rabid rat once, remember? Didn't even get any treatment for it—and look at me."

"That's why I asked, dear."

The cats were obviously used to being fed, and the real danger came from tripping over them as they vied for our attention. By the time I got halfway to the woods, I had a live leg warmer wrapped around each ankle. A few of the persistent pussies even followed us into the dense undergrowth at the woods' edge. Finally the going got so tough, even they became discouraged and turned back.

"Melvin, you said there was a trail."

"There is, Yoder. Can't you see it?"

"I can barely see you—not that I'm complaining."

"See that? I carved that notch into that tree when I was just a kid. That was over thirty years ago and it's still there. Look, there's another."

I didn't see a thing except dying leaves and brambles. At one point, while trying to protect my face, my still-sore right hand snagged on a blackberry vine. If Melvin hadn't sounded so cocksure, I would have turned back and joined the pussies. A bird in the hand might be worth two in the bush, but a hand in a bush—well, that can be mighty painful.

There simply isn't all that much woods between the Block House and the ridge, so Melvin must have led me in concentric circles. It got to the point where I wouldn't have been surprised if we suddenly stumbled onto the Pacific Ocean. A sweating Stoltzfus and a scratched Sacagawea, that's what we were.

The panting mantis finally stopped, and I came within inches of smacking into him. "It used to be right there."

"What? Where?"

He pointed at the ground just in front of him. "The cave, you idiot. I swear that's where it was."

That's when I first noticed that we were standing at the base of a sheer rock wall. Funny how I hadn't noticed the ridge through the trees. At any rate, there was nothing to see where Melvin pointed except leaf clutter and a few half-rotted branches. It was what one might expect on the floor of any dense woods.

"How can you be sure this is the spot?" A terrifying thought had just occurred to me. Sure, Melvin had managed to find the cliff, but by way of San Francisco. No doubt it would be ten times harder to find our way back to the Block House. We might even get so lost we could wander over the border into Maryland, a situation for which we were not prepared. After all, one should never venture into Maryland without provisions.

"I'm positive this is the right spot, Yoder, because there're my initials again. I carved them into the rock with the knife Mama gave me for my ninth birthday."

"Elvina Stoltzfus gave *you* a pocket knife?" It's a good thing nobody else knew that at the time, or Melvin's mama would surely have been cited for child endangerment.

"Don't be ridiculous, Yoder. It was a table knife—but it did have a serrated edge."

I shuffled through the leaves and sticks to get a closer look. While I couldn't be certain Melvin had carved them, there were indeed initials.

MS loves MY.

"Who's MY? Mabel Yutzy?"

Unable to decipher Melvin's low mumble, I guessed again.

"Marilyn Yost?"

"Don't be mean, Yoder. I was just a kid."

"I'm not being mean. Marilyn Yost is a beautiful, talented woman. It's too bad she can't seem to stay married. And just in case you're getting ideas—remember that you're married."

"It wasn't Marilyn Yost, damn it, it was you!"

I recoiled right into a veritable thicket of blackberry vines. So shocked was I that I forgot to chide Melvin for swearing. In fact, I didn't even feel the pain of a thousand thorns.

"What did you say?"

"You heard me. But like I said, I was just a kid, and you were so—uh, well, magnificent."

I thrashed free of the thorns. Try saying that five times in rapid succession. Perhaps then you can imagine what it was like for me to spit out anything coherent.

"B-but I'm eleven years older than you. I would have been a twenty-year-old woman."

"Yeah," he said, sounding wistful. "And what a woman. Smart, funny, sexy—"

"Aack!" I clamped bloody hands over my ears, but a fat lot of good that did.

"I mean it, Yoder. You are—I mean, were—everything I wanted in a woman."

"A carpenter's dream?"

"I like flat-chested women. I married Susannah, didn't I?"

Oh what a laugh the Good Lord must be having. The same Magdalena Portulacca Yoder who never had a date in either high school or college, and who had come to think of herself as the poster woman for maiden ladies everywhere, was really a sex goddess.

"Melvin, please tell me you no longer feel that way about me."

He brayed like a donkey, which was, to say the least, disconcerting. There are no wild asses in Pennsylvania, and it was still a good two months until deer season, but some hunters break the rules. And neither of us was wearing red—although one of us was starting to see that color.

"What's so funny?" I demanded.

"You got to be kidding. Of course I don't feel that way now."

"Oh?" It's much nicer to be lusted after than laughed at.

"It's because you've gotten arrogant, Yoder."

"That's not true! I've always been conceited."

"You think you're so much smarter than me. You're always putting me down. Susannah, on the other hand, builds me up. Makes me feel like a man."

"I never realized she was such a hard worker."

"You see what I mean?"

Sometimes I think I'm diagonally parked in a parallel universe. Even just this morning I would have thought this entire scenario was about as likely to happen as—well, me allowing a pig to live in the inn. And almost as surprising was the fact that I wanted to argue with Melvin, to convince him that I was still worthy of his affection. Not that I was attracted to him, mind you, but isn't it human nature to want to be liked? Yes, I'd detested the man all these years (in a loving, Christian sort of way), but I hadn't known there was a time when we could have actually been civil to each other.

But instead of making a fool of myself, or lapsing into familiar sarcasm, I decided to practice random acts of intelligence and senseless acts of self-control. At least until we got back to the safety of civilization. And believe you me, eighteen wheelless cars and a hundred-odd cats were starting to seem pretty normal.

"Melvin, dear, perhaps the cave and your initials are farther apart than you remembered. After all, you were a little boy."

He grunted, which I took as agreement. I began to follow the cliff face in one direction, and he in another. After about fifty yards I gave up, but only because the sheer wall had given way to a steep, but wooded slope. The terrain no longer jibed at all with Melvin's description.

When I returned to our starting point, I learned that he had not been successful either. "It's a trick, Yoder."

"What is?"

He nodded in the direction of the initials. "I know I carved them above the entrance, so this isn't the place. Must have been Buffalo Mountain I was remembering—like you said, I was just a kid back then. Must have carved my initials in two places."

"Melvin, only a goat kid would confuse Buffalo Mountain with Stucky Ridge. Even you—" I've bitten my tongue so many times, that I have permanent indentations for my teeth. In fact, it doesn't even hurt anymore.

"You see, Yoder? This is what I mean. When you were twenty, you weren't mean like this."

That, however, hurt. "I wasn't trying to be mean. I was backing you up. If you remembered there being a cave here, there must have been one."

He snorted, sounding more like a horse now than a donkey. "Caves don't just disappear," he said. "It's not like there was a magic rock you rolled over the opening."

"Yes, but there could be another explanation." I stared at rock face and the ground in front of it. Just a solid expanse of rock and wet leaves—suddenly my heart was beating even faster than it had on my wedding night to that cad Aaron Miller. "Melvin, when is the last time it rained?"

"How should I know? I'm not a meteorologist."

"You'll be seeing stars if you don't give me a quick answer."

"August—but I don't know when. Like I said, I'm not a weatherman."

"Are you sure it hasn't rained since August?"

"Positive. Every Labor Day my Sweetie Pot Pie and I spend the night in the backyard. It's kinda a tradition, I guess. We put up our pup tent just in case it rains, but if it's really nice we—well, some things are more exciting if they're done outside. Not that you'd understand, Yoder."

"And I don't want to," I wailed. "Now, can we get back to the task on hand?"

"You're the one who asked."

"Look at those leaves," I ordered. "The ones by the wall, just below your initials. Do you see what I see?"

"You mean ugly wet leaves?"

"Exactly. But if it hasn't rained for at least a couple of weeks, how did they get wet?"

I may as well have been asking sheep geometry questions. The mantis's minuscule brain couldn't even begin to think of an answer. His left eye stared at me balefully, while his right eye studied the tops of his shoes.

"I give up, Yoder. How?"

"Because those leaves were on the bottom of the forest litter until very recently." I found a sturdy stick and turned over a patch of dry leaves some distance from the cliff. Sure enough the leaves next to the ground were wet and clumped together like cold broad noodles. "See what happens?"

One of the lights went on in my nemesis's noggin. "Yeah, I see what you mean. But what does it prove?"

I strode back to the cliff. "The leaves here are a bit deeper. It's a wonder we didn't notice it before, but they look as if they've been piled up. See how they slope away from where I'm standing?"

Another light switched on. "But, Yoder, the entrance to the cave wasn't just a crack along the ground."

"It might not have seemed that way to a little boy. Here, help me." I started to push leaves aside with hands that felt like I'd run them through a blender. Unless you tried it yourself, you wouldn't believe the number and variety of creepy crawly things that inhabit piles of rotting vegetation.

Melvin just stood there.

"Help me," I said.

"Can't, Yoder. I have allergies. Leaf mold exacerbates them."

"If you don't help, you won't get any credit for what we discover."

He dug like a dog that smelled a bone—one with a three-pound steak attached to it. Because the leaves had recently been disturbed and the heavy wet bottom layer redistributed, we cleared the ground at the base of Lovers' Leap in no time.

"Still no cave," Melvin moaned, as we used our feet to scrape away the last of the fallen foliage.

"But look—fresh dirt! There definitely is something here that's been covered."

Because my modesty precludes the wearing of fingernails that resemble painted claws, I had nothing to lose by digging in the soil with my hands—except for my last remaining shreds of skin.

Melvin, who does wear clear polish—thanks to Susannah's influence—was again reluctant to dig.

"Melvin, you have to help me."

"Your shoes are the size of boats, Yoder. Why don't you use one for a shovel?"

He needed incentive. "When I describe this to the newspapers, I might accidentally refer to you as a sissy."

He dug like a dog again. Within minutes we had uncovered what was indeed the entrance to a small cave. At least a small entrance to something. It was perhaps six feet long, but only eighteen inches high. When I stepped back a few paces, it appeared to be nothing more than a dark gash at the cliff's base.

"Oh yeah," Melvin said, in a maddeningly offhand manner, "it was kind of a tough squeeze at that. Funny how your mind plays tricks on you."

"I guess it has to amuse itself somehow in all that empty space." I got down on all fours and peered into the darkness. Darkness was all I saw. "What does your mind have to say about the size of the cave itself?"

"You don't need to be rude, Yoder. That I remember as clear as day. It may not be the biggest cave around, but it's plenty big enough for a bear to hibernate in."

"Bear?" I backed away from the opening and struggled to my feet. Thank heavens I realized my foolishness before Melvin did. "The entrance was disguised, dear. Do bears generally do that before, or after, they crawl in?"

"How should I know?"

Bears, or not, we were running out of daytime. September sunsets can take one by surprise, especially on mild days like this. But we weren't going to get any more work done here without a light source.

"By any chance would you happen to have a flashlight on you?"

"Of course not."

"Me either," I grumbled. "How stupid could we have been?"

"Speak for yourself, Yoder. At least I have one back at the car."

"Be a dear and get it, will you please?"

My gallant brother-in-law charged into the trees. I tapped a long, slender foot—more like a canoe than a boat—as I counted. Before I got to five, he'd returned.

"Very funny, Yoder."

"I do my best. How about matches? Do you have any of those? Or better yet, a cigarette lighter?"

"You know I haven't smoked since I've been married."

"That's right. Since you set Susannah's veil on fire. Well, we're just going to have to come back tomorrow with flashlights."

"Guess again, Yoder. We have a job to do. And anyway, there's no point. I searched all over that cave—even took a pickax to the floor. Read my lips: There isn't any treasure."

"But there could be a body," I said quietly.

Melvin stared at me. Then he stared at the mouth of the cave. In the deepening shadows it looked as if someone had painted the rock face with a swath of India ink.

"Let's get the heck out of here, Yoder."

20

Grilled Breaded Veal Chops

4 veal rib or loin chops, each about
   ¾-inch thick
Salt and whole white pepper in a
   pepper mill
Whole nutmeg in a grater
Grated zest from 1 lemon

1 tablespoon chopped parsley
¼ cup all-purpose flour
1 egg, lightly beaten
1 cup dry bread crumbs
4 tablespoons butter, melted
1 lemon, cut into 8 wedges

If you are using rib chops, scrape the meat and fat from the long end of the bone, leaving only the meaty eye of the chop attached. Set the scraps aside for broth. With a mallet or scaloppine pounder, lightly beat the chops until the meat is about a ½-inch thick. (If you are using loin chops, beat the tougher loin side well to tenderize it.) Sprinkle both sides liberally with salt, several grindings of white pepper, a generous grating of nutmeg, lemon zest, and parsley. Lightly press the seasonings into the meat.

Put the flour, egg, and crumbs into separate shallow bowls. Lightly roll each chop first in the flour, then dip it in the egg until it is well coated and roll it in the crumbs. Lay the chops on a wire rack and let the crumbs set for at least 30 minutes.

Prepare a grill with hardwood coals or preheat the broiler for at least 15 minutes. When the coals are glowing red but lightly ashed over, spread them and position a rack about 5 inches above them (in the broiler, about 5 inches below the heat source). Brush one side of the chops lightly with the butter and put them on the grill, buttered side toward the heat. Grill/broil until the crumbs are toasted golden brown, about 3 minutes. Brush the uncooked side with butter, turn, and grill until they are evenly browned, about 3 minutes more for medium rare. If you prefer the veal more done, move the rack a couple of inches away from the heat and grill/broil about 1 to 2 minutes more per side for medium. Don't overcook them or they will be tough. Serve hot, garnished with lemon wedges.

SERVES 4

21

Melvin and I agreed to meet at the Block House at seven in the morning. We would both bring flashlights. In addition, he would bring rope and I would bring provisions. I wanted to be prepared in case the cave was larger inside than he remembered, and we accidentally ventured over the state line into Maryland. I was, however, anything but prepared for what greeted me at the inn. The second I set foot over the threshold of the kitchen door, Gabriel grabbed me by an arm and pulled me the rest of way in.

"Where have you been?" he demanded.

"Gabe! What are *you* doing here?"

"You want someone should starve?" A raspy female voice answered.

I glanced around the room, seeing no one. Then I lowered my eyes a few feet. Ida Rosen was standing at Freni's stove, her back turned to me. She appeared to be stirring something. If it hadn't been for that movement, I would have dismissed her as an apron, or a tea towel, tucked dangerously into the handle of the oven door. Even I know that a talking tea towel makes no sense, but it had been a long day.

"Good evening, Mrs. Rosen," I said. I stretched every syllable Tennessee thin to give myself time to cool down. It was the same as counting to ten.

"Sure, maybe for you." She turned to face me. "But it is not such a good evening for me, or for my Gabriel."

"Ma!" Gabe protested, but the old woman shot him down with a look that should be studied more closely by the Pentagon.

"I vas across the road cooking my boy a normal meal, and he gets this call from the little one asking what she should make for supper. Vhat was I supposed to do?"

"Alison called?"

"Nu, is there another child in this house?"

"But there's plenty for her to eat that doesn't require cooking."

Ida waved her spatula at the refrigerator. "You call that food? A dog should eat better than that."

"I'll pass that along to Freni."

"First you fire her, and now you vant to hurt her feelings. Go figure."

"I did not fire her!"

"Ma!" Gabe complained, a convenient three seconds too late.

My future mother-in-law turned back to the stove. Looking over her head I could see that a frying pan and two large saucepans had been pressed into use. A little red light above indicated that the burners were on.

"That looks like an awful lot of food," I observed.

She waved the spatula above her head. "Just a nice brisket I brought over. And some potato pancakes, green beans, tzimmes, and a kugel."

"A what and a what?"

"A stewed carrot dish and a kind of noodle pudding," Gabe said, but he wouldn't look me in the eye.

"That's still an awful lot of food for one girl, even if she is a teenager." I stifled a gasp. "Unless you two are planning to eat with her."

"Ve already ate," Ida snapped. "At the proper time."

Gabe took a hesitant step in my direction. "Don't worry, hon. She said that with Freni being gone, and you unable to cook—"

"Say what?"

"Alison said—"

There was no point in hearing him out, not when I could hear it from the horse's mouth.

I found the horse's mouth alarmingly close to the pig's mouth. Alison was sitting on my bed, holding Babe in her lap, when I barged into the room. I think she'd been about to kiss his spouted little snout, because she flushed with embarrassment.

"Mom, don'tcha believe in knocking first?"

"Not when it's my room, dear."

"Well, before ya go ragging on me, he's clean. I bathed him, remember?"

"We'll talk about you kissing a pig later. I want to know what Mrs. Rosen is really doing in my kitchen."

"Oh that. Ya said if I made 'em supper," she said, referring to the guests, "that you would double my allowance."

"That, I did. But I didn't mention Ida Rosen."

"Yeah, I know, but I got to thinking. I could make them soup and sandwiches, or scrambled eggs or something—but that's kinda boring even for me. Besides, doubling my allowance ain't such a big deal, since ya don't hardly give me nothing to begin with."

"But there isn't anything in town to spend it on!"

"That don't stop you from wanting to make money."

"Yes, but I tithe. I give ten percent to the church, and a whole bunch more to charities."

"That's what I plan to do with my two hundred bucks."

"Your *what*?"

Alison grinned happily. Her pig appeared to smile as well.

"I asked them guests if they had ever had authentic Jewish cooking. Guess what? They all said no. So I told them they could have a meal if they paid an extra twenty-five dollars, and they all said yes. Then I called Grandma Ida and told her I was hungry. She said she'd be right over to fix me supper on account of I'm neglected."

"But you're not neglected!" I wailed.

"Yeah, but she thinks I am. Anyway, ya know how she always

cooks too much food? I asked her if I could keep the leftovers, see. And she said sure thing, seeing as how ya fired Freni and I'm likely to starve to death, on account ya ain't the world's best cook—"

"I didn't fire Freni! Alison, you have got to stop telling tales—wait a minute. Do you mean to say you're selling our guests leftovers for twenty-five dollars a head, and it isn't costing you a thing, *and* Mrs. Rosen is doing all the work?"

She nodded. "Ya ain't too mad, are ya?"

"Mad? You go, girl!" I said, and gave her the high five.

Of course, she wasn't expecting the gesture, but she's a quick study, and smacked her hand against mine. I yelped with pain.

"What's the matter, Mom?"

"Nothing permanent, dear. I'll be fine. By the way, where are the guests now? This place is as silent as the hospital morgue."

"Ah, they're taking a walk."

"A walk? Where?"

"Herniahenge."

I gasped, depleting the room of its oxygen, the end result of which was that Alison and Babe the pig gasped as well. Herniahenge is strictly off-limits to outsiders.

Lest you think that by now I have permanently flipped my prayer cap, please allow me to explain. Herniahenge is our equivalent of Stonehenge. Geologically it is a cluster of giant boulders, one almost as big as my inn, that some experts claim were pushed into placed by advancing glaciers tens of thousands of years ago. Since the world was created no more than six thousand years ago, I find that theory highly unlikely.

More likely, if you ask me, is the growing speculation that these rocks were erected by aliens and serve as a navigational landmark of some kind. I know, many devout people deny the existence of extraterrestrials. But that's only because they have yet to meet the Mishler twins, who at age eighty-seven saunter naked around their yard (although in the winter there is really no point). Nor have these doubting Thomases met Wanda Hemphopple, with her potentially lethal hairdo that threatens to topple at every toss of her ornery head. Or what about Zelda Root, who keeps her face together with spackle and is the leader of a cult of Melvin worshippers? And speaking of the Stoltzfus, where do you think John Gray got his idea for men being from Mars?

At any rate, only we locals know about this unusual placement of rocks, and we want to keep it this way. After Stucky Ridge, this is our second favorite spot to picnic and cavort (not me, of course, since I am not the cavorting kind). Thankfully, this geological oddity remains hidden by deep woods—although we did come mighty close to sharing it with the world.

You see, the land upon which these rocks sit used to belong to Aaron Miller Sr., my pseudo ex-father-in-law. At one time he wanted to sell the land to the commonwealth for development as a park. He suggested calling it Herniahenge, or some such similar nonsense. A few of our wealthier citizens (need I say who?) banded together and made Mr. Miller an offer he couldn't refuse. But he was a cantankerous old geezer and did refuse.

Finally, when "Pop," as he still wanted me to call him, began to grope his way through the dark halls of dementia, he suggested that we play a game. If any of us succeeded at the game, we could buy the acreage in question for a dollar each. The object of this farce was to dislodge some smaller rocks that occurred naturally atop one of the tallest and steepest monoliths in the group. We were each assigned a small boulder, visible from the ground, but we were forbidden to use any sort of projectiles, such as catapults, slingshots, etc. Alas, none of us succeeded in getting our rocks off.

But neither could the commonwealth afford Pop's asking price. The situation might have become very interesting, probably even involved a lawsuit, had not Hermoine Liverbottom, an old flame of Pop's, shown up on the scene like an angel sent from heaven. She convinced Pop to sell her the property for a siren's song and a few thousand dollars. Hermoine was forced to make a verbal agreement that she would never sell the property to a resident of Hernia, but that turned out to be a moot point. Three weeks after the deed passed into her hands, Hermoine conveniently died. Shortly thereafter the townsfolk were overjoyed to learn that she had left her entire estate to the town—the only caveat being that the property be called, in perpetuity, Herniahenge.

"Alison," I said sharply, "you can't be sending folks to Herniahenge."

"But it's such a cool place. And anyway, I didn't send them—I led them. They paid me ten bucks each to be the tour guide."

When a smile and frown compete for face space, they can give the impression one desperately needs to use the bathroom. I was forced to look away from Alison, since she has told me on more than one occasion that I am full of it.

"Still, if word gets out—why, we could be overrun by tourists." Even worse, I thought, although I did not say it, my inn could accommodate only a small percentage of the influx.

"Ya worry too much, Mom, ya know that? I said I led them there. I meant that literally. I made them all wear blindfolds and hold hands."

My heart nearly burst with pride. I doubt if a flesh and blood daughter could have made me any happier.

"How will they get back, dear?"

"I'm supposed to pick them up—but of course, Grandma Rosen wants me to eat first." She set the pig on her bed and hopped to the window. "Holy guacamole, it's almost dark already."

"That it is. Look dear, you eat, and then get rid of Ida Rosen as fast as you can. In the meantime I'll lead the troops home."

"Thanks, Mom!" Not to be outdone, Babe squealed his gratitude as well.

I basked in the glow of combined filial and porcine love for a full minute. "Just one thing, dear," I finally said.

She skipped back to our bed. "Yeah?"

"Ida Rosen is not your grandmother. I'd appreciate it if you didn't refer to her as that."

Alison exhaled so hard Babe's ears blew back flat against his head. "Whew, that's a relief. 'Cause I already got me a grandma back in Minnesota, and I don't really want another one."

"Then why do you call her that?"

"She told me to, that's why."

"Well, we'll just see about that," I said, and turned on my narrow heels.

But Alison's role model is not as stupid as she looks. I had no intention of speaking with Ida Rosen until after my guests were fed.

There have been recent rumors of Bigfoot prowling about Hernia and environs, but since the tales were generated by Alison and are, in fact, based on yours truly, I don't put much stock in them. Still, I was somewhat startled to see three shadowy figures stagger out of the woods on the Herniahenge side of the road. Although I was carrying a flashlight, it wasn't so dark that I would stumble. Therefore I decided against turning it on. One must save energy whenever one can, right?

But it is always okay to pray. "Lord, if one of them wants to breed with me, please don't let him be too ugly."

Immediately one of the creatures broke ranks and advanced toward me at an astonishingly fast pace. "Miss Yoder, is that you?"

The voice was unmistakenly female in timbre, so even if it was an attractive Bigfoot bearing down on me, there would be no horizontal hootchy-kootchy in the vicinity of Herniahenge. I must say I was a mite disappointed.

"Miss Yoder, it *is* you!" Octavia Cabot-Dodge's assistant grabbed me by my right arm and pulled me down Hertlzer Road like I was her toy wagon. I tried to dig my heels into the asphalt, but it was a waste of good leather.

"Miss Miller," I protested, "I'm quite capable of walking on my own."

"Yes," she hissed, "but we must stay ahead of them."

"Oh, I get it. You want us to lose them—sort of like a game, right?"

"Don't be ridiculous, Miss Yoder. I have something to say to you that is a matter of life and death."

22

"I'm all ears," I cried. Now it was me who was pulling her. "What's this all about?"

"Your fleecing of America."

"I read that book!"

"I'm not talking about a book. I'm referring to all the ways you have of extorting cash from your guests. It doesn't seem at all like the Mennonite way to me."

I am the first to admit that I don't fit the profile of the typical Mennonite. That doesn't bother me. But there are areas in which I fit the mold quite well. Mennonites are supposed to be humble in their dealings with the world, and quite frankly I am proud of my humility.

"Man does not live on bread alone," I said, quoting the Good Lord himself, and then, because I speak to Him on a daily basis, I felt free to add a few words on my own. "And woman requires meat, fruits, vegetables, and a warm, dry place to sleep. That all takes money."

"Which my employer does not have."

"Get out of town! I mean, I knew Miss Cabot-Dodge is a has-been, but I thought surely she'd managed to sock away some moola in her heyday, brief though it was."

"She tries to maintain that image, but it's getting harder and harder. Have you looked closely at the limousine?"

"No, but if you've seen one, you've seen them all, right?" But even I knew that wasn't true. Colonel Custard, who had the unfortunate experience of dying in my inn recently, owned a limo, the seats of which were covered with the foreskins of stillborn whales.

"Miss Yoder, that limousine is twelve years old. It is in need of new tires. The dress my employer wore to dinner the other night—well, just between you and me, she bought that in a Hollywood thrift shop."

"You don't say. Well, you certainly didn't seem to be bothered by my rates when you booked the rooms."

"I was under orders to conduct business as usual. In the film industry image is everything. No one wants to hire a desperate actress—not one her age, at any rate."

"You mean she plans to make another movie?"

"Can you keep a secret?"

"Are my eyes blue?"

"I don't know, Miss Yoder. They just look dark and beady to me."

"Well, they *are* blue. Yes, I can keep a secret."

She glanced over her shoulder, but at the pace we were walking, there was no way her boss could be close enough to hear us. "Miss Cabot-Dodge is up for a part in a sitcom."

"You mean like *Green Acres*? Now that was a show worth watching."

Augusta Miller snorted, not the wisest way to express oneself on a road heavily trafficked by Amish buggies. They weren't any Amish out and about at that hour, but had there been, we both might have found ourselves behind traces.

"My employer's sitcom—and I have no doubt she'll get the part—is much more sophisticated than that. It's called *Clone on the Range,* and she'll be playing a wealthy widow on a Wyoming ranch who has herself cloned. But you see, the clone—and they're hoping to get Jennifer Aniston for the part—turns out nothing like the donor. That sounds like a winner, doesn't it?"

"Well, frankly—"

"But the thing is, she doesn't have the part *yet.* So all these extra expenses you keep coming up with are proving to be an embarrassment. She feels she has no choice but to say yes, in order to maintain her image as a star."

"Point taken," I said charitably. "I'll only pretend to charge her for the extra privileges. As for you and the chauffeur—well, I'll just say I've changed my policy and servants are no longer allowed to mingle with the rest of us."

"I am hardly a servant!"

I wrenched free from talons capable of eviscerating a marble antelope. "Now, if you'll excuse me, I was headed the other way. The folks at the rocks are going to need help getting back."

By the time I reached Herniahenge the woods were as black as Aaron Miller's heart. Fortunately my big feet knew every twist and turn in the path. When Aaron and I were courting we—never you mind. Suffice it to say, I reached the rocks without as much as stubbing my toes. Apparently, I was pretty silent in my approach as well.

"Of course it's a rip-off." Bibi Norton's voice boomed through the night air. "But Father and I were just saying that we really don't mind paying her exorbitant prices, because of the convenient location."

"They are not such high prices," Terri said softly. "In Japan many hotels cost this much. But Miss Yoder is so—how do you say—bossy?"

At least three people laughed. I couldn't identify the culprits in the dark, but believe you me, I was going to pay special attention the next time we were together in a well-lit situation and someone told a joke.

"She told me the place was haunted," Capers drawled, adding eight more syllables than were necessary. "But I still haven't seen her grandmother's ghost. Now, if she came to my house in Charleston, I could personally introduce her to several specters."

"You're joking, right?" If I hadn't recognized Chuck Norton's voice, I probably would have thought it was a barking dog I heard.

"Oh, no," Buist said. "In the eighteen hundreds a pirate was hanged virtually in our front yard. He had a peg leg, but they took it away from him before they strung him up. I guess it was an early form of recycling. Anyway, we've seen and heard him many times. Usually in the upstairs hallway."

"What do you mean you heard him?" Terri's voice had risen an octave.

"When you first see him he appears out of nowhere, leaning on a cane and asking for his leg back. Keeps asking for it, in fact, until you say 'here it is.' Then he turns and walks away, and you can hear both the cane and his leg clumping down the hall—but you can't see him anymore."

"You never actually see the peg leg," Capers said in a mere eleven syllables.

"There are many ghosts such as this?" Terri asked, now sounding properly terrified.

"They're everywhere," Buist said. "Walk down any street late at night, and half the people you think you see, aren't really there. At least not in a flesh and blood way."

"Remind me not to go to Charleston," Chuck said, and then laughed nervously.

"Oh, that one-legged pirate likes to follow us around. Once he even showed up in our hotel room on Maui. So much for the theory that ghosts can't travel over water."

"I'm not saying that I don't believe you," Bibi blared, "but if you ask me, Miss Yoder embellishes everything. Why, just look at those brochures we got in the mail—'comfortable accommodations in a quaint, authentic Mennonite setting.' Ha! It wouldn't surprise me if those dowdy clothes she wears are just part of her act."

That did it. If the farmer's wife wanted to see acting, she was in for a treat. I played Brunhilde the Barbarian in a fourth-grade production, and everyone said I was a natural. I would have tried out for Ghengis Kahn in the fifth grade, but that's the year Susannah was born, and I was forced to wash cloth nappies by hand while Mama napped.

The first thing I needed to do was to get my ungrateful guests' attention. I did that by moaning. My brief, but bogus, marriage to Aaron had honed both my acting and moaning skills.

Terri responded first. "What was that?"

"Probably just an owl," Buist said.

I moaned again. A long, low sound, quite unlike any owl I've heard. For Aaron it had been a signal that it was time to wrap things up and get the ordeal over with.

Southern owls must have their own vocabulary. "Yes, ma'am, that's just an owl," Buist said. "He's probably just upset that all our talk is chasing away his prey."

It was time to crank things up a notch. "I want my peg leg."

"What was *that*?" Capers managed to spit that out in just four syllables.

Bibi grunted. "I didn't hear anything."

"I w-a-a-a-nt my p-e-e-e-g l-e-e-e-g."

I think it was Terri who screamed first, but if so, she was joined a millisecond later by the other two women, and at least one of the men.

"And I want it now!" I turned the flashlight on for the first time. I held it so that the business end was pointed up at the underside of my chin. No doubt my shnoz, silhouetted as it was, resembled a peg leg—of course one that hovered well over five feet above the ground. At any rate, the screams were practically deafening now, and involved both men.

A really rude person would have laughed far longer than I did. But really polite guests wouldn't have cursed me either. Eventually we calmed down enough to have a near civil discussion, and I informed them that I had been privy to the harsh comments about me. I'd been hurt to the quick, I said, and it would take me years of therapy to recover. There was no reason to add that the therapist's name was Mr. Hershey and that we had been having a bittersweet relationship for decades. Before that I been just plain nuts about him.

"I am so sorry, Miss Yoder," Terri said. In fact, she must have said it a dozen times.

I shone my flashlight in each of their faces by turn. The only one who didn't look at least a mite chagrined was Bibi Norton. She stared placidly at me, like a cow on antidepressants—not that I've seen many of those, mind you. Her brown plastic barrettes glinted like an extra pair of eyes. In a childish fit of pique, I wanted to rip the doodads from her hair and fling them among the scree.

Instead I prayed for patience. Imagine my surprise when I opened my mouth and discovered my prayer had been answered.

"Here, you take this," I said to Chuck, and handed him the flashlight. "A big strong man like you should be leading the way. Just follow this little footpath, and don't worry about getting lost, because I won't let you. And you others be sure to keep up right behind him—hold hands if you must. Mrs. Norton and I will bring up the rear, won't we, dear? We have so much to talk about, both being farm women and all."

Chuck didn't hesitate a second. That surprised me, although I can't say I blamed him. And once he was a couple of yards down the path, you can be sure the others fell right in behind.

Meanwhile I laid a hand gently on Bibi's arm, just in case she bolted. If it hadn't been for her skin temperature, I might have thought I'd grabbed hold of steel cable. You know, a thick one, like they use on the bridges in Pittsburgh.

"Miss Yoder—"

"Oh, you're perfectly safe with me, dear. We won't lag far behind. Besides I thought we might use this occasion to get to know each other better."

"But I suffer from night blindness. Miss Yoder, I could hurt myself."

"Nonsense, dear. Here, take my hand, and follow along right behind me."

This was, of course, a great sacrifice on my part. I eschew the custom of shaking hands, on the grounds that it is the number-one way in which the common cold is spread. And as if the mere thought of manual interdigitation wasn't enough to give me the heebie-jeebies, her hand felt exactly like a pinecone. Perhaps it was a pinecone she'd proffered me, but if so, it seemed to be attached to an arm. I made a mental note to examine the woman closer when we got back to the inn. After all, if pirates can have peg legs, why can't farmers' wives have cone hands?

"Now, dear," I said, when it seemed like we were making progress in our walking, "tell me all about yourself."

Bibi grunted. "Not much to tell. I'm just a simple farm woman from Inman, Kansas."

"What do you farm?"

"Mostly corn and hogs. Although Father put in a few acres of soybeans this year. Said he read in a journal that within ten years, everyone in America will have switched from cow's milk to soybean milk."

"That will never happen," I assured her. "Can you imagine going to your neighbor's house for tea, and they ask if you want lemon or beans in your brew?"

She grunted again. "Don't care for it much myself, but the small farm these days has to diversify."

"I'm sure that's the case. So tell me, Mrs. Norton—or should I call you Mother?" Okay, so that was wicked of me, but a gal can't be perfect, can she?

"Mrs. Norton is fine."

"Then Mrs. Norton it is. Tell me, dear, is this the first time you've been to Pennsylvania?"

"First time I've been west of the Mississippi."

"That would be east, dear—but never mind. Why did you pick Hernia?"

I can't say I preferred her snorts over her grunts. "Why, that ad in *Condornest*—the one I mentioned reading when I called for reservations. Father and I never had much opportunity to travel, on account our sons are too busy with their own farms to look after ours. But now that June Bug—that's Father's youngest brother—has been laid off from the Kmart, we finally have the time. June Bug is just itching to prove himself on Father's new combine, so bringing in the corn won't be a problem, and as for taking care of the hogs, well, Prissy Mae—that's June Bug's second wife, was raised on a hog farm over by Hutchinson. His first wife, Udmillia, lost her head in a threshing accident. Never could find it, until Horace Grubb—that's the man who bought the hay—opened a bale to feed his horses. Anyway, Prissy Mae was Miss Hog-Calling Champion of 1983. Both she and June Bug are like children to us. They didn't have any of their own, see, on account of Bug's sperm never learned to swim—"

I let go of the pinecone to clap both hands over my ears. "T.M.I.!"

Perhaps it was my outcry, or the fact that I let go of her hand, but Bibi Norton was suddenly at a loss for words. That's not to say that she was silent. She thrashed about in the bushes like a spastic sumo wrestler. If there had been any bears in the vicinity, they were now halfway to the Maryland border. I hoped they remembered to take their provisions with them.

"Mrs. Norton, dear, give me your hand."

Groping desperately, she managed to grab my person—in a very personal spot. Had it been Susannah, no doubt Bibi would have had at least one finger bitten off. I managed to remove Bibi's hand before we had no excuse *but* to progress to a first-name basis.

"So," I said, just as smoothly as if nothing untoward had happened, "what are your impressions of Pennsylvania?"

"It's very hilly," she said, taking the smooth cue from me. "And there are so many trees."

"Actually, these are mountains, not hills."

"They look like hills to me."

"But you're from Kansas," I said. "I have wrinkles in my sheets that are higher than any hills you have there. So, what do you think of our Amish?"

"We have Amish in Kansas too."

"Any named Hostetler, or Hochstetler, or any variation thereof?"

"I'm sure I wouldn't know. I don't go around asking their names."

I pretended to think for a minute. It was harder work than I remembered.

"You look somewhat like my cousin Delphia Hostetler," I said. And that wasn't a lie, given that they both had the general human shape—Bibi more so than Delphia, I'm loath to admit. "Wouldn't it be interesting if you and I were related?"

"But you're a Yoder."

"Prick a Yoder and a Hostetler bleeds. If you have any Amish ancestors—any at all, you and I are undoubtedly cousins."

"Well, that isn't the case." She didn't sound the least bit disappointed.

"How about your husband? I know Norton isn't one of our names, but maybe through his mama—or his paternal grandmother."

"I think the Nortons were English all the way back. But neither my husband nor I are interested in genealogy."

"That's a shame, because you never know when a little knowledge of your family history can reap dividends. Take the Hostetlers, for instance. There are family legends that mention a huge fortune, just waiting to be found."

"Ha, legends!" She lost her footing and thrashed a bit more. She was panting when she spoke again. "Every family has their legends, but I wouldn't bet the farm on any of them."

I was at my wit's end. "Are you sure you're not a Hostetler? You're just as stubborn as one."

"Miss Yoder, there is no need for you to be rude."

I gave up. "Fine. Then don't tell me anything about yourself. But you can't blame a hostess for showing interest in her guests. Why, even that nixnux Buzzy Porter was more forthcoming than you."

"Mr. Porter was no mere nixnux. That man had a mean streak a mile long. I couldn't stand him."

Shocked by what I'd just heard, I stopped dead in my tracks. Because I lack brake lights on my heinie, Bibi Norton rammed into me. They say the bigger they are, the harder they fall. Well, I may be tall, but I'm also rail thin, so I fell like a ton of feathers. I may even have floated to the ground, had not sturdy Bibi been determined to land on me.

"Ding dang," I cried as my probing proboscis penetrated the porous forest floor.

"You clumsy oaf," Bibi bellowed.

I didn't mind being called a name. At least now that I finally had a real suspect.

23

I thought of pinning Bibi to the ground while I interrogated her. But given her muscles, and my lack of them, physical restraint would be about as useless as it would be for me to enter the Miss America pageant. Instead, I decided to use the darkness that surrounded us to my advantage.

"What's that?" I gasped.

"I don't hear anything."

"It sounded an awful lot like a bear."

"Are they dangerous?" She sounded like she was already convinced this was the case.

Somewhere I read that grizzly bears—and we have no wild ones in Pennsylvania—are one of the most dangerous animals on the planet. Eastern black bears, on the other hand, would sooner run from you than attack. Of course there are always exceptions. I addressed the exception.

"Their claws could fillet you like a fresh salmon."

She pawed me with her pair of pinecones. She might be incapable of cutting open a fish with her nails, but I had no doubts she could mince meat.

"Come on, Miss Yoder, let's get out of here."

"In a minute, dear. Where did you learn the word nixnux?"

"I don't know what you mean."

"Just now, when I called Buzzy a nixnux—well, you knew exactly what I meant."

"It's an Amish word, isn't it?"

"Exactly!"

"So maybe I picked it up from our Kansas Amish."

"The ones whose names you don't even know? Look, Mrs. Norton—if that is indeed your name—we're going to stay right here, come hungry bears or high water, until you spill everything."

Thank heavens the woods are filled with obliging creatures who prefer to move around at night. The noise we heard next sounded like a large male deer crashing through the underbrush. Apparently they don't have many bounding bucks in the middle of Kansas because Bibi was all over me like gravy on Doc's mashed potatoes.

"All right," she screeched, louder than any owl I've heard. "I'll tell you every damn thing."

"Ah, ah, ah, no swearing, dear."

I doubt if she heard me, as fired up as she was to unburden herself of the truth. "My maiden name is Kauffman. Both my parents have Hostetler blood. And yes we have a family story about the Hochstetler treasure, but it isn't a legend—it's true!"

"And where is it supposed to be buried?"

"Buried?"

"Otherwise known as interment. Something that will not happen to either of us if that bear is really hungry."

"I know what the word means," she growled, "but the treasure isn't buried."

"It's not?"

"It's a city. You can't bury that."

"Ah, the Bern story."

"Zurich," she snapped. "Every last acre under that city is ours, and what's on top of it too. That includes the banks, you know."

I was tempted to throw my arms around her in the dark, but didn't want the gesture to be misconstrued. Here was a woman after my own heart—a woman who dared to think big. Who cared about Bern and its billions, when there was Zurich and its trillions to be had?

"Bibi, dear," I said, now that we were kissing cousins—just not in that way, "tell me something. Isn't there supposed to be a buried deed somewhere?"

An amateur might have thought hyenas had been imported to Hernia. "Haaaaa! The deed's not buried, it's in a Bible."

"It *is*?"

"The Hochstetler family Bible. The one that belonged to our Great-great-great-great-great-great-great-grandfather Jacob."

"Add a few greats for me, dear. I'm not quite as old as you."

"Anyway, by my calculations, that Bible is supposed to be here in Hernia."

"How do you know that?"

"I lied to you, Miss Yoder. I am into genealogy."

"No duh," I said softly.

"What was that?"

"Uh—I was just talking to myself. So, if the deed is in a Bible somewhere around here, what brings you into town just as we are about to unearth our time capsule?"

"Because the owner of that Bible is mentioned in a document that is buried in the time capsule."

Leave it to a relative to split hairs so thin they couldn't be seen on a bald man under a spotlight. "So you were after the time capsule."

Her anger emboldened her. Either that, or her eyes had adjusted to the dark. At any rate, she pushed away from me. She even bared her teeth—unless a dozen fireflies, in an unprecedented act of cooperation, had aligned themselves in two straight rows.

"I did not kill Mr. Porter. I'm not saying I'm sorry he died, but neither I, nor Chuck, had anything to do with his death. Our plan was simply to buy the document. Barring that, just to get a good look at it."

"You keep mentioning this document. What sort of document is this?"

"A list of the founding fathers."

"What?"

"My grandmother was there when they buried the time capsule. She was just a little girl, of course. She said that she remembers there being an argument about whose name should be on this list. There was one person everyone wanted to omit, because his descendants refused to let anyone have a peek at their Bible—the one in which the deed to the Hochstetler family fortune is recorded."

I must admit that this particular family legend sounded more plausible than most. The Bibles of my ancestors were filled with annotations of a personal nature: genealogies, birthdays, even a hand-written marriage contract in my grandmother's well-worn tome. Why not a deed? Indeed, it made a great deal of sense.

"How old did you say your grandmother was when the capsule was buried?"

"Let's see, she was born in ninety-four—*1894*."

"But then she would have been only ten. How could she remember something so grown up as a list of founding fathers?"

"Oh, she didn't remember that. Her mother filled her in on that later. She remembered the fistfight."

"You're kidding!"

"The fight was quite famous. I'm surprised you haven't heard of it. One man had his jaw broken—by the one who kept insisting his ancestor should be included. Anyway, we already know— thanks to our genealogical and historical research, who the all the founding fathers were. Now we just need to know who is *not* on the list. Then we can track down the Bible, buy it, and the fortune is ours." The last words were delivered as a sigh, the sort one might emit after a particularly satisfying dinner.

"Well, is that all?" I said. Yes, I was about to lie, and yes, I had a good reason. I also had enough of a conscience to recognize the impending error of my ways. "You should have just asked me for the list when you registered."

Her eyes glowed with greed. Either that, or there truly was a large wild animal in the vicinity.

"*You* have the list?"

"Of course." At least I had *a* list. Like any good Mennonite woman, I keep a pad and paper in the bathroom, in the little stand that holds my collection of *Reader's Digest*. Who knows when inspiration is going to strike or I might want to jot down a shopping list for my next trip to Mystery Lovers bookstore in Pittsburgh.

Her mission almost accomplished, Bibi wrenched herself free from my grip, ready to take on the monsters of the night if need be.

"Miss Yoder," she practically bellowed, "I'm sure we can make a deal."

In for a penny, in for a pound—of sin, I mean. Instead of answering her, I hauled myself to my feet and resumed my trek to the inn. Bibi crashed along behind me.

"So, do we have a deal?"

"Eighty, twenty," I said.

"Don't be ridiculous. I'm the one who did all the research. I'll give you ten percent."

"I'm afraid you have it wrong, dear. I'm offering you the twenty percent."

"What?" she barked.

"Look, I have the list. And I have all the same genealogy books. I probably don't even need them, because all the founders are buried in Settlers' Cemetery up on Stucky Ridge. All I have to do is peruse the graveyard. Their headstones are specially marked. Anyway, it shouldn't take me more than a few minutes."

"Fifty, fifty."

"Hmm, that would make us equal partners."

"Not quite," she snapped. "Father and I have to share our half."

"As well you should. The two of you are married, after all. One flesh that no man should put asunder, or whatever the vows say. So, do we have a deal?"

She mumbled her assent. Still, it was loud enough to send roosting birds shrieking from the treetops.

"Good. But now that we're partners—fifty, fifty—we have to be absolutely straight with each other."

"I did not kill Mr. Porter, if that's what you're getting at. And neither did Father."

"You sure? I mean, if you did—well, what's one paltry human life compared to that much moola?" I tried to sound casual, but probably didn't. In our tradition there is no justifiable reason to take another human life. Our ancestor's wife was scalped because he refused to defend her when the Delaware attacked on the evening of September 19, 1757. Of course, Bibi's blood had been diluted—at least I assumed it was. She was clearly not of the faith.

"Miss Yoder, if we had killed Mr. Porter, we would have the list now, wouldn't we? There would be no use for this conversation."

I finally believed her. And if Bibi Norton was innocent, so was her husband, Chuck. That left just six suspects, five if you counted the Littletons as a unit. No doubt all five were now back at the inn with my precious Alison, who had only a pig to protect her—assuming that Babester and his meddling mama had gone home like they were supposed to.

"Come on, dear," I cried. "There's no time to waste!"

I charged down the trail with all the intensity of an infuriated rhino. These beasts, I am told, have difficulty seeing. Well, I couldn't see the trail either, and although my feet are used to it, they are also used to operating under much calmer circumstances. I made a few wrong moves, smacked into the odd bush or tree, but emerged onto Hertlzer Road without losing Bibi and having suffered only minor cuts and scrapes. Trust me, my engine was still only getting revved when I burst through the kitchen door.

"What do you mean she refuses to leave? She doesn't have any choice. This is my house, and I want her out—at least for now."

Gabe squirmed. "Shhh. Ma's in the kitchen. She'll hear you."

"Hear, schmeer. The two of you are supposed to be out of here. As in gone home."

"We couldn't leave when we found out about the pig."

"The pig isn't any of her business."

"Magdalena, you don't understand."

"Then enlighten me." I had already ascertained that Alison was safe in my room, trading swine-raising tips over the phone with Donna Wylie.

Gabe grabbed me by a narrow shoulder and tried to steer me out of the dining room, where we'd been standing, and into the parlor. The guests, thank heavens, had all gone upstairs to dress for dinner. I allowed him to pull me as far as the foyer, where I keep my little office.

"You see, Magdalena, pigs aren't kosher."

"I know that, but your mother doesn't keep kosher. And it's not like I'm asking her to eat it."

"Yes, but it goes beyond that. A lot of foods aren't kosher, but ham and pork have become symbolic of what is forbidden. Historically our enemies have used pigs to torment us. In some cases Jews have been forced to either eat pork or be killed."

"That's horrible. But I still don't see how I can ask Alison to give up her pet. She'll see me as a double-crosser."

"You can't be sure of that. She's a very bright girl."

"But I can't risk it, either. She's just now beginning to trust me—she's been betrayed so many times. Gabe, I just can't do it."

His fingers slid off my shoulder. They felt like icicles.

"Does this mean you're choosing a pig over me?"

"That's not at all what I said!" Gabe had taken my words and twisted them like a pretzel. A master baker couldn't have done a better job. And some women have the nerve to think of men as simple-minded creatures.

"Shall I take that as a 'yes'?"

"What does letting Alison keep her pet have anything to do with choosing, or not choosing, you?"

"Because I already told Ma that she could live with us. And I can't go back on my word, either, Magdalena. She's my mother— my *flesh and blood* mother."

That did it. That hiked my hackles so high they scratched my armpits.

"Are you trying to tell me that Alison doesn't count because she's not my biological daughter?"

"Don't put words in my mouth. But as long as you've brought the subject up, whose biological daughter is she?"

"You know the answer to that. She's Aaron's—and his wife's. His first wife."

"Enough said."

I had plenty more to say, and believe me, I would have said every regrettable word, had not Ida Rosen burst into the room. Pausing only long enough to look up and see where I was, she came right at me, like an angry pit bull.

"So now she stabs me in the back." Her eyes were on me, but her words obviously directed to her son.

"Ma, I told you I'd take care of this."

"Stay out of this, Gabey."

Gabey?

"Ma!"

Ida was all eyes and no ears. She glared at me as she poked me in the sternum with a finger no longer than a Vienna sausage.

"I make supper for your little one, and you vant to repay me by letting her sell the leftovers to your guests?"

"Who squealed?" I squealed. "Alison?"

"Don't blame her, Miss Yoder. But she is in the kitchen now, putting my leftovers into serving bowls. Big money, she says, she'll get for my food."

"Well, you are a good cook."

The Babester didn't poke me with a finger, but he glared at me as well. "How could you take advantage of my mother like that?"

"She wasn't supposed to find out," I wailed. "What she didn't know wasn't supposed to hurt her."

Gabe put a strong tanned arm protectively around his mother's shoulders. "Come on, Ma. I'll take you home."

"But vhat about my food?"

"Forget about it. You can make some more at home."

"Vhat? And let this gonef keep it?"

I stamped a long, narrow foot. "Take that back, Mrs. Rosen!"

"You see, she vants I should take it back, Gabey."

"I meant the name. I keep the food—rather, Alison does. You made it for her."

"I take back nothing, and *I* keep the food."

"She has a legal right," Gabe said. "She paid for it."

"But she gave it away. Besides, you're a doctor, not a lawyer."

"Yes, a doctor," Ida said, shaking her head like a terrier with a rat in its mouth. "He could have had his pick of women back in the city. Good Jewish girls too."

"Instead he retired to the country to become a paperback writer. And now he's engaged to a simple Mennonite woman. That must really get to you, doesn't it, Mrs. Rosen?"

"Magdalena," Gabe said sharply. "That's my mother you're speaking to. Your future mother-in-law."

"Not anymore," I said. I tried to wrench the football-size sapphire and diamond ring off my finger, but it wouldn't budge. Oh well, it was the gesture that counted, right?

"Yes," Ida Rosen hissed. If she got any giddier, she was in danger of floating away, like a stubby helium-filled balloon.

Gabriel had nothing more to say. However, he did help his mother carry a small mountain of food back across Hertlzer Road. It took them three trips, and it wasn't until I heard the door slam for the fourth time that I realized the enormity of the situation. In the meantime, I sat in Granny Yoder's rocking chair in the parlor, my head in my hands, trying to look as dejected as possible (well, except for occasional peeks out the window). With any luck Granny Yoder's ghost would come to my rescue and knock sense into the Babester's head. Barring that, the Babester might stick his head into the room, and seeing me look so pitiful, send his mama packing and cleave to me, and me alone, like a proper husband was meant to do. At any rate, it wasn't until that final slam that I looked up to see Alison standing in the doorway.

"Mom," she said quietly, "was this all my fault?"

"Heavens no, dear. That woman and I—well, Gabe will see the light. Don't you worry."

"You mean you're really not breaking up with him?"

"Of course not, dear. He's breaking up with his mother—he

just doesn't realize it yet. Men sometimes need a little push, that's all."

"Yeah, men. Go figure." She sucked in her lower lip. "Mom, I hate ta tell ya this, but we got ourselves a worse problem now than guys."

I smiled. "And what would that be?"

"Well, I just came to tell you that some of the guests have started to pack."

"They *what*?"

"They claim you're trying ta starve them. That stuck-up old movie star says she's already got herself motel reservations somewhere else."

"But that's impossible. Every motel in Bedford is booked up."

"Yeah, but she's willing to go all the way over to Somerset. She's dragging those slaves of hers with her. Some of the others said they'd be going too."

I stamped a long narrow foot so hard that I left a permanent groove in the floor. The entire house shook. If I didn't do something about reigning in my temper, one of these days the roof was going to fall down around my head—a situation most likely not covered under my homeowner's insurance.

"We'll just see about that!" I roared. "Alison, call your auntie Susannah and tell her to get over to Freni's fast. Tell her she has my permission to drive like a bat out of—uh, a very hot cave. Have her tell Freni that the peasants are rebelling, and I need her help in the kitchen *now*."

"But Freni is really ticked at you, Mom. She quit, remember?"

"Details, dear. Tell Auntie Susannah to tell her that I apologize. That I'm down on my hands and knees begging."

"Cool. But why don't you call Auntie Susannah yourself."

"Because I'm going upstairs to put a stop to this nonsense. Guests checking out early, indeed!"

"Oh, Mom, can I watch? Please?"

"Sweetie, I'm not going to hit them or anything."

"I know, but ya do the best hollering in the whole wide world. If ya sold tickets, ya would be famous, ya know?"

I can't help it if my bony chest swelled with pride. My inflated thorax did not, of course, enhance my bosoms, but it did fill out my dress somewhat.

"Thank you, dear, for the compliment, but I'm not going to yell at them—well, I'm certainly not going to holler. Just the same, you go call your auntie Susannah and then you can come up and watch."

The girl moved like lightning. I did as well. Unfortunately I went straight upstairs like I said I would. A wise Magdalena, on the other hand, would have put her bony butt behind the steering wheel of her car and taken off for a week's R and R somewhere. Somewhere far away and really exotic, like Cincinnati, Ohio.

24

I rounded up all eight rats before they could jump ship and herded them into the parlor. If I were really a policewoman, and they were official suspects, I could simply have ordered them not to leave town. But I was only a pretend policewoman, and they were only pseudosuspects. My only power, as usual, lay in my lingua.

To my credit I didn't holler, but my frown muscles got such a workout that my forehead hurt as much as my hands. And with all that skin bunched above my eyes, there was hardly enough left on the lower half of my face to allow me to open my mouth. "You really don't want to book rooms in Somerset, dears," I grunted. "There's a tunnel between here and there. If it gets blocked—if there's an accident—well, it will take you forever to get to Hernia on the back roads. You'll miss out on some of the festivities to be sure."

"With all due respect," Capers cooed, "the odds are against an accident in the tunnel."

"Tell that to Mama and Papa," I snapped. But then, because she had not meant any disrespect and was really a rather pleasant woman, I had to force my frown lines into a smile. "Whatever you think you'll find in Somerset, I'm sure I can provide for you here."

"How about some decent food?"

I wanted to wipe young Stanley's smirk off his face—with a piece of sandpaper. Instead I forced the corners of my mouth into unnatural positions. No doubt I looked like a constipated fox.

"That issue is being addressed as we speak. Mrs. Hostetler will be here momentarily to fix you an authentic Pennsylvania Dutch meal."

"Cold cuts and salads?"

So frustrated was I, that I actually thought of ripping out my own tongue and lashing the arrogant youth with it. But, of course, in order to do that, I would have had to open my mouth a lot wider.

"It will be a full, hot meal. I promise."

Octavia Cabot-Dodge cleared her throat to speak—eight times in all. "Miss Yoder," she finally said, "it isn't just the food—or lack thereof—that we find unsatisfactory. Quite frankly, we are tired of your games."

"Games?" I had yet to insist we play a rousing game of Scrabble or a death-match tournament of Chinese checkers. When it comes to games, with the exception of face cards, we Mennonites are known to excel.

"This A.L.P.O. nonsense and whatnot. The very idea of charging more to do janitorial work. These games might work on some of your unfortunate guests, but we do not find them amusing."

My face burned with shame. "That's because you are all descendants of Jacob—or else married to one, which is almost the same thing. Real English guests wouldn't have minded one bit."

Terri Mukai's face glowed. I'm sure she was quite pleased to be included unequivocally in my ancestral clan.

"Yoder-san, may we speak privately?"

"In a minute, dear. Just as soon as we sort out this silly little matter."

"Bilking the public is hardly trivial," Bibi burbled.

"Yoder-san," Terri said softly, "in my country, now would be the time to be generous."

"*Generous?*"

"Perhaps a reduction in price." She whispered this time.

"Lower my prices?" I bellowed. You would have thought I was Bibi.

Fifteen eyes fixed on me. One of Stan's eyes remained on Terri. She was, after all, a rather attractive girl.

Buist Littleton is a very handsome man, except when he chooses to take sides against me. "The Wagon Wheel Lodge in Somerset," he drawled, "charges only fifty-nine ninety-nine for a double. And they have cable TV."

"Yes, but does that include meals?"

"Like your ridiculous fee does," Octavia Cabot-Dodge mumbled.

"It does in theory," I wailed. "I can't help it that my cook quits at the drop of a saucepan."

"I bet no one has ever been murdered at the Wagon Wheel Lodge," Augusta said.

Stan smirked again and held that look until I shot him a special look of my own—one that has been known to wither watermelons on a rainy day. "Mr. Porter was *not* murdered in this inn."

Chuck Norton, whom I almost thought of as an ally now that we'd chased pigs together, cocked his head. "But have there been other murders here?"

"No fair! The town is full of gossips, so what? I'll have you know that lots of people have survived their stays here."

"Just how many murders have there been?" And I thought I could count on Capers!

"Your prices," Terri said softly. To her credit, the girl was just trying to be helpful.

I threw up my hands in resignation. "Okay, there is no need for anyone to get their knickers in a knot—and believe you me, you all better be wearing some. I'll cut my rates by a third, and you won't have to pay for the privilege of cleaning your rooms."

"Ridiculous," someone snorted. Had there been a collection of horses present, I would have guessed it was the Clydesdale. Under the circumstances I was forced to conclude that it was the diva who was still not satisfied.

"All right," I conceded. "You get fifty percent off, but count yourselves lucky. A lot of people are happy to pay big bucks to stay in a place where there have been so many—uh, I mean, where there is so much ambience."

"Ha!" Bibi put her hands on her hips, which is a very un-

Mennonite gesture and was therefore a testament to her mixed blood. "Either you match the Wagon Wheel's rates—including meals and maid service, or we're all out of here." She turned to the others. "Right?"

They nodded in unison, even Terri. And I thought the Japanese were supposed to be polite.

"But I have no maid to service you! I can't possibly ask a seventy-five year old Amish woman to do all that *and* cook."

"Then do it yourself," Augusta retorted.

"*Moi?* But I'm the proprietress!"

"You look sturdy enough to me—maybe a little on the skinny side. We're only talking about normal, everyday housekeeping."

For a soul-threatening second I had a vision of me mopping the floor, or perhaps scrubbing toilets, with Augusta Miller's graying locks, her head still attached. I took a deep breath, begged the Good Lord for forgiveness, and tarried on along that narrow, re-strictive road of righteousness.

"I give up," I cried. "You have a deal. But you each have to sign a paper saying you'll never disclose these terms to anyone. If words gets out—" Too late I clamped a plate-size paw across the lips that had just sunk my own ship.

"Yoder-san," the Japanese Judas said, her voice still elegant and breathy, "perhaps you should let us stay for free. Otherwise there may be great temptation to—how does one say?—send you the dark mail."

"You mean blackmail, dear?"

"Yes. And Yoder-san, there is still the matter of my clothes."

"We're doing what we can to recover your luggage," I said, perhaps a bit too brusquely. "It is not my responsibility to reim-burse you."

"I'm hungry," Stan whined.

"Supper's coming right up, dear."

I fled the room before I found myself in a situation in which I was supposed to pay *them*. Forget the waivers; my inn's reputation would survive somehow. Sometimes it is better to settle than to fight for one's rights. Besides, I'd fix their wagons with my chuck.

I'm the first to admit that I'm a terrible cook. The only cook I ever knew whose food tasted worse than mine, died from eating her own grub. While my victuals are usually not lethal, they have been known to do permanent damage to unsuspecting taste buds.

Operation Gag was underway.

My scorched potato soup and rubbery grilled-cheese sandwiches would have done the trick nicely, had not Susannah taken me at my word. She must have driven a hundred miles an hour. Poor Freni was so shaken by her wild ride, that her knees buckled with every other step.

"Freni," I implored, "please sit for a minute and catch your breath."

"Ach, not if the English are revolting."

"I heard that," Bibi blared. The woman had the nerve to be eavesdropping on a private family conversation.

"Freni," I chuckled, "that wasn't such a nice thing to say, now was it?"

"Maybe. But that is what Susannah said."

My sister rolled her eyes. "I was just repeating Alison's message, sis."

I shook my head. "But what I said was—ah, yes. I said that the guests were rebelling, *not* revolting. Revolting has more than one meaning."

"English," Freni muttered, referring to the language that is not quite her mother tongue. "It has too many meanings, yah?"

"We'll discuss linguistics some other time, dear. Now, pop into the kitchen and work magic with those fingers of yours."

Her bottle-thick lenses magnified the horror in her eyes. "Magic? Magdalena, the Bible forbids us to practice this. It is a sin."

I sighed patiently. "I'm well aware of that. What I meant is that your fingers are capable of producing the best food in all of Bedford County."

She gazed with awe at her own stubby digits. "Yah? You think so?"

"Without a doubt." So perhaps it was a slight exaggeration. But what harm was there in that? The Bible also instructs us to encourage each other.

"These fingers," she murmured. "The best cook in the county—ach! Magdalena, you lead me into temptation."

"But you came willingly!"

"You people are weird," Bibi said. "No wonder my branch of the family moved West."

"Then keep moving," I said kindly, "like to your room or the parlor, so that our cooking whiz here can do her stuff."

Bibi's stomach must have overruled her tongue, because she actually cooperated. And while the meal Freni whipped up couldn't have compared favorably to one of Doc's worst creations, it was far better than anything I could have produced—even by accident.

Much to my amazement, all eight guests went to bed satisfied. The sound of their snores—audible even from the ground floor—confirmed that at least some of them had Hochstetler blood. If not diluted too much, the Hochstetler gene has the ability to induce such sound sleep, that more than a few of the clan have confessed that they are fearful of missing the Second Coming.

The Yoder gene, on the other hand, has the opposite effect. And by the way, this is the more dominant gene of the two. When they should be sleeping, Yoders tend to replay in their heads every conversation they'd had through throughout the day. A few of us, due to excessive inbreeding, are capable of recalling conversations that may, or may not, have taken place twenty years earlier.

Alas, I am one of the unfortunate who suffers from diarrhea of the mind. What sleep I might have gotten was robbed from me by a pig and a hog. The pig had hooves and squealed when I accidentally rolled over on him. The hog was my foster daughter who, thanks to her Hochstetler blood, was sound asleep the entire time and continuously wrested the covers from yours truly.

I gave up on dreamland just after four a.m. My plan was to try and grab a few winks on the love seat in the parlor. What I did not plan on was an encounter with Grandma Yoder. After all, the woman died when I was twelve.

But sure enough, there she was, sitting in a hardback chair, looking every bit as warm and welcoming as the statues on Mount Rushmore—which is about twice as friendly as she was in life. I know, you probably don't believe in ghosts. If, however, the vision was just the product of a fertile imagination, then my gray cells could make the entire Sahara desert bloom. That's how real she seemed to me.

"Sit down, Magdalena," she snapped. "I don't want to have to look up at you."

"I prefer to stand, Grandma."

"Then stand straight, with your shoulders back. But don't stick your chest out too much, because that would be immodest—well, I guess not in your case."

"Grandma!"

"It's true, child. You've got the Yoder mind, but not the Yoder bosoms. Must be that Lehman blood that found its way into your mother's side of the family. I told your father he should have married Rebecca Miller instead. Good bone structure, that girl had."

"There was nothing wrong with Mama."

"I didn't come to talk about your mama, child."

"Then what do you want, Grandma? I brush my teeth three times a day, just like you taught me, and I say my prayers every night before I go to bed."

"Not tonight, you didn't."

"That's because the English were revolting. Just ask Freni."

"Freni doesn't need me, child. You do."

"I'm not a child anymore, Grandma. In fact, I'm about to get married."

"Indeed you are. And for the second time, I might add."

"But I didn't know Aaron was married. Besides, since it wasn't legal, it doesn't count."

"Are you telling me it's all right to sleep with a man who isn't your husband? Why, Magdalena, soon you'll be telling me it's okay to dance."

"I never said that, Grandma!"

"Good, because it isn't, you know. There's a special place in You-Know-Where for folks who dance." Grandma sighed, and she sounded like wind blowing through the Allegheny tunnel. "There used to be lots of room in You-Know-Where. Now I hear it's getting filled up with Presbyterians."

"Are you saying that Hell is filled with—"

"Heavens, no, child. I'm talking about Mt. Olive Retirement Home. Used to be almost all shimmying Methodists and a few hard-drinking Baptists, but now the predestination crowd is taking over."

It was my turn to sigh. "Grandma, can we get to the point? Why are you here? I mean, don't you have a harp lesson or something you should be attending?"

"Been there, done that. Graduated from harp school with an A+ average. I don't start Cloud Making 101 until next week. We have plenty of time to chat."

Since Grandma Yoder never had a funny bone in her body—I think she even lacked a humerus—she was dead serious about the classes. But she still hadn't answered my question.

"What, specifically, is it that you want to lecture me about?"

"It's that Jewish man."

"Grandma, don't even start. Jesus was a Jew, you know."

"I know that very well. And what I've come to tell you is that you should marry this one. Don't let his mother stand in the way."

"But she runs his life. If I marry Gabriel, she'll not only run my life too—she'll ruin it."

"And if you don't marry him, will she ruin it then?"

"So what are you saying? I should make Alison give away the pig?"

"Don't worry, child. She'll give it away on own her account. Pigs and teenage girls weren't meant to live together."

"But, Grandma, that woman is domineering."

"So are you, child. Has no one ever told you that?"

"Of course not. True, I may have some strong opinions, but that's because I know I'm right. Take that time when Gabriel insisted that—"

But Grandma had vanished. Ghosts do that, you know. They appear and disappear at the most inconvenient times, and usually when I have a lot on my mind. Mama's ghost does that too. It's like they have a conspiracy to meddle in my personal affairs.

After waiting politely a few minutes, just to make sure Grandma wasn't roaming around the rest of the inn and planning to return, I curled up on the love seat. But sleep was not forthcoming, and after about an hour I gave up on this elixir altogether, dressed, and went in search of the one thing that was sure to see me through the travails of the coming day.

25

Grill-Broiled Green Tomatoes

4 medium or 2 large green
   tomatoes
Salt
2 tablespoons bacon drippings or
   extra-virgin olive oil

Whole black pepper in a pepper
   mill

Prepare a grill with hardwood coals and light them, or position a rack about 5 inches from the heat source and preheat the oven broiler for at least 15 minutes before you are ready to cook the tomatoes. Cut the tomatoes in half crosswise, lightly sprinkle the cut side with salt, and invert them in a colander set over the sink. Drain them for 30 minutes.

When the coals are ready or the broiler is very hot, wipe the cut side of the tomatoes dry. Lightly brush them with the drippings or oil, then sprinkle them with several generous grindings of pepper. (If you are using the oven broiler, skip to step 3.) Put tomatoes on the grill cut side down and grill until they are lightly browned, about 6 to 8 minutes. Lightly brush them with more drippings or oil, turn them, and continue grilling until the tomatoes are tender, about 8 minutes more.

If you are using the oven broiler, put the tomatoes cut side up into a broiling pan fitted with a rack. Position the rack under the broiler within 6 inches of the heat source and place the tomatoes on it. Broil until the cut side is nicely browned, about 8 minutes. Turn them carefully, brush lightly with more drippings or oil, and continue broiling until the tomatoes are tender, about 8 minutes more.

SERVES 4

26

Doc opened the door even before I knocked. I have hard knuckles and he claims he's too old to refinish wood.

"Blue heard you again," he said, reading my mind. "I'm afraid I just got up myself, but if you don't mind watching, I'll make you a proper breakfast. If you're in a real hurry, there's a box of cereal somewhere around here, if you want to help me find it. Was Belinda's."

Since Belinda was Doc's wife, and she's been dead for over twenty years, I elected to wait. Besides, comfort food was what I'd come for.

Doc's idea of comfort that morning was broiled grapefruit halves oozing with melted brown sugar, Spanish omelets, genuine English-style kippers, lemon zest scones, and a large pot of home-made hot chocolate. Ignoring my protestations, he piled the latter high with fresh whipped cream, sprinkled with nutmeg.

Ever the gentleman, Doc waited until I was satiated before getting down to what he considered business. "So, do we have a dinner date every Saturday night until Christmas?"

"They're just dinners, not dates!"

"Aha! So I was right. Well, how many were there?"

"Too many. Even the Japanese girl, for crying out loud. And, Doc, if I keep my word, Gabriel is going to be really sore with me. It's bad enough the way things are."

"Problems in paradise?"

"*Problem*. In short, it's Ida, his mother." Under normal circumstances I would have laughed at my little joke.

"Ah, the woman you want me to date. Thanks to you, I took a second look at her. She's a stunner, all right."

"I beg your pardon?"

"A fine-looking woman."

"Very funny, Doc. Tell me another."

"I mean it." His expression told me that he did.

"But she'd not your type!" An honest Magdalena would share that she was experiencing bizarre feelings of jealously. But Doc was an eighty-six-year-old man for pete's sake. And I still had a shot at the hunky Gabe. What was there to be jealous of?

Doc grinned. "But you're exactly the same. Grant it, you don't look alike, but when you get to be my age it's what's inside a woman that stokes the fire inside a man's furnace. Sure, we still get turned on by the usual things—"

"No details, please!"

His grin widened. "But what you might think is a plain woman when you're young, can look mighty fine a few decades later if she's got that certain spark."

I knew he meant me. But as much as I love to talk about myself, I had to steer the conversation back to Ida. "Doc, you wouldn't mind it if I fixed you up with Mrs. Rosen?"

He didn't hesitate a second. "I'd like that mighty fine."

"But if I do, you have to let me out of my promise to have dinner with you every Saturday night."

Doc nodded vigorously.

"You don't have to agree so quickly."

Doc stopped nodding, but his eyes glittered. "Face it, Magdalena, you really wouldn't want an old codger like me. So, are you really going to fix me up with the Rosen woman?"

"If you let me have another scone and a little more hot chocolate. I'm supposed to meet Melvin Stoltzfus in a few minutes for some police work. We're hiking out to the base of Lovers' Leap. There's a cave there that might be important to the investigation. You ever been there, Doc?"

"Never at the bottom of the leap, only at the top," he said with a twinkle in his eye. "Been on top many times."

"At any rate, this may be my last meal."

"Then take a few scones with you. And a thermos full of chocolate."

"Thanks, Doc. I will."

"How long do you think you'll be?"

"I don't know. That depends on what we find. Shouldn't take us more than two hours, I'd guess."

"Stoltzfus is a nutcase. If I don't hear from you by noon, Blue and I are coming in after you. Where did you say this trail is?"

"I didn't. But it's behind the Block House. You know, the place with a zillion cats."

"Dang people should have been thrown in jail, letting them cats multiply like that. You know, Magdalena, I would have spayed and neutered them for free, but my eyesight is not what it used to be." He winked. "Except for a pretty woman."

I chose to interpret the wink as a compliment directed at me. Or it could have been merely a tick generated by his deteriorating eyesight. Whatever the reason, it was a high note on which to leave.

Melvin, as usual, was a low note. "Where have you been, Yoder?"

I glanced at my watch. "It's seven o'clock on the dot."

"It's eight, Yoder. I've been waiting here for half an hour. I was about to come and get you."

I grabbed his spindly wrist. "Melvin, *dear*, Mickey's thumb is on the seven. Pay no attention to the rest of that big fat glove. And if you've been waiting here for half an hour, then by your own cockeyed means of telling time, you're the one who is late."

Melvin can change subjects faster than a teenager. "Your sister is driving me crazy," he said, apropos of nothing.

"You mean this is the first time?"

"She can't decide what to wear to my inauguration."

We started into the woods. "I thought she had decided on fifteen feet of filmy fuchsia fabric. Isn't that what she always wears to any important occasion?"

"Until you talked her out of it. 'Be more conservative,' you said."

"Yes, and I suggested a nice opaque polyester."

"Exactly. But then she got to thinking—"

"Another first?" I know, that wasn't nice. And I owed Susannah, especially after what she did for me last night. But sometimes I just can't stop this tart tongue of mine.

"No, she's thought several times before this," Melvin said. *He* was dead serious, and there was admiration in his voice. "Anyway, she finally decided that if the material has to be opaque, she may as well wear body paint instead."

"Excuse me?"

"Are you hard of hearing, Yoder? I said paint."

"I know what you said, but it didn't make any sense. What do you mean by 'instead'?"

"You serious?"

"As serious as a hernia at a weight-lifters competition." I wasn't speaking from personal experience, mind you. This just seemed like a good metaphor.

Melvin thrashed on ahead, delighted to be in the position of enlightening me. "It's kind of a new fad. We get a lot of these pictures over the Internet. Anyway, instead of wearing real clothes, the person wears clothes that are painted on. You know, like a tuxedo, or a swim suit, or whatever."

"But over their sturdy Christian underwear, yes?"

"Over nothing, Yoder. Zip, zilch, nada."

"You mean they're naked?"

"If you don't count the paint."

The shock of his words was too much for me. Both knees buckled just as surely as if someone had punched them from behind, and I collapsed onto a tangle of blackberry brambles. The second flesh met thorns, I was up again, but my head was spinning like it does when I step off the Tilt-A-Whirl at the county fair. I sat down a few more times—once on Melvin, I believe. Finally I got to the point where I could lean against the fissured bark of a walnut tree while I tried to put a positive spin on things.

"But you said she's still deciding, right?"

"She's positive about the paint job. What she's trying to decide on is a pink outfit, or a yellow one. She's going to call it a gown designed by Sherwin Williams. "

I took several deep cleansing breaths. There was no need to get my knickers in a knot over this nonsense. Melvin had as much chance of becoming President as I did at winning the International Patience Championships. And besides, there was always my not-so-secret weapon.

"Tell Susannah that if she wears anything *but* fifteen feet of filmy fuchsia, I'm cutting off her credit line at the Material Girl over in Bedford. I'll be calling all the paint stores too. If I have to, I'll cut off her allowance altogether."

"Gee, thanks, Yoder. I owe you one."

Melvin meant it. Between that point and the base of Lovers' Leap, he led the way. No blackberry bush was too mean for my protector, no sycamore sapling too savage. The stalwart Stoltzfus was unflappable—well, he may have flapped a few times, but after all, mantises do have wings.

Once we got to the cave, however, Melvin turned into Milquetoast. "Yoder, you have a flashlight. You look in there first."

"You have a flashlight too, dear. I think you should have the honor."

"Ladies first, Yoder."

"All right. All right." Fear, I have discovered, can make me a mite irritable.

I got down on all fours, then arching my behind like a puppy begging to play, I lowered my front half until I was leaning on my elbows.

"You see anything?" Melvin demanded.

"I haven't turned on my light," I snapped. "And if you even think of looking up my skirt—"

"Gag me with a spoon, Yoder. I'd rather rip out my own fingernails."

"Which of these two procedures would you prefer, dear?"

"Very funny, Yoder. Now turn on the light and tell me what you see."

I pushed the switch, but my brain lagged behind the beam of light. It took me forever to focus on what lay in a far corner of the cavern. In fact, I had to crawl all the way in to make sure that my peepers weren't lying to me. Alas, they weren't.

27

"It's Buzzy Porter," I said weakly. I'd backed out of the entrance and was sitting in the damp leaves. Who cared if bugs crawled up my skirt? In the grand scheme of things, what did that matter? They'd soon be crawling in and out of Buzzy until he returned to dust. At least I was assured of my salvation. As for Buzzy, I had no idea where he stood on that issue. For all I knew, by the time the worms played pinochle on his snout, his soul would be dancing with the Devil.

"Are you sure?"

"Don't be such a wuss, and look for yourself."

"I'm not a wuss. I need to stay out here and protect you."

"Then call for backup."

"Zelda?"

"No, Santa and his reindeer. Of course, Zelda. Tell her to get the Amstutz brothers out here. They can carry Mr. Porter out. Heaven knows, they've carried enough deer out of these woods. And, of course, call the hospital and get that ambulance out to the Block House lickety-split."

"Don't be ridiculous, Yoder. The man is dead. He's not going anywhere."

"Don't be so sure. He's already done a fair amount of traveling in this condition. And this time have him taken to the county morgue."

"What about the sheriff?"

"What about him?"

"Yoder, if the sheriff gets involved—well, you know."

It is possible to be just too tired, too frazzled, to care anymore about the consequences of one's words. Trust me, I've been to that breaking point more than once. I think '83 and '96 were also watermark years.

"Enough about this stupid election, Melvin. You're never going to win, so put aside your pride and do your job for a change."

I could have knocked the Mantis over with one of the dead leaves I was sitting on. His mandibles moved mutely, while his entomological brain searched for words—any words.

Sadly, I didn't have the patience to wait. "Face it, Melvin, there's no grain in your silo."

"Huh? I don't have a silo. But Mama does, and it's plenty full."

"Let me try again," I said kindly. "Your antenna doesn't pick up all the channels."

"That's because we have cable."

"Touché. Then let me put it this way, your belt doesn't go through all the loops."

"Yes, it does. Susannah looped it for me."

I was running out of analogies. "Your dogs aren't all on the same leash!"

He shook his head in pity. "We've only got the one, Yoder. And you know Susannah carries it around in her bra. As soon as the Amstutz brothers get here, have somebody drive you into Hernia so you can see a shrink. Personally, I recommend Dr. Frawd."

To my credit, I kept my cool. "For your information, it's Freud, not Frawd, and he's been dead for well over sixty years."

"Don't be an idiot. I see Dr. George Frawd every week."

That was jaw-dropping news, but I tried not to let even my teeth show. The Mantis in therapy? Perhaps there was hope for the world. But poor Dr. Frawd. I would definitely put him on my prayer list.

"Melvin, allow me to be as straightforward as possible. Nobody's going to vote for you—except maybe Susannah."

"Yoder, you're nuts, you know that?"

I saw that there was no point in continuing the conversation. What would Jesus do? I wondered. It seemed like he was forever breaking bread and passing it around. I didn't have any bread with me, of course, but I did have Doc's scones. And hot chocolate.

"Melvin, are you hungry?"

"Starved, Yoder. We ate all the cornflakes last night for supper. But what's it to you?"

Perhaps it sounds callous, eating and drinking, when Buzzy Porter lay moldering in a cave just feet away, but that's what we did. For the record, that was the first time I ever felt close to my bothersome brother-in-law.

Sheriff Hobson is a kind and competent man. He took over with grace and skill that amazed me. Melvin remained officially in charge of the case, but from now it would be the sheriff and his deputies that would do the actual work—the detecting if you would. Melvin would still get the credit when the case was solved. If there never was a resolution, my nemesis could blame it on the county. If not exactly a win-win situation, he certainly had nothing to lose.

Having turned the matter into Hobson's hands, I headed straight for the PennDutch and Big Bertha. She's my one vice, now that I have given up sitting on my Kenmore. Big Bertha—that's her catalog name—is a 125 gallon, 30 jet-spray, whirlpool bathtub.

I know, a lot of people prefer showers, and 125 gallons is a lot to waste on a single bath, but I think the Good Lord wouldn't have allowed such a luxury to exist if he didn't approve of it. After all, this particular tub is practically deep enough for one to be baptized in—although we Mennonites prefer the more sedate method of "pouring."

I have only recently acquired this tub, and I had to send all the way to Sin City for it. Fortunately, the Philadelphia vendor was skilled in remodeling, because we had to rip out one of the walls to get the tub in. Susannah says it's big enough for six people—and not for a religious occasion either. Only a Presbyterian would think of such a thing.

At any rate, much to my relief, Alison was busy outside playing with her pig, Freni was in the kitchen trying to decide if broccoli was a dairy product since she normally serves it with a cheese sauce, and the guests had all gone to the Blough farm to observe the hay-baling contest. At least for the moment, I was deliciously alone.

When I slipped into the swirling bubbles late that morning, it felt so good it had to be a sin. I turned the bathroom radio to a gospel channel, just to keep Big Bertha from giving me impure thoughts. As far as I'm concerned, the streets of Heaven don't need to be paved in gold, just as long as my suite contains a Big Bertha tub. And just for the record, it took only half the jets to make me feel this way.

Who knows how long my bliss would have lasted, had it not been for a hiss.

"Psst, Magdalena, are you decent?"

"What?" I jerked my sleepy head out of the suds.

"Ach, it's that Rosen woman," Freni said.

I turned off the radio and the jet sprays. "What about her?"

"She bothers me again. 'Make it this way,' she says. 'Make it that.' Do you want that I should quit, Magdalena?"

I sat ramrod straight. Thank heavens the tub was deep enough, and there were still enough bubbles, that my bosoms, such as they are, remained covered.

"Of course I don't want you to quit! I never want you to quit. Quitting is always your idea."

"Then you must make her leave. Magdalena, this woman is a horn in my side."

Freni learned Pennsylvania Dutch before she learned English, and her idioms sometimes need clarification. It is possible she meant that Ida Rosen was a thorn in her side, *or* she could have meant that Gabe's mother was goring her—metaphorically, of course. Either way, my kinswoman cook was not a happy camper.

"Give me a minute to get dressed, dear. Then I'll tell that buttinsky to get her buttocks back across Hertlzer Road."

"Ach!" By the gleam emanating from behind her thick lenses, Freni was both horrified and delighted by my strong language. "Yah, you tell her."

"Tell me vhat?"

I looked across the vast expanse of the tub, where my eyes locked on to those of Ida Rosen. Our peepers were on the same level.

"What on earth are *you* doing in my bathroom?" I demanded.

"Making sure she doesn't tell any lies."

"Ach, I do not lie!"

"Ladies!" I screamed. "Out, out, out!"

"I go nowhere until you tell me vhat you vere going to say."

"Yah, I stay too. Maybe she tells lies about me."

The two stout women glared at each other. Surely they were sisters under the skin. Put Freni's glasses on Ida, smear Ida's pink lipstick on Freni's pouting lips, and who could tell the difference? And both were equally guilty of violating the sanctity of my bath.

For a few very wicked seconds I fantasized about jumping out of the tub and throwing both uninvited guests in. I might even have done so, had I not remembered that Freni couldn't swim. And Big Bertha had a deep end. Also, I had no clue about Ida's aquatic skills. Although both women were blessed with natural flotation devices, if they found themselves floating on their stomachs, they might well choke to death on lavender-scented bubbles.

"Okay, ladies," I said, "stay. But at your own risk. I may get out of this tub at any minute, and believe me, it's not a pretty sight."

"Yah, I know. I helped raise you, remember?"

"So, vhat do I care either? You see one naked lady, you see them all."

"Enough! Okay, Mrs. Rosen, I told Freni I was going to tell you to stay away from the PennDutch."

"The buttocks," Freni hissed. "Tell her about the buttocks."

"Vhat about my buttocks? Yours are such a pretty sight?"

"Ach!"

"Just that you should keep them home where they belong," I

hastened to explain. "I mean, what happens over here is really not your business."

"My Gabriel is my business, and if he changes his mind and marries you—oy, the heartache vill be too much."

"Marries me? Gabe and I aren't even speaking now—thanks to you. Besides, even if we do work things out, you wouldn't be losing a son, Mrs. Rosen. You'd be gaining a daughter. *And*," I added, playing my trump card, "you could be gaining a boyfriend—well, a man friend."

Both elderly women snapped to attention. Surely they were once conjoined twins, separated at birth. Amish, Jewish, what did it matter? Both were descended from Eve and that apple-eating husband of hers.

"A man friend?" they said in unison.

"I happen to know that Doc Shafor wants to ask you out."

If Ida's beam was brighter it was only because she didn't wear glasses. "A doctor? Is he Jewish?"

"A chunk," Freni said, and licked her lips wistfully. A sin for a happily married woman, if you ask me.

"That's hunk, dear. And yes, he is a doctor of sorts—he's a genuine veterinarian. As for his religion, does it really matter? It's not like you two would ever raise a family together."

"Vhat does he look like?"

"A real woman-killer," Freni said. She licked her lips again.

"She means a lady-killer."

"So he's a looker?"

I don't find Doc physically attractive, but I know plenty of women who do. "That's the general consensus. Anyway, he wants to ask you out. Says he's had his eye on you for quite some time now."

"Vell then"—Ida patted her hair, as if it were possible that a strand had broken loose from the lacquered helmet—"perhaps I say yes."

"Ach!" Freni cried in distress, then clamped a stubby hand over a mouth that had betrayed her.

Ida Rosen smiled victoriously. Dating Doc was one thing that she could certainly do better than Freni. That smile, however, was directed at me.

"You see, Magdalena, how it pays to keep yourself up?"

"I think it's the aerosol spray, dear." Trust me, what Botox can't achieve, enough hair spray usually does. I see it in my guests all the time.

"Vhat is that supposed to mean?"

I answered her question with one of my own. "What time would you like Doc to pick you up Saturday night?"

"Seven thirty," she said without a moment's hesitation. "Tell him to make the dinner reservation for eight. And I do not like to be late."

"Uh—you'll probably be eating in."

"You mean he vants that I should cook for him?" She didn't sound the least put off by the idea.

"I think it's the other way around."

Ida recoiled—well, as much as it is possible for a woman of her stature to do so. "A man who cooks?"

"Not just cooks, dear. He lives to cook. What's more, he savors every bite he eats."

A fuming Freni flapped her arms futilely; she was never going to achieve liftoff. "Ach," she squawked, "a sin!"

Ida did a little victory dance of a sort. She resembled a drunken chicken—not that I've seen very many of those, mind you. She too would never be airborne by her own power.

"Is it a sin to enjoy good food?"

"Like you should know," Freni said. These were strong words for a pious Amish woman.

Ida countered with even stronger words, but they came out in Yiddish. Freni must have understood them, because she lobbed them right back in Pennsylvania Dutch. Although separated by centuries of linguistic changes, both languages are based on German and bear similarities, enough at least to cause even further misunderstandings.

"Take it out in the hallway, will you, dears?"

They ignored me.

I stood up in the tub. "Get out," I bellowed in a voice worthy of Bibi Norton.

They stared at me for a second, and then turned as one. It wasn't a silent departure by any means. With every step the voices grew louder. Not that it mattered.

I turned the gospel music back on, even before getting out of the tub and locking the door. Then I turned on the jets. All *thirty* of them.

Refreshed and reattired, I wandered downstairs to see how lunch preparations were coming. Freni had wanted to make a pork roast, but I'd made her promise to hold off on hog until our little piggy went to market—so to speak. Instead, my stalwart cook made roast chicken and dressing.

"The hens are a little tough, yah? But I soak them in Vermont, so they get tender like pullets."

"Vermont?"

"Yah. It is a special recipe."

"It sounds special, indeed—given that Vermont is hundreds of miles away. How did you manage to pull that one off, and how does soaking them in another state make them tender?" I wasn't being facetious. The wonders of cooking—even Freni's—are beyond my ken.

"Ach, Magdalena, you talk such nonsense." She opened a cabinet, withdrew a tall bottle, and thrust it into my hands. "*This* is Vermont."

I reeled in shock. "That says vermouth, not Vermont!"

"But it also good for soaking chicken, yah? Marionette, they call it."

"That's *marinade*, dear. And vermouth is anything but a state. It's a kind of—uh . . ." I bit my tongue. What was the point in telling a seventy-six-year-old Amish woman that she was cooking with alcohol? The shock could kill someone her age. Did I want to have her death on my hands as well? Besides, wasn't vermouth a kind of wine? And Jesus turned water into wine at the wedding in

Cana, didn't He? Perhaps He turned it into vermouth. Except that when Reverend Schrock preaches on that story he is always careful to add that the translation must be in error, and that in his opinion the beverage served at that biblical wedding was really grape juice.

Freni was waiting for my approval. "It smells good, yah?"

"Delicious. Where did you get the vermouth?"

"That nice English woman, the one who speaks slowly. She gives me the recipe. And she brings me the bottle from a special store in Bedford."

I am certainly no expert on spirits. Before I lectured Freni on using ingredients supplied by guests, I owed it to the both of us to sample the contents of this bottle and determine if indeed it was prohibited by my faith. Yes, I know, there was a label on the bottle, but one can't trust everything one reads, you know. Why, just get on the Internet if you don't believe me; half the stuff on there is rubbish. Besides, the print on that label was so small I risked going cross-eyed, which would not be a flattering look for me, given my prominent proboscis.

Therefore, being ever the responsible daughter my pious parents raised, I filled a small glass with the amber liquid. It certainly smelled sweet and innocuous. Then, breathing a prayer for forgiveness, lest it turn out to be forbidden, I sampled the stuff.

Sweet, definitely. Perhaps a woody undertone—not that I chew on much wood, mind you. It didn't taste like I imagined wine to taste. But then how was I to know? And if it really was wine, I had better memorize that taste, so as not to inadvertently imbibe on some other occasion. It was practically my Christian duty to sample it again.

Due to the fact that I am an earnest woman, who really does try to do the right thing, I sometimes find it hard to make decisions. It was because I was trying to be fair that I drank the entire glass. In the end I concluded that the jury would remain out until I had the time, and was feeling well enough, for further sampling.

You see, the hot bath with the thirty jets had left me feeling a bit light-headed. In fact, I felt a definite need for fresh air.

"Hairy on," I said to Freni. "I mean, carry on. I'm going outside for a minute."

"Magdalena, are you all right?"

"I'm fine as frog chair, dear. Oops, make that frog hair. Although that expression has never made sense to me, since frogs don't have any. Hair—that is. Or chairs either, I presume." I giggled pleasantly. "At any rate, do what you do best."

Freni flushed. "Ach! What I do at home, with my Mose, is not your business."

"Cook," I cried gaily. "I was talking about cooking. Although, after all these years of marriage, if you and Mose are still doing the mattress mambo, then more power to you. Just remember—no dancing!" I chortled at my own wit.

"Dancing!"

"Yes, dancing, the worst of all sins." Feeling suddenly frisky, I grabbed a broom from the corner and pretended to dance with it. Having never seen the shameful act, I had no idea how to imitate it. But I shrugged my shoulders and waggled my hips in what I imagined to be lascivious gyrations.

"Ach!" Freni fled into the dining room. Who knew she could be so sensitive?

"It was only with a broom," I called after her. "It doesn't count. It's not like it was a vacuum cleaner."

By then I really did need fresh air. I dropped the broom and waltzed to the back door. Flinging it open, I shimmied into the sunshine.

"Woo-hoo, look at me, I'm dancing," I called to the world at large. And why not? Since everyone always thought the worst about me, why not enjoy the sins about which I had no doubt already been accused? Surely, the sharp-tongued Schrock had accused me of doing the hokeypokey before. And if not—well, this was equal to any two other sins on her list.

Alas, the world was not paying attention. While I shimmied and shook, Hernia was too busy watching sweaty farmers bale hay. Even Alison and her pig were too engrossed playing in a nearby field to notice me.

"This is your last chance!" I shouted to the sparrows in the trees. "If you want to see me shake my booty, you better look now."

That language, by the way, was courtesy of Susannah. To me a booty has always been nothing more than an infant's foot covering.

"And a might fine booty it is," one of the sparrows said in a surprisingly deep voice.

"Why, thank you—although it is a little on the skinny side, don't you think?"

"I like it just the way it is."

I whirled. That was certainly no sparrow. Not with that vaguely East Coast accent.

28

"Gabe!" My beloved stood not six feet away, a moon-size grin on his face.

"Hi, babe. Don't tell me you didn't know I was here."

"I had no idea! How long have you been standing there?"

"Long enough to see you strut your stuff. And you told me you didn't dance."

"I don't." The vermouth-induced feeling of liberation was now a distant memory. "This was the first time—and my last."

Gabe planted a long, lingering kiss on my lips. This is what Susannah calls getting to first base. I allow it because we are engaged. I don't know exactly what getting to second and third base entail, but I can guarantee that my fiancé is going to keep his bat in the dugout until after we're married.

"Hey," he said, finally pulling back, "I thought you were a teetotaler."

"I am. Totally tea!" What possible harm could one more little lie do? It was basically the truth.

Gabe winked. "Tastes a little bit like you've been hitting the sauce as well."

"Marionette sauce," I explained quickly. "I mean marinade. Freni is roasting some old hens."

"What's in this marinade?"

"Well, I'm not really sure—okay, so maybe there's a little vermouth."

"Was it the sauce you sampled, or did you chug it straight from the bottle?"

"I didn't chug anything! I merely sipped. And does it matter? Because I'm never doing that again either. From now on, I'm flying straight as an arrow. Not that I'm flying now, mind you. Not high like a kite or anything. Definitely not high at all. Anyway, I promise never to do those things again."

His brown eyes twinkled. "Then that will be a shame. I was getting to like your wild side."

"But I can be wild in other ways. You should see me play Florida golf." I was referring to a Mennonite card game that is said to have originated in Sarasota, Florida, a long-time watering hole of Mennonite and Amish retirees. This game, by the way, uses Skip-Bo cards, and not the sinful face cards found in regular decks.

"I'd love to," Gabe said. His face became serious for a moment. "What's this I hear about you fixing Ma up on a date?"

"He's one of Hernia's most respected citizens," I hastened to explain. There was no need to mention Doc's reputation as a womanizer. If Ida Rosen was lucky, she'd find that out soon enough.

Gabe gave me a peck on the forehead. Believe me, not many men are tall enough to do that.

"My tone was supposed to be kidding. I think it's a wonderful idea."

"You do?"

"Absolutely. Mags, hon, I know how controlling she can be. Don't think I like it, because I don't. I put up with it because—well, I don't want to be disrespectful. And since Pa died, she doesn't have anyone else to order around."

"How about your sisters in New York?"

"Sarah and Dafna won't listen to a word Ma says. Never have. Ma needs someone to push around."

"Oops. I think Doc may be a pusher himself. He's definitely not a pushover."

"All the better. Neither was Pa. Ma likes to push just so hard and then get it right back at her. The trouble is, unlike my sisters, I go the opposite direction. Conflict avoidance, I guess you'd call it."

Too bad. Truth be told, I can be a wee bit pushy myself—well, not exactly pushy, but I do have strong opinions. That's what one can expect from someone who is generally right about things. It's not my fault I'm well informed.

"Gabe, you might not have noticed, but—"

"You're the pushiest woman, besides Ma, in Bedford County?"

"Hey, no fair! What about Lodema Schrock?"

"She's not pushy, she's merely obnoxious. Don't get me wrong, hon. I don't like it in Ma—too much history—but in you it's charming."

"It is?"

"You bet. Now, what the heck are you doing over there by the barn? Putting in a swimming pool?"

His words made no sense. Hernians don't build swimming pools. Our summers aren't long enough or hot enough to justify the expense. Besides, with a plethora of farm ponds and creeks about, why bother?

"Of course I'm not building a pool."

"Then why all the digging?"

I looked past Gabe's shoulder to the east corner of the barn. To the left, where yesterday there had been nothing but a low, decomposing blanket of *haufa mischt,* there was now an immense pile of dirt. Anyone but a blind or very drunk person would have noticed the change in topography.

"Ding dang dong dung!" Thanks to an endless series of stressful situations, I could now swear like a trooper.

The Babester laughed. "Well, it was dung, wasn't it?"

Ignoring his crude remark, I trotted over to inspect the damage to my property. Believe me, by now any trace of the vermouth was well on its way to Vermont. I could think as clearly as Sean Penn.

And I needed every wit about me to process the awful sight. This wasn't just a pile of dirt; it was a wall of dirt that encircled what had been the perimeter of my manure heap. In the center was a hole, perhaps ten feet square and some three feet deep. As for the *haufa mischt*, it was scattered hither, thither, and yon around the farmyard. In fact, I was stepping in some that very moment. Thank heavens it was well rotted and beyond the smelling stage.

"Well, it looks like a good start on a swimming pool anyway," Gabe said. "Of course, it needs to be much longer if you plan to swim laps. And maybe another foot deeper. Plus, you'd do well to forget about installing a diving board, no matter how deep you make it. Private pools produce a lot of broken necks—even the ones that are supposedly deep enough."

"This isn't a pool," I wailed, furious at myself for not having figured it out sooner. "It's a treasure pit."

"Come again?"

"It's a family legend. The key to the Hochstetler fortune is supposed to be hidden somewhere in and around Hernia. Possibly buried. Only the descendants can claim it. Anyway, I cleverly planted the idea in two of my guests' heads—Capers and Teruko—that the treasure was buried under my manure pile. They obviously fell for the bait."

"Do you think they found it?"

A brunette can be just as dense as a blonde—which shouldn't be a surprise, I guess, since most blondes started out that way. I tried not to give my beloved a pitying look.

"Of course there wasn't treasure there, or I would have dug it up myself. I just wanted to get the manure turned over this fall, so I could have a nice fertile vegetable plot next spring. Carrots grown in well-rotted *haufa mischt* are the deepest orange you've ever seen. But my real objective to planting this idea was to see if either of these guests believed strongly enough in the legend to follow any lead." I peered down into the hole. Too bad it wasn't a lot deeper. How handy it would be to lower a long rope and hoist up freshly cooked Chinese food. Guests wouldn't rebel then.

"They may have fallen for the bait," Gabe said quietly, "but that doesn't mean they were the primary rats."

"I beg your pardon?"

"Your guest—Mr. Porter, right?—was murdered before this hole was dug. And he was found near another hole, from which the time capsule went missing. One can't make any reasonable conclusions from that. Different guests could have made different holes."

"Don't poke pins in my balloon," I wailed. "And anyway, Miss Mukai and the Littletons are awfully chummy. That very first night, when the taxi drove off with Miss Mukai's luggage, Capers Littleton offered to lend the girl some of her clothes. What do you make of that?"

Gabe shrugged. "That Mrs. Littleton is a gracious Southern lady?"

"Cahoots!" I cried. "They're in cahoots!"

Gabe threw up his hands. "You're the expert, hon. Whatever you say."

"Don't patronize me, Gabriel Ephraim Rosen."

"Oh, the full-name treatment, is it? Well, two can play that game, Magdalena Portulacca Yoder."

"Maybe, but my mother doesn't tuck me in at night."

"That's being childish," he had the chutzpah to say.

Well, I could be just as childish if I put my mind to it. Probably even more so. Instead, I put my hands on my hips and stamped a long, narrow foot.

"You're right, I *am* the expert. So just go home and do whatever it is you do to fill your days. Write those silly little mysteries, for all I care."

"Fine. In the meantime you can make this hole even deeper. Hey, I know, why don't you give it a name—like the Great Hole of Hernia? I bet you could charge admission."

"Just maybe I will. I'm sure I'll make more money from it than you will from your books—*if* you ever manage to sell one."

"That was a low blow." His voice was barely more than a whisper, but he may as well have been shouting. Without even giving me an angry glare, he turned and walked away.

"You idiot!" I said. "What do you know about relationships? Nothing, that's what. Don't be a total fool. Apologize this minute."

I was talking to myself. Gabriel Ephraim Rosen was the best thing that had ever happened to me. Okay, he was a bit of a mama's boy, but so what? Doc was going to take care of that. Why, then, was I so irritated with him? Because he had stated the obvious about my conclusions? That they were invalid? Did this mean I was no more competent than my nemesis, the Mantis?

Well, the truth hurts, as they say. In order that my ego didn't have to suffer alone, I kicked one of the mounds of dirt that surrounded the "Great Hole of Hernia." My toe hit a stone.

Angrily, I kicked a second pile with my other foot. Then another pile. There were eight piles in all—*eight* piles? I counted them three times. Sure enough, eight was the magic number. But that had to be a coincidence. Even if Capers and Terri had shared my misinformation with Octavia Cabot-Dodge—well, a woman her age couldn't possibly have dug a hole this large by herself. And if by some miracle she had, surely there would be another clue.

I circled the pit like a hawk over a field fire, one intent on catching mice. What was I missing? Nothing, that's what. There was nothing untoward that I could see about that pit and the eight piles of dirt—well, except that one was a tad smaller than the others. Wait, a minute. One was also considerably larger than the others. But they all had stones.

Stones! That was it. The dirt on my farm does contain stones, but it's not like I live in a gravel pit. Yet each pile appeared peppered with stones. My heart raced as I began to count the stones on the nearest pile. Just as I suspected; there were eight on the first pile. Eight on the second. Eight on all eight piles, and not a stone more.

"Aha," I said, as the lightbulb went on in my otherwise empty head. Given my pale eyes, it probably shone right through them, bestowing on me the look of one possessed.

"Mom!"

Bless Alison's heart. I hadn't seen the child approach. But to be fair, I was every bit as startled by her sudden appearance as she was by my glowing peepers.

"Not to fear, dear," I assured her. "Your old mom just had an epiphany."

"Mom, do we have to talk about religion now? Babe just ate my hair."

"What?"

"My hair!" she shrieked. "What's the matter, ya blind?"

When the girl first came to live with me, her head was decked out in spiked hair the color of a ripe eggplant. The first thing I made her do—after losing the body-piercing jewelry—was to undo the spike and get her locks back to their original color, a rich shade of chestnut brown. Over the past eight months it had grown to the point where it no longer attracted undo attention.

"Alison, I don't see—" I gasped. A huge chunk of hair from the left side of her head was missing.

"Ya see now, don'tcha?"

"The pig did that?"

"Yeah, and I was just getting to like my hair that way."

"Why did you let him—I mean, how did that happen?"

"Well, I kind of fell asleep out there in the meadow. And the next thing I knew he was chewing away. Mom, I hate him."

At least there was a bright side to this catastrophe. "As a matter of fact, dear, I was just about to suggest that we reconsider—"

"And he peed in your bed."

"*What?*"

"When I woke up this morning you were gone and the bed was all wet. I know I didn't do it, so it had to be him." She put her hands on hips that were just beginning to round. "Unless it was you."

"*Moi?*" I put my hands where my hips should have been. "I'll have you know, young lady, that I haven't wet the bed since high school."

"See? So it was him. Mom, I hope ya don't get mad or anything—like holler real loud—but I'd kind of like to . . . well, get rid of him."

"Oh." It was all I could do to not jump up and down with joy.

"Actually," she said, averting her eyes, "I was more like hoping you would let me sell him."

"Child of my heart!" I cried and clutched her to my bony chest.

She pushed out of my embrace and then glanced at the road behind me. I turned just in time to see two cars, the Littletons' and the Nortons', pull into my driveway. Heaven forbid anyone saw a kid being hugged by her mom—even a foster one.

"Ya don't have ta get all weird on me."

"Sorry. It was probably just an electrical impulse beamed down on me from a satellite. Where's the little monster now?"

"In the barn. So, it's all right with you? Selling him, I mean."

"Sell away," I said happily.

"And I get to keep the money, right?"

"Right as rain. Unless you want me to invest it for you."

"Nah." It was obvious she couldn't wait to get into the house and start making her calls. Not that she would get a lot of money for a single piglet in a farming community, but knowing Alison as I did, I had no doubt the critter would fetch a lot more than it was worth.

I would have insisted that Alison stay long enough to hear at least the short version of the "saving money speech." But before I could open my nagging trap, the most incredible thing happened.

29

"Will you look at that!"

Alison was already halfway to the house and the nearest phone. No doubt visions of a shopping trip into Bedford danced through her head.

Never mind. I don't mind talking to myself. After all, I find that I am my own best listener. And rarely do I interrupt myself.

"What on earth is that down-on-her-luck diva doing with the Littletons? She has her own chauffeur, for crying out loud. Well, she doesn't look too happy, that's for sure. Then again, when has she looked happy? Slap that woman's mug on a jar of pickles, and it will sell itself. Now there is a business opportunity I should seriously consider. I could call the company Cabot-Dodge Dill Pickles. My slogan could be 'The taste so tart it's guaranteed to wipe the smile off your face.' Should go over well at church suppers across the country. And if dour diva refused to sell rights to her likeness, I could always try one of my own photographs."

Although I rather enjoy my private conversations, seldom do my questions get definitive answers. Therefore, I trotted over to greet my guests to give them the third degree. Unfortunately, they saw me coming and all but one of them hightailed it into the house. The only reason I was able to catch the diva is because she was trapped in her stair-counting ritual.

"Miss Cabot-Dodge," I said, mustering the fake cheer that comes with years of inn keeping, "where are your staff?"

"Ha!" she barked. "Staff. That's a joke if I ever heard one." Then, because she'd lost count, she retreated to the bottom step.

"They are planning to show up for lunch, aren't they?"

"Whether or not they miss lunch is not my concern, Miss Yoder."

"But it is mine. If I have to throw away a lot of food—"

"Well, I paid for it, didn't I?"

"Yes, but—"

"The nerve of those two, after all I've done for them. Always complaining that their wages are too low. But where would they be if I hadn't supported them all these years, tell me that?"

"Somewhere different?"

"Ragsdale to riches, that's what she thought it would be." The diva sat to deliver the rest of her diatribe. "But she didn't have the talent. I did. And she certainly didn't have the skills to be my manager. Kept saying the parts weren't coming in, but a good manager would have known how to bring them to me. At least get me a competent agent. But no, not Augusta. Like Jacob and Esau, Mama always said. From the very beginning I had a hunch that things wouldn't work out. I should have followed my instincts and gone it alone. Now look where I am."

"Sitting on my front steps?"

"Blood maybe thicker than water, Miss Yoder. But at least you can drink water."

My legs were shaking so hard I found myself forced to sit on the opposite side of the steps. "Where are they now?"

"Running their own errands—and in *my* limousine."

"Miss Cabot-Dodge, are you and Augusta twins?"

It's a good thing the Good Lord created cartilage, because her reworked skin could not have held those jaws together by itself. That's how wide her mouth opened. For the record, Octavia Cabot-Dodge has had her tonsils removed.

"How did you know?"

"That Jacob and Esau reference. Plus the fact that you were obviously both born in August. You know, Octavia—Augusta." I slapped my forehead, but gently of course. My hands may be bony, but they can deliver quite a punch. Plus my palms still hurt. But why hadn't I seen that connection before?

"Ha! For all you know, I was named after Mark Antony's wife."

"Yes, but in Hernia that would make you Elizabeth Taylor. We're not the most sophisticated folks, you know."

"What makes you think I'm from Hernia?"

"You just said you were. 'Ragsdale to Riches' you said."

She glared at me. "Ha! You must think you're really clever, Miss Yoder."

"Only some of the time. Right now I'm having a hard time coming up with a reason for your visit. Nostalgia, I can understand. But if that's it, why not be open about your roots—small town girl makes good, that kind of thing?"

"Coming here was my sister's idea, not mine. She thought it would make me grateful for how far I've come."

"Has it?"

Her glare intensified. "Surprisingly so. I'm grateful to have left this narrow-minded community behind. And you know as well as I do, Miss Yoder, that Hernians do not consider being a movie star a badge of success."

"Narrow minds keep the devil away," I said, quoting my mother. I didn't agree, but Mama's mind was so narrow, she had room for only one thought at a time, and I'm sure it was never put there by the man with the pitchfork.

"Ha!"

"Miss Cabot-Dodge, did you drive all the way from California?"

"Of course not! My chauffeur did. Airline fares are ridiculous these days."

"You could have flown by yourself."

"Ha! You don't know Augusta." She had nothing further to say. And although it must have been humiliating, especially under the circumstances, she completed her ritual and climbed the stairs.

I turned away to give her privacy. Besides, now that all the pieces were finally falling into place, I was back on the job. But before I rolled up my sleeves (to a modest elbow length) I had to run my theory past the person in Hernia who was best suited to answer my one remaining question.

Doc put the plate in front of me almost shyly. "It's not much, I'm afraid. Blue's radar must be down. Anyway, it's just some chicken and walnut salad with a bleu cheese dressing. Avocado wedges and ripe tomatoes—those are late tomatoes from my own garden, by the way. At least these," he said, placing a basket of crescent rolls in the center of the table, "are made from scratch. Not out of those tubes. I know, folks say it's a lot of trouble to make fresh ones, and you can't tell the difference from the tube ones, but I say they're wrong. Take one—tell me what you think."

I voted by taking two. That was just the first round. Altogether I had six rolls and three helpings of the chicken salad, but just one slice of the quadruple chocolate cake with mocha icing, and real chocolate-covered coffee beans on top for decoration.

"You should enter that cake in the Bake-Off, Doc."

"I plan to. Got to be there at two sharp. That's why lunch isn't anything to write home about."

"But it's really good, nonetheless. This is the tastiest chicken salad I've ever eaten. Really moist."

"That's because it's beer butt chicken."

"I beg your pardon."

"Grilled it this morning. You see, you stick a can of beer up— never mind. I'm sure the only thing you need to know is that the alcohol cooks off."

Like it did with Freni's Vermont chicken. But if I'd drunk the beer straight from the can—well, there was no point dwelling on past sins.

"Doc, you know a lot about human diseases, don't you?"

He cocked his head. "Not as much as that handsome young stud of yours. Why don't you save your question for him?"

"Because Gabriel and I—" I sighed. "Because we're not communicating well at the moment, that's why."

"How about his mother? Did you communicate with her?"

"The woman is hot to trot," I said, borrowing one of Susannah's seemingly meaningless phrases.

Doc rubbed his hands together. "Excellent!"

"Glad to be of service," I said, as I swallowed more irritation than salad. "Now that I've gotten you lined up with a date, how about answering my question."

"Which is?"

"What do you know about Obsessive-Compulsive Disorder?"

"So it's finally gotten that bad, has it?"

"I beg your pardon?"

"Don't worry, Magdalena, your secret is safe with me."

"But I don't have a secret," I wailed. "I'm not talking about me."

He smiled encouragingly. "Let's pretend you're not. I just want you to know that they have ways of treating this disorder these days. Some of those antidepressant drugs are said to be very useful, especially in conjunction with talk therapy. It's certainly nothing to be ashamed of. You come by it honestly, you know."

"I do? I mean, I don't—because I don't have it."

"Your mama—now there was a fine specimen of a woman— always had to put her right stocking and shoe on first."

"How on earth do you know that?" I clapped my hands over my ears, dreading the answer. But not so tight that I couldn't hear it.

"Because your papa was always teasing her. Also said she had to check the gas stove ten times before she left the house."

"Well, I'm not Mama, and I only check it twice. I asked the question because of one of my guests, not me."

He took a sip of coffee and leaned back in his chair. "I'm listening."

"Her name is Octavia, because she was born in August, and apparently she has this thing about the number eight. Especially when it comes to stairs, but I've seen her doing it at other times as well."

"Go on."

"Well, I planted a false clue—to two other guests, not her—about the Hochstetler treasure being buried under my manure pile."

Doc's coffee exited in a fine spray. "That's my girl. Magdalena, I sure as heck hope this Rosen woman is half as interesting as you."

"Thanks—I think. Anyway, this morning the *haufa mischt* had been scattered and the ground beneath it dug up. Into eight piles. And each pile had eight stones pressed into it."

"Were the stones randomly placed, or in recognizable groupings?"

"Random. I didn't notice them at first. And what's more, Doc, the piles weren't all the same size. Close maybe, but not the same."

He dabbed at his shirt with a crisp linen napkin. "Well, like I said, I'm not a people doctor, but if you want my guess—for what's worth—it looks like a setup. Anyone who was compulsive enough to put the dirt in eight piles would make them as even as possible. As for that stone bit, it's over the top."

"That's what I thought. It's like someone is purposely calling attention to the eight piles. To direct suspicion away from themself."

"Exactly."

"Ah, so you know who it is?"

"I have my theory."

"But you're not going to act on it alone, right?"

"Absolutely not. Trust me, Doc, I've learned my lesson."

He sighed. "Yeah, I bet. Promise me that if you get in over your head, you'll call the sheriff, not the dummkopf."

"Aye, aye, Captain—I mean Doc."

But if life throws you a curveball, and you don't have any of your own—curves, that is—you take what you can get. I was on my way to the inn, fully intending to give the sheriff a call if things got out of hand, when I spotted Octavia's limo. It was headed not back to PennDutch, but in the other direction, toward the road that leads up Stucky Ridge. It was my duty to follow it, at a discreet distance, of course, to see if the occupants were up to any mischief. They were, after all, on the wrong side of town for both the hay-baling and the Bake-Off.

When they turned on the winding lane to the summit, I stuck with them. Yes, I know it should have been the sheriff I dialed on my cell phone. But in my defense, Melvin does live on this side of town. Besides, I still had no proof.

"What now?" he snapped. I was right to assume that our Chief of Police would take the day off when the town was overflowing with visitors. There were probably a million—okay, maybe half a dozen—fender benders, and no one available to write up citations. Not unless Zelda could be convinced to give up her vacation. Perhaps I should give her a call next and entice her with the probability that at least one of the fender benders was going to result in fisticuffs. Breaking up a fight was an activity she was bound to enjoy.

"I think I know who did it," I said calmly.

"Don't tell me, you idiot. Unless, of course, it was Erica Kane."

"Are you watching that soap opera again?"

"It's not a soap; it's a televised drama. So you don't know who, do you?"

"Augusta Miller and Stanley Dalrumple. She's Octavia's twin sister. I'm not sure what Mr. Dalrumple's connection is, other than chauffeur."

"Don't be an idiot, Yoder. They're not even in the story line."

"Listen to me you—you—" Fortunately I sputtered out of steam before I called him a name. I took a deep, cleansing breath. "I'm talking about the murders of Buzzy Porter and Ron Humphrey."

"Yeah, those names I recognize."

If my arms were skinnier I could reach through a phone line and grab Melvin by his equally scrawny neck. I was, however, on my cell phone.

"Melvin, dear," I said dripping so much sarcasm I feared for the floorboards of my car, "if you can't remember the last several days, then perhaps you should indeed consider the presidency. Or maybe big business."

"Thanks, Yoder—hey, that wasn't a compliment, was it?"

I watched the limo make the last turn before reaching the summit. "No, it wasn't. But if you want a chance to exercise your strongest muscle—maybe even redeem yourself—meet me up on Stucky Ridge. Pronto."

"I'm a married man, Yoder."

I considered the source. "The suspects are in the limo. I'm pretty sure they don't know they're being followed. Meet me just before the top, at the last bend. We'll go the rest of the way on foot."

"Okay, Yoder, but you better be onto something. *One Life to Live* comes on next."

"Summit!" I hissed and then hung up.

30

Author's note: Pious people should avoid this recipe, which involves both alcohol and the business end of a chicken. However, yielding to temptation does reward one with a delectable treat.

Jim and Jan Langdoc's Beer Butt Chicken

Hickory- or mesquite-scented wood chips
1 can beer
Commercial or homemade "rub."

1 whole chicken, thoroughly washed and patted dry
Vegetable oil as needed

Homemade Rub

¼ cup salt (sea or kosher)
⅓ cup brown sugar (light or dark)

¼ cup paprika (sweet or hot)
3 tablespoons freshly ground pepper

Soak hickory- or mesquite-scented wood chips for 30 minutes in half of the beer, leaving the other half of the beer in the can. Spread soaked chips over hot coals in the grill (or if using gas, put in smoker box).

Sprinkle 1 teaspoon of rub into cavity of chicken. Oil the outside of the chicken and sprinkle with 1 tablespoon of the rub. Rub in well.

Put about 1½ tablespoons of rub directly into tab opening of the beer can. Punch 2 additional holes in the can, using a sharp object (such as grilling fork). Insert the beer can into the cavity of the chicken.

Place can and chicken on grill, so that the legs and can form a tripod to support the chicken. Cook until meat thermometer reaches 180 degrees without touching bone (between 1 and 1½ hours). The steam from the beer keeps the bird moist and succulent, as well as giving it character. Let the chicken rest 5 minutes before serving.

31

The limo stopped soon after it reached the summit, which surprised me. It did not surprise me, however, to see both Augusta Miller and Stanley Dalrumple hop out. Stanley was carrying a coil of rope over his shoulder. Augusta had a pair of binoculars hung around her neck. I was able to spot these accouterments because I keep a pair of binoculars of my own in the glove compartment. Don't ask me what I use them for, and you'll be spared an answer that might embarrass you.

At any rate, neither of them glanced my way, and if they had, they probably wouldn't have seen me anyway. I'd stopped my car the second I saw their brake lights come on, and had advanced on foot. Now I was hiding behind a tree trunk, which is yet another advantage of being rail thin.

I could hear their conversation, thanks to a gentle breeze that was blowing in my direction. Still, it was faint, so I cupped both hands behind my ears.

"You should have marked the spot where you threw the shovel over." At that distance Augusta's voice sounded identical to that of her sister. Why hadn't I noticed that before?

"But, Grandma," Stanley whined, "it's not like I had the time. That jogger was onto us, and my prints were all over the handle."

Grandma! So that was Augusta's relationship to the boy. I crept closer.

"You should have worn gloves, Stanley, like I told you."

"So I forgot them. You didn't remember either, and this whole damn thing was your idea, not mine."

"Don't you swear in front of me," Augusta snarled. "And switching the bodies at the morgue was most certainly not my idea."

"You got to admit, that was brilliant thinking on my part. Kept them confused long enough so that we could dispose of Buzzy."

She sighed. "It wasn't supposed to turn out this way. Buzzy was my grandson too. But oh no, he had to jump the gun—get all the treasure for himself. Didn't I tell you from the beginning that he was high-risk? Just like that no-good magician father of his, who sole my youngest daughter off to Vegas."

"Yeah, but Grandma, you said yourself that Buzzy probably heard the treasure story a million times before Auntie Vera and Uncle Ray died in that accident."

It was a bizarre time for her to laugh, but that didn't stop her. "I guess we should be glad that my dotty old sister has been too stuck on herself all these years to see the boy even once. She didn't even blink when they were introduced Sunday."

Stanley snickered. "You can bet the cops would have blinked if they'd had more time with his body. I look just like him when I take off my glasses."

"Don't flatter yourself, Stanley. Just thank your lucky stars I remembered that little cave at the bottom of Lovers' Leap."

"Yeah, but I had to lower his body through these trees and then push all them leaves up against the cave."

"Well, I couldn't exactly get down there myself now, could I? I'm not a spring chicken anymore, you know."

"You were supposed to run over the jogger, but you didn't. So then I had to shoot him."

"Stanley, are you getting cheeky with me?"

"I'm just saying, seems to me I've had to do all the work. So what if I had a little fun along the way?"

"You're just like your cousin, Stanley. You know that? You

could have been caught, and that would have been the end of everything."

The lad giggled. "Yeah, but Buzzy is dead, and I'm not. Man, I'd give anything to hear what went on in that rinky-dink morgue when they discovered the switch. But you can bet it wasn't one of the staff. They were as dumb as bricks."

Augusta snorted. "They couldn't sew shut a Thanksgiving turkey if their lives depended on it. No, it had to be that busybody, Ms. Yoder."

"Needle Nose?"

Needle Nose? Why, the nerve of that boy! And she was no better—busybody indeed. I crept closer so as not to miss a disparaging word. Unfortunately, it is hard to put a size eleven shoe—even a narrow one—down on any surface without making a noise. It is especially hard to do so when skirting a woods. The branch that cracked under my foot must have been as dry as tinder, because the report was as loud as a sonic boom.

Stanley and Augusta wheeled in unison, as if they had choreographed the scene. He was a holding a gun, which appeared to be aimed right at me, and she already had the binoculars pressed to her face.

"It's her," she said. "Needle Nose. Under that sycamore."

Intellectually I knew that small handguns are notoriously inaccurate, especially at a distance. If I ran, particularly in a zigzag pattern, my chances of escaping unharmed were good. And since I stood at the edge of the woods, they were, in fact, excellent. Alas, my brain refused to communicate this knowledge to my legs, which had suddenly become columns of overcooked pasta. Mountains of mushy macaroni. Rebellious rigatoni. Spastic spaghetti. Limp linguini. Choose your carbohydrate, but you get the picture.

This cowardly reaction is quite unlike me, I assure you. Under normal circumstances I might well have charged the deadly duo and then nudged them off the cliff with my infamous shnoz. These were not normal circumstances, however, because when I stepped on the crackling branch, I had placed my tootsie no more than an inch away from a snake.

It was a small snake, not more than a foot and a half long, but from the pattern on its back, not to mention its telltale tail, I could see at once that it was some form of rattler. It was coiled when I first saw it, but almost immediately it began to unwind in a quest to slither away to safety. It was, however, directionally challenged, and in its haste to escape, slithered directly over my foot.

I can't blame the poor thing for mistaking my black brogan for just another boulder. I'm sure it was as confused and scared as I was. It took only a second or two for the reptile to cross my foot, but those precious seconds were all Stanley Dalrumple needed. As the snake disappeared under the litter of leaves that blanketed the ground, the chauffeur and would-be heir closed the gap that was my margin of safety.

"Take one step, Miss Yoder, and I'll blow your refrigerator head off." He actually used a far cruder expression, one that bears no repeating.

My legs were still not under my command, although my tongue was. "Your grandmother should wash your mouth out with soap."

By now Augusta was close enough to hear what I said. "My grandson's language is none of your business, Miss Yoder."

"Some grandmother you are. You don't seem the least bit saddened by your other grandson's death. That bogus fortune means more to you."

"It isn't bogus," Stanley snapped. "Tell her, Grandma."

Augusta's face, when viewed closely, was not a pretty sight. Please don't misunderstand, there is nothing wrong with wrinkles. Her skin, however, was so dry and so crisscrossed with creases, that it resembled the soles of my feet in the dead of winter.

"We found a map in the time capsule."

"Map?"

"Don't pretend you're stupid, Miss Yoder. It's a map that shows where the Hochstetler family treasure is buried."

"I honestly don't know anything about a treasure map. If any-

thing, the capsule was supposed to contain a list of the founding
fathers. Sort of a code as to which family Bible to look in."

"Ah, Bibi Norton's theory. Well, she's wrong. As simple as that.
It's a map, and we have it now."

"Get out of town!"

"We plan to, just as soon as we figure out how to read it."

"Show it to her, Grandma."

I was dying of curiosity. "Yes, please show it to me."

To my astonishment Augusta reached into the front of her dress
and withdrew from her bosom an ancient piece of paper. Mama
used to keep a clean handkerchief in her cleavage, and Susannah
keeps a dog where her bosom should be, so this was definitely a
family trait. It's just that I didn't really expect there to be a map.

"You help us find it," she said, "and we won't kill you."

"But she'll squeal," Stanley squealed. He sounded just like our
soon-to-be-ex-pet pig.

I shook my head vigorously. My legs had regained their
strength and I was feeling feisty again—well, at least foolish.

"Split it three ways, and I won't tell a soul."

"Why, the nerve," Augusta said, but her eyes shone with admiration.

"Show me." I held out my right hand.

Augusta opened the document with great care. "I remembered
the cave, but not all the area landmarks."

She wouldn't let me touch it, but she did let me get close
enough to get a good look. It was all I could do to keep from laughing. In fact, a sort of bray escaped my lips before I could will them
closed. The map, you see, was not a treasure map at all, but the sit-
ing plan for an outdoor toilet. An outhouse, as we used to call
them.

This particular sketch was not for your run-of-the-mill outhouse, but the famous six seater that Great-grandpa Milo Yoder
built on the family farm. It was hailed as the largest outhouse east
of the Mississippi, and some wag on the Bedford newspaper even
dubbed it the Eighth Wonder of the Underworld. I know, it must
sound ostentatious to have such a grand bathroom, even if it was

detached from the house and lacked plumbing. But you see, my great-grandparents had eleven children. An ordinary two seater just wouldn't do. Besides, Great-grandpa Milo was of the philosophy that the family that sprayed together, stayed together. Trust me, I hadn't an inkling that the plans for this incredible structure (which was sadly destroyed by fire in my lifetime) had been deemed important enough to be included in Hernia's time capsule.

"Is something funny, Miss Yoder?" Stanley looked like he wanted to snatch the map from his grandmother's hands and away from my mocking eyes.

"Oh, nothing in the least," I managed to say with a straight face. "It's just that I recognize everything on this map." That, incidentally, was the truth. The large rectangle was our barn, the square was our house, and the long narrow rectangle with the row of small circles in it, the famous six seater. There were even two scalloped circles to represent the pair of large maples that still stand in my front yard.

"Okay, you're in," Augusta said. She handed me the map.

I shall always regret what I did next. I honestly believe I intended no harm to these killers, merely a way for me to escape so that I could be reunited with my loved ones. And anyway, we were a long way from Lovers' Leap, and the drop-off wasn't more than thirty feet at that point. Besides, the ledge below the cliff was covered with small trees and bushes, so that if anyone did go over, they might be badly scratched and break a few bones, but they surely wouldn't die from the experience.

"That," I said, pointing to the rectangle that represented the barn, "is Murphy's Mountain over there to the southwest. And that"—I pointed to the box that marked my house—"is Buffalo Mountain, which is behind us."

"Don't look like mountain symbols to me," Stanley said.

I flashed him a smile, which, if genuine, would have rotted his teeth in a nanosecond. "That's because in those days a triangle was considered vulgar, imitating as it does the female bosom."

Augusta nodded, as if she remembered "those days." Perhaps she did.

"And what about these two scalloped circles?" she asked.

"Ah, well, this one is the Neunschwander farm, and the other one is the Berkey place. They're just on there as points of reference. What's important is this long narrow rectangle with six circles in it."

They stared at the design for great-grandpa's outhouse. "What does it mean?" Augusta demanded. Her breath was as hot as any August day, although not nearly as sweet.

"You see," I said, praying for inspiration, "this long skinny rectangle is Stucky Ridge. That, of course, is where we're standing right now. The circle on this end is the cave just below Lovers' Leap—but you already know all about that one. There are five caves just like it, only they're harder to find. "Now this"—I tapped the slanted line that indicated the location of the outhouse door—"tells us which cave contains the treasure."

"You said there wasn't a treasure map," Stanley said. The boy was far smarter than I gave him credit for. "Now you tell us you know where the treasure is buried. Grandma, I think she's conning us."

Where in tarnation was the Stoltzfus? What were the chances he'd sneaked up on us and was lurking in the underbrush, just seconds away from being my hero? Frankly, it was about as likely as Charlie Sheen joining the NRA. No doubt Melvin was still at home, lollygagging about in his La-Z-Boy recliner, watching *One Life to Live*. If I got out of this predicament alive, I would pull strings with the finance company he used and get his TV repossessed.

However, now was not the time to appear anything but serene. I tapped the map again.

"This circle is right below a rock feature we call The Old Man. If we get closer to the edge you can look down and see his nose. It's almost as big as mine."

"I don't remember a rock called that," Augusta said.

"Well, it has other names as well. But look, there it is."

I'd been stepping sideways toward the cliff, and they, unwittingly, had been moving with me. Just a few more steps and I might be able to trip or push one of them, and send him or her crashing into the foliage below.

"I don't see a nose," Augusta said, craning her neck. "Do you, Stanley?"

"Maybe it's because I'm taller than either of you," I said, "but I can see it. I'm sure you will too, if you get closer."

They each took a couple of steps forward. In fact, they were now nearer the edge than I was. When opportunity knocks, you either open the door or rue the day you didn't. This was my opportunity, so I took it.

32

I pushed Stanley. Because of his youth and testosterone, he was the biggest threat to me. Besides, he was the one holding the gun. And it was Stanley who had shot Ron Humphrey when Augusta found herself unable to run the jogger over with her car.

Alas, the youth had the reflexes of a cat. One foot went over the edge, but he managed to whip around and grab my left arm. Using me as a fulcrum, he pivoted so that both his feet were back on the cliff. Then, instead of being generous of spirit, he pushed *me* off the cliff.

"Sayonara," I heard him say, as I sailed out over the abyss.

Okay, so it was a rather short cliff, but you try falling thirty feet, even if there are trees in the way to block your fall. To this day I thank the Good Lord that I have never given in to the temptation to wear slacks. My broadcloth skirt contains almost as much material as your average parachute. And in addition to my sturdy Christian underwear, I am never without a slip. These modest garments saved my life.

To say that I floated into the trees below would be an overstatement, but at least I didn't crash. In fact, I never even made it to the ground. The hem of my frock caught on a bare branch, in two places, and just feet below the ledge. I continued to fall a couple of feet more, so that when I jerked to a stop, both skirt and petticoat were up around my face.

I saw this as God's mercy. If I was to be shot at close range, at least I would not have to see the actual pulling of the trigger.

"Thank You, Lord," I said. "Thank You for all the blessings You've given me throughout my life. I truly am grateful. But please don't let this be a painful death—although I probably deserve it for grilling my guests like weenies. I'm not really big on pain, You see. Even if it hadn't been against Your will, I still would not have pierced my ears. And whenever the dentist works on my teeth, I make him use laughing gas—oops, that's not a sin, Lord, is it? Well, I guess I better sign off and let the Angel of Death do his stuff. Oh, just one more thing, please tell Mama and Papa I'll be seeing them real soon."

No sooner had I finished my brief prayer than the gun fired. In fact, it fired several times. There was nothing I could do but close my eyes and try to relax as much as possible while the bullets zinged through me. Perhaps they wouldn't hurt so much if my flesh was pliable. I was, after all, a sitting duck—make that a hanging woman. Cooperation with my killers would well be the last gift I gave myself.

There was shouting as well, but I did my best to tune it out. The quicker I left this world and its concerns behind, the quicker I entered Heaven. In fact, I was starting to get excited. What fun to be fitted for my celestial robes. I sure hoped we got fitted for halos as well, because it would be hard to find a ready-made halo my size. And I could hardly wait to see my mansion. Just as long as I wasn't expected to play a harp. I tried playing Susannah's guitar once and got blisters on my fingertips. Perhaps St. Peter would issue me an oboe instead.

The gunfire ceased. Well, now that was a big surprise; dying wasn't half-bad. I mean, it hadn't hurt at all. My wedding night with Aaron—well, never you mind. Trust me, dying was a lot more pleasant.

I opened my eyes. What on earth was my skirt still doing in front of my eyes? And why weren't my feet resting on golden streets? Metallic avenues had always seemed a mite dangerous to me, but I was willing to give them a try.

"Help me, Lord," I implored. "Help me to at least die right."
The Good Lord had a surprisingly high-pitched laugh. "I see
London, I see France, I see Yoder's underpants."

"Don't tease me, Lord—hey, you're not God at all! Are you?"

"Your sister seems to think so."

"*Melvin Stoltzfus!*"

"Quit horsing around Yoder. Get back up here and give me a
hand."

"If I could get back up, I'd give you a flock of birds, Melvin."
You see what having a trash-mouthed sister has done to me?

"Then go hang yourself," he said.

"I did *not* say that." Melvin punctuated his statement by giving me
the evil eye with his right orb. Meanwhile his left eye was surveying the Founder's Day Picnic, which, I shudder to mention, had
hastily been renamed Melvin Stoltzfus Day.

The mouthwatering smells emanating from dozens of portable
barbecue grills did nothing to ameliorate the bitter taste of jealousy.
I had done all the work, and now the Mantis was reaping the glory.
How fair is that? The time capsule, which truly did contain nothing more interesting the oversized outhouse plans, had been safely
returned from the trunk of Octavia's limo.

"You left me hanging, Melvin, and you know it."

Susannah, who was standing next to me, and whose fifteen feet
of filmy fuchsia fabric was flapping in my face, had to open her big
yap. "That's because my Babykins had to drive the two killers,
which he handcuffed all by himself, down to the jail. Really, Mags,
you should be grateful."

"Well, he wouldn't have had to do it all himself if he'd come
straight up here when I called for backup."

Melvin forced his left eye to leave the crowd of picnickers and
focus on me. "I already I told you, I had just gotten the call from
the Harrisburg police."

"Right. But *they* caught the cabdriver who stole Miss Mukai's
clothes; you didn't have anything to do with it."

Gabe's fingers encircled my biceps. "Hon, can I speak to you for a minute?"

"Yes, but first—"

My on-again, off-again, fiancé pulled me away from my family's grill. Melvin couldn't boil water if given written directions, yet he somehow manages to excel on a grill. It must be a guy thing—one that includes male mantises. That day he was cooking a side of ribs that smelled so delicious, half of Hernia was leaning our way, inhaling the breeze.

"I'm sorry," Gabe said, without a preamble. "From now on I'm putting you first."

"I'm sorry too. And you don't *always* have to put me first. After all, Ida is your mother—I mean, Alison is my daughter, and there might be times when I—"

You should have heard the collective gasp as hundreds of Mennonites and Amish assembled on that ridge saw the Babester silence me with a kiss. On the lips, no less. First base, right out there in the open, in broad daylight. They could have been more shocked only had we broken into a jig. Or maybe the highland fling.

"Ooh," Susannah squealed, "how come you never kiss me like that, Babykins?"

"But I do, Sugar Poodle."

"I think I'm gonna be sick." I recognized the voice as belonging to Alison.

"Hon," Gabe said to me, "do you want me to do it again?"

Of course I did! Just not in front of the entire town.

"Yes, let's talk."

Gabe grabbed my hand and ushered me through the gaping crowd. Neither of us said anything until we reached the cemetery. This was, incidentally, the least populated spot on the ridge. The wooded area in which Buzzy was found dead was full of teenagers. Because of their youth, no one cared if *they* got to first base. And believe me, Cornelia Unruh and one of the Bontrager boys (they all look alike) had just rounded second and looked eager to press on to third. But the cemetery, for the most part, remained the domain of its long-term residents.

My beloved knew me well enough to keep away from my parents' plots. We sat on the grass next to Ebeneezer Schrock's headstone. This man, by the way, was no relation to Lodema or her husband. Ebeneezer Schrock was an itinerant preacher who had no business being buried on Stucky Ridge. This unfortunate event happened well over a century ago, and nobody alive is quite sure of the circumstances. My point is that since Ebeneezer has no descendants in Hernia, his plot is seldom visited.

"Hon," Gabe said, when our privacy was assured, "for your own sake, you have got to let go of this."

"But it's Melvin," I wailed. "For years I've done all his work for him, and now, suddenly, he's gets lucky and ends up a hero."

"He did single-handedly apprehend Augusta Miller and her grandson."

"He shot her in the toes when his gun accidentally discharged!"

"Nevertheless, this is his shining moment, and you're a big enough person to let him have it."

"But I'm not! And it just isn't fair."

"What's not fair," Gabe said, his lips so close to mine that I could feel their heat, "is that I didn't meet you twenty-five years ago."

"But I—"

I fully intended for Gabe to silence me again with a kiss. He seemed happy to comply.